The Dragon In The Sea

In the endless war between East and West, oil has become the ultimate prize. Nuclear-powered subtugs brave enemy waters to tap into hidden oil reserves. Psychologist John Ramsay has gone undercover aboard a Hell Diver subtug where, hunted relentlessly by the enemy, the crew find themselves isolated in a claustrophobic undersea prison, struggling for survival against the elements . . . and themselves.

The Santaroga Barrier

Santaroga seemed to be nothing more than a prosperous farm community. But there was something . . . different . . . about Santaroga. Maybe Santaroga was the last outpost of American individualism. Maybe they were just a bunch of religious kooks . . . Or maybe there was something extraordinary at work in Santaroga. Something far more disturbing than anyone could imagine.

The Dosadi Experiment

Generations of a tormented human-alien people, caged on a toxic planet, conditioned by constant hunger and war – this is the Dosadi Experiment, and it has succeeded too well. For the Dosadi have bred for Vengeance as well as cunning, and they have learned how to pass through the shimmering God Wall to exact their dreadful revenge on the Universe that created them . . .

D1603225

Also by Frank Herbert

Novels

The Dragon in the Sea (1956)
Dune (1965)
Destination: Void (1966)
The Eyes of Heisenberg (1966)
The Green Brain (1966)
The Heaven Makers (1968)
The Santaroga Barrier (1968)
Dune Messiah (1969)
Whipping Star (1970)
The Godmakers (1972)
Soul Catcher (1972)
Hellstrom's Hive (1973)
Children of Dune (1976)
The Dosadi Experiment (1977)
The Jesus Incident (with Bill Ransom) (1979)
God-Emperor of Dune (1981)
The White Plague (1982)
The Lazarus Effect (with Bill Ransom) (1983)
Heretics of Dune (1984)
Chapterhouse: Dune (1985)
Man of Two Worlds (with Brian Herbert) (1986)
The Ascension Factor (with Bill Ransom) (1988)

Short Story Collections

The Worlds of Frank Herbert (1970)
The Book of Frank Herbert (1973)
The Best of Frank Herbert: 1952–1964 (1977)
The Best of Frank Herbert: 1965–1970 (1977)
The Priests of Psi (1980)
Eye (1985)

Frank Herbert

SF GATEWAY OMNIBUS

THE DRAGON IN THE SEA
THE SANTAROGA BARRIER
THE DOSADI EXPERIMENT

GOLLANCZ
LONDON

The right of Frank Herbert to be identified as the author
of this work has been asserted by him in accordance with the
Copyright, Designs and Patents Act 1988.

First published in Great Britain in 2013 by Gollancz
An imprint of the Orion Publishing Group
Orion House, 5 Upper St Martin's Lane, London WC2H 9EA
An Hachette UK Company

A CIP catalogue record for this book
is available from the British Library

ISBN 978 0 575 10110 4

1 3 5 7 9 10 8 6 4 2

Typeset by Input Data Services Ltd, Bridgwater, Somerset

Printed and bound by CPI Group (UK) Ltd, Croydon, CR0 4YY

The Orion Publishing Group's policy is to use papers
that are natural, renewable and recyclable products and
made from wood grown in sustainable forests. The logging
and manufacturing processes are expected to conform to
the environmental regulations of the country of origin.

www.orionbooks.co.uk

CONTENTS

ENTER THE SF GATEWAY . . .

Towards the end of 2011, in conjunction with the celebration of fifty years of coherent, continuous science fiction and fantasy publishing, Gollancz launched the SF Gateway.

Over a decade after launching the landmark SF Masterworks series, we realised that the realities of commercial publishing are such that even the Masterworks could only ever scratch the surface of an author's career. Vast troves of classic SF & Fantasy were almost certainly destined never again to see print. Until very recently, this meant that anyone interested in reading any of those books would have been confined to scouring second-hand bookshops. The advent of digital publishing changed that paradigm for ever.

Embracing the future even as we honour the past, Gollancz launched the SF Gateway with a view to utilising the technology that now exists to make available, for the first time, the entire backlists of an incredibly wide range of classic and modern SF and fantasy authors. Our plan, at its simplest, was – and still is! – to use this technology to build on the success of the SF and Fantasy Masterworks series and to go even further.

The SF Gateway was designed to be the new home of classic Science Fiction & Fantasy – the most comprehensive electronic library of classic SFF titles ever assembled. The programme has been extremely well received and we've been very happy with the results. So happy, in fact, that we've decided to complete the circle and return a selection of our titles to print, in these omnibus editions.

We hope you enjoy this selection. And we hope that you'll want to explore more of the classic SF and fantasy we have available. These are wonderful books you're holding in your hand, but you'll find much, much more . . . through the SF Gateway.

www.sfgateway.com

INTRODUCTION
from The Encyclopedia of Science Fiction

Frank Herbert (1920–1986) was a US writer born in Tacoma, Washington, and educated at the University of Washington, Seattle; he was Brian Herbert's father. Herbert worked as a reporter and editor on a number of West Coast newspapers before becoming a full-time writer. He began publishing SF with "Looking for Something?" in 1952, and during the next decade was an infrequent contributor to the SF magazines, producing fewer than twenty short stories (which nevertheless constituted a majority of his short fiction; he never made a significant impact with work below novel length); much of this material was assembled in various collections, including *The Book of Frank Herbert* (1973) and *The Best of Frank Herbert* (1975). At this time he also wrote one novel, *The Dragon in the Sea* (1956), a much praised SF thriller concerning complex psychological investigations aboard a submarine of the Near Future whose mission is to steal oil from America's foes.

His emergence as a writer of major stature commenced with the publication in Analog from December 1963 to February 1964 of "Dune World", the first part of his Dune series. It was followed by "The Prophet of Dune" (January-May 1965 Analog); the two were amalgamated into *Dune* (1965), which won the first Nebula for Best Novel, shared the Hugo, and became one of the most famous of all SF novels.

Dune is a novel of extraordinary complexity. It encompasses intergalactic Politics of a decidedly feudal nature, the development of Psi Powers, Religion – specifically the reluctant but inevitable evolution of its protagonist into a Messiah – and Future War. Its primary impact, however, lay in its treatment of Ecology, a theme which it brought into the forefront of modern SF readers' and writers' awareness. The desert planet Arrakis, with its giant sandworms and its Bedouin-like human inhabitants, the Fremen, clinging to the most precarious of ecological niches through fanatical scrupulousness in water conservation, is possibly the most convincing Planetary-Romance environment created by any SF writer. With its blend (or sometimes clash) of complex intellectual discourse and Byzantine intrigue, *Dune* provided a template for Herbert's significant later work. Sequels soon began to appear which carried on the arguments of the original in testingly various manners and with an intensity of discourse seldom encountered in the SF field. *Dune Messiah* (1969) elaborates the intrigue at the cost of other elements, but *Children of Dune* (1976) recaptures much of the strength of the original work and addresses another recurrent theme in Herbert's work – the Evolution of Man, in this case into Superman.

God Emperor of Dune (1981), set after 3500 years under the idealistic sway of the sandworm-cum-emperor Leto Atreides II, was followed by *Heretics of Dune* (1984) and *Chapter House Dune* (1985). The last volume of the sequence may have the recapitulary air of a long coda, but *God Emperor of Dune* and *Heretics of Dune*, like the enormously extended sonata-form development section in the first movement of a great symphony, work and rework the initial material into more and more elaborate presentations of the initial themes. As a whole, the sequence almost fully justified Herbert's decision – certainly astute in marketing terms – to so comprehensively draw out his original inspiration. A set of Sequels by Brian Herbert (Frank Herbert's son) with Kevin J Anderson has not seriously diminished the effect of the original series.

Although Dune dominated his career from 1965, Herbert began in the mid-1960s to publish other novels and series with admirable regularity. *The Green Brain* (1966) features mutated insects which achieve corporate intelligence. *Destination: Void* (1966), a clotted novel on a Cybernetics theme, concentrates on the construction of an AI aboard a starship, where it comes to the conclusion that it is God. The Pandora sequence, all written with Bill Ransom – *The Jesus Incident* (1979), *The Lazarus Effect* (1983) and *The Ascension Factor* (1988) – follows on from *Destination: Void*, exploring in exhaustive detail the implications of the earlier book, while placing in a Planetary-Romance frame the complex and developing relationship between God-"protected" human stock and the natives of Pandora. *The Eyes of Heisenberg* (1966) is about Genetic Engineering and Immortality, and *The Heaven Makers* (1968) again copes with immortality. *The Santaroga Barrier* (1968), describing a higher order of Intelligence evolved within an isolated, near-Utopian community, served to emphasize the thematic centrality of intelligence throughout Herbert's work, in which consistent attempts are made not only to suggest different, or evolved, types of intelligence but to describe them in detail. Among contemporary SF writers only Ian Watson has addressed this theme as frequently and as convincingly.

Alien intelligence is further examined in the Jorj X McKie/Consentiency sequence comprising "The Tactful Saboteur" (short story, 1964), *Whipping Star* (1970) and *The Dosadi Experiment* (1977) – the last of which, orchestrated through a plot of multi-levelled intrigue, searchingly describes several different alien species in detail, examines the effect of an experiment in extreme Overpopulation, and gifts its hero and heroine with advanced Psi Powers, including total mind transference.

Herbert's other SF novels include: *The God Makers* (1972), in which a god is reified through human endeavours; the rather surly *The White Plague* (1982), in which a man driven into mad misogyny destroys the women of the world; and the minor *Man of Two Worlds* (1986) with his son Brian Herbert. More important than any of these, however, is *Hellstrom's Hive* (1973), which derives its title from the film *The Hellstrom Chronicle* (1971) but otherwise has little connection with it. Arguably Herbert's most successful novel after *Dune*, this presents in persuasive detail an Underground colony of humans selectively bred, on insect-hive principles, into various specializations. In this society the individual's existence is of minor importance; the continuation of the hive as a functioning entity is paramount. The novel points up the contradictions of a society which in its own terms is a successful Utopia, but which from an outside human viewpoint is horrific.

Much of Herbert's work taxes the reader, mostly for good reasons. His ideas were genuinely developed concepts, not merely decorative notions, but they were sometimes embodied in excessively complicated plots and articulated in prose which did not always match the level of thinking, so that much of his writing seemed dense and opaque. His best novels, however, were the work of a speculative intellect with few rivals in modern SF, and were passionate with thought. He was posthumously inducted into the Science Fiction Hall of Fame in 2006.

It is sometimes easy to forget that Herbert wrote *Dune* (and its sequels) in the course of a long, industrious, highly competent career, and that everything he wrote was about something. He was a hard arguer, and it is a joy to revisit some of his battlefields, as the three books selected here demonstrate. *The Dragon in the Sea,* which is over half a century old, remains dangerous: an atomic sub, with a spy on board, is stealing oil from America's enemies, because we have almost depleted the planet of natural resources. The action is unrelenting, but the depths of the sea, which evoke Jungian psychology, bring redemption to the tough crew. Behind *The Santaroga Barrier* lives a society as enclosed as any submarine, its virtues enforced by drugs, its analysis of the consumption-driven Dystopian world outside savagely telling all the same: it is a world we recognize. And again, similar but entirely different, we find in *The Dosadi Experiment* yet another prison, this time an entire world in which a cohort of humans has been dumped, with memories or resources, as a Thought Experiment in survival. They survive. The galaxy, engined by sentient stars, takes notes. But we as readers do not need to, because Herbert speaks directly and urgently to us. He teaches us how exciting a good thought can be, if a good story tells it.

For a more detailed version of the above, see Frank Herbert's author entry in *The Encyclopedia of Science Fiction*: http://sf-encyclopedia.com/entry/herbert – frank

Some terms above are capitalised when they would not normally be so rendered; this indicates that the terms represent discrete entries in *The Encyclopedia of Science Fiction.*

THE DRAGON IN THE SEA

*To the 'special' men of the United States
Submarine Service – chosen as crewmen on
the first atomic submarines – this story
is respectfully dedicated*

The blonde WAVE secretary at the reception desk took the speaker cup of a sono-typer away from her mouth, bent over an intercom box.

'Ensign Ramsey is here, sir,' she said.

She leaned back, stared up at the redheaded officer beside her desk. His collar bore the zigzag of electronics specialist over the initials BP – Bureau of Psychology. He was a tall man, round-faced, with the soft appearance of overweight. Freckles spotted his pinkish face, giving him the look of a grown-up Tom Sawyer.

'The admiral's usually a little slow answering,' said the receptionist.

Ramsey nodded, looked at the door beyond her. Gold lettering on a heavy oak panel: *CONFERENCE ROOM – Sec. I.* Security One. Above the clatter of office sounds, he could hear the tooth-tingling hum of a detection scrambler.

Through his mind passed the self-questionings he could never avoid, the doubts that had made him a psychologist: *If they have a rough job for me, can I do it? What would happen if I turned it down?*

'You can rest that here on the desk,' said the receptionist. She pointed to a black wooden box, about a foot on a side, which Ramsey carried under his left arm.

'It's not heavy,' he said. 'Maybe the admiral didn't hear you the first time. Could you try again?'

'He heard me,' she said. 'He's busy with a haggle of braid.' She nodded toward the box. 'Is that what they're waiting for?'

Ramsey grinned. 'Why couldn't they be waiting for me?'

She sniffed. 'Enough braid in there to founder a subtug. *They* should be waiting for an *ensign*. There's a war on, mister. You're just the errand boy.'

A wave of resentment swept over Ramsey. *You insolent bitch*, he thought. *I'll bet you don't date anything less than a full commander.* He wanted to say something biting, but the words wouldn't come.

The receptionist returned the sono-typer cup to her mouth, went back to her typing.

5

I've been an ensign so long I'll even take lip from a WAVE yeoman, he thought. He turned his back on her, fell to musing. *What do they want with me? Could it be that trick on the* Dolphin? *No. Obe would have said. This might be important, though. It could be my big chance.*

He heard the receptionist behind him take a sheet of paper from her machine, replace it.

If I got a big assignment and came back a hero, she'd be the kind who'd try to beat Janet's time with me. The world's full of 'em.

Why do they want me in Sec. I?

Obe had just said to bring the telemetering equipment for the remote-control vampire gauge and show up on the Sec. I doorstep at 1400. Nothing more. Ramsey glanced at his wrist watch. A minute to go.

'Ensign Ramsey?' A masculine voice sounded behind him. Ramsey whirled. The conference-room door stood open. A gray-haired line captain leaned out, hand on door. Beyond the captain, Ramsey glimpsed a long table strewn with papers, maps, pencils, overflowing ash trays. Around the table sat uniformed men in heavy chairs, almost like fixtures. A cloud of blue tobacco smoke hung over the scene.

'I'm Ensign Ramsey.'

The captain glanced at the box under Ramsey's arm, stepped aside. 'Will you come in, please?'

Ramsey skirted the reception desk, entered the room. The captain closed the door, indicated a chair at the foot of the table. 'Sit there, please.'

Where's the boss? Ramsey wondered. His gaze darted over the room; then he saw Obe: a hollow-cheeked little civilian, straggly goatee, thin bird features, seated between two burly commodores like a prisoner under guard. The little civilian's radiation-blinded eyes stared straight ahead. The mound of a radar bat-eye box atop one shoulder gave him a curious unbalanced appearance.

Ramsey sat down in the chair indicated, allowed himself an inward chuckle at the thought of the two commodores guarding Dr Richmond Oberhausen, director of BuPsych. *Obe could reduce them to quivering jelly with ten words.*

The captain who had admitted Ramsey took a chair well down the table. Ramsey moved his black box to his lap, noted eyes following the movement.

Obe has briefed them on my little invention, he thought.

The hum of the detection scrambler was strong in the room. It made Ramsey's teeth ache. He closed his eyes momentarily, blanked off the pain, opened his eyes, stared back at the men examining him. He recognized several of the faces.

Very high braid.

Directly opposite at the other end of the table sat Admiral Belland, ComSec, the high mogul of Security, a steely- eyed giant with hook nose, thin slit of a mouth.

He looks like a pirate, thought Ramsey.

Admiral Belland cleared his throat in a hoarse rumble, said, 'This is the ensign we've been discussing, gentlemen.'

Ramsey's eyebrows went up a notch. He looked to Dr Oberhausen's impassive face. The BuPsych chief appeared to be waiting.

'You know this ensign's Security rating,' said Belland. 'It's presumed we can talk freely in front of him. Would any of you care to ask him—'

'Excuse me, please,' Dr Oberhausen arose from between the two commodores with a slow, self-assured movement. 'I have not acquainted Mr Ramsey with any of the particulars of this meeting. In view of the assignment we have in mind, it would appear more humane if we did not treat him like a piece of dry goods.' The sightless eyes turned toward Belland. 'Eh, Admiral?'

Belland leaned forward. 'Certainly, Doctor. I was just coming to that.'

The admiral's voice carried a tone somewhere between fear and deference.

Ramsey thought: *Obe is running this meeting pretty much as he wants, and without these birds being certain they're outmaneuvered. Now, he probably wants me to pick up a cue and help him apply the clincher.*

Dr Oberhausen sank back into his chair with a stiff, stick-like gesture. A punctuation.

Belland's chair rasped on the floor. He got to his feet, went to the side wall at his left, indicated a north-polar projection map. 'Ensign Ramsey, we've lost twenty subtugs in these waters over the past twenty weeks,' he said. He turned to Ramsey altogether like a schoolteacher about to propound a problem. 'You're familiar with our pressing need for oil?'

Familiar? Ramsey restrained a wry smile. Through his mind sped the almost interminable list of regulations on oil conservation: inspections, issuance forms, special classes, awards for innovations. He nodded.

The admiral's bass rumble continued: 'For almost two years now we've been getting extra oil from reservoirs under the marginal seas of the Eastern Powers' continental shelf.' His left hand made a vague gesture over the map.

Ramsey's eyes widened. *Then the rumors were true: the sub services were pirating enemy oil!*

'We developed an underwater drilling technique working from converted subtugs,' said Belland. 'A high-speed, low-friction pump and a new type of plastic barge complete the general picture.'

The admiral's mouth spread into what he probably imagined as a disarming grin. It succeeded only in making him appear even more piratical. 'The boys call the barge a *slug*, and the pump is a *mosquito*.'

Dutiful chuckles sounded through the room. Ramsey smiled at the forced response, noted that Dr Oberhausen maintained his reputation as Old Stone Face.

Admiral Belland said, 'A *slug* will carry almost one hundred million barrels of oil. The EPs know they're losing oil. They know how, but they can't always be sure of where or when. We're outfoxing them.' The admiral's voice grew louder. 'Our detection system is superior. Our silencer planes—'

Dr Oberhausen's brittle voice interrupted him. 'Everything we have is superior except our ability to keep them from sinking us.'

The admiral scowled.

Ramsey picked up his cue, entered the breach. 'What was the casualty percentage on those twenty subtugs we lost, sir?'

An owl-faced captain near Belland said dryly, 'Of the last twenty missions, we lost all twenty.'

'One hundred percent,' said Dr Oberhausen. The sightless eyes seemed to look across the room at a beet-faced lieutenant commander. 'Commander Turner, would you show Mr Ramsey the gadget your boys found?'

The lieutenant commander pushed a black cylinder about the size of a lead pencil down the table. Hands carried the object along until it reached Ramsey. He studied it.

'Mr Ramsey's work, of course, involves electronics,' said Dr Oberhausen. 'He's a specialist with the instruments used for detecting traumatic memories.'

Ramsey caught this cue, also. He was the omniscient BuPsych electronics expert. The Man Who Knows Your Innermost Thoughts. *Ergo:* You don't have Innermost Thoughts in this man's presence. With an ostentatious gesture, Ramsey put his black box onto the table. He placed the cylinder beside it, managing to convey the impression that he had plumbed the mysteries of the device and found them, somehow, inferior.

What the devil is that thing? he wondered.

'You've probably recognized that as a tight-beam broadcaster,' said Belland.

Ramsey glanced at the featureless surface of the black cylinder. *What would these people do if I claimed X-ray vision?* he asked himself. *Obe must have hypnotized them.*

Belland transferred his tone of deference-fear to Ramsey. 'The EPs have been getting those things aboard our subtugs. We think there's a delayed-action device which turns them on at sea. Unfortunately, we've been unable thus far to dismantle one without exploding the anti-tamper charge.'

Ramsey looked at Dr Oberhausen, back to Belland, implying without words: 'Well, if they'd turn these problems over to BuPsych ...'

The admiral rallied some of his Pride of Department, said, 'Turner believes he has it solved, however.'

Ramsey looked at the beet-faced lieutenant commander. *And you'll be a rear-rank swabby if you fail,* he thought. The lieutenant commander tried to make himself inconspicuous.

The commodore to Dr Oberhausen's right said, 'Enemy agents aboard the tugs could be turning them on.'

Dr Oberhausen said, 'To make a long story short, these devices have been leading the enemy to our secret wells.'

'The real trouble,' said Belland, 'is that we're shot through with sleepers – people the EPs planted years ago – long before the war – with orders to wait for the right moment. People in the damnedest places.' He scowled. 'Why, my driver—' He fell silent, turned the scowl on Ramsey. 'We're reasonably certain you're not a sleeper.'

'Reasonably certain?' asked Ramsey.

'I am reasonably certain no one in this room is a sleeper,' growled Selland. 'But that's all I am.' He turned back to the wall map, pointed to a position in the Barents Sea. 'This is the island of Novaya Zemlya. Off the west coast is a narrow shelf. The edge is in about one hundred fathoms. It's steep. We've a well into the flank of that shelf tapping one of the richest oil reservoirs we've ever encountered. The EPs don't even know it's there – yet.'

Dr Oberhausen put a bony hand on the table, tapped a finger once. 'We must make certain Mr Ramsey understands the morale factor.' He turned toward Ramsey. 'You understand that it has been impossible to keep our losses completely secret. As a result, morale in the subtugs has dropped off to almost nothing. We need *good* news.'

Belland said, 'Turner, take it from there.' The admiral returned to his chair, lowered himself into it like a battlewagon settling into dry dock.

Turner focused watery blue eyes on Ramsey, said, 'We've screened, screened and rescreened our subtug crews. We've found one that looks good. They're at Garden Glenn Rest Camp now and will be coming out in five weeks. However, they do not have an electronics officer.'

Ramsey thought: *Great Grieving Freud! Am I going to be palmed off as a submariner?*

As though he had read Ramsey's thought, Dr Oberhausen said, 'That's where you come in, Ramsey.' He nodded to Turner. 'Please forgive me, Commander, but we're taking too much time with this.'

Turner shot a glance at Belland, sank back into his chair. 'Of course, Doctor.'

Dr Oberhausen arose, again with that air of vast assurance. 'This is my field, anyway. You see, Ramsey, the previous electronics officer suffered a psychotic blowup at the termination of their last mission. It's the same problem you were working on with the men of the *Dolphin*. Amplified. The subtugs are smaller, a complement of only four men. The focal symptoms point to a kind of induced paranoia.'

'The captain?' asked Ramsey.

'Precisely,' said Dr Oberhausen.

We are now impressing the natives with our mysterious knowledge, thought Ramsey. He said, 'I noticed similar conditions in the battle-fatigue syndrome when I was on the *Dolphin*.' He patted the box in front of him. 'The captain's emotional variations were reflected in varying degrees all through the ship's personnel.'

'Dr Oberhausen outlined your work with the men of the *Dolphin*,' said Turner.

Ramsey nodded. 'I'm troubled by one point here. You say this crew rates high. That doesn't check if the captain is a border-line psychotic.'

'Again, that's where you come in,' said Dr Oberhausen. 'We were about to beach this captain. But now Battle-Comp tells us he and his crew have far and away the highest chance of success in this mission to Novaya Zemlya. But only if certain other conditions are present.' He paused, tugged at an ear lobe.

Ramsey caught the signal, thought: *Ah, there's the bite. Somebody important hasn't agreed to this arrangement and it's vital to Obe that I get on that subtug crew. Who are we playing to? The admiral? No, he'd go himself if Obe said the word.* Ramsey's eyes abruptly caught the scowling glare of the commodore on Dr Oberhausen's left, and at the same moment he noted for the first time the tiny sunburst on the commodore's collar. *A presidential aide! That would be the one.*

'One of the other conditions would be that they have secret psychological monitoring,' said Ramsey. 'How had you planned to link in my remote-control vampire gauge to this pivotal captain without his knowing?'

'An ingenious solution has been proposed by Admiral Belland,' said Dr Oberhausen. 'Security has a new type of detector to combat those spy-beam transmitters. A speaker pellet is surgically imbedded in the neck and tuned to wave scanners which are similarly imbedded beneath the armpits. Micro-instrumentation would permit us to include with the speaker the recorders you need.'

Ramsey nodded toward the admiral. 'Clever. You'd rig this subtug skipper that way, send me along to keep him in balance.'

'Yes,' said Dr Oberhausen. 'However, there has been some objection raised.' The sightless eyes seemed to peer down at the commodore on his left. 'On the grounds that you have no extended deep-tug combat experience. It's a specialized service.'

The commodore grunted, glared at Ramsey. 'We've been at war sixteen years,' he said. 'How is it you've escaped combat?'

Old school tie, thought Ramsey. He turned his telemeter box until one flat surface faced the commodore, squinted at the officer over it. *When in doubt, fire a broadside.*

'Every man we preserve for combat brings victory that much nearer,' said Ramsey.

The commodore's leathery face grew dark.

'Mr Ramsey has a special combination of training – psychology and electronics – which have made him too valuable to risk,' said Dr Oberhausen. 'He has made only the most essential cruises – such as that with the *Dolphin* – when that was absolutely required.'

'If he's so valuable, why're we risking him now?' demanded the commodore. 'This all seems highly irregular!'

Admiral Belland sighed, started at the commodore. 'The truth is, Lewis, this new emotional-telemetering equipment which Mr Ramsey developed can be used by others. However, his inventive talents are the very things which make his services so essential at this time.'

'You may think me rude,' said the commodore, 'but I'd like to know also why this young man – if he's as good as all that – is still' – he flicked a glance at Ramsey's collar bars— 'an ensign.'

Dr Oberhausen held up a hand, said, 'Permit me, my dear Admiral.' He turned to the commodore. 'It is because there are people who resent the fact that I have been able to keep myself and my top department heads out of uniform. There are those who do not see the necessity for this essential separation. It is regrettable, therefore, that those of my people in the lower echelons, who are required to wear uniforms, sometimes find it difficult to gain advancement no matter how talented they may be.'

The commodore looked as though he were about to explode.

'By rights,' said Dr Oberhausen, 'Mr Ramsey should be at least a commodore.'

Several fits of coughing broke out simultaneously around the table.

Ramsey suddenly wished he were anywhere else but under the eyes of this commodore. The latter said, 'Very well, my objection is withdrawn.' The tone of voice said: *I will pass sentence in my own court.*

'I have planned,' said Dr Oberhausen, 'upon completion of this mission, to have Mr Ramsey released from the service and installed as head of a new department devoted to problems of submariners.'

A harsh smile pulled at the corners of the commodore's mouth. 'If he lives through it,' he said.

Ramsey swallowed.

As though he had not heard, Dr Oberhausen said, 'The training will be a problem, but we have five weeks plus the full facilities of BuPsych.'

Belland heaved his bulk from the chair, stepped to one side. 'If there are no more questions, gentlemen, I believe we are all satisfied with Mr Ramsey.' He glanced at his wrist watch. 'The medics are waiting for him now, and he's going to need every minute of the next five weeks.'

Ramsey got to his feet, took his telemeter box under his arm, a question in his eyes.

'You're also going to be rigged as a walking detection system,' said Belland.

Dr Oberhausen appeared to materialize beside Ramsey. 'If you'll come with me, please, John.' He took Ramsey's arm. 'I've had the essential material about Commander Sparrow – he's the captain of this subtug – and the other two crewmen reduced to absolute minimum. We've set aside a special ward at the bureau for you. You're going to be our prize patient for . . .'

Ramsey heard Turner speaking behind him. 'Dr Oberhausen called that ensign John. Is he the *Long John* Ramsey who . . .'

The rest was blurred as Dr Oberhausen raised his voice. 'It's going to be rough on you, John.' They stepped into the outer corridor. 'Your wife has been notified.' Dr Oberhausen lowered his voice. 'You handled yourself very well in there.'

Ramsey suddenly realized that he was allowing himself to be guided by a blind man. He laughed, found that he had to explain the laughter. 'It was the way you handled that brassy commodore,' he said.

'You don't lie at all well,' said Dr Oberhausen. 'But I'll let it pass. Now, about the commodore: he's a member of the board which passes upon promotions for BuPsych men.'

Ensign Ramsey abruptly found that laughter had left him.

Ramsey often referred to his five weeks' training for the subtug mission as 'The time I lost twenty pounds.'

They gave him three rooms in the sound wing of Unadilla Naval Hospital: blank white enclosures furnished in rattan and cigarette-scarred mahogany, a functional TV set, equally functional hospital bed on high legs. One room was set up for training: hypnophone, wall diagrams, mockups, tapes, films.

His wife, Janet, a blond nurse, received a weekend schedule for visits: Saturday nights and Sundays. Their children, John Junior, age two, and Peggy, age four, were not permitted in the hospital, had to be packed off to their grandmother's at Fort Linton, Mississippi.

Janet, wearing a one-piece red dress, came storming into the sitting room of Ramsey's suite on their first Saturday night. She kissed him, said, 'I knew it!'

'Knew what?'

'That sooner or later the Navy and that awful Obe would be regulating our sex life.'

Ramsey, aware that everything he said and did in the hospital was being monitored, tried to shush her.

'Oh, I know they're listening,' she said. She threw herself onto the rattan couch, crossed her legs, lighted a cigarette, which she puffed furiously. 'That Obe gives me the creeking creeps,' she said.

'That's because you let him,' said Ramsey.

'And because that's the effect he wants to give,' she countered.

'Well . . . yes,' admitted Ramsey.

Janet jumped to her feet, threw herself into his arms. 'Oh, I'm being a fool. They said I wasn't to upset you.'

He kissed her, rumpled her hair. 'I'm not upset.'

'I told them I couldn't upset you if I tried.' She pushed away from him. 'Darling, what is it this time? Something dangerous? It isn't another one of those horrible submarines?'

'I'm going to be working with some oilmen,' he said.

She smiled. 'Oh, that doesn't sound bad at all. Will you be drilling a well?'

'The well's already drilled,' he said. 'We're going to see about increasing production.'

Janet kissed his chin. 'Old efficiency expert.'

'Let's go to dinner,' he said. 'How're the kids?'

They went out, arm in arm, chatting about the children.

Ramsey's weekday routine began at 0500 when the nurse entered with his wake-up shot to rouse him from the hypnophone drugs. High-protein breakfast. More shots. Blood test.

'This is going to hurt a little.'

'Owoooooooch! Whatta y' mean a little? Next time warn me!'

'Don't be a big baby.'

Diagrams. Floor plans of Hell Diver Class subtugs.

They turned him over to a large subtug expert from Security. Clinton Reed. Bald as an egg. Thin eyes, thin nose, thin mouth, thick skin. Sense of duty as solid as his neck. Absolutely no sense of humor.

'This is important, Ramsey. You have to be able to go anywhere on this vessel, man any control blindfolded. We'll have a mock-up for you in a couple of days. But first you have to get a picture of it in your mind. Try flashing these plans and then we'll test your memory.'

'Okay. I've finished the general layout. Try me.'

'Where's the pile room?'

'Ask me something hard.'

'Answer the question.'

'Oh, all right. It's forward in the bulb nose; first thirty-two feet.'

'Why?'

'Because of the teardrop shape of this class, and for balance. The nose gives the most room for shielding.'

'How thick is the radiation wall behind the pile room?'

'I missed that.'

'Twelve feet. Remember it. Twelve feet.'

'Well, I can tell you what it's made of: hafnium, lead, graphite, and poroucene.'

'What's on the aft face of the radiation wall?'

'Direct-reading gauges for the reactor. Repeaters are in the control room, forward bulkhead to the right of the first-level catwalk. Then there are lockers for ABG suits, tool lockers, doors to the tunnels leading into the pile room.'

'You're getting it. How many tunnels into the pile room?'

'Four. Two top; two bottom. Not to be entered for more than twelve minutes at a time unless wearing an ABG suit.'

'Fine. What's the rated horsepower?'

'Two hundred and seventy-three thousand, reduced to about two hundred and sixty thousand by the silencer planes behind the screw.'

'Excellent! How long is the engine room?'

'Uh . . . nope. That one's gone, too.'

'Look, Ramsey, these are important. You have to remember these distances. You have to get a feeling for them. What if you don't have any lights?'

'Okay. Okay. How long is the damned thing?'

'Twenty-two feet. It fills the whole midship section. The four electric engines are set two to a level with the gearbox for the drive below center aft.'

'Gotcha. Here, let me take a flash of the aft section. Okay. Now try me.'

'How many catwalks in the engine room and where located?'

'Look, I just flashed the *aft* section.'

'How many catwalks and—'

'Okaaaay. Let's see: one center of the control deck going forward. One off center into machine stores on the second level below. One called A level into top stores. Same for bottom level: called B level. Short bridging catwalks from A and B levels to the engines and oxy tanks. And one very short to the conning-tower-retracted which lifts into a section of steps when the tower is extended.'

'Good. You see, you can do this if you set your mind to it. Now, tell me how the four staterooms are placed.'

'Staterooms yet.'

'Stop dodging the question.'

'Wise guy! Let's see: captain is top-level starboard behind the electronics shack. First officer portside behind the recreation room-sick bay. Engineering officer starboard below the captain's quarters and behind the machine shop. Electronics officer portside below the first officer and aft of galley stores. That's the place for me. Gonna cut me a private door into galley stores.'

'Where's the galley?'

'That one I can answer. It's far port, top level, entered through the wardroom. Selector controls for the prepackaged meals are against the bulkhead separating galley and wardroom. The galley-wardroom unit is between control deck and rec room.'

'What's behind the staterooms?'

'Machinery of the Palmer induction drive.'

'Why an induction drive?'

'Because at the dive limit for Hell Divers, there can be no weak points in the hull, therefore no shaft through the hull.'

'You're getting the drive on the hypnophone tonight. Every man blindfolded. There'll be a model for you to work on day after tomorrow.'

'Oh goody!'

'What's the pressure hull limit for Hell Divers?'

'Three thousand and ten pounds to the square inch or 7000 feet.'

'Stick to your first answer. Pressure varies with different water conditions. You'd be okay at 7100 feet in one place, dead at 6900 another. Learn to depend on your static pressure gauge. Now let's go to the atmosphere composition. What's a vampire gauge?'

'A little device worn on your wrist during deep dives. Needle goes into your vein, tells you if your CO_2 diffusion is fast enough so you won't crock out. It also tattles on nitrogen.'

'What's minimum diffusion?'

'When you get below .200 on CO_2 you get the jeebies. If your blood CO_2 count goes to four percent you're in trouble. With nitrogen it's different. The subtug atmosphere is supposed to be entirely cleared of it. A small quantity of helium is substituted.'

'How do you get by with the high atmospheric pressure?'

'Aerobic carbonic anhydrase is fed into the atmosphere by the ventilator system. This speeds up the CO_2 loading and unloading of the blood, prevents gas bubbles forming.'

'You're good on that. Did you know it before?'

'My emotional telemeter is just a glorified vampire gauge.'

'Oh, sure. Now, why is the electronics officer so important?'

'Contact with the exterior control motors is by coded wave pulse. If the E-system breaks down when a subtug is submerged, it stays submerged.'

'Right. Now, let's go through the plans again.'

'Not again!'

'Start with the reactor room. In detail.'

'Slave driver!'

The nightly hypnophone sessions flooded Ramsey's mind with the new knowledge: pressure hull, resonating hull, tank hull ... pressure compensating system ... header box ... reactor controls ... search and sounding ... diving plane controls ... valve controls ... pile check-off ... sonoran automatic-navigation board ... atmosphere controls ... automatic timelog, Mark IX ... external and internal TV eyes, specifications for servicing of ... gyro controls ... tow controls ... plastic barge, oil, components of ... needle torpedoes, external racking system ... torpedo homing systems ... scrambler systems ... systems ... systems ... systems ....

There were times when Ramsey's head felt filled to the bursting point.

Dr Oberhausen appeared in Ramsey's quarters on the fourth day of training. The doctor's unpressed clothes gave him the appearance of a bedraggled robin. He came in quietly, sat down beside Ramsey, who was seated in a viewerscope-sequence training hookup.

Ramsey pulled the fitted faceplate away from his eyes, turned to Dr Oberhausen. 'Ah, the chief of the inquisition.'

'You are comfortable, Johnny?' The sightless eyes seemed to stare through him.

'No.'

'Good. You are not supposed to be comfortable.' The doctor's chair creaked as he shifted his weight. 'I have come about the man Garcia who is engineering officer of this crew.'

'What's wrong with him?'

'Wrong? Have I said anything was wrong?'

Ramsey completely disengaged the viewerscope, sat back. 'Come to the point.'

'Ah, the impatience of youth.' Dr Oberhausen sighed. 'Do you have a file on Garcia?'

'You know I have.'

'Get it please, and read me what you have.'

Ramsey leaned to his right, took a file folder from the bottom ledge of his coffee table, opened it. Garcia's picture on the inside front cover showed a short man – about five feet seven inches – slim. Latin features – dark. Black curly hair. Sardonic half smile. The picture managed to impart a sense of devil-may-care. Under the photograph a note in Ramsey's handwriting: 'Member Easton championship water-polo team. Likes handball.'

'Read to me,' said Dr Oberhausen.

Ramsey turned the page, said, 'Age thirty-nine. Came up from ranks. Ex-CPO machinist. Ham radio license. Born Puerto Madryn, Argentina. Father cattle rancher Jose Pedro Garcia y Aguinaldo. Mother died at birth of daughter when Garcia age three. Religion: Catholic. Wears rosary around neck. Takes blessing of priest before each mission. Wife: Beatrice, age thirty-one.'

'Do you have her picture?' asked Dr Oberhausen.

'No.'

'A pity. I am told she is quite beautiful. Continue, please.'

Ramsey said, 'Educated at New Oxford. That accounts for his British accent.'

'I grieved when the British Isles were destroyed,' said Dr Oberhausen. 'Such a lovely culture, really. So basically solid. Immovable. But that is weakness, also. Continue, if you please.'

'Plays bagpipes,' said Ramsey. He looked at the doctor. 'Now there's something: a Latin American playing the bagpipes!'

'I see nothing wrong with that, Johnny. For certain moods, nothing is more soothing.'

Ramsey raised his gaze to the ceiling. 'Soothing!' He looked back at the BuPsych chief. 'Why am I reading this?'

'I wanted to get the full flavor of Garcia in mind before imparting the latest morsel from Security.'

'Which is?'

'That Garcia may be one of these *sleepers* who are giving Security so many *sleepless* nights.'

Ramsey snorted. 'Garcia! That's insane! As well as suspect me!'

'They are still investigating *you*,' said Dr Oberhausen. 'As to Garcia – perhaps; perhaps not. Counter-Intelligence has turned up the description of a sleeper supposed to be in the subtugs. The description fits Garcia. Security almost called off the mission. I convinced them to go ahead by suggesting that you be primed to watch Garcia.'

Ramsey returned to the color photograph in his file folder, observed the sardonic smile. 'I say we're chasing shadows. And that may be what the EPs really want. If it's carried to its illogical extreme, certain Security-thinking is first cousin to paranoia – dementia praecox type.'

Dr Oberhausen lifted himself from the rattan chair. It gave off a reedy creaking. 'Do not say that to the Security gentlemen when they come to brief you on Garcia,' he said. 'Oh, and one other thing: the commodore is sharpening knives with which to carve you if there is some error on this mission.'

'I have you to thank for that,' said Ramsey.

'I take care of my own,' said Dr Oberhausen. 'Fear not on that score.' He waved toward the viewerscope. 'Continue with your studies. I have other work.'

Ramsey waited for the door to close, threw the file folder back onto the coffee table, took twenty deep breaths to calm his nerves. Presently, he leaned to the right, captured the folders on the other two crew members, scanned them.

Commander Harvey Acton Sparrow. Age forty-one. Picture of a tall, thin man with balding sandy hair, a face of sharp planes, stooped shoulders.

He looks like a small-town college professor, thought Ramsey. *How much of that is conditioned on his early desire to teach mathematics? Does he resent the fact that his hard-crust Navy family forced him to follow in the old man's footsteps?*

Father: Rear Admiral Acton Orwell Sparrow, lost with subcruiser *Plunger* in Battle of Irish Sea, 16 October 2018. Mother: Genene Cobe Sparrow. Invalid (heart), lives at Waters Point Government Rest Home. Wife: Rita. Age thirty-six. Blonde? Childless.

Does Sparrow know that his wife is unfaithful? Ramsey asked himself. *Most of their friends are aware of it.*

Qualifications: navigator – superior; gunnery officer – superior;

medical officer (advanced first aid and pressure syndrome) – excellent; general submarine competence – superior.

Ramsey turned to the other folder.

Lieutenant Commander Leslie (none) Bonnett. Age thirty-eight. Picture of a heavy-bodied man (just under six feet) with brown wavy hair (artificial wave?), aquiline nose, overhanging eyebrows, the look of a brooding hawk.

Orphan foundling. Raised at Cape Neston Home for the Unwanted.

For the Unwanted! thought Ramsey.

Married four times. Two children – one by each of first two wives. Maintains marriage relationship with wife number four: Helene Davis Bonnett. Age twenty-nine. Miss Georgia of 2021.

The Unwanted, thought Ramsey. *He's carrying out an unconscious revenge pattern against women, getting even with the mother who deserted him.*

Qualifications: navigator – good; supply officer – excellent; gunnery officer – superior (top torpedo officer of subtugs four years running); general submarine competence – excellent plus.

Ramsey looked at the note in the psych record: 'Held from advancement to his own command by imperfect adjustment to deep-seated insecurity feelings.'

The Unwanted, he thought. *Bonnett probably doesn't want advancement. This way, his commander supplies the father authority lacking in his youth.*

Ramsey tossed the folders back onto the coffee table, leaned back to think.

An association of twisted and tangled threads.

Sparrow and Bonnett were Protestants, Garcia a Catholic.

No evidence of religious friction.

These men have evolved a tight working arrangement. Witness the fact that their subtug has the highest efficiency rating in the service.

What has been the effect of losing Heppner, the other electronics officer? Will they resent his replacement?

Damn! Heppner was the wrong one to go! A case history with no apparent clues. Quiet childhood. Calm home life. Two sour notes: a broken love affair at age twenty-four; a psychotic blowup at age thirty-two. It should have been someone like Bonnett. The Unwanted. Or Captain Sparrow. The frustrated mathematician.

'Sleeping?'

It was Reed, the constant tutor.

'It's three o'clock,' he said. 'I brought a layout plan of the electronics shack on these Hell Divers.' He handed a blueprint to Ramsey, pointed as he spoke. 'Bench here. Vise there. Wrench kit. Micro-lathe. Vacuum pumps. Testing-board plugs.'

'Okay, I can read.'

'You have to be able to plug into that test board in total darkness,' said Reed. He sat down squarely in the rattan chair lately occupied by Dr Oberhausen. 'Tomorrow you're going to start training on a mock-up.'

'Tomorrow's Saturday, Clint!' Ramsey glared at him.

'You don't get out of here before 1800,' said Reed. He bent forward over the plan. 'Now, concentrate on that plug layout. This here is emergency lighting. You'll be expected to find it the first time.'

'What if it takes me two tries?'

Reed leaned back, turned his flinty gaze on Ramsey. 'Mr Ramsey, there's something you should understand so thoroughly that it's second nature to you.'

'Yeah? What's that?'

'There is no such thing as a *minor* accident on a submarine.'

Commander Sparrow trotted down the ramp from the tube landing, slowed as he stepped into the cavernous, floodlighted gloom of the underground submarine moorage. A fine mist of condensation from the rock ceiling far away in upper blackness beat against his face. He picked his way through the pattern of scurrying jitneys, darting, intent people. Ahead of him, the bulbous whale mound of his subtug rose above the pier; a 140-foot Wagnerian diva center stage beneath banks of floodlights.

Instructions from the final Security session jangled through his mind.

'Your crew has the top Security rating of the service, but you must remain alert for sleepers.'

'In my crew? Hell, man, I've known them all for years. Bonnett's been with me eight years. Joe Garcia and I served together before the war. Heppner and—' His face had crimsoned. 'What about the new E-officer?'

'You won't need to worry about him. Now, the inspectors assure us there are no enemy signal devices aboard your boat.'

'Then why this gadget in my neck?'

'That's just an added precaution.'

'What about this new man? What's his E-rating?'

'He's one of the best in the service. Here, look at his record.'

'Limited combat experience in gulf patrol! He's practically a dryback!'

'But look at his E-rating.'

'Limited combat!'

A jitney driver shouted at Sparrow, bringing him out of his reverie. He glanced at his wrist watch: 073 8 – twenty-two minutes until castoff. His stomach tightened. He quickened his steps.

Damn Security's last minute details!

Across the ebony velvet of the mooring pool he could see the glow tubes outlining the marine tunnel. Down the 160-mile slant of that tunnel, out into the underwater deeps of De Soto Canyon and the Gulf of Mexico – and beyond – ranged the enemy. An enemy grown suddenly, terrifyingly, one hundred, percent effective against vessels such as his.

It came to Sparrow that the marine tunnel formed a grotesque birth canal. This cavern carved under a Georgia mountain was nestled in the earth like a fantastic womb. When they took their vessel out to do battle they were born into a terrible world that they did not want.

He wondered what BuPsych would think of an idea like that. *They'd probably rate it as an indication of weakness,* he thought. *But why shouldn't I have a weakness? Something about fighting a war a mile and a half under the ocean – the unrelenting pressure of water all around – exposes every weakness in a man. It's the pressures. Constant pressures. Four men isolated in pressure, held in a plasteel prison as they are held in the prisons of their souls.*

Another jitney scurried across Sparrow's path. He dodged, looked up at his boat. He was close enough now to make out the name plate on the retractable conning tower high above him: *Fenian Ram S1881.* The boarding ramp swooped down from the tower in a long, graceful curve.

The dock captain, a moonfaced lieutenant commander in fatigues, hurried up to Sparrow, a check list in his hands.

'Captain Sparrow.'

Sparrow turned without stopping. 'Yes? Oh, hullo, Myers. Are all the ready crews off?'

Myers fell into step beside him. 'Most of them. You've lost weight, Sparrow.'

'Touch of dysentery,' said Sparrow. 'Got some bad fruit up at Garden Glenn. Has my new electronics officer showed up?'

'Haven't seen him. His gear came along earlier. Funny thing. There was a sealed box with his stuff. About so by so.' He gestured with his hands. 'Cleared by Admiral Belland.'

'ComSec?'

'None other.'

'Why was it sealed?'

'It's supposed to contain some highly delicate instruments to monitor your new long-range search equipment. It was sealed so no zealous searcher could foul the works.'

'Oh. I take it the new long-range gear is installed?'

'Yes. You're battle-checking it.'

Sparrow nodded.

A cluster of men at the foot of the boarding ramp snapped to attention as the two officers approached. Sparrow and Myers stopped. Sparrow said, 'At ease.'

Myers said, 'Sixteen minutes, Captain.' He held out his hand, shook with Sparrow. 'Good luck. Give 'em hell.'

'Right,' said Sparrow.

Myers headed for the foot of the dock.

Sparrow turned toward a heavy-bodied, hawk-faced man beside the ramp, First Officer Bonnett. 'Hi, Les.'

'Good to see you, Skipper,' said Bonnett. He tucked a clip board under his left arm, dismissed three ratings who were with him, turned back to Sparrow. 'Where'd you and Rita go after the party?'

'Home,' said Sparrow.

'So'd we,' said Bonnett. He hooked a thumb toward the submarine behind him. 'Final safety inspection's completed. Spare gear checked out. But there's a bit of a delay. Heppner's replacement hasn't reported.'

Sparrow cursed inwardly, felt a stomach-gripping surge of frustration-anger. 'Where is he?'

Bonnett shrugged. 'All I know is that Security called and said there might be some delay. I told them—'

'Security?'

'That's right.'

'Suffering Jesus!' barked Sparrow. 'Do they always have to wait until the last minute? They had me—' He broke off. That was classified.

'They said they'd do their best,' said Bonnett.

Sparrow pictured the complicated arrangements which would pass the *Fenian Ram* through their own defense network outward bound.

'It could take another day to set up a new passage time.'

Bonnett glanced at his wrist watch, took a deep breath. 'I told them 0800 was the latest. They wouldn't answer a damned one of my—' He fell silent as the ramp beside them rattled to descending footsteps.

Both men looked up, saw three figures coming down: two ratings carrying heavy-duty electronics detection gear, followed by a short, wiry man with dark Latin features. He wore stained service fatigues, carried a small electronic search box under his right arm.

'Don José Garcia,' said Sparrow.

Garcia shifted the search box to his left arm, stepped down to the dockside. 'Skipper! Am I glad to see you!'

Sparrow moved back to permit the ratings to pass with their load, looked questioningly at the search box under Garcia's arm.

Garcia shook his head. 'For God and Country,' he said. 'But sometimes I think I overdraw my account with God.' He crossed himself. 'The Security chaps have had us at this floating sewer pipe half the night. We've been over it from stem to stern four distinct times. Not a blip. Now, I say to you: they want me to make another search after we get underway down tunnel!' He raised his eyebrows. 'I ask you!'

'We'll have to do it,' said Sparrow. 'I've allowed time before our first contact point for total deep-dive inspection.'

'I say,' said Garcia. He grinned. 'You know, I've already gone and rigged for it.'

Sparrow answered the grin, felt some of the tensions inside him begin to unknot.

Bonnett glanced significantly at his watch. 'Twelve min—'

The whine of a command jitney's electric motor intruded upon him. All three men turned toward the sound. It came down the dark line of mooring slots, its single light casting an erratic Cyclops gleam upon the damp concrete. The jitney swerved up to the ramp, jerked to a stop. A redheaded man with round, innocent face sat beside the driver, clutching his uniform cap in his hands.

Sparrow saw ensign's bars on the man's collar, thought: *That will be my new E-officer.* Sparrow grinned at the man's obvious relief up on a safe arrival. The recklessness of the base jitney drivers was a standard service joke.

The new man put his cap over his red hair, stepped out of the jitney. The machine rebounded from his weight. The driver whirled the jitney back the way they had come.

The ensign stepped up to Sparrow, saluted, said, 'I'm Ramsey.'

Sparrow returned the salute, said, 'Glad to have you aboard.'

Ramsey handed his service record to Sparrow, said, 'No time to send these through channels.'

Sparrow passed the papers to Bonnett, said, 'This is Mr Bonnett, first officer.' He turned to Garcia. 'Mr Garcia, engineer.'

'Good to meet you,' said Ramsey.

'We'll soon dissuade you of that illusion,' said Garcia.

Sparrow smiled, offered his hand to Ramsey, was surprised to feel strong muscle in the new man's grip. The fellow just *looked* soft. Bonnett and Garcia also shook hands.

23

Ramsey was busy cataloguing his first visual impressions of the three men in the flesh. It seemed strange to be meeting these people for the first time when he felt that he already knew them. And that, he knew, would have to be concealed. Odd bits of knowledge about the personal lives of these men – even the names of their wives – could not be in the memory of a new man.

'Security said you might be delayed,' said Sparrow.

'What's got Security on its ear?' asked Ramsey. 'I thought they were going to dissect me.'

'We'll discuss that later,' said Sparrow. He rubbed at the thin scar on his neck where the Security surgeons had imbedded the detection-system speaker. 'Castoff is 0800. Mr Garcia will take you aboard. Get into fatigues. You'll be assisting him in a final spy-beam inspection as we get underway.'

'Yes, sir,' said Ramsey.

'Your gear came along hours ago,' said Garcia. He took Ramsey's arm, propelled him toward the ramp. 'Let's get with it.' They hurried up the ramp.

Ramsey wondered when he could break away to examine his telemeter box. He felt an anxiety – a need to study the first records on Sparrow.

That mannerism of rubbing his neck, thought Ramsey. *Extreme nervous tension well concealed. But it shows in the tight movements.*

On the pier, Sparrow turned to look across the mooring basin at a string of moving lights. 'Here comes our tow, Les.'

'Do you think we'll make it, Skipper?'

'We always have.'

'Yes, but—'

'"For now is our salvation nearer than when we believed,"' said Sparrow. '"The night is far spent, the day is at hand: let us therefore cast off the works of darkness, and let us put on the armour of light."' He looked at Bonnett. 'Paul wrote that to the Romans two thousand years ago.'

'A pretty wise fellow,' said Bonnett.

A bos'n's whistle sounded at the head of the dock. A swifty crane came darting up to take away the boarding ramp. Ratings hurried to attach the hooks, looked inquiringly at the two officers.

Men hurried along the pier, a new purposefulness in their movements. Sparrow swept his gaze over the scene. 'We're being asked to perform,' he said. He gestured for Bonnett to precede him up the ramp. 'Like the man said: Let's get with it.'

They climbed to the conning tower. Bonnett ducked for the cable rack which mounted the float for their TV periscope. As a matter of routine, he glanced at the housing, saw that it was secured for dive. He grasped the ladder arms, slid down into the subtug.

Sparrow remained topside. Around him, the mooring basin appeared a vast lake. He looked at the rock ceiling's blackness.

There should be stars, he thought. *Men should get one last look at stars before they go under the sea.*

On the pier below, scurrying figures moved to cast off the magnetic grapples. For a moment, Sparrow felt like a useless pawn being thrown into a sacrifice position. There had been a time, he knew, when captains conned their vessels away from the dock, shouting orders through a megaphone. Now, it was all automatic – done by machines and by men who were like machines.

A surface tug swung up to their bow, slapped its tow grapples onto them. White water boiled from beneath the tug's stern. The *Fenian Ram* resisted momentarily, as though reluctant to leave, then began a slow, ponderous movement out into the basin.

They cleared the slot, and another tug slid alongside their stern. The magna-shoe men leaped onto the *Ram's* silencer planes, hitched the tow and guide cables of the long plastic tube which stretched out across the dark water of the basin. Their shouts came up to Sparrow in the tower like the clear noise of children. He tasted a sudden oil-tainted breeze and knew they had crossed the path of a ventilator duct.

No special fanfare, no brass bands, no ceremony for the departure of a raider, he thought. *We are as a reed shaken with the wind. And what go we out into the wilderness to see? No John the Baptist awaits us. But it's a kind of baptism all the same.*

Somewhere in the darkness a klaxon hooted. *Turn and identify the man next to you. Another Security scheme: Show your identification when the horn sounds. Damn Security! Out here I identify myself to my God and none other.*

Sparrow looked astern at the set of the tow. *Oil. War demanded the pure substance born in the sediment of rising continent. Vegetable oil wouldn't do. War was no vegetarian. War was a carnivore.*

The tow tug shifted to the side of the *Ram* and now the sub was being nosed into the traveler rack which would carry it down to the underwater canyon and the gulf.

Sparrow looked at the control console in the conning tower, and the green *clear-away* light. He flashed the standby signal to the tug below him and, with a practiced motion, touched the controls to retract the tower. It slid smoothly into the sub, its plasteel lid twisting into the groove seats.

A chest microphone hung beside the tower console. Sparrow slipped it on, spoke into it: 'Rig for dive.'

He focused his attention on the dive board in front of him.

Back came Bonnett's voice, robbed of life by the metallic mutes of the intercom: 'Pressure in the hull.'

One by one, the lights on Sparrow's dive board shifted from red to green. 'Green board,' he said. 'Stand by.' Now he could feel the hull pressure and another pressure in his stomach. He closed the signal circuit which told the outside crews that the subtug was ready to go down tunnel.

The *Ram* shifted, lurched. A dull clang resonated through the boat. Across the top of the dive board amber lights flashed: they were in the grip of the tunnel elevator. Twenty hours of free ride.

Sparrow grasped a handhold beside the dive board, swung down and out onto the engine-room catwalk. His feet made a slithering sound on the catwalk padding as he made his way aft, crawled through the control-room door, dogged it behind him. His gaze paused for a moment on the hand-etched brass plate Heppner had attached beside the door – a quotation from some nineteenth-century pundit:

'No one but a crazy man would waste his time inventing a submarine and no one but a lunatic would go down in it if it were invented.'

Through the gulf shelf in the Florida elbow, De Soto Canyon slashes the soft peninsula limestone like a railroad cut: fourteen fathoms where it starts in Apalachee Bay, more than two hundred and sixty fathoms where it dives off into the ocean deeps south of Cape San Blas and east of Tampa.

The gulf exit of the marine tunnel opens into the canyon wall at fifty fathoms: a twilight world of waving fan kelp, red fingers of gorgonian coral, flashing sparkles of reef- dwelling fish.

The *Fenian Ram* coasted out of the dark hole of the tunnel like a sea monster emerging from its lair, turned, scattering the fish, and slanted down to a resting place in the burnt-umber mud of the canyon bottom. A sonar pulse swept through the boat. Detectors in the triple hulls responded, registered on control gauges of the navigation deck.

Garcia's clipped accent – oddly squeaking in the oxygen-high atmos-phere – repeated the check list as he watched the Christmas tree lights of the main board. ' . . . no leaks, trim weights balanced, external salvage air clear and pressure holding, atmosphere free of nitrogen, TV eyes clear and seeing, TV periscope surfaced and seeing; periscope gyro checks with—' His laughter echoed through the intercom: 'Seagull! It tried to land on the peri-box as I started to reel in. Lit on its fanny in the water.'

Bonnett's crisp tones interrupted: 'What's it like topside, Joe?'

'Clear. Just daybreak. Going to be a good day for fishing.'

Sparrow's voice rasped over the speakers: 'Enough of that! Was there anyone up there to spot the gull's flop? They could've seen our box.'

'Negative, Skipper.'

Sparrow said, 'Les, give me the complete atmosphere check. Vampire gauges everyone. Follow the check. Report any deviations.'

The patient inspection continued.

Ramsey interrupted. 'I'm in the induction-drive chamber. A lot of static here as I entered.'

Garcia said, 'Did you go back by the lower shaft tunnel?'

'Lower.'

'I noticed that myself earlier. We'll rig a ground for the scuff mat. I think that'll fix it.'

'I grounded myself before entering.'

Sparrow said, 'Run that down, Joe. Les, where are you?'

'Second-level catwalk in the engine room.'

'Relieve Joe on the main board. Ramsey, get into your shack. Contact with base in eleven minutes.'

'Aye, Skipper.'

Sparrow moved from his position on the control deck below Garcia to a point at the first-level door which was open to permit visual inspection of the big gauges forward on the radiation wall. *That room in the bow,* he thought. *That's what worries me. We can see into it with our TV eyes; gauges tell us what's happening. But we can't touch it with our bare hands. We don't have a real feeling for that place.*

He mopped his forehead with a large red handkerchief. *Something, somewhere is wrong.* He was a subtug skipper who had learned to depend on his feeling for the boat.

A string of Spanish curses in Garcia's voice, rendered metallic by the intercom, interrupted his reverie.

Sparrow barked: 'Joe! What's wrong?' He turned toward the stern, as though to peer through the bulkheads.

'Wiper rag in the rotor system. It was rubbing the induction ring every revolution. That's Ramsey's static.'

'Does it look deliberate?'

'Did you ever come across a *silk* wiping rag?' The sound of a grunt came over the intercom. 'There, by heaven!'

Sparrow said, 'Save that rag.' Then: 'Ramsey, where are you?'

'In the shack warming up the transmitter.'

'Did you hear Joe?'

'Yes.'

'Tell base about that rag. Tell them—'

'Skipper!' It was Garcia's voice. 'There's oil in the atmosphere back here!'

Sparrow said, 'A mist of oil plus static spark equals an explosion! Where's that oil coming from?'

'Just a minute.' A clanking of metal against metal. 'Open pet-cock in the lube system. Just a crack. Enough to squirt a fine spray under full drive.'

Sparrow said, 'Ramsey, include that in the report to base.'

'Aye, Skipper.'

'Joe, I'm coming back there,' said Sparrow. 'We're going over that drive room with a microscope.'

'I've already started.'

Bonnett said, 'Skipper, would you send Ramsey up here after he gets off the contact? I'll need help checking the main board.'

'Hear that, Ramsey?' asked Sparrow.

'Aye.'

'Comply.'

'Will do.'

Sparrow went aft, dropped down to the lower level, crawled through the shaft tunnel and into the drive room – a cone-shaped space dominated by the gleaming brass induction ring, the spaced coils. He could smell the oil, a heavy odor. Garcia was leaning into the coil space, examining the induction ring by magnifying glass.

'They're just little things,' said Sparrow. 'But taken together – boom!'

Garcia turned, his eyes glittering in the harsh work lights. 'I don't like the feel of things, Skipper. This is a bad beginning. This is starting like a *dead-man* mission.'

Sparrow took a deep breath, exhaled slowly. With an abrupt motion, he thumbed the button of his chest mike. 'Ramsey, when you contact base, request permission to return.'

'Aye, Skipper.'

Ramsey's thoughts leaped. *What will that do to morale? The first raider in months turns back without getting out of the gulf. Bad.* He stared at the wavering fingers of the dial needles. His contact timer hit the red line, buzzed. He rapped out the first pulse with its modulated message: 'Able John to Red Hat. Over.'

The speaker above his head hissed with background noise like a distant surf. Presently, a voice came out of it, overriding the noise: 'This is Red Hat. Over.'

'Able John to Red Hat: We've discovered sabotage aboard. A silk rag was put in the motor system of our drive room. A static spark from the rag could've blown us out of the bay. Over.'

'Red Hat to Able John. Stand by, please. We are routing your message to Bird George.'

'*Security!*'

Again the speaker came to life. 'Bird George to Able John. This is Teacher. What is the situation? Over.'

Clint Reed! Ramsey could almost see the humorless face of his Security teacher. *Teacher Reed. Impromptu code.* Ramsey bent over his own mike: 'Teacher, this is Student.' He repeated the story of sabotage.

'Teacher to Student. What's your suggestion? Over.'

'Student to Teacher. Permit us to go on with inspection out here. There's less chance for an unknown factor. Just the four of us aboard. If we check safe, allow us to continue the mission. Bad for morale if we came back. Over.'

'Teacher to Student. That's the way we see it. But stand by.' Pause. 'Permission granted. How much time do you need? Over.'

Ramsey turned on his intercom microphone. 'Skipper, base suggests we continue the inspection here and not return if we check secure.'

'Did you tell him what we'd found?'

'Yes, sir.'

'What'd they say?'

'That there's less chance for a Security slip out here. Fewer personnel. They suggest we double-check each other, give every—'

'Suffering Jesus!'

'They want to know how much time we'll need.'

Silence.

'Skipper, they—'

'I heard you. Tell them we'll need ten hours.'

Ramsey turned back to his transmitter. 'Student to Teacher. Skipper says give us ten hours. Over.'

'Teacher to Student. Continue as ordered. We'll clear new check points for you. Over and out.'

Ramsey sat back, thought: *Now, I've really stuck my neck out. But Obe said this one has to go through.*

Bonnett's voice rasped over the intercom: 'Ramsey! If that contact's over, get your ass up here and help me on this board!'

'Coming.'

In the drive room, Sparrow hefted a socket wrench, looked at Garcia crouched under the secondary coils. 'They want this one to go through, Joe. Very badly.'

Garcia put a contact light on two leads. It glowed. 'Yes, and they give us a green hand like that Ramsey. A near dryback.'

'His service record says limited combat in gulf Security patrols.'

'Get the priest and the parish!' He shifted to a new position. 'Something odd about the chap!'

Sparrow opened the plate over a condenser. 'How so?'

'He strikes me like a ringer, a chap who pretends to be one thing when he's actually something else.'

'Where do you get that idea?'

'I really couldn't say, Skipper.'

Sparrow shrugged, went on with his work. 'I dunno, Joe. We'll go into it later. Hand me that eight-inch flex wrench, please.'

Garcia reached up with the wrench, turned back to his own work. Silence came over the little room, broken only by the sound of metal on metal, buzzing of test circuits.

Sparrow ducked through the door into the control room, stood silently as Bonnett and Ramsey reinstalled the final cover plate of the main board.

Bonnett straightened, rubbed the back of his neck. His hand left a grease smear. He spoke to Ramsey: 'You're a boy, Junior. We may make a submariner out of you yet. You've just gotta remember that down here you never make the same mistake once.'

Ramsey racked a screw driver in his tool kit, closed the kit, turned, saw Sparrow. 'All secure, Skipper?'

Sparrow didn't answer at once. He looked around the control room, sniffed the air. Faint smell of ozone. A distant humming of standby machinery. The round eyes of the indicator dials like symbiotic extensions of himself. The plucking disquiet remained within him.

'As secure as mortals can make it – I hope,' he said. 'We'll repair to the wardroom.' Sparrow turned, ducked out the way he had entered.

Ramsey put his tool kit into its wall rack. Metal grated against metal. He shivered, turned. Bonnett was going through the door. Ramsey stepped across the control room, ducked through the door, followed Bonnett into the wardroom. Sparrow and Garcia already were there, Garcia seated to the right, Sparrow standing at the opposite end of the table. Ramsey's eyes widened. An open Bible lay on the table before Sparrow.

'We invoke the help of the Almighty upon our mean endeavors,' said Sparrow.

Bonnett slipped into a chair at the left.

Sparrow indicated the seat opposite himself. 'Will you be seated, please, Mr Ramsey?'

Ramsey lowered himself into the chair, rested one hand on the green felt of the table cover. Sparrow towered above them at the other end of the table. *The Giver of the Law with hand upon the Book.*

Religious services, thought Ramsey. *Here's one of the binding forces of this crew. Participation Mystique! The consecration of the warriors before the foray.*

'What is your religion, Mr Ramsey?' asked Sparrow.

Ramsey cleared his throat. 'Protestant Episcopal.'

'It's not really important down here,' said Sparrow. 'I was merely curious. We have a saying in the subtugs that the Lord won't permit a *live* atheist to dive below a thousand feet.'

Ramsey smiled.

Sparrow bent over the Bible. His voice rumbled as he read: '"Woe unto them that call evil good, and good evil: that put darkness for light, and light for darkness; that put bitter for sweet, and sweet for bitter! Woe unto them that are wise in their own eyes, and prudent in their own sight!"'

He closed the Bible, lifted his head. It was a movement of power, of authority. Ramsey received an impression of deep strength.

'We do our job with what we have at hand,' said Sparrow. 'We do what we believe to be the *right* thing. Though it grieve us, we do it. We do it that the godless shall perish from the earth. Amen.'

Sparrow turned away, placed the Bible in a case against the bulkhead. With his back still turned to them, he said, 'Stations, everyone. Mr Ramsey, contact base, tell them we are ready to go. Get the time for the first check point.'

Ramsey got to his feet. Foremost in his thoughts was the almost physical need to examine the first telemeter record on Sparrow. 'Yes, sir,' he said. He turned, ducked through the door to the companionway and across into his shack, contacted base.

First check point in four hours.

Ramsey relayed the information to Sparrow.

'Zero the automatic timelog,' said Sparrow. 'Check in, everyone.'

'Garcia here. Drive and tow secure.'

'Bonnett here. Main secure.'

Ramsey looked at his board in the electronics shack. A queer sensation of belonging here passed over him. A sense of familiarity, of association deeper and longer than the five weeks of training. 'E-board secure,' he said. 'Two atmospheres in the hull.' He looked to the vampire gauge on his wrist. 'Diffusion normal-plus. No nitrogen.'

Back came Sparrow's voice over the intercom: 'Les, slide off.'

Ramsey felt the subtug lurch, then a faint whispering pulse of power. The deck assumed a slight upward incline, leveled. Presently, it tipped down.

We're headed into the deeps, thought Ramsey. *Physically and mentally. From here on it's up to me.*

'Mr Ramsey, come to the control deck,' Sparrow ordered.

Ramsey closed down his board, went forward. Sparrow stood, hands behind his back, feet braced slightly apart almost precisely in the center of the control deck. He appeared framed in a background maze of pipes, wheels, levers, and dials. To his right, Garcia worked the tow controls; to his left, Bonnett held the high-speed pilot wheel. The big static pressure gauge high in the control bulkhead registered 1,310 pounds, increasing; they were below 3,000 feet.

Without turning, Sparrow asked, 'What's in that little box that came aboard with your effects, Mr Ramsey?'

'Monitoring equipment for the new search system, sir.'

Sparrow's head moved to follow the flickering of a tow-control dial; he turned back. 'Why was it locked?'

'It's extremely delicate and packed accordingly. They were afraid someone—'

'I'll want to see it at the first opportunity,' said Sparrow. He stepped over behind Bonnett. 'Les, is that a leak in compartment nine?'

'There's no moisture or pressure variant, Skipper. It has to be condensation.'

'Keep an eye on it.' Sparrow stepped back beside Ramsey.

I'm going to find out quick if that disguise system in the box satisfies his curiosity, thought Ramsey.

'What's your hobby?' he asked Ramsey.

Ramsey blinked. 'Astronomy.'

Bonnett spoke over his shoulder: 'That's a peculiar hobby for a submariner.'

Before Ramsey could reply, Sparrow said, 'There's nothing wrong with astronomy for a man who goes to sea.'

'The basis of navigation,' said Ramsey.

Sparrow glanced sidelong at Ramsey, returned his gaze to the board. 'I was thinking as we moved out across the mooring basin back at base that we were entitled to a last look at the stars before going under the sea. They give one a sense of orientation. One night before we left Garden Glenn I was struck by the clarity of the sky. The constellation of Hercules was—' He broke off as the *Ram*'s nose tipped upward.

A down hands moved over his controls to correct for the deflection.

'Hercules,' said Ramsey. 'Do you mean the Kneeler?'

'Not many call him that any more,' said Sparrow. 'I like to think of him up there all these centuries, guiding mariners. The Phoenicians used to worship him, you know.'

Ramsey felt a sudden wave of personal liking for Sparrow. He fought it down. *I must remain clearheaded and objective*, he told himself.

Sparrow moved to the left to get a clearer view of the pilot gauges. He studied them a moment, turned to Ramsey. 'Has it ever occurred to you, Mr Ramsey, that these Hell Diver subtugs are the closest things to spaceships that mankind has developed? We're completely self-contained.' He turned back to the control board. 'And what do we do with our spaceships? We use them to hide under the liquid curtain of our planet. We use them to kill one another.'

Ramsey thought: *Here's a problem – a morbid imagination vocalized for the benefit of the crew.* He said, 'We use them in self-defense.'

'Mankind has no defense from himself,' said Sparrow.

Ramsey started to speak, stopped, thought: *That's a Jungian concept. No man is proof against himself.* He looked at Sparrow with a new respect.

'Our underground base,' said Sparrow. 'It's like a womb. And the marine tunnel. A birth canal if I ever saw one.'

Ramsey thrust his hands into his pockets, clenched his fists. *What is going on here?* he asked himself. *An idea like that should have originated with BuPsych. This man Sparrow is either teetering on the ragged edge or he's the sanest man I've ever met. He's absolutely right about that base and the tunnel and we've never spotted the analogy before. This bears on our problem. But how?*

Sparrow said, 'Joe, secure the tow board on automatic. I want you to go with Mr Ramsey now and test out the new detection gear. It should be ranged on our first check point.' He looked to the big sonoran auto-nay chart on the forward bulkhead and the red dot showing their DR position. 'Les, surface the peri-box and get a position reading.'

'Right, Skipper.'

Garcia closed the final switch on his board, turned to Ramsey. 'Let's go, Junior.'

Ramsey looked at Sparrow, a wish to be part of this crew uppermost in his mind. He said, 'My friends call me Johnny.'

Sparrow spoke to Garcia. 'Joe, would you also initiate Mr Ramsey into the idiosyncrasies of our atmospheric system? The carbonic anhydrase phase regulator would be a good place to start.'

Ramsey felt the rejection of his first name like a slap, stiffened, ducked through the aft door and into the companionway.

Garcia followed, dogged the door behind them, turned, said, 'You'd better know something about the subtugs, Ramsey. A new hand is always known by his last name or anything else the crew feels like calling him until after the first combat. Some guys hope they *never* get called by their first name.'

Ramsey cursed inwardly. Security had missed that point. It made him appear like a green hand. Then he thought: *But this is a natural thing. A unit compulsive action by the crew. A bit of magic. Don't use the secret name of the new man lest the gods destroy him . . . and his companions.*

In the control room, Bonnett turned to Sparrow, sniffed. He rubbed a hand across the back of his neck, turned back to the control board. 'He's green,' he said.

'He appears willing, though,' said Sparrow. 'We can hope for the best.'

Bonnett asked, 'Aren't you worried about that last-minute Security check-up on the guy?'

'Somewhat,' said Sparrow.

'I can't help it,' said Bonnett. 'The guy – something about him – I dunno. He strikes me as a wrongo.' Bonnett's shaggy brows drew down in thought.

'It could've been routine,' said Sparrow. 'You know the going over they gave us.'

'I'm still going to keep an eye on him,' said Bonnett.

'I've some paper work,' said Sparrow. 'Steady as she goes. Call me before the first check point.'

'What's the watch schedule?' asked Bonnett.

'That's what I'm going to be working on,' said Sparrow. 'I want to set it up so I can spend some time with Ramsey while we're still in comparatively safe waters. I don't want him goofing when the chips are down.'

Sparrow ducked for the aft door, went down the companionway and into the wardroom. The first thing that struck him as he entered was the color of the wardroom table cover – a cover and a color he had seen thousands of times.

Why is it that Navy wardrooms always have green table covers? he asked himself. *Is it a little of the color of the growing land? Is it to remind us of home?*

In the electronics shack, Garcia and Ramsey closed down the board after testing the detection gear.

'What now?' asked Ramsey.

'You'd better log a little sack time,' said Garcia. 'It's Les's watch. The skipper's probably setting up the schedule right now. You may be called next. Things are pretty loose the first day or so.'

Ramsey nodded, said, 'I am tired.' He turned aft, said, 'See you later.'

Garcia's 'Righto,' floated after him.

Ramsey hurried to his room, dogged the door, dragged out the tele-meter box, unlocked it, extracted the first record strips, sat back to examine them.

Pituitra and adrenaline high points showed early on the scrolls. Ramsey noted that one was before he arrived and the other coincided with the moment pressure was first bled into the hull.

The first tense moments, he thought. *But that's normal.*

He reeled the scrolls of telemeter tape forward to the moment the sabotage was discovered, double-checked the timed setting, scanned backward and forward across the area.

Nothing!

But that can't be!

Ramsey stared at the pattern of rivets on the bulkhead opposite him. The faint whispering of the drive seemed to grow louder. His hand on the blanket beside him felt every tuft, every thread. His nostrils sorted out the odors of the room: paint, oil, soap, ozone, perspiration, plastic . . .

Is it possible for a person to go through anxiety without glandular changes? he asked himself. *Yes, under certain pathological circumstances, none of which fit Sparrow.*

Ramsey remembered the sound of the captain's voice over the inter-com during the period of stress: higher pitched, tense, clipped.

Again, Ramsey examined the tape. *Could the telemeter be wrong?*

He checked it. Functioning perfectly. Could there be dysfunction in the mechanism within Sparrow's flesh? Then the other fluctuations would not have registered.

Ramsey leaned back, put a hand behind his head, thought through the problem. Two major possibilities suggested themselves: *If Sparrow knew about the wiper-rag-oil-spray thing then he wouldn't be anxious. What if he planted the rag and set that lube-system petcock himself? He could've done it to disable the ship and stop the mission because he's lost his nerve or because he's a spy.*

But there would've been other psychomotor indications which the telemeter would have registered.

This led to the other possibility: *In moments of great stress Sparrow's automatic glandular functions are taken over by the higher cortical centers. That could tie in with the known paranoiac tendencies. There could be a systematic breakdown of normal function under stress: such a turning away from fear that the whole being believes there could be no danger.*

Ramsey sat bolt upright. *That would fit the pattern of Sparrow's religious attitude. An utter and complete faith would explain it. There had been religious paranoiacs before. They'd even tried to hang the label on Christ.* Ramsey frowned. *But of course Schweitzer made the ones who tried look like fools. Tore their arguments to shreds.*

A sharp rap on Ramsey's door interrupted his thoughts. He slipped the tapes into the false bottom of the telemeter box, closed the lid, locked it.

Again the rap. 'Ramsey?' Garcia's voice.

'Yes?'

'Ramsey, you'd better take a couple of anti-fatigue pills. You're scheduled for the next watch.'

'Right. Thanks.' Ramsey slipped the box under his desk, went to the door, opened it. The companionway was empty. He looked at Garcia's door across the companionway, stood there a moment, feeling the ship around him. A drop of moisture condensing from the overhead fell past his eyes. Abruptly, he had to fight off a sense of depression. He could almost feel the terrible pressure of water around him.

Do I know what it is to be truly afraid? he asked himself.

The *Ram* moved to the slow rhythm of the undersea currents, hiding under every cold layer her crew could find because the cold water damped the sound of her crew; creeping between the walls of underwater canyons like a great blimp with a tail because the canyon walls stopped the sound of her passage.

Watches changed, meals were eaten. A chess game started between Sparrow and Garcia. The automatic timelog's hands swept around, around, around and around, clocking off the deadly dull routine of danger. The red dot marking their position on the sonoran chart crept around the tip of Florida, up the Atlantic coast and out into the ocean – a mite creeping toward Iceland.

Five days, thirteen hours, twenty-one minutes from point of departure.

Sparrow entered the control room, stooping for the door, pausing inside to sweep his gaze over the dials – his *other* sense organs. Too much moisture in the atmosphere. He made a mental note to have Garcia check that on his watch. Now, it was Bonnett's watch. The main board was set up for remote control. A repeater board was missing from its rack.

On the sonoran chart, their position marker stood almost due east of the northern tip of Newfoundland, and on a line south from the southernmost tip of Greenland: course sixty-one degrees, twenty minutes. The static pressure gauge registered 2360 pounds to the square inch: about 5500 below the surface.

Sparrow stepped across the control room, ducked through the door and out onto the engine-room catwalk. The catwalk padding felt soft under his feet.

Bonnett stood on the lower catwalk, back to Sparrow, staring down to the left. Sparrow followed the direction of his first officer's gaze: the door sealing one of the emergency tunnels into the reactor room.

Something odd about Bonnett's movements, thought Sparrow. *Looks like he's counting.*

Then Sparrow recognized the motion: Bonnett was sniffing the air. Sparrow took an experimental whiff himself, smelled the omnipresent stink of their recirculated air plus the ozone and oil normal to the engine room. He strode out onto the catwalk, bent over the railing. 'Something wrong, Les?'

Bonnett turned, looked upward. 'Hi, Skipper. Don't know. I keep smelling something rotten in here.'

Sparrow's lips twisted into a half smile. 'How can you tell in this stinkpot?'

'I mean actually rotten,' said Bonnett. 'Carrion. Rotting meat. I've been getting it for several days – every time I go past here.'

'Has anybody else noticed it?'

'They haven't said.'

'It's probably your imagination, Les. After five days in this floating sewer pipe everything stinks.'

'I dunno, Skipper. I can sort out most of the smells. This one doesn't fit.'

'Just a minute.' Sparrow stepped to the connecting ladder, dropped down to Bonnett's level.

'Take a sniff, Skipper.'

Sparrow drew in a deep breath through his nose. There *was* a faint carrion odor in the air, but then meat got high quickly in the heavy oxygen of a subtug's atmosphere. 'Could it be a dead rat?' he asked.

'How would it get aboard? Besides, we went over the *Ram* with a fine-tooth comb. A mosquito couldn't—' He broke off, turned, stared at the radiation bulkhead.

'There's one place we didn't comb,' said Sparrow.

'Still, we looked it over with the internal eyes,' said Bonnett. 'There—' He fell silent.

'Let's take another look,' said Sparrow.

He led the way back to the control room, keyed the master screen to the reactor-room scanners, one by one.

'Nothing,' said Bonnett. He looked at Sparrow, shrugged.

Sparrow glanced at his wrist watch. 'Joe went off standby about an hour ago.' He looked at the now blank screen. 'Get him up to that tunnel door anyway. Put Ramsey on stand by here in the control room. I'm going forward.' He stooped for the forward door, went out onto the catwalk, dropped down to the lower level.

In the control room, Bonnett went to the communications panel, buzzed Garcia. A sleepy voice came on the speaker. 'Yeah?'

'Skipper wants you forward. Number-one reactor-room tunnel.'

'What's up?'

'He'll tell you.'

Bonnett closed the circuit, opened the call network. 'Ramsey.'

'Aye. In the rec room.'

'Stand by on the control deck.'

'Right away.'

Bonnett clicked the call switch off, joined Sparrow at the tunnel door forward. Garcia was with them almost immediately, still buttoning his shirt, black hair tumbled over his forehead. 'Something wrong?'

Sparrow said, 'You made the last pile check, Joe. Did you open the tunnel doors?'

'Sure. But I didn't go inside. The Security crew gave us a clean—'

'That's okay. Did you smell something?'

Garcia frowned. 'You mean like with my nose?'

'That's right.'

'I don't believe so.' Garcia scratched his head. 'Why?'

'Take a sniff,' said Bonnett.

Garcia wrinkled his nose, inhaled. Again. 'Rotten.'

'Les has been smelling it for a couple of days.'

'Has anybody checked the ventilator duct?' asked Garcia.

'First thing,' said Bonnett. 'I couldn't be certain. Far enough in there it'd be a race between bacteria and sterilizing radiation.'

'With the bacteria winning as soon as we hit high oxy,' said Sparrow. He pointed to the screened outlet of the tunnel vent. 'It's worst right there. Joe, get me a length of our spare high-pressure tubing.'

'How long?'

'About twenty feet. Something that'll bend for the center dip of the tunnel and reach out into the open section.'

'Righto.' Garcia went aft and into machine stores.

Sparrow turned to a wall rack, broke out a portable TV eye and spotlight. 'All of us have a blind spot on the reactor room. We don't like to think about it. We count on the stationary eyes being arranged for maximum inspection. This way we'll lose one portable eye and one spotlight when they get hot, but we'll see into the odd corners.'

Garcia returned with the tubing. 'What're you going to do?'

'Rig a portable eye and light on the end,' said Sparrow.

Garcia blushed. 'I didn't think of that.'

'Like I was telling Les,' said Sparrow. 'Our minds don't function right on—'

Ramsey's voice came from the speaker on the bulkhead above them. 'I have you on my screen here. What's doing?'

Bonnett thumbed his chest mike. 'Something rotten in this pile-room tunnel.'

Sparrow looked up from where he was rigging the TV eye and light to the tubing. 'Have him take it from the portable board you left up there on the catwalk railing. We may need his help.'

Bonnett relayed the order.

Presently, Ramsey came out on the catwalk above them, checked the portable control board. He leaned over the railing, looked down at them. 'I just smelled it,' he said. 'Do you think it's a rat?'

'Don't know,' said Bonnett.

'Here.' Sparrow passed the tubing to Garcia, turned to the tunnel door, undogged it, paused. He looked up at Ramsey. 'Take that board back a ways.'

Ramsey complied, moving about ten feet back along the catwalk.

Sparrow nodded to Bonnett. 'Les, move over a bit.'

Bonnett stepped back out of line of the door. 'What're you expecting?'

Sparrow nodded toward the fixed radiation counter above the tunnel door. 'It may be a little warm. Keep an eye on that thing.'

Garcia brought a portable radiation snooper from its wall rack, stood beside Sparrow.

'Okay,' said Sparrow. 'Here goes.' He pulled the door open.

Garcia gagged.

'Wheee-ew!' gasped Sparrow.

'If you'll excuse the pun,' said Bonnett, 'I don't like the smell of that.'

Ramsey leaned over the railing. 'That's no rat,' he said. 'Too much of it.'

Sparrow took the length of tubing, snapped on the light. It was turned so that its beam flashed full into Ramsey's eyes, blinding him moment-arily. When Ramsey's vision returned, Sparrow had the tube pushed into the tunnel. Garcia was bent over the portable receiver beside the door, staring into the screen.

Ramsey tuned one of his own circuits to the portable unit, gasped as Garcia barked, 'Skipper! Look at this!'

The screen showed part of the downward curve of the tunnel floor. Just within view were the soles of a man's shoes and part of his legs. The picture stopped just below the knees.

Bonnett looked at Ramsey, who caught a glimpse of staring eyes under the shaggy brows. Sweat glistened on the first officer's forehead. 'You getting this on your screen?' he asked.

Ramsey nodded. Because of the angle of view, the men below him had a foreshortened, gnome-like appearance. A trick of acoustics brought their voices to Ramsey with a faint ringing quality. He felt like a man observing a marionette show.

Bonnett turned back to examine the fixed meter above the door. 'Radiation's up slightly,' he said.

'Nothing the filters can't take care of,' said Garcia.

Sparrow was bending over to maneuver the TV eye and light farther into the tunnel. Garcia moved the portable receiver back where Bonnett could see it.

'Anything?' asked Sparrow.

'More leg,' said Bonnett.

Ramsey became conscious of a low murmuring, realized that Garcia was whispering: 'Holy Mary, Mother of God . . .' The engineering officer's hands were tolling the Rosary under his shirt.

Sparrow gave the tubing a gentle twist.

'Knife!' blurted Bonnett.

Ramsey saw it on his panel. The hilt of a knife projected from the chest of the man in the tunnel.

'Get a record camera on this,' ordered Sparrow.

'I have it up here,' called Ramsey. He pulled the camera from its rack beside the control board, hung it over the receiver screen.

Sparrow pushed the tubing farther into the tunnel until the scanner picked up the man's face. 'Anybody recognize him?'

'I think I've seen him,' said Garcia. 'That's a rating uniform. Looks like atomic tech insignia.' He shook his head. 'But he's not one of the Techs I let aboard for the final embarkation check.'

Sparrow turned, looked up at Ramsey. 'How about you, Ramsey?'

'He's a special Security officer attached to Admiral Belland's office,' said Ramsey. 'His name's Foss or Foster. Something like that.'

'How do you know?' asked Bonnett.

Ramsey suddenly realized he had committed a tactical error. 'When I was with the gulf patrol,' he said. 'This bird was our Security liaison.'

The lie came easily. He remembered the last time he had seen the man: Belland's outer officer, Teacher Reed performing the introductions.

'Do you know what he was doing here?' asked Sparrow.

Ramsey shook his head. 'I can guess. He was probably making a special check when somebody caught him.'

'Caught him at what?' asked Garcia.

With an abrupt intake of breath, Ramsey recalled that Garcia was the suspected sleeper.

'It was probably the other way around,' said Bonnett. 'This Security officer caught somebody doing something and—'

'Doing what?' barked Sparrow. He turned to a locker to the left of the tunnel. 'Joe, help me into an ABG suit.' He opened the locker, pulled out a suit.

Garcia moved to help him.

Presently, Sparrow's voice came to them over the suit communicator: 'Les, get a contamination bag and a lead box for this man's effects. Leave it at the hatch here. Joe, get into another suit to help me when I bring him out. Ramsey, monitor me and get a still record of the items I hold up for you. Get a repeater on my suit's radiation snooper. I may be too busy to watch it.'

'Right,' said Ramsey.

Garcia already was pulling on another suit. Bonnett was moving aft toward the door into machine stores.

Sparrow ducked for the door, clambered clumsily into the tunnel. Immediately, the radiation-snooper repeater on Ramsey's board picked up the count.

'It's hot in there,' said Ramsey. 'I read it 5000 milli-R here.'

'I see it,' said Sparrow. 'Tune to my helmet scanner.'

Ramsey tuned another screen on his board to the scanner on Sparrow's helmet. The screen showed a gloved hand: Sparrow's. The hand moved out of range and revealed a portion of the dead man's uniform.

'Note,' said Sparrow. 'He left a note. Get a voice record of this as I read it and then photograph it. It's dated April 16, time 0845.'

Our embarkation day, thought Ramsey. *At that time we were in the marine tunnel.*

Sparrow's voice continued: '"To Captain H. A. Sparrow from Lieutenant Arthur H. Foss, SYO-2204829. Subject: Extra Security inspection subtug *Fenian Ram* this date."'

The captain cleared his throat, continued: '"Pursuant to new Security policy, I was making a special investigation of your atomic components following the regular check by the pile crew. This was to be a quick tunnel crawl for a look at the end plate and manuals. I did not wear an ABG suit because of the anticipated short time of the check and to maintain secrecy."'

Garcia had moved up to the tunnel mouth, hovering over it in his ABG suit like some other-world monster. 'You want me in there, Skipper?' he asked.

'Wait out there, Joe,' said Sparrow. He went on reading: '"My snooper's switch was accidentally turned off as I crawled through the tunnel and I received no warning that it was hot."' (Sparrow's voice quickened.) '"I found that one of your hafnium damper rods had been taken from the pile in the secondary bank and hidden in the tunnel. I was directly on top of it before I noticed it. There was no mistaking what it was. I turned on my snooper and immediately saw that I'd had a lethal overdose."'

Sparrow paused. 'May the Lord be merciful to him,' he said. He continued with the note: '"It was obvious that the damper rod had been selected for a timed overload, but the timing was not immediately apparent. It could have been set to blow at the base. Therefore, I made haste to slip the rod back onto the pile-room manuals and replaced it. I also repaired the alarm-system wiring where it had been cut to hide the sabotage."'

Sparrow stopped and Ramsey saw the note (through the scanner) change position as the Skipper shifted. 'Joe, did you notice any peculiar reaction from the alarm system?' asked Sparrow.

'Not a thing,' said Garcia.

Sparrow grunted, continued with the note: '"When the damper had been replaced, I looked for the communicator box at the pile end. It had been smashed. I then crawled back, thinking I'd get the medics to ease my dying. The tunnel hatch had been dogged from the outside and I was trapped. I tried to attract attention by calling through the vent, but there was no response. My own portable communicator would not work inside the shielding of the reactor wall."'

Sparrow's voice stopped. 'That explains it,' he said.

Ramsey bent over his panel mike. 'Explains what?'

'This tunnel vent opens from the inside. It should've been closed. But if it'd been closed we wouldn't have noticed—' He fell silent.

Ramsey's thoughts went to the actions of that Security officer: alone in the tunnel with the certain knowledge he was dying and nothing could save him. Spending his last minutes to guard the safety of others.

Would I have been as brave? he wondered.

Sparrow said, 'He put the knife in himself rather than go out the slow way alone in here. He says he doesn't know who sabotaged the pile and tripped him.'

'He could've attracted somebody,' said Ramsey. 'If he'd shorted one of—'

'And he'd have chanced shorting the wrong circuit and kicking every damper rod out onto the pile-room floor,' said Garcia.

'But the gravity catches—'

'How could he know what'd been fouled up in there?' demanded Garcia. His voice was choked with emotion. 'But suicide!'

Sparrow said, 'Joe, who were the last dock crewmen aboard?'

'Two snoopers I let aboard. I believe you saw them leave.'

Ramsey thought: *Garcia again.* He leaned over the catwalk railing, called down to Garcia. 'Joe, who were—'

Then he remembered that Garcia's suit would damp out the sound and turned back to his mike: 'Joe, who were those men?'

The blank faceplate of Garcia's suit tipped upward toward Ramsey. 'Two new ones. Their names are on the gangway check list.'

Sparrow said, 'Record this from the note, Ramsey.' He read: '"Whoever sabotaged your pile was hoping it would blow while this subtug was in the marine tunnel. Such a blowup would eliminate the subtug base until a rerouted tunnel section could be built. Obviously, the enemy knows of the existence of this base. Security should be notified at once."' The skipper's voice lowered. '"Please tell my wife that my last thoughts were of her."'

Garcia said, 'Those dirty, evil—' He choked.

Sparrow held up the note for his suit scanner while Ramsey photographed it.

'Is there anything else?' asked Ramsey.

'A notebook filled with what looks like Security code. Yes, here's a notation from Lieutenant Foss: "See that Security Section Twenty-Two gets this notebook".'

Ramsey saw the book through Sparrow's suit scanner.

Sparrow said, 'Record the pages as I hold them up, Ramsey.' He flipped through the pages for the scanner, said, 'I have the contents of his pockets. I'm coming out.' He backed out to the tunnel entrance.

Bonnett returned from the rear storeroom dragging a bulky contamination bag and a small lead box. He looked up at Ramsey, said, 'I listened in on the storeroom portable while I was getting this stuff. Lord, how I'd like to have my hands on the rats who scragged that poor guy!'

'You mean who almost scragged us,' said Ramsey. He bent over his panel mike: 'Joe, you'd better get that stuff from Les. He shouldn't go any closer to the tunnel without a suit.'

Garcia's voice issued from the speaker: 'Righto.' He went back to the engine-room floor to Bonnett, returned to the tunnel with the contamination bag and lead box.

Sparrow emerged from the tunnel, turned, said, 'Ramsey, record these items as I put them in the box. One Mark XXVII hand-snooper, one wrist-type communicator, one flashlight, one wallet with the following items: a picture of woman and child inscribed "All our Love, Nan and Peggy," one ID card issued to Lieutenant Senior Grade Arthur Harmon Foss, SYO- 2204829, one base gate pass, one mess-hall pass, one driver's license, currency and coins to sixteen dollars and twenty-four cents.'

He turned back to the tunnel, picked up another bundle tied in a handkerchief, untied the handkerchief clumsily with his heavily gloved hands. 'Here's some more: one fountain pen, one key ring with four keys, one fingernail clipper, one minicamera. The telltale's turned red: film's been ruined by radiation. One pocket recorder with wire blank.'

Sparrow dropped the bundle into the box. Garcia sealed it.

Ramsey glanced at his wrist watch, noted the time. *The telemeter record of Sparrow's reactions: what will it show for this period?* he asked himself.

Garcia straightened from the lead box. 'What's the pile end like?' he asked.

Sparrow nodded his head toward the tunnel mouth, a grotesque gesture in the bulky suit. 'Just as he described it. Everything back as it should be. All except the communicator box. Smashed. Why?'

'Maybe whoever did it anticipated the inspection,' said Garcia.

'Maybe.'

Ramsey's hands moved over his portable control panel, compensating for a minor course deflection caused by an upward current. When they were back on true, he looked over the railing. Garcia and Sparrow were just sealing the Security officer's body into the contamination bag.

Sparrow said, 'Les, when we get him out of here, flush this area out with the detergent hoses. Let me know what the radiation count is.'

Ramsey punched the switch on his panel mike: 'Skipper, that note could've been faked to throw us off. Did you think of that? It strikes me the man would've used his recorder.'

Garcia said, 'And taken the chance of having his message accidentally erased? No sir.' He dragged the sacked body under an engine-room hoist.

Sparrow said, 'Les, when you get this place cleaned, get into a suit and make another inspection of the end plate and manuals of that tunnel. I'm eight minutes from my limit.'

Bonnett acknowledged.

Garcia passed a snooper over the contamination bag. 'Hot,' he said. 'We'll have to get him overboard within twelve hours. Otherwise, I wouldn't be responsible for the filters clearing our air.' He racked the snooper, turned back, rigged a net under the bag.

Meanwhile, Bonnett had gone down the starboard side of the engine room, donned an ABG suit from that side and moved to the detergent hoses at the tunnel mouth.

Garcia took the slack out of the hoist line, turned toward Sparrow. 'Skipper, why don't you get Les to help you here and let me crawl the tunnel? That's my department.'

The faceplate on Sparrow's suit turned toward Bonnett, who hesitated beside the tunnel door. 'Okay, Joe. Les, give me a hand here.'

Bonnett stepped to Sparrow's side.

Garcia went to the tunnel door, turned back and looked up at Ramsey. The quartz viewplate gave him the appearance of a one-eyed monster. He turned back to the tunnel, bending down as he snaked his way inside. Presently, his voice came over the speaker to Ramsey: 'You with me, Junior?'

'I read you.'

'My suit snooper says it's hotter than a two-dollar pistola where the shield curve ends here. I'm at the halfway mark. Here's the tunnel communicator box. It's a mess.' (Pause.) 'I'm now at the manuals.' (Long pause.) 'The mirrors show no visible evidence of sabotage on this face of the pile. All secure. I'm coming out.'

In Ramsey's mind a single thought: *If Garcia's really a sleeper, what's he actually doing in there? Why was he so anxious to make that inspection?*

Ramsey wondered if he could think up an excuse to make a personal inspection of that tunnel.

Probably not, he thought. *Sparrow wouldn't risk having three of his crewmen take a near-limit dosage. He'd have no reserve if something else made it necessary to crawl one of the tunnels.*

Ramsey resolved to make as thorough an inspection as possible using the internal scanners.

Sparrow and Bonnett were hoisting the contamination bag up to the discharge tubes below the retracted conning tower. Sparrow said, 'Ramsey, take your board back against the aft bulkhead. That bag's leaking some.'

Ramsey complied, racking his board on the catwalk rail.

Sparrow left the hoist to Bonnett, stepped into the decontamination chamber against the port pressure hull, emerged without his ABG suit. He looked up to Ramsey, his long face drawn into serious lines. 'Is Joe on his way out?'

'He's on his way,' said Ramsey.

'Foss's ID card shows he was Catholic,' said Sparrow. 'Ask Joe if he'll read the service for the dead.'

Ramsey relayed the request.

Garcia, emerging from the tunnel, paused. 'He couldn't have been Catholic,' he said. 'Either that, or he was murdered. A good Catholic doesn't commit suicide.'

Sparrow heard Garcia's voice on the speaker, said, 'Suffering Jesus! He's right.' He looked thoughtful for a moment, found his chest mike, asked, 'Will you read the service?'

Garcia said, 'Under the circumstances, yes.' He closed the tunnel door, dogged it, stepped into a decontamination chamber and emerged without a suit.

Bonnett swung up to the central catwalk, anchored the hoist's load with a side line, returned to the lower deck and reeled out the detergent hoses. He began to spray the area.

Sparrow and Garcia mounted to the catwalk beside Ramsey.

'We'll surface at midnight local time for burial,' said Sparrow. He went aft through the number-one door without glancing up at the bundle swinging from the hoist.

Ramsey, watching Bonnett at work below him, again had the feeling of looking at a marionette show. *Last act, scene one.*

Garcia, beside him, said, 'My watch coming up. I'll take it on the main control deck.' He released Ramsey's portable board from the rail, carried it up to the central catwalk, ducked through the door in the aft bulkhead.

Ramsey followed, turned at the door for one last look at the long bundle swaying in the hoist net: a body in a sack. He turned, passed through the control room, went directly to his quarters and pulled out the telemeter tapes.

No significant deviations!

He coded the tapes for identification, placed them in the false bottom, lay back on his bunk. Around him he could feel the faint vibrations of the subtug: a feeling as of life. He seemed to fit into the pattern of the room, one with the crisscross of pipes overhead, the ventilator ducts, the repeaters for the electronics-shack instruments, wall mike and speaker.

Presently, he fell asleep, dreamed that he was a deep-dwelling fish trying to figure out a way to climb to the light of the surface far away above him.

The problem was that a terrible pressure held him trapped in the deeps.

At midnight they committed the body of Lieutenant Foss to the ocean. A cold, starless night, a high-running sea. Ramsey stood shivering on the deck while Garcia mumbled the service for the dead.

'Into Thy hands we commend this spirit.'

For Lieutenant Arthur Harmon Foss; last act, last scene.

Afterward, they homed into the depths as though fleeing the scene of a crime. Ramsey was startled by the faraway look in Sparrow's eyes, heard the captain whispering the lines from the first chapter of Genesis:

'" . . . and darkness was upon the face of the deep. And the Spirit of God moved upon the face of the waters . . . "'

From some recess in his memory, Ramsey recalled the next lines: '"And God said, Let there be light: and there was light."'

Ramsey thought: *If there is a God, let Him make things right for that brave guy.* It was his nearest approach to a prayer since childhood. He was surprised at the stinging sensation in his eyes.

Then another thought mingled with the memory of Garcia's voice: *And what if Garcia is the sleeper?*

The thought spurred him to hurry into the electronics shack, examine the contaminated tunnel through the internal scanners. The scanners showed only the pile-room end. Nothing appeared amiss. Ramsey activated one of the control-room scanners to check on Garcia. The engineering officer was bent over the portside grab rail, knuckles white from the pressure of his grip upon the rail, his forehead pressed against the cold metal of the pressure hull.

He looks ill, thought Ramsey. *I wonder if I should go down and relieve him?*

As Ramsey watched, Garcia straightened, slammed a fist against the hull surface so hard his knuckles bled. The *Ram* took this moment to tip slightly from the thrust of an undersea current. Garcia whirled to the controls, corrected for the deflection. Ramsey could see tears streaming down his face.

Abruptly, Ramsey switched off his screen, feeling that he had eavesdropped upon the workings of a man's soul and that it was wrong to have done so. He stared at his hands, thought: *Now that's a strange reaction for a psychologist! What's come over me?* He reactivated the screen, but now Garcia was calmly going about the business of his watch.

Ramsey returned to his quarters with the strong sense that he had blinded himself to something vital. For almost an hour, he lay awake on his bunk, unable to resolve the problem. When he fell asleep it was to sink again into the dream of the fish.

He awoke to his next watch with the feeling of not having slept at all.

●

There had been a time when people thought it would solve most seafaring problems to take ocean shipping beneath the surface storms. But, as had happened so many times in the past, for every problem solved a new one was added.

Beneath the ocean surface flow great salt rivers, their currents not held to a horizontal plane by confining banks. The 600 feet of plastic barge trailing behind the *Ram* twisted, dragged, and skidded – caught by currents flowing through 60 degrees at right angles to their course. If the current set downward, the *Ram* tipped upward and had to fight against the climb. If a current took the tow upward, the *Ram* headed down. Variations often gave the subtug's deck a stately rolling and tipping as though the vessel were beset by a slow-motion storm.

Automatics took care of most of the deflections, but many were sufficient to cause wide course error. Because of this, a portable gyro repeater always accompanied the man on duty.

Bonnett carried such a repeater on his remote-control panel as he prowled the engine room during his watch. The little timelog repeater beside the gyro dial showed seven days, eight hours, and eighteen minutes from departure. The *Ram* had moved forward deep into the ocean no man's land south of Iceland.

Maybe it'll be a milk run, he thought. *For all our detectors have shown, we could be alone in the whole damned ocean.* He fell to remembering the night before departure, wondered if Helene was really faithful to him. *So damned many Navy wives ...*

An amber light glowed at the upper corner of his board, the signal that someone had entered the control room. He spoke into his chest mike: 'I'm on the second-level catwalk in the engine room.'

Sparrow's voice came out of the board speaker: 'Continue as you are. I'm just restless. Thought I'd look around.'

'Right, Skipper.' Bonnett turned to examine the master control gauges on the reactor bulkhead. Ever since they'd found the dead Security officer, Bonnett had been nursing an uneasy feeling about the room in the subtug's nose.

A sudden needle deflection on his control board caught his attention. The outside water temperature had dropped ten degrees: a cold current.

Ramsey's voice came over the intercom: 'This is Ramsey in the shack. My instruments show a sharp ten-degree temperature drop outside.'

Bonnett thumbed his mike switch: 'What're you doing up and about, Junior?'

'I'm always nervous when it's your duty,' said Ramsey. 'I couldn't sleep, so I came in here to run an instrument check.'

'Wise guy,' said Bonnett.

Sparrow's voice joined them: 'Find out how deep it is, Ramsey. If it doesn't extend below our limit, we can hide under it and pick up speed. Ten degrees will cloud a lot of noise.'

'Right, Skipper.' Pause. 'Sixty-eight hundred feet, give or take a few.'

'Les, take her down,' said Sparrow.

Bonnett racked his control console onto the catwalk railing, took electronic hold of the diving planes. Abruptly, his static pressure gauge repeater showed what his sense of balance already had told him: they were going down too fast; an upcurrent was following them, lifting the tow. Bonnett fought it until they were inclined at a safe three degrees.

The *Ram* leveled at 6780 feet.

In the shack, Ramsey looked at his own repeater for the master pressure gauge: 2922 pounds to the square inch. Instinctively, his gaze went to the pressure hull beside him – a small length of it seen through a maze of pipes and conduits. He tried to fight away from the thought of what would happen if the hull should implode: bits of protein pulp floating amidst shattered machinery.

What was it Reed had said? It came back to Ramsey clearly, even to the impersonal tones of his instructor's voice: 'An implosion of external equipment at extreme depths may set up a shock wave which will split your hull wide open. Of course, it'd be all over for you before you'd hardly realized what happened.'

Ramsey shivered.

What is Sparrow's reaction to the increased danger? he wondered. Then: *I don't really care as long as his ability keeps me safe.*

This thought shocked Ramsey. He suddenly looked around his electronics shack as though seeing it for the first time, as though he had just awakened.

What kind of a psychologist am I? What have I been doing?

As though answering a question from outside himself his mind said: *You've been hiding from your own fears. You've been striving to become an efficient cog in this crew because that way lies a measure of physical safety.*

What am I afraid of? he asked himself.

Back came the answer: *You're afraid of your own personal extinction.*

'It'd be as though I'd died *en utero*,' he said, speaking the thought softly to himself. 'Never born at all.'

He found that he was trembling, bathed in perspiration. The plug holes of the test board in front of him seemed to stare back – a hundred demanding eyes. He suddenly wanted to scream, found he couldn't move his throat muscles.

If there was an emergency now, I'd be helpless, he thought. *I couldn't move a finger.*

He tried to will the motion of the index finger of his right hand, failed.

If I move I'll die!

Something touched his shoulder and he almost blanked out in frozen panic. A voice spoke softly beside his ear and it was as though the voice had shouted loud enough to split his eardrums.

'Ramsey. Steady, boy.'

'You're a brave man, Ramsey. You took it longer than most.'

Ramsey felt the trembling of his body had become so violent that his vision blurred.

'I've been waiting for this, Ramsey. Every man goes through it down here. Once you've been through it, you're all right.'

Deep, fatherly voice. Tender. Compassionate.

With all his being, Ramsey wanted to turn, bury his head against that compassionate chest, sob out his fears in strangled emotion.

'Let it go,' said Sparrow. 'Let it come. Nobody here but me, and I've been through it.'

Slowly at first, then in gasping sobs, the tears came. He bent over the bench, buried his face in his arms. All the time, Sparrow's hand upon his shoulder, a feeling of warmth from it, a sense of strength.

'I was afraid,' whispered Ramsey.

'Show me the man who isn't afraid and I'll show you a blind man or a dolt,' said Sparrow. 'We're plagued with too much thinking. It's the price of intelligence.'

The hand left Ramsey's shoulder. He heard the shack door open, close.

Ramsey lifted his head, stared at the test board in front of him, the open intercom switch.

Bonnett's voice came from the speaker: 'Ramsey, can you give us a sound-distance test now?'

Ramsey cleared his throat. 'Right.' His hands moved over the board, slowly, then with rapid sureness. 'There's enough cold stuff above us to blanket force speed,' he said.

The speaker rumbled with Sparrow's voice. 'Les, give us force speed. Ramsey, we are within ninety pounds of pressure limit. Remain on watch with Les until you are relieved.'

The humming of the *Ram's* electric motors keened up a notch, another.

'Right, Skipper,' said Ramsey.

Garcia's voice came over the intercom. 'What's up? I felt the motors.'

'Cold layer,' said Sparrow. 'We're gaining a few knots while we can.'

'Need me?'

'Come up here on standby.'

Ramsey heard the voices over the intercom with a peculiar clarity, saw the board in front of him with a detail that amazed him: tiny scratches, a worn plug line.

Back came the memory of his blue funk and with it, a detail his mind had avoided: Sparrow calling to him over the intercom to make the sound-distance test.

And when I didn't answer, he came immediately to help me.

Another thought intruded: *He knows how green I am – has known it all along.*

'Ramsey.'

Sparrow stood in the shack doorway.

Ramsey stared at him.

Sparrow entered, sat down on the bench stool beside the door. 'What are you, Ramsey?'

He cleared his throat. 'What do you mean?'

'Every man has to wrestle with his shadow down here. You held out a long time.'

'I don't understand you.'

'This life makes you face your fears sooner or later.'

'How did you know I was afraid?'

'Every man's afraid down here. It was just a matter of waiting until you found out you were afraid. Now, answer my question: What are you?'

Ramsey stared past Sparrow. 'Sir, I'm an electronics officer.'

A faint smile touched Sparrow's eyes and mouth. 'It's a sad world we live in, Ramsey. But at least Security picks its men for their courage.' He straightened.

Ramsey accepted this silently.

'Now, let's have a look at that little box of yours,' said Sparrow. 'I'm curious.' He stood up, went out into the companionway, turned aft.

Ramsey followed.

'Why not keep it in the shack?' asked Sparrow.

'I've been using my off time to check it.'

'Don't wear yourself out.' Sparrow dropped down to the lower level, Ramsey behind him. They entered Ramsey's room. The humming of the induction drive came through the bulkhead.

Ramsey sat down on his bunk, brought out the box, put it on his desk and unlocked it. *Can't let him look too close*, thought Ramsey. He noted that the disguise system was working.

Sparrow peered into the box with a puzzled frown.

What's he expect to find? Ramsey wondered.

'Give me a rundown,' said Sparrow.

Ramsey pointed to a dial. 'That monitors the sweep of the primary search impulse. The first models were plagued by feedback echo.'

Sparrow nodded.

Ramsey indicated a group of signal lights. 'These separate the pulse frequencies. They flicker red when we're out of phase. The particular light tells me which circuit is bouncing.'

Sparrow straightened, shot a searching glance at Ramsey.

'Tapes inside make a permanent record,' said Ramsey.

'We'll go into it at greater length some other time,' said Sparrow. He turned away.

He expected some Security gadget, thought Ramsey.

'Why'd Security plant you on us?' asked Sparrow.

Ramsey remained silent.

Sparrow turned, stared at him with a weighing look. 'I won't force this issue now,' he said. 'Time enough for that when we get home.' His face took on a bitter expression. 'Security! Half our troubles can be traced to them.'

Ramsey maintained his silence.

'It's fortunate you're a good electronics officer,' said Sparrow. 'Doubtless you were chosen for that quality.' A sudden look of indecision passed over his features. 'You *are* a Security man, aren't you?'

Ramsey thought: *If he believes that, it'll mask my real position. But I can't just admit it. That'd be out of character.* He said, 'I have my orders, sir.'

'Of course,' said Sparrow. 'Stupid of me.' Again the look of indecision. 'Well, I'll be getting—' Abruptly, he stiffened.

Ramsey, too, fought to keep from showing surprise. The pellet imbedded in his neck had just emitted a sharp *ping!* He knew that the identical equipment in Sparrow also had reacted to a signal.

Sparrow whirled to the door, ran forward to the control deck, Ramsey on his heels. They stopped before the big master board. Garcia turned from his position at the monitor controls. 'Something wrong, Skipper?'

Sparrow didn't answer. Through his mind was running a senseless rhyme born of the twenty kills the EPs had made in the previous months: *Twenty out of twenty is plenty ... twenty out of twenty is plenty ...*

Ramsey, standing behind Sparrow, was extremely conscious of the charged feeling in the control room, the stink of the atmosphere, the questioning look on Garcia's face, the clicking of automatic instruments, and the answering response of the deck beneath his feet.

The pellet in his neck had begun sending out a rhythmic buzzing.

Garcia stepped away from the board. 'What's wrong, Skipper?'

Sparrow waved him to silence, turned right. Ramsey followed.

The buzzing deepened. Wrong direction.

'Get a signal snifter,' said Sparrow, speaking over his shoulder to Ramsey.

Ramsey turned to the rear bulkhead, pulled a snifter from its rack, tuned it as he rejoined Sparrow. The instrument's speaker buzzed in rhythm to his neck pellet.

Sparrow turned left; Ramsey followed. The sound of the snifter went up an octave.

'Spy beam!' said Garcia.

Sparrow moved toward the dive board, Ramsey still following. The sound from the snifter grew louder. They passed the board and the sound deepened. They turned, faced the board. Now, the signal climbed another octave.

Ramsey thought: *Garcia was in here alone. Did he set up a signal device?*

'Where's Les?' asked Sparrow.

'Forward,' said Garcia.

Sparrow seemed to be trying to look through the wall in front of him.

He thinks it may be Bonnett sending that signal, thought Ramsey. With a sudden despair, he wondered: *Could it be?*

Sparrow spoke into his chest microphone: 'Les! To the control room! On the double!'

Bonnett acknowledged and they heard a clang of metal as he slipped on the catwalk; then he shut off his microphone.

Ramsey frowned at his snifter. The signal remained stationary although Bonnett was moving. But then a signal device could have been left hidden forward. He moved the snifter to the right, aiming it toward the center of the dive board. The signal remained constant.

Sparrow had followed the motion.

'It's in the board!' shouted Ramsey.

Sparrow whirled toward the board. 'We may have only a couple of minutes to get that thing!'

For a mind-chilling instant, Ramsey visioned the enemy wolf packs converging for another kill – twenty-one.

Garcia slammed a tool kit onto the deck at their feet, flipped it open, came out with a screw driver. He began dismantling the cover plate.

Bonnett entered. 'What's wrong, Skipper?'

'Spy-beam transmitter,' said Sparrow. He had found another screw driver, was helping Garcia remove the cover plate.

'Should we take evasive action?' asked Ramsey.

Sparrow shook his head. 'No, let them think we don't know about it. Steady as she goes.'

'Here,' said Garcia. 'Pull on that end.'

Ramsey reached forward, helped pull the cover plate away from the board, revealing a maze of wiring, transistors, high-pressure tubes.

Bonnett picked up the snifter, passed it in front of the board, stiffened as the signal increased in front of the tube bank.

'Joe, stand by on the auxiliary dive board,' said Sparrow. 'I'm shutting down this whole section.'

Garcia darted across to the auxiliary board on the opposite side of the control room. 'Auxiliary operating,' he called.

'Wait,' said Bonnett. He held the search box steady before a tube, reached in with his free hand and pulled the tube from its socket. The signal continued, but now it emanated from Bonnett's hand as he waved the tube in front of the snifter.

'A self-contained power unit in that little thing!' gasped Ramsey.

'Suffering Jesus save us,' muttered Sparrow. 'Here, give it to me.' He took the tube from Bonnett's hand, gritted his teeth at the heat of the thing.

Bonnett shook the hand which had held the tube. 'Burned me,' he said.

'It was in the Z02R bank,' Ramsey said.

'Smash it,' said Garcia.

Sparrow shook his head. 'No.' He grinned mirthlessly. 'We're going to gamble. Les, take us up to discharge depth.'

'Six hundred feet?' asked Bonnett. 'We'll be sitting ducks!'

'Do it!' barked Sparrow. He turned to Ramsey, extended the tube. 'Anything special about this you could use to identify it?'

Ramsey took the tube, turned it over in his hand. He reached into his breast pocket, pulled out a tiny record camera, began photographing the tube from all angles.

Sparrow noted the ready availability of a record camera, but before he could comment on it, Ramsey said, 'I'll have to look at the enlargements.' He glanced up at Sparrow.

'Do we have time to give this thing a more thorough going-over in the shack?'

Sparrow looked to the static pressure gauge. 'About ten minutes. Whatever you do, don't stop that signal.'

Ramsey whirled, hurried to the shack, Sparrow behind him. He heard Sparrow speaking into a chest mike as they ran.

'Joe, get a garbage disposal container and ready a tube to discharge that spy beam. With any luck at all, we're going to send the EPs chasing after an ocean current.'

Ramsey put a piece of soft felt on his workbench, placed the tube on it.

'If you've ever prayed, pray now,' said Sparrow.

'Nothing this small could have an internal power source to give off that much signal,' said Ramsey.

'But it does,' said Sparrow.

Ramsey paused to wipe perspiration from his hands. A thought flitted through his mind: *What will the telemeter record show on Sparrow's endocrine balance this time?*

'Devilish thing!' muttered Sparrow.

'We're playing a big gamble,' said Ramsey. He placed calipers over the tube, noted the measurements. 'Standard size for the Zo2R.' He put the tube in a balance scale with another of the same make. The spy tube sank, unbalancing the scale.

'It's heavier than the standard,' said Sparrow.

Ramsey moved the balance weights. 'Four ounces.'

Bonnett's voice came over the bulkhead speaker above their heads: 'Estimating discharge depth in four minutes. We've picked up a free ride on a current.'

Sparrow said, 'Do you think you can find out anything else about that thing?'

'Not without tearing it down,' said Ramsey. 'Of course, there's a possibility X-ray would show some internal detail we could figure out.' He shook his head.

'There'll be more of those aboard,' said Sparrow. 'I know there will.'

'How?'

Sparrow looked at him. 'Call it a hunch. This mission has been marked.' He glared at the tube on the bench. 'But by all that's sacred, we're going to come through!'

'Two minutes,' said Bonnett's voice over the speaker.

Ramsey said, 'That's it. Let me examine what we already have.'

Sparrow scooped up the tube, said, 'Move out to full limit.'

'They may detect our pulse,' said Ramsey, then colored as he felt the metronomic response of the speaker in his neck.

Sparrow smiled without mirth, turned, stooped for the door, and disappeared down the companionway. Presently, his voice came over the intercom: 'We're at the tube and ready to blow this thing, Les. Give me the static gauge readings.'

Back came Bonnett's voice: 'Four-ninety, four-seventy, four-forty . . . four hundred even!'

Ramsey heard the faint 'chug!' of the discharge tube, the sound carried to him through the hull.

Sparrow's voice rang over the intercom: 'Ride the vents!'

The *Ram*'s deck tipped sharply. The humming of the motors climbed through a teeth-grating vibration.

Ramsey looked to the dial showing their sound-transmission level. Too high. The silencer planes would never cover it.

Sparrow's voice boomed from the speaker: 'Ramsey, take over the internal-pressure system on manual. Overcompensate for anticipated depth. We'll worry about Haldane charts and depth sickness later. Right now, I want that cold level and 7000 feet over us.'

Ramsey acknowledged, his hands moving to the controls as he spoke. He glanced at the vampire gauge on his wrist. Diffusion rate low. He stepped up the release of carbonic anhydrase into the atmosphere.

Sparrow again: 'Ramsey, we've fired a salvo of homing torps on our back path. Delayed timing. Track the signal if any of them blow.'

'Aye, Skipper.' Ramsey plugged a monitor phone into one of the board circuits ahead of him, glanced to the telltale above it. As he did, he noted that the pellet in his neck had almost lost the sound of the tube behind them. His hands continued to move the internal pressure ahead of the depth requirement. The outside pressure repeater above his head showed 2600 pounds to the square inch, still climbing. Abruptly, the temperature recorder responded to their entrance into the cold current.

Ramsey spoke into his chest mike: 'We're in the cold, Skipper.'

Back came Sparrow's voice: 'We have it here.'

Ramsey's pressure repeater climbed through 2815 pounds, steadied. He felt the deck beneath him come up to level. Relays clicked, a bank of

56

monitor lights flashed green. He sensed the ship around him – a buoyant, almost living thing of machines, plastics, gases, fluids … and humans. He could hear Sparrow's voice over the open intercom giving orders in the control room.

'Force speed. Change course to fifty-nine degrees, thirty minutes.'

The secondary sonoran chart at Ramsey's left noted the course change. He looked at the red dot marking their position: almost due south of the western tip of Iceland, directly on the sixtieth parallel of latitude. Automatic timelog reading: seven days, fourteen hours, twenty-six minutes from start of mission.

'Ramsey, anything on those fish we sent back?'

'Negative, Skipper.'

'Stick with the shack. We're going to start tearing down the board. We'll have to check every tube for deviation from standard weight.'

'We'll have to go over the shack and the E-stores, too,' said Ramsey.

'Later.' Sparrow's voice conveyed a calm surety.

Ramsey glanced at his wrist watch, correlated it with the timelog. *What will the telemeter show?* he asked himself. Again, he felt that his mind had made a failing grasp at an elusive piece of essential knowledge. Something about Sparrow. Ramsey's gaze ranged over the board in front of him. His ears felt tuned for the slightest sound over the monitor phones. He glanced at the oscilloscope in the right bank: only background noise. For a fleeting instant, Ramsey felt that he was one with the ship, that the instruments around him were but extensions of his senses. Then it was gone and he could not recapture the feeling.

In the control room, Sparrow fought down the twitching of a cheek muscle. He replaced a tube in the sonoran system, extracted another, read the code designation from the tube's side: 'PY4X4.'

Garcia, beside him, ran a finger down a check list: 'Fifteen ounces plus.'

Sparrow checked it on a balance scale. 'Right on.' He replaced the tube, said, 'You know, when I was in high school they were saying that someday they'd run systems like this with transistors and printed circuits.'

'They did for a while,' said Garcia.

'Then we got into sweep circuits,' said Sparrow. He pulled out an octode cumulator tube, read off the code, checked the weight.

'We could still get by with lighter stuff if it weren't for high atmospheric pressures.' He went on to another tube. 'What we need is a dielectric as tough as plasteel.'

'Or an armistice,' said Garcia. 'Then deep-tug equipment would be specialty stuff.'

Sparrow nodded, pulled another tube from its socket.

'Skipper, what is that Ramsey?' asked Garcia.

Sparrow paused in the process of weighing a tube, looked at Garcia. 'I *think* he's a Security man planted on us.'

'That occurred to me,' said Garcia. 'But have you asked yourself yet who planted the spy beam on us? He could be a sleeper. He could be, Skipper.'

Sparrow's hand trembled as he reached for another tube to weigh. He brought back his hand empty, wiped the palm on his shirt, looked down at Garcia. 'Joe—' He broke off.

'Yes?'

'Has it ever occurred to you that humanity's basic problem is all wrapped up in the idea of Security?'

'That's a big mouthful, Skipper.'

'I mean it, Joe. Look, I know what I am. I can even tell you what my conception of myself is. How you have nothing to fear from me. Les can do the same thing. And you. And Ramsey.' He wet the corners of his mouth with his tongue, stared wide-eyed at Garcia. 'And any one of us or all of us could be lying.'

'That's not a Security problem, Skipper. That's a problem in communications. Ramsey's department.'

Sparrow turned back to the board without answering, went on with his patient inspection.

'I'd like to know what that last-minute Security inspection of Ramsey was all about,' said Garcia.

'Shut up!' barked Sparrow. 'Until there's proof positive to the contrary, he's one of us. So are you and Les. And so am I.' His mouth twisted in faint amusement. 'We're all in the same boat.' The lips thinned. 'And we've a bigger and more immediate problem.' He balanced a tube on the scales, replaced it. 'How can we break radio silence to notify home base of what we've discovered?'

A distant dull thump pounded through the hull. A second one.

Ramsey's voice over the intercom: 'Skipper! Two hits! Blast pattern identical to our fish!' His voice rose in pitch: 'Breaking up noises! Two sources. Skipper! We got two!'

'God forgive us,' said Sparrow. 'God forgive us.'

More thudding sounds resonating through the hull, a strange double beat.

'Anti-torp seekers,' said Ramsey. 'They've knocked out the rest of our fish.'

'Those men didn't stand a chance,' said Sparrow. His voice lowered, became almost inaudible. '"He that smiteth a man, so that he die, shall be surely put to death. And if a man lie not in wait, but God deliver him into his hand; then I will appoint thee a place whither he shall flee. But if a man come presumptuously upon his neighbour, to slay with guile; thou shalt take him from mine altar, that he may die."'

Across from him, Bonnett held up a tube. 'Joe, what's standard on a GR5?'

Garcia glanced at Sparrow, who turned abruptly back to his examination of the board. 'Eight ounces,' said Garcia.

'That's what I make it,' said Bonnett. 'But this one tops thirteen.' A tone of suppressed excitement vibrated in his voice.

Sparrow looked aft, lips trembling.

'I think I have one, Skipper,' said Bonnett.

Garcia had stepped across to Bonnett's side. He took the tube from the first officer.

'There should be a better way to live and a better way to die,' said Sparrow. He shuddered, stabbed a glance at Bonnett. 'Well, set it aside and see if there are any more!'

Bonnett appeared about to reply, but remained silent. He reclaimed the tube from Garcia, deposited it gently in a padded tray of his tool box.

Sparrow passed a hand across his forehead. His head ached strangely. *Is there a spy aboard?* he asked himself. *Is it Ramsey? Is it Les? Is it Joe? The EPs are hoping we lead them to the well.* He looked blankly at the open wiring before him. *Then why set off a tracer now? To test our alertness? The obvious time for a signal with be when we're sitting on top of the well.*

A strange vibration inside his head distracted Sparrow. He was startled to discover he'd been grinding his teeth. *When we're sitting on the well! God help me! How will I prevent it? I can't remain awake the whole time.*

'That's the last one,' said Garcia. He indicated a tube which Sparrow had automatically placed in the balance scales.

Sparrow shuddered, drew himself back to the present. 'Put it back,' he said.

Garcia complied.

Sparrow looked at Bonnett. 'Les, start checking the spares in E-stores.'

'Aye,' said Bonnett.

Sparrow spoke to Garcia: 'Stay on watch here.'

Garcia nodded. 'Are you going to rest, Skipper?'

Sparrow shook his head from side to side. 'No. No, I have to go back to the shack and help Ram—' He stopped, glanced at Garcia. 'We've engaged the enemy and come through.' Sparrow stepped to the door leading aft. 'I'm going to help *Johnny* check out the tubes in the shack.'

'What about that?' Garcia indicated the tube Bonnett had left in the tray of his tool box.

Sparrow returned, picked up the tube, went back to the door, examining the tube. 'We'll have a look. Maybe it'll tell us something.' He glanced at Garcia. 'You be thinking about how we can contact base.'

He was gone through the door.

Garcia clenched his fists, turned to face the master board. His gaze fell on the sonoran chart and its marker: a red insect creeping across vastness. *Where? Where's the well?*

Ramsey looked up from his instruments as Sparrow entered. 'Anything new, Skipper?'

'Les found this.' Sparrow placed the tube on the felt padding of Ramsey's bench. 'It's five ounces over.'

Ramsey looked at the tube without touching it. 'Has it occurred to you that thing could be set to explode on tampering?'

'Some of the old Salem sea captains used to attend their own funerals before embarking,' said Sparrow. 'Figuratively, I'm in the same frame of mind.'

'That's not what I mean,' said Ramsey. 'A half ounce of nitrox could get us both. Maybe you'd better leave me alone with it.'

Sparrow frowned, shrugged. He thumbed his chest mike: 'Joe, Les – hear this. This tube may be booby-trapped. If anything happens to Johnny and me, you two drop the tow and head for home. That's an order.'

Johnny! thought Ramsey. *He called me Johnny!* And then he remembered: *We've met the enemy. The old magic is dead. Enter the new magic.*

'We'll want a record of this,' said Sparrow. He took a camera from a drawer, racked it above the bench, focused it. 'Okay,' he said. 'You're the expert on these gadgets.'

Ramsey spoke without looking up from the tube: 'A half hour of just looking at this thing, studying all the angles, could mean the difference between success and failure.'

'What're we looking for?'

'I don't really know. Something different. Something that hits a sour note.'

Sparrow bent over the bench, grabbed a handhold as the *Ram*'s deck slanted to the upflow of an undersea current. Ramsey steadied the tube with one hand, brought up folds of the felt padding to keep the tube from rolling. The amber light of the temperature-gadget indicator on the board ahead of them flashed off, on, off.

Ramsey switched on the thermo repeater above the light: thirty-four degrees.

Sparrow nodded at the repeater. 'The Arctic bottom drift. It's full of food. There'll be a sonic curtain of sea life above us.' He smiled. 'We can breathe a bit easier.'

Ramsey shook his head. 'Not with that thing to solve.' He stared at the tube on the bench. 'If you were going to trigger that to explode, how would you do it?'

'A tiny wire maybe. Break it and—'

'Maybe,' said Ramsey. 'A better way would be to set a trigger keyed to pressure change – if the vacuum breaks . . .' He straightened. 'First some infra and X pictures. Then we'll rig a vacuum jar with remote controls, handle the tube in the vacuum. After that we'll break the seal.'

Sparrow touched the tube with one long finger of his left hand. 'Looks like standard heavy-pressure glass.'

'I don't understand something,' said Ramsey. He spoke as he worked, setting up the portable infra camera on the bench. 'Why did this thing start when it did? That wasn't smart. The clever thing would've been to wait until we reached the well.'

'My idea exactly,' said Sparrow.

Ramsey focused the camera. 'How much longer until we reach it?'

The casual way of the question caught Sparrow off balance. He looked up to the shack room sonoran chart, started to say, 'Well, it's on the flank of—' He froze.

Ramsey made an exposure, turned the tube to a new angle.

He's too casual, thought Sparrow.

'You were saying.' Ramsey spoke without looking up from the tube.

'Mr Ramsey, a subtug's destination is known only to its commander until the immediate area of that destination is reached.'

Ramsey straightened. 'That's a stupid order. If something happened to you we couldn't go on.'

'Are you suggesting I should confide our destination in you?'

Ramsey hesitated, thought: *I already know it. What would happen if I indicated that to Sparrow? That'd confirm his opinion that I'm Security.*

'Well ?'

'Skipper, I asked you a civil question. Phrased a bit loosely, perhaps. What I want to know is how much longer until we reach Novaya Zemlya?'

Sparrow held himself in rigid control, thinking: *Security? A spy trying to draw me out with a clever guess?* He said, 'I don't see where it's your concern how long it takes us to get anywhere.'

Ramsey returned his attention to the tube. *Is he convinced that I'm a Security officer?*

I could ask him for the exact coordinates, thought Sparrow. *But would it prove anything if he doesn't know them? Or if he does know them?*

Ramsey set up a bell jar and vacuum pump, the tube resting on the black mastic sealer inside the jar. He removed the jar, arranged a small remote-control console, replaced the jar.

Sparrow watched carefully, still undecided about Ramsey.

'This is going to be slow,' said Ramsey.

Lord in heaven, if I only knew! thought Sparrow. *Is he a spy? How can I tell? He doesn't really act like one.*

Ramsey locked a stool in place before the bench, sat down. 'Slow and easy,' he said.

Sparrow studied him. *It could be a clever act. I'll get busy checking the shack tubes, watch him.* He said, 'I'll start checking out your tubes.' He removed a cover plate at the left, found scales, began removing tubes, weighing them.

Minutes ticked away – an hour, two hours ... two hours and forty minutes. Inside the bell jar, the parts of the tube were laid out in rows. Sparrow long since had finished his job, was watching the work at the bench.

'No booby trap,' said Ramsey. He activated a magnet arm inside the jar, lifted a grid section. 'And I still don't see how they rigged this thing to go off. This looks like standard stuff.' He rotated the part on the magnet. 'There's nothing arranged to fuse with an overload. Nothing extra at all except that micro-vibrator and its capacitor power source.' He replaced the grid section. 'Our boys are going to want to see that.' He picked up a cathode segment, turned it over, set it down. 'No trigger. How was it done?'

Sparrow looked to the camera which had been capturing every movement of the examination, turned back to Ramsey. 'We have another problem.'

'What's that?' Ramsey straightened, rubbed the small of his back.

Sparrow slid off his stool. 'How're we going to get word of this back to base? If the EPs get us, the things we've discovered are lost. But I have an ironclad order against breaking radio silence.'

Ramsey stretched his back. 'Do you trust me, Skipper?'

Before he could stop himself, Sparrow said, 'No.' He frowned.

Ramsey grinned. 'I'm still the one with the solution to your problem.'

'Let's have it.'

'Put the whole story onto a squirt repeater and—'

'Squirt repeater?'

Ramsey bit his lip, coughed. *Damn! Another BuPsychSecurity secret.* It had slipped out.

'I've never heard of a squirt repeater,' said Sparrow.

'It's something new in . . . uh . . . electronics. You code a message onto ultra-stable slow tape, then speed up the tape. You set the message to repeat – over and over – a little squirt of sound. It's recorded at the receiver end, slowed for playback and translation.'

'That's still breaking radio silence.'

Ramsey shook his head. 'Not if the message is broadcast by a little set in a floater rigged to start transmitting long after we've gone.'

Sparrow's jaw fell. He snapped his mouth shut. Then 'Could you rig it?'

Ramsey looked around him. 'We have all the essentials right here.'

Sparrow said, 'I'll send Garcia in to help you.'

Ramsey said, 'I won't need any help with—'

'He'll help you anyway.'

Again Ramsey grinned. 'That's right. You don't trust me.'

In spite of himself, Sparrow grinned back at the amusement in Ramsey's face; then wiped the grin from his features and from his thoughts. His brows drew together. *Is this all an act on Ramsey's part?* he wondered. *Amuse me. Throw me off guard. It could be.*

Ramsey glanced at the wall chrono. 'My watch.' He indicated the parts in the bell jar. 'This'll keep.'

'I'll stand your watch,' said Sparrow. He thumbed his chest mike. 'Joe, come to the shack. Johnny's figured out how to get a message to home base. I want you to help him.'

'This shouldn't take more than a couple of hours,' said Ramsey. 'It's really a simple rig. I'll report in as soon as we've finished.'

Sparrow pursed his lips in thought, stared solemnly at Ramsey. 'There's something else. I'm instituting a new watch procedure: two men on duty at all times, never to leave actual sight of each other.'

Ramsey's eyes widened. 'There are only four of us, Skipper.'

'It'll be rough,' said Sparrow. 'We'll stagger the watches, change the second man in mid-watch.'

'That's not what I meant,' said Ramsey. 'It'll be more than rough. There are only four of us. Isolated. Under your plan, we'll obviously be watching each other. When you watch another man it tends to make you suspicious. Suspicion sets up a paranoiac situation where—'

'Your reluctance to accept an order for the general safety is being noted and will be entered in the log,' said Sparrow.

Ramsey's face took on a look of watchful remoteness. He thought: *Take it easy. This is the paranoiac learning that Obe mentioned.* He said, 'Efficiency will suffer if we're—'

'I'm still the captain of this vessel,' said Sparrow.

'Yes, *Captain*,' said Ramsey. He made the title sound faintly reproachful.

Sparrow's lips thinned. He whirled, left the shack, hurried aft to his quarters, bolted the door behind him. He sat down on his bunk, swung the folding desk into position. The faint whispering of the induction drive resonated through the wall behind him. The *Ram* had an uncertain, shifting motion; the bottom turbulence of the Arctic Current.

He thought: *We've a spy aboard. It's obvious someone activated that spy beam. I wish I'd had Joe checking Ramsey when he opened that tube. He says there was no internal trigger system in the thing, but he could've hidden something from me.*

From a recess in his desk, Sparrow removed his private log, opened it to a clean page, smoothed the log flat. He took his pen and, in a neat cramped hand, wrote the date, then: 'This date Ensign John Ramsey made objection to a Security procedure designed to . . .'

He paused, remembering that he'd ordered Garcia to the shack. He thumbed the switch on his chest mike: 'Joe, are you in the shack?'

Garcia's voice came out of the wall speaker. 'Righto.'

'Just checking,' said Sparrow. 'Would you have a look at that spy beam, see if there's anything about it we may have missed?'

'Righto, Skipper. Been doing just that.'

'That's all,' said Sparrow. He turned back to his log.

In the shack, Garcia looked up from the bell jar. 'You're dead right, Johnny-O. No trigger.'

'What's that thing look like to you?' asked Ramsey. 'Only one thing it could be,' said Garcia. 'A relay amplifier.'

Ramsey nodded. 'Right. The actual signal's coming from someplace else.'

'It'd have to be close,' said Garcia. 'Just giving you a freehand estimated-type guess, I'd say within ten feet.'

Ramsey rubbed the back of his neck.

'What're you wearing a phone for?' asked Garcia. He nodded toward the monitor phone in Ramsey's left ear.

'Monitor on the seismo,' said Ramsey. 'If another spy beam goes off—'

'Good idea.'

Ramsey brought his hand around to the side of his neck, passing it over the faint scar which covered the pellet. 'What'd you find in the spare?' he asked.

Garcia shook his head. 'Nothing.'

'Skipper checked the shack while I was dismantling that tube,' said Ramsey. 'Negative here, too.'

'Hadn't you better get started?' asked Garcia.

'Huh?'

'Building your little gadget.'

'Sure.' Ramsey turned back to his bench. As he turned, the speaker above the seismoscope rasped to an upper-range sound. Ramsey's eyes snapped to the scope. The pulsing green line made a sharp upsweep, repeated.

Bonnett's voice came over the speaker from the control deck: 'Skipper.'

Sparrow's bass tones: 'What is it, Les?'

'Seismic shock somewhere astern.'

'I have it here,' said Ramsey. 'Torp blast. It's in the same range as the EPs' 24-K fish.' He scribbled some figures on a note pad, picked up a slide rule, set it, read it. 'About a hundred miles astern. Well within range of drift for that little package we left behind us.'

'Would they waste a torp on that little thing?' asked Sparrow, then answered his own question. 'What's the matter with me? Of course they would. All they'd see on their gear would be the signal. They'd think it was us lying doggo.'

'That's the way I figure it,' said Ramsey. He looked at Garcia. 'What do you say, Joe?'

Garcia was trembling, face pale. He shook his head. Ramsey stared at him questioningly. He appeared extremely agitated.

Sparrow's voice boomed from the speaker: 'All hands: as soon as I am finished with work here, I will relieve Mr Bonnett.' There was the sound of a throat being cleared.

Ramsey glanced at the wall chrono. 'About time. Les has been on three straight watches.'

The skipper's voice continued: 'At that time I will post a new watch schedule in the wardroom. It is to go into effect immediately.'

Garcia had brought himself under control. He said, 'What's eating the skipper? He sounds angry.'

Ramsey outlined the new watch schedule.

'What the bloody!' said Garcia. 'As if we weren't nuts enough already!'

Ramsey stared at him. *That was an odd reaction for an engineering officer,* he thought. *For a psychologist, okay. But not for Garcia.*

In his quarters, Sparrow wrote: 'I must make certain there is no opportunity for anyone to activate a spy signal when we reach the well.' He penned his signature, made the final period an exclamation point, closed the log, and returned it to its hiding place.

The timelog repeater on his cabin bulkhead showed seven days, nineteen hours, twenty-three minutes from point of departure.

Sparrow stood up slowly, left his room, closing the door meticulously behind him. He turned, strode forward to the wardroom. As he passed the shack, he heard Ramsey saying: 'This stabilizes the micro-timing of the take-up spool. It has to be right on.'

Garcia's answer was lost to Sparrow as he stepped into the wardroom, closing the door meticulously behind him.

●

They dropped the signal squirter in the next watch. Sparrow noted the time – seven days, twenty hours, forty-eight minutes from departure – and entered it in the main logbook. He added the position from the sonoran chart: sixty-one degrees, fifty-eight minutes North Latitude, seventeen degrees, thirty-two minutes West Longitude. The squirter was set for a four-hour delay.

'Very good, Johnny,' he said. There was no warmth in his tone.

Ramsey said, 'We make do with what we have.'

'Let us pray that it works,' said Sparrow. He looked at Garcia. 'But we won't count on it.'

Garcia shrugged. 'It *could* work,' he said. 'If anybody hears it.' He stared coldly at Ramsey.

Sparrow thought, *Joe's suspicious. Oh, Lord! If Ramsey's a spy, he'd key that squirter to a wave length the EPs are listening to. It'll tell them we're on to the spy beam and they'll redouble their patrols!*

'Am I relieved now?' asked Ramsey.

'Until your watch,' said Sparrow. He stared after Ramsey.

In his quarters, Ramsey brought out the telemeter box, examined the tapes. Sweeping disturbance lines hit his eyes. Now Sparrow was reacting. But what reaction! They reminded Ramsey of a feedback record. Each succeeding wave worse than the one before. The whole area from the discovery of the spy beam was a scrambled record of disturbance.

The room seemed to grow smaller around Ramsey, pressing in upon him.

Sparrow's losing touch with reality. I'll have to do something. But what?

He took deep breaths to calm himself, forced his mind to orderly channels.

I've been with Sparrow a week. I've observed him in all manner of stress. The big elements should be in my hands by now: enough to make some kind of a plan of action. What do we have here?

He made a mental list:

We started out with evidence of rigid self-control.

But only after we knew that he could react.

There is some indication of religious paranoia.

A tendency to paranoiac type was Obe's earlier classification.

But there are things that don't fit the pattern.

He thinks clearly in a stress situation where you'd expect a breakdown.

Extremely masculine type. A leader.

But not totally despotic, or even nearly so.

And he's a brilliant submariner. At times you'd think the boat was a part of him or vice versa. That he was a built-in component: Captain, Submariner type: Mark I. Portable.

Ramsey's back stiffened. *Part of the boat. Mechanical. What better way to describe rigid self-control?*

He recalled his own feeling of synchronous intermingling with the boat. Fleeting as that had been – one instant in the shack. And then gone beyond recapture.

It'd be a strong survival adaptation.

Captain, Submariner type: Mark I. Portable. That may be closer than I'd imagined.

He rubbed at a burning sensation in his eyes, glanced at his wrist watch. Two hours until his next watch and he was aching with fatigue. He put away the telemeter, flopped sideways onto his bunk. Almost immediately, he was asleep and dreaming.

A giant surgeon with Sparrow's face bent over him in his dream. Little wires. Nerves. One here. One there. Soon he'll be built into the boat.

Electronics officer, Submariner type: Mark I. Portable.

It was Garcia's watch.

Timelog reading: eight days, four hours, and nineteen minutes from point of departure.

Bonnett on stand by, dozing on a tall stool in front of the control search board.

The *Ram* at cruising speed making twenty knots.

Garcia lounged against the guardrail in front of the valve master control, eyes idly taking in the gauges, now and then a glance at the autopilot indicator.

The search board emitted a soft buzzing.

Bonnett's head snapped up. He looked to the green face of the scope at his left, kicked the switch which automatically silenced the *Ram*'s motors.

They coasted quietly.

'What is it?' asked Garcia.

'Metal. Big. Coming our way.'

'One?'

'Dunno yet.'

'Is it an EP?'

His hand adjusted a dial and he looked to a gauge above it. 'One. Coming fast like she owned the ocean. In these waters that means EP. Buzz the skipper.'

Garcia pushed a button on the call board.

Presently, Sparrow joined them, bending his tall figure for the aft doorway. He buckled his belt as he stepped across the control deck.

Bonnett nodded toward the search board.

The *Ram*'s deck had been slowly tipping to starboard as she lost headway. Now, she was pointing down by the nose and the starboard incline was steep enough that Sparrow had to steady himself on the main grab-rail. He swept his gaze across the search board, asked, 'How far to bottom?'

'Too far,' said Bonnett.

Garcia, one hand on the valve-board rail, turned toward them. 'I hope you two decide what we're going to do before we turn turtle. We're almost at a standstill.'

Sparrow's gaze again went to the search gauges. The other sub was less than three miles distant, coming fast. As he looked, the detection equipment suddenly resolved its signal into two images.

'Two of them traveling tandem,' said Sparrow.

Through his mind sped a quotation from the tactical handbook: 'Submarines stalking each other under the sea are like blindfolded adversaries with baseball bats, locked in a room together, each waiting for the other to strike.'

'They're going to pass inside of a thousand yards,' said Bonnett.

'If they hold their present course,' said Sparrow. 'And that could be a trick to throw us off guard.'

'They must be asleep not to've spotted us before this,' whispered Garcia.

'Their metal-detection gear isn't too hot,' said Sparrow. He turned to Garcia. 'Joe, drop four homing torps, five minutes delay, set to swing around in front of them. Then give us just enough push to get underway and take us down to absolute.'

Garcia's hands moved over the control board, adjusting a vernier, setting a dial. He slapped one hand against a switch, turned to the drive controls. The *Ram* picked up speed slowly, nose pointing into the depths. The deck righted.

Sparrow and Bonnett watched the detection gear.

'Drift,' said Sparrow.

Bonnett's hand swept over his drive switch. They floated downward silently.

'Give us a little more,' said Sparrow.

Again the engines took up their slow turning.

Garcia whispered: 'They're not blind; they're deaf!'

Sparrow held up a hand to silence him. He glanced up to the big static pressure gauge; 2790 pounds to the square inch ... 2800 ... 2825 ...

Slowly, the indicator hand swept around: 2900 ... 2925 ...

Above the gauge, the flat bronze plate stamped with the *Ram*'s weight and specifications. Someone had used red paint to fill the indentations showing pressure limit: 3010 pounds.

The hand of the dial pointed to 2975 ... 3000 ...

Perspiration stood out on Garcia's face. Bonnett pulled nervously at an ear lobe. Sparrow stood impassively, feeling the boat around him. 'Ease her off,' he whispered. He wet his lips with his tongue.

The knowledge of the outside pressure was like an actual physical weight pressing inward against his skull. He fought against showing his feelings.

The dial steadied at 3008, slowly climbed to 3004, stayed there.

Bonnett whispered, 'They're almost on top of our—'

A dial fluttered wildly and they felt the *whump!* of a detonation through the hull. Sparrow's glance darted to the static pressure gauge: it made a stately fluctuation through 3028, back to 3004.

Garcia whispered, 'I heard that the *Barracuda* took 3090 before she imploded.'

'There's a bigger safety factor than that,' said Bonnett.

Sparrow said, 'May the Lord take their souls and grant them mercy. Even as it may come to pass with us. God forgive us that we do this not in anger, but out of need.'

Garcia fingered the beads of his Rosary through his shirt.

A sudden thought passed through Sparrow's mind. He looked down at his first officer. 'Les, what do you do when the heat is on?'

'Huh?' Bonnett glanced up at him, back to the dials.

'What do you think about?'

Bonnett shrugged. 'I remind myself I been married four times – four beautiful babes. What more could a man ask?'

'Every man to his own philosophy,' said Sparrow.

Ramsey entered the control room, took in the scene, whispered, 'The silence woke me up. Are we hunting something?'

'And vice versa,' said Garcia. 'Get in here and help me on the board.'

'You were not called to duty,' said Sparrow.

Ramsey hesitated.

'Get in here with Les,' said Sparrow. 'I'll stand by with Joe.' He backed away from the controls.

Ramsey stepped into the vacated spot.

Sparrow moved up to stand beside Garcia.

Bonnett looked at Ramsey out of the corners of his eyes. 'I'll clue you in on something, Junior,' he said. 'This is too much like playing grab-tail with a panther for me ever to become addicted to it.'

Sparrow said, 'We can't be traced from the track of our fish. They were on a curving course before they could've been detected.'

'That second boy out there could've gotten a shock-wave echo from the blast,' said Bonnett. 'He's just drifting now. He's already put out his anti-torp volley and it should—'

Three shock waves washed over them in rapid succession.

'That would be our fish being knocked out,' said Sparrow. 'Any breaking up noises from that EP?'

'Negative,' said Bonnett.

'Then they have our position now from the echo,' said Sparrow. 'Send out a detection scrambler and get our antitorp volley off.' He slapped Garcia on the back, said, 'Evasive action. Force speed.'

Ramsey standing beside Bonnett hit a series of switches with the heel of his hand. A cloud of tiny torp-homing exploders swept out from the *Ram*.

Bonnett kicked the control which sent out a dummy torpedo carrying signal equipment to scramble detection systems.

'Why couldn't I have taken a nice safe job in a nitrox factory?' Garcia moaned.

'You guys who want to live forever make me sick,' said Bonnett. 'Here you are in a nice perambulating sewer pipe with ple—'

'Up!' barked Sparrow. 'If we get into close quarters I want a bigger pressure margin.'

Garcia complied. The deck slanted upward.

Ramsey said, 'What makes you think ...'

'We're coming out of that scrambler's field,' said Bonnett.

'Fire another along our forward path,' said Sparrow. Again he slapped Garcia's shoulder. 'Right rudder and drift.'

Garcia pulled the wheel right, straightened it, shut down the drive. Slowly, the *Ram* lost headway. Again the deck tilted to starboard.

'We've gotten sloppy on our trim,' said Sparrow.

Bonnett leaned toward Ramsey, whispered, 'That guy's a genius. We coast along the edge of the first scrambler's field. The one we just sent out will leave a track for the other boys to follow and they'll—' He broke off, staring at the detection system, eyes widening. 'Skipper!' he husked, voice hanging on the edge of horror. 'They're right on top of us – force speed. Going overhead now. Not more than one hundred feet!'

Sparrow shouldered Garcia aside, kicked the *Ram* into force speed, swerved it into the wake of the other sub. To Bonnett, he said, 'Keep us on their tail. Gently, friend ... gently.'

Garcia whispered, 'I heard of this happening once with old *Plunger*, but I never thought I'd see it myself.'

Ramsey said, 'Their blind spot. They can't hear us in the turbulence of their own wake.'

Bonnett's voice came calm and steady: 'Two degrees port.'

Sparrow swerved the *Ram* to follow.

Ramsey pointed to the oscilloscope.

Bonnett followed the direction, said, 'Skipper, off to starboard is a whole wolf pack. They're converging on that last scrambler we sent out.'

'Too close for comfort,' said Sparrow. With one hand he eased down drive speed; with the other he punched the controls to arm a torpedo. 'Give me minimum range,' he said. 'This has to be fast. As soon as the blast reaches us, fire scramblers to the four points of the compass.'

Bonnett acknowledged. 'One hundred yards,' he said. 'One twenty-five ... one fifty ... one seventy ...' He glanced to the secondary scope. 'Any second now that pack will be getting two signals from us and one of the signals won't fit IFF. Two fifty ... two seventy-five ...'

Sparrow fired the single torpedo, killed the drive, began counting: 'One, two, three, four, five, six, seven, eight, nine, ten, elev—'

The concussion shook the *Ram*.

Bonnett fired the scramblers.

Ramsey's ears were ringing.

Sparrow kicked on drive to force speed, brought the *Ram* about in a tight circle, coursing upward. With one hand, he pushed Garcia into the control position, stepped back. 'They'll be expecting us to dive,' he said. 'Blow the tanks.'

Garcia palmed the switches and the *Ram* bounced to the lift.

Sparrow said, 'Les, give me a fifty-foot warning on the edge of the scrambler field.'

'Right,' said Bonnett. 'We've a ways to go yet.'

Bonnett caught the puzzled look on Ramsey's face, said, 'They taught you things in subschool, but they never taught you this, did they?'

Ramsey shook his head.

'We're going to float up,' said Bonnett. 'We may be walking on the ceiling before we get there, but we're going to do it silently.'

Sparrow looked to the static pressure gauge: 1200 pounds – above the 0003-foot level. He glanced inquiringly at Bonnett, who shook his head.

The seconds ticked away.

Bonnett said, 'Now!'

Garcia killed the drive.

Sparrow wiped his face with his hands, looked startled when his hand came away bloody. 'Nosebleed,' he said. 'Pressure change was too rapid. Haldane tablets, everyone.' He fished a flat green pill from a pocket, popped it into his mouth. As always, his reaction was sudden nausea. He grimaced, held the pill down by willpower, shuddered.

Ramsey choked on his pill, coughed, fought it down.

Bonnett spat into his handkerchief, said, 'Human beings weren't meant to take this kind of a beating.' He shook his head.

The *Ram* began to tip gently to the right.

Sparrow looked at Ramsey, said, 'Johnny, go over to the left there.'

Ramsey complied, thinking: *What a way to get on a first-name basis! I'd sooner stay a dryback.*

As he passed Garcia, the engineering officer spoke the thought aloud: 'Bet you wish you were still Junior Ramsey.'

Ramsey smiled faintly.

The deck's tipping slowed, but did not stop.

Sparrow nodded to Bonnett. 'Hand pump. Start shifting some water. Slow and easy.'

Bonnett stepped to the aft bulkhead, swung out a crank handle. Sparrow took over the search-board position. Slowly, they steadied on an even keel, but now the nose began to sink. Then the deck began to slant slowly to the left. Sparrow glanced at Ramsey, nodded toward the aft bulkhead on his side. 'Take over fore-and-aft stabilization. Easy does it. No noise.'

Ramsey moved to obey. He looked at the pressure gauge: 840 pounds. They were above the 2000-foot level.

'We can maintain some sort of trim until we hit wave turbulence,' said Sparrow. 'Then we may have to risk the drive.'

Gently, the *Ram* drifted upward, tipping, canting.

Ramsey found the rhythm of it. They couldn't hold her in exact trim. But they could rock her to a regular teeter-totter rhythm. He grinned across at Bonnett on lateral stabilization.

The deck suddenly stopped a leftward countermotion and heeled far right, came back again, nose rising; again she heeled to the right. A hissing sound resonated through the hull.

The screen on the forward bulkhead – tuned to the conning TV eye – showed milky green.

Sparrow stood at the controls, one hand on the rail. He stared upward at the screen.

When's he going to give us headway? Ramsey wondered.

This time the *Ram* heaved far over to the left.

For one frightening moment, Ramsey looked directly down into the pipe and conduit maze against the port pressure hull. *We're going over*, he thought.

But the *Ram* came back sluggishly, righting. The bulkhead screen broke free of foam, cleared to reveal fog and long, white-capped rollers. The *Ram* pitched and bobbed in the seas.

'I agree with you, Skipper,' said Bonnett. 'One way of dying is as good as another. They'd have heard us sure.'

Garcia worked his way along the handrail, fighting the uneasy motion of the deck. 'If we could rig a sea anchor,' he said.

'We already have one,' said Sparrow.

Garcia blushed. 'The tow!'

'Thank you, Lord, for the lovely fog,' said Bonnett.

The *Ram* swung downwind from her tow in a wide, rolling arc, jerking against the lines like a wild horse at a snubbing post.

'More line on the tow,' said Sparrow. He nodded to Garcia, who jumped to obey.

The motion of the deck smoothed.

Sparrow kept his gaze on the detection gear. 'What's our heading, Joe?'

'Near fifty-eight degrees.'

'Wind's favorable,' said Sparrow. 'And those boys down under haven't changed course.'

'They're still snooping after our last scrambler,' said Garcia.

'Time for you to go off watch, Joe,' said Sparrow. 'I am relieving you.'

'Want me to bring up some sandwiches before I sack down?' asked Garcia.

'Ham and cheese,' said Bonnett.

'No, thanks,' said Sparrow. He studied the sonoscope on the search board. 'We'll drift with the wind until we no longer get signals from that pack.'

Ramsey yawned.

Sparrow hooked a thumb toward the aft door. 'You, too. That was a good job, Johnny.'

Ramsey said, 'Aye.' He followed Garcia down the companionway, muscles aching from the unaccustomed exercise at the ballast pumps.

Garcia turned at the wardroom door, looked at Ramsey. 'Chow?'

Ramsey steadied himself with one hand against the bulkhead. Beneath him, the deck rolled and dipped.

'These tubs weren't designed for the surface,' said Garcia. 'What breed of sandwich?'

The thought of food suddenly made Ramsey's stomach heave. The long companionway appeared to gyrate in front of him, rolling counter to the motion of the deck. He capped his mouth with a hand, raced for his quarters. He reached the washbasin just in time, stood over it retching.

Garcia followed him, pressed a blue pill into his hand, made him swallow it.

Presently, the surging of Ramsey's stomach eased. 'Thanks,' he said.

'In the sack, Junior.'

Garcia helped him grope his way into his bunk, pulled a blanket over him.

Seasick! I'll never live it down! thought Ramsey. He heard Garcia leave. Presently, he remembered the telemeter. But he was too weak, too drowsy. He drifted off to sleep. The motion of the *Ram* became a soothing thing.

Rockaby ... rockaby ...

He could almost hear a voice. Far away. Down a tunnel. In an echo chamber.

'The boat is my mother. I shall not want ...'

When he awakened it was the call to watch and he had a scant moment in which to glance at the telemeter tapes.

Sparrow had returned to the pattern of rigid control.

It was as though Ramsey's subconscious had been working on a problem, chewing it, and these were the final data. The answers came spewing up to his conscious level.

He knew what he had to do.

●

Twenty-three hours the *Ram* drifted downwind, angling away from Iceland to the northeast. A gray speck on gray and foam. And behind her, barely submerged, the green surge of their tow, a sea monster escaped from the deep.

In Ramsey's second watch they passed within two miles of a radio-active iceberg, probably broken from the skerries of the northeast Greenland coast. Ramsey kept radiation snoopers tuned to the limit until they were out of range. The berg, its random contours catching the wind like a sail, was almost quartering the gale. It pulled away from the *Ram*, like a majestic ship.

Ramsey noted in the log: 'Current setting easterly away from our course. We did not cross the berg's path.'

Outside radiation: 1800 milli-R.

Garcia came across the control room. 'Safe yet?'

'Clear,' said Ramsey.

Garcia looked to the screen on the control bulkhead, the view of gray rollers. 'Moderating.'

'If the fog will just hold,' said Ramsey.

Sparrow came through the aft door, his lank form seemingly more loose-jointed than usual.

He's relaxed, thought Ramsey. *That fits. What EP commander would dream of looking for us up here? We're too low in the water to show on a shore screen.*

'All quiet, Skipper,' he said.

'Very good,' said Sparrow. He looked to the timelog: nine days, three hours, and forty-seven minutes. 'Joe, how long since you've had a signal from our friends?'

'Not a sign of them for almost ten hours.'

Sparrow glanced at the sonoran chart. The red dot stood at sixty-six degrees, nine minutes, twenty seconds North Latitude, two degrees, eleven minutes West Longitude. He nodded to Ramsey. 'Get us under-way, if you please. Surface speed. Quarter throttle. Keep us under eight knots.'

Ramsey moved to obey.

The *Ram* shuddered to a wave impact, fought up the slope of a sea. They gathered headway, sluggishly.

'She answers the helm, sir,' said Ramsey.

Sparrow nodded. 'Course thirteen degrees. We've drifted a bit too close to the Norwegian coastline. The EPs have shore-based listening posts there.'

Ramsey brought the subtug around on her new heading.

'We'll stay on the surface as long as we have fog,' said Sparrow.

'Our guardian angels are working overtime,' said Garcia.

'I wonder if they have a union?' asked Ramsey.

Sparrow looked to the timelog: nine days, four hours even. He caught Garcia's attention, nodded toward the timelog and then the helm. 'Take over, if you please, Joe.'

Garcia took the helm from Ramsey.

'You are relieved,' said Sparrow.

Ramsey felt a wave of fatigue sweep through him. He remembered what he had to do, fought down the tiredness. 'We'll be there soon,' he said.

Sparrow frowned.

'None too soon for me,' said Ramsey. 'I feel like we're living on borrowed time. I want our payment in the bank – a whole load of that sweet oil.'

'That will be enough,' said Sparrow.

'You afraid I'm going to give away a nasty old Security secret?' asked Ramsey.

Garcia darted a puzzled glance at him.

'Go to your quarters,' said Sparrow.

'Righto,' said Ramsey, copying Garcia's accent. He made his tone as insolent as possible without coming to actual insubordination, turned toward the aft door.

'I'll wish to speak with you before your next watch,' said Sparrow. 'We're long overdue for an understa—' He broke off as a red warning light flashed on the reactor system's scram board. The light winked green, then red, then green.

Garcia saw it, too.

Ramsey turned back to the control bulkhead, caught the last flash from red to green.

'Something's loose in the pile room,' said Sparrow.

'That torpedo shock we took,' said Ramsey.

'More likely the pounding we've had from these seas,' said Garcia.

'That's circuit "T" of the secondary damper controls,' said Sparrow. 'Right side forward. Get Les up here on the double.'

Garcia pushed the alarm buzzer.

'Try the screens,' said Sparrow.

Ramsey moved back to the helm, took it. Garcia glanced at him, moved to the screen controls, began hitting switches.

Bonnett entered. 'What's up?'

'Something loose in the pile room,' said Sparrow. 'It's "T" circuit.'

'Right side forward,' said Bonnett. He moved to get a better view of the screens, caught the handrail to steady himself against the rolling of the deck.

Sparrow said, 'I'm going forward.' He looked at the scram board. The light winked at him: red, green, red, green, red, green … 'Les, come forward with me and help me into a suit. I'll have to crawl the right-side tunnel, use the manuals and mirrors.'

'Just a minute, Skipper,' said Garcia. 'Look at that.' He pointed at a screen.

Sparrow stepped to his side.

'Central damper controls,' said Garcia. 'See. When we pitch into the trough of a wave it seems to – There!'

They all saw it. The long hanging arm of the manual damper control swung free like the multi-jointed leg of an insect. It exposed a break at the top elbow hinge. The upper bracing flapped outward to the sway of the boat.

'It was wedged against the hinge,' said Garcia. 'Now it's broken free again.' He looked at the scram board. Red, green, red, green, red …

Each time the light flashed red, the swinging arm touched a control-circuit cable. A blue arc of electricity splashed upward.

Garcia pointed to the lower half of the screen which showed the base of the control system. 'There's the real trouble. The whole control base is twisted. See those sheared bolts?'

Sparrow whirled to the forward hatch, undogged it. 'Les, I've changed my mind. Stay here with Johnny on the main board. Joe, come with me.' He glared at Ramsey, hesitated, then said, 'Take us down below wave turbulence.'

Ramsey's hands went to the controls: diving planes two degrees, compensating system open, hull pressure holding. He found that it was better to let his body react, to accept the results of his training, secure in the knowledge that this way he would be right.

Sparrow went through the door, out onto the engine- room catwalk. Garcia followed.

Ramsey activated the engine-room scanners to follow their movements. *What a time I picked to go into my act,* he thought. He gave a mental shrug. *But one time's as good as another.*

'We're going to make it,' said Bonnett. 'Nothing can stop us.'

Startled, Ramsey darted a glance at the first officer.

Bonnett was staring at the screen. Ramsey followed the direction of his gaze. Sparrow and Garcia were scrambling down the ladder to the right-side tunnel. Sparrow jerked open the door to the bulkhead locker, swung out an ABG suit on its traveler rack.

'The EPs are crazy to think they can beat him,' said Bonnett. 'He's like a god!'

Something in Bonnett's voice . . .

Ramsey fought down a shudder.

The screen showed Garcia helping Sparrow into the bulky suit.

Ramsey turned back to his controls as the subtug steadied. He found the need to say something, said, 'We're out of wave turbulence.'

Bonnett looked at him. 'Do tell.' He turned his attention back to the screen.

Ramsey adjusted the controls, brought the deck to level.

Now, Sparrow was completely sealed into his suit. He turned clumsily, helped Garcia.

What does the telemeter show? Ramsey wondered. *Is Sparrow under control? Or is the wild feedback starting?*

In the heavy suit, Sparrow felt the perspiration begin to roll off him. His fingers seemed unwilling to obey him as he assisted Garcia. *Damned sweat suits! There!* The final seal went into place.

Sparrow took a deep breath, spoke into his suit mike: 'Testing . . . testing. Do you read me, Les?'

The captain's voice boomed out of the speaker on the control deck. Ramsey turned down the volume.

Bonnett spoke into his chest mike: 'Loud and clear.'

'Joe,' said Sparrow. 'Are you receiving me?'

'Righto, Skipper.'

'Now get this, Les,' said Sparrow. 'If that damper arm swings out too far it'll begin clubbing the side of the pile. Monitor me on your screen. I might not be able to see a position change soon enough.'

Bonnett looked to the screen showing the reactor room.

'It's quiet now, Skipper. Resting against the first-stage clamps.'

'Those bolts are sheared off, though,' said Sparrow. 'The whole unit could fall over onto the pile.'

Bonnett studied the screen. 'Skipper, there's a chance you could catch the main drive bar with the grapple of the forward manuals.' He bent closer to the screen. 'It'll be a near thing. You'll have to snake past that broken hinge.'

'How much clearance?'

'Maybe six inches. No more. The mirror's at a bad angle.'

'Talk me in,' said Sparrow. 'We can do it.' He turned, undogged the tunnel hatch and snapped on his helmet light. 'Joe, stay here unless I call you.' He reached a hand into the tunnel, found the filter-system switch, started it. He plugged his suit hose into the traveler, tested the air.

Garcia said, 'I'll time you. Have Les monitor the tunnel radiation.'

Bonnett, listening to the conversation over the intercom, said, 'I'll give you the time-over-radiation from here.' He twisted a dial, plugged in a jack, tested the circuit.

'I'm going in,' said Sparrow. He bent, slid into the tunnel. 'I'll give you a running commentary when I reach the manuals, Les. Get everything on tape. Base will want a complete record of this.'

'Take it slow and easy, Skipper,' said Bonnett.

Sparrow said, 'Joe, dog that tunnel door behind me. If that base falls to the right it'll smash the end plug. There'd be hot stuff all over the place.'

'Righto.'

A faint thump behind Sparrow and a feeling of pressure change told him when Garcia had complied. Sparrow felt the isolation like a physical band tightening on his forehead. Perspiration rolled down his cheeks, down his nose. His clothes were damp with it, clinging to him.

Garcia's voice came over the phones like a sound from another world. 'What do you see, Skipper?'

'Tunnel's clear. Nothing hot yet.' His helmet light cut a bright path through the metallic darkness.

It's another birth canal, he thought. And he remembered all the times he had crawled the mock-up tunnel at training school without ever encountering that thought. *There's a first time for everything: a first time to be born, a first time to die.* He longed to wipe the perspiration from his forehead. *Lest ye be born again ye shall not enter . . .*

The light picked up the safety door near the end of the tunnel. This was the limit of the bulkhead. Beyond that was the lead soda straw jutting into the pile room. And at the end: the manuals. He undogged the door, swung it back into its recess.

Pile-room floodlights cast their blue glare onto the tunnel floor ahead of him, reflected through the mirror system in a weird splotching of brilliance and shadows. Sparrow inched his way into the glare.

'I am at the manuals,' he said. He turned onto his back, fighting against the terror that threatened to overwhelm him. Out there in the blue glare of the pile room was . . . what? The world and all its threats.

Garcia's voice came over the intercom: 'Are you okay, Skipper?'

Sparrow took a deep breath. 'Yes.'

I'll pretend I'm still in school, he thought. *This is a test. I have to pass or take a black mark. They've yanked the control units free of their base and I have to make repairs under simulated action conditions. Old Lieutenant Maurey is back at the tunnel mouth hoping I'll fail. That's not really a reactor out there; it's just a mock-up. They wouldn't risk an unimportant student with the real thing. They have to wait until you've had all that expensive training and it's cost something to lose you. Then —*

'Skipper,' Les's voice, metallic in the phones.

'Yes?'

'Are you ready?'

'Just a moment, Les.'

'Right.'

Sparrow slipped his hands into the fitted grips of the manual controls, pulled the stud which hooked him into the grapple. He pulled back with his right hand, watched in the mirror as the grapple came into lift position.

'Les?'

'I see it, Skipper. Bring it up about three feet. Line it up with the spring bar, but keep it back away from the broken hinge.'

Sparrow pulled down on the right grip, turned it slightly to bring the hydraulic booster into play. The grapple darted upward. *Too fast!* Sweat popped out on his forehead.

'A little slower,' said Bonnett.

Sparrow whispered, '"Lord, I am like David. I am in a great strait: let us fall now into the hand of the Lord; for his mercies are great: and let me not fall into the hand of man. Stay now thine hand. I have sinned and I have done wickedly: but these sheep, what have they done? Put thine hand over mine, Lord. Guide me."'

Steadiness came to him.

'Did you say something, Skipper?' asked Bonnett.

'I'm all set, Les. Guide me in.'

'Okay. You have to come up about six inches and to the left about an inch. Take it slow.'

Sparrow lowered the thrust of the hydraulic booster, put his muscle into the grip. The manual arm went up slowly, paused, shifted to the left.

'Right on, Skipper. Bring it forward three feet and lock it while you lift the rear hinge section into place.'

The grapple moved as though it were a part of his body. He twisted his left grip to lock the end section, eased the next element of the grapple arm into alignment.

'How's that?'

'Perfect. Now, can you lift the whole arm about an inch? You're a little close to that broken hinge.'

'I can't see the end of the grapple and the next element at the same time, Les. I'd better watch the element.'

'Okay. Fine it down and bring the grapple end up a quarter of an inch at a time.'

Sparrow grunted as he made the first lift.

'That was a half inch, Skipper. One more exactly like it.'

Again Sparrow grunted as he moved the grip.

'A hair over, Skipper, but you still have clearance.'

'Do you want me to fine it down?'

'No. Let it stand there. Now bring the grapple end past the hinge. One straight push about three feet.'

Sparrow twisted his head to get a view of the grapple in the mirrors. It looked as though it would smash directly into the broken hinge. *Poor angle of view*, he thought. *How'd a piece of bad planning like that get by?* He lifted his right hand grip. The grapple surged forward, stopped.

'Hold it right there a second, Skipper.'

Sparrow heard mumbling over the phones.

Bonnett's voice returned: 'You'll have to get three elements of the grapple arm past that break before you can drop the tip. Better align the next element.'

Sparrow brought up the next hinged section, straightened it. 'How's the alignment?'

'Right on. Bring it forward.'

He complied, his hands moving the controls with increased sureness. The next element came up, was aligned, sent forward.

'Another foot forward, Skipper.'

He moved the grapple arm.

'Now comes the ticklish part. Drop the end at number-three joint. Take it down slowly and stop when I tell you.'

Sparrow bent the end elements downward. He thought that it was almost as though he could feel the moving part as he could feel his own arm. He sensed the position and stopped it while Bonnett was forming the order on his lips. The grapple end now was out of sight below the control base. It would take four adjustments of the mirrors to bring it back into view.

'You're about ten inches above the main drive bar. To reach it, you'll have to angle down with that section spanning the broken hinge.'

'I don't dare jar that hinge,' said Sparrow. 'There's a lot of leverage that far up. I could break it right off.'

'I've used the calipers on the screen,' said Bonnett. 'You'll have about an inch to spare.'

Sparrow felt the fatigue in his wrists and forearms, whispered, 'Just a little longer, Lord. We're making it.'

'You ready?' asked Bonnett.

'Yes. Talk me down.'

'Okay. Take the tip toward you about four inches.'

Sparrow moved the grapple.

'Now down six inches.'

Sparrow eased the tip downward, felt the sureness of his control, said, 'How's the lateral alignment?'

'Half inch to the right.'

He shifted the descent angle, continued down with the tip. 'How's the upper clearance?'

'You still have two inches.'

He felt the grapple jaws touch the drive bar, lowered them onto it, gripped the bar.

'Skipper, you couldn't have done that better if you'd had your own hand out there.'

Sparrow locked the grapple into position, brought up secondary grapples to brace it. He slid backward down the tunnel until he could reach the manual controls at number-two position, reached up with a short grapple and clamped it onto the broken unit. The control shivered.

'Lordy,' said Bonnett. 'It would've gone right over without the bracing on that drive bar.'

Sparrow swung an extension torch into place above the broken hinge, locked it into position, lifted the broken end until the sheared sections touched. He started the torch.

'Fuse it solid at the hinge. Only thing I can do now. There's enough play in the other elements to almost compensate for the lost mobility. We'll be able to cover more than eighty percent of this pile face. The manuals will cover the rest.'

'What're you going to do, Skipper?'

'What about the base?'

'I'm going to knock the sheared bolts right on through into the catch basin.' He lowered the torch, playing its flame onto the sheared hinge. At the molten moment, he cut the torch, crushed the broken elements together. The repair formed a wedge-shaped cup. He sprayed the inside with brazing flux, brought up the brazing rod, and filled the cup.

'That looks like it'll hold,' said Bonnett, 'I've been examining the base. It doesn't appear to be warped, but it's out of alignment. You'll need a spreader jack at the aft end.'

'Right. What's the inclination?'

'About one degree. Put the replacement bolts along the inside face first. They'll hold it while you drop the drive bar.'

'I've a better idea,' said Sparrow. 'Watch closely and tell me if anything starts to go wrong.'

'What're you going to do?'

'Drop the bolts into place along the inner face, then throw a little torque into the drive bar. The thrust against the grapple will push the base back into position.'

'That's risky.'

'No worse than thrusting a jack against the base of the pile to horse that thing into position. This way we don't touch the pile.'

Sparrow continued to speak as he worked. 'Rule one of pile-room repair should be: Don't touch the reactor unless you absolutely have to.'

'You have nine minutes, Skipper,' said Bonnett. 'You should be on your way out in five minutes.'

'That's another reason for doing it my way,' said Sparrow.

'Couldn't Joe finish it?'

'Only if he has to. Best not to have two of us on the cooling-off list.'

He touched the drive-bar switch. The control base rocked against its grapple braces. Metal protested. Two of the bolts dropped into position. Sparrow slipped nuts onto them, drove them tight with a motor wrench. Again he rocked the base with the drive bar. The remaining bolts slipped home.

Sparrow's fingers flew over the manual controls as he completed the job. He disengaged the grapples, swung the repaired control arm out of the way, clamped it.

'Two minutes, Skipper. On your way, right now!'

Sparrow released the last temporary brace, dropped it, slid backward down the tunnel, closed and dogged the door at the bulkhead limit. His helmet light was a pale flame after the blue glare of the tunnel end. He crawled backward, heard Garcia undog the door behind him, felt the other man's suited hands on his legs helping him the last few feet.

Bonnett's voice came over the phones: 'You went about a minute over. Get down to the sick bay and take your shots.'

Sparrow grinned: It was good for Les to give orders; eased his tensions.

'On the double, Skipper,' said Bonnett. 'Every second's delay means that much more time cooling off for you.'

Sparrow fought down a feeling of irritation. Under Rule Ninety, Bonnett was technically in command when his superior officer had taken an overdose of radiation. But one minute!

Garcia ran a snooper over him, working silently, gesturing for Sparrow to turn. The engineering officer straightened, racked the snooper. 'Into that decon chamber.' He unhooked Sparrow's hose from the tunnel system, closed the door and dogged it.

Sparrow climbed into the decontamination chamber, felt the surge of foaming detergent around him.

'Joe, what's the delay?' Bonnett again.

'He's in decon now, Les. Thirty seconds more.'

'Cut it short, Joe. Ramsey is on his way down with the needle to give him his shots there. It'll save a couple of minutes.'

Ramsey came out on the catwalk above them, carrying a radiation-first-aid kit under his arm. He dropped down to their level, helped Garcia break the seal on his suit.

Sparrow came out of the chamber without his suit, frowned at the kit in Ramsey's hand.

'Bend over, Skipper,' said Ramsey.

Sparrow obeyed, dropped his trousers, winced at the needle. 'Just don't enjoy yourself, Johnny,' he said.

Ramsey extracted the needle, wiped the bare skin with disinfectant. 'That does it and I hope you never have to do the same for me.'

The lifting of tension about Sparrow was an almost physical thing.

Ramsey replaced the hypodermic in the kit, sealed it.

'Let's go,' said Sparrow.

Garcia hung his ABG suit in its locker, followed them up the ladder.

Ramsey thought: *What's on the telemeter? Lord, I thought he'd never come out of that tunnel.*

They stepped out onto the center catwalk, headed for the control room. Abruptly, the giant motors around them fell silent. Sparrow broke into a run, ducked through into the control room. Ramsey sprinted after him, went through the door on Sparrow's heels.

Bonnett stood at the search board, one hand on the drive controls. His eyes were on the oscilloscope of the limit sono-finder. He spoke without turning: 'Signal. At extreme range. We've lost it.'

'By now they must have a rough idea of our course,' said Sparrow. 'They're quartering the area. What's the depth?'

'We're over the sub-arctic shallows,' said Bonnett. 'Bottom's about 350 fathoms.'

'Too shallow for us to lie doggo,' said Sparrow. 'They would range too close for—'

'There it is again,' said Bonnett. He nodded toward the scope, adjusted two flanking dials. 'Northeast. A pack by the noise. Damn! Lost them again. That's probably a school of fish between us.'

'Head for the Norway basin,' said Sparrow. 'We need deep water.' He glanced at the sonoran chart. 'Course nine degrees.'

Bonnett engaged the drive, swung the helm to the left until they were on the new course.

Sparrow stepped to his nav-plot board, bent over it, figuring. Presently, he straightened. 'Estimating time of arrival two hours and six minutes.' He turned. 'Johnny, stay with search here. We've the range on them, but not so much that we can afford to get careless.'

Ramsey moved to the search board.

Garcia stepped through the door from the engine room. 'The real danger is an EP that lies doggo until we're in range,' he said.

'It's a big ocean,' said Sparrow.

'And a small world,' said Garcia.

Sparrow looked at the radiation kit which Ramsey had placed on one of the control-board stools. He glanced at his wrist watch. 'Does someone have a timer set for my next shots?'

'I have,' said Ramsey.

'Get what rest you can, Skipper,' said Bonnett. 'I'll have a look at you as soon as we find a sitting spot.'

'I can do it,' said Garcia.

Bonnett nodded. 'Okay.'

'Timer's in the kit,' said Ramsey.

Garcia picked up the sealed box, gestured for Sparrow to precede him aft.

They're worried about me, thought Sparrow. *But one minute over isn't that important.*

Ramsey noted the proprietary attitude of Garcia and Bonnett toward Sparrow, realized abruptly that he shared it. *He's our skipper*, he thought.

Sparrow and Garcia went aft.

The *Ram* crept onward.

'It's a little deeper,' said Ramsey. 'We're over the hump.'

'Sill depth across here runs 400 to 600 fathoms,' said Bonnett. 'When we reach 600 we'll be close to the basin slope.'

'It's 450 now.'

'A bad stretch,' said Bonnett. 'You'd expect the EPs to be ranging this area in net formations.'

Garcia slipped into the control room. 'Les.'

'How is he?'

'Are you sure it was just one minute over?'

'Certainly I'm sure. What's wrong?'

'Very low white count. It looks like closer to half an hour over.'

'Any burns?'

'No indications yet.'

'It could be that he didn't recover well from handling that Security lieutenant,' said Ramsey.

'That's what I was thinking,' said Garcia. 'I gave him a sedative and a booster shot of de-sulph and de-carb.'

'Good.' Bonnett turned to Garcia. 'Stick by him until I call you.'

'Righto.' Garcia ducked back through the door.

Bonnett's in command, thought Ramsey. *We never thought of that. Can he adjust to the job?* And then another thought: *Good Lord! What if he's the sleeper?* He studied the first officer covertly out of the corners of his eyes.

The *Ram* sped onward.

'Depth 550 fathoms,' said Ramsey.

Bonnett shifted the *Ram*'s diving planes, took them down to 500 fathoms in a low glide. He brought the deck level when the pressure gauge read 1300 pounds to the square inch.

'Twenty minutes,' said Ramsey.

'Give or take a few,' said Bonnett. 'What's wrong with Joe? Why doesn't he let us know how the skipper is?'

'You didn't tell him to,' said Ramsey.

'Yes, but—'

'There's most likely nothing to report. It's too soon.'

'Get him on the intercom.'

Ramsey shrugged, thumbed the switch on his chest mike: 'Joe?'

'Here.'

'How's the skipper?'

'Still sleeping. I'd give a pretty to know what the overdose actually was.'

'Did you check his suit dosometer?'

'Right after he got out of the tunnel. Slight overage, just as Les said.

You know, I'm no medical chap, but I'd bloody well swear that he'd gotten contaminated atmos.'

'How?'

'I don't know, really. I saw him check suit pressure before going in. It was still holding when he came out. I'm certain there were no leaks.'

'Did you snoop the tunnel filter system?'

'That's what I'm worried about, Johnny. I naturally assumed—'

Bonnett interrupted, speaking into his own microphone: 'Can you leave the skipper?'

'Yes. He's resting quietly.'

'Get forward and snoop that filter.'

'I'm on my way.'

Bonnett turned to Ramsey. 'There's a lesson for you and I'm ashamed to say it of Joe: Never assume anything. You have to know!'

'Couldn't he assume that the tunnel's filter system was okay?'

'Well . . .'

'We assume a lot of things about our little world.'

'The perfect ecology,' muttered Bonnett. 'Self-sustaining.'

Garcia slipped into the control room, went out the forward door without speaking.

'If that filter system is leaking,' said Bonnett, 'I'll—'

'Signal!' Ramsey slapped the cut-off switch, silencing the drive. The *Ram* drifted. 'Quartering to the east.' He narrowed down the tuning band. 'Pack. There's more behind us!' He rotated the finder band. 'More at 340.'

'Boxed!' said Bonnett. 'Have they spotted us?'

'Can't be certain. No collision courses.'

'What's the depth?'

'Reading now 680 fathoms. We're on the edge of the basin.'

Bonnett engaged the drive, eased them forward at minimum speed. 'Tell me the instant you detect a change of course from one of those signals.'

'Aye.'

Garcia's voice came over the intercom. 'Les?'

'What is it?'

'Filter's cool, but the inner hose line shows a slight leakage.'

'How much?'

'Sixty m-r. I make it a thirty-eight-minute overdose.'

'Where's the leak?'

'Inside somewhere. Maybe that broken control arm slapped something. I can't tell from here.'

'Dog the hatch and come up here. We're ranging an EP signal.'

'Righto. I heard you slip the drive.'

Bonnett turned to Ramsey. 'Depth?'

'Something over 7200 feet. Shelving off rapidly. Les! That pack behind us has changed course.' Ramsey worked over his dials. 'They've closed the angle, but they're not headed for us.'

'It could be a trick! We can't chance it.' He fed more power to the drive. The *Ram* picked up speed.

'They're on us! They've altered course, increased speed.'

Bonnett pushed the drive control to its limit. They felt the straining of the giant engines.

Garcia stepped into the control room, wiped a spot of grease from his hand, looked at the searchscope. 'Have we had it, chaps?'

Bonnett ignored him. 'Depth?'

'A little over 1500 fathoms. I'd make it about 9100 feet.' Ramsey reset a dial beside the searchscope. 'The pack to our east has changed course. They are now on collision heading.'

'It was nice knowing you, gentlemen,' said Garcia.

'We can't turn east or south,' said Bonnett. 'Bottom is 2000 feet below our limit.'

'I'm getting an interference reading at 8400 feet,' said Ramsey. 'Seamount. Heading 215 degrees.'

'It might just as well be 84,000 feet,' said Garcia. 'That'd be something like 3600 pounds to the square inch, almost 600 over our limit.'

'They'll be in firing range within a half hour,' said Ramsey. He glanced at Bonnett. 'What happens to the pressure hull coefficient if we boost internal pressure beyond ten atmos?'

'We wouldn't be alive to enjoy it,' said Garcia.

'Maybe,' said Ramsey. He slipped his vampire gauge from its belt case, locked it onto his wrist, shot the needle into his vein. 'How long would it take to draw everything but the oxy out of our atmos?'

'Pure oxy?' Garcia appeared startled.

'What's on your mind?' asked Bonnett.

Ramsey said, 'Put the anhydrase generation on manual and balance it by sight.' He nodded toward the gauge on his wrist.

'What do the medics say about that?' asked Garcia.

'Nothing certain,' said Ramsey. 'I've heard it argued both ways.' He glanced at the scope in front of him. 'I think it may be our only chance.'

'Joe, take over here,' said Bonnett. He stepped away from the controls as Garcia took hold of the helm.

'What're you going to do, Les?'

'Unhook the governor from the anhydrase generator system.'

Garcia's head jerked around. 'You're not paying serious attention to this punk's suggestion!'

Bonnett already was removing the cover plate from the atmosphere controls. 'I am.'

'That's suicide.'

Bonnett looked to the scope in front of Ramsey. 'We're already dead. What do we have to lose?'

He put the cover plate carefully on the deck, returned to the maze of wiring which had been revealed.

'It's those red primaries at the top,' said Garcia.

'I know,' said Bonnett. He reached in with cutter pliers, snipped the wires. 'Do you think the skipper's all right?'

'This is no time to worry about that.'

Bonnett nodded, adjusted a pump control. 'Johnny, what's the helium reading?'

'Point four.'

Bonnett took out his own vampire gauge, adjusted it on his wrist. 'Joe, take us down. Heading 215 degrees. Johnny, how far to that seamount?'

'Six minutes.'

Bonnett's head snapped up. 'You been working time-over-distance in your head?'

Ramsey busied himself with the search controls as the *Ram*'s deck slanted downward. 'Yes.'

'We'll make a submariner out of him yet,' said Garcia. He looked at Bonnett. 'Are you sure it wouldn't be better to try floating up again?'

'They're too close,' said Bonnett. 'Besides, I'm afraid to take another chance on rolling. We sheared off the damper-control base in there.' He nodded toward the bow. 'No telling what we did to the pile base.'

Garcia wet his lips with his tongue.

'Won't they hear us go down?' asked Ramsey.

'They know our depth limit,' said Bonnett.

'This was your idea,' said Garcia. 'Are you getting cold feet?'

Ramsey swallowed.

'Their metal detection is poor,' said Bonnett. 'I'm counting on their thinking we've taken the deep six rather than risk their fish.'

'They won't hear any breaking up noises,' said Garcia.

'We hope,' said Ramsey.

Garcia paled.

Ramsey looked to the big static pressure gauge. 'Outside pressure 2900 pounds.' He glanced at Bonnett, 'Skipper.'

'We have only one skipper,' said Bonnett. 'He's aft in sick bay.'

'No, I'm not!'

They whirled. Sparrow stood in the aft doorway, hand on the metal rim, face pale and beaded with perspiration. 'What is the situation, Les?'

Bonnett told him.

Sparrow turned a searching look on Ramsey. 'This was your idea?'

Ramsey nodded. *How long was he standing there?* he wondered.

'What are your orders?' asked Bonnett.

'Carry on,' said Sparrow. 'You are in command.'

Bonnett turned back to the pressure controls. 'Helium below detection range,' he said. 'Shall we go sit in the mud, Joe?'

'The medics say it's theoretically possible for the human body to take 400 pounds under pure oxy and carbonic anhydrase conditions,' said Ramsey.

'Do all of them say that?' asked Bonnett.

'No, only some of them.'

'I can see it, now,' said Garcia. 'An account of the reactions of four human bodies to 400 pounds atmospheric pressure in a Hell Diver Class submarine, with technical commentary on the autopsies.'

Ramsey shivered, looked at the red center dial on the static pressure gauge showing the *Ram*'s internal pressure: 297 pounds to the square inch. He glanced at the vampire gauge on his wrist, said, 'CO_2 diffusion is now .266. We have .054 to go under present conditions.'

Bonnett said, 'I'll give us 350 pounds internal as a starter.' He opened a valve, increased the anhydrase pump setting.

'Two minutes to bottom,' said Ramsey. 'It's a long thin seamount, ridge running parallel with our course. About ten miles.'

'Pressure is holding,' said Bonnett. 'How long until that pack ranges us?'

'Fifteen minutes.'

Behind them, Sparrow said, 'Now we're going to find out how well these Hell Divers are built.'

'I'm more interested in how well I'm built,' said Garcia.

'I'd say the good Lord did an excellent job, all things considered,' said Bonnett.

Ramsey thought: *Now that was a strange remark from him. More what I'd have expected from Sparrow.*

'Lord, we beg your indulgence upon us,' said Sparrow. 'We who have no right to ask it. Amen.'

'Flatten the glide angle,' said Bonnett.

Garcia brought up the nose.

'Give us the nose eyes and two searchlights.'

The main screen above them came alive, showing a path of light through green water. Pale phosphorescent shapes ranged beyond the limits of the light.

Ramsey looked at the internal-pressure reading: 400 pounds even.

'Ease her down,' said Bonnett.

The deck tipped.

Outside pressure passed through 3400 pounds ... 3420 ... 3440 ... Ramsey found himself unable to tear his gaze away from the dial. 3500 ... 3520 ... 3540 ...

'Diffusion is normal,' said Bonnett. 'Is anyone feeling ill effects?'

'I feel silly,' said Garcia.

'Steady,' said Bonnett.

'Be alert for oxygen intoxication,' said Sparrow.

The pressure dial passed 3600 pounds ... 3620 ...

'Flatten the glide,' said Bonnett.

Garcia complied.

'How far to the bottom?'

Ramsey forced himself to look at his instruments.

'Fifty feet.'

'Down,' said Bonnett.

Again the deck tipped.

Now, they watched the big screen below the pressure gauge.

'There!' said Garcia.

It seemed to come at them out of a green fog; a long pie cut of red ooze slashed from the darkness by the searchlights. A uniform ripple pattern stretched diagonally across the ooze. It showed not a sign of sea life.

Garcia eased up the bow planes and the *Ram* grounded gently, stirring up a fog of the red ooze which clouded the screen.

'Kill the drive,' said Bonnett.

Garcia's hand already was on the switch. The motors fell silent.

Ramsey whispered, 'It's 8460 feet.'

'A new world's record,' said Garcia.

Sparrow stepped forward onto the control deck. 'Thank you, Lord,' he said.

'I've come to a decision,' said Ramsey. 'I'm just a natural-born coward. Nothing ever came so easy to me in all my life.'

'Is anybody feeling ill effects from the pressure?' asked Sparrow.

'I'm still feeling silly,' said Garcia.

'Anybody else?'

Ramsey shook his head, studied the search instruments in front of him.

'Diffusion is .214,' said Bonnett. 'We're still rid of it faster than we take it in.'

Ramsey said, 'Great God in heaven!'

'Where else would you expect him to be?' asked Garcia.

'There's a cold current moving in,' said Ramsey. 'Right over us.'

'God spreads his cloak upon us,' said Sparrow.

'Pack ranging over us to the south,' said Ramsey. 'Eight thousand yards.'

Bonnett said, 'Any indication that they smell us?'

'No.'

'They won't look where they don't believe we can be,' said Garcia. He grinned. 'And that's not strange. I don't believe I'm here, either.'

'I'm losing 'em through that cold layer,' said Ramsey.

'Skipper an' God are buddies,' said Garcia. 'Good close buddies. Do favors for each other alla time.' He staggered slightly.

Ramsey grabbed Garcia's wrist, looked at his vampire gauge. 'Diffusion normal. What's—'

'Oxygen reactions vary,' said Bonnett.

'What's wrong with you chaps?' Garcia's head wobbled. He peered at them owlishly.

'Take it easy, Joe,' said Sparrow.

'Easy?' He squinted up at Sparrow. 'I know you, Skipper. You're King David all over again. I've heard you.' He shook his head loosely, lifted his right hand. '"In my distress I called upon the Lord, and cried to my God: and he did hear my voice out of his temple, and my cry did enter into his ears."'

'All right, Joe. Let's go back and hit the sack.' Sparrow took Garcia's elbow, urged him toward the aft door.

'Leggo me,' said Garcia. He shook off Sparrow's hand, staggered, caught his balance, turned, and stared deliberately at Ramsey. 'I know all about you, Mr Long John Ramsey. You look down your long nose at me! Think you know somethin' bout me. You don't know nothin'. Nothin'!'

'That will be quite enough, Mr Garcia.' Sparrow's voice had iron in it, a harsh note of command.

'Sorry, Skipper.' He turned toward the door. 'Le's go. 'M tired.'

Sparrow stared at Ramsey, then turned, urged Garcia out the door.

In the control room there was silence for a moment broken only by the faintest murmuring of standby machinery. Then Bonnett said, 'Long John? How'd you get a nickname like that?'

Ramsey studied his instrument before turning toward Bonnett. *That damned nickname! It could mean only that Garcia knew about his past – his real past.*

Bonnett said, 'I asked—'

'Yes, I heard you. A supply officer christened me. Said I was a worse pirate than the original Long John Silver. That's all.'

'Pirate? Why?'

'For scrounging extra equipment. Moonlight requisition.'

Bonnett smiled. 'I don't see why that'd put Joe on his ear. Unless he's jealous of someone better at it than he is.'

And Ramsey was thinking: *Garcia will tell the skipper. Sure as hell he will.*

'Is it extra hot in here?' asked Bonnett.

Ramsey looked at the beads of perspiration on Bonnett's face, glanced at his vampire gauge. Blood temperature normal. He looked at the dial of the thermo-system monitor on his board, said, 'Seventy-one degrees.'

'My skin feels itchy,' said Bonnett.

Ramsey resisted the impulse to scratch at his own forearm, said, 'I've been noticing the same thing.'

Bonnett glanced at the exposed wiring of the atmosphere controls, checked a dial setting. 'Anhydrase generation is double the normal. Gas volume twenty cc's per cubic meter.'

'We're off in a wild unknown,' said Ramsey.

'We shouldn't be,' said Bonnett. 'We've had carbonic anhydrase for forty years.'

Ramsey reset a kick-out meter on his sono-board, looked up at the primary oscilloscope.

'Hear anything?'

Ramsey shook his head. 'This C-A is funny stuff, Les. We've pushed chimpanzees to 400 pounds with it for extended periods. Some lived. Some didn't. A few of the bright boys think they know why.'

'Why?'

'Well, the theory is that C-A acts on a rather nebulous central nervous system thing called the "metabolic governor" in such a way as to keep us from burning up when available oxygen is increased. They think sometimes the governor gets a little bit off – out of timing kind of – and the organism gets caught in a feedback situation: oscillates to death.'

'Why?'

'That they don't know. Maybe the "metabolic governor" gets tired.'

'What're the chances one of us'll get caught that way?'

Ramsey shot a sharp glance at him, looked at the search board. 'That's a stupid question, Les.'

Bonnett colored. His jaw set.

'If you're trying to get me to reassure you, no dice,' said Ramsey. 'All I know is we're still alive, even if we are a bit uncom— Signal!' He slapped the switch on the ranging computer, read the dial. 'Five hundred yards. They're quartering southwest.'

'Do we still have God's cold cloak over us?'

Ramsey caught a jibing cynicism in Bonnett's voice he had never noted before. He glanced at the thermocouple dial. 'It's been over us periodically. Gone now. I think this seamount acts like a barrier to the Arctic Current. Probably sets up complex whorl patterns.' He looked back to the ranging dials. 'The EPs are holding course. They're drawing away now.'

'Was there any doubt that they would?' asked Bonnett.

'What do you mean?'

'You've some things to learn yet about our skipper,' said Bonnett. 'Joe wasn't joking. There's an unca—'

The *Ram* gave an abrupt lurch and the deck tipped two degrees left.

Ramsey caught the rail in front of his board. 'What the—'

'The tow,' said Bonnett. 'Current's playing with it.'

'I felt it nudge us when we sat down,' said Ramsey. 'But the bumpers—'

They lurched another degree to the left.

'Just pray it doesn't drag us off this mountain,' said Bonnett. 'We couldn't take the extra 500 feet.'

'How do you know?' asked Ramsey. He studied the search board.

'I feel the mountain under my feet all foggy.'

Ramsey looked up. 'What'd you say?'

'I feel all foggy in the head,' said Bonnett. He leaned against the grab-rail. 'Fall off the mountain. Hate the fog.' He forced himself upright. 'Not thinking straight. Take over, Mr Ramsey. I'm . . . I'm—' He sat down on the deck, one hand above him still clinging to the rail.

An abrupt correlation interlocked in Ramsey's mind. He glanced one more time over his search board, turned away, forced himself to walk calmly across to Bonnett. He bent over the first officer, checked Bonnett's vampire gauge. CO_2 diffusion .228. Above normal by .016. He dropped Bonnett's wrist, stood up and made a minute micro-meter-gauge reduction in anhydrase generation.

'What's wrong with Les?' Sparrow stood in the aft door, gaze sweeping over the control deck. He stepped through the door as Ramsey turned.

'Take it slow,' said Ramsey.

'Wha—' Sparrow hesitated in midstride.

Ramsey bent over Bonnett, again checked his vampire gauge, compared it with the one on his own wrist. No change. Too soon. He said, 'I've just formed the Ramsey Theory on why some chimpanzees died and some didn't.'

Sparrow again moved forward, bent over Bonnett. 'What chimpanzees?'

'The chimps Med. I put under 400 pounds with peak anhydrase. My advice is for you not to overexert, get excited, nervous, or—'

'I know about the chimps,' said Sparrow. 'Do you think—' He hesitated.

'Some kind of glandular upset,' said Ramsey. 'What more likely than an emotional trigger, maybe coupled to physical activity?'

Sparrow nodded.

Ramsey noted the vampire-gauge needles sinking toward normal. He began massaging Bonnett's left arm. 'You're okay, Les. Just relax and take it easy. The crisis is over. Take it easy ... take it easy ... take it easy ...'

Bonnett's head rocked groggily.

'We have to avoid excitement,' said Ramsey. 'Our bodies are walking a tight wire down here. An uneasy balance.'

Sparrow stood up, went to the search board. 'I gave Joe a sedative. He was crying, raving. Maybe I—' He fell silent.

Bonnett opened his eyes.

'Remain calm,' said Ramsey. 'Do you hear me, Les?'

The first officer nodded.

'There's no danger if you relax.'

'You can't force a man to relax,' said Sparrow.

Ramsey reached around Bonnett's head, found the nerve line on the back of his neck, massaged it. 'You're feeling better already.'

Bonnett wet his lips with his tongue. ''M okay. Get back to your board.'

'Breathe slow and easy,' said Ramsey. He stood up.

Bonnett swallowed, spoke as though past a thickened tongue. 'It was like quicksand. Feelin' better now.'

Ramsey turned toward Sparrow. 'He'll be okay now.'

Sparrow glanced down at Bonnett. 'Stay where you are, Les, until you feel like getting up.' He turned to Ramsey. 'I've been on the eyes. The current has pulled our tow to a forty-five-degree angle across our stern.

If we slack off the top towline we'll right but that might free the tow for a further shift.'

'Best leave well enough alone,' said Ramsey.

'How near the edge of this seamount are we? The eyes don't show it.'

'Maybe seventy-five yards. For the tow, that is. We were angling away from the edge when we sat down.'

Sparrow looked at the ranging computers. 'Intermittent signal near extreme range.'

'That cold layer is waving over us like a fan,' said Ramsey.

Sparrow backed away from the board, looked around him, brought his attention back to Ramsey. There was something in the way he looked at Ramsey of the same attention he gave to his boat's instruments. 'What's this "Long John" business? Joe doesn't make sense.'

Ramsey repeated what he had told Bonnett.

'Did the *Ram* benefit from this acquisition propensity of yours?'

'Not this trip, Skipper.'

Sparrow glanced upward to the row of reactor-room telltales. 'Maybe next trip.'

Bonnett spoke from his position on the deck. 'We're gonna have a next trip, too. If we don't crack up like poor Hepp.'

'We won't,' said Sparrow.

Bonnett heaved himself to his feet. 'I'm glad we have God's word on that.'

Sparrow gave him a searching stare, said, 'I'm reassuming command, Les. The circumstances warrant it. I'm in no immediate danger from that radiation overage.'

'Of course, Skipper.' There seemed a sigh of relief in Bonnett's voice.

Sparrow said, 'I'm going back now and have another look at Joe. I'm leaving Johnny on the search board. All clear?'

'All clear, Skipper.'

Sparrow turned his angular form slowly, went out the aft door.

'He's an automaton,' said Ramsey, addressing the empty air where Sparrow had stood.

'He's under more pressure than the submarine,' said Bonnett. He took a deep breath. 'Let's you pay attention to that board.'

Ramsey frowned, returned his attention to his gauges and dials.

Silence hung between them.

Presently, Bonnett said, 'Thanks, Johnny. Maybe you saved my life.'

Ramsey shrugged, remained silent.

'I heard what you told the skipper. It feels right. Come to think of it, maybe you saved all of our lives.'

'Be damned lonesome down here all alone,' said Ramsey.

'You'd probably prefer three well-stacked blondes,' said Bonnett. 'Come to think of it, that'd get my vote, too.'

'Another signal at outer range,' said Ramsey. 'Six subs in net-search spacing. They'll pass out of range in the southeast quadrant.'

'They just ain't looking where nobody could possibly be,' said Bonnett. 'Can't say that I blame them. I still don't believe I'm here.' He glanced up at the static pressure gauge, looked quickly away.

'No need for two of us here,' said Ramsey.

'Nothing except the skipper's double-team orders.'

'Stupid orders,' said Ramsey.

'Take it easy, lad,' said Bonnett. 'You can't fight the Navy chain of command and you can't fight God.' He shrugged. 'And when the two are on the same team—'

'What makes you believe that nonsense?' asked Ramsey.

Bonnett froze. 'I make jokes, boy. That's one thing. What you just said is another thing.' He shook his head. 'I've been forty missions with that Savvy Sparrow guy. Don't talk to me about nonsense. I know what I've seen.'

And you know what you want to believe, thought Ramsey.

Somewhere a faint dripping caught his attention: condensation on the pipes. The *Ram* suddenly assumed a cold empty feeling around him. *We're not going to make it*, he thought. *A thousand alert enemy subs ranging across our track. It was crazy to send us out. A desperation move.*

The lights of his thermocouple monitor winked blindly on the instrument board.

God's cold cloak waving over us! Maybe that's the best thing to believe. Knowledge is the course of our lives. We eat the apple and we learn just enough to make us afraid.

The *Ram* shuddered briefly as the current tugged at her tow. The deck tilted back toward level.

'If we raise a big mud patch on the surface – stirring up the bottom like a mud pie – they'll spot it,' said Bonnett. 'They'll have a sky full of buzzards this close to their own shores.'

'How'll they see it in the fog?' asked Ramsey. He felt a sudden lightening of his spirits.

'Fog topside? How can you tell?'

'Skipper arranged it with God,' said Ramsey.

'You think you're joking,' said Bonnett. He looked at Ramsey. 'You do, don't you?'

Ramsey reset the ranging computer in front of him. 'A man has to live with his boat – be a part of it,' he said, speaking lightly. He felt the sudden undertow pull of thought below the words. It was like stepping outside his body and watching it function. 'This boat believes in God,' he said.

The counter hands of the timelog swept around . . . around . . . around. . . . The watches changed as the *Ram* snuggled into the mud of the seamount.

Eleven days, thirty-two minutes from point of departure.

Sparrow stood at the control board with Ramsey, sharing the last half of the electronics officer's watch. The sense of excess pressure outside their hull had become a thing accepted.

'How long since you've heard one of their packs?' asked Sparrow.

'Over six hours.'

'How's the tow?'

Ramsey checked the line telltales, switched on the stern eyes one by one. 'Laying to starboard about thirty degrees. Towlines clear.'

Sparrow tested the drive controls, switched on the motors. A humming sense of expectancy came over the sub-tug. Ramsey felt it tingle through his body, starting in his feet against the deck.

'Let's go get that oil,' said Sparrow. He threw in the drive switch, threw it off. 'Just to stir up the mud around us. Drop four waist torpedoes, Johnny. We'll need buoyancy.'

'What about the tow? It's not carrying enough pressure to blow at this depth.'

'We're going to jerk it off the bottom. Pay out line until we get a good run on.'

Ramsey pushed down the flat black toggles which dropped the torpedoes from the waist belt.

The *Ram* bobbled upward. Sparrow again threw power into the drive. The subtug slanted upward, towline reeling out behind them.

'Snub it,' said Sparrow.

Ramsey locked the magnetic brakes on the outside reel drums. The tug came almost to a full stop, motors straining. Slowly they struggled ahead.

'Line stretching,' said Ramsey. 'That slug's in solid.'

Sparrow shook his head. 'How much more line?'

'Eight hundred feet more or less.'

'Give us some more.'

The *Ram* again angled upward. Sparrow circled left, came back to the right in a snake track, barely moving.

'Operational depth,' said Ramsey. 'Outside pressure 2994 pounds.'

'Snub towlines and blow number-one tank,' said Sparrow.

Again Ramsey stopped the outside reels. His right hand went out to the red handle marked 'high pressure air.' He set it over number one, flicked on the safety toggle, started bleeding air into the number-one tank.

'Give it everything,' said Sparrow.

Ramsey turned the valve two revolutions.

Sparrow put full power into the drive. The *Ram*'s bow tipped up to almost ten degrees. By inches, they climbed, twisting soggily.

'She's off,' said Ramsey.

'How's the slug's compensator system?'

Ramsey looked to the tow board. 'Following the pressure curve.'

'Blow the slug's bow and stern tanks,' said Sparrow.

'She's not at—'

'Blow them anyway. Water pressure will hold the air until we reach operational depth. We're going to need all the help we can get and as soon as we can get it.'

Ramsey's hands moved over the tow board carrying out his orders.

They inched upward. Ramsey stared at the red dials of the slug's pressure system. 'Bow tank's beginning to bubble.'

They could feel it in the deck: a return to normal climb gradient, speed picking up.

'Bow tank just blew,' said Ramsey. 'There goes the stern.' He wiped perspiration from his forehead.

'That was the thing Les should have considered,' said Sparrow. 'Now we know we can get off. As long as we have external weight which we can drop for the initial buoyancy.'

'How do you know that Les didn't—'

'I know my shipmates,' said Sparrow. 'Learn something from this, Johnny, and you'll make a good submariner. Never head into anything with a sub unless you have already worked out a plan for coming out the other side.'

Ramsey chose his words carefully. 'What's your plan for making the big come-out on the other side – with the oil?'

'Not just one plan,' said Sparrow. 'I have plans for every contingency I can think of. And for some maybe I shouldn't have thought of.'

'Like for instance?'

Sparrow turned and looked full at him. 'Like for instance my crew going psychotic, one by one.'

Ramsey's eyes widened. The words leaped out before he could stop them. 'And what about yourself?'

Sparrow's eyes glittered. 'That's one of the ones maybe I shouldn't have thought of,' he said. He swung back to the controls.

He's like a piece of machinery, thought Ramsey. *Great God in heaven, what went into making a man like that?*

Bonnett entered carrying a hypodermic, its needle covered by a sterile pad. 'Time for your shot, Skipper.'

'In my left arm?' asked Sparrow.

'Well—'

'Don't I get to keep any dignity?' asked Sparrow.

Ramsey grinned.

'I swear you guys take a perverse delight in this,' growled Sparrow.

'It's really too much for your arm,' said Bonnett. He glanced up at the static gauge. 'Six thousand feet! What're we doing up here in the shallows?'

Sparrow chuckled. 'Okay, take my mind off my troubles.' He backed away from the board. 'Take over here, Johnny.' Ramsey stepped into control position. Behind him, he heard Sparrow grunt. 'Easy, Les!'

'Easy as I could, Skipper. There. Have Joe check you on his watch. You seem to be coming along okay.'

'I should be. I've three nursemaids.'

Sparrow moved up beside Ramsey. 'Hold us on course sixty-four degrees, forty-five minutes.'

Ramsey turned the helm, looked up at the sonoran chart. 'That'll bring us around Nordkapp.' He did some mental figuring, glanced at the shaftlog counter. 'About twenty-six and a half hours.'

Sparrow looked startled.

'He's good with figures,' said Bonnett.

'He's also too interested in where we're going to be and when,' said Sparrow.

'That Security pap is for the birds,' said Ramsey.

'I wish to remind you that we found a dead man aboard this vessel, that we've been sabotaged right and left, that—' He broke off, staring at Ramsey.

It was Bonnett's turn to look startled.

And now I'm in over my head, thought Ramsey. *My plan had better be right or I won't . . . come out the other side.*

Sparrow looked at the timelog. 'Time for Les to go on watch now.' He gestured for Bonnett to take the helm. 'Put us on auto-pilot. Steady as she goes.'

Ramsey went to the aft door, found Sparrow staring at him. The captain turned deliberately away, moved closer to Bonnett. 'Stand by the search board as soon as we're on auto-pilot.'

'Aye, Skipper.'

Ramsey went out the door, swung it almost closed behind him, stood there with his ear to the crack.

Bonnett said, 'How's Joe?'

'He's all right. He'll stand his regular watch.'

'What's with this Long John Ramsey? Skipper, could he be a phony?'

'No doubt of it,' said Sparrow. 'The only question in my mind is: What kind of phony?'

'Could he be a—'

'He very definitely could be. Someone loaded us with spy beams and trapped that Security officer.'

'But Ramsey wasn't aboard then.'

'That's what bothers me. Unless there was something wrong with the Security man's timing. That would explain it.'

'I'll watch him, Skipper.'

'You do that. I'm also alerting Joe.'

Ramsey tiptoed away from the door. *Well, I did it*, he thought. *I'd better be right*. He shuddered, turned at the end of the companionway, dropped down to his cabin level. He paused in front of Garcia's cabin, looked at the blank metal of the door. Again the thought passed through his mind: *I'd better be right*.

He went into his cabin, closing the door softly behind him, locking it. Then he brought out the telemeter, unreeled the tapes.

There was response for Sparrow's time in the tunnel repairing the pile controls, but now Sparrow was under rigid control. The wave patterns on the tapes were like the path of a rubber ball bouncing between two walls.

I have to be able to crack that control at will, thought Ramsey. *He has to fail – just once. At the right time and at the right thing.*

And another part of his mind said: *That's a helluva way to make someone well.*

He fought down that thought. *It has to be. It's accepted practice. It works.*

Most of the time.

Sparrow's advice came back to him: '*Never head into anything unless you have already worked out a plan for coming out the other side.*'

Ramsey sat down on his bunk, reset the telemeter, sealed it, slid it back beneath his desk.

What if my plan doesn't work? What's my alternative for that contingency?

He lay back on his bunk, staring at the rivet pattern overhead. Around him, the muted throbbing and humming of the subtug took on a fantasy life. As though it knew where it was going and how to get there.

Ramsey fell into a troubled sleep, awoke for his next watch to find his body soaked in perspiration, a disturbing half memory of a dream – no, a nightmare – which he could not bring to consciousness.

The automatic timelog read twelve days, seven hours, and five minutes from departure. Last half of Garcia's watch, first half of Bonnett's. The red dot on the sonoran chart stood well into the shore off Nordkapp: shallow water with the *Ram* creeping along the bottom in one hundred fathoms.

In the control room, a brightly lighted sweep of bulkhead, telltales flashing, heavy shadows on the undersides of levers and valve wheels. Wavering admonitions of dial needles. The two men bent over their work like laborers in a metal cave.

Bonnett looked up to the static pressure: 260 pounds to the square inch. 'What's the skipper thinking of, coming in close like this?'

'Don't ask so many questions.' Garcia made a minute adjustment in the bow planes, watched the depth repeater. 'We're twenty feet from bottom.'

Sparrow ducked through the door from the aft companionway. 'Anything showing on the search board?' His voice was husky with a sense of fatigue. He coughed.

'Negative,' said Bonnett.

'This is their water,' said Sparrow. 'They've no shore stations along the north coast; only along the Norway reaches.'

'This is still awful close,' said Bonnett. Again he looked to the depth gauge. 'And awful shallow.'

'You don't think this is a safe place for us?' asked Sparrow.

'No.'

'Good. That means they don't either. They know this is a *deep* tug. They're out scouring the Norwegian basin. The sill depth there is right on our known limit.'

'So?'

'So we're going to shoot right across the shallows.' He glanced at Garcia, then up to the sonoran chart. 'Course seventy degrees, Joe.'

Garcia swung the helm, watched the compass until they were heading true, then he, too, looked at the chart. 'Novaya Zemlya,' he whispered.

'We're shallow enough to start taking outside samples,' said Sparrow. 'Les, look for an isobaric surface running almost parallel with our course. We could use the shielding of some cold water.'

Bonnett pulled down a density-gradient chart for the area, checked the isobaric differences, ran a siphon sample of the exterior water. 'Give us sixty-nine degrees for five minutes,' he said.

Garcia touched the helm. They watched the thermocouple repeater. Suddenly, it dipped fifteen degrees. 'Resume course,' said Sparrow.

The *Ram* returned to seventy degrees, cruising under the sheltering mask of the cold current which spilled down around them.

'Steady as she goes,' said Sparrow. 'Push search to limit. It's a straight run from here on in.'

'It's Novaya Zemlya, isn't it?' asked Garcia.

Sparrow hesitated, then: 'It's obvious anyway. Yes.'

'That's an EP rocket-testing base,' said Bonnett. 'It'll be bristling with buzzards and snoopers.'

'We dug the well right under their noses,' said Sparrow. 'If we could dig without their hearing us, we ought to be able to drain it dry undetected.'

'Are they tapping the reservoir, too?'

Sparrow grinned wolfishly, his long face glistening in the multi-hued lights of the control board. 'That's the beauty of it. They don't even know it's there.'

'Lord,' whispered Bonnett. 'A fresh well. What're we looking for in the way of landmarks?'

Again Sparrow hesitated while his eyes sought out the red dot on the sonoran chart. *It wouldn't even be a secret from the EPs if they spotted us here*, he thought. *Now, we're in God's hands for sure.*

'We're looking for a narrow fault fissure,' he said. 'It's called the gut and it slants right up into the island shelf. You can't miss it once you range across it. Depth down to 3600 feet and only 400 feet across.'

'Fissure is right,' said Garcia. 'Do we go down into that thing?'

'No. It's our trail. We track it in.' Again he looked at the chart. 'Thirty-three hours at this rate.' He turned to the aft door. 'Call me if anything develops.'

And he was gone down the companionway.

'If anything develops,' muttered Bonnett. 'We're sitting ducks. The only development we'll get is a fish in our belly. That'll wake him!'

'I think he's right,' said Garcia. 'They're all out in the deeps looking for us. This is going to be a milk run.'

'I'm curdled already,' said Bonnett. He fell silent, watching the search board.

The *Ram* drove onward, headlong across the shallows like a frightened fish. The hands of the timelog swept around, around.

'Relieving Mr Garcia on watch.' Ramsey spoke as he ducked through the door into the control room. He could sense the immediate stiffening of the two men on the board, the mounting tension.

Garcia made an attempt at casual banter. 'Look who's gone all Navy formal on us.'

Ramsey took up his position beside Garcia. 'What course?'

'Seventy degrees.' Garcia surrendered the helm.

'Busting right across the shallows,' said Ramsey. 'If we make this, I'm going to burn a candle to St. Cuthbert.'

'That's not good talk,' said Bonnett.

'Have you heard what the EPs have done now?' asked Ramsey. 'They've put engines in Novaya Zemlya. When we get close they're going to move it right out of our way, let us go lumbering off into Siberia.'

'Clever chaps,' said Garcia.

'Skipper's going to run us right into an EP trap net,' said Ramsey. 'We'll spend the rest of the war in a prison camp being brainwashed while they take the *Ram* apart bolt by—'

'Button your bloody lip,' said Garcia. 'We're going to pull this one off. And when we set foot on that blessed dock I'm going to take an obscene pleasure in pushing you—'

'That will be enough!' said Bonnett. 'This is no time for fighting among ourselves.'

'You wouldn't say that if you knew all about this wise guy,' said Garcia. 'The superior brain: knows all, sees all, tells nothing!'

'Hit the sack, Joe,' said Bonnett. 'That's an order.'

Garcia glowered at Ramsey, turned away, went out the aft door.

'What're you trying to prove, Johnny?'

'How do you mean?'

'Baiting Joe like that.'

'He baits easy.'

Bonnett stared at him. 'One way to wreck a ship is to destroy crew morale,' he said. 'There will be no more such actions from you on this cruise.'

'You sound like one of the old ladies of Security,' said Ramsey.

Bonnett's face darkened. 'Knock it off, Mr Ramsey. This won't work with me.'

It's already working, thought Ramsey. He said, 'This is going to be a really gay bunch when we get to Novaya Zemlya. All of us looking over each other's shoulders.'

'How do you know where we're headed?' gritted Bonnett. 'You weren't here when Skipper announced our destination.'

'I read tea leaves.' Ramsey nodded toward the depth-gauge graph tape. 'Are we looking for that?'

Bonnett snapped his attention back to the tape. A sharp line broke off the tape, came back on after a brief interval.

'That's a *development*,' said Bonnett. 'Buzz the skipper.'

Ramsey depressed the black toggle of the number-one call button. 'Shall I hold course?'

'No. Quarter back on – Signal!' He slapped the button for the range computer, shut off the drive. 'Eighteen miles. Intercept course.'

Ramsey whirled the helm to the right. 'Have they heard us?'

'There's no telling,' said Bonnett. They coasted silently while he watched the pips on his screen.

Sparrow entered the control room. 'Signal?'

'Heading 270 degrees,' said Bonnett.

'What's the depth here?'

'Four hundred feet, give or take a few.'

'You're forgetting something,' said Ramsey. He pointed to the tape record of the deep fissure.

'Hide in that thing?' Bonnett's voice rose half an octave. 'We couldn't maneuver. Straight down the alley and they'd have us bottled up.'

The *Ram*'s deck began to tip to the left as they lost way.

'Give us headway,' ordered Sparrow.

Ramsey eased in the drive. He watched the pulse-reader showing bottom depth below them. Abruptly, it fell off beyond the meter setting. Without being told, Ramsey brought the helm up to left until they were over the fissure.

'Down into it,' said Sparrow.

'What if it narrows down to nothing?' asked Bonnett.

'We couldn't back out without fouling our towlines. We'll be—'

'Watch your board,' ordered Sparrow.

The oscillations on the screen damped down, then blanked out.

'Full speed,' said Sparrow. 'Down farther, Johnny!'

Ramsey felt the excitement gripping his stomach. 'The walls of this fissure are hiding our sound!'

'If we hit something, we've had it,' said Bonnett.

Sparrow glanced at the big static pressure gauge: 1240 pounds. 'Give us a pulse sweep on those walls – fifth-second intervals.'

'Whatta you think I'm doing?' muttered Bonnett.

Sparrow grinned. He put a hand on Ramsey's shoulder. 'Ease her up.'

'Speed?'

'No, depth. Set us level.'

Ramsey brought up the bow planes. The *Ram*'s deck came up to level.

'One degree right,' said Bonnett.

Ramsey swung the helm.

'We're doing twenty-two knots,' said Sparrow. 'If we can just put—'

'Two degrees right,' said Bonnett.

'Coax a little more speed out of her,' said Sparrow.

Ramsey fined down the setting on the magnometer for the induction drive.

'Open the silencers,' said Sparrow.

'But—'

Sparrow's fingers dug into Ramsey's shoulder. 'Do it!'

Ramsey's hand went out, jerked down the big red handle above the helm. They could feel the added surge of power.

'Twenty-eight knots,' said Sparrow. 'There's life in the old girl yet.'

'Two degrees left,' said Bonnett.

Ramsey complied.

'An EP subcruiser can do forty-five knots,' said Bonnett. 'Are you trying to run away from them?'

'How fast were they closing us at our last known position?' asked Sparrow.

'Estimated search speed of twenty knots,' said Bonnett. 'Say forty-five or fifty minutes unless they were on us and upped speed when we went out of sound. Then maybe only a half hour.'

Sparrow looked at the timelog. 'We'll count on a half hour.' He waited silently.

'Two degrees left,' said Bonnett.

Ramsey brought the helm over, straightened them out on the new course.

'She's narrowing down,' said Bonnett. 'No more than 300 feet wide here.' He reset the ranging computer. 'Now it's down to 250. Here's – Two degrees left!'

Ramsey swung the helm.

'We're all right if we don't scrape the slug off on the walls of this hole,' said Sparrow.

'Three degrees right.'

Ramsey obeyed.

'Two hundred feet,' said Bonnett. 'Minus ... minus ... 185 ... 200 ... 215 – Two degrees right.'

The *Ram* tipped to the rudder response.

'Give us the silencer planes,' said Sparrow.

Ramsey pushed up the big red handle. They could feel the drag.

'Half speed,' said Sparrow. 'How far to the canyon rim?'

'I can only guess,' said Bonnett. 'Too sharp an angle to get a difference reading.'

'Well, guess then.'

'Eighteen hundred feet.'

'Hear anything behind us?'

'Negative.'

'Motors off,' said Sparrow.

Ramsey silenced the drive.

'Now, do you hear anything?'

Bonnett fussed with his instruments. 'Negative.'

'Full speed,' said Sparrow. 'Two degrees on the bow planes.'

'Two degrees on the bow planes,' acknowledged Ramsey. He brought up the planes, eased in the drive, sent them surging upward.

'One degree left,' said Bonnett.

Ramsey swung the helm.

Sparrow looked at the pressure reading: 860 pounds. They were above 2000 feet. Still the *Ram* coursed upward. 'Half speed,' said Sparrow.

Ramsey brought back the throttle control to the mid-notch.

'I can give you a rim reading,' said Bonnett. 'About ninety fathoms.'

'Five hundred and forty feet,' translated Sparrow. 'Are you sure of that still depth?'

Bonnett rechecked his instruments. 'Reasonably sure. I can give you a better reading in a minute.'

Again Sparrow looked to the pressure gauge: 600 pounds.

'Make it eighty fathoms,' said Bonnett. 'I was getting angular distortion.'

'Four hundred and eighty feet,' said Sparrow. 'Less than a thousand to go. Quarter speed, if you please.'

Again Ramsey brought the throttle bar back a full notch.

'Hear anything, Les?'

'Negative.'

The pressure gauge climbed past 400 pounds to the square inch: above 1000-foot depth.

'I make that canyon rim in 460 feet of water,' said Bonnett.

'Anything on the phones yet?'

'Still quiet.'

'Give us full power until we reach maximum speed,' said Sparrow. 'Then shut everything down and coast up onto the rim. Set us down gently as you can.'

Ramsey's eyes widened.

'Now,' said Sparrow.

Ramsey shot the throttle forward. The subtug leaped ahead. They watched the pitlog sweep through twenty-three knots.

'Now!' barked Sparrow.

Ramsey killed the drive, freed the induction system to allow the propeller to spin free. He jockeyed the planes to keep them on an even keel with the least drag.

'We're over,' said Bonnett.

Ramsey watched the pitlog, began counting off the time-over-distance until he was certain the tow had cleared. Then he brought the bow planes down.

They grounded in mud with almost no headway.

'I'm hearing them, Skipper,' said Bonnett. 'About ten miles behind us and to the—'

'What's wrong?'

'Lost 'em.'

'They've gone into the gut after us,' said Ramsey.

'Lift us,' said Sparrow. 'Force speed!'

Ramsey jerked into motion, fed power into the drive, eased them off the bottom, pushed the throttle to the final notch.

Sparrow watched the timelog. Five minutes. 'Kill the drive.'

'Still silent,' said Bonnett.

'Five minutes more,' said Sparrow.

Ramsey again sent them shooting ahead. Five minutes. Drift and listen. Five minutes. Drift and listen. Five minutes. Drift and listen.

'Set us into the mud again, Johnny.'

The *Ram* slanted down, grounded on a ripple surface of black manganese pebbles.

'We've come eight miles from the gut,' said Bonnett. He looked at the pressure gauge: 300 pounds. 'It's only 700 feet deep here.'

'What do we care?' asked Ramsey. 'They think we're in that slot. They'll be scraping the bottom of it.'

Sparrow said, 'And there goes the whole shooting match.'

Ramsey looked at him sharply. 'What do you mean?'

'They spotted us too close to target. And right on the trail leading to the well.'

'How do they know it wasn't a feint?'

'No. They know we were hiding. They know—' He fell silent.

'You mean we're going to slink home empty-handed?' It was Bonnett, voice bitter.

'I wouldn't give them the satisfaction.' The voice came from the aft door: Garcia.

The three in the control room whirled.

Garcia stepped fully onto the control deck. 'We've *got* to thumb our noses at them, Skipper.'

'How long've you been there?' asked Sparrow.

Garcia frowned. 'Maybe ten minutes. I heard the shift in speed and felt—' He broke off. 'Skipper, we've come too far to—'

'Relax,' said Sparrow. 'We're going through.'

'How?'

'We're going to sit here.'

'How long?' asked Ramsey.

'Maybe a day; maybe longer. Until they get tired of looking or decide they've missed us.'

'But they're sure to leave a stakeout around here on just that chance,' protested Bonnett.

'Let's just pray that they do,' said Sparrow. 'Les, take over the controls and standby search. Johnny, you and Joe come with me.' Sparrow led the way across to the chart board. He swept his earlier work aside, pulled out a fresh sheet of scratch paper, began drawing cyclic curves across it. He took a second sheet, repeated the performance.

Ramsey watched, puzzled, Garcia bent close to the work.

Presently, Sparrow straightened. 'What do I have here, Johnny?'

'It could be a sonic curve, but—'

'It's the modulated beat of one of our A-2 fish,' said Garcia.

Sparrow nodded. 'Now watch this.' He lifted one of the sheets, placed it over the other, held both to a light and adjusted them. He clipped the sheets together, still holding them up to the light, began to draw a new freehand curve, a broken scrawl on the surface 'That's rough,' he said, 'but it gives the idea.'

'A silencer-damped screw beat from the *Ram*,' said Ramsey.

'Two of our A-2 fish hooked in tandem and their screws set to resonate,' said Sparrow.

'It might fool an EP until he got close enough to detect the difference in mass,' said Ramsey.

Sparrow nodded. 'And what if our pair of fish carried a scrambler set to go off before they could detect mass difference?'

Ramsey stepped back from the board, stared at Sparrow.

'These are shallow waters,' he said. 'The EPs would blanket the distortion area and flood it with seeker fish and—'

'And they'd get a very satisfactory explosion,' said Sparrow.

'This is all very well, but how're we going to rig our fish out there when we're in 700 feet of water and unable to start our engines?' asked Garcia.

'We've a perfect stabilizer,' said Sparrow. 'The slug. We bleed air into our tanks until we gain enough buoyance to lift; then we pay out towline until we reach 300 feet where we can go outside and do our work. The slug anchors us.'

'Balance on the four points of the towlines,' muttered Garcia. 'It'll bloody well work. It will.' He looked up at Sparrow. 'Skipper, you're a genius.'

'Can you two rig those fish to fake the sound of our screw?' asked Sparrow.

Ramsey grinned. 'Just let us out there.'

'One more thing,' said Sparrow. 'I'll want you to alter the drive speed controls like this—' Again, he bent over the chart board, scribbling on the scratch pad.

Ramsey shook his head. 'Just a minute, Skipper.'

Sparrow stopped, looked up at Ramsey.

The electronics officer took the pencil from Sparrow's hand. 'To the devil with speed only. That's too complicated. What you want is a sound variation: first the *sound* of a Hell Diver subtug under quarter speed, then half speed, and then full speed to simulate flight.' He sketched in a series of matched harmonics. 'We'll just change the resonating factor and—'

'The adjustments to change resonance won't give it much increase in speed,' said Garcia.

'It'll be enough,' said Sparrow. 'They won't be looking for refinements. Johnny's plan is simpler, less likely to break down.' He put a hand on the sketch pad. 'Can you two do it?'

Garcia nodded. 'Get us up there.'

Sparrow turned back to the control board, strode across to Bonnett. 'You hear that, Les?'

'Enough to get the idea.' He tilted his head toward the search board. 'Still no sound of those boys.'

'Let's hope they run right up onto Novaya Zemlya,' said Sparrow. 'Give us a half a percent buoyancy in the bow tank.'

Bonnett stepped to his left, turned a valve wheel a fraction of a degree, watched a dial above it, closed the valve.

'Joe, play us up on the towlines,' said Sparrow.

Garcia moved to the tow controls, released the magnetics clutch on the big master reel. Slowly, almost imperceptibly, the *Ram* lifted off the bottom, slid upward.

They watched the static pressure gauge climb through 200 pounds to the square inch, 180 ... 160 ... 140 ...

'Slow us down,' ordered Sparrow.

Garcia fed a little power into the magnetic brakes. 130 ... 120 ... 115 ...

'Snub us,' ordered Sparrow.

The needle stopped on 110 pounds.

'That's close enough to 250 feet,' said Sparrow. 'Joe, Johnny, this is your show.'

Garcia secured the tow board. 'Better watch the balance on these lines,' he said. 'If the current shifts—'

'That's our worry,' said Sparrow. 'I'd blow tanks before I'd pull you two down into high pressure.'

Garcia smiled wanly. 'Sorry, Skipper. You know how I feel about—'

'You've a good electronics man with you,' said Sparrow. He nodded toward Ramsey, looked significantly at Garcia.

'I'm with you, Skipper,' said Garcia.

Ramsey thought: *Why doesn't he just say 'Keep an eye on this suspicious character?'* He looked at Garcia. 'You afraid of the water?'

Garcia's dark features paled.

'That will be enough,' said Sparrow. 'You've a job to do.'

Ramsey shrugged. 'Let's go swimming,' he said, turned toward the forward door and led the way out onto the engine-room catwalk, up the ladder to the escape hatch.

The sea suits and aqua lungs were in a slide locker beside the hatch. Ramsey yanked one set out, stepped aside for Garcia, fitted himself for the sea. Finished, he undogged the hatch, climbed inside and leaned against the ring rail.

Garcia followed, checked his mouthpiece, pulled it aside and glared at Ramsey. 'Somewhere, someday, someone is going to thump your head for you.'

'Yeah, head thumper.'

Ramsey stared at the engineering officer. 'What do—'

'You psycho boys are all alike,' said Garcia. 'You think you're the custodians of deep, dark knowledge . . . sole custodians.'

'I don't—'

'Come off that,' said Garcia.

'But I thought you—'

'Yes?' Garcia grinned at him – a mirthless expression.

'Well, I—'

'You thought I had you pegged for a spy, a jolly old sleeper,' said Garcia. He shook his head. 'None such. I'm quite certain you're not.'

'What gives you the idea I'm a psych man?'

'We're wasting time,' said Garcia. He jammed his mouthpiece into place, pulled up the hatch and dogged it.

Ramsey put the cold rubber of the mouthpiece between his teeth, tested the air. It tasted of chemicals, bitter.

Garcia spun the sea valve.

Cold water rushed in around them, spewing upward onto the circular walls, whirling in swift currents.

A kick of fin flippers took Ramsey to the open hatch. Outside was utter blackness broken only by the glow from the escape compartment and the small hand lamp carried by Garcia. The long Arctic night on the surface and the cover of water conspired to create an utter absence of light. In spite of the reflecting layers of his sea suit, Ramsey could feel the chill of the water begin to bite into him.

Garcia held to the hatch guard with one hand as he rigged a safety line onto his belt. The hand lamp clipped to his wrist pointed down toward the waist rack of torpedoes: thin deadly shapes stuck through the metal guide slots like bullets in a belt.

Ramsey fastened his own belt clip to the safety line.

Garcia pointed his hand lamp back into the hatchway, indicated another line snaking out of the green gloom of the escape compartment. Ramsey pulled on the line, brought out a tool kit.

A current caught at Ramsey, pulled him away from the hatch. He was snubbed short by the safety line, swam back and caught up the kit.

Garcia kicked off the hull, swam down toward the torpedo rack. Ramsey turned for one look upward toward the night-cloaked surface, followed. The engineering officer stopped at a torpedo low down on the rack, keeping well clear of the finned arming rotor on the torpedo's nose. Yellow stripes behind the arming rotor identified it as a short-range, low-blast model for infighting.

Row on row of the deadly metal fish extended upward around the *Ram*'s waist.

Garcia patted the torpedo, looked at Ramsey.

Ramsey shook his head, pointed to one below it: red stripes – a long-range seeker.

Garcia nodded.

They dropped down to the torpedo, cautiously disarmed it. Ramsey noted the number: fourteen, pointed to it. Garcia nodded.

Ramsey unhinged the side plate, motioned for the light. Its beam shone into the torpedo. He had already figured out the changes necessary: disconnect seeker circuit, reset for level course; drive-timer coupling racked back to new control order – 400 revolutions, 600 ... 800. He forgot to worry about Garcia in the concentration of work.

Presently, it was done. They dropped down to another torpedo of the same model, repeated the changes except for the calculated resonance factor. Then it was time to disconnect the upper torpedo, lower it down beside the second, link the two carefully with swivel bolts.

Below the altered torpedoes, Ramsey sought out the solid yellow and red nose of a scrambler model, inserted the seeker capsule from the first unit they had changed. He tied this torpedo to the other two with a length of light cable.

Toward the last he found himself working in less and less light. He seated the final cable clamp, looked up the hull.

Garcia floated high along the rack; now he was swimming toward the escape compartment. Swimming fast. The sea's darkness swept down around Ramsey.

Is he going to trap me out here? Close the hatch against me?

Panic washed over him. He flailed the fin flippers, swept up toward the receding light.

Garcia could wait in the compartment until he was almost out of air, knowing I'd be in the same fix. Then he could go inside to safety. I'd drown before they could come back out. He'd have a plausible story about me disappearing.

Garcia's light sank into the escape compartment, leaving the darkness behind.

I'm not going to make it!

The safety line abruptly snubbed him up short. Ramsey tugged at it. Fouled on something! He fought the belt connection, freed it, resumed his flailing progress toward the hatch, a faint glow from Garcia's light against the blackness.

Now, he was over the hatch. Ramsey grabbed the rail, felt a hand take his, pull him inside. Garcia! Ramsey felt a wave of relief. The light in the compartment showed that Garcia had been reeling in the safety line. It stretched taut between reel and hatch. The snag. Garcia pointed toward the hatch.

He wants me to go out and free it, thought Ramsey. He shook his head.

Again Garcia pointed toward the hatch.

Again Ramsey shook his head.

Garcia hesitated, then swung up the line and out the hatch, taking the portable light with him. Presently, he returned and the line sagged. He reeled it onto its drum, sealed the outside hatch.

Ramsey opened the high-pressure air valve. The water level began to lower.

When it reached their shoulders, they unhooked the face connections of the aqua lungs. Garcia's mouth held a subtle hint of amusement.

He knows he frightened me, thought Ramsey. *He did it deliberately.*

The last of the water swished out of the sea cock. Garcia undogged the inner hatch, led the way out onto the upper catwalk of the engine room. Silently, they stripped the suits from their bodies, returned to the control deck.

Sparrow met them at the door. 'Well?'

'All done,' said Garcia. 'Fourteen is linked to twenty-two. They'll both fire on twenty-two's stud. They'll seek a northerly course and hold about ten fathoms off bottom.'

Sparrow looked at Ramsey, who nodded. The skipper turned back to Garcia. 'Run into any trouble?'

'Johnny's the electronics man. He did all the work.'

Sparrow turned to Ramsey.

'It was fairly easy.'

Garcia said, 'Johnny's safety line snagged on the way in, but I freed it. Outside of that, it was a quiet swim.'

'All quiet in here, too,' said Sparrow. He nodded toward a cot on the far side of the control room, Bonnett stretched out on it. 'Les is getting some shut-eye. You two had better do the same. We're going to sit here for a while.'

'Righto,' said Garcia. 'The swim made me tired. Let's go, Johnny boy.' He ducked through the door, went down the companionway, Ramsey following.

Garcia stopped at the door of his room, turned and smiled at Ramsey. 'Pleasant dreams ... head thumper.'

Ramsey brushed past him into his own room, locked the door behind him, and leaned against it. He could feel his heart thumping heavily.

Damn that man!

He fought himself into a semblance of calmness, went to the telemeter box, examined the new lengths of tape. Sparrow was still locked in icy control.

Ramsey reset the box, turned off his lights, fell into his bunk and into a restless sleep. It seemed that he had just closed his eyes when he was aroused by the buzzer. He got up stiffly, went forward to the control deck. The others already were there.

'Take over the search board,' said Sparrow. He waited for Ramsey to comply, depressed the firing-board stud at number twenty-two.

Immediately, Ramsey picked up the beat of it on his instruments. He felt Sparrow move into position beside him. Together, they stared at the scope.

'Good job,' said Sparrow. 'Looks just like our pip.'

Ramsey rotated the outside bell-detector of the ranging system. 'No sign of a stakeout,' he said.

'That would be a bitter one,' said Garcia. 'All of our yeoman efforts out there gone for nought. I'd almost ra—'

'There he is,' said Ramsey. 'Northeast and coming fast.'

'Interception course,' said Sparrow.

'And there's the first speed increase in our decoy,' said Ramsey.

'Couldn't have been better timing,' said Bonnett.

'Another signal to the west,' said Ramsey. 'Our stakeout has called his pals.'

'And there's full-speed simulation,' said Sparrow. 'Wonderful job, Johnny!'

They waited, watching the signals merge. Abruptly, the instruments gyrated wildly as the decoy's scrambler system was activated.

Again they waited.

A distant double thump resonated against the *Ram*'s hull and simultaneously, the scrambler signal stopped.

'Now track every one of them,' said Sparrow. 'If those EPs all leave, we've made it.'

Ramsey watched the signals. 'Pack quartering over the explosion area. Four departing.' He waited. 'Two more. Courses southwest. There go the last ones.'

He tracked them until they went off his instruments, turned with a triumphant smile and looked at Sparrow. 'Just as you planned it, Skipper.'

'Ummmm, yes.' He turned away, 'We'll wait here another four hours before going on into the well area.'

The *Ram* crept up the fissure at quarter speed, lifted out in six hundred feet of water and slid upslope like a giant fish seeking its dinner in the bottom mud. Inside, Sparrow stood at the helm, Garcia with him.

'There's the ledge,' said Sparrow. He nodded toward the screen above them. It showed a pie slice of illumination cut from the dark waters by the bow lights, a rocky outcropping.

'Shall I call the others?' asked Garcia.

'Yes.'

Garcia pressed the call button. Ramsey acknowledged from the electronics shack.

'What are you doing in the electronics shack?' asked Sparrow.

'I couldn't rest, so I—'

'My orders that we were to work only in double teams didn't interest you?'

'Skipper, I had an idea about—'

'Just a moment.' Sparrow pointed to the screen above him, a starfish-shaped mound. 'Right on, Joe.' He disengaged the drive, drifted up on the mound, past it, grounded.

'Two hundred and five pounds even, Skipper.'

Sparrow nodded, plugged in the side-eyes, examined the bottom, 'Plenty of mud for ballast.'

Bonnett entered. 'Skipper, are we—'

'We've arrived,' said Sparrow. 'Les, will you go aft to the shack and check on Johnny?'

'Isn't he—'

'He's been in the shack for some time ... alone!'

Bonnett whirled around, disappeared down the companionway.

'I will not be responsible for revealing the site of this well,' said Sparrow.

'What do you mean?' asked Garcia. 'You don't think I—'

Sparrow froze him with a look. 'Mr Garcia, we've been shipmates since you were a chief machinist and I was a dry-back ensign; but right now I wouldn't trust you as far as I could see you. One of Security's men was trapped and killed aboard my ship. The EPs got spy beams aboard us. Someone did it. Do I make myself clear?'

'Yes, sir.' Garcia turned back to the search board.

In the electronics shack, Ramsey held up the tube on which he had been working. *This has to be how they set off their spy beam*, he thought. *And it means they could have another one ready to go any second.*

His hand trembled as he reached out to plug the tube into a test socket. The hand was abruptly knocked aside and a fist crashed into the side of his jaw.

'You dirty spying bastard!' growled Bonnett. Again his fist crashed into Ramsey's jaw.

Ramsey – bent backward over the bench – tried to dodge aside. 'Les, wait! I—'

'Gonna save us the price of a trial,' gritted Bonnett. He crashed an elbow into Ramsey's mouth, lifted a knee to the groin.

My God! He means to kill me! thought Ramsey. He fought back desperately, chopping an arm at Bonnett's throat. Nausea from the groin blow clutched him.

Bonnett dodged Ramsey's blow, sent another fist into the electronics officer's mouth.

'For God's sake!' screamed Ramsey. 'I'm no spy!'

'You dirty, lying, sneaking—' Bonnett stepped back, chopped the side of his hand into the curve of Ramsey's neck, sent a fist crashing into Ramsey's jaw.

Ramsey felt himself going blank, waved his arms futilely in front of him. Something crashed against the side of his head. He felt a sledgehammer blow over his heart and blacked out.

Voices.

They came to Ramsey from somewhere at the top of a long black hole. He tried to ignore them, moved his head. Pain shot through him.

'I think he's coming around.' Garcia.

'Here. Make him drink this.' Sparrow.

'Why waste it?' Bonnett.

'I'm not satisfied that you're correct.' Sparrow.

'I tell you, Skipper, I saw him putting that spy-beam tube into a socket and—'

'How do you know it was a spy beam? One of you stepped on it and crushed it during that fracas.'

'It looked damned suspicious, Skipper.'

'Looked . . . schmooked.' Garcia.

Hand under his neck. Something acid and biting in his mouth, burning his throat.

Choking, coughing.

Ramsey gagged, retched.

Again the liquid was forced past his lips. He shuddered, managed to keep it down. His body felt like one large ache.

'Can you talk, Johnny?' Sparrow.

Ramsey opened his eyes. Sparrow bent over him, supporting his shoulders.

Bonnett and Garcia stood beyond.

Ramsey's eyes focused on the rest of his surroundings: rec room, cot, table, and first-aid kit.

Back to Bonnett and Garcia.

Bonnett glowering, perhaps a bit uncertain.

Garcia faintly worried.

Ramsey groped toward his jaw with one hand, felt a lance of fire shoot through his head. 'I c'n talk a li'l,' he said.

Sparrow brought some pillows up behind Ramsey, eased him back onto them. 'What were you doing in the shack?'

The tube! Spy beam!

Ramsey forced the words past his thickened lips. 'Think I found out how spy beam triggered.'

Sudden interest in the eyes of Sparrow and Garcia. More uncertainty in Bonnett's expression.

'By someone on board?' asked Sparrow.

'No. This's urgen', Skipper. Don' raise th' peri-box.'

'Why?'

'Piping in a signal.'

'The air's full of stuff. What—'

'This's special. You gave me idea.' Ramsey passed his tongue over his thickened lips, forced himself to speak clearly. 'Go'to un'erstan'me,' he said. 'Resonance. EPs are sending out a harmonic on th' plate frequency of our L-4 tubes. Eventually, it breaks 'em down so they become microphonic. Th' tubes we found were just amplifiers. Spy beam actually comes from th' L-4s.'

'But if we've taken out all the amplifiers—'

'Enough L-4s sending and they'd interact in feedback,' said Garcia. 'Wouldn't need an amplifier. They'd set up a howl that could be heard anywhere.'

'Why the peri-box?' asked Sparrow. Then he said, 'Of course: they have to get a clear strong signal into us and the peri-box is the only road that isn't damped by a plasteel hull.'

He shook his head. 'Granting that you're telling the truth and that this is so, how can—'

'Rig a substitute for the L-4s,' said Garcia. 'That's the weak spot in the system.'

'That's what I was testing when Les jumped me,' said Ramsey.

Bonnett scowled. 'This could be a trick, Skipper.'

Garcia said, 'Can it, Les.'

'Dammit all!' shouted Bonnett. 'Yesterday you were both telling me how suspicious—'

'We'll discuss it another time,' said Sparrow. He turned to Garcia. 'What do you think, Joe?'

'It sounds right, Skipper.' Garcia held up a hand, ticked off items on his fingers. 'It has the advantage of simplicity: all they'd have to know is the plate frequency factor of a suitable tube and they could channel all their efforts toward breaking down that one unit. If the actual signal originates with them and is merely rebroadcast from our system, they'd have the essential elements of a sonoran system: pin-point accuracy in locating us. And what would be harder to detect? Their broadcast would be a constant sound in the ether; so every time we raised our peri-box, our board filters would automatically cut out that signal as non-dangerous and we wouldn't be listening at all on the wave length that would be likely to give us away!'

Even Bonnett was nodding in agreement as Garcia finished.

Garcia looked at Ramsey. 'Is that the way you had it figured?'

'Yes.'

'I could probably figure out a substitute system to eliminate the L-4s,' said Garcia, 'but you're the electronics expert. How?'

'Schematic on shack workbench,' said Ramsey.

'Les, check that,' ordered Sparrow. 'If it's true, it's one more item to confirm his story.'

Bonnett went out the door.

Ramsey shut his eyes, tried to slide off the pillows and stretch out flat on the cot.

'Better not,' said Sparrow. He held Ramsey upright. 'Joe, steady him here a moment while I look at that nose.'

Garcia held Ramsey's shoulders.

Sparrow touched Ramsey's nose gently.

'Ouch!' Ramsey jerked back.

'Doesn't appear to be broken,' said Sparrow. He reached out, put a thumb on Ramsey's left eyelid, held up the lid while he flashed a hand light into the eye. 'Maybe a slight concussion.'

'How long was I out?' asked Ramsey.

'About an hour,' said Sparrow. 'You—'

Bonnett entered carrying a grease-stained sheet of note paper. He passed the paper to Garcia, who removed one hand from Ramsey's shoulder to take the paper.

'What do you say, Joe?' asked Sparrow.

Garcia studied the paper silently, nodded once, passed it to Sparrow. 'A clever adaptation. Simple. It'll work and it uses a tube with a different plate frequency.'

'What does this mean?' asked Bonnett.

'It means you batted out, old chap,' said Garcia. 'In the vernacular, you goofed.'

Bonnett's voice was dangerously low. 'Is that so?'

'As a matter of honest fact, we've all goofed,' said Garcia. 'You were the overt instrument of our dereliction.'

Bonnett looked down at Ramsey. 'If I made a mistake, I apologize.' He glanced at Sparrow, who was still studying Ramsey's schematic diagram. 'But I reserve the right to my own opinion.'

Sparrow straightened from beside Ramsey's bunk, looked at Garcia. 'Keep him awake for a couple of hours, Joe.' He turned away. 'Come along, Les. We've a slug to fill and some tube-jockeying. No time to waste.'

'Do you want me to do the electronics work?' asked Garcia.

'You stick with him,' said Sparrow. He pushed in the doorway, stared speculatively at Ramsey, turned and left, followed by Bonnett.

'Do you think they could break down those L-4s without piping through the peri-box?' asked Garcia.

'In time,' said Ramsey. 'But they'd have to increase signal strength by several factors to get a return signal unamplified unless our box were on the surface.'

'Clever devils,' muttered Garcia. 'How'd you spot it?'

'Skipper gave me the idea with his scheme for faking the sound of our screw.'

'Got you thinking about resonance,' said Garcia.

'About building signals with harmonics,' corrected Ramsey.

'Same thing.' Garcia came around in front of Ramsey. 'Boy, he really worked you over.'

'I guess he did.'

'Your own fault, though.'

Ramsey jerked his head up to stare at Garcia, winced at the sudden motion. 'Why do you say that?'

'For some reason, you've deliberately set out to make the skipper suspicious of you. But you forgot one thing: suspicion is contagious.'

'The pressure's cooking your brains,' said Ramsey.

'I wish I knew what you were trying to prove,' said Garcia. 'Maybe you're trying to beach the skipper.'

'Nuts! You have too much imagination.'

'We're alike there, Johnny. And time drags in a subtug. There's time for a good imagination to run wild.' He stared at the bulkhead a moment. 'That's the skipper's problem, too, really.'

'That's a rare piece of insight,' said Ramsey.

Garcia acted as though he had not heard. 'Imagination is a weakness when too much responsibility hangs on your shoulders.'

They felt the *Ram* move, stop.

'We're seating the pump onto that well cap,' said Garcia. 'It'll take us a couple of days to fill the slug, then home we go.'

'If it were only that easy,' said Ramsey.

Garcia turned, strode across to the rec-room bookshelf, found a book, searched in it for a moment, and brought it back to Ramsey. 'I think you'd better read this, Johnny. It's Savvy Sparrow's favorite passage.'

He handed Ramsey a Bible, pointing to the beginning of a chapter, said, 'Isaiah, twenty-seven, one and two.'

Ramsey read it through silently, then reread it aloud:

'"In that day the Lord with his sore and great and strong sword shall punish leviathan the piercing serpent, even leviathan that crooked serpent; and he shall slay the dragon that is in the sea."'

Garcia continued the quotation from memory:

'"In that day sing ye unto her, A vineyard of red wine."'

Ramsey stared at the passage, shook his head. 'What's it mean to him?'

Garcia said, 'And he shall slay the dragon that is in the sea.' He reached down, took back the Bible. 'To Savvy Sparrow, we're the dragon in the sea.'

'Here, let me have that,' said Ramsey. He took back the Bible. 'Think I'll read for a while.'

'Look out, or you'll get religion,' said Garcia.

'No chance,' said Ramsey. 'My teachers always said if you want to understand a subject, study the basic source. This is it for our captain.'

'For a great many people,' said Garcia softly. 'And a psychologist who does not have an intimate knowledge of that book is a doctor without instruments. And blind, to boot.'

Ramsey looked at Garcia over the top of the book. 'When are you going to give up that line?'

'When you wake up,' said Garcia.

Ramsey hid a frown behind the Bible, opened it again to the passage Garcia had pointed out, soon lost himself in the fury of Isaiah and the woe of Hezekiah and the thundering messages of prophecy.

In the cold Arctic waters outside the *Ram*, pumps turned, hose nozzles sought out bottom muck for ballast. The plastic slug began to swell with its cargo of oil – like a live thing drinking at a jugular in the earth.

The hands of the timelog swept around, around. Fifty-one hours at the well.

Full slug. It stretched out on the bottom behind the *Ram*, turgid with its cargo, now almost a mile long, held in delicate hydrostatic balance so that it would tow beneath the surface.

Ramsey and Garcia entered the control room together. Sparrow and Bonnett already were there.

Garcia nodded at something Ramsey had said. 'You're right. We'd better—'

'Right about what?' asked Sparrow.

'Johnny was just saying that the slug's compensator system would drop ballast if we try to pull that deep-dive maneuver on the way home.'

'He's right,' said Sparrow. 'And if we don't compensate, we'll rupture the slug.'

'And bleed oil all over the surface,' said Bonnett. 'Wouldn't that be lovely, now.'

'There might be a way to pull it off,' said Sparrow. 'But let's hope we don't have to try it.' He turned to the control board. 'Les, lift us off. Minimum headway. Take us right down into the gut. We're going to use it for cover as long as we're able.'

'Aye.' Bonnett's hands moved over the controls.

'Wouldn't they be likely to lay for us in a place like that?' asked Ramsey.

'We're dead, remember?' said Garcia.

Sparrow said, 'Joe, take over auxiliary search and keep us down the center of that canyon. Johnny, get on standard search and watch for enemy pips.' He folded his arms in front of him. 'The Lord has been kind to us, gentlemen. We're going home.'

'A milk run,' said Garcia.

'For mad dogs and Englishmen,' said Bonnett.

The *Ram*'s deck tilted upward, hung there for a moment. Slowly, the slug lifted behind them, followed. They slanted down into the gut.

'One degree right,' said Garcia. 'Steady as she goes.'

'Steady as she goes,' sang Bonnett.

'Here's where we thank our lucky stars that the slug will track us in sections of hull length,' said Ramsey. 'If we scrape the side wall—'

'Two degrees left,' said Garcia.

'Two degrees left,' acknowledged Bonnett.

Sparrow glanced at Ramsey. 'You were saying.'

'I was just making talk.'

'Let's save the talk for rest camp,' said Sparrow. He turned back to the board in front of Bonnett. 'We will take fatigue shots in three hours and at four-hour intervals until we've cleared the Arctic Circle. Let me know immediately if any of you show a Larson reaction from them.'

Bonnett said, 'They tell me those shots lop the sleepless hours off your life expectancy. Wonder if there's anything in that?'

'I once heard the moon was made of green cheese,' said Garcia.

'Shall we pay attention to business, gentlemen?' asked Sparrow.

Ramsey smiled. He could sense the increased vital drive in the crew like a strong outpouring of elation. He rubbed at the sore spot on his jaw where Bonnett had hit him, thought: *It came at me from an unexpected angle, but Catharsis Number One has come and gone. AND I'm still alive. And Sparrow's still functioning.*

The captain cleared his throat. 'As soon as we've cleared the Norwegian basin we should be out of immediate danger. Their search packs should be ranging the Iceland passage now and they won't be expecting someone from behind them. Our chief worry is picket tugs, line replacements moving up: the chance passerby.'

'I've decided I'm going to die of old age,' said Garcia. 'That's my chief worry.'

'You're getting old before your time,' said Bonnett.

'One degree left,' said Garcia.

'One degree left,' acknowledged Bonnett.

Deep in the underwater canyon, the *Ram* coursed generally westward. At the sill of the Norwegian basin, they lost the gut as it shoaled, crept along the basin rim, course 276 degrees. The bottom depth crept upward. They were in 200 fathoms when they swung south to parallel the Norwegian coastline, course 201 degrees.

Eighty-one hours, fifty-eight minutes from the well, still two degrees above the Arctic Circle. Ramsey said, 'Signal!' and slapped the switch which silenced their motors.

'Course, distance, and direction?' asked Sparrow.

'Southeast, ranging westerly and maybe a bit south. I'm just getting them on the outer limits of the long-range system: say thirty-five miles.'

'Resume speed,' said Sparrow. 'They have nothing that'll reach that far.'

'They'll be off my board in a minute at present course,' said Ramsey.

'We'll play it safe anyway,' said Sparrow. 'Ten minutes run due east, then resume course.'

Garcia at the helm, acknowledged. The *Ram* changed course.

'Lost them,' said Ramsey.

'Resume course,' said Sparrow.

Again they came around to parallel the Norwegian coast. South they went, and then west-southwest to gain greater distance from the shore stations along the southern reaches of Norway. And again bearing to the south, and again westerly to give the Faeroes a wide berth. Now they were at the edge of the deeps southeast of Iceland. Watch and standby: Ramsey and Sparrow on the control deck.

'You certainly called the shot,' said Ramsey.

'Don't brag your luck,' said Sparrow. 'It'll change.'

'What makes mariners so superstitious?' asked Ramsey.

'Awareness of the limits of our knowledge,' said Sparrow. 'And experience with the reality of luck.'

'It's a wonder we don't have government-issue rabbits' feet.'

'I'll suggest it when we—'

'Pack!' Ramsey slapped the silencer switch. 'They're onto us, Skipper! They were lying doggo!'

Sparrow kicked the alarm buzzer, brought the engines to life.

'They're right in our path,' said Ramsey. 'Range fifteen miles.'

'Sure-kill range,' said Sparrow. He brought the subtug and tow around to the northeast, pulled the power bar to its last notch.

Bonnett and Garcia hurried into the control room.

'A pack on us,' said Ramsey.

'On the controls, you two,' said Sparrow.

Bonnett and Garcia moved into their battle stations, Bonnett at the helm, Garcia on the torpedo board. Sparrow stepped to Ramsey's side.

'There's bottom at 8800 feet,' said Ramsey.

'We'll have to chance it,' said Sparrow. 'Les, take us down. Johnny, monitor the atmosphere.'

Ramsey opened the control valve on the anhydrase generator one notch.

The subtug's deck slanted downward.

'Joe, call the depths,' said Sparrow.

'Sixty-eight hundred feet and 2880 pounds ... 7000 feet and 3010 pounds ... 7500 and 3235 ... 8000 and 3440 ... 8500 and 3655—'

'Coast in,' said Sparrow.

Bonnett silenced the drive.

Garcia's voice continued: '—8600 and 3700 ... variation, Skipper—'

'Noted.'

'—8700 and 3750 ... that's nine pounds over normal, Skipper—'

'Noted.'

'—8750 and 3780 ... that's eighteen pounds over ...'

'Noted. Les, flatten the glide angle and give us the bow eye on the main screen.'

'Bottom is forty feet,' said Ramsey. 'The pack is closing fast. Range about eleven miles.'

The big screen above their heads showed its pie slice of light and, abruptly, bottom mud.

'Drop the slug in first,' said Sparrow.

Bonnett brought up the bow planes until they felt the drag of the slug behind them. The *Ram* settled onto bottom mud in 8800 feet. The big static pressure gauge read 3804 pounds even: twenty pounds above normal for the depth.

'Pack range nine miles and fanning out,' said Ramsey. 'I count sixteen of them.'

'Fanning out,' said Sparrow. 'That means they're confused by our—'

'Two breaking away toward the surface,' said Ramsey. 'They think we've floated up.'

'Over normal pressure,' said Sparrow. 'There's a cold density layer above us confusing our sound pattern. Unless they detect metal, we're safe.'

'Unless we implode,' said Bonnett.

'If we had some ham we'd have some ham and eggs if we had some eggs,' said Ramsey.

Garcia chuckled.

'The important thing is for us all to relax,' said Sparrow. 'We don't want the same complications we had last—'

'Complishmashuns,' said Garcia. 'Alla time talk-talk-talk-talk. So he can psycho . . . psy – So he can find out what makes us go tick-tick-tick-tick-tick-tick. Don't y', Johnny boy?'

Ramsey raised his eyebrows, looked at Sparrow. Sparrow shrugged, said, 'Come along, Joe. You need a shot.'

'Need a whole bottle,' said Garcia. 'Need a shycoan'lyst like Johnny boy here. Don' I, Johnny boy?'

'I'm ordering you to come with me, Joe,' said Sparrow.

Tears welled up in Garcia's eyes. 'I need a conscience,' he sobbed. 'I wanna confess, but no one—'

'Come along!' Sparrow grabbed Garcia's arm, jerked him toward the aft door.

'Easy, Skipper,' said Ramsey.

Sparrow took a deep breath. 'Right.'

'I'll come quietly,' said Garcia. 'No need get excited. I don' wanna be any trouble. I been enough trouble. I been terrible trouble. Never forgive me. Never.'

He allowed himself to be led out the door, still mumbling, 'Never ... never ... never ... never ...'

'Quoth the raven,' said Ramsey. He rubbed absently at the still-sensitive bruise on his jaw where Bonnett had hit him.

'That figures,' said Bonnett.

'Huh?'

'Head thumper. BuPsych rang you in on us.'

'Not you, too, Brutus,' said Ramsey.

'Sure it figures,' said Bonnett. 'Hepp went loco, so they rang you in on us to find out why.'

'What?'

'Sure. You want to see which of us is next.'

'Me, if I hear any more of this nutty talk. I've—'

'Otherwise you're a spy,' said Bonnett. 'I guess you're not that.'

'Of all the—'

'I'm trying to apologize,' said Bonnett. 'It isn't easy. Basically, I don't like head thumpers. You screw doctors are all alike. Superior ... know-it-all. Explanations for everything: Religion is a manifestation of deep-seated anxieties which—'

'Oh, knock it off,' said Ramsey.

'What I'm trying to say is that I've felt better ever since I pounded you. Call it a cathartic. For a minute I had the enemy in my own hands. He was an insect I could crush.'

'So?'

'So I've never had the enemy in my hands before.' He held up his hands and looked at them. 'Right there. I learned something.'

'What?'

'This may sound asinine.'

'Say it anyway.'

'Maybe I'd better not.'

'Nothing was ever more important than for you to focalize that thought,' said Ramsey. And he thought: *No matter what I do, I'm cast in the role of analyst!*

Bonnett rubbed his hands against his shirt, looked at the control board. 'When you meet your enemy and recognize him and touch him, you find out that he's like yourself: that maybe he's part of you.' He shook his head. 'I'm not saying this right.'

'Try.'

'I can't do it.' Bonnett lowered his head, stared at the deck.

'What's it like? Try a comparison.'

In a low, almost inaudible voice, Bonnett said, 'It's like when you're the youngest and weakest kid on the playground. And when the biggest kid smacks you, that's all right because he noticed you. That means you're alive. It's better than when they ignore you.' He looked up at Ramsey. 'Or it's like when you're with a woman and she looks at you and her eyes say you're a man. Yeah, that's it. When you're really alive, other people know it.'

'What's that have to do with having the enemy in your hands?'

'He's alive,' said Bonnett. 'Dammit all, man, he's alive and he's got the same kind of aliveness that you have. Each of us is the enemy' – Bonnett's voice grew firmer – 'to the other and to himself. That's what I mean: I'm the enemy within myself. Unless I master that enemy, I always lose.'

Ramsey stared at Bonnett in amazement.

'Not the kind of thinking you'd expect from me,' said Bonnett.

Ramsey shook his head.

'Why not? I feel things just like anybody else. So I hide it most of the time. Who am I hiding it from?' He sneered. 'Me. That's who.'

'What set you off?'

'I found someone I could talk to, someone who had to keep his professional mouth shut because—'

'Just a minute.' Ramsey's gaze, never off the search-board instruments for more than a few seconds, had caught a sharp needle deflection. 'Sonic search blast. There's another. If they're spaced on us, our hull will stick up like a sore thumb: a fat metal finger.'

'They won't look for us down here.'

'Don't count on it. There's anoth—'

'What's going on?' Sparrow ducked through the door into the control room.

'Sonic search bombs,' said Ramsey. 'The EPs are looking for a metallic bounce labeled *Fenian Ram*.'

Sparrow moved closer to stand at Ramsey's shoulders. 'And here comes one ranging over us.'

'Fast,' said Ramsey. He put his hand on the anti-torp volley switch.

'Leave that alone,' said Sparrow. 'They won't use a fish on an unidentified bump.'

'He's inside of a mile,' said Ramsey. 'In the six-thousand-foot level. There goes another search bomb.'

They felt the dull bump of it through the hull.

'If one of our external fittings implodes, the shock wave'll crack us like—'

'We've all read the manual, Les,' said Sparrow. He turned away from the board, bent his head. 'Lord, we who have no right to ask it, do plead for your mercy. Thy will be done. . . . Whatever.'

'He's turning away,' whispered Ramsey.

'Lord, turn not away from thy—'

'That EP sub,' said Ramsey. 'He's turning away.'

Sparrow lifted his head. 'Thank you, Lord.' He looked at Bonnett. 'Joe's under sedation. Go back and stay with him.'

Bonnett went out the aft door.

Sparrow again moved to stand beside Ramsey. 'That was a good thing you did for Les.'

Ramsey stiffened.

'I stood outside the door until he'd shed the load on his chest,' said Sparrow. 'You're a much deeper man than I'd suspected, Johnny.'

'Oh, for Heaven's sake!'

'Yes, for Heaven's sake,' said Sparrow. 'You're a devious one.'

Ramsey closed his eyes in exasperation, opened them. *I'm the father-confessor whether I like it or not*, he thought. 'Garcia is off his rocker,' he said.

'I've shipped with Joe for quite a number of years,' said Sparrow. 'I've seen him drunk before. Pressure drunkenness is no different. He's not the kind to make false accusations. That would be bearing false witness against—'

'He's just talking to—'

'He's troubled in the spirit,' said Sparrow. 'He needs someone like you – a confessor. Did you ever stop to think that you boys are like priests in the way—'

'I've heard it mentioned,' said Ramsey, and realized he had made a confession of identity.

Sparrow smiled. 'Always have a way out the other side, Johnny. Have your safe line of retreat prepared. Joe hates you right now because he doesn't want to admit he needs you.'

Ramsey thought: *Who's the doctor and who's the patient here?* He said, 'Are you suggesting I copper my bets in the religious gamble?'

'No bet-coppering there,' said Sparrow.

'Yeah, I guess you're right,' agreed Ramsey. His mouth twisted into a wry smile. 'That's like telling your psychoanalyst, "I'm going to get married as soon as my analysis is finished." You'll never finish.' And he thought: *Well, the mask is off. Why do I feel relieved? That's suspicious. I shouldn't feel relieved.*

Sparrow studied the search board. 'They're almost out of range.' He began to hum, then in a low voice sang, 'You'll never get to heaven on roller skates! You'll roll right past those pearly gates.'

'"I ain' gonna grieve my Lord no more,"' said Ramsey.

'What?' Sparrow turned away from the board.

'That's what you were singing: "I ain' gonna grieve my Lord no more."'

'So I was.' Sparrow cocked his head toward the search board. 'They're going out of range in the northeast quadrant. Surface currents set northeast here. That means they've decided we floated up. Give them an hour out of range.'

Ramsey checked the sonic pickup monitor on the board, said, 'All accounted for in that quadrant, Skipper. No stakeouts.'

'Certain?'

Ramsey nodded toward the monitor tape.

'They're flustered and that means bad judgment every time,' said Sparrow. 'Remember that, Johnny. Keep calm no matter what and you'll—'

'Skipper!' It was Bonnett at the door behind them.

They whirled.

'Joe's blood pressure. It's going up, then down, wider and wider. He acts like he's in shock and—'

Sparrow turned back to the board. 'They're beyond range. Slide off, Johnny. Take us to 6000 feet. Fast!' He hurried toward the door. 'Les, come with me.'

'What about the slug?' called Ramsey.

Sparrow stopped in mid-stride, turned back to Ramsey. 'I should listen to my own advice. Les, do what you can for Joe. Johnny, free the clutch on the tow cables.' Sparrow moved to the main controls. 'We'll have to lift the *Ram* and leave the slug on the bottom until we reach cable limit.'

'Then try to jerk it off,' said Ramsey.

'If we can get it started up, the compensator system will keep it coming,' said Sparrow.

'If,' said Ramsey.

'Drop two of our fish,' said Sparrow.

Ramsey depressed two of the red-banded torpedo switches.

The subtug shifted, remained on the bottom.

'Two more,' said Sparrow.

Again Ramsey selected two matched torpedo switches, depressed them.

The subtug's nose lifted gently seemed to hesitate, resumed its rise.

The tail came up. Ramsey fed power into the drive, raised the bow planes.

The *Ram* slid upward. They could feel the faint rumbling of the giant cable reel into the outer hull.

At 1700 feet, Sparrow said, 'Try the brake.'

Ramsey put pressure on the reel hub. The *Ram* strained against the lines.

'Five hundred feet more cable,' said Ramsey.

Sparrow threw full power into the drive. 'Lock the reel.'

Ramsey closed the switch on the magnetic brake.

The subtug came almost to a full stop, then slowly resumed its climb. Ramsey watched the tow board. 'That freed her, Skipper. Now, how much mud are we going to lose out of the compensator system?' He leaned to the right to adjust the atmosphere controls. 'If we lose ballast, it'll be—'

'Skipper.' It was Bonnett at the aft door.

Sparrow spoke without turning away from the controls. 'How is he?'

'Resting easier.' Bonnett looked at the big static pressure gauge. 'It's only 2790 pounds now. We got off okay.'

'Not okay yet,' said Sparrow. 'Take over the helm.' He turned the wheel over to Bonnett, moved across to Ramsey's station.

'What course?' asked Bonnett.

'Steady on 197 degrees.'

'Steady on 197 degrees,' acknowledged Bonnett.

'We need some more luck,' said Ramsey.

'St. Christopher is already getting overtime on this trip,' said Bonnett.

'She seems to be maintaining hydrostatic balance,' said Ramsey.

'Stay with that board,' said Sparrow. 'It's too soon to tell.'

'Compartment twenty-seven is fluctuating a little,' said Ramsey.

'How much?'

'Maybe five percent.'

'Keep an eye on it.' Sparrow went back to Bonnett's station. He stared up at the sonoran chart. 'That pack left us in the corner of the northeast quadrant.'

'They made a bad guess,' said Bonnett.

Sparrow said, 'Are you sure Joe is all right?'

'Everything was back to normal when I left him.'

'Mmmm, hmmm.' Sparrow nodded. 'Don't sell that enemy commander short. He had inadequate information. The surface currents set that way.' Sparrow pointed to the lower portion of the chart. 'That's radioactive water to the south – contaminated by the British Isles. He knows we wouldn't turn east into the range of their shore station. *Ergo:* We went with the current.'

Bonnett pointed to the red-outlined radioactive area west of the British Isles. 'There are deep cold currents setting south into that area, Skipper.'

'You're reading my mind,' said Sparrow.

'They wouldn't be as hot as the surface layers,' said Bonnett.

'It depends on how well we're able to follow the thermal layer,' said Sparrow.

'It'd be like nosing into a one-way pipe,' said Ramsey. 'We'd have to follow the thermal current of uncontaminated water. And what would happen if we had to come up through all that hot water? Uh, uh.'

Sparrow said, 'Let me figure this.' He took a sheet of paper from his pocket, scribbled on it, stared at it, scribbled some more, again examined his work. 'Steady as she goes on 197 degrees,' he said. 'It's our best chance.'

Bonnett said, 'What about Joe?'

'I'll go back and check him now. Stay here with Johnny. Let me know if outside water goes above 1000 milli-R.'

'Aye.'

The *Ram* coursed southeast, moving closer and closer to the blighted Scottish coast, rising to shallower and shallower waters. The relatively radiation-free thermal current thinned until it was not quite twice the *Ram*'s hull diameter from top to bottom: about 120 feet.

Sparrow returned from the rec room. 'He's okay now. No residual effects.' He stepped across to the tow board. 'Any more fluctuation in compartment twenty-seven?'

'Negative. We haven't been in one depth long enough for me to get a check on the pressure constant.' Ramsey looked at the search board, watched the green face of the ranging scope. 'Not a pip out of those EP packs.' He turned to Sparrow. 'Could we risk a slave pulse inside the slug? I'd like to get something positive on the relative densities.'

Sparrow pulled at his lower lip, looked at the ranging scope. 'Okay. Just one.'

Ramsey set up the recording dials on the tow board, pushed the sonar-pulse button. Dial needles surged: the time-over-density counter buzzed.

Sparrow said: 'Ballast compartment's slow forward.'

Ramsey compared the outer and inner time recordings. 'Oil in the ballast,' he said. 'There's a pressure break on the inside.'

'And we're painting an oily path on the surface!' barked Sparrow. 'If the EPs have an air patrol over this area they'll spot the slick. They might just as well have an engraved chart of our course.'

Ramsey turned to the timelog. 'Four hours to daylight topside. What's the Security word on EP air patrols over these hot waters?'

'Dunno. I wish they'd—'

'What's wrong?' Garcia stood in the aft door.

Sparrow said, 'You're not supposed to be up. Get back to sick bay.'

'I'm okay.' He stepped onto the control deck. 'What's going on?'

'We're leaking oil,' said Bonnett.

Garcia's gaze darted to the sonoran chart. 'Holy Mother! What're we doing down here?'

Sparrow said, 'Les, take us up. Johnny, monitor the outside radiation. Mark each 1000 milli-R increase. Let me know immediately if that ruptured oil compartment starts to blow.' He turned toward Garcia, studied him for a minute. 'Joe, do you feel up to rigging us for slug repair?'

Garcia shrugged. 'Why not? I've just had a good rest. What'd I do this time?'

'A cheap drunk,' said Bonnett. 'Where'd you hide the bottle?' He bent to turn the wheel on the bow planes.

'Two degrees! No more,' barked Sparrow.

'Two degrees,' acknowledged Bonnett.

Garcia moved forward, went through the door onto the engine-room catwalk.

'Reading 2200 milli-R,' said Ramsey. 'Pressure 690 pounds to the square inch.'

Sparrow said, 'Oil loss?'

'Fifty-five gallons a minute. Constant.'

Sparrow said, 'I'll take over here, Johnny. Go forward and help Joe.'

'Aye.' Ramsey surrendered his position, went to the forward door, stepped through onto the catwalk. The electric engines were four droning hives around him, the gray metal of their casings gleaming dully in the standby lights. Through the webwork of girders, catwalks, and ladders, Ramsey could see Garcia high above him near the escape hatch unreeling a safety line, readying it for the outside spools.

Ramsey mounted the ladders, came up behind Garcia. 'Looks like I'm going swimming again, Joe.'

Garcia glanced back, returned his attention to his work. 'This one's on me.'

Ramsey bent over, steadied the spool. 'Why?'

'I'm the best swimmer aboard. It stands to—'

'Somehow I got the idea you might be afraid of the water.'

Garcia grinned, then frowned. 'I was responsible for a man dying in a water-polo game. Broke his neck. That was supposed to be a game. This is business.'

'But you just got up from pressure sickness.'

'I've had a good rest.' He straightened. 'Hand me down that patching kit from the bulkhead rack. That's a good fellow.'

Ramsey turned to the bulkhead, found the underwater patch kit, removed it. Behind him, he heard Garcia on the intercom.

'Is it compartment twenty-seven?'

'Yes. Why?' Sparrow's voice impersonalized by the speaker system.

'How'm I going to fix—'

'I'm doing this one, Joe. That's—'

'I'm rested, Skipper, and I feel fine. Remember me? Swimming champ?'

Silence. Then: 'Are you sure you feel okay?'

'Tiptop, Skipper. Never better.'

'Ramsey.'

Ramsey turned, then grinned at the reaction, pushed the button on his chest mike. 'Here, Skipper.'

'How's Joe look?'

Ramsey looked at Garcia. 'Same as ever.'

'Okay, Joe. But if you start feeling funny, come back in immediately. That's an order.'

'Righto, Skipper. How much oil we losing?'

'It's been going down as we climbed. Now it's about thirty gallons a minute. Have Ramsey rig you in a detergent suit. That oil is mucky stuff to work in.'

Garcia said, 'Remember in refresher school when your suit system failed? You looked like a—'

'All right, Joe. Some other time.'

'How hot is it out there, Skipper?'

'You can take it for about one hour, Joe. That means you would be starting back within forty minutes.'

'That's cutting it close, Skipper. Is there a margin?'

'I don't think so. Watch your suit counter. We're stabilized now at 150 feet. We'll slip down and balance on the pumps. Outside pressure is sixty-six pounds to the square inch. Milli-R . . . 9050. You're on, Joe. Be careful.'

Ramsey said, 'Shouldn't I go out with him, Skipper?'

'I don't want two of us on the radiation-limit list if I can help it,' said Sparrow. 'Get yourself rigged and stand by for an emergency call.'

'Aye.' Ramsey pulled a detergent suit from its locker, helped Garcia into it, tested the seals.

Garcia spoke over his suit system. 'Make sure I'm tight. The suit will give me a little margin.'

Again Ramsey went over the seals. 'You're tight.'

'Control deck, do you read me?'

'Loud and clear, Joe.'

'I'm going into the hatch now.'

'We'll follow you on the eyes. Be careful.'

'Righto.' Garcia swung open the escape hatch, clambered through, closed the hatch behind him.

Ramsey heard the water pouring into the locker chamber. He turned, pulled out another detergent suit, donned it. His own suit seals came in for a double check. He could hear Bonnett's voice over the intercom: 'Lock pressure equalized. Outer door open . . . closed.'

Sparrow's voice: 'Johnny?'

'Aye.'

'Into the lock as soon as the water's out of it. Seal the hatch and stand by to flood it.'

High-pressure air roared and the green light beside the hatch flashed clear. 'In I go,' said Ramsey. He worked the outside dog controls, breached the hatch, climbed inside the escape chamber, sealed the hatch behind him. The flood-valve release light blinked on. He leaned against the ring rail within reach of the valve, settled down to wait.

'Keep an open talk switch,' said Sparrow.

'You mean me?' asked Ramsey.

'Yes. Joe's out of range of the stern eyes now.'

Ramsey watched the water dripping from the damp flood-valve control, glanced at his suit snooper. Some residual radiation: about twenty-three-hour dosage. He looked around the oval compartment, up to the egg dome of the outside hatch. Garcia was out there, probably through the stricture valve by now and into the viscous crude of compartment twenty-seven. Ramsey could imagine the patient search by feel in the black muck of oil. His eyes began to get heavy and he opened the oxy regulator on his lung suit a crack.

The hands of the timelog swept around: fifty-five minutes.

'Ramsey!'

He snapped up, realized he had been dozing. 'Aye, Skipper.'

'We've given Joe all the time we're able. Really too much. Go see what's wrong . . . and be careful.'

'Right.' Ramsey spun the big wheel of the flood valve, felt the gush of water around his ankles. It surged up about him, tugging at his suit. The warning light and buzzer of his snooper came on simultaneously. The red needle swung into the seventy-minute zone.

Compartment pressure equalized. Ramsey undogged the outside hatch, swung it clear and locked it in the open position. They could free the magna-lock inside if they had to and this would save time. He pulled a hand light from its wall rack, kicked his fin flippers, and drifted out the hatch opening. Immediately, he felt a wave of aloneness. No intercom out here where signals could be heard by the enemy.

The hand light picked out Garcia's safety line snaking away in the darkness. Ramsey hooked his suit ring to it, struck out along the line. The water had an inky quality that swallowed the glow of the light. He sensed the bulk of the slug ahead and above him before he could actually see it and was struck by the oddity of the feeling. The line ran aft along the plastic wall, looped upward onto an external knob.

Ramsey tugged at the line. No response. He swam up to the knob. A coil of the line was caught in a half hitch around the projection, the end disappearing into a tiny hole through the slug's surface.

Fouled control on the stricture valve. Ramsey freed the half hitch, again tugged on the line. He grabbed the projection, felt the valve control through it, pulled downward and turned.

A gush of oil shot out around the safety line as the hole expanded. The oil diffused upward, leaving a darker shape within its cloud. The darker shape moved toward Ramsey's light trailing an oily smudge. Ramsey closed the stricture valve, reached out and touched the moving shape. A hand gripped his shoulder through the suit: once, twice, three times.

All well.

They turned together, swam back with the safety line. The hatch light glowed out of darkness and they followed it in. Ramsey unhooked the safety line while Garcia was entering the compartment, dragged the coil in behind him. Garcia brought the hatch down, dogged it. Ramsey cracked open the high-pressure air line, turned to face Garcia.

'Are you okay in there?' Sparrow's voice over the intercom.

Ramsey said, 'Apparently, Skipper.'

'Joe's had a twenty-five-minute overdose,' said Sparrow.

Ramsey looked at the oil-dripping shape across from him. The last water swept out of the compartment with a sucking roar. Ramsey opened the detergent nozzles, felt the hard thudding of the pressure streams. The oil swept off their suits, disappeared down the flush-out.

'Okay, Joe,' he said.

Garcia remained motionless.

'Come on, Joe, let's go.'

Still he remained motionless.

'Something's wrong with him, Skipper.'

No answer.

Ramsey motioned toward the hatch between their feet.

Garcia nodded, stepped aside. Ramsey undogged the hatch. It swung back with an assist from outside and Ramsey saw Sparrow peering up at him. Sparrow motioned toward Ramsey's throat.

Then Ramsey recognized the silence. Dead mike switch. He fumbled for it with his suited hand, caught Sparrow in mid-roar. ' . . . sick bay on the double, Joe!'

'Detergent spray turned off my mike,' explained Ramsey.

'You've got to watch that,' said Sparrow. 'Come down out of there.'

Ramsey followed Garcia, helped Sparrow strip the suit from the engineering officer. The skipper helped Garcia up onto the catwalk mounting, peeled off the flipper sections. Ramsey stepped back, pulled off his headgear.

'Tired,' said Garcia. 'Knew somebody'd come for me. Coulda cut my way out in 'mergency.' He slid off the catwalk mounting, led the way down the stairs.

Ramsey stripped off his own suit, put both suits away, went down the stairs. Garcia and Sparrow had disappeared through the control-room door. The motors came to life as Ramsey dropped to the control room.

Bonnett stood at the helm, alone in the maze of control arms and dials. He spoke without turning. 'Get on the board and help me find that thermal.'

Ramsey moved to his station, checked the outside temperature reading. The radiation counter caught his eye. 'Who shut off the alarm?'

'Skipper. He had his eyes glued to it.'

'Were we in that?'

'No. You had the hatch sealed before the count went up.'

Ramsey shivered, stared at the dial: 42,000 milli-R. 'That's almost at a self-sustaining level. Would be if it weren't for current diffusion.'

'Where's that thermal?' asked Bonnett.

Ramsey tried a short-range pulse, checked the back wave. 'Try two degrees starboard . . . right.'

'My, we're salty,' said Bonnett.

'We're in it,' said Ramsey. 'Radiation dropped, too.' He looked at the big pressure gauge: 262 psi.

The *Ram*'s deck remained tilted downward.

'We're in it,' repeated Ramsey. 'Let's level out.'

'Buoyancy in the tow,' gritted Bonnett. He flicked the button on his chest mike: 'Skipper, buoyancy in the tow.'

Back came Sparrow's voice: 'What's our depth?'

'We're in the thermal – about 600 feet.'

'Bring us around to westward – make it 260 degrees even.'

'What if we lose the thermal?'

'Just see that we don't.'

'How's Joe?' asked Ramsey.

'Full of needle holes,' said Sparrow.

Bonnett spun the helm, brought up the bow planes, dropped them, found the stabilizing point. The deck inclined forward at an uneasy three degrees.

'She wants to coon dog on us,' said Ramsey.

'Why couldn't oil be a nice heavy substance like lead?' asked Bonnett. He changed the pitch on the rear planes, readjusted the bow planes, glanced at the pitlog. 'The drag's cutting our speed in half.'

Sparrow ducked through the door into the control room, looked to the rear plane setting, swept his glance across the control reading dials.

Ramsey abruptly realized that in the one sweeping glance Sparrow had familiarized himself with the facts of his vessel's life.

He's part of the machine, thought Ramsey.

'The tow's riding stern-heavy,' said Bonnett. 'We lost ballast from the bow. What we need is some nice nonradioactive bottom muck to replenish ballast.'

Ramsey looked at the sonoran chart. The red dot on their position stood north of the blighted Scottish skerries, course line pointing toward Newfoundland. 'Seamount Olga is right in our path,' he said. 'Its west slope would be scoured by clean currents and—'

'It may be hotter than our damper rods,' said Sparrow. 'But it's a good chance. That's why we changed course.'

'Outside radiation's up a few points, Skipper. The thermal's thinner than our diameter here.'

'Steady as she goes,' said Sparrow. 'The tank hull took a near-limit dose back there. It'll have to go through decon anyway. Our concern now is to get that oil home.'

'It's hot, too,' said Bonnett.

'But usable,' Ramsey reminded him.

Sparrow said, 'The immediate problem is how to get that ballast off the bottom when we can't go down to it. I think we're going to have to waste another fish.' He turned to Ramsey. 'Johnny, do you feel hot enough on the remotes to snag our ballast hose in the fin prongs of one of our Con-5 fish?'

Ramsey remembered Teacher Reed at the torpedo base on Boca Raton. He had patted the agate smooth skin of a thin torpedo. '*This is the Con-5. Those buttons in the nose are radar and TV eyes. Through them, you sit right in the nose of this baby while you guide her into the target.*' And he had turned then to a black radio case with a stub antenna protruding from it. '*Here are the controls. Let's see what you can do. This one's a dud, so you can make lots of errors.*'

'Well, what do you think?' asked Sparrow.

'Once that baby's out of her rack, she's charged and ready to blow. If I smack the pin into something near the hull, we've had it.'

'You don't think you can handle it?'

'I didn't say that.' Ramsey looked at his hands. They were steady. 'I can do it if anybody can but—'

'Youth is what it takes,' said Sparrow. 'Les and I are growing old.'

'Howdy, Grandad,' said Bonnett.

'I'm serious,' said Sparrow. 'The end of that ballast hose sticks out only about a foot. The Con-5 will have to be moving better than fifteen knots to snag the hose tightly. That means—'

'That means I'd better be right,' said Ramsey.

'Right the first time,' said Bonnett.

Ramsey shrugged. 'Well, at Boca Raton they said I took to the Con-5 like it was—'

'Boca Raton?' asked Sparrow. 'What's at Boca Raton?'

And Ramsey realized he had made another error. Boca Raton was a torpedo school . . . for Security specialists.

'Isn't that a Security school?' asked Bonnett.

'I missed out on my regular class because of illness,' said Ramsey. 'So they sent me there.' He said a silent prayer that his lie would be believed.

'We'll be over Olga in twenty minutes,' said Bonnett.

'I'm going back for another look at Joe,' said Sparrow. He turned, went out the aft door.

'Garcia's trying for homestead rights on the sick bay,' said Ramsey.

'I hope he's okay,' said Bonnett. 'I don't think the skipper should've let him make that slug repair. I could've done it.'

'Even I could've done it,' said Ramsey. 'But I guess the skipper had his reasons.' He frowned. 'Only I'd like to know his reason for picking me to do this snag job.'

'Did you ever get into a Con-5 game?' asked Bonnett.

Ramsey suddenly grinned. 'Sure. My instructor thought he was a hotshot. So he said we'd take these two Con-5s, him controlling one, me the other. It was a touch match in the bay, first nose-hit the winner. You know, I took—'

'All right, all right,' said Bonnett. 'I'm just trying to make a point. I don't want a blow by blow. That's a young man's game, or at least a school game. We've been a long time out of school. You haven't.'

'Oh.'

Bonnett chuckled. 'I used to be pretty good at it, too. Tell you what: when we get back let's hunt up a fish school and I'll challenge you to a snag match. There's the fun.'

Ramsey sobered. 'The skipper doesn't make mistakes, does he?'

'Not about people,' said Bonnett. 'Or about machines, either.' He stopped to correct the setting on the bow planes. 'And when we get back home they'll have him on the carpet for wasting too many fish. And what about all those spare parts?'

Ramsey thought: A *first-year psych man knows the leader of a group is the integrative force … the logos. Of course this crew has the top rating. Sparrow is—*

'It makes my blood boil when I think about it,' said Bonnett.

Sparrow came through the doorway onto the control deck. 'What makes your blood boil?'

'All the stupid red tape back at base.'

'It's supposed to make your blood boil. That's why it exists. How far to that seamount?'

'Five minutes.'

'Okay, Johnny. Let's see how good you are at Con-tag.' Sparrow gestured toward the torpedo board at Bonnett's left.

'How's Joe?' asked Bonnett.

'I just shot him full of de-carb. If that hot stuff settles in his bones, he's a cooked engineer.'

Ramsey approached the torpedo board slowly.

Bonnett said, 'We caught him in time. He'll be as good as new in a couple of days. No calcium, no carbonate, no—'

'Just call him rubber bones,' said Ramsey. 'Now how about a little quiet?'

'The maestro is about to perform,' said Bonnett.

Ramsey stared up at the banks of red-handled switches, the guide screens, arming triggers. And there in front of him was the little blue stick that made a Con-5 perform. He chose one off the top of the rack, keyed it to the controls, said, 'Standing by. How far is down?'

'Twenty-two hundred feet,' said Bonnett. 'You can go any time now.

It's directly under us.' He slowed the engines until they were barely moving.

'We'll have hose to spare,' said Sparrow.

'Shall I make a recon down to that bottom to see if I can get some muck for our hull snooper?' asked Ramsey.

'No. We have to make this one fast. An EP may pick up our control pulse. If the bottom's hot, then we'll have hot oil and they can use it to lube atomic engines.'

'Now?' asked Ramsey.

'Take her away,' said Sparrow. 'Les, put the side lights on that hose reel.'

'They're already on,' said Bonnett.

Ramsey turned the guide screen to the nose eye in his Con-5, activated the multi-wave projector beside the nose eye. The screen showed a pattern outline for the hull of the *Ram*, picked up in waves beyond the normally visible spectrum. Superimposed was the faint glow of the side light illuminating the hose reel. A second superimposition showed the relative positions of the *Ram* and the tiny Con-5.

'A little more ship speed, please,' said Ramsey. 'It'll steady us.'

Bonnett moved the throttle bar forward a fractional notch and the *Ram* picked up speed.

Ramsey brought the deadly torpedo in closer. He could not see the fin prongs on his torpedo, but he knew where they were – forward projecting edges of the stabilizing fins, designed for hydrostatic balance and set just back of the needle curve of the torpedo's nose.

'Blink the side light,' said Ramsey.

Bonnett winked the light switch off, on, off, on.

The glow on Ramsey's guide screen went on and off to the movement of the switch.

'Wanted to make sure that was the correct light,' said Ramsey. He flashed the Con-5 in close and hovered it over the light. The hose projection was visible ahead, jutting at a forty-five-degree angle from the reel base.

'Okay,' he said. 'Here goes.' He dropped the Con-5 back ten feet, threw full power into the torpedo's drive. It surged ahead, swooped down onto the hose, seemed to hesitate, then ranged away from the *Ram*.

'You got it,' said Bonnett.

'What else?' asked Ramsey. He slacked off the speed of his torpedo, looked at the counter dial which showed how fast the hose was unreeling. Abruptly, the dial showed a slowing down, slacked off to zero.

'Lost it,' said Sparrow.

Ramsey brought the Con-5 around in a sweeping curve. The snaky line of the hose was the superimposed outline now. He brought the little torpedo in fast, tipped it at the last minute like a hungry shark and again had the hose in tow. 'Got a better hold on it that time.'

'I'm bringing us around on that seamount,' said Bonnett. 'I have you on the search board. I'll warn you one hundred feet from bottom. You can take it in visually from there.'

'I picked up the hose about ten feet from the end that last time,' said Ramsey. 'Get the pump going the minute I touch the nozzle into the muck; that'll hold her there. I don't want to hold that firing pin any closer to a target any longer than I have to.'

'Pump ready,' said Sparrow.

Ramsey glanced sideways, saw Sparrow at the tow board. Sparrow's hands moved over the controls. 'Line checks clear to the ballast compartment,' he said.

Ramsey visualized the ballast connections running aft, through the tow controls and into the web mesh which linked *Ram* and slug. If that linkage remained sound ... if he could plug that hose end into ballast muck ... if ...

'One hundred feet,' said Bonnett. 'You're bearing along the east face of the seamount.'

'I have its outline,' said Ramsey, eyes on screen.

He maneuvered the torpedo closer to the bottom.

'Ledge,' he said. 'That'll have muck.'

'Pray it's cool,' said Sparrow.

'Pray it's ballast,' said Ramsey.

He edged the torpedo and its hose end closer to the bottom, closer, closer ...

'She's in!'

'Pump on and ... holding,' said Sparrow.

Ramsey tipped the Con-5, freed it from the hose, brought it up away from the bottom.

'Stand by with that thing,' said Sparrow. 'We may have to move the hose.'

They waited.

'The slug's bow is coming down,' said Sparrow. He hit the switch of a ballast snooper. 'It's cool.'

Slowly, as the *Ram* circled over the seamount, the slug came to hydrostatic balance. Presently, Sparrow said, 'Okay, Johnny, find some deep bottom for that Con-5, set it down, disengage and leave it. Don't let it blow.'

'Aye.' Ramsey took the little torpedo down along the flank of the seamount, found a deep ledge and set the deadly metal fish down. He shut down the remote-control system, stepped back.

'Hose coming in,' said Sparrow. 'Take us down into that thermal, Les. Course 260. Johnny, how about looking in on Joe?'

'Aye, Skipper.' He felt suddenly exhausted, but buoyed by an inner nervous exhilaration.

'Then get some rest,' said Sparrow.

Ramsey turned aft, went to the door, stepped through, and went to the rec room – sick bay.

Garcia lay on the sun-lamp cot clad only in a pair of shorts. He was on his back, one brown arm thrown across his eyes. Dots of perspiration glistened on his dark skin. As Ramsey entered the room, Garcia lifted the arm from his eyes, peered from under it.

'Oh, it's you.'

'Who'd you expect? The surgeon general?'

'Aren't we funny!'

Ramsey put the back of his hand against Garcia's forehead. 'Fever?'

Garcia cleared his throat. 'Some. Those damned decalcification shots.'

Ramsey glanced at the chart Sparrow had taped to the bulkhead above the cot. 'You're due for another shot right now. De-carb and de-phos. Another de-sulf in an hour.' He turned away, went to the pharmacy locker across the room, saw that Sparrow had set out the hypodermics in sterile seals, labeled them.

'What have we been doing?' asked Garcia.

Ramsey turned with the hypo for the shot, said, 'Getting a new cargo of ballast for the slug. Turn over.'

'This one in the left arm,' said Garcia. He held out the arm, watched while Ramsey swabbed the area, administered the injection, returned the hypo to the pharmacy rack.

Garcia spoke behind him. 'Have you and your little black box finally got the skipper figured out?'

Ramsey's muscles locked. He took a deep breath to quiet his nerves, turned. 'What do you mean?'

Garcia's face bore a twisted smile. 'Don't play it innocent, Johnny. Remember me? I'm the guy who's capable of taking over the electronics shack if you crock out.'

'But—'

'My hobby is breaking and entering,' said Garcia. He put his hands under his head, winced as he moved his left arm. 'You've heard about Pandora's box?' He managed a shrug by lifting his eyebrows and making the slightest movement of shoulders. 'You shouldn't put temptation like that in front of a guy like me.'

Ramsey wet his lips with his tongue. 'You mean the test equipment for the long-range—'

'Really, old boy, don't you know when the jig's up?' He stared at Ramsey, a calculating look. 'The gear in that box is tied to the skipper someway. I don't know how, but—'

'Oh, come off that,' said Ramsey. 'You—'

'I put it to the acid test,' said Garcia.

'Acid test?'

'You're a deuced reluctant type, Johnny. If I didn't—'

'Start at the beginning,' said Ramsey, tiredly. 'I want to know what you think.'

'Fair enough,' said Garcia. He wriggled into a more comfortable position on the cot.

Ramsey brought up a stool, sat down.

'In the first place,' said Garcia, 'you didn't offer to introduce me to the intricacies of your little black box. That was a mistake. Any normal E-man would've been all eager to share his gadget with another man aboard who could talk shop.' The smile tugged at the corners of Garcia's mouth. 'You, by the way, don't talk shop.'

'So?'

'So there's nobody else aboard who talks your particular brand of shop.'

'Is that when you figured me for a spy?'

Garcia shook his head. 'I've never figured you for a spy.' He frowned. 'Sorry about that. Maybe I could've saved you a bad time with Les. I've been certain all along that you weren't a spy.'

'How could you be?'

'Too inept.' Garcia hesitated. 'And besides, my wife is a cousin of Commander Gadsen of the *Dolphin*. Gad was very impressed by a fellow named Long John Ramsey from BuPsych who pulled them out of a nasty spot when their oxy system went sour. He says this man Ramsey improvised a special vampire gauge and pulled some stunts with anhydrase that weren't in the books. Seemed to think this Ramsey saved their lives.'

'So you figured me for this same Ramsey.'

'Gad was *extremely* impressed by this Long John Ramsey except one thing: he said the redheaded bastard got on your nerves with his know-it-all attitude!'

'The world's full of redheaded—'

'Uh, uh!' Garcia shook his head. 'You're BuPsych. Two things on this floating sewer pipe interest you more than anything else: the skipper and that black box in your room. So I opened the box.'

Ramsey forced himself to remain impassive. 'And?'

An enigmatic grin captured Garcia's features. 'There's a separate set of recording instruments in it keyed to the timelog. I copied four of your tapes, checked back on what we'd been doing.'

'What'd that prove?'

'Whenever the skipper's asleep, your graphs flatten. Every time.'

Ramsey shrugged, remained silent.

'But I needed the clincher,' said Garcia. 'Two times when the skipper hurt himself – a barked shin and one electric shock – I logged the exact time. The squiggles on a couple of your tapes go wild at exactly those moments.'

Ramsey recalled the tape gyrations, his own cautious questioning to elicit the reasons. 'Clever.'

'Thank you, old chap. I thought so myself.'

'What's all this prove?'

Garcia raised his eyebrows. 'It proves you're making some kind of record of the skipper's internal chemistry. Only one type of fellow is that interested in why people tick.'

'Yes?'

'He's vulgarly referred to as a head thumper.'

In spite of himself, Ramsey grinned. *So I'm all washed up*, he thought. *So I'm in good company.*

'I don't believe I'm going to give you away yet,' said Garcia. 'This show hasn't played itself out. I must remember to thank BuPsych, too, for one of the most entertaining cruises I've ever had.'

'I suppose you want into the act,' said Ramsey.

'Good heavens, no! I already have my part to play. Just one thing, old fellow. Don't sell our Captain Savvy Sparrow short.'

'Oh?'

'He's the director of this show. Whether you know it or not, he controls the script.'

Ramsey fought down the vague tuggings of disquiet. 'Is that why you're not giving me away?'

'You obviously mean well,' said Garcia. His voice went lower, more harsh. 'Now, give me my other shot and get the hell out of here! Your air of superiority is beginning to wear on me.'

Ramsey felt the hot blood suffusing his features. He took two quick breaths, surged to his feet.

Garcia deliberately turned over, spoke with his mouth muffled slightly by the pillow. 'Left buttock this time, old thing. Try not to work your temper out on me while you're about it.'

Ramsey went to the pharmacy locker, returned with the hypo, administered the shot, replaced the hypo in its rack.

'That was very gentle,' said Garcia. 'Good control.'

Ramsey walked across the room, stood over the cot. 'What air of superiority?' he demanded.

Garcia rolled onto his back, grimaced, said, 'I don't mind your dislike of me or Les, but by Heaven, you owe your life to—'

'That's enough!' barked Ramsey. 'You talk about superior! Every damned one of you has been so superior it—'

'Oh, I say!' Garcia stared up at him. 'We all have our soft spots. Evidently the junior ensign—'

'You've had your inning,' gritted Ramsey.

'So I have.' Garcia nodded. 'Maybe you've just wanted to be one of the gang. In spite of—' He fell silent.

'In spite of what?'

'Your other job.'

'Maybe because of it,' said Ramsey.

Garcia digested this. 'I never thought of that. But it makes sense. You psych boys must be pretty lonely. All your friends – outside the profession, that is – always on guard lest you pounce.'

Ramsey shoved his hands into his hip pockets. 'Where'd you get this low opinion of psych?'

'Watching you operate, Doctor.'

Ramsey sniffed. 'You've never seen me operate.' He kicked the stool closer to Garcia's cot, sat down. 'You're going to talk shop.'

Garcia raised on one elbow. 'Now see here, old thing, I really—'

'Your secret's showing,' said Ramsey.

Garcia's face went blank. 'What ... did ... you ... mean ... by ... that?'

'You act like a man under some contra-survival threat greater than the fear of death. You keep making sacrificial gestures, as though you were seeking to excuse—' Ramsey fell silent, staring at Garcia.

'Well?'

'I never brought it into concrete focus before, Joe. Did you have anything to do with the death of that Security lieutenant?'

Garcia sank back onto his pillow. 'No.'

'Even indirectly?'

'I didn't know a thing about him until we found him!'

Ramsey started to nod, then thought: *Wait a minute! That's not a direct answer. A clever evasion phrased like an answer.* He said, 'Wouldn't an outright lie be preferable?'

Garcia stared at the ceiling, mouth held in a harsh line.

'Okay, we'll talk about something else, Joe.'

'Why don't you go talk by yourself?'

'You're such pleasant company I can't bear to leave. Tell me, Joe, outside of psych men who look through your sham wall of inadequate defenses—'

'Look, fellow!' Garcia turned his head on the pillow until he was staring directly at Ramsey. 'So you came out after me when I was caught in the slug. That was your boy-scout good deed for the day and I thanked you nicely when we got back, but—'

'Thanked me?'

'Oh, I forgot, you goofed with the detergent jet and had your hearing aid turned off. No matter. I was about to say that your gesture wasn't necessary. I could've cut myself out of the slug if the need arose. So we're—'

'What with?'

'Huh?'

'You stripped your pockets before getting into the lung suit. Your knife was right there on the suit ledge when I got ready to go out. What were you going to cut yourself out with – the patch scraper?' Garcia's dark features grew pale.

'You're welcome,' said Ramsey.

'You've suddenly built your part up greater than it first appeared, Johnny. Who does your scripts?'

'It's just that you've never really seen me operate,' said Ramsey. 'Now, I started to ask you a question. I'd like a straight answer and we'll call it even. Okay?'

Garcia smiled thinly. 'Righto.'

'What is it about this service that really gripes a submariner?'

'Nothing gripes us,' said Garcia. 'We love our work. There's really nothing in this whole wide world to compare with the subtugs. It has playing grab-tail with a panther pushed completely off the jolly map. Now, you take—'

'I'm serious, Joe. I'm looking for something that's bottled up way inside you. I think I know what it is, but I want to hear it from someone else. Someone like you who knows people and submarines. I think we've been looking in the wrong direction.'

'What do you want to know?'

'I'm not going to put the words in your mouth. I want to know what it is about this service that really burns your country ass – the thing you don't even talk about among yourselves?'

Again Garcia lifted himself on one elbow. He grimaced as he moved the arm which had received the earlier shots. 'All right, Johnny boy. You deserve a straight answer for being such an observant chap – about knives and such. You saw how we shoved off?'

'Yes.'

'Sneaking off. You know – just routine.'

'That's Security.'

'Stuff Security. Do these fatheads imagine the EPs are ignorant of the location of our bases?'

Ramsey shook his head. 'Well, Security can be sure the EPs know where *our* home base is. They can be sure if they got our squirt message, that is.'

'They should be sure without our message! This cops-and-robbers routine is an ache in the bustard. Air cover and sea patrol are the real reasons there aren't wolf packs waiting at the outlets of all five of our—'

'Five?'

'Five bases, Johnny. Every submariner knows about 'em. The sub skippers know; so the men know. That's survival and Security can go blow that out its bloody bum—'

'I don't get you, Joe. Sorry.'

'Johnny, let's say you're the only man aboard able to operate the boat. The rest of us are all gowed up somehow or other. Say a pile flare-up. It's survival, Johnny, for you to know that the radiation medical center is at the other end of the Charleston short tunnel and that the tunnel opens into Charleston harbor just inside the mole and a hundred feet left.'

'I see what you mean. So we have five bases.'

'We used to have six. Then the EPs sabotaged one of our sub-cruisers and it blew while going down the tunnel – like we almost did. That's the Corpus Christi crater you've—'

'Wait a minute!' Ramsey shook his head. 'That was an EP war rocket. It was aimed at—'

'Swamp mud! It won't wash, Johnny. That doesn't explain how the alleged war rocket pierced our "perfect" robo-slave defenses and hit smack on that tunnel.'

'What tunnel?'

'Johnny, I've been up that tunnel. So've a lot of other fellows in the sub service. Security may peddle its pap to somebody else, not to us. You can't tell me a rocket launched in Siberia can center on a hole in the ground in Texas – even by accident. That's stretching probability or accuracy.' He sank back onto his pillow.

'Let's grant your argument,' said Ramsey. 'What's that have to do with my original question?'

'You still want to get way inside my head?'

'I'd like an answer to my original question.'

Garcia stared at the ceiling. 'Right, Johnny. The answer you want goes something like this: there are men all through the services – not just the subs – who are so sick of war – year after year after year after year of war – so sick of living with fear constantly that almost anything else is preferable. Death? He's an old friend – a neighbor just beyond the bulkhead there. Lots of things become preferable. Fouling up the works, for instance, to let the other side win. Just so somebody wins and that puts a stop to the thing – the bloody, foolish, never-ending thing.' His voice trailed off and he turned, stared emptily at the bulkhead behind Ramsey.

'That's insane,' whispered Ramsey.

'Certainly it is,' said Garcia faintly. 'But you're not going to argue that war is sane. We're human beings, whatever that means. If insanity is the pattern, that's us and you'll find damned little that's contradictory. Just little scratches of sanity where the blood runs through a different color.'

'Oh?'

'Like the skipper. You've seen him pray for the souls of the men he kills. That's a scratch of sanity. You can feel it.' He turned a fierce glare on Ramsey. 'Do you ever wonder what they're like – those other fellows? Perdition! They can't be so very much different from us. They have wives, kids, sweethearts, hopes, fears. I know as certainly as I know I'm here now that there are people over there who feel the same way about this stupid war as we do.' His voice rose. 'Anything! Just to get this damnable thing over with! It's like a pain that's way inside your chest and it won't stop. It goes on and on and on and—'

'Easy, Joe.'

Garcia relaxed. 'Okay.'

'That's battle pressure,' said Ramsey. 'I was thinking of something else.' He hesitated. 'No, maybe you were talking about the same thing.'

'Such as?'

'It has to do with death instincts, Joe.'

'Oh, and it's too deep for the likes of me.'

'I didn't say that.'

'You implied it, Johnny. Some more of your esoteric nonsense. I've had a normal amount of psych study. I've read the old masters and the new: Freud, Jung, Adler, Freeman, Losi, Komisaya. I went looking for answers and found double-talk. I can speak the jargon.'

'So you know what a death instinct is.'

'Sure, Johnny. The EPs and us – we're moving blindly toward our mutual destruction. Is that what you wanted me to say?'

'I guess not. I had something else in mind. Maybe I'm wrong.'

'Or maybe I like to be blind, too.'

'Yes. We were on another track earlier, Joe. You didn't answer. Are you ready to tell me if the EPs have ever approached you to do their dirty work?'

Garcia looked at him coldly. 'I hope to see you in hell,' he said, enunciating the words precisely.

Ramsey got to his feet. 'You've been a big help, Joe. But you're really supposed to be resting.' He pulled a light blanket from a wall hanger, threw it over Garcia, turned away and went to the door.

Garcia said, 'Do you think I'm a sleeper?'

Without turning, Ramsey said, 'Would a sleeper have taken an overdose of radiation to keep us hidden from the EPs?'

'Maybe,' said Garcia. 'If he didn't like his job and was as tired of this war as I am.'

And that, thought Ramsey, *is precisely the answer I was afraid of.* He said. 'Get some rest.'

'Bit players hamming up their parts,' said Garcia.

Ramsey stepped out into the companionway and it was a cold gray corridor suddenly – leading nowhere in either direction. He thought: *My world's gone completely schizoid. Security! Its job is to make us even more schizoid – to break down as many lines of communication as possible.* He turned and looked back at Garcia on the cot. The engineering officer had turned on his side, facing the bulkhead. *That's why it's so important to belong to Savvy Sparrow's group. That's the scratch of sanity.*

And he remembered Heppner, the electronics officer who had gone mad. *If you can't belong and you can't leave: What then?*

The shape and substance of things began to reform in Ramsey's mind. He turned up the companionway, went to the control deck. The room seemed to greet him as he stepped through the door: warmth, flashing of red and green lights, a sibilant whispering of power, a faint smell of ozone and oil riding on the background of living stink which no filters could completely eliminate.

Sparrow stood at the helm, an almost emaciated figure with rumpled clothes hanging loosely upon him. Ramsey was suddenly startled by the realization that Sparrow had lost weight when there didn't seem to be any place from which he could lose it.

'How's Joe?' Sparrow spoke without turning.

Saw my reflection in the dive-board glass, thought Ramsey. *Nothing escapes him.*

'He's going to be all right,' said Ramsey. 'His vein-counter shows negative absorption. He may lose a little hair, be nauseated for a while undoubtedly.'

'We ought to set him into Charleston,' said Sparrow. 'The vein-counter doesn't tell you what's happening in the bone marrow. Not until it's too late.'

'All the signs are good,' said Ramsey. 'Calcium leaching out and being replaced by non-hot. Sulphate's negative. He's going to be okay.'

'Sure, Johnny. It's just that I've sailed with him for a long time. I'd hate to lose him.'

'He knows it, Skipper.'

Sparrow turned, smiled, a strangely plaintive gesture. 'I guess he does at that.'

And Ramsey thought: *You can't tell a man you love him – not if you're a man. That's a problem, too. We don't have the right word – the one that leaves out sex.*

He said, 'Where's Les?'

'Getting some rest. We hit the Arctic stream twenty minutes ago.'

Ramsey moved up to the search-board station, rested a hand on the wheel to external salvage air beside the board. His mind was full of moving thoughts. It was as though the conversation with Garcia had tapped a well – or had dropped head pressure and allowed what was underneath to come to the surface.

'Les will take the next watch in an hour,' said Sparrow. 'I can handle her now. You come on in three hours. We'll need a tighter schedule without Joe.'

'Aye, Skipper.'

He turned, went aft to his quarters, and was suddenly aware of a bone weariness. It was too much trouble to get out the telemeter and inspect its tapes. Besides, he knew what it would show: the iron-hard inner control that simulated normality. Or maybe it *was* normality. He fell asleep on the bunk without undressing.

The *Ram* bore southwest toward home waters, and the timelog reeled off the days. A monotonous succession of watches amidst the cold pipes, dials, wheels, levers, blinking lights, and telltale buzzers. The same faces and the same danger.

Even peril can grow boring.

A distant sound of propellers in an area where all such sounds mean *hunter.*

Wait and listen. Creep ahead a few knots. Wait and listen. Creep ahead a few knots. Wait and listen. The distant sound is gone. The *Ram* picks up speed while red-rimmed eyes watch the ranging and sonar gear.

Garcia was up and about on the fourth day – a man grown strangely morose and sullen when Ramsey was present.

Still the subtug moved steadily nearer to safety, towing the turgid slug: a prize wrested from death itself.

And a special tension – a new pressure – crept into the actions of the *Ram*'s crew. It was a tension that said: 'We're going to make it ... We're going to make it ... We're going to make it ...

'Aren't we?'

Ramsey, asleep in his bunk, wrestled with a silent nightmare in which Sparrow, Garcia, and Bonnett suddenly turned to face him – all with the features of mad Heppner.

Slowly, the nightmare lifted and left him peaceful in the womb-like stillness of the boat.

Stillness!

Ramsey sat bolt upright in his bunk, wide awake, every sense crying out against the strange new element: quiet. He reached behind him and snapped on his bunk light. It was dim – showing that they were on emergency batteries.

'Johnny!' It was Sparrow's voice over the wall speaker.

'Here, Skipper.'

'Get up to your shack on the double. We're having pile trouble.'

'I'm on my way!'

His feet hit the deck, fumbled into shoes. He snapped off his bunk light, ran out the door, up the ladder two steps at a time, down the companionway and into his shack station, talk switch open. 'On station, Skipper. Is it serious?'

Bonnett's voice came back. 'Full-scale flare-up.'

'Where's the skipper?'

'Forward with Joe.'

'Joe shouldn't be anywhere near that! He's still on the hot list!'

'It was Joe's watch. You know how—'

'Johnny!' Sparrow's voice over the intercom.

'Here.'

'Secure the shack for minimum power drain and come forward.'

'Right.' Ramsey found that his hands knew automatically which switches to hit. He blessed the long hours of patience with the mock-up board. This was what Reed had meant: '*There is no such thing as a minor emergency aboard a submarine.*' He made the conventional glance-around double check: standby light glowing amber, jacks out, main switch up, relay circuit to control room plugged in and green. He thumbed his chest mike: 'Les, she's all yours.'

'On your way.'

He ran out the door, turned right up the companionway, through the control room without glancing at Bonnett, and out onto the central catwalk. The laboring hum of one engine turning slowly on battery power to give them headway permeated the engine room.

Garcia stood beside the tunnel hatch down forward to the left, his hands fumbling with the zipper of an ABG suit.

Ramsey's first thought was: *What's wrong with Sparrow? He can't let Joe go in there!* Then he understood the significance of the scene.

The nozzle of a detergent hose was racked beside Garcia. Sparrow stood about twenty feet away on the lower catwalk. The space between them showed raw splashes of detergent spray. As Sparrow took a step forward, Garcia stopped working with the zipper, put a hand on the nozzle.

'Stay where you are, Skipper!'

Garcia's voice was metallic and seemed to echo in the engine room and Ramsey realized the man was talking into the open mike of his ABG suit.

Garcia lifted the hose nozzle, pointed it at Sparrow. 'One step more and I'll let you have another taste of this.'

Ramsey went to the left hand-ladder, dropped down to Sparrow's level. He saw that the front of Sparrow's uniform was dripping with detergent, and winced at the thought of what that high-pressure jet spray could do to a man.

'Shall we rush him, Skipper?' he asked. 'I could drop down to—'

'Well, if it isn't the head thumper,' said Garcia. The zipper on his suit suddenly unjammed and he pulled it closed, reached back and folded the hood forward over his head, sealed it. The quartz-plate front gleamed at them like a malignant Cyclops eye.

Sparrow glanced at Ramsey, turned back to Garcia. 'We couldn't move an inch against that hose. We have to reason with him.'

'Let the head thumper reason with me,' said Garcia, his voice booming from the bulkhead speaker above them. 'That's his department.'

'He's only four days from a radiation overdose,' said Ramsey.

'This is my show,' said Garcia. 'This is my big scene. I'm going to crawl that tunnel and there's nothing you can do to stop me. Besides, I know this end of the ship better than any of you.'

Ramsey looked down at the open door to the tunnel, realized abruptly that it was the same tunnel in which they had found the dead Security officer.

Garcia half turned toward the door.

'Joe, stop!' barked Sparrow. 'That's an order!' He made a sudden dash forward, was bowled over backward by a hard stream of detergent spray.

Behind him, Ramsey caught part of the spray, slipped to his knees. By the time they had scrambled to their feet, Garcia had disappeared into the tunnel, closing the door behind him.

Sparrow said, 'He took a wrecking bar with him. He's going to jam the hatch dogs inside so we can't follow him.' They heard metal banging on metal.

Garcia's voice came over the bulkhead speaker. 'That's right, Skipper. Can't have you fellows trying to steal my scene. You have front-row seats; enjoy the show.'

'Has he gone off his rocker?' asked Ramsey.

Sparrow slipped down to the tunnel door, tested the dogs. 'Jammed!'

'Has he gone psychotic?' asked Ramsey.

'Of course not!' barked Sparrow. 'There's a full-scale flare-up in that pile room. He's gone in to do what he can.'

Ramsey looked at the snooper above the tunnel door, saw that its needle was jammed in the red. 'Skipper! It's hot here!'

Sparrow slapped the snooper with one hand and the needle swung back into the seven-hour-limit zone. 'Jammed when he opened the door.' He turned to the tool rack beside the door. 'Joe! Do you hear me?'

'Sure, Skipper. No need to shout. I'm almost at the tunnel curve.'

'Joe, defiance of orders is a serious offense.'

Garcia's laughter roared from the speaker. 'So sue me!'

'What happened in the pile room?' asked Ramsey.

Sparrow began pulling tools from the rack. 'Our repairs didn't hold. Tie bolts sheared. The whole reactor slipped to the left, jammed the remote-control bank.' He glanced at his wrist watch. 'The batteries will give us steerage control for about another thirty minutes. When we lose steerage, the planes won't be able to hold us level and over we go. Over goes the pile. If we're lucky it'll reach critical mass. If we're unlucky, the whole boat will be contaminated and us with it. That'll be the slow way out.'

'And if Joe lives through this, you'll have his hide,' said Ramsey. 'Even though he's risking—'

'You blasted idiot!' shouted Sparrow. 'What do you mean *if he lives?* Don't you know there's only one way to get that pile back onto its base?'

All Ramsey could think was: *I did it! I cracked through that iron control! Now his emotions can take a normal –*

'Skipper!' It was Bonnett's voice over the intercom.

Sparrow spoke into his chest mike. 'Yes?'

'I'm tuned to the portside pile-room eye over the tunnel plates. They're moving out toward – Good God! Joe! Get out of there! Skipper! He's in the pile room!'

'That's what I meant,' murmured Sparrow. 'Our Father, protect him.' He stared at the tunnel door. '"The Lord is my shepherd; I shall not want. He maketh me to lie down in green pastures: He leadeth me beside the still waters. He restoreth my soul: He leadeth me in the paths of righteousness for His name's sake. Yea, though I walk through the valley of the shadow of death, I will fear no—"'

'Now hear this.' It was Garcia's voice from the bulkhead speaker. 'I can last maybe fifteen minutes. When I get the remote-control bank cleared, be ready to take over.'

'Sure, Joe,' whispered Sparrow. He swung open a panel on the forward bulkhead, revealing the direct controls to the left-side bank. The telltale lights glowed red when he threw in the switch.

'He's a dead man already,' said Ramsey.

'Quiet!' barked Sparrow. 'Tune that bulkhead screen above us to that pile-room eye.'

Ramsey jumped to obey. The screen came to life. It showed Garcia's figure bulky in an ABG suit. He was bent over, rigging jacks to force the reactor onto its foundation. As they watched, Garcia began to turn the screws. Slowly, the deadly block inched toward its proper position. They could feel Bonnett adjusting the planes to accommodate for the shifting weight.

Sparrow bent over the tools he had removed from the bulkhead rack, hefted a big Stillson wrench. 'Let's try one of those dogs,' he said.

'The only way he could've jammed it is from the bottom,' said Ramsey. 'If we force it down, break it off and—'

Sparrow fitted the wrench to the upper dog, said, 'They drilled you well for your little job.'

Now, what's he mean by that? thought Ramsey.

'Here, give me a hand,' said Sparrow.

Ramsey took told of the wrench.

Together, they bore down on the handle. Abruptly, the dog twisted, snapped off. Ramsey took a punch and hammer from the stack of tools, knocked the fitting through the door into the tunnel.

Sparrow had the wrench fitted to the other dog.

Ramsey glanced up at the screen. The reactor was back on its foundation, and Garcia was securing it with new lag bolts.

'Let's go,' said Sparrow.

They snapped off the other dog, heard a clatter of metal in the tunnel as Garcia's wrecking bar fell away. Sparrow pried the door open, swung it wide.

The snooper's needle jammed in the red.

'Suits,' said Sparrow. He motioned toward the locker.

'Skipper.' It was Garcia's voice from the speaker. 'Tell my wife she doesn't have to be afraid any more. She'll understand.'

'Sure, Joe.'

'Tell her to go someplace and change her name.'

'Why?'

Ramsey passed him an ABG suit, began scrambling into his own.

'Johnny'll understand.'

Sparrow slipped into the suit, looked at Ramsey. 'Well?'

Ramsey shook his head, unable to speak.

Sparrow spoke into his mike as he sealed the hood in place. 'Joe, we've forced the door. I'm bringing in the detergent hose and a cool suit. Come out of there.'

'I'm too hot,' said Garcia. 'Leave me here.'

'Come out or I'll come in after you,' said Sparrow.

Ramsey handed Sparrow a fresh ABG suit, glanced up at the bulkhead screen. It showed Garcia's squat-suited figure, standing beside the tunnel plates. Above him, one of the giant remote-control manuals swung outward. At the same time, Bonnett's voice came over the intercom. 'The control bank's free, Skipper. I can take it from here. Get that damned fool out of there. He may still have a chance.' Bonnett was almost sobbing.

'I'm coming in after you,' said Sparrow.

'You don't understand,' shouted Garcia. 'Stay out of here, Skipper!'

'I'm coming,' repeated Sparrow. He freed the detergent hose from its reel clip.

Garcia's voice rose almost to a scream. 'Skipper! I'm your spy! Don't be a fool!'

'You're my engineering officer,' said Sparrow. He bent for the tunnel, slid into it, dragging hose and ABG suit behind him.

Garcia's voice came to them: 'You can't—' He fell silent, choked, coughed, collapsed onto the reactor-room floor.

Around Ramsey in the engine room, lights brightened, the four motors resumed their normal humming. He could feel the *Ram's* response through his feet as though it were a report from someone outside himself. He was unable to tear his gaze from the screen. The giant manual arm swung out over Garcia's prone figure, clasped him gently, lifted him into the tunnel, replaced the cover plates.

'I've got him,' said Sparrow. A gush of detergent washed out the mouth of the tunnel.

Ramsey jumped to the bulkhead console, started a pump removing the hot fluid.

'Johnny!' Sparrow's voice.

He spoke into his suit mike. 'Here, Skipper.'

Sparrow's voice lowered. 'You don't have to help in this, Johnny. Get away from the tunnel mouth if you value your virility. Joe's hot. Very hot.'

'I've already got two kids,' said Ramsey. 'Bring him out.'

'Here he is.'

Garcia's limp body was extruded from the tunnel mouth like an insect from its burrow. Ramsey eased him to the deck. Sparrow followed.

'I almost drowned him in detergent getting him into his suit. It's already too hot.'

Ramsey bent over, unzipped the front of Garcia's suit. Sparrow helped him pull the limp figure from it. They hustled Garcia into the decontamination chamber. Sparrow removed his own suit, went in with Garcia. Ramsey took the suits, stuffed them into the tunnel mouth, stripped off his own and pressed it in after the others. He closed the door, wedged it with the Stillson wrench.

The door to the decon chamber popped open. Sparrow emerged nude, dragging Garcia after him in like condition. 'We'll have to replace every drop of his blood,' said Sparrow. 'Get in there and shed your clothes, then come up to the rec room.' He stooped, lifted Garcia over his shoulder and went up the ladder to the catwalk, muscles knotting on his legs and back with the strain of the load.

Ramsey paused to speak into his chest mike. 'Les, Skipper is bringing Joe up. Better lend a hand.' Then he ducked into the decon chamber, slapped the medium-jet control. The harsh streams, designed for a man in a protective suit, bit into his flesh with a stinging pressure. Ramsey shucked out of his clothes, kicked them into a corner, stopped the spray, went out and followed Sparrow's wet footprints up the ladder.

He was afraid to look back at the snooper above the tunnel door. Jammed in the red. *We've had it, but good,* he thought.

Bonnett was still at the helm as Ramsey entered the control room. 'Wouldn't let me help,' he said. He motioned toward the door aft.

Ramsey continued after the line of wet footprints. *Naked of soul, naked of body,* he thought. *Now we're down to the simplest essentials.*

In the rec room, Sparrow had Garcia stretched out on a cot, a plasma bottle hung above him, its tube leading into a vein. Sparrow was setting up a blood-exchange unit on the opposite side of the cot, adjusting the vein and artery taps, the flow meters, the height of the armrest.

Ramsey went to the live-blood storage, checked the automatic circulation and revitalization systems, found them operative.

'Blood ready,' he said. He turned.

Sparrow said, 'Right.' He plugged the blood exchange into the live-blood circulating system, put a hand on the valve. 'Monitor what we pump out of him.'

Ramsey went to the head of the blood-exchange unit, glanced at the taps which Sparrow had adjusted to Garcia's arm. The engineering officer's breath was coming in slow, shallow rhythm, the movement of his chest discernible. The skin of his face and chest had a mottled blue cyanotic appearance.

Sparrow opened the exchange valve. Blood from Garcia's body began to flow into the unit's lead-lined storage system as the new blood was pumped into his body. Immediately, Ramsey's monitor snooper swung far right, stuck there.

'He's off the meter, Skipper.'

Sparrow nodded. 'Shall I use it all?'

'What do you mean?'

'There won't be any blood left for us.'

Ramsey's memory flashed back to a vision of the tunnel snooper jammed in the red. 'We'll get by with plasma,' he said.

'My thought. I'm glad you agree.' He came around the cot, unhooked the plasma tube from Garcia's left arm. 'If we need it, that is. And I'm more apt to than you are. I was in that tunnel.'

'Let's save a couple of changes for you,' said Ramsey. 'You never can—'

'I'll be all right.'

Ramsey fell silent, watching the monitor dial. It stayed against the right-hand pin.

'I got his shots into him and took my own before you came up,' said Sparrow. 'We'd better check you now.'

'Go ahead,' said Ramsey. He held out his left arm, kept his gaze on the monitor dial. 'Three changes through him by now for sure and he's still off the meter. Skipper, I've never heard of—'

'This is the de-carb,' said Sparrow. 'It'll hurt.' He grasped Ramsey's arm, injected the serum precipitate into the muscle. 'Don't worry about Joe. He's in God's hands, now.'

'Aren't we all,' said Ramsey.

'Skipper!' It was Bonnett's voice over the intercom.

Sparrow stepped to a wall mike, flipped the switch. 'Go ahead.'

'I've just checked out the pile. All secure.'

'Set course for Charleston,' said Sparrow. 'Force speed.'

'Aye. How's Joe?'

'It's too soon to know.'

'Tell me if—'

'We will.' Sparrow closed the switch.

Garcia stirred on the cot; his lips moved and he twisted his head from side to side. Suddenly, he spoke, his voice surprisingly strong. 'I've gotta do it, Bea! They'll get at me through our kids, don't you understand?'

He seemed to be listening.

'I can't tell anybody! They'd shoot me!'

'Easy, Joe,' said Sparrow.

Garcia's eyes flickered open, closed, opened. He stared blankly at Sparrow. 'Where's Bea! Did they hurt her?'

'She'll be all right,' said Sparrow.

Garcia shuddered. 'If we could've just gone somewhere and changed our name. That's all.' He closed his eyes.

'Do you know where you are?' asked Sparrow.

Garcia nodded. 'Nightmare.'

'He's on the meter,' said Ramsey. 'But so far into the probable fatal that—'

'Be quiet,' said Sparrow. He checked the change-count dial in the blood system. 'Eight down.'

'And sixteen to go,' said Ramsey.

Sparrow reduced the rate of flow.

'You should've left me in there,' said Garcia.

'Don't talk foolish,' said Sparrow.

'I was trained Buenos Aires spy school,' said Garcia. 'Twenty years ago. Then I came up here an' met Bea. So I quit. Easy. They'd taught me how to hide in plain sight.'

'He shouldn't be talking,' said Ramsey. 'Blood pressure's up.'

'Gotta talk,' said Garcia. 'They found me six months ago, said, "Come through, or else!" Our kids. Y' understand?'

'Sure, Joe,' said Sparrow. 'Now, please be quiet. Save your strength.'

'First time in my life I ever belonged anywhere – really belonged – was with your crew,' said Garcia. 'With Bea, sure. But that's different.'

'You have to conserve your strength,' said Sparrow.

'Why? So Johnny Security can take me back to stand trial?'

'I'm not Security, Joe.'

'He's a BuPsych,' said Sparrow. 'They put him on to ride herd on me.'

Ramsey's mouth dropped open.

'I spotted that the day we first went down overlimit,' said Sparrow. 'It was the way he treated Les.'

'Security, too,' said Garcia.

'Only by adoption,' said Ramsey. 'And I can't—'

'If you spill this,' said Sparrow, 'I'll—'

'I was about to say that I can't hear so well,' said Ramsey. He grinned, then frowned and looked down at Garcia. 'Did you have anything to do with the death of that Security inspector?'

'Nothing, so help me God,' said Garcia.

'How about the sabotage?'

'That was my old friends just being doubly sure.' He shook his head. 'I was just supposed to tip off the location of the well when we reached it. Instead, I set it off while we were still in our own waters. Thought they'd just force us up, capture us.'

'How'd you do it?' asked Sparrow.

'By stepping up the sono-pulse system, keyed to weak tube plate.'

'When did you decide not to tip them to the well?'

'I never decided *to* do it.'

Sparrow seemed to relax.

'I told Bea to take our kids and go to Security as soon as we were out of pursuit range with the *Ram*.' He fell silent.

'Try to rest,' said Sparrow.

Garcia sniffed. 'What's the needle say now, Johnny?'

Ramsey looked at Sparrow, who nodded assent.

'P-F,' said Ramsey.

'Probable fatal,' translated Garcia.

'The needle has come down some,' said Ramsey.

'Do you want to chance an overdose of de-phos and de-calse?' asked Sparrow.

Garcia looked up at him. 'Carry on the jolly battle a little longer, eh?'

He smiled. 'If you say so, Skipper. But keep me under morph, will you?' His grin became tight, like a death's head. 'Convulsions are so messy!'

Sparrow took a deep breath, hesitated.

'It's his only chance,' said Ramsey. 'If you can call that a chance.'

'All right,' said Sparrow. He stepped to the pharmacy rack, readied the shots, returned.

'The morphine,' reminded Garcia.

Sparrow held up an ampule.

'Thanks for everything, Skipper,' said Garcia. 'One favor: Will you look after Bea and the kids?'

Sparrow nodded curtly, bent and administered the injections – one, two, three.

They watched the morphine take effect.

'Eight more blood changes left in the machine,' said Ramsey.

'Give him maximum flow rate,' said Sparrow.

Ramsey adjusted the valve.

'Now, Johnny, I want the whole story from you,' said Sparrow. He spoke without taking his gaze from Garcia.

'Evidently, you already know it,' said Ramsey.

'Not in detail. That's what I want now.'

Ramsey thought: *The cloak-and-dagger role is a farce. Sparrow's had me spotted for some time – and that's probably Garcia's doing. I've been flying blind and didn't know it. Or did I?* He thought back over his vague feelings of misgiving.

Sparrow said, 'Well?'

Stalling for time to think, Ramsey said, 'How much detail?'

'Start from the beginning,' said Sparrow.

Ramsey mentally crossed his fingers, thought: *This is the crisis. If Sparrow's really psycho, he'll blow. But I have to chance it. I don't know how much he's discovered. I can't pull any punches.*

'You can start right now,' said Sparrow. 'That's an order.'

Ramsey took a deep breath, began with the message from Dr Oberhausen and the conference with Admiral Belland in Sec. I.

'This telemetering equipment,' said Sparrow. 'What does it tell you about me?'

'That you're like a part of this submarine. You react like one of its instruments instead of like a human being.'

'I'm a machine?'

'If you want.'

'Are you sure of your little black box?'

'The body's own juices don't lie.'

'I suppose they don't. But interpretations can be mistaken. For instance, I don't think you've correctly evaluated the adjustment we have to make to exist down here in the deeps.'

'How do you mean?'

'Do you recall the day you broke down in the shack?'

Ramsey remembered his fear, his inability to move, the reassuring influence of Sparrow. He nodded.

'What would you call that experience?'

'A temporary psychotic break.'

'Temporary?'

Ramsey stared at Sparrow. 'What's that supposed to mean?'

'Would you say that all of your actions aboard the *Ram* have been completely sane?'

Ramsey colored, feeling the hot flush of blood in his face. 'What kind of a machine are you now, Skipper?'

'A computing machine,' said Sparrow. 'Now listen to me and listen carefully. Here in the subtugs, we have adapted to about as great a mental pressure as human beings can take and still remain operative. We have *adapted*. Some to a greater degree than others. Some one way and some another. But whatever the method of adaptation, there's this fact about it which remains always the same: viewed in the light of people who exist under lesser pressures, our adaptation is not sane.'

'How do you know?'

'I've had to know,' said Sparrow. 'As you've observed, my particular adaptation has been machine-like. Considered in the light of human normality, you psych people have a name for that adaptation.'

'Schizoid.'

'So I've compartmentalized my life,' said Sparrow. 'I have a part of me – call it a circuit if you want – which keeps me going down here. It believes in the hereafter because it has to—'

Ramsey caught the third-person reference to self; he tensed.

'Who's to deny me the right to be whatever I have to be down here?' asked Sparrow. He rubbed the side of his jaw with his long-fingered hand. 'I had to know what it was I was doing. So I studied me. I analyzed me. I computed me against every background I could think of. It was completely ruthless with me.' He fell silent.

Cautiously, Ramsey said, 'And?'

'I'm nuts,' said Sparrow. 'But I'm nuts in a way which fits me perfectly to my world. That makes my world nuts and me normal. Not sane. Normal. Adapted.'

'You're saying the world's schizoid, fragmented.'

'Hasn't it always been?' asked Sparrow. 'Where are there completely unbroken lines of communication? Show me complete social integration.' He shook his long head from side to side in a slow negation. 'It's the pressure, Johnny.'

Ramsey made a minute adjustment on the flow meter controlling the exchange of blood in Garcia's body. He looked down at the drugged engineering officer. Face relaxed, peaceful. Pressures gone for the moment.

'We look to a Utopian existence as sanity,' said Sparrow. 'No pressures against survival. That's why we get a dreamy nostalgia about us when we think of the old South Seas. Minimum threat to survival.' Again he shook his head. 'Whatever the pressure and whatever the adaptation, that adaptation is definable by your science as non-sane. I sometimes think that's the proper interpretation of the biblical phrase: "A child shall lead them." Children generally don't have survival pressures. *Ergo:* They're more sane than adults.'

'They have their pressures,' said Ramsey.

'Of a different character,' said Sparrow. He bent, felt Garcia's pulse. 'How many changes left?'

'Two.'

'What's the radiation reading?'

Ramsey's head jerked as he turned to stare fully at the dial. 'Fifty-fifty.'

'He'll live,' said Sparrow. His voice carried a tone of absolute decision, an irrevocable judgment.

Ramsey fought down an unaccountable irritation. 'How can you be so damned sure?'

'You were startled when you focused on the meter,' said Sparrow.

'It's a miracle he's come this far.' In spite of himself, Ramsey's voice betrayed his irritation.

'That's right, a miracle,' said Sparrow. 'Listen to me, Johnny. In spite of all your science and your medicine, there's something you people often refuse to admit.'

'Which is?' Now his voice was openly hostile.

'There's such a thing as being on God's side. Being right with the world. That's really the thing behind miracles. It's quite simple. You get in ... well, phase. That's the mechanical way of saying it. You ride the wave instead of bucking it.' Sparrow's voice carried a tone of calm detachment.

Ramsey pressed his lips together to keep from speaking his thoughts. And over it all, his own psychological training was feeding data to a train of thought: *Religious fanaticism. Fragmentation. Impenetrable belief in own righteousness. The evidence for a diagnosis of paranoiac type is very strong.*

'Your particular adaptation is dictation by your psychological training,' said Sparrow. 'You have a function: to keep operating. Call it normal. You have to believe I'm insane and that your diagnosis of insanity type is accurate. That way, you're on top; you're in control. It's your way to survival. You can guide me and direct me like the proper animal that I am, and I'll take you back where the pressures are reduced.'

'This is nonsense,' barked Ramsey. 'Psychological nonsense! You don't know what you're talking about!'

'If your diagnosis is correct, what's the probable course of my life?' asked Sparrow.

Before he could stop himself, Ramsey said, 'You'll go completely psychotic! Completely—' He broke off.

Sparrow laughed. He shook his head. 'No, Johnny. I'll go back where the pressures are less. And I'll take a deep breath. And play a little poker at Garden Glenn. And I'll get drunk a time or two because it's expected of me. I'll have another honeymoon with my wife. She'll be very nice to me. Very contrite because of all the times she's cuckolded me while I've been away. That's her adaptation. It doesn't really hurt me. Why should it?'

Ramsey stared at him.

'And, of course, I'll do some more wondering: What's this all about? What are we human animals? What's the meaning behind all this? If there is a meaning. But my roots are solid, Johnny. I've seen miracles.' He nodded toward Garcia. 'I've known the outcome of events before even the events. That gives me a—'

The warning buzzer sounded on the blood-exchange unit. Ramsey slapped the transfer switch. Sparrow moved around the cot, disengaged the artery and vein taps.

'Sixty-forty,' said Ramsey.

'We'll be at Charleston in twenty-two hours,' said Sparrow. He looked at Ramsey. 'What do you intend to tell Admiral Belland's boys about Joe?'

'I don't remember anything about Joe worth telling Belland,' said Ramsey.

A slow smile formed on Sparrow's lips. 'That's normal,' he said. 'Not sane, but normal.'

Ramsey sniffed. Why *am I irritated?* he asked himself. And his psychological training gave him the unavoidable answer: *Because I'm not facing something about myself. There's something I don't want to see.*

'Let's talk about Heppner,' said Sparrow.

Ramsey suppressed an urge to shout: *For Christ's sake! What for?*

'He got to wondering about sanity,' continued Sparrow. 'And one day the truth dawned on him that I'm not particularly sane. Then he got to wondering: What is sanity? He talked about some of his thoughts. And he found he couldn't define sanity. Not for sure. Which meant to him that he himself was off balance.' Sparrow closed his eyes.

'So?' whispered Ramsey.

'So he applied for a transfer out of the subtugs. He gave me the application to submit when we landed. That last trip.'

Ramsey said, 'He cast himself adrift.'

Sparrow nodded. 'And he'd already admitted to himself that he had no anchor, no point of reference from which to navigate.'

Ramsey felt a curious internal stimulation, as though he were on the brink of a great revelation.

'And that,' said Sparrow, 'is why I have to train another new electronics officer. You have to go back to BuPsych where you have your roots. That's an ocean in which you can navigate.'

Ramsey could contain the question no longer. 'What's your definition of sanity, Skipper?'

'The ability to swim,' said Sparrow.

Ramsey felt a cold shock, as though he had been immersed suddenly in freezing water. He had to force himself to continue breathing normally. As though from a great distance, he heard Sparrow's voice:

'That means the sane person has to understand *currents*, has to know what's required in different waters.'

Ramsey heard a heavy thundering, counterpoint to Sparrow's matter-of-fact tones.

'Insanity is something like drowning,' said Sparrow. 'You go under; you flounder without direction; you – Johnny! What's wrong?'

He heard the words, but they lacked meaning. The room was a spinning centrifuge with himself at the rim ... faster ... faster ... faster. ... He caught at the blood-exchange unit, missed, crashed to the floor. A detached part of him sensed hands on his face, a finger lifting an eyelid.

Sparrow's voice squeaked insanely down an inverted funnel: 'Shock!'

Thud! Thud! Thud! Thud! footsteps slamming of cabinet door clinking of glass

He floated in a gelatin hammock, bound in upon himself. A miniature stage opened before his eyes. Sparrow, Garcia, and Bonnett stood arm in arm, doll figures staring across Lilliputian footlights.

Puppets.

In a dull monotone, the miniature Sparrow said, 'I am a Commander, Submarine, Portable, Mark I.'

The miniature Garcia said, 'I am an Engineering Officer, Submarine, Portable, Mark I.'

The miniature Bonnett said, 'I am a First Officer, Submarine, Portable, Mark I.'

Ramsey tried to speak, but his lips would not respond.

On the doll stage, Sparrow said, 'I am not sane; he is not sane; you are not sane; we are not sane; they are not sane.'

Garcia said, 'I regret to report the failure of a component: myself.' He dissolved, leaving Sparrow and Bonnett separated by a space.

Bonnett said, 'That Ramsey is a catalyst.'

Sparrow said, 'I cannot help you; he cannot help you; we cannot help you; they cannot help you; you cannot help yourself.'

Garcia's voice came from the empty space: 'I regret that I cannot thank you in person.'

Bonnett said, 'My generation doesn't believe in vampires.'

Again Ramsey tried to speak, but no sound came.

In unison, Sparrow and Bonnett began to recite: 'Be quiet ... be quiet ... be quiet ... be quiet ... be quiet ... be quiet ...'

fainter

fainter

fainter

Garcia's voice was a faint echo, slightly off beat.

deep enfolding darkness

an amniotic darkness

Ramsey felt movement, a humming: the motors. Bonnett's voice: 'I think he's coming around.'

Sparrow: 'Can you hear me, Johnny?'

He didn't want to answer. That would take energy. It would give substance to the world. His years of psychological training abruptly said to him: *You are in a tight fetal position.*

Sparrow: 'Let's try to straighten him out. That may help.'

Bonnett: 'Break it to him gently, Skipper.'

Hands touched his legs, his arms, pulling him from the curled ball. He wanted to resist, but his muscles felt like weak putty.

Break what gently?

Sparrow's voice was imperative: 'Johnny!'

Ramsey wet his dry lips with a reluctant tongue. *Break what gently?* His voice came out faintly: 'Yeah.'

'Open your eyes, Johnny.'

He obeyed, looked straight up into a crosshatch of pipes and conduits. Control room. He sensed Sparrow beside him, turned. The skipper looked down at him, a worried frown tensing the long face. Beyond him, Bonnett stood at the controls, back to them.

'Wha's – wha's—' He tried to clear his throat.

Sparrow said, 'We brought you in here where we could keep an eye on you. We're almost at Charleston.'

Ramsey sensed the life pulse of subtug around him, sank into it momentarily. *Break what gently?* He said, 'What happened?'

'You reacted to something,' said Sparrow. 'Maybe the decalcification shot. It may have had something to do with our overpressure dives, increased anhydrase. How do you feel?'

'Lousy. How's Joe?'

Sparrow seemed to retreat within himself. He took a deep breath. 'Joe ran out of red cells. Nothing we could do.'

And there went your miracle, thought Ramsey. He said, 'I'm sorry, Skipper.'

Sparrow passed a hand over his eyes. 'Perhaps it was for the best.' He shrugged. 'He was too—'

'I have something on the ranging scope,' said Bonnett. He keyed the IFF circuits, tested them. 'It's a Monitor. One of ours. Coming fast.'

Sparrow whirled, went to the communications board, tested the relays from the shack. 'Are we close enough for voice?'

Bonnett studied his instruments. 'Yes.'

Sparrow turned a rheostat, closed the microphone key. 'This is Able John. Repeat. This is Able John. We have a full slug. One crewman down with radiation sickness. Request clearance for Charleston. Over.'

A voice came from the wall speaker with the eerie wavering of pulse modulation. 'Hello, Able John. You're a bit hot. Stand by for snooping. Over.'

Bonnett depressed the drive bar and their speed slackened.

From his position on the cot, Ramsey could see the ranging scope, blip lines growing deeper and deeper as the Monitor approached.

Again the eerie voice wavered from the speaker. 'Monitor to Able John. You'll pass, Able John. Proceed at entrance depth. We will flank you. Over.'

Bonnett pulled up the drive bar. The *Ram* surged ahead.

'Give us the bow eyes,' said Sparrow.

The big screen above the search board came to life. Green water and occasional kelp.

Sparrow turned toward Ramsey. 'We'll have you in good hands soon, Johnny. Before you know it.'

Ramsey felt a strange dragging at his senses. He tried to imagine the Charleston tunnel entrance – a black hole in the wall of an underwater canyon. His mind sheered away. *Why was that?* he asked himself. Then: *Break what gently?* Part of him seemed to be standing off, making clinical notes. You *don't want to go back. Why? A bit ago you were in a rolled-up ball. Remember? Very interesting.*

He sensed an answer, said, 'Skipper.'

'Yes, Johnny?'

'I went catatonic, didn't I? Catatonic shock?'

Sparrow's voice became brisk. 'Just shock.'

The tone told Ramsey what he wanted to know. The clinical part of his mind said, *Catatonic. Well, well.* He was suddenly very aware of the cot beneath him, pressure of his own weight against his back. In the same instant, pieces of his puzzle started clicking into place. He took a deep breath.

'Just take it easy,' said Sparrow.

Bonnett glanced back, a look of wariness about his eyes.

'I'm all right,' said Ramsey. And he was surprised at the full extent of truth in that statement. Strength was pouring into him. 'I went into a full retreat,' he said. 'But now I know why.'

Sparrow stepped to the side of the cot, put the back of his hand against Ramsey's forehead. 'You should try to relax.'

Ramsey repressed an urge to laugh. 'Joe told me, Skipper, but I didn't believe him.'

Sparrow's reply was little more than a whisper: 'What did Joe tell you?'

'That you've had this situation pegged and under control all along.' He nodded. 'That marine tunnel's a birth canal. Going through it is like being born. This sub is a perambulating womb looking for a place to spew us out.'

Sparrow said, 'Maybe you hadn't better talk now.'

'I want to talk. We're born into another set of realities. There's one kind of insanity down here; another up there. Just look at the old *Ram* here. An enveloped world with its own special ecology. Damp atmosphere, ever present menace from the outside, a constant rhythm in motion—'

'Like a heartbeat,' said Sparrow quietly.

Ramsey smiled. 'We're afloat in amniotic fluid.'

'How's that?'

'Salt water. It's chemically almost identical with the fluid surrounding an unborn baby. The unconscious knows. And here we are headed for birth.'

'You make a more detailed comparison than I ever have,' said Sparrow. 'What's our umbilical cord?'

'Experience. The kind of experience that ties you to your boat, makes you a part of it. Petite perception. You're the perfect symbiote. We become siblings, brothers, with all the emotional ties and rivalry that—'

'First check point,' said Bonnett flatly. 'Now on heading for the Charleston mole. Do you want to take over, Skipper?'

'Take her in, Les,' said Sparrow. 'You've earned the right.'

Bonnett reached up, adjusted the range-response dial. His shoulders seemed to take on a new, more positive set. Ramsey realized abruptly that Bonnett had come of age on this voyage, that he was ready to cut his own cord. The thought gave Ramsey a tug of possessive fondness for Bonnett, an emotion touched by nostalgia at the thought of separation.

Truly like brothers, he thought.

Sparrow looked down at Ramsey. 'Why don't you transfer out of BuPsych and into the subtugs?' asked Sparrow.

'Yeah,' echoed Bonnett. 'We need good men.'

Sadness tightened Ramsey's chest. 'That's the finest compliment I've ever received,' he said. 'But I can't. I was sent out here to solve a problem: Why were submariners breaking down? You gave me the answer. Now, I'll have to take a hand in applying that answer.' He swallowed a lump in his throat. 'Dr Oberhausen of BuPsych has promised me my own department dealing with problems of submariners.'

Sparrow said, 'That's wonderful, Johnny! A big-time shore job.'

'We're going to hate losing you,' said Bonnett. 'Will you still talk to the likes of us when you're an important brass type?'

'Never fear,' said Ramsey.

'What is this solution?' asked Sparrow.

'The breakdowns are a rejection of birth by men who have unconsciously retreated into the world of prebirth. What child would seek birth if he knew that pain and fear – a constant menace – awaited him on the other side?'

'There's menace down here,' said Sparrow.

'But our little world under the sea fools and confuses the unconscious,' said Ramsey.

Bonnett spoke up, faint note of sarcasm in his voice. 'That makes sense even to me ... I think.' He kept one hand on the wheel, stepped aside to adjust the tow controls.

'We have to make the complete cycle desirable,' said Ramsey. 'I'm going to recommend a whole new procedure: the best quarters for submariners. A big jump in pay for each mission.'

'That's for me!' said Bonnett.

'There are going to be some changes made,' said Ramsey.

'Johnny, do me a favor,' said Sparrow.

'Name it.'

Sparrow looked away, swallowed. 'It sounds like you're going to be a VIP and—' He hesitated. 'Will you do what you can to cushion things for Joe's wife?'

'Anything I can do,' said Ramsey. 'I promise.' He took a deep breath. 'Who's going to get the dirty job of telling her?'

'I will,' said Sparrow. 'I'll break it to her as gently as I can.'

A sudden chill swept over Ramsey's body. *Break it gently!* He cleared his throat. 'Skipper, that reminds me. I heard Les say something about breaking a bit of news to me. What?'

Sparrow wet his lips with his tongue, looked across at Bonnett working with the controls.

'Break what gently?' repeated Ramsey.

'Joe's death.'

'But—'

'Each time we tried to bring you out of shock, you—'

'Each time?'

'We tried four or five times. Each time you raved for Joe to come back. We guessed it was delirium, but—'

Silence fell between them.

'The unconscious senses many things,' said Ramsey. He felt a deep emptiness and suddenly recalled his nightmare. Garcia's voice: '*I regret that I cannot thank you in person.*'

For what?

Ramsey said, 'We had a lot in common. Joe understood me. He saw right through my act ... said so. I guess I resented it. Joe was better at my game than I was.'

'He admired you,' said Sparrow.

Ramsey's eyes burned and smarted.

'He was awake at the end,' said Sparrow. 'Worried about you. He said he'd given you a raw deal by feeding our suspicions. Joe thought you had the makings of a top submariner.'

Ramsey turned away.

'Will you do what you can for his wife?' asked Sparrow.

Ramsey nodded, unable to speak.

'We're approaching the mole,' said Bonnett, his voice oddly casual. 'Bottom marked number two coming up.' He indicated the screen above him.

Through a green haze of water, two high-piercement lights keyed to their IFF circuits winked at them.

'Are we set for the automatic pickup?' asked Sparrow.

'All set,' said Bonnett.

'We've brought home the bacon,' said Ramsey.

Bonnett's voice took on an unconscious mimicry of Garcia's bantering accent: 'We're a bunch of bloody heroes!'

●

It was peaceful in Dr Oberhausen's Charleston office. The wizened BuPsych chief sat behind a desk like all other BuPsych office desks, leaning back with his hands steepled beneath his goatee. His bat-eye radar box, disconnected from its shoulder harness, rested on the patterned wood of the desk top. Dr Oberhausen's sightless ball-bearing eyes seemed to be staring at Ramsey, who sat across the desk from him.

Ramsey rubbed a hand over his head, feeling the stubble of returning hair. 'That's pretty much the story,' he said. 'Most of it was in my notes. You've had those, even though the medics wouldn't let you talk to me.'

Dr Oberhausen nodded silently.

Ramsey leaned back in his chair. It creaked and Ramsey suddenly realized that Dr Oberhausen purposely surrounded himself with creaking chairs – reassuring signals for a blind man.

'A close thing with you, Johnny. Radiation sickness is a peculiar thing.' He passed a hand across his own radiation-blinded eyes. 'It is fortunate that BuPsych agents are virtually indestructible.'

'Does this check with my notes and the telemeter tapes?' asked Ramsey.

Dr Oberhausen nodded. 'Yes, it checks. Sparrow became almost literally a part of his boat, sensitive to everything about it – including his crew. An odd mating of the right mentality and the right experiences has made him a master psychologist. I'm going to see about taking him into the department.'

'What about my recommendation for preventing those psychotic breaks?'

Dr Oberhausen pursed his lips, tugged at his goatee. 'The old Napoleonic fancy-uniform therapy: fanfare coming and going.' He nodded. 'Security will kick and scream that it will prevent secrecy of departures, but they've already made one concession.'

'What?'

'They've announced officially that we're pirating oil from the EPs.'

'That was a senseless secret anyway.'

'They were reluctant.'

'We'd be better off without Security,' muttered Ramsey. 'We should be working to get rid of it. Security stifles communication. It's creating social schizophrenia.'

Dr Oberhausen gave a negative shake of his head. 'No, Johnny, we shouldn't get rid of Security. That's an old fallacy. Use Captain Sparrow's analogy: In an insane society, a crazy man is normal. Security has the kind of insanity that's normal for wartime. Normal and needed.'

'But *after* the war, Obe! You know they're going to keep right on!'

'They'll try, Johnny. But by that time we'll have Security under the control of BuPsych. We'll be able to nullify them quite effectively.'

Ramsey stared at him, then chuckled. 'So that's why you've been moving in on Belland.'

'Not just Belland, Johnny.'

'You scare me sometimes, Obe.'

Dr Oberhausen's goatee twitched. 'Good. That means my pose of omnipotence is effective even with those who know better.' He smiled.

Ramsey grinned, stirred in his chair. 'If that's all, Obe, I'd like to get away. They wouldn't let Janet and the kids anywhere near me while I was in the hospital, and now that—'

'I waited, too, Johnny. BuMed's little dictatorship halted even the great BuPsych. There's an area of autonomy in radiation medicine that—' He shook his head slowly.

'Well?' asked Ramsey.

'The impatience of youth,' said Dr Oberhausen. 'There are just a few more points to be cleared up. Why do you believe we never saw the need for this fancy-uniform therapy?'

'Partly Security,' said Ramsey. 'But it really wasn't obvious. Wrong symptoms. Napoleon was looking to build up enlistments and stop his gunners from going over the hill. We've never had that trouble. In fact, our submariners seemed eager to return to duty. That's the paradox: they found threat in both spheres – ashore and at sea. When they were ashore they seemed to forget about the menace of the sea because the subconscious masked it. The boat spelled enveloping safety, a return to the womb. But when the men came ashore, that was birth: exposure. The sky's a hideous thing to men who want to hide from it.'

Dr Oberhausen cleared his throat. His voice took on a crisp, business-like tone. 'Now, I'd like to go back to your notes for just a moment. You say BuPsych should emphasize religious training. Explain your reasoning.'

Ramsey leaned forward and the telltale chair creaked. 'Because it's sanity, Obe. That's the—'

'It smacks of a panacea, Johnny. A nostrum.'

'No, Obe. A church provides a common bond for people, a clear line of communication.' He shook his head. 'Unless BuPsych can uncover telepathy or absolute proof of the hereafter, it can't substitute for religion. The sooner we face that, the sooner we'll be able to offer—'

Dr Oberhausen slapped his hand on the desk top. 'Religion is not scientific! It's faith!' He said *faith* as he might have said *dirty*.

He's needling me, thought Ramsey. He said, 'Okay, Obe. All I'm saying is this: We don't have a substitute for religion. But we're offering our so-called science as a substitute. That's all I'm—'

'So-called?'

'How many distinct schools of psychology can you name?'

Dr Oberhausen smiled thinly. 'At least as many as there are distinct religions.'

'We're following the pattern even there,' said Ramsey.

The BuPsych chief chuckled. 'Did I interrupt a chain of thought?'

Ramsey paused. 'Only that I've never met a psychoanalyst who didn't – at least subconsciously – offer his system as a substitute for religion. Present company included. We set ourselves up as little gods – all-knowing, all-healing. People resent that and rightly. We have polite labels for our failures. We agree among ourselves that anything bearing one of those labels is, of course, incurable.'

Dr Oberhausen's voice held a sense of remoteness. 'That's quite an indictment, Johnny. Do I take it that you've been *converted* by our good Captain Sparrow?'

Ramsey leaned back, laughed. 'Hell, no! I'm just going to stop posing as a messiah.'

Dr Oberhausen took a deep breath. 'That's encouraging.'

'And I guess I'll go on poking around inside people's minds. If that describes whatever it is we do.' He smiled. 'I'll keep on being a psychologist.'

'What do you expect to find?'

Ramsey was silent a moment, then: 'A good scientist doesn't *expect* to find anything, Obe. He reports what he sees.'

Dr Oberhausen clasped his hands. 'If you find God, please let me know.'

'I'll do that.' Ramsey forced briskness into his voice. 'As long as we're clearing up loose ends, what about me? When do I get out of this damned uniform and into my nice new department of BuPsych?'

Dr Oberhausen pushed his chair back, resting his hands on the edge of the desk. He tipped his head down, appeared to be staring at the bat-eye box. 'First, you'll have to play out your hero role. The president's going to pin medals on all of you. That's Belland's doing. By the way, the admiral has given Mrs Garcia a job in his department, his polite way of keeping her under surveillance. But it works out for the best of all concerned.'

'In this best of all possible worlds,' said Ramsey. He sensed hesitancy in Dr Oberhausen's manner. 'But when *do* I get out of the service?'

Dr Oberhausen lifted his chin. 'I may not be able to get you out immediately, Johnny.'

Ramsey felt pressure building up inside him. 'Why?'

'Well, you're a hero. They'll want to exploit that.' The BuPsych chief cleared his throat. 'Some things are difficult even for BuPsych. Look, I couldn't even get past BuMed and in to see you while—'

'You promised me a—'

'And I'll keep my promise, Johnny. In time.' He leaned back. 'Meanwhile, there's a commodore on the board of classification and promotion. He's a presidential errand boy and he needs an – an aide-de-camp.'

'Oh no!' Ramsey stared at Dr Oberhausen.

The little doctor shrugged. 'Well, Johnny, he found out that you're the clever Long John Ramsey who improvised a vampire gauge from a hypodermic and two glass tubes and saved the *Dolphin* during that training-mission breakdown. He wants—'

Ramsey groaned.

'You'll be jumped to lieutenant,' said Dr Oberhausen.

'Thanks,' said Ramsey bitterly. He curled his lips, copied Dr Oberhausen's voice: 'Sure, Johnny. You'll have your own department.'

'You're young,' said Dr Oberhausen. 'There's time.'

'He'll have me polishing his shoes.'

'Oh no. He's quite impressed by your talents. Says you're too good for BuPsych. Bringing home that oil has done nothing to reduce his admiration.' Again the BuPsych chief cleared his throat. 'And while you're with the commodore, there are some things about this department that I'd like you to—'

'So that's it!' barked Ramsey. 'Another of your damned spy jobs! You want me to ferret out the dope on the commodore so you can move in on him. I'll bet you set this job up yourself.'

'I'm sure you see the necessity,' said Dr Oberhausen. 'That way lies sanity.'

'I'm not so sure,' said Ramsey.

'I like your Captain Sparrow's analogy about sanity and swimming,' said Dr Oberhausen. 'But I would add to it, the swimmer must be prepared at all times to grasp a paddle.'

Ramsey smiled even as he realized that Dr Oberhausen was amusing him to ease the tension between them. 'Okay, Obe. One more. But I'm telling you now: that's all.'

'Fair enough, Johnny. Now, if you'll just—'

A door slammed in the outer hall behind Ramsey. He heard a flurry of sounds. A woman's voice shouted: 'You can't stop me from going in there!'

Janet!

His pulse quickened.

The woman's voice mounted almost to a scream: 'I know he's in there with that damned Dr Oberhausen! And by Heaven I'm going in!'

The office door behind Ramsey burst open. He turned. It was a secretary. 'Please excuse me,' she said. 'There's—'

'Let her come in,' said Dr Oberhausen.

Ramsey stood up, feeling suddenly giddy. Janet came rushing through the door and into his arms. A familiar perfume. The contours of a familiar face pressing against his cheek, a familiar body against his own.

'Johnny! Oh, Johnny!'

He heard Dr Oberhausen get up, saw him walk past him toward the office door, fastening the bat-eye box to his shoulder as he went.

'Johnny, I missed you so.'

'I missed you, too,' he said.

'I never knew it would be so dangerous. Why, they told me—'

'It wasn't bad, Janet. Really.'

'But you were so long in the hospital!'

Dr Oberhausen paused at the door, a figure in new perspective, grown suddenly smaller, giving off a sense of loneliness. Ramsey wanted to call out something but didn't know what. He said, 'Obe.'

The BuPsych chief turned.

'We'll see you soon,' said Ramsey.

The doctor smiled, nodded, went out, closing the door behind him.

And then Ramsey had to explain to Janet why he wanted to include 'that awful old Obe' in their reunion plans.

THE SANTAROGA BARRIER

1

The sun went down as the five-year-old Ford camper-pickup truck ground over the pass and started down the long grade into Santaroga Valley. A crescent-shaped turn-off had been leveled beside the first highway curve. Gilbert Dasein pulled his truck onto the gravel, stopped at a white barrier fence and looked down into the valley whose secrets he had come to expose.

Two men already had died on this project, Dasein reminded himself. Accidents. *Natural* accidents. What was down there in that bowl of shadows inhabited by random lights? Was there an accident waiting for him?

Dasein's back ached after the long drive up from Berkeley. He shut off the motor, stretched. A burning odor of hot oil permeated the cab. The union of truckbed and camper emitted creakings and poppings.

The valley stretching out below him looked somehow different from what Dasein had expected. The sky around it was a ring of luminous blue full of sunset glow that spilled over into an upper belt of trees and rocks.

There was a sense of quiet about the place, of an island sheltered from storms.

What did I expect the place to be? Dasein wondered.

He decided all the maps he'd studied, all the reports on Santaroga he'd read, had led him to believe he knew the valley. But maps were not the land. Reports weren't people.

Dasein glanced at his wristwatch: almost seven. He felt reluctant to continue.

Far off to the left across the valley, strips of green light glowed among trees. That was the area labeled 'green-houses' on the map. A castellated block of milky white on an outcropping down to his right he identified as the Jaspers Cheese Cooperative. The yellow gleam of windows and moving lights around it spoke of busy activity.

Dasein grew aware of insect sounds in the darkness around him, the swoop-humming of air through night-hawks' wings and, away in the distance, the mournful baying of hounds. The voice of the pack appeared to come from beyond the Co-op.

He swallowed, thinking that the yellow windows suddenly were like baleful eyes peering into the valley's darker depths.

Dasein shook his head, smiled. That was no way to think. Unprofessional. All the ominous nonsense muttered about Santaroga had to be put aside. A scientific investigation could not operate in that atmosphere. He turned on the cab's dome light, took his briefcase from the seat beside him. Gold lettering on the brown leather identified it: 'Gilbert Dasein – Department of Psychology – University of California – Berkeley.'

In a battered folder from the case he began writing: 'Arrived Santaroga Valley approximately 6:45 p.m. Setting is that of a prosperous farm community . . .'

Presently, he put case and folder aside.

Prosperous farm community, he thought. How could he know it was prosperous? No – prosperity wasn't what he saw. That was something he knew from the reports.

The real valley in front of him now conveyed a sense of waiting, of quietness punctuated by occasional tinklings of cowbells. He imagined husbands and wives down there after a day of work. What did they discuss now in their waiting darkness?

What did Jenny Sorge discuss with her husband – provided she had a husband? It seemed impossible she'd still be single – lovely, nubile Jenny. It was more than a year since they'd last seen each other at the University.

Dasein sighed. No escaping thoughts of Jenny – not here in Santaroga. Jenny contained part of Santaroga's mystery. She was an element of the Santaroga Barrier and a prime subject for his present investigation.

Again, Dasein sighed. He wasn't fooling himself. He knew why he'd accepted this project. It wasn't the munificent sum those chain stores were paying the university for this study, nor the generous salary provided for himself.

He had come because this was where Jenny lived.

Dasein told himself he'd smile and act normal, *perfectly normal*, when he met her. He was here on business, a psychologist detached from his usual teaching duties to make a market study in Santaroga Valley.

What was a perfectly normal way to act with Jenny, though? How did one achieve normalcy when encountering the paranormal?

Jenny was a Santarogan – and the normalcy of this valley defied normal explanations.

His mind went to the reports, 'the known facts.' All the folders of data, the collections of official pryings, the second-hand secrets which were the stock in a trade of the bureaucracy – all this really added up to a single 'known fact' about Santaroga: There was something extraordinary at work here, something far more disturbing than any so-called market study had ever tackled before.

Meyer Davidson, the soft looking, pink fleshed little man who'd presented himself as the agent of the investment corporation, the holding company behind the chain stores paying for this project, had put it in an angry nutshell at the first orientation meeting: 'The whole thing about Santaroga boils down to this – Why were we forced to close our branches there? Why won't even *one* Santarogan trade with an outsider? That's what we want to know. What's this Santaroga Barrier which keeps us from doing business there?'

Davidson wasn't as soft as he looked.

Dasein started the truck, turned on his headlights, resumed his course down the winding grade.

All the data was a single datum.

Outsiders found no houses for rent or sale in this valley. Santaroga officials said they had no juvenile delinquency figures for the state's statistics.

Servicemen from Santaroga always returned when they were discharged. In fact, no Santarogan had ever been known to move out of the valley.

Why? Was it a two-way barrier?

And the curious anomalies: The data had included a medical journal article by Jenny's uncle, Dr Lawrence Piaget, reputedly the valley's leading physician. The article: 'The Poison Oak Syndrome in Santaroga.' Its substance: Santarogans had a remarkable susceptibility to allergens when forced to live away from their valley for extended periods. This was the chief reason for service rejection of Santaroga's youths.

Data equaled datum.

Santaroga reported no cases of mental illness or mental deficiency to the State Department of Mental Hygiene. No Santarogan could be found in a state mental hospital. (The psychiatrist who headed Dasein's university department, Dr Chami Selador, found this fact 'alarming.')

Cigarette sales in Santaroga could be accounted for by transient purchasers.

Santarogans manifested an iron resistance to national advertising. (An un-American symptom, according to Meyer Davidson.)

No cheese, wines or beers made outside the valley could be marketed to Santarogans.

All the valley's businesses, including the bank, were locally owned. They flatly rejected outside investment money.

Santaroga had successfully resisted every 'pork barrel' government project the politicians had offered. Their State Senator was from Porterville, ten miles behind Dasein and well outside the valley. Among the political figures Dasein had interviewed to lay the groundwork for his study, the State Senator was one of the few who didn't think Santarogans were 'a pack of kooks, maybe religious nuts of some kind.'

'Look, Dr Dasein,' he'd said, 'all this mystery crap about Santaroga is just that – crap.'

The Senator was a skinny, intense man with a shock of gray hair and red-veined eyes. Barstow was his name; one of the old California families.

Barstow's opinion: 'Santaroga's a last outpost of American individualism. They're Yankees, Down Easters living in California. Nothing mysterious about 'em at all. They don't ask special favors and they don't fan my ears, with stupid questions. I wish all my constituents were as straightforward and honest.'

One man's opinion, Dasein thought.

An isolated opinion.

Dasein was down into the valley proper now. The two-lane road leveled into a passage through gigantic trees. This was the Avenue of the Giants winding between rows of *sequoia gigantea.*

There were homes set back in the trees. The datum-data said some of these homes had been here since the gold rush. The scroll work of carpenter gothic lined their eaves. Many were three stories high, yellow lights in their windows.

Dasein grew aware of an absence, a negative fact about the houses he saw: No television flicker, no cathode living rooms, no walls washed to skimmed-milk gray by the omnipresent tube.

The road forked ahead of him An arrow pointed left to 'City Center' and two arrows directed him to the right to 'The Santaroga House' and 'Jaspers Cheese Co-op.'

Dasein turned right.

His road wound upward beneath an arch: 'Santaroga, The Town That Cheese Built.' Presently, it emerged from the redwoods into an oak flat. The Co-op loomed gray white, bustling with lights and activity behind a chain fence on his right. Across the road to his left stood Dasein's first goal here, a long three-storey inn built in the rambling 1900 style with a porch its full length. Lines of multipaned windows (most dark) looked down onto a gravel parking area. The sign at the entrance read: 'Santa-roga House – Gold Rush Museum – Hours 9 a.m. to 5 p.m.'

Most of the cars nosed to a stone border parallel to the porch were well-kept older models. A few shiny new machines were parked in a second row as though standing aloof.

Dasein parked beside a 1939 Chevrolet whose paint gleamed with a rich waxy gloss. Red-brown upholstery visible through the windows appeared to be hand-tailored leather.

Rich man's toy, Dasein thought.

He took his suitcase from the camper, turned to the inn. There was a smell of new mown lawn in the air and the sound of running water. It reminded Dasein of his childhood, his aunt's garden with the brook along the back. A strong sense of nostalgia gripped him.

Abruptly, a discordant note intruded. From the upper floors of the inn came the raucous sound of a man and woman arguing, the man's voice brusk, the woman's with a strident fishwife qualify.

'I'm not staying in this godforsaken hole one more night,' the woman screamed. 'They don't want our money! They don't want us! You do what you want; I'm leaving!'

'Belle, stop it! You've ...'

A window slammed. The argument dimmed to a muted screeching-mumbling.

Dasein took a deep breath. The argument restored his perspective. Here were two more people with their noses against the Santaroga Barrier.

Dasein strode along the gravel, up four steps to the porch and through swinging doors with windows frosted by scroll etching. He found himself in a high-ceilinged lobby, crystal chandeliers overhead. Dark wood paneling, heavily grained like ancient charts enclosed the space. A curved counter stretched across the corner to his right, an open door behind it from which came the sound of a switchboard. To the right of this counter was a wide opening through which he glimpsed a dining room – white tablecloths, crystal, silver. A western stagecoach was parked at his left behind brass posts supporting a maroon velvet rope with a 'Do Not Touch' sign.

Dasein stopped to study the coach. It smelled of dust and mildew. A framed card on the boot gave its history: 'Used on the San Francisco-Santaroga route from 1868 to 1871.' Below this card was a slightly larger frame enclosing a yellowed sheet of paper with a brass legend beside it: 'A note from Black Bart, the Po-8 Highwayman.' In sprawling script on the yellow paper it read:

'So here I've stood while wind and rain
Have set the trees a-sobbin'
And risked my life for that damned stage
That wasn't worth the robbin'.'

Dasein chuckled, shifted his briefcase to his left arm, crossed to the counter and rang the call bell.

A bald, wrinkled stick of a man in a black suit appeared in the open doorway, stared at Dasein like a hawk ready to pounce. 'Yes?'

'I'd like a room,' Dasein said.

'What's your business?'

Dasein stiffened at the abrupt challenge. 'I'm tired,' he said. 'I want a night's sleep.'

'Passing through, I hope,' the man grumbled. He shuffled to the counter, pushed a black registry ledger toward Dasein.

Dasein took a pen from its holder beside the ledger, signed.

The clerk produced a brass key on a brass tag, said: 'You get two fifty-one next to that dang' couple from L.A. Don't blame me if they keep y' awake arguing.' He slapped the key onto the counter. 'That'll be ten dollars ... in advance.'

'I'm hungry,' Dasein said, producing his wallet and paying. 'Is the dining room open?' He accepted a receipt.

'Closes at nine,' the clerk said.

'Is there a bellboy?'

'You look strong enough to carry your own bag.' He pointed beyond Dasein. 'Room's up them stairs, second floor.'

Dasein turned. There was an open area behind the stagecoach. Scattered through it were leather chairs, high wings and heavy arms, a few occupied by elderly men sitting, reading. Light came from heavy brass floor lamps with fringed shades. A carpeted stairway led upward beyond the chairs.

It was a scene Dasein was to think of many times later as his first clue to the real nature of Santaroga. The effect was that of holding time securely in a bygone age.

Vaguely troubled, Dasein said: 'I'll check my room later. May I leave my bag here while I eat?'

'Leave it on the counter. No one'll bother it.'

Dasein put the case on the counter, caught the clerk studying him with a fixed stare.

'Something wrong?' Dasein asked.

'Nope.'

The clerk reached for the briefcase under Dasein's arm, but Dasein stepped back, removed it from the questing fingers, met an angry stare.

'Hmmmph!' the clerk snorted. There was no mistaking his frustration. He'd wanted a look inside the briefcase.

Inanely, Dasein said: 'I ... uh, want to look over some papers while I'm eating.' And he thought: *Why do I need to explain?*

Feeling angry with himself, he turned, strode through the passage into the dining room. He found himself in a large square room, a single massive chandelier in the center, brass carriage lamps spaced around walls of dark wood paneling. The chairs at the round tables were heavy with substantial arms. A long teak bar stretched along the wall at his left, a wood-framed mirror behind it. Light glittered hypnotically from the central chandelier and glasses stacked beneath the mirror.

The room swallowed sounds. Dasein felt he had walked into a sudden hush with people turning to look at him. Actually, his entrance went almost unnoticed.

A white-coated bartender on duty for a scattering of customers at the bar glanced at him, went back to talking to a swarthy man hunched over a mug of beer.

Family groups occupied about a dozen of the tables. There was a card game at a table near the bar. Two tables held lone women busy with their forks.

There was a division of people in this room, Dasein felt. It was a matter of nervous tension contrasted with a calmness as substantial as the room itself. He decided he could pick out the transients – they appeared tired, more rumpled; their children were closer to rebellion.

As he moved farther into the room, Dasein glimpsed himself in the bar mirror – fatigue lines on his slender face, the curly black hair mussed by the wind, brown eyes glazed with attention, still driving the car. A smudge of road dirt drew a dark line beside the cleft in his chin. Dasein rubbed at the smudge, thought: *Here's another transient.*

'You wish a table, sir?'

A Negro waiter had appeared at his elbow – white jacket, hawk nose, sharp Moorish features, a touch of gray at the temples. There was a look of command about him all out of agreement with the menial costume. Dasein thought immediately of Othello. The eyes were brown and wise.

'Yes, please: for one,' Dasein said.

'This way, sir.'

Dasein was guided to a table against the near wall. One of the carriage lamps bathed it in a warm yellow glow. As the heavy chair enveloped him, Dasein's attention went to the table near the bar – the card game

... four men. He recognized one of the men from a picture Jenny had carried: Piaget, the doctor uncle, author of the medical journal article on allergens. Piaget was a large, gray-haired man, bland round face, a curious suggestion of the Oriental about him that was heightened by the fan of cards held close to his chest.

'You wish a menu, sir?'

'Yes. Just a moment ... the men playing cards with Dr Piaget over there.'

'Sir?'

'Who are they?'

'You know Dr Larry, sir?'

'I know his niece, Jenny Sorge. She carried a photo of Dr Piaget.'

The waiter glanced at the briefcase Dasein had placed in the center of the table. 'Dasein,' he said. A wide smile put a flash of white in the dark face. 'You're Jenny's friend from the school.'

The waiter's words carried so many implications that Dasein found himself staring, open-mouthed.

'Jenny's spoken of you, sir,' the waiter said.

'Oh.'

'The men playing cards with Dr Larry – you want to know who they are.' He turned toward the players. 'Well, sir, that's Captain Al Marden of the Highway Patrol across from Dr Larry. On the right there, that's George Nis. He manages the Jaspers Cheese Co-op. The fellow on the left is Mr Sam Scheler. Mr Sam runs our independent service station. I'll get you that menu, sir.'

The waiter headed toward the bar.

Dasein's attention remained on the card players, wondering why they held his interest so firmly. Marden, sitting with his back partly turned toward Dasein, was in mufti, a dark blue suit. His hair was a startling mop of red. He turned his head to the right and Dasein glimpsed a narrow face, tight-lipped mouth with a cynical downtwist.

Scheler of the independent service station (Dasein wondered about this designation suddenly) was dark skinned, an angular Indian face with flat nose, heavy lips. Nis, across from him, was balding, sandy-haired, blue eyes with heavy lids, a wide mouth and deeply cleft chin.

'Your menu, sir.'

The waiter placed a large red-covered folder in front of Dasein.

'Dr Piaget and his friends appear to be enjoying their game,' Dasein said.

'That game's an institution, sir. Every week about this hour, regular as sunset – dinner here and that game.'

'What do they play?'

'It varies, sir. Sometimes it's bridge, sometimes pinochle. They play whist on occasion and even poker.'

'What did you mean – *independent* service station?' Dasein asked. He looked up at the dark Moorish face.

'Well, sir, we here in the valley don't mess around with those companies fixin' their prices. Mr Sam, he buys from whoever gives him the best offer. We pay about four cents less a gallon here.'

Dasein made a mental note to investigate this aspect of the Santaroga Barrier. It was in character, not buying from the big companies, but where did they get their oil products?

'The roast beef is very good, sir,' the waiter said, pointing to the menu.

'You recommend it, eh?'

'I do that, sir. Grain fattened right here in the valley. We have fresh corn on the cob, potatoes Jaspers – that's with cheese sauce, very good, and we have hot-house strawberries for dessert.'

'Salad?' Dasein asked.

'Our salad greens aren't very good this week, sir. I'll bring you the soup. It's borscht with sour cream. And you'd like beer with that. I'll see if I can't get you some of our local product.'

'With you around I don't need a menu,' Dasein said. He returned the red-covered folder. 'Bring it on before I start eating the tablecloth.'

'Yes, sir!'

Dasein watched the retreating black – white coated, wide, confident. Othello, indeed.

The waiter returned presently with a steaming bowl of soup, a white island of sour cream floating in it, and a darkly amber mug of beer.

'I note you're the only Negro waiter here,' Dasein said. 'Isn't that kind of type casting?'

'You asking if I'm their *show* Negro, sir?' The waiter's voice was suddenly wary.

'I was wondering if Santaroga had any integration problems.'

'Must be thirty, forty colored families in the valley, sir. We don't rightly emphasize the distinction of skin color here.' The voice was hard, curt.

'I didn't mean to offend you,' Dasein said.

'You didn't offend me.' A smile touched the corners of his mouth, was gone. 'I must admit a Negro waiter is a kind of institutional accent. Place like this ...' He glanced around the solid, paneled room. ' ... must've had plenty of Negro waiters here in its day. Kind of like local color having me on the job.' Again, that flashing smile. 'It's a good job, and my kids are doing even better. Two of 'em work in the Co-op; other's going to be a lawyer.'

'You have three children?'

'Two boys and a girl. If you'll excuse me, sir; I have other tables.'

'Yes, of course.'

Dasein lifted the mug of beer as the waiter left.

He held the beer a moment beneath his nose. There was a tangy odor about it with a suggestion of cellars and mushrooms. Dasein remembered suddenly that Jenny had praised the local Santaroga beer. He sipped it – soft on the tongue, smooth, clean aftertaste of malt. It was everything Jenny had said.

Jenny, he thought. *Jenny ... Jenny ...*

Why had she never invited him to Santaroga on her regular weekend trips home? She'd never missed a weekend, he recalled. Their dates had always been in mid-week. He remembered what she'd told him about herself: orphaned, raised by the uncle, Piaget, and a maiden aunt ... Sarah.

Dasein took another drink of the beer, sampled the soup. They did go well together. The sour cream had a flavor reminiscent of the beer, a strange new tang.

There'd never been any mistaking Jenny's affection for him, Dasein thought. They'd had a *thing*, chemical, exciting. But no *direct* invitation to meet her family, see the valley. A hesitant probing, yes – what would he think of setting up practice in Santaroga? Sometime, he must talk to Uncle Larry about some interesting cases.

What cases? Dasein wondered, remembering. The Santaroga information folders Dr Selador had supplied were definite: 'No reported cases of mental illness.'

Jenny ... Jenny ...

Dasein's mind went back to the night he'd proposed. No hesitant probing on Jenny's part then – Could he live in Santaroga?

He could remember his own incredulous demand: 'Why do we have to live in Santaroga?'

'Because I can't live anywhere else.' That was what she'd said. 'Because I can't live anywhere else.'

Love me, love my valley.

No amount of pleading could wring an explanation from her. She'd made that plain. In the end, he'd reacted with anger boiling out of injured manhood. Did she think he couldn't support her any place but in Santaroga?

'Come and see Santaroga,' she'd begged.

'Not unless you'll consider living outside.'

Impasse.

Remembering the fight, Dasein felt his cheeks go warm. It'd been finals week. She'd refused to answer his telephone calls for two days ... and he'd refused to call after that. He'd retreated into a hurt shell.

And Jenny had gone back to her precious valley. When he'd written, swallowed his pride, offered to come and see her – no answer. Her valley had swallowed her.

This valley.

Dasein sighed, looked around the dining room, remembering Jenny's intensity when she spoke about Santaroga. This paneled dining room, the Santarogans he could see, didn't fit the picture in his mind.

Why didn't she answer my letters? he asked himself. *Most likely she's married. That must be it.*

Dasein saw his waiter come around the end of the bar with a tray. The bartender signaled, called: 'Win.' The waiter stopped, rested the tray on the bar. Their heads moved close together beside the tray. Dasein received the impression they were arguing. Presently, the waiter said something with a chopping motion of the head, grabbed up the tray, brought it to Dasein's table.

'Doggone busybody,' he said as he put the tray down across from Dasein, began distributing the dishes from it. 'Try to tell me I can't give you Jaspers! Good friend of Jenny's and I can't give him Jaspers.'

The waiter's anger cooled; he shook his head, smiled, put a plate mounded with food before Dasein.

'Too doggone many busybodies in this world, y' ask me.'

'The bartender,' Dasein said. 'I heard him call you "Win."'

'Winston Burdeaux, sir, at your service.' He moved around the table closer to Dasein. 'Wouldn't give me any Jaspers beer for you this time, sir.' He took a frosted bottle from the tray, put it near the mug of beer he'd served earlier. 'This isn't as good as what I brought before. The food's real Jaspers, though. Doggone busybody couldn't stop me from doing that.'

'Jaspers,' Dasein said. 'I thought it was just the cheese.'

Burdeaux pursed his lips, looked thoughtful. 'Oh, no, sir. Jaspers, that's in all the products from the Co-op. Didn't Jenny ever tell you?' He frowned. 'Haven't you ever been up here in the valley with her, sir?'

'No.' Dasein shook his head from side to side.

'You *are* Dr Dasein – Gilbert Dasein?'

'Yes.'

187

'You're the fellow Jenny's sweet on, then.' He grinned, said: 'Eat up, sir. It's *good* food.'

Before Dasein could collect his thoughts, Burdeaux turned, hurried away.

'*You're the fellow Jenny's sweet on,*' Dasein thought. Present tense ... not past tense. He felt his heart hammering, cursed himself for an idiot. It was just Burdeaux's way of talking. That was all it could be.

Confused, he bent to his food.

The roast beef in his first bite lived up to Burdeaux's prediction – tender, juicy. The cheese sauce on the potatoes had a flowing tang reminiscent of the beer and the sour cream.

The fellow Jenny's sweet on.

Burdeaux's words gripped Dasein's mind as he ate, filled him with turmoil.

Dasein looked up from his food, seeking Burdeaux. The waiter was nowhere in sight. *Jaspers.* It was this rich tang, this new flavor. His attention went to the bottle of beer, the non-Jaspers beer. *Not as good?* He sampled it directly from the bottle, found it left a bitter metallic aftertaste. A sip of the first beer from the mug – smooth, soothing. Dasein felt it cleared his head as it cleared his tongue of the other flavor.

He put down the mug, looked across the room, caught the bartender staring at him, scowling. The man looked away.

They were small things – two beers, an argument between a waiter and a bartender, a watchful bartender – nothing but clock ticks in a lifetime, but Dasein sensed danger in them. He reminded himself that two investigators had met fatal accidents in the Santaroga *Valley – death by misadventure* ... a car going too fast around a corner, off the road into a ravine ... a fall from a rocky ledge into a river – drowned. *Natural* accidents, so certified by state investigation.

Thoughtful, Dasein returned to his food.

Presently, Burdeaux brought the strawberries, hovered as Dasein sampled them.

'Good, sir?'

'Very good. Better than that bottle of beer.'

'My fault, sir. Perhaps another time.' He coughed discreetly. 'Does Jenny know you're here?'

Dasein put down his spoon, looked into his dish of strawberries as though trying to find his reflection there. His mind suddenly produced a memory picture of Jenny in a red dress, vital, laughing, bubbling with energy. 'No ... not yet,' he said.

'You know Jenny's still a single girl, sir?'

Dasein glanced across to the card game. How leathery tan the players' skin looked. *Jenny not married?* Dr Piaget looked up from the card game, said something to the man on his left. They laughed.

'Has ... is she in the telephone directory, Mr Burdeaux?' Dasein asked.

'She lives with Dr Piaget, sir. And why don't you call me Win?'

Dasein looked up at Bordeaux's sharp Moorish face, wondering suddenly about the man. There was just a hint of southern accent in his voice. The probing friendliness, the volunteered information about Jenny – it was all faintly southern, intimate, kindly ... but there were undertones of something else: a questing awareness, harsh and direct. The psychologist in Dasein was fully alert now.

'Have you lived very long here in the valley, Win?' Dasein asked.

''Bout twelve years, sir.'

'How'd you come to settle here?'

Burdeaux shook his head. A rueful half-smile touched his lips. 'Oh, you wouldn't like to hear about that, sir.'

'But I would.' Dasein stared up at Burdeaux, waiting. Somewhere there was a wedge that would open this valley's mysteries to him. *Jenny not married?* Perhaps Burdeaux was that wedge. There was an open shyness about his own manner, Dasein knew, that invited confidences. He relied upon this now.

'Well, if you really want to know, sir,' Burdeaux said. 'I was in the N'Orleans jailhouse for cuttin' up.' (Dasein noted a sudden richening of the southern accent.) 'We was doin' our numbers, usin' dirty language that'd make your neck hair walk. I suddenly heard myself doin' that, sir. It made me review my thinkin' and I saw it was kid stuff. Juvenile.' Burdeaux mouthed the word, proud of it. 'Juvenile, sir. Well, when I got out of that jailhouse, the high sheriff tellin' me never to come back, I went me home to my woman and I tol' Annie, I tol' her we was leavin'. That's when we left to come here, sir.'

'Just like that, you left?'

'We hit the road on our feet, sir. It wasn't easy an' there was some places made us wish we'd never left. When we come here, though, we knew it was worth it.'

'You just wandered until you came here?'

'It was like God was leadin' us, sir. This place, well, sir, it's hard to explain. But ... well, they insist I go to school to better myself. That's one thing. I can speak good standard English when I want ... when I think about it.' (The accent began to fade.)

Dasein smiled encouragingly. 'These must be very nice people here in the valley.'

'I'm going to tell you something, sir,' Burdeaux said. 'Maybe you can understand if I tell you about something happened to me here. It's a thing would've hurt me pretty bad one time, but here ... We were at a Jaspers party, sir. It was right after Willa, my girl, announced her engagement to Cal Nis. And George, Cal's daddy, came over and put his arm across my shoulder. "Well there, Win, you old nigger bastard," he said, "we better have us a good drink and a talk together because our kids are going to make us related." That was it, Mr Dasein. He didn't mean a thing calling me nigger. It was just like ... like the way we call a pale blonde fellow here Whitey. It was like saying my skin's black for identification the way you might come into a room and ask for Al Marden and I'd say: "He's that red-headed fellow over there playing cards." As he was saying it I knew that's all he meant. It just came over me. It was being accepted for what I am. It was the friendliest thing George could do and that's why he did it.'

Dasein scowled trying to follow the train of Burdeaux's meaning. Friendly to call him nigger?

'I don't think you understand it,' Burdeaux said. 'Maybe you'd have to be black to understand. But ... well, perhaps this'll make you see it. A few minutes later, George said to me: "Hey, Win, I wonder what kind of grandchildren we're going to have – light, dark or in between?" It was just a kind of wonderment to him, that he might have black grandchildren. He didn't care, really. He was curious. He found it interesting. You know, when I told Annie about that afterward, I cried. I was so happy I cried.'

It was a long colloquy. Dasein could see realization of this fact come over Burdeaux. The man shook his head, muttered: 'I talk too much. Guess I'd better ...'

He broke off at a sudden eruption of shouting at the bar near the card players. A red-faced fat man had stepped back from the bar and was flailing it with a briefcase as he shouted at the bartender.

'You sons of bitches!' he screamed. 'You think you're too goddamn' good to buy from me! My line isn't good enough for you! You can make better ...'

The bartender grabbed the briefcase.

'Leggo of that, you son of a bitch!' the fat man yelled. 'You all think you're so goddamn' good like you're some foreign country! An *outsider* am I? Let me tell you, you pack of foreigners! This is America! This is a free ...'

The red-headed highway patrol captain, Al Marden, had risen at the first sign of trouble. Now, he put a large hand on the screamer's shoulder, shook the man once.

The screaming stopped. The angry man whirled, raised the briefcase to hit Marden. In one long, drawn-out second, the man focused on Marden's glaring eyes, the commanding face, hesitated.

'I'm Captain Marden of the Highway Patrol,' Marden said. 'And I'm telling you we won't have any more of this.' His voice was calm, stern . . . and, Dasein thought, faintly amused.

The angry man lowered the briefcase, swallowed.

'You can go out and get in your car and leave Santaroga,' Marden said. 'Now. And don't come back. We'll be watching for you, and we'll run you in if we ever catch you in the valley again.'

Anger drained from the fat man. His shoulders slumped. He swallowed, looked around at the room of staring eyes. 'I'm glad to go,' he muttered. 'Nothing'd make me happier. It'll be a cold day in hell when I ever come back to your dirty little valley. You stink. All of you stink." He jerked his shoulder from Marden's grasp, stalked out through the passage to the lobby.

Marden returned to the card game shaking his head.

Slowly, the room returned to its previous sounds of eating and conversation. Dasein could feel a difference, though. The salesman's outburst had separated Santarogans and transients. An invisible wall had gone up. The transient families at their tables were hurrying their children, anxious to leave.

Dasein felt the same urgency. There was a pack feeling about the room now – hunters and hunted. He smelled his own perspiration. His palms were sweaty. He noted that Burdeaux had gone.

This is stupid! he thought. *Jenny not married?*

He reminded himself that he was a psychologist, an observer. But the observer had to observe himself.

Why am I reacting this way? he wondered. *Jenny not married?*

Two of the transient families already were leaving, herding their young ahead of them, voices brittle, talking about going 'on to the next town.'

Why can't they stay here? he asked himself. *The rates are reasonable.*

He pictured the area in his mind: Porterville was twenty-five miles away, ten miles outside the valley on the road he had taken. The other direction led over a winding, twisting mountain road some forty miles before connecting with Highway 395. The closest communities were to the south along 395, at least seventy miles. This was an area of National Forests, lakes, fire roads, moonscape ridges of lava rock – all of it sparsely inhabited except for the Santaroga Valley. Why would people want to travel through such an area at night rather than stay at this inn?

Dasein finished his meal, left the rest of the beer. He had to talk this place over with his department head, Dr Chami Selador, before making another move. Burdeaux had left the check on a discreet brown tray – three dollars and eighty-six cents. Dasein put a five dollar bill on the tray, glanced once more around the room. The surface appeared so damn' normal! The card players were intent on their game. The bartender was hunched over, chatting with two customers. A child at a table off to the right was complaining that she didn't want to drink her milk.

It wasn't normal, though, and Dasein's senses screamed this fact at him. The brittle surface of this room was prepared to shatter once more and Dasein didn't think he would like what might be revealed. He wiped his lips on his napkin, took his briefcase and headed for the lobby.

His suitcase stood atop the desk beside the register. There was a buzzing and murmurous sound of a switchboard being operated in the room through the doors at the rear corner. He took the suitcase, fingered the brass room key in his pocket – two fifty-one. If there was no phone in the room, he decided he'd come down and place his call to Chami from a booth.

Feeling somewhat foolish and letdown after his reaction to the scene in the dining room, Dasein headed for the stairs. A few eyes peered at him over the tops of newspapers from the lobby chairs. The eyes looked alert, inquisitive.

The stairs led to a shadowy mezzanine – desks, patches of white paper. A fire door directly ahead bore the sign: 'To Second Floor. Keep this door closed.'

The next flight curved left, dim overhead light, wide panels of dark wood. It led through another fire door into a hall with an emergency exit sign off to the left. An illuminated board opposite the door indicated room two fifty-one down the hall to the right. Widely spaced overhead lights, the heavy pile of a maroon carpet underfoot, wide heavy doors with brass handles and holes for old-fashioned passkeys gave the place an aura of the Nineteenth Century. Dasein half expected to see a maid in ruffled cap, apron with a bow at the back, long skirt and black stockings, sensible shoes – or a portly banker type with tight vest and high collar, an expanse of gold chain at the waist. He felt out of place, out of style here.

The brass key worked smoothly in the door of two fifty-one; it let him into a room of high ceilings, one window looking down onto the parking area. Dasein turned on the light. The switch controlled a tasseled floor lamp beside a curve-fronted teak dresser. The amber light revealed a partly opened doorway into a tiled bathroom (the sound of water dripping there), a thick-legged desk-table with a single straight chair pushed against it. The bed was narrow and high with a heavily carved headboard.

Dasein pushed down on the surface of the bed. It felt soft. He dropped his suitcase onto the bed, stared at it. An edge of white fabric protruded from one end. He opened the suitcase, studied the contents. Dasein knew himself for a prissy, meticulous packer. The case now betrayed a subtle disarray. Someone had opened it and searched it. Well, it hadn't been locked. He checked the contents – nothing missing.

Why are they curious about me? he wondered.

He looked around for a telephone, found it, a standard French handset, on a shelf beside the desk. As he moved, he caught sight of himself in the mirror above the dresser – eyes wide, mouth in a straight line. Grim. He shook his head, smiled. The smile felt out of place.

Dasein sat down in the straight chair, put the phone to his ear. There was a smell of disinfectant soap in the room – and something like garlic. After a moment, he jiggled the hook.

Presently, a woman's voice came on: 'This is the desk.'

'I'd like to place a call to Berkeley,' Dasein said. He gave the number. There was a moment's silence, then: 'Your room number, sir?'

'Two fifty-one.'

'One moment, please.'

He heard the sound of dialing, ringing. Another operator came on the line. Dasein listened with only half his attention as the call was placed. The smell of garlic was quite strong. He stared at the high old bed, his open suitcase. The bed appeared inviting, telling him how tired he was. His chest ached. He took a deep breath.

'Dr Selador here.'

Selador's India-*cum*-Oxford accent sounded familiar and close. Dasein bent to the telephone, identified himself, his mind caught suddenly by that feeling of intimate nearness linked to the knowledge of the actual distance, the humming wires reaching down almost half the length of the state.

'Gilbert, old fellow, you made it all right, I see.' Selador's voice was full of cheer.

'I'm at the Santaroga House, Doctor.'

'I hear it's quite comfortable.'

'Looks that way.' Through his buzzing tiredness, Dasein felt a sense of foolishness. Why had he made this call? Selador's sharp mind would probe for underlying meanings, motives.

'I presume you didn't call just to tell me you've arrived,' Selador said.

'No ... I ...' Dasein realized he couldn't express his own vague uneasiness, that it wouldn't make sense, this feeling of estrangement, the separation of Santarogans and Outsiders, the pricklings of warning fear. 'I'd like you to look into the oil company dealings with this area,' Dasein said. 'See if you can find out how they do business in the valley. There's apparently an independent service station here. I want to know who supplies the gas, oil, parts – that sort of thing.'

'Good point, Gilbert. I'll put one of our ...' There was a sudden crackling, bapping sound on the line. It stopped and there was dead silence.

'Dr Selador?'

Silence.

Damn! Dasein thought. He jiggled the hook. 'Operator. Operator!'

A masculine voice came on the line. Dasein recognized the desk clerk's twang. 'Who's that creating all that commotion?' the clerk demanded.

'I was cut off on my call to Berkeley,' Dasein said. 'Could you ...'

'Line's out,' the clerk snapped.

'Could I come down to the lobby and place the call from a pay phone?' Dasein asked. As he asked it, the thought of walking that long distance down to the lobby repelled Dasein. The feeling of tiredness was a weight on his chest.

'There's no line out of the valley right now,' the clerk said. 'Call can't be placed.'

Dasein passed a hand across his forehead. His skin felt clammy and he wondered if he'd picked up a germ. The room around him seemed to expand and contract. His mouth was dry and he had to swallow twice before asking: 'When do they expect to have the line restored?'

'How the hell do I know?' the clerk demanded.

Dasein took the receiver away from his ear, stared at it. This was a very peculiar desk clerk ... and a very peculiar room the way it wavered and slithered with its stench of garlic and its ...

He grew aware of a faint hissing.

Dasein's gaze was drawn on a string of growing astonishment to an old-fashioned gaslight jet that jutted from the wall beside the hall door.

Stink of garlic? Gas!

A yapping, barking voice yammered on the telephone.

Dasein looked down at the instrument in his hand. How far away it seemed. Through the window beyond the phone he could see the Inn sign: *Gold Rush Museum.* Window equaled air. Dasein found muscles that obeyed, lurched across the desk, fell, smashing the telephone through the window.

The yapping voice grew fainter.

Dasein felt his body stretched across the desk. His head lay near the shattered window. He could see the telephone cord stretching out the window. There was cool air blowing on a distant forehead, a painful chill in his lungs.

They tried to kill me, he thought. It was a wondering thought, full of amazement. His mind focused on the two investigators who'd already died on this project – accidents. Simple, easily explained accidents … just like this one!

The air – how cold it felt on his exposed skin. His lungs burned with it. There was a hammering pulse at his temple where it pressed against the desk surface. The pulse went on and on and on …

A pounding on wood joined the pulse. For a space, they beat in an insane syncopation.

'You in there! Open up!' How commanding, that voice. *Open up*, Dasein thought. That meant getting to one's feet, crossing the room, turning a door handle …

I'm helpless, he thought. *They could still kill me.*

He heard metal rasp against metal. The air blew stronger across his face. Someone said: 'Gas!'

Hands grabbed Dasein's shoulders. He was hauled back, half carried, half dragged out of the room. The face of Marden, the red-haired patrol captain, swung across his vision. He saw the clerk: pale, staring face, bald forehead glistening under yellow light. There was a brown ceiling directly in front of Dasein. He felt a rug, hard and rasping, beneath his back.

A twanging voice said: 'Who's going to pay for that window?' Someone else said: 'I'll get Dr Piaget.'

Dasein's attention centered on Marden's mouth, a blurred object seen through layers of distortion. There appeared to be anger lines at the corners of the mouth. It turned toward the hovering pale face of the desk clerk, said: 'To hell with your window, Johnson! I've told you enough times to get those gas jets out of this place. How many rooms still have them?'

'Don't you take that tone with me, Al Marden. I've known you since …'

'I'm not interested in how long you've known me, Johnson. How many rooms still have those gas jets?'

The clerk's voice came with an angry tone of hurt: 'Only this'n an' four upstairs. Nobody in the other rooms.'

'Get 'em out by tomorrow night,' Marden said.

Hurrying footsteps interrupted the argument. Dr Piaget's round face blotted out Dasein's view of the ceiling. The face wore a look of concern. Fingers reached down, spread Dasein's eyelids. Piaget said: 'Let's get him on a bed.'

'Is he going to be all right?' the clerk asked.

'It's about time you asked,' Marden said.

'We got him in time,' Piaget said. 'Is that room across the hall empty?'

'He can have 260,' the clerk said. 'I'll open it.'

'You realize this is Jenny's fellow from the school you almost killed?' Marden asked, his voice receding as he moved away beside the clerk.

'Jenny's fellow?' There was the sound of a key in a lock. 'But I thought . . .'

'Never mind what you thought!'

Piaget's face moved close to Dasein. 'Can you hear me, young fellow?' he asked.

Dasein drew in a painful breath, croaked, 'Yes.'

'You'll have quite a head, but you'll recover.'

Piaget's face went away. Hands picked Dasein up. The ceiling moved. There was another room around him: like the first one – tall ceiling, even the sound of dripping water. He felt a bed beneath his back, hands beginning to undress him. Sudden nausea gripped him. Dasein pushed the hands away.

Someone helped him to the bathroom where he was sick. He felt better afterward – weak, but with a clearer head, a better sense of control over his muscles. He saw it was Piaget who'd helped him.

'Feel like getting back to bed now?' Piaget asked.

'Yes.'

'I'll give you a good shot of iron to counteract the gas effect on your blood,' Piaget said. 'You'll be all right.'

'How'd that gas jet get turned on?' Dasein asked. His voice came out a hoarse whisper.

'Johnson got mixed up fooling with the valves in the kitchen,' Piaget said. 'Wouldn't have been any harm done if some idiot hadn't opened the jet in your room.'

'I coulda sworn I had 'em all turned off.' That was the clerk's voice from somewhere beyond the bathroom door.

'They better be capped by tomorrow night,' Marden said.

They sounded so reasonable, Dasein thought. Marden appeared genuinely angry. The look on Piaget's face could be nothing other than concern.

Could it have been a real accident? Dasein wondered.

He reminded himself then two men had died by accident in this valley while engaged in the investigation.

'All right,' Piaget said. 'Al, you and Pim and the others can clear out now. I'll get him to bed.'

'Okay, Larry. Clear out, all of you.' That was Marden. 'I'll get his bags from the other room.' That was a voice Dasein didn't recognize.

Presently, with Piaget's help, Dasein found himself in pajamas and in the bed. He felt clearheaded, wide awake and lonely even with Piaget still in the room.

Among strangers, Dasein thought.

'Here, take this,' Piaget said. He pressed two pills into Dasein's mouth, forced a glass of water on him. Dasein gulped, felt the pills rasp down his throat in a wash of water.

'What was that?' Dasein asked as he pushed the glass away.

'The iron and a sedative.'

'I don't want to sleep. The gas ...'

'You didn't get enough gas to make that much difference. Now, you rest easy.' Piaget patted his shoulder. 'Bed rest and fresh air are the best therapy you can get. Someone'll look in on you from time to time tonight. I'll check back on you in the morning.'

'Someone,' Dasein said. 'A nurse?'

'Yes,' Piaget said, his voice brusk. 'A nurse. You'll be as safe here as in a hospital.'

Dasein looked at the night beyond the room's window. *Why the feeling of danger now, then?* he wondered. *Is it reaction?* He could feel the sedative blurring his senses, soothing him. The sense of danger persisted.

'Jenny will be happy to know you're here,' Piaget said. He left the room, turning off the light, closing the door softly.

Dasein felt he had been smothered in darkness. He fought down panic, restored himself to a semblance of calm.

Jenny ... Jenny ...

Marden's odd conversation with the clerk, Johnson, returned to him ' *... Jenny's fellow from the school ...'*

What had Johnson thought? What was the thing Marden had cut short?

Dasein fought the sedative. The drip-drip of water in the bathroom invaded his awareness. The room was an alien cell.

Was it just an accident?

He remembered the fragmented confusion of the instant when he'd focused on that hissing gas jet. Now, when the danger was past, he felt terror.

It couldn't have been an accident!

But why would Johnson want to kill him?

The disconnected telephone call haunted Dasein. Was the line really down? What would Selador do? Selador knew the dangers here.

Dasein felt the sedative pulling him down into sleep. He tried to focus on the investigation. It was such a fascinating project. He could hear Selador explaining the facets that made the Santaroga Project such a glittering gem —

'Taken singly, no item in this collection of facts could be considered alarming or worthy of extended attention. You might find it interesting that no person from Cloverdale, California, could be found in a mental hospital. It might be of passing interest to learn that the people of Hope, Missouri, consumed very little tobacco. Would you be alarmed to discover that all the business of Enumclaw, Washington, were locally owned? Certainly not. But when you bring all of these and the other facts together into a single community, something disturbing emerges. There is a difference at work here.'

The drip of water in the bathroom was a compelling distraction. *Dangerous difference,* Dasein thought. *Who'll look in on me?* he wondered.

It occurred to him to ask himself then who had sounded the alarm. The breaking window had alerted someone. The most likely person would be Johnson, the room clerk. Why would he bring help to the person he was trying to kill? The paranoia in his own thoughts began to impress itself on Dasein.

It was an accident, Dasein thought. *It was an accident in a place of dangerous difference.*

Dasein's morning began with a sensation of hunger. He awoke to cramping pains. Events of the night flooded into his memory. His head felt as though it had been kicked from the inside.

Gently, he pushed himself upright. There was a window directly ahead of him with the green branch of an oak tree across it. As though his muscles were controlled by some hidden force, Dasein found himself looking up at the door to see if there was a gas jet. Nothing met his questing gaze but a patch on the wallpaper to mark the place where a jet had been.

Holding his head as level as possible, Dasein eased himself out of bed and into the bathroom. A cold shower restored some of his sense of reality.

He kept telling himself: *It was an accident.*

A bluejay was sitting on the oak branch screeching when Dasein emerged from the bathroom. The sound sent little clappers of pain through Dasein's head. He dressed hurriedly, hunger urging him The bluejay was joined by a companion. They screeched and darted at each other through the oak tree, their topknots twitching. Dasein gritted his teeth, faced the mirror to tie his tie. As he was finishing the knot, he saw reflected in the mirror the slow inward movement of the hall door. A corner of a wheeled tray appeared. Dishes clattered. The door swung wider.

Jenny appeared in the doorway pushing the tray. Dasein stared at her in the mirror, his hands frozen at the tie. She wore a red dress, her long black hair caught in a matching bandeaux. Her skin displayed a healthy tan. Blue eyes stared back at him in the mirror. Her oval face was set in a look of watchful waiting. Her mouth was as full as he remembered it, hesitating on the edge of a smile, a dimple flickering at her left cheek.

'Finish your tie,' she said. 'I've brought you some breakfast.' Her voice had a well-remembered, throaty, soothing tone.

Dasein turned, moved toward her as though pulled by strings. Jenny abandoned the cart, met him half way. She came into his arms, lifting her lips to be kissed. Dasein, feeling the warmth of her kiss and the familiar pressure of her against him, experienced a sensation of coming home.

Jenny pulled away, studied his face. 'Oh, Gil,' she said, 'I've missed you so much. Why didn't you even write?'

He stared at her, surprised to silence for a moment, then: 'But I did write. You never answered.'

She pushed away from him, her features contorted by a scowl. 'Ohhh!' She stamped her foot.

'Well, I see you found him.' It was Dr Piaget in the doorway. He pushed the cart all the way into the room, closed the door.

Jenny whirled on him. 'Uncle Larry! Did you keep Gil's letters from me?'

Piaget looked from her to Dasein. 'Letters? What letters?'

'Gil wrote and I never got the letters!'

'Oh.' Piaget nodded. 'Well, you know how they are at the post office sometimes – valley girl, fellow from outside.'

'Ohhh! I could scratch their eyes out!'

'Easy, girl.' Piaget smiled at Dasein.

Jenny whirled back into Dasein's arms, surprised him with another kiss. He broke away slightly breathless.

'There,' she said. 'That's for being here. Those old biddies at the post office can't dump *that* in the trash basket.'

'What old biddies?' Dasein asked. He felt he had missed part of the conversation. The warmth of Jenny's kisses, her open assumption nothing had changed between them, left him feeling defenseless, wary. A year had passed, after all. He'd managed to stay away from here for a year – leaning on his wounded masculine ego, true, fearful he'd find

Jenny married ... lost to him forever. But what had she leaned on? She could've come to Berkeley, if only for a visit.

And I could've come here.

Jenny grinned.

'Why're you grinning?' he demanded. 'And you haven't explained this about the post office and the ...'

'I'm grinning because I'm so happy,' she said. 'I'm grinning because I see the wheels going around in your head. Why didn't one of us go see the other before now? Well, *you're* here as I knew you would be. I just *knew* you would be.' She hugged him impulsively, said: 'About the post office ...'

'I think Gilbert's breakfast is getting cold,' Piaget said. 'You don't mind if I call you Gilbert?'

'He doesn't mind,' Jenny said. Her voice was bantering, but there was a sudden stiffness in her body. She pushed away from Dasein.

Piaget lifted a cover from one of the plates on the cart, said: 'Jaspers omelette, I see. *Real* Jaspers.'

Jenny spoke defensively with a curious lack of vitality: 'I made it myself in Johnson's kitchen.'

'I see,' Piaget said. 'Yes ... well, perhaps that's best.' He indicated the plate. 'Have at it, Gilbert.'

The thought of food made Dasein's stomach knot with hunger. He wanted to sit down and bolt the omelette ... but something made him hesitate. He couldn't evade the nagging sense of danger.

'What's this Jaspers business?' he asked.

'Oh, that,' Jenny said, pulling the cart over to the chair by the desk. 'That just means something made with a product from the Co-op. This is our cheddar in the omelette. Sit down and eat.'

'You'll like it,' Piaget said. He crossed the room, put a hand on Dasein's shoulder, eased him into the chair. 'Just let me have a quick look at you.' He pinched Dasein's left ear lobe, studied it, looked at his eyes. 'You're looking pretty fit. How's the head?'

'It's better now. It was pretty fierce when I woke up.'

'Okay. Eat your breakfast. Take it easy for a day or two. Let me know if you feel nauseated again or have any general symptoms of lethargy. I suggest you eat liver for dinner and I'll have Jenny bring you some more iron pills. You weren't in there long enough to cause you any permanent trouble.'

'When I think of that Mr Johnson's carelessness, I want to take one of his cleavers to him,' Jenny said.

'We *are* bloodthirsty today, aren't we,' Piaget said.

Dasein picked up his fork, sampled the omelette. Jenny watched him, waiting. The omelette was delicious – moist and with a faint bite of cheese. He swallowed, smiled at her.

Jenny grinned back. 'You know,' she said, 'that's the first food I ever cooked for you.'

'Don't rush him off his feet, girl,' Piaget said. He patted her head, said: 'I'll leave you two for now. Why don't you bring your young man along home for dinner? I'll have Sarah make what he needs.' He glanced at Dasein. 'That all right with you?'

Dasein swallowed another bite of the omelette. The cheese left a tangy aftertaste that reminded him of the unpasteurized beer Burdeaux had served. 'I'd be honored, sir,' he said.

'Honored, yet,' Piaget said. 'We'll expect you around seven.' He glanced at his wristwatch. 'It's almost eight-thirty, Jenny. Aren't you working today?'

'I called George and told him I'd be late.'

'He didn't object?'

'He knows ... I have a friend ... visiting.' She blushed.

'Like that, eh? Well, don't get into any trouble.' Piaget turned, lumbered from the room with a head-down purposeful stride.

Jenny turned a shy, questioning smile on Dasein. 'Don't mind Uncle Larry,' she said. 'He darts around like that – one subject then another. He's a very real, wonderful person.'

'Where do you work?' Dasein asked.

'At the Co-op.'

'The cheese factory?'

'Yes. I'm ... I'm on the inspection line.'

Dasein swallowed, reminded himself he was here to do a market study. He was a spy. And what would Jenny say when she discovered that? But Jenny posed a new puzzle. She had a superior talent for clinical psychology – even according to Dr Selador whose standards were high. Yet ... she worked in the cheese factory.

'Isn't there any work ... in your line here?' he asked.

'It's a good job,' she said. She sat down on the edge of the desk, swung her legs 'Finish your breakfast. I didn't make that coffee. It's out of the hotel urn. Don't drink it if it's too strong. There's orange juice in the metal pitcher. I remembered you take your coffee black and didn't bring any ...'

'Whoa!' he said.

'I'm talking too much I know it,' she said. She hugged herself. 'Oh, Gil, I'm so happy you're here. Finish your breakfast and you can take me across to the Co-op. Maybe I can take you on the guided tour. It's a fascinating place. There are lots of dark corners back in the storage cave.'

Dasein drained his coffee, shook his head. 'Jenny, you are incorrigible.'

'Gil, you're going to love it here. I know you are,' she said.

Dasein wiped his lips on his napkin. She was still in love with him. He could see that in every look. And he ... he felt the same way about her. It was still *love me love my valley*, though. Her words betrayed it. Dasein sighed. He could see the blank wall of an unresolvable difference looming ahead of them. If her love could stand the discovery of his true role here, could it also stand breaking away from the valley? Would she come away with him?

'Gil, are you all right?' she asked.

He pushed his chair back, got up. 'Yes. I'm ...'

The telephone rang.

Jenny reached behind her on the desk, brought the receiver to her ear. 'Dr Dasein's room.' She grinned at Dasein. The grin turned to a scowl. 'Oh, it's you, Mr Pem Johnson, is it? Well, I'll tell you a thing or two, Mr Johnson! I think you're a criminal the way you almost killed Dr Dasein! If you'd ... No! Don't you try to make excuses! Open gas jets in the rooms! I think Dr Dasein ought to sue you for every cent you have!'

A tinny, rasping noise came from the phone. Dasein recognized only a few words. The grin returned to Jenny's face. 'It's Jenny Sorge, that's who it is,' she said. 'Don't you ... well, I'll tell you if you'll be quiet for a minute! I'm here bringing Dr Dasein what the doctor ordered for him – a good breakfast. He doesn't dare eat anything you'd have prepared for him It'd probably have poison in it!'

Dasein crossed to a trunk stand where his suitcase had been left, opened it. He spoke over his shoulder. 'Jenny, what's he want, for heaven's sake?'

She waved him to silence.

Dasein rummaged in the suitcase looking for his briefcase. He tried to remember what had been done with it in the confusion of the previous night, looked around the room. No sign of it. Someone had gone to the other room for his things. Maybe whoever it was had missed the brief-case. Dasein thought of the case's contents, wet his lips with his tongue. Every step of his program to unravel the mystery of the Santaroga Barrier was outlined there. In the wrong hands, that information could cause him trouble, throw up new barriers.

'I'll tell him,' Jenny said.

'Wait a minute,' Dasein said. 'I want to talk to him.' He took the phone from her. 'Johnson?'

'What do you want?' There was that twangy belligerency, but Dasein couldn't blame him after the treatment he'd received from Jenny.

'My briefcase,' Dasein said. 'It was in the other room. Would you send up someone with a key and . . .'

'Your damned briefcase isn't in that room, mister! I cleaned the place out and I ought to know.'

'Then where is it?' Dasein asked.

'If it's that case you were so touchy about last night, I saw Captain Marden leave with something that looked like it last night after all the commotion you caused.'

'I caused?' Outrage filled Dasein's voice. 'See here, Johnson! You stop twisting the facts!'

After only a heartbeat of silence, Johnson said: 'I was, wasn't I? Sorry.'

Johnson's abrupt candor disarmed the psychologist in Dasein. In a way, it reminded him of Jenny. Santarogans, he found, displayed a lopsided reality that was both attractive and confusing. When he'd collected his thoughts, all Dasein could say was: 'What would Marden be doing with my case?'

'That's for him to say and you to find out,' Johnson said with all his old belligerence. There was a sharp click as he broke the connection.

Dasein shook his head, put the phone back on its hook.

'Al Marden wants you to have lunch with him at the Blue Ewe,' Jenny said.

'Hmmm?' He looked up at her, bemused, her words taking a moment to register. 'Marden . . . lunch?'

'Twelve noon. The Blue Ewe's on the Avenue of the Giants where it goes through town . . . on the right just past the first cross street.'

'Marden? The Highway patrol captain?'

'Yes. Johnson just passed the message along.' She slipped down off the desk, a flash of knees, a swirl of the red skirt. 'Come along. Escort me to work.'

Dasein picked up his suitcoat, allowed himself to be led from the room.

That damn' briefcase with all its forms and notes and letters, he thought. *The whole show!* But it gave him a perverse feeling of satisfaction to know that everything would be out in the open. *I wasn't cut out to be a cloak and dagger type.*

There was no escaping the realization, though, that revelation of his real purpose here would intensify Santaroga's conspiracy of silence. And how would Jenny react?

2

Dasein's first impression of the Jasper Cheese Cooperative with the people at work in and around it was that the place was a hive. It loomed whitely behind its fence as Jenny led him from the Inn. He found it an odd companion for the Inn, just across the road, nestled against a steep hill, poking odd squares and rectangles up onto an outcropping. The previous night's brooding look had been replaced by this appearance of humming efficiency with electric carts buzzing across the yard, their platforms loaded with oblong packages. People walked with a leaning sense of purpose.

A hive, Dasein thought. There must be a queen inside and these were the workers, guarding, gathering food.

A uniformed guard, a police dog on a leash beside him, took Dasein's name as Jenny introduced him. The guard opened a gate in the chain-link fence. His dog grinned wolfishly at Dasein, whined.

Dasein remembered the baying he'd heard when he'd first looked down into the valley. That had been less than fourteen hours ago, Dasein realized. The time felt stretched out, longer. He asked himself why dogs guarded the Co-op. The question bothered him.

The yard they crossed was an immaculate concrete surface. Now that he was close to the factory, Dasein saw that it was a complex of structures that had been joined by filling the between areas with odd additions and covered walkways.

Jenny's mood changed markedly once they were well inside the grounds. Dasein saw her become more assertive, sure of herself. She introduced Dasein to four persons while crossing the yard – Willa Burdeaux among them. Willa turned out to be a small husky-voiced young woman with a face that was almost ugly in its tiny, concise sharpness. She had her father's deeps-of-darkness skin, a petite figure.

'I met your father last night,' Dasein said.

'Daddy told me,' she said. She turned a knowing look on Jenny, added: 'Anything I can do, just tell me, honey.'

'Maybe later,' Jenny said. 'We have to be running.'

'You're going to like it here, Gilbert Dasein,' Willa said. She turned away with a wave, hurried across the yard.

Disturbed by the undertones of the conversation, Dasein allowed himself to be led down a side bay, into a wide door that opened onto an aisle between stacked cartons of Jaspers Cheese. Somewhere beyond the stacks there was a multiplexity of sounds – hissings, stampings, gurgling water, a clank-clank-clank.

The aisle ended in a short flight of wide steps, up to a loading bay with hand trucks racked along its edge. Jenny led him through a door marked 'Office.'

It was such an ordinary place – clips of order forms racked along a wall, two desks with women seated at them typing, a long counter with a gate at one end, windows opening onto the yard and a view of the Inn, a door labeled 'Manager' beyond the women.

The door opened as Dasein and Jenny stopped at the counter. Out stepped one of the card players from the Inn's dining room – the balding sandy hair, the deeply cleft chin and wide mouth – George Nis. The heavily lidded blue eyes swept past Dasein to Jenny.

'Problems in Bay Nine, Jenny,' Nis said. 'You're needed over there right away.'

'Oh, darn!' Jenny said.

'I'll take care of your friend,' Nis said. 'We'll see if we can't let you off early for your dinner date.'

Jenny squeezed Dasein's hand, said: 'Darling, forgive me. Duty and all that.' She blinked a smile at him, whirled and was back out the door, the red skirt swirling.

The women at their typewriters looked up, seemed to take in Dasein with one look, went back to their work. Nis came to the gate in the counter, opened it.

'Come on in, Dr Dasein.' He extended a hand.

The handshake was firm, casual.

Dasein followed the man into an oak-paneled office, unable to get his mind off the fact that Nis knew about the dinner date with Jenny. How could the man know? Piaget had extended the invitation only a few minutes before.

They sat down separated by a wide desk, its top empty of papers. The chairs were padded, comfortable with sloping arms. In large frames behind Nis hung an aerial photograph of the Co-op and what appeared to be a ground plan. Dasein recognized the layout of the yard and front of the building. The back became heavy dark lines that wandered off into the hill like the tributaries of a river. They were labeled with the initial *J* and numbers – *J-5* ... *J-14* ...

Nis saw the direction of Dasein's gaze, said: 'Those are the storage caverns – constant temperature and humidity.' He coughed discreetly behind a hand, said: 'You catch us at an embarrassing moment, Dr Dasein. I've nobody I can release to show you through the plant. Could Jenny bring you back another day?'

'At your convenience,' Dasein said. He studied Nis, feeling oddly wary, on guard.

'Please don't wear any cologne or hair dressing or anything like that when you come,' Nis said. 'You'll notice that our women wear no makeup and we don't allow female visitors from outside to go into the cave or storage areas. It's quite easy to contaminate the culture, give an odd flavor to an entire batch.'

Dasein was suddenly acutely aware of the aftershave lotion he'd used that morning.

'I'll be pure and clean,' he said. He looked to the right out the windows, caught suddenly by motion there on the road between the Co-op and the Inn.

A peculiar high-wheeled vehicle went lurching past. Dasein counted eight pairs of wheels. They appeared to be at least fifteen feet in diameter, big ballooning doughnuts that hummed on the pavement. The wheels were slung on heavy arms like insect legs.

In an open cab, high up in front, four leashed hounds seated behind him, rode Al Marden. He appeared to be steering by using two vertical handles.

'What in the devil is that?' Dasein demanded. He jumped up, crossed to the window to get a better look at the machine as it sped down the road. 'Isn't that Captain Marden driving it?'

'That's our game warden's bush buggy,' Nis said. 'Al acts as game warden sometimes when the regular man's sick or busy on something else. Must've been out patroling the south hills. Heard there were some deer hunters from outside messing around there this morning.'

'You don't allow outsiders to hunt in the valley, is that it?' Dasein asked.

'*Nobody* hunts in the valley,' Nis corrected him. 'Too much chance of stray bullets hitting someone. Most of the people around this area know the law, but we occasionally get someone from down south who blunders in. There're very few places the buggy can't get to them, though. We set them straight in a hurry.'

Dasein imagined that giant-wheeled monstrosity lurching over the brush, descending on some hapless hunter who'd blundered into the valley. He found his sympathies with the hunter.

'I've never seen a vehicle like that before,' Dasein said. 'Is it something new?'

'Sam, Sam Scheler, built the bush buggy ten, twelve years ago,' Nis said. 'We were getting some poachers from over by Porterville then. They don't bother us anymore.'

'I imagine not,' Dasein said.

'I hope you'll forgive me,' Nis said. 'I do have a great deal of work and we're short-handed today. Get Jenny to bring you back later in the week ... after ... well, later in the week.'

After what? Dasein wondered. He found himself strangely alert. He'd never felt this clearheaded before. He wondered if it could be some odd after effect of the gas.

'I'll, ah, let myself out,' he said, rising.

'The gate guard will be expecting you,' Nis said. He remained seated, his gaze fixed on Dasein with an odd intensity until the door closed between them.

The women in the outer office glanced up as Dasein let himself through the counter gate, went back to their work. A gang of men was loading hand trucks on the ramp when Dasein emerged. He felt their eyes boring into him as he made his way down the dock above them. A sliding door off to the left opened suddenly. Dasein glimpsed a long table with a conveyor belt down its middle, a line of men and women working along it, sorting packages.

Something about the people in that line caught his attention. They were oddly dull-eyed, slow in their actions. Dasein saw their legs beneath the table. The legs appeared to be held in stocks.

The door closed.

Dasein continued out into the sunshine, disturbed by what he had seen. Those workers had appeared ... mentally retarded. He crossed the yard wondering. Problems in Bay 9? Jenny was a competent psychologist. More than compewnt. What did she do here? What did she *really* do?

The gate guard nodded to him, said: 'Come again, Dr Dasein.' The man went into his little house, lifted a telephone, spoke briefly into it.

'*The gate guard will be expecting you,*' Dasein thought.

He crossed to the Inn, ran lightly up the steps and into the lobby. A gray-haired woman sat behind the desk working at an adding machine. She looked up at Dasein.

'Could I get a line out to Berkeley?' he asked.

'All the lines are out,' she said. 'Some trouble with a brush fire.'

'Thanks.'

Dasein went outside, paused on the long porch, scanned the sky. Brush fire? There wasn't a sign or smell of smoke.

Everything about Santaroga could appear so natural, he thought, if it weren't for the underlying sense of strangeness and secrecy that made his neck hairs crawl.

Dasein took a deep breath, went down to his truck, nursed it to life.

This time, he took the turn to 'City Center.' The Avenue of the Giants widened to four lanes presently with homes and business mixed at seeming random on both sides. A park opened on the left – paved paths, central bandstand, lower borders. Beyond the park, a stone church lifted an imposing spire into the sky. The sign on its lawn read: 'Church of All Faiths ... Sermon: "Intensity of God response as a function of anxiety."'

Intensity of God response? Dasein wondered. It was quite the oddest sermon announcement he had ever seen. He made a mental note to try and catch that sermon on Sunday.

The people on the streets began to catch Dasein's attention. Their alertness, the brisk way they moved, was a contrast to the dullness of the line he'd seen in the Co-op. Who were those dull creatures? For that matter, who were these swiftly striding folk on the streets?

There was vitality and a happy freedom in the people he saw, Dasein realized. He wondered if the mood could be infectious. He had never felt more vital himself.

Dasein noted a sign on his right just past the park: A gamboling sheep with the letters 'Blue Ewe' carved in a scrolling script. It was a windowless front faced with blue one, an impersonal façade broken only by wide double doors containing one round glass port each.

So Marden wanted to have lunch with him there. Why? it seemed obvious the patrol captain had taken the briefcase. Was he going to pull the 'go-and-never-darken-my-door' routine he'd used on the hapless salesman in the dining room of the Inn? Or would it be something more subtle designed for 'Jenny's friend from the school'?

At the far end of the town, the street widened once more to open a broad access to a twelve-sided service station. Dasein slowed his truck to admire the structure. It was the largest service station he had ever seen. A canopy structure jutted from each of the twelve sides. Beneath each canopy were three rows of pumps, each row designed to handle four vehicles. Just beyond it, separated from the giant heel of the station, stood a building containing rows of grease racks. Behind the station was a football-field-sized parking area with a large building at the far end labeled 'Garage.'

Dasein drove into the station, stopped at an outside row of pumps, got out to study the layout. He counted twenty grease racks, six cars being serviced. Cars were coming and going all around him. It was another hive. He wondered why none of the datum-data mentioned this complex. The place swarmed with young men in neat blue-gray uniforms.

One of the neat young men came trotting up to Dasein, said: 'What grade, sir?'

'Grade?'

'What octane gas do you want?'

'What do you have?'

'Eighty, ninety and a hundred-plus.'

'Fill it with ninety and check the oil.'

Dasein left the young man to his labors, walked out toward the street to get a better perspective on the station. It covered at least four acres, he estimated. He returned to the truck as the young man emerged from beneath the hood holding the dipstick.

'Your oil's down a bit more than a quart,' the young man said.

'Put in thirty-weight detergent,' Dasein said.

'Excuse me,' he said, 'but I heard this clunker drive in. We carry an aircraft grade of forty weight. I'd recommend you use it. You won't burn quite as much.'

'What's it cost?'

'Same as all the others – thirty-five cents a quart.'

'Okay.' Dasein shook his head. Aircraft grade at that price? Where did *Mr Sam* buy it?

'How do you like Santaroga?' the young man asked, his voice bright with the invitation for a compliment.

'Fine,' Dasein said. 'Beautiful little town. You know, this is the biggest service station I've ever seen. It's a wonder there haven't been any news-paper or magazine articles about it.'

'Old Sam doesn't cotton to publicity,' the attendant said.

'Why's it so damn' big?' Dasein asked.

'Has to be big. It's the only one in the valley.' The young man worked his way around the engine, checking the water in the radiator, the level in the battery. He grinned at Dasein. 'Kinda surprises most outsiders. We find it handy. Some of the farmers have their own pumps and there's service at the airport, but they all get their supplies through Sam.' He closed the hood.

'And where does Old Sam get *his* supplies?'

The attendant leveled a probing stare at Dasein. 'I sure hope you haven't taken on a sideline with one of the big oil companies, sir,' he said. 'If you're thinking of selling to Sam, forget it.'

'I'm just curious,' Dasein said. The attendant's choice of words was puzzling. *Sideline?* Dasein chose to ignore it for the moment, intent on the larger question.

'Sam orders his supplies once a year on open bid,' the attendant said. He topped off the truck's gas tank, returned the hose to its holder. 'This year it's a little company in Oklahoma. They truck it up here in convoys.'

'That so?'

'I wouldn't say it if it weren't so.'

'I wasn't questioning your word,' Dasein said. 'I was registering surprise.'

'Don't see much to get surprised about. Person ought to buy where he gets the most value for his money. That'll be three dollars and three cents.'

Dasein counted out the change, said: 'Is there a pay phone around here?'

'If you're making a local call, there's a phone inside you can use, Dr Dasein,' the attendant said. 'The pay phones are over there beside the rack building, but no sense wasting your time if you're calling outside. Lines are down. There was a fire over on the ridge.'

Dasein went, to full alert, glared at the attendant. 'How'd you know my name?' he demanded.

'Heck, mister, it's all over town. You're Jenny's fellow from the city. You're the reason she sends all the locals packing.'

The grin that went with this statement should have been completely disarming, but it only made Dasein more wary.

'You're going to like it here,' the attendant said. 'Everybody does.' The grin faded somewhat. 'If you'll excuse me, sir. I've other cars to service.'

Dasein found himself staring at a retreating back. *He suspected I might represent an oil company,* Dasein thought, *but he knows my name . . . and he knows about Jenny.* It was a curious disparity and Dasein felt it should tell him something. It could be the simple truth, though.

A long green Chrysler Imperial pulled into the empty space on the other side of the pumps. The driver, a fat man smoking a cigarette in a holder, leaned out, asked: 'Hey! This the road out to 395?'

'Straight ahead,' Dasein said.

'Any gas stations along the way?'

'Not here in the valley,' Dasein said. 'Maybe something outside.' He shrugged. 'I've never been out that way.'

'You damn' natives,' the driver growled. The Imperial shot ahead in a surge of power, swerved out onto the avenue and was gone.

'Up yours,' Dasein muttered. 'Who the hell you calling a native?'

He climbed into his truck, turned back the way he had come. At the fork, he headed up the mountain toward Porterville. The road climbed up, up – winding its way out of the redwoods and into a belt of oaks. He came at last to the turn off where he'd taken his first long look at the valley. He pulled out and parked.

A light smokey haze obscured details, but the Co-op stood out plainly and the slash burner of a sawmill off to the left. The town itself was a patch of color in the trees – tile roofs – and there was a serpentine river line out of the hills straight across from him. Dasein glanced at his wristwatch – five minutes to ten. He debated going out to Porterville and placing his call to Selador there. That would crowd him on the date with Marden, though. He decided to post a letter to Selador, have the 'burned out phone lines' story checked from that end.

Without his briefcase and notes, Dasein felt at a disadvantage. He rummaged in the glove compartment, found a small gas-record note-book and stub of pencil, began setting down his observations for later formal entry in his report.

'The township itself is small,' he wrote, 'but it appears to serve a large market area. There are a great many people about during the day. Note twelve double pumps in service station. Transients?

'Odd alertness about the natives. Sharpness of attitude toward each other and *outsiders*.

'Question local use of Jaspers products. Why won't the cheese travel? What's the reason for the decided local preference? It tastes different than what I bought outside. What about aftertaste? Subjective? What relationship to the beer?

'Investigate use of Jaspers as a label. Adjective?'

Something big was moving through the trees on the hill beyond the Co-op. The movement caught Dasein's attention. He studied it a moment. Too many trees intervened to permit a clear look.

Dasein went around to the camper back, found his binoculars there. He focused them on the movement in the trees. The donut-wheeled bush buggy leaped into view. Marden was driving. It threaded its way through trees and buck brush. The thing appeared to be herding some-thing ... or someone. Dasein scanned ahead for a clearing, found one, waited. Three men in hunting clothes emerged, hands clasped over their heads. Two dogs flanked them, watchful, guarding. The hunters appeared angry, frightened.

The group angled down into a stand of redwoods, was lost to view.

Dasein climbed back into the cab, made a note on what he had seen.

It was all of a pattern, he thought. These were things that could be resolved by natural, logical explanations. A law enforcement officer had picked up three illegal hunters. That was what law enforcement officers were supposed to do. But the incident carried what Dasein was coming to recognize as a Santaroga twist. There was something about it out of phase with the way the rest of the world operated.

He headed his truck back into the valley, determined to question Marden about the captive hunters.

3

The Blue Ewe's interior was a low-key grotto, its walls painted in varying intensities of pastel blue. Rather ordinary banquette booths with tables flanked an open area of tables and chairs. A long bar with a mirror decorated by dancing sheep occupied the back wall.

Marden awaited him in one of the booths. A tall iced drink stood in front of him. The patrol captain appeared relaxed, his red hair neatly combed. The collar tabs of his uniform shirt carried the double bars of a captain. He wore no coat. His eyes followed Dasein's approach with an alert directness.

'Care for a drink?' he asked as Dasein sat down.

'What's that you're having?' Dasein nodded at the iced drink.

'Kind of an orange beer with Jaspers.'

'I'll try it,' Dasein said.

Marden raised a hand toward the bar, called: 'Another ade, Jim.' He returned his attention to Dasein. 'How's your head today?'

'I'm fine,' Dasein said. He found himself feeling edgy, wondering how Marden would bring up the subject of the briefcase. The drink was put in front of him. Dasein welcomed it as a distraction, sipped it. His tongue encountered a sharp orange flavor with the tangy, biting overtone of Jaspers.

'Oh, about your briefcase,' Marden said.

Dasein put down his drink with careful deliberation, met Marden's level, measuring stare. 'Yes?'

'Hope it hasn't inconvenienced you, my taking it.'

'Not too much.'

'I was curious about technique mostly,' Marden said. 'I already knew why you were here, of course.'

'Oh?' Dasein studied Marden carefully for a clue to the man's mood. How could he know about the project?

Marden took a long swallow of the orange beer, wiped his mouth. 'Great stuff, this.'

'Very tasty,' Dasein agreed.

'You've laid out a pretty routine approach, really,' Marden said. He stared at Dasein. 'You know, I've the funny feeling you don't realize how you're being used.'

There was amusement in Marden's narrow face. It touched off abrupt anger in Dasein, and he struggled to hide his reaction. 'What's that supposed to mean?' he asked.

'Would it interest you to know you've been a subject of discussion before our Town Council?' Marden asked.

'Me?'

'You. Several times. We knew they'd get to you sooner or later. Took 'em longer than we expected.' Marden shook his head. 'We circulated a photograph of you to key people – waiters, waitresses, bartenders, clerks . . .'

'Service station attendants,' Dasein said. The pattern was becoming clear. He made no attempt to conceal his anger. How dared they?

Marden was sweet reasonableness. 'They were bound to get wind of the fact that one of our girls was sweet on you,' he said. 'That's an edge, you understand. You use any edge you can find.'

'Who's this *they* you keep referring to?' Dasein demanded.

'Hmmmm,' Marden said.

Dasein took three deep breaths to calm himself. He had never really expected to hide his purpose here indefinitely, but he had hoped for more time, before exposure. What the devil was this crazy patrol captain talking about?

'You pose quite a problem,' Marden said.

'Well, don't try tossing me out of the valley the way you did that stupid salesman last night or those hunters you got today,' Dasein said. 'I'm obeying the law.'

'Toss you out? Wouldn't think of it. Say, what would you like to eat? We did come here for lunch.'

Dasein found himself psychologically off balance, his anger diverted by this sudden change of subject, his whole attitude hampered by feelings of guilt.

'I'm not hungry,' he growled.

'You will be by the time the food gets here. I'll order for both of us.' Marden signaled the waiter, said: 'Two salads Jaspers on the special lunch.'

'I'm not hungry,' Dasein insisted.

'You will be.' Marden smiled. 'Hear a big two-fisted outsider in a Chrysler Imperial called you a native today. Did that tick you off?'

'News certainly gets around here,' Dasein said.

'It certainly does, Doc. Of course, what that fellow's *mistake* says to me is that you're just a natural Santarogan. Jenny didn't make any mistake about *you.*'

'Jenny has nothing to do with this.'

'She has everything to do with it. Let's understand each other, Doc. Larry needs another psychologist and Jenny says you're one of the best. We can make a good place here in the valley for a fellow like you.'

'How big a place?' Dasein asked, his mind on the two investigators who'd died here. 'About six feet long and six feet deep?'

'Why don't you stop running away from yourself, Dasein?'

'I learned early,' Dasein said, 'that a good run was better than a bad stand.'

'Huh?' Marden turned a puzzled frown on him.

'I'm not running away from myself,' Dasein said. 'That's what I mean. But I'm not going to stand still while you order my life for me the way you ordered those salads.'

'You don't like the food you don't have to eat it,' Marden said. 'Am I to understand you won't consider the job Larry's offering?'

Dasein looked down at the table, absorbing the implications of the offer. The smart thing would be to play along, he knew. This was his opportunity to get behind the Santaroga Barrier, to find out what really went on in the valley. But he couldn't escape the thought of the Town Council at its meetings, questioning Jenny about him, no doubt, discussing *preparations* for the Dasein invasion! The anger wouldn't stay down.

'You and Jenny and the rest, you have it all figured out, eh?' he asked. 'Throw the poor sucker a bone. Buy him off with a . . .'

'Slack off, Doc,' Marden said. The voice was level and still with that tone of amusement. 'I'm appealing to your intelligence, not to your greed. Jenny says you're a very sharp fellow. That's what we're counting on.'

Dasein gripped his hands into fists beneath the table, brought himself under control. So they thought he was a poor innocent jerk to be maneuvered by a pretty female and money!

'You think I'm being used,' he said.

'We *know* you're being used.'

'You haven't said by whom.'

'Who's behind it? A group of financiers, Doc, who don't like what Santaroga represents. They want in and they can't get in.'

'The Santaroga Barrier,' Dasein said.

'That's what they call it.'

'Who are *they*?'

'You want names? Maybe we'll give them to you if that suits our purposes.'

'You want to use me, too, is that it?'

'That isn't the way Santaroga runs, Dasein.'

The salads came. Dasein looked down into an inviting array of greens, diced chicken and a creamy golden dressing. A pang of hunger gripped him. He sampled a bite of chicken with the dressing, tasted the now familiar tang of a Jaspers cheese in it. The damned stuff was ubiquitous, he thought. But he had to admit it was delicious. Perhaps there was something in the claim that it wouldn't travel.

'Pretty good, isn't it?' Marden asked.

'Yes, it is.' He studied the patrol captain a moment. 'How does Santaroga run, Captain?'

'Council government with Town Meeting veto, annual elections. Every resident above age eighteen has one vote.'

'Basic Democracy,' Dasein said. 'Very nice when you have a community this size, but ...'

'We had three thousand voters and fifty-eight hundred proxies at the last Town Meeting,' Marden said. 'It can be done if people are interested in governing themselves. We're interested, Dasein. That's how Santaroga's run.'

Dasein gulped the bite of salad in his mouth, put down his fork. Almost nine thousand people over age eighteen in the valley! That was twice as many as he'd estimated. What did they all do? A place like this couldn't exist by taking in each others' wash.

'You want me to marry Jenny, settle here – another voter,' Dasein said. 'Is that it?'

'That's what Jenny appears to want. We tried to discourage her, but ...' He shrugged.

'Discourage her – like interfering with the mails?'

'What?'

Dasein saw Marden's obvious puzzlement, told him about the lost letters.

'Those damn' biddies,' Marden said. 'I guess I'll have to go down there and read them the riot act, But that doesn't change things, really.'

'No?'

'No. You love Jenny, don't you?'

'Of course I love her!'

It was out before Dasein could consider his answer. He heard his own voice, realized how basic this emotion was. Of course he loved Jenny. He'd been sick with longing for her. It was a wonder he'd managed to stay away this long – testimony to wounded masculine pride and the notion he'd been rejected.

Stupid pride!

'Well, fine,' Marden said. 'Finish your lunch, go look around the valley, and tonight you talk things over with Jenny.'

He can't really believe it's that simple, Dasein thought.

'Here,' Marden said. He brought Dasein's briefcase from the seat, put it on the table between them. 'Make your market study. They already know everything you can find out. That's not really how they want to use you.'

'How *do* they want to use me?'

'Find out for yourself, Doc. That's the only way you'll believe it.'

Marden returned to his salad, eating with gusto.

Dasein put down his fork, asked: 'What happened to those hunters you picked up today?'

'We cut off their heads and pickled them,' Marden said. 'What'd you think? They were fined and sent packing. You want to see the court records?'

'What good would that do?'

'You know, Doc,' Marden said, pointing a fork at Dasein, 'you're taking this much the same way Win did – Win Burdeaux.'

Taking what? Dasein wondered. But he asked: '*How* did Win take it?'

'He fought it. That's according to pattern, naturally. He caved in rather quickly, though, as I remember. Win was tired of running even before he got to Santaroga.'

'You amateur psychologists,' Dasein sneered.

'That's right, Doc. We could use another good professional.'

Dasein felt baffled by Marden's unassailable good nature.

'Eat your salad,' Marden said. 'It's good for what ails you.'

Dasein took another bite of the chicken drenched in Jaspers sauce. He had to admit the food was making him feel better. His head felt clear, mind alert. Hunger crept up on one at times, he knew. Food took off the pressures, allowed the mind to function.

Marden finished eating, sat back.

'You'll come around,' he said. 'You're confused now, but if you're as sharp as Jenny says, you'll see the truth for yourself. I think you'll like it here.'

Marden slid out of the booth, stood up.

'I'm just supposed to take your word for it that I'm being used,' Dasein said.

'I'm not running you out of the valley, am I?' Marden asked.

'Are the phone lines still burned out?' Dasein asked.

'Darned if I know,' Marden said. He glanced at his watch. 'Look, I have work to do. Call me after you've talked to Jenny.'

With that, he left.

The waiter came up, started collecting dishes.

Dasein looked up into the man's round face, took in the gray hair, the bent shoulders. 'Why do you live here?' he asked.

'Huh?' The voice was a gravelly baritone.

'Why do you live in Santaroga?' Dasein asked.

'You nuts? This is my home.'

'But why this place rather than San Francisco, say, or Los Angeles?'

'You are nuts! What could I get there I can't get here?' He left with the dishes.

Dasein stared at his briefcase on the table. Market study. On the seat beyond it, he could see the corner of a newspaper. He reached across the table, captured the paper. The masthead read: 'Santaroga Press.'

The left-hand column carried an international news summary whose brevity and language startled Dasein. It was composed of paragraph items, one item per story.

Item: 'Those nuts are still killing each other in Southeast Asia.'

It slowly dawned on Dasein that this was the Vietnam news.

Item: 'The dollar continues to slip on the international money market, although this fact is being played down or suppressed in the national news. The crash is going to make Black Friday look like a picnic.'

Item: 'The Geneva disarmament talks are disarming nobody except the arrogant and the complacent. We recall that the envoys were still talking the last time the bombs began to fall.'

Item: 'The United States Government is still expanding that big hidey hole under the mountain down by Denver. Wonder how many military bigshots, government officials and their families have tickets into there for when the blowup comes?'

Item: 'France thumbed its nose at the U.S. again this week, said to keep U.S. military airplanes off French airbases. Do they know something we don't know?'

Item: 'Automation nipped another .4 percent off the U.S. job market last month. The bites are getting bigger. Does anyone have a guess as to what's going to happen to the excess population?'

Dasein lowered the paper, stared at it without seeing it. The damned thing was subversive! Was it written by a pack of Communists? Was that the secret of Santaroga?

He looked up to see the waiter standing beside him.

'That your newspaper?' the man asked.

'Yes.'

'Oh. I guess Al must've given it to you.' He started to turn away.

'Where does this restaurant buy its food?' Dasein asked.

'From all over the valley, Dr Dasein. Our beef comes from Ray Allison's ranch up at the head of the valley. Our chickens come from Mrs Larson's place out west of here. The vegetables and things we get at the greenhouses.'

'Oh. Thanks.' Dasein returned to the newspaper.

'You want anything else, Dr Dasein? Al said to give you anything you want. It's on his bill.'

'No, thank you.'

The waiter left Dasein to the paper.

Dasein began scanning through it. There were eight pages, only a few advertisements at the beginning, and half the back page turned over to classified. The display ads were rather flat announcements: 'Brenner and Sons have a new consignment of bedroom furniture at reasonable prices. First come, first served. These are all first quality local.'

'Four new freezer lockers (16 cubic feet) are available at the Lewis Market. Call for rates.' The illustration was a smiling fat man holding open the door of a freezer locker.

The classified advertisements were mostly for trades: 'Have thirty yards of hand-loomed wool (54 inches wide) – need a good chain saw. Call Ed Jankey at Number One Mill.'

'That '56 Ford one-ton truck I bought two years ago is still running. Sam Scheler says its worth about $50 or a good heifer. William McCoy, River Junction.'

Dasein began thumbing back through the paper. There was a garden column: 'It's time to turn the toads loose in your garden to keep down the snails.'

And one of the inside pages had a full column of meeting notices. Reading the column, Dasein was caught by a repetitive phrase: 'Jaspers will be served.'

Jaspers will be served, he thought. *Jaspers ... Jaspers ...* It was everywhere. Did they really consume that much of the stuff? He sensed a hidden significance in the word. It was a unifying thing, something peculiarly Santarogan.

Dasein turned back to the newspaper. A reference in a classified ad caught his eye: 'I will trade two years' use of one half of my Jaspers Locker (20 cubic feet in level five of the Old Section) for six months of carpenter work. Leo Merriot, 1018 River Road.'

What the devil was a Jaspers Locker? Whatever it was, ten cubic feet of it for two years was worth six months' carpentry – no small item, perhaps four thousand dollars.

A splash of sunlight brought his head up in time to see a young couple enter the restaurant. The girl was dark haired with deeply set brown eyes and beautiful, winged eyebrows, her young man fair, blue-eyed, a chiseled Norman face. They took the booth behind Dasein. He watched them in the tilted bar mirror. The young man glanced over his shoulder at Dasein, said something to the girl. She smiled.

The waiter served them two cold drinks.

Presently, the girl said: 'After the Jaspers, we sat there and listened to the sunset, a rope and a bird.'

'Sometime you should feel the fur on the water,' her companion said. 'It's the red upness of the wind.'

Dasein came to full alert. That haunting, elusive quality, of almost-meaning – it was schizophrenic or like the product of a psychedelic. He strained to hear more, but they had their heads together, whispering, laughing.

Abruptly, Dasein's memory darted back more than three years to his department's foray into LSD experiments and he recalled that Jenny Sorge, the graduate student from Santaroga, had demonstrated an apparent immunity to the drug. The experiments, abandoned in the glare of sensational LSD publicity, had never confirmed this finding and Jenny had refused to discuss it. The memory of that one report returned to plague Dasein now.

Why should I recall that? he wondered.

The young couple finished whatever they'd ordered, got up and left the restaurant.

Dasein folded the newspaper, started to put it into his briefcase. A hand touched his arm. He looked up to find Marden staring down at him.

'I believe that's my paper,' he said. He took it from Dasein's hand. 'I was halfway to the forks before I remembered it. See you later.' He hurried out, the paper tucked under his arm.

The casual bruskness, the speed with which he'd been relieved of that interesting publication, left Dasein feeling angry. He grabbed up his briefcase, ran for the door, was in time to see Marden pulling away from the curb in a patrol car.

To hell with you! he thought. *I'll get another one.*

The drugstore on the corner had no newspaper racks and the skinny clerk informed him coldly that the local newspaper could be obtained 'by subscription only.' He professed not to know where it was published. The clerk in the hardware store down the street gave him the same answer as did the cashier in the grocery store across from where he'd parked his truck.

Dasein climbed into the cab, opened his briefcase and made notes on as many of the paper's items as he could recall. When his memory ran dry, he started up the truck and began cruising up and down the town's streets looking for the paper's sign or a job printing shop. He found nothing indicating the *Santaroga Press* was printed in the town, but the signs in a used car lot brought him to an abrupt stop across the street. He sat there staring at the signs.

A four-year-old Buick bore the notice in its window: 'This one's an oil burner but a good buy at $100.'

On a year old Rover: 'Cracked block, but you can afford to put a new motor in it at this price: $500.'

On a ten-year-old Chevrolet: 'This car owned and maintained by Jersey Hofstedder. His widow only wants $650 for it.'

His curiosity fully aroused, Dasein got out and crossed to Jersey Hofstedder's Chevrolet, looked in at the dash. The odometer recorded sixty-one thousand miles. The upholstery was leather, exquisitely fitted and tailored. Dasein couldn't see a scratch on the finish and the tires appeared to be almost new.

'You want to test drive it, Dr Dasein?'

It was a woman's voice and Dasein turned to find himself face to face with a handsome gray-haired matron in a floral blouse and blue jeans. She had a big, open face, smooth tanned skin.

'I'm Clara Scheler, Sam's mother,' she said. 'I guess you've heard of my Sam by now.'

'And you know me, of course,' Dasein said, barely concealing his anger. 'I'm Jenny's fellow from the city.'

'Saw you this morning with Jenny,' she said. 'That's one fine girl there, Dr Dasein. Now, if you're interested in Jersey's car, I can tell you about it.'

'Please do,' Dasein said.

'Folks around here know how Jersey was,' she said. 'He was a gol-danged perfectionist, that's what. He had every moving part of this car out on his bench. He balanced and adjusted and fitted until it's just about the sweetest running thing you ever heard. Got disc brakes now, too. You can see what he did to the upholstery.'

'Who was Jersey Hofstedder?' Dasein asked.

'Who ... oh, that's right, you're new. Jersey was Sam's chief mechanic until he died about a month ago. His widow kept the Cord touring car Jersey was so proud of, but she says a body can only drive one car at a time. She asked me to sell the Chevvy. Here, listen to it.'

She slipped behind the wheel, started the motor.

Dasein bent close to the hood. He could barely hear the engine running.

'Got dual ignition,' Clara Scheler said. 'Jersey bragged he could get thirty miles to the gallon with her and I wouldn't be a bit surprised.'

'Neither would I,' Dasein said.

'You want to pay cash or credit?' Clara Scheler asked.

'I ... haven't decided to buy it,' Dasein said.

'You and Jenny couldn't do better than starting out with Jersey's old car,' she said. 'You're going to have to get rid of that clunker you drove up in. I heard it. That one isn't long for this world unless you do something about those bearings.'

'I ... if I decide to buy it, I'll come back with Jenny,' Dasein said. 'Thank you for showing it to me.' He turned, ran back to his truck with a feeling of escape. He had been strongly tempted to buy Jersey Hofstedder's car and found this astonishing. The woman must be a master salesman.

He drove back to the Inn, his mind in a turmoil over the strange personality which Santaroga presented. The bizarre candor of those used car signs, the ads in the *Santaroga Press* – they were all of the same pattern.

Casual honesty, Dasein thought. *That could be brutal at the wrong time.*

He went up to his room, lay down on the bed to try to think things through, make some sense out of the day. Marden's conversation over lunch sounded even more strange in review. A job with Piaget's clinic? The hauntingly obscure conversation of the young couple in the restaurant plagued him. Drugged? And the newspaper which didn't exist – except by subscription. Jersey Hofstedder's car – Dasein was tempted to go back and buy it, drive it out to have it examined by an *outside* mechanic.

A persistent murmuring of voices began to intrude on Dasein's awareness. He got up, looked around the room, but couldn't locate the source. The edge of sky visible through his window was beginning to gray. He walked over, looked out. Clouds were moving in from the northwest.

The murmur of voices continued.

Dasein made a circuit of the room, stopped under a tiny ventilator in the corner above the dresser. The desk chair gave him a step up onto the dresser and he put his ear to the ventilator. Faint but distinct, a familiar television jingle advertising chewing gum came from the opening.

Smiling at himself, Dasein stepped down off the dresser. It was just somebody watching TV. He frowned. This was the first evidence he'd found that they even had TV in the valley. He considered the geography of the area – a basin. To receive TV in here would require an antenna on one of the surrounding hills, amplifiers, a long stretch of cable.

Back onto the dresser he went, ear to the ventilator. He found he could separate the TV show (a daytime serial) from a background conversation between three or four women. One of the women appeared to be instructing another in knitting. Several times he heard the word 'Jaspers' and once, very distinctly, 'A vision, that's all; just a vision.'

Dasein climbed down from the dresser, went into the hall. Between his door and the window at the end with its 'Exit' sign there were no doors. Across the hall, yes, but not on this side. He stepped back into his room, studied the ventilator. It appeared to go straight through the wall, but appearances could be deceiving. It might come from another floor. What was in this whole rear corner of the building, though? Dasein was curious enough now to investigate.

Downstairs he trotted, through the empty lobby, outside and around to the back. There was the oak tree, a rough-barked patriarch, one big branch curving across a second-floor window. That window must be his, Dasein decided. It was in the right place and the branch confirmed it. A low porch roof over a kitchen service area angled outward beneath the window. Dasein swept his gaze toward the corner, counted three other windows in that area where no doors opened into a room. All three windows were blank with drawn shades.

No doors, but three windows, Dasein thought.

He set a slower pace back up to his room. The lobby was still empty, but there were sounds of voices and the switchboard from the office behind the desk.

Once more in his room, Dasein stood at the window, looked down on the porch roof. The slope was shallow, shingles dry. He eased open the window, stepped out onto the roof. By leaning against the wall, he found he could work his way sideways along the roof.

At the first window, he took a firm grip on the ledge, looked for a gap in the curtain. There was no opening, but the sound of the TV was plain when he pressed his ear against the glass. He heard part of a soap commercial and one of the women in the room saying: 'That's enough of this channel, switch to NBC.'

Dasein drew back, crept to the next window. There was a half-inch gap at the bottom of the shade. He almost lost his balance bending to peer in it, caught himself, took a firm grip on the ledge and crouched to put his eyes to the gap.

The swimming wash of cathode gray in a shadowy room met his gaze. He could just make out a bank of eight TV receivers against the wall at his right. Five women sat in comfortable arm chairs at a good viewing distance from the screens. One of the women he noted with some satisfaction was knitting. Another appeared to be making notes on a shorthand pad. Yet another was operating some sort of recorder.

There was a businesslike women-at-work look about the group. They appeared to be past middle age, but when they moved it was with the grace of people who remained active. A blonde woman with a good figure stood up on the right, racked a clip-board across the face of the top right-hand screen, turned off the set. She flopped back into her chair with an exaggerated fatigue, spoke loudly:

'My God! Imagine letting that stuff pour uncensored into your brain day after day after day after ...'

'Save it for the report, Suzie!' That was the woman with the recorder.

Report? Dasein asked himself. *What report?*

He swept his gaze around the room. A row of filing cabinets stood against the far wall. He could just see the edge of a couch directly under the window. A pull-down stairway of the type used for access to attics occupied the corner at the left. There were two typewriters on wheeled stands behind the women.

Dasein decided it was one of the most peculiar rooms he had ever seen. Here were all the fixtures of normalcy, but with that odd Santaroga twist to them. Why the secrecy? Why eight TV receivers? What was in the filing cabinets?

What report?

From time to time, the women made notes, used the recorder, switched channels. All the time, they carried on casual conversations only parts of which were audible to Dasein. None of it made much sense – small talk: 'I decided against putting in pleats; they're so much trouble.' 'If Fred can't pick me up after work, I'll need a ride to town.'

His exposed position on the roof began to bother Dasein. He told himself there was nothing else to be learned from a vigil at the window.

What explanation could he give if he were caught here?

Carefully, he worked his way back to his room, climbed in, closed the window. Again, he checked the hall. There just was no door into that strange room at this level. He walked down to the exit sign, opened a narrow door onto a back landing. An open stairway with doweled railing wound up and down from the landing. Dasein peered over the railing, looked down two stories to a basement level. He looked up. The stairwell was open to a skylight above the third floor.

Moving quietly, he climbed to the next level, opened the landing door onto another hall. He stepped in, looked at the wall above the secret room. Two steps from the landing there was another door labeled 'Linen Supplies.' Dasein tried the handle – locked.

Frustrated, he turned back to the landing. As he stepped from the hall, his right foot caught on a loose edge of carpeting. In one terrifying instant, Dasein saw the railing and the open stairwell flash toward him. His right shoulder hit the rail with a splintering crash, slowing his fall but not stopping it. He clutched at the broken rail with his left hand, felt it bend out, knew then that he was going over – three stories down to the basement. The broken rail in his hand made a screeching sound as it bent outward. It all seemed to be happening in a terrible slow motion. He could see the edges of the descending stairway where they had been painted and the paint had run in little yellow lines. He saw a cobweb beneath one of the risers, a ball of maroon lint caught in it.

The broken rail came free in one last splintering crack and Dasein went over. In this deadly instant, as he saw in his mind his own body splattered on the concrete three floors down, strong hands grabbed his ankles. Not quite realizing what had happened, Dasein swung head down, released the broken rail and saw it turn and twist downward.

He felt himself being pulled upward like a doll, dragged against the broken edges of the railing, turned over onto his back on the landing.

Dasein found himself looking up into the scowling black face of Win Burdeaux.

'That were a mighty close one, sir,' Burdeaux said.

Dasein was gasping so hard he couldn't answer. His right shoulder felt like a giant ball of pain. The fingers of his left hand were bent inward with an agonizing cramp from the strength with which he had gripped the rail.

'I heard someone try the supply closet door,' Burdeaux said. 'I was in there, sir, and I came out. There you were going through the railing, sir. How did that happen?'

'Carpet,' Dasein gasped. 'Tripped.'

Burdeaux bent to examine the area at the landing door. He straightened, said: 'I'll be blessed if that carpet isn't torn there, sir. That's a very dangerous situation.'

Dasein managed to straighten his cramped fingers. He took a deep breath, tried to sit up. Burdeaux helped him. Dasein noted that his shirt was torn. There was a long red scratch on his stomach and chest from being dragged across the broken rail.

'You best take it easy for a few minutes, sir,' Burdeaux said. 'You want for me to call the doctor?'

'No ... no, thank you.'

'It wouldn't take but a minute, sir.'

'I'll ... be all right.'

Dasein looked at the torn carpet, a jagged edge of maroon fabric. He remembered the piece of railing as it had tumbled away into the stairwell and found it strange that he had no recollection of hearing the thing hit the bottom. There was another picture in his mind, equally disturbing: the fatal accidents of the two previous investigators. Dasein pictured himself dead at the bottom of that stairwell, the investigation – all very natural, regrettable, but natural. Such things happened.

But were they accidents?

His shoulder was beginning to throb.

'I'd better get down to my room ... and change,' Dasein said. The pain in his shoulder, intense now, told him he had to have medical attention. He could feel some instinct in himself fighting the idea, though, even as he struggled upright.

Burdeaux reached out to help him to his feet, but Dasein pulled away, knowing the irrationality of the act as he did it.

'Sir, I mean you no harm,' Burdeaux said. There was a gentle chiding in the tone.

Was my fear of him that obvious? Dasein asked himself.

He remembered then the strong hands grabbing his ankles, the life-saving catch at the brink of the stairwell. A feeling of apology overcame Dasein.

'I ... know you don't,' he said. 'You saved my life. There aren't words to thank you for that. I ... was thinking about the broken rail. Shouldn't you see about fixing that?'

Using the wall as a support, Dasein gained his feet. He stood there panting. The shoulder was a massive agony.

'I will lock this door here, sir,' Burdeaux said, his voice gentle, but firm. 'I am going to call the doctor, sir. You are favoring your shoulder. I suspect there is much pain in it. Best the doctor see you, sir.'

Dasein turned away, wondering at his own ambivalence. A doctor had to see the shoulder – yes. But did it have to be Piaget? Hugging the wall for support, Dasein moved down the steps. Piaget ... Piaget ... Piaget. Had Piaget been called on the two fatal *accidents?* Movement sent fiery pain through the shoulder. Piaget ... Piaget ... How could this incident on the stairs have been anything except an accident? Who could have predicted he'd be in that particular place at that particular moment?

There came the sound of the door being closed and latched above him Burdeaux's heavy footsteps sounded on the stairs. The vibration sent more pain through the aching shoulder. Dasein clutched the shoulder, paused on the second floor landing.

'Sir?'

Dasein turned, looked up at the dark Moorish face, noting the expression of concern.

'It will be best, sir,' Burdeaux said, 'if you do not go out on the roof again. You may be subject to falls, sir. A fall from that roof would be very dangerous.'

4

The rain storm hit the valley just before dark. Dasein was settled into a heavy old-fashioned chair in the Piaget house by then, his shoulder immobilized by a firm bandage, Jenny sitting across from him on a hassock, an accusing look on her face.

A gentle, unswerving Burdeaux had driven him to the clinic adjoining Piaget's house and had seen him into the antiseptic atmosphere of a tiled emergency room before leaving.

Dasein didn't know what he'd expected – certainly not the cold professional detachment with which Piaget had set about treating the shoulder.

'Torn ligaments and a slight dislocation,' Piaget had said. 'What were you trying to do – commit suicide?'

Dasein winced as a bandage was drawn tightly into place. 'Where's Jenny?'

'Helping with dinner. We'll tell her about your damn foolishness after we have you repaired.' Piaget secured the end of a bandage. 'You haven't told me what you were up to.'

'I was snooping!' Dasein growled.

'Were you now?' He adjusted a sling around Dasein's neck, set it to immobilize the arm. 'There, that should hold you for awhile. Don't move that arm any more than you have to. I guess I don't have to tell you that. Leave your coat off. There's a covered walkway to the house – right through that door. Go on in and I'll send Jenny to entertain you until dinner.'

The covered walkway had glass sides and was lined with potted geraniums. The storm struck as Dasein was making his way between the pots and he paused a moment to look out at a new-mown lawn, rows of standard roses, a lowering blue-gray sky. The wind whipped rain down a street beyond the roses, bending the branches of a line of white birches. There were people hurrying along the sidewalk beside the birches. The damp hems of their coats lashed their legs in each gust.

Dasein felt a bit light-headed, chilled in spite of the walkway's protection. *What am I doing here?* he asked himself. He swallowed in a dry throat, hurried on to the door of the house and into a paneled living room full of big furniture. There was the faint smell of a coal fire in the room. His shoulder was a place of dull throbbing. He made his way across the room, past a sideboard full of massive cut-glass pieces, lowered himself carefully into a deep, soft chair of corded green upholstery.

The lack of movement and its temporary easing of pain filled him with a momentary sense of relief. Then the shoulder began throbbing again.

A door slammed – hurrying feet.

Jenny burst upon him through a wide archway to the left. Her face was flushed. A damp wisp of hair strayed at her temple. She was wearing a simple orange dress, a shocking splash of color in the dull tones of the big room. With an odd sense of detachment, Dasein remembered telling her once that orange was his favorite color. The memory filled him with an unexplainable wariness.

'Gil, for heavens sake!' she said, stopping in front of him, hands on hips.

Dasein swallowed.

Jenny looked at his open shirt, the edge of bandages, the sling. Abruptly, she dropped to her knees, put her head in his lap, clutching at him, and he saw she was crying – silent tears that spread shiny dampness across her cheeks.

'Hey!' Dasein said. 'Jenny ...' The tears, the lack of contortion in her face – he found it embarrassing. She filled him with a sense of guilt, as though he'd betrayed her in some way. The feeling overrode his pain and fatigue.

Jenny took his left hand, pressed her cheek against it. 'Gil,' she whispered. 'Let's get married – right away.'

Why not? he wondered. But the guilt remained ... and the unanswered questions. Was Jenny bait in a trap that had been set for him? Would she even know it if she were? Did the worm know it was impaled on the hook to lure the trout?

A soft cough sounded from the archway to Dasein's left.

Jenny pulled back, but still held his hand.

Dasein looked up to find Piaget there. The man had changed to a blue smoking jacket that made him look even more the mandarin. The big head was tipped slightly to the right with an air of amusement, but the dark eyes stared out speculatively.

Behind Piaget, amber wall sconces had been turned on in a dining room. Dasein could see a large oval table set with three places on white linen, the gleam of silver and crystal.

'Jenny?' Piaget said.

She sighed, released Dasein's hand, retreated to the green ottoman, sat down with her legs curled under her.

Dasein grew aware of the smell of roasting meat savory with garlic. It made him acutely aware of hunger. In the heightening of his senses, he detected an enticing tang, recognized the *Jaspers* odor.

'I think we should discuss your susceptibility to accidents,' Piaget said. 'Do you mind, Gilbert?'

'By all means,' Dasein said. He sat watching the doctor carefully. There was an edge of caution in Piaget's voice, a hesitancy that went beyond a host's reluctance to engage in an embarrassing conversation.

'Have you had many painful accidents?' Piaget asked. He strode across the room as he spoke, crossing to a quilted leather chair behind Jenny. When he sat, he was looking across Jenny's shoulder at Dasein and Dasein had the abrupt suspicion that this position had been chosen with care. It aligned Piaget and Jenny against him.

'Well?' Piaget asked.

'Why don't we trade answers?' Dasein countered. 'You answer a question for me and I answer a question for you.'

'Oh?' Piaget's face relaxed into the bemused smile of a private joke.

Jenny looked worried.

'What's your question?' Piaget asked.

'A bargain's a bargain,' Dasein said. 'First, an answer. You ask if I've been involved in many accidents. No, I have not. That is, not before coming here. I can recall one other – a fall from an apple tree when I was eight.'

'So,' Piaget said. 'Now, you have a question for me.'

Jenny frowned, looked away.

Dasein felt a sudden dryness in his throat, found his voice rasping when he spoke: 'Tell me, Doctor – how did the two investigators die – the ones who came before me?'

Jenny's head snapped around. 'Gil!' There was outrage in her voice.

'Easy, Jenny,' Piaget said. A nerve began ticking on the broad plane of his left cheek. 'You're on the wrong track, young man,' he growled. 'We're not savages here. There's no need. If we want someone to leave, he leaves.'

'And you don't want me to leave?'

'Jenny doesn't want you to leave. And that's two questions from you. You owe me an answer.'

Dasein nodded. He stared across Jenny at Piaget, reluctant to look at her.

'Do you love Jenny?' Piaget asked.

Dasein swallowed, lowered his gaze to meet a pleading stare in Jenny's eyes. Piaget knew the answer to that question! Why did he ask it now?

'You know I do,' Dasein said.

Jenny smiled, but two bright tears beaded her eyelashes.

'Then why did you wait a year to come up here and tell her so?' Piaget asked. There was an angry, accusatory bite in his voice that made Dasein stiffen.

Jenny turned, stared at her uncle. Her shoulders trembled.

'Because I'm a damn' stubborn fool,' Dasein said. 'I don't want the woman I love to tell me where I have to live.'

'So you don't like our valley,' Piaget said. 'Maybe we can change your opinion about that. You willing to let us try?'

No! Dasein thought. *I'm not willing!* But he knew this answer, visceral and instinctive, would come out petulant, childish. 'Do your damnedest,' he muttered.

And Dasein wondered at himself. What were his instincts telling him? What was wrong with this valley that put him on guard at every turn?

'Dinner's ready.'

It was a woman's voice from the archway.

Dasein turned to find a gaunt gray female in a gray dress standing there. She was a Grant Woods early American come to life, long-nosed, wary of eye, disapproval in every line of her face.

'Thank you, Sarah,' Piaget said. 'This is Dr Dasein, Jenny's young man.'

Her eyes weighed Dasein, found him wanting. 'The food's getting cold,' she said.

Piaget lifted himself out of his chair. 'Sarah's my cousin,' he said. 'She comes from the old Yankee side of the family and absolutely refuses to dine with us if we eat at a fashionable hour.'

'Damn' foolishness, the hours you keep,' she muttered. 'My father was always in bed by this time.'

'And up at dawn,' Piaget said.

'Don't you try to make fun of me, Larry Piaget,' she said. She turned away. 'Come to table. I'll bring the roast.'

Jenny crossed to Dasein, helped him to his feet. She leaned close, kissed his cheek, whispered: 'She really likes you. She told me so in the kitchen.'

'What're you two whispering?' Piaget demanded. 'I was telling Gil what Sarah said about him.'

'Oh, what'd Sarah say?'

'She said: "Larry isn't going to browbeat that young man. He has eyes like Grandpa Sather."'

Piaget turned to study Dasein. 'By George, he has. I hadn't noticed.' He turned away with an abrupt cutting-off motion, led the way into the dining room. 'Come along, or Sarah will change her good opinion. We can't have that.'

To Dasein, it was one of the strangest dinners of his life. There was the pain of his injured shoulder, a steady throb that impelled him to an alertness that made every word and motion stand out in sharp relief. There was Jenny – she had never looked more warmly feminine and desirable. There was Piaget, who declared a conversational truce for the meal and plied Dasein with questions about his courses at the University, the professors, fellow students, his ambitions. There was Sarah, hovering with the food – a muttering specter who had soft looks only for Jenny.

With Sarah, it's what Jenny wants, Jenny gets, Dasein thought.

Finally, there was the food: a rib roast cooked to a medium rare perfection, the Jaspers sauce over peas and potato pancakes, the local beer with its palate-cleansing tang, and fresh peaches with honey for dessert.

Beer with dinner struck Dasein as strange at first until he experienced the play of tastes, a subtle mingling of flavor esters that made individual savors stand out on his tongue even as they were combining to produce entirely new sensations. It was a crossing of senses, he realized – smells tasted, colors amplifying the aromas.

At the first serving of beer, Piaget had tasted it, nodded. 'Fresh,' he said.

'Within the hour just like you ordered,' Sarah snapped. And she'd cast a strange probing stare at Dasein.

It was shortly after 9:30 when Dasein left.

'I had your truck brought around,' Piaget said. 'Think you can drive it, or shall I have Jenny take you back to the hotel?'

'I'll be all right,' Dasein said.

'Don't take those pain pills I gave you until you're safely in your room,' Piaget said. 'Don't want you running off the road.'

They stood on the broad verandah at the front of the house then, street lights casting wet shadows of the birches onto the lawn. The rain had stopped, but there was a chilled feeling of dampness in the night air.

Jenny had thrown his coat around his shoulders. She stood beside him, a worried frown on her face. 'Are you *sure* you'll be all right?'

'You ought to know I can steer with one hand,' he said. He grinned at her.

'Sometimes I think you're a terrible man,' she said. 'I don't know why I put up with you.'

'It's chemistry,' he said.

Piaget cleared his throat. 'Tell me, Gilbert,' he said. 'What *were* you doing on the hotel roof?'

Dasein felt an abrupt pang of fear, a sense of incongruity in the timing of that question.

What the hell! he thought. *Let's see what a straight answer does.*

'I was trying to find out why you're so all-fired secret about your TV,' he said.

'Secret?' Piaget shook his head. 'That's just a pet project of mine. They're analyzing the silly infantilisms of TV, producing data for a book I have in mind.'

'Then why so secret?' Dasein felt Jenny clutching his arm, ignored the fear he sensed in her reaction.

'It's consideration for the sensibilities of others, not secrecy,' Piaget said. 'Most TV drives our people wild. We monitor the news, of course, but even that is mostly pap, sugar-coated and spoon-fed.'

There was a ring of partial truth in Piaget's explanation, Dasein felt, but he wondered what was being left out. What else were those women *researching* in that room.

'I see,' Dasein said.

'You owe me an answer now,' Piaget said.

'Fire away.'

'Another time,' Piaget said. 'I'll leave you two to say good night, now.' He went inside, closed the door.

Presently, Dasein was headed down the street in his truck, the tingling sensation of Jenny's kiss still warm on his lips.

He arrived at the wye intersection to the hotel shortly before ten, hesitated, then bore to the right on the road out of the valley to Porterville. There was an odd feeling of self-preservation in the decision, but he told himself it was just because he wanted to drive for awhile . . . and think.

What is happening to me? he wondered. His mind felt abnormally clear, but he was enveloped by such a feeling of disquiet that his stomach was knotted with it. There was an odd broadening to his sense of being. It made him realize that he had forced himself inward with his concentration on psychology, that he had narrowed his world. Something was pushing at his self-imposed barriers now, and he sensed things lurking *beyond*, things which he feared to confront.

Why am I here? he asked himself.

He could trace a chain of cause and effect back to the university, to Jenny ... but again he felt the interference of things outside this chain and he feared these things.

The night sped past his truck and he realized he was fleeing up the mountain, trying to escape the valley.

He thought of Jenny as she'd appeared this night: an elf in orange dress and orange shoes, lovely Jenny dressed to please him, her sincerity and love all transparent on her face.

Bits and pieces of the dinner conversation began coming back to him. *Jaspers.* 'This is the old Jaspers – deep.' That had been Jenny tasting the sauce. 'Almost time to put down a new section of Jaspers in number five.' That had been Sarah bringing in the dessert. And Piaget: 'I'll talk to the boys about it tomorrow.'

Now, recalling this, Dasein realized there'd been a faint, familiar tang even in the honey. He wondered then about the way *Jaspers* figured so often in their conversations. They never strayed far from it, seemed to find nothing unusual in the constancy of it. They talked Jaspers ... and at the oddest moments.

He was at the pass out of the valley now, trembling with an ambivalent feeling of escape ... and of loss.

There'd been a fire across the slopes through which Dasein was now descending. He smelled damp ashes on the wind that whipped through the ventilators, recalled the reported trouble with telephone lines. Clouds had begun to clear away here outside the valley. Dead trees stood out on the burned slopes like Chinese characters brushstroked on the moon-lighted hills

Abruptly, his mind clamped on a logical reason for coming out of the valley: *The telephone! I have to call Selador and confer. There are no lines out of the valley, but I can call from Porterville ... before I go back.*

He drove steadily then, his being suspended, static, held in a curious lack of emotion – nothing on his mind. Even the pain of his shoulder receded.

Porterville loomed out of the night, the highway becoming a wide main street with a blue and white 'Bus Depot' sign on the left over an all-night cafe – two big truck-trailer rigs there beside a little convertible and a green and white Sheriff's car. An orange glow across the street was 'Frenchy's Mother Lode Saloon.' The cars at the curb conveyed a general decrepit look, depressingly alike in their battered oldness.

Dasein drove past, found a lonely phone booth beneath a street light at the corner of a darkened Shell station. He turned in, stopped beside the booth. The truck's engine was hot and tried to go on running with a clunking, jerking motion after he shut off the ignition. He stopped the motion with the clutch, sat for a moment looking at the booth. Presently, he got out. The truck creaked with distress at his movement.

The Sheriff's car drove past, its headlights casting enormous shadows on a white fence behind the phone booth.

Dasein sighed, went into the booth. He felt strangely reluctant to make the call, had to force himself.

Presently, Selador's precise accent came on the line: 'Gilbert? Is that you, Gilbert? Have they repaired the deuced telephone lines?'

'I'm calling from Porterville, just outside the valley.'

'Is something wrong, Gilbert?'

Dasein swallowed. Even at long distance, Selador managed to remain perceptive. *Something wrong?* Dasein delivered a brief recital of his accidents.

After a prolonged silence, Selador said: 'That's very odd, Gilbert, but I fail to see how you can construe these incidents as other than accidents. With the gas, for example, they put out a great effort to save you. And your tumble – how could anyone possibly have known you'd be the one to pass that way?'

'I just wanted you to know about them,' Dasein said. 'Piaget thinks I'm accident prone.'

'Piaget? Oh, yes – the local doctor. Well, Gilbert, one should always discount pronouncements that go outside one's specialty. I doubt Piaget's qualified to diagnose an accident prone, even if there were such a syndrome – which I sincerely disbelieve.' Selador cleared his throat. 'You don't seriously think these people have malignant designs against you?'

Selador's sane, level tones had a soothing effect on Dasein. He was right, of course. Here, removed from the valley, the events of the past twenty-four hours took on a different shade of meaning.

'Of course not,' Dasein said.

'Good! You've always struck me as a very level head, Gilbert. Let me caution you now that you may have intruded upon a situation where people are being genuinely careless. Under those circumstances, the Inn might be an extremely dangerous place, and you should leave.'

'To go where?' Dasein asked.

'There must be other accommodations.'

Carelessness at the Inn? Dasein wondered. Then why were no others injured? A dangerous place, yes – but only because it was part of the valley. He felt a strong reluctance to agree with Selador. It was as though his own reluctance were based on data unavailable to Selador.

Abruptly, Dasein saw how the loose carpet could have been aimed at him He thought of a baited trap. The bait? That was the TV room, of course – an odd place certain to arouse his curiosity. Around the bait would be several traps, all avenues covered. He wondered what trap he had missed on the roof. As he thought about it, Dasein recalled how the stair rail had broken.

'Are you there, Gilbert?'

Selador's voice sounded thin and distant.

'Yes – I'm here.'

Dasein nodded to himself. It was so beautifully simple. It answered all the vague uneasiness that had plagued him about the accidents. So simple – like a child's drawing on a steamy window: no excess lines or unnecessary data. Bait and traps.

Even as he saw it, Dasein realized Selador wouldn't accept this solution. It smacked of paranoia. If the theory were wrong, it would be paranoia. It implied organization, the involvement of many people, many officials.

'Is there something else you wanted, Gilbert? We're paying for some rather costly silence.'

Dasein came to himself suddenly. 'Yes, sir. You recall Piaget's article about Santarogans and allergens?'

'Quite.' Selador cleared his throat.

'I want you to query the public health officials and the department of agriculture. Find out if they have chemical analyses of the valley's farm products – including the cheese.'

'Public health ... agriculture ... cheese,' Selador said. Dasein could almost see him making notes. 'Anything more?'

'Perhaps. Could you get to the attorneys for the real estate board and the chain store people? I'm sure they must've explored possibilities of legal recourse on the leased land they ...'

'What're you driving at, Gilbert?'

'The chain stores leased the property and built their expensive installations before discovering the Santarogans wouldn't trade with them. Is this a pattern? Do Santaroga realtors trap unwary outsiders?'

'Conspiracy to defraud,' Selador said. 'I see. I'm rather inclined to believe, Gilbert, that this avenue already has been exhausted.'

Hearing him, Dasein thought Selador's usual acuteness had been blunted. Perhaps he was tired.

'Most likely,' Dasein said. 'It wouldn't hurt, though, for me to see what the legal eagles were thinking. I might get some new clues on the scene.'

'Very well. And, Gilbert, when are you going to send me copies of your notes?'

'I'll mail some carbons tonight from Porterville.'

'Tomorrow will be all right. It's getting late and ...'

'No, sir. I don't trust the Santaroga post office.'

'Why?'

Dasein recounted Jenny's anger at the women in the post office. Selador chuckled.

'They sound like a veritable band of harpies,' Selador said. 'Aren't there laws against tampering with the mails? But, of course, determined people and all that. I hope you found Miss Sorge in good health.'

'As beautiful as ever,' Dasein said, keeping his voice light. He wondered suddenly about Selador. *Miss* Sorge. No hesitation, no question at all about her being unmarried.

'We're exploring the source of their petrol supply,' Selador said. 'Nothing on that yet. Take care of yourself, Gilbert. I shouldn't want anything to happen to you.'

'That makes two of us,' Dasein said.

'Good-bye, then,' Selador said. His voice sounded hesitant. A click signaled the breaking of the connection.

Dasein hung up, turned at a sound behind him A Sheriff's car was pulling into the station. It stopped facing the booth. A spotlight flashed in Dasein's eyes. He heard a door open, footsteps.

'Turn that damn' light out of my eyes!' Dasein said.

The light was lowered. He discerned a bulky shape in uniform standing outside the booth, the gleam of a badge.

'Anything wrong?' It was an oddly squeaky voice to come from that bulk.

Dasein stepped out of the booth, still angry at the way they had flashed the light in his eyes. 'Should there be?'

'You damn' Santarogans,' the deputy muttered. 'Must be important for one of you to come over to make a phone call.'

Dasein started to protest he wasn't a Santarogan, remained silent as his mind was caught by a flow of questions. What made outsiders assume he was a Santarogan? The fat man in the Chrysler and now this deputy. Dasein recalled Marden's words. What was the identifying tag?

'If you're through, you best be getting home,' the deputy said. 'Can't park here all night.'

Dasein saw an abrupt mental image of his gas gauge – it was faulty and registered almost empty even when the tank was full. Would they believe he had to wait for the station to open in the morning? What if they roused an attendant and found his tank took only a few gallons?

Why am I debating petty deceptions? Dasein wondered.

It occurred to him that he was reluctant to return to Santaroga. Why? Was living in the valley turning him into a Santarogan?

'That's a real artistic bandage you're wearing,' the deputy said. 'Been in an accident?'

'Nothing important,' Dasein said. 'Strained some ligaments.'

'Good night, then,' the deputy said. 'Take it easy on that road.' He returned to his car, said something in a low voice to his companion. They chuckled. The car pulled slowly out of the station.

They mistook me for a Santarogan, Dasein thought, and he considered the reactions which had accompanied that mistake. They'd resented his presence here, but with an odd kind of diffidence ... as though they were afraid of him. They hadn't hesitated to leave him alone here, though – no question of his being a criminal.

Disturbed by the incident and unable to explain his disturbance, Dasein climbed back into his truck, headed for Santaroga.

Why had they assumed he was a Santarogan? The question kept gnawing at him.

A bump in the road made him acutely conscious of his shoulder. The pain had settled into a dull ache. His mind felt clear and alert, though, poised on a knife-edge peak of observation. He began to wonder about this sensation as he drove.

The road flowed beneath him, climbing ... climbing ...

As though part of the road's pattern, disconnected images began flowing through his mind. They came with words and phrases, madly jumbled, no thought of order. Meaning eluded him. Feeling suddenly light-headed, he tried to grapple with the sensations –

Cave ... limping man ... fire ...

What cave? he wondered. *Where have I seen a limping man? What fire? Is it the fire that destroyed the telephone lines?*

He had the sudden impression that he was the limping man. Fire and cave eluded him.

Dasein felt he wasn't reasoning, but was pawing through old thoughts. Images – labels summoned objects before his mind's eye: *Car.* He saw Jersey Hofstedder's polished old machine. *Fence.* He saw the chain-link fence around the Co-op. *Shadows.* He saw bodiless shadows.

What's happening to me?

He felt trembly with hunger ... sweaty. Perspiration rolled off his forehead and cheeks. He tasted it on his lips. Dasein opened his window, allowed the cold wind to whip around him

At the turn-off where he'd stopped the first evening, Dasein pulled onto the gravel, shut off engine and lights. The clouds were gone and an oblate silver moon rode low on the horizon. He stared down into the valley – widely spaced lights, blue-green from the greenhouses far to his left, the bustle and stir from the Co-op off to the right.

Up here, Dasein felt removed from all that, isolated. The darkness enclosed him.

Cave? he wondered.

Jaspers?

It was difficult to think with his body behaving in this oddly erratic fashion. His shoulder throbbed. There was a nodule of aching in his left lung. He was aware of a tendon in his left ankle – not pain, but knowledge of a weakness there. He could trace in his mind the fiery line of scratches down his chest where Burdeaux had dragged him across the broken bannisters.

A picture of the map on George Nis's wall flashed into his mind, was gone.

He felt *possessed*. Something had taken over his body. It was an ancient, frightening thought. Mad. He gripped the steering wheel, imagined that it writhed, jerked his hands away.

His throat was dry.

Dasein took his own pulse, staring at the luminous dial on his wrist-watch. The second hand jumped oddly. It was either that or his pulse was rapid and erratic. Something was distorting his time sense.

Have I been poisoned? he wondered. *Was there something in Piaget's dinner? Ptomaine?*

The black bowl of the valley was a forbidding hand that could reach up and grab him.

Jaspers, he thought. *Jaspers.*

What did it really mean?

He sensed a oneness, a collective solitude focusing on the cooperative. He imagined something lurking outside there in the darkness, hovering at the edge of awareness.

Dasein put a hand to the seat. His fingers groped across the briefcase with its notes and documents, all the things that said he was a scientist. He tried to cling to this idea.

I'm a scientist. This uneasiness is what Aunt Nora would've called 'the vapors.'

What the scientist had to do was very clear in Dasein's mind. He had to insinuate himself into the Santaroga world, find his place in their oneness, live their life for a time, think as they thought. It was the one sure way to plumb the valley's mystery. There was a Santaroga state of mind. He had to put it on like a suit of clothes, fit it to his understanding.

This thought brought the sensation that something intruded on his inner awareness. He felt that an ancient being had risen there and examined him It filled his whole subconscious, peering, urgent, restless – sensed only by reflection, indistinct, blurred . . . but real. It moved within him, something heavy and blundering.

The sensation passed.

When it was gone, there was an emptiness in Dasein such that it explained the whole concept of being empty. He felt himself to be a floating chip lost on an endless sea, fearful of every current and eddy that moved him.

He knew he was projecting. He was afraid to go back down into the valley, afraid to run away.

Jaspers.

There was another thing he had to do, Dasein knew. Again, he pictured the map on George Nis's wall, the black tributary lines, the ganglia pattern.

Cave.

He shivered, stared toward the distant bustling that was the Co-op. What lay hidden there behind the chain fence, the guards, the dogs and the prowling bush buggy?

There could be a way to find out.

Dasein stepped from the truck, locked the cab. The only weapon he could find in the camper was a rusty hunting knife with a mildewed sheath. He slipped the sheath onto his belt, working clumsily one-handed, feeling more than a little foolish, but aware also of that inner sense of danger. There was a penlight, too. He pocketed it.

The movement set his shoulder throbbing. Dasein ignored the pain, telling himself it would be too easy to find a physical excuse for not doing what he knew he had to do.

A narrow game trail led down the hill from the upper end of the guard fence. Dasein picked his way down the trail, marking the path in the moonlight until it descended into brush-choked shadows.

Branches pulled at his clothing. He bulled his way through, guiding himself by the moon and the bustle of the Co-op, which was visible whenever he topped a ridge. Whatever the Santaroga mystery, Dasein knew, the answer lay there behind that chain fence.

Once, he stumbled and slid down a hillside into a dry creekbed. Following the creekbed brought him out onto a tiny alluvial plain that opened onto a panoramic view of the Co-op and the valley beyond bathed in moonlight. Twice, he startled deer, which went bounding and leaping off into the night. There were frequent scampering sounds in the brush as small creatures fled his blundering approach.

Holding to a narrow game trail, he came at last to a rock ledge about a thousand yards from the Co-op's fence and five hundred feet above it. Dasein sat down on a rock to catch his breath and, in the sudden silence, heard a powerful engine laboring somewhere to his right. A light swept the sky. He crept back into a low copse of buck brush, crouched there.

The sound of the engine grew louder, louder. A set of giant wheels climbed out against the stars to occupy a hill above him. From some-where above the wheels, a light flashed on, swept across the brush, probing, pausing, darting back and forth.

Dasein recognized the bush buggy, a monster vehicle some two hundred feet away. He felt exposed, naked with only a shield of thin brush between him and that nightmare creation. The light washed over the leaves above him.

Here it comes, he thought. *It'll come right down the hill onto me.*

The sound of the engine had grown muter while the bush buggy paused to search its surroundings. It was so near Dasein heard a dog whining on it, remembered the dogs that had accompanied Marden.

The dogs will smell me, he thought.

He tried to draw himself into as tight a ball as possible.

The engine sounds grew suddenly louder.

Dasein moved a branch, ventured a look through the brush, preparing himself to leap up and run. But the big machine turned up the ridge upon which it had emerged. It passed across the hills above Dasein, the noise and light receding.

When it was gone, he took a moment to calm himself, crept out to the lip of the rock ledge. Dasein saw then why the buggy had not come down upon him. This was a dead end, no trail down from here. He would have to climb up where the machine had emerged upon the hill, backtrack on it to find a way down.

He started to turn away, paused at sight of a black gash in the floor of the ledge off to his right. Dasein crossed to the break in the rock, looked down into darkness. The break in the rock wasn't more than three feet across, opening out to the face of the ledge, narrowing to a point about twenty feet to his right. Dasein knelt, risked a brief flash of his penlight. The light revealed a smooth-walled rock chimney leading down to another ledge. What was more important, he could see a game trail down there in the moonlight.

Dasein slid his feet over the edge of the chimney, sat down there with his legs hanging into the darkness, considered the problem. The injured shoulder made him hesitate. Without that, he'd have gone right over, worked his way down, back against one side, feet against the other. Dangerous, yes – but a thing he had done many times in mountains rougher than these. The other ledge was no more than fifty feet down there.

He looked around him, wondering if he dared risk it. In this instant, his mind offered up the datum that he had forgotten to mail off the carbons of his notes to Selador. It was like a cold dash of water in the face. He felt that his own body had betrayed him, that he had conspired against himself.

How could I have forgotten? he wondered. There was anger in the thought, and fear. Perspiration bathed his palms. He glanced at the luminous dial of his wristwatch: almost midnight. There came over him then the almost overpowering desire to retrace his way back to the road and the camper.

He was suddenly more afraid of what his own body might do to him than he was of any danger which could come out of the night or of the climb down this simple rock chimney. Dasein sat there trembling, recalling his feeling that he was *possessed.*

This was madness!

He shook his head angrily.

There was no turning back; he had to go down there, find a way into that Co-op, expose its secrets. While the strength of anger was upon him, Dasein probed across the chimney with his feet, found the other side, slid off his perch and began working his way down. At each movement of his back, his shoulder stabbed him with pain. He gritted his teeth, felt his way down through the darkness. Rock scraped across his back. Once, his right foot slipped and he strained with the left for purchase.

The floor of the chimney when he found it was almost an anticlimax, a slope of loose rock which slid from beneath his feet and cascaded him out onto the game trail he had seen from above.

Dasein lay there a moment regaining his breath, allowing the fire in his shoulder to subside to a dull throb.

Presently, he struggled to his feet, marked where the moonlighted trail led down to his right. He picked his way down through a screen of brush onto a sloping meadow dotted with the dark shapes of oaks. Moonlight gleamed on the fence beyond the meadow. There it was, the boundary of the Co-op. He wondered if he could climb that fence one-handed. It would be galling to come this far only to be stopped by a fence.

As he stood there examining the meadow and the fence, a deep humming sound impressed itself on him. It came from off to his right. He searched for the source of the sound, eyes hunting through shadows. Was that a gleam of metal down there, something round emerging from the meadow? He crouched low in the dry grass. There was a heavy odor of mushrooms all around. He recognized it abruptly – the smell of *Jaspers*. It came over Dasein that he was staring at a ventilator.

Ventilator!

He lifted himself to his feet, trotted across the meadow toward the sound. There was no mistaking that sound nor the wash of Jaspers-saturated air that enveloped him. There was a big fan at work down there under the earth.

Dasein stopped beside the ventilator outlet. It was about four feet across, stood approximately the same distance above the meadow topped by a cone-shaped rain hood. He was about to examine the fastenings of the hood when he heard a snuffling sound and crackling of brush from the direction of the fence. He ducked behind the ventilator as two uniformed guards emerged from the brush beyond the fence, dogs sniffing hungrily ahead of them, straining at their leashes.

If they get my scent, Dasein thought.

He crouched behind the ventilator breathing softly through his mouth. There was a tickling sensation on the back of his tongue. He wanted to cough, clear his throat, fought down the impulse. Dogs and guards had stopped directly below him.

A glaring light washed across the ventilator, swept the ground on both sides. One of the dogs whined eagerly. There was a rattling sound, a sharp command from one of the guards.

Dasein held his breath.

Again, something rattled. The sounds of guards and dogs moved along the fence. Dasein ventured a quick glance around the ventilator. They were flashing a light along the base of the fence, looking for tracks. One of the guards laughed. Dasein felt the touch of a light breeze on his cheeks, realized he was downwind from the dogs, allowed himself to relax slightly. The rattling sound came once more. Dasein saw it was one of the guards dragging a stick along the fence.

The casual mood of the guards caused him to relax even more. He took a deep breath. They were going over a low hill now, down the other side. The night swallowed them.

Dasein waited until he no longer could hear them before straightening. His left knee was trembling and it took a moment for this to subside.

Guards, dogs, that big bush buggy – all spoke of something important here. Dasein nodded to himself, began examining the ventilator. There was a heavy screen beneath the rain cap. He ventured a flash of the penlight, saw hood and screen were a welded unit held to the ventilator by heavy sheet metal screws.

Dasein brought out his hunting knife, tried one of the screws. Metal screeched against metal as he turned it. He stopped, listened. His ears detected only the sounds of the night. There was an owl somewhere in the brush above him. Its mournful call floated across the night. Dasein returned to the screw. It came out in his hand and he pocketed it, moved on to the next one. There were four in all.

When the last screw was out, he tried the screen. It and the hood lifted with a rasping metallic protest. He flashed his penlight inside, saw smooth metal walls going straight down about fifteen feet before curving back toward the hills.

Dasein returned the screen and hood to their normal position, went searching under the oaks until he found a fallen branch about six feet long. He used this to prop the hood and screen; peered once more down the ventilator with the penlight.

It was going to take two hands getting in there, he realized. No other way. Gritting his teeth, he removed the sling, stuffed it into a pocket. Even without the sling, he knew the arm wasn't going to be much use ... except perhaps in an emergency. He felt the rim of the ventilator – sharp, rough metal. *The sling,* he thought. He brought it out, rolled it into a pad for his hands. Using this pad, he hauled himself across the lip of the ventilator. The pad slipped and he felt metal bite his stomach. He grabbed the edge, swung himself inward. Metal ripped buttons off his shirt. He heard them clatter somewhere below. His good hand found a purchase over a bit of the sling; he dropped down, pain screaming in his injured shoulder, swung his feet to the opposite side, turned and braced himself. Feet and back held. He slipped the hunting knife out of its sheath, reached up, knocked the limb prop aside.

Screen and hood came down with a clang he felt must have been heard for a mile. He waited, listening.

Silence.

Slowly, he began inching his way down.

Presently, his feet encountered the curve. He straightened, used the penlight. The ventilator slanted back under the hill at a gentle slope of about twenty degrees. There was something soft under his left foot. The light revealed the sling. He picked it up. The front of his shirt was sticking, to his skin. He turned the light on it, saw red wetness, a section of skin scraped off by the lip of the ventilator. The pain was as a minor scratch compared to his shoulder.

I'm a mess, he thought. *What the hell am I doing here?*

The answer was there in his mind, clear and disturbing. He was here because he had been maneuvered into a one-way passage as direct and confining as this ventilator tube. Selador and friends formed one side of the passage; Jenny and fellow Santarogans formed the other side.

And here he was.

Dasein lifted the sling. It was torn but still serviceable. He gripped one end in his teeth, managed to restore it to a semblance of its former position.

There was only one way to go now. He dropped to his knees, crawled backward down the ventilator, using his light occasionally to probe the darkness.

The Jaspers odor filled the confined space. It was a tangy essence of mushrooms here. He received the distinct impression it cleared his head.

The tube went on and on and on ... He took it one step at a time. It curved slowly toward what he felt was south and the slope steepened. Once, he slipped, slid downward for twenty feet, cutting his left hand on a rivet. He wasn't positive, but he thought the sound of the fan motor grew louder.

Again, the tube turned – and again. Dasein lost all sense of direction in the confining darkness. Why had they constructed this ventilator with so many turns? he wondered. Had they followed a natural fault in the rock? It seemed likely.

His left foot encountered an edge of emptiness.

Dasein stopped, used the penlight. Its feeble glow illuminated a flat metal wall about six feet away and a square of shadows beneath it. He turned the light downward, exposed a box-like opening about five feet deep with a heavy screen for one side. The sound of the fan motor came from somewhere behind the screen and it definitely was louder here.

Bracing himself with a hand in the screen, Dasein lowered himself into the box. He stood there a moment examining his surroundings. The wall opposite the screen appeared different from the others. There were six round-head bolts in it held by flanged metal keepers as though they'd been designed to stay in that position while nuts were tightened from the outside.

Dasein pried up one of the flanges with his knife, turned the bolt. It moved easily, too easily. He pulled back on it, turned it once more. That took more effort and he was rewarded by having the bolt work backward into his hand. The nut dropped outside with a sound of falling on wood.

He waited, listening for a response to that sound.

Nothing.

Dasein put his eye to the bolt hole, peered out into an eerie red gloom. As his eye grew accustomed to it, he made out a section of heavy screen across from him, packages piled behind the screen.

He drew back. Well, Nis had said this was a storage cave.

Dasein applied himself to the other bolts. He left the bolt in the upper right corner, bent the metal out and swung it aside. There was a wooden catwalk immediately below him with three wing nuts on it. He slipped out to the catwalk, scooped up the wing nuts. The other nuts obviously had dropped through the space between the boards of the walk. He looked around, studying what he saw with care, absorbing the implications of this place.

It was a troglodyte cave illuminated by dim red light. The light came from globes beneath the catwalk and above it, casting enormous shadows on a rock wall behind the ventilator panel and over stacked tiers of cage-walled compartments. The cages were stuffed with packages and reminded Dasein of nothing more than a public freezer locker.

The richly moist odor of Jaspers was all around him.

A sign to his right down the catwalk labeled this area as 'Bay 21–D-1 to J-5.'

Dasein returned his attention to the ventilator, restored three of the bolts, forcing the cover plate back into position. A crease remained in the metal where he had bent it, but he thought it would pass casual inspection.

He looked up and down the catwalk.

Where would he find one of these compartments he could open to examine the contents? He crossed to the one opposite the ventilator plate, looked for a door. Could he find a compartment left unlocked by a careless Santarogan ... provided he could find the door? There apparently was no door on the first compartment he inspected. The lack of a door filled Dasein with unease. There had to be a door!

He stepped back, studied the line of compartments, gasped as he saw the answer. The fronts of the compartments slid aside in wooden channels ... and there were no locks. Simple peg latches held them.

Dasein opened the front of a compartment, pulled out a small cardboard box. Its label read: 'Auntie Beren's spiced crab apples. Ex. April '55.' He replaced the box, extracted a salami-shaped package. Its label read: 'Limburger exposed early 1929.' Dasein replaced the limburger, closed the compartment.

Exposed?

Methodically, Dasein worked his way, down the line in Bay 21, examining one or two packages in each compartment. Most of the time it was written 'Ex' with a date. The older packages spelled it out.

Exposed.

Dasein sensed his mind racing. *Exposed. Exposed to what? How?*

The sound of footsteps on the lower catwalk behind him brought Dasein whirling around, muscles tense. He heard a compartment door slide open. Papers rustled.

Softly, Dasein worked his way along the catwalk away from the sound. He passed steps, one set leading up, one down, hesitated. He couldn't be certain whether he was going deeper into the cave complex or out of it. There was another catwalk above him, a rock ceiling dimly visible above that. There appeared to be at least three tiers of catwalks below him.

He chose the steps going up, lifted his head slowly above the floor level of the next walk, glanced both ways.

Empty.

This level was like the one below except for the rock ceiling. The rock appeared to be a form of granite, but with oily brown veins.

Moving as silently as he could, Dasein climbed out onto the walk, moved back in the direction of the ventilator listening for the person he had heard on the lower level.

Someone was whistling down there, an idiot tune repeated endlessly. Dasein pressed his back against a cage, peered down through the openings in the walk. There came a scraping of wood against wood. The whistling went away to his left, receded into silence.

That probably was the way out, then.

He had heard the person down there but hadn't been able to see him – a fact which could work both ways.

Placing his feet carefully, Dasein moved along the walk. He came to a cross way, peered around it. Empty both ways. The gloom appeared a little thicker to the left.

It occurred to Dasein that up to this point he hadn't felt the need to worry about how he was going to get out of the cave complex. He had been too intent on solving the mystery. But the mystery remained ... and here he was.

I can't just go marching out, he thought. *Or can't I? What could they do to me?*

His throbbing shoulder, memory of the gas jet, the knowledge that two previous investigators had died in this valley – these were sufficient answer to the question, he thought.

Wood slammed against wood off to the front and below. Footsteps pounded along a catwalk – at least two pair of feet, possibly more. The running stopped almost directly beneath him. There came a low-voiced conversation, mostly unintelligible and sounding like instructions. Dasein recognized only three words – ' ... back ...' ' ... away ...' and a third word which set him in motion running softly down the dim side passage to his left.

'... ventilator ...'

A man beneath him had said 'ventilator' sharply and distinctly.

The pounding of feet resumed down there spreading out through the catwalks.

Dasein searched frantically ahead for a place to hide. There was a sound of machinery humming somewhere down there. The catwalk turned left at about a fifteen degree angle, and he saw the cave walls were converging here – fewer tiers below and smaller compartments on each side. The walk angled more sharply to the right and there was only his walk and the one below, single compartments on each side.

He had put himself into a dead-end side passage, Dasein realized. Still, there was the sound of machinery ahead.

His catwalk ended in a set of wooden stairs going down. There was no choice; he could hear someone running behind him.

Dasein went down.

The stairs turned left into a rock passage – no compartments, just the cave. There was a louvered door on the right, loud sound of an electric motor in there. His pursuer was at the head of the steps above.

Dasein opened the door, slipped through, closed the door. He found himself in a rectangular chamber about fifty feet long, twenty feet wide and some fifteen feet to the ceiling. A row of large electric motors lined the left wall, all of them extending into round metal throats with fanblades blurring the air there. The far wall was one giant metal screen and he could feel air rushing out of it toward the fans.

The right wall was piled high with cardboard cartons, sacks and wood boxes. There was a space between the pile and the ceiling and it appeared darker up there. Dasein scrambled up the pile, crawled along it, almost fell into a space hollowed out of boxes and sacks near the far end. He slid into the hole, found himself on what felt like blankets. His hand encountered something metallic, which groping fingers identified as a flashlight.

The louvered door slammed open. Feet pounded into the room.

Someone scrambled up the far end of the pile. A woman's voice said: 'Nothing up here.'

There came the sound of someone dropping lightly to the floor.

There'd been something familiar about the woman's voice. Dasein was willing to swear he'd heard it before.

A man said: 'Why'd you run this way? Did you hear something?'

'I thought so, but I wasn't sure,' the woman said.

'You sure there's nothing on top of the stores?'

'Look for yourself.'

'Doggone, I wish we could use real lights in here.'

'Now, don't you go doing something foolish.'

'Don't worry about me. Doggone that Jenny anyway, getting herself mixed up with an outsider!'

'Don't pick on Jenny. She knows what she's doing.'

'I guess so, but it sure makes a lot of stupid extra work, and you know what's liable to happen if we don't find him pretty soon.'

'So let's hurry it up.'

They went out, closed the door.

Dasein lay quietly absorbing the import of what they'd said. Jenny knew what she was doing, did she? What would happen if they didn't find him?

It felt good to stretch out on the blankets. His shoulder was a steady aching throb. He brought up the flashlight he'd found here, pressed its switch. The thing produced a dull red glow. The light revealed a tight little nest – blankets, a pillow, a canteen half full of water. He drank some of it thirstily, found it heavy with Jaspers.

He supposed nothing in the cave could escape that flavor.

A fit of shivering took over his muscles. The canteen's cap rattled as he replaced it. When the trembling passed, he sat staring at the canteen in the dim red light.

Nothing in the cave could escape the Jaspers flavor!

That was it!

Exposed!

Something that could exist in this cave – a mould or a fungus, something related to mushrooms and dark places, something that wouldn't travel ... a *Jaspers* something invaded anything exposed to this environment.

But why was it so important to keep this fact secret? Why the dogs and the guards?

He heard the louvered door open, close, turned off the red flashlight. Someone ran lightly across the rock floor to a point just below him.

'Gilbert Dasein!' a voice hissed at him.

Dasein stiffened.

'It's Willa Burdeaux,' the voice hissed. 'It's Willa, Jenny's friend. I know you're in there, in the place Cal made for us. Now, you listen. Amulf will be right back from the upper end and I have to be out of here before that. You don't have much time. There's too much Jaspers in here for someone who's not used to it. You're breathing it and it's going in your pores and everything.'

What the hell? Dasein thought.

He crawled up out of the nest, leaned out and looked down at Willa Burdeaux's dark, harshly-beautiful face.

'Why can't I take too much of it?' he asked.

'Hasn't that Jenny explained anything to you?' she whispered. 'Well, no time now. You have to get out of here. Do you have a watch?'

'Yes, but ...'

'There's no time to explain; just listen. Give me fifteen minutes to get Amulf out of the way. He's such a prig. In fifteen minutes you come out of this room. Turn left the way you came in, but go down instead of up. Take the second crossway to your left and after that keep to your left. It's easy to remember. Left turns only. You want the ramp out of Bay 2-G. I've left the ramp's door unlocked. Lock it after you. It'll be about twenty steps straight in front of that door to an emergency gate. The gate's unlocked. Go out and lock it after you. The Inn's right across the road. You ought to be able to make that on your own.'

'Apparently, you've been rather busy.'

'I was in the office when they sounded the alarm. Now, get down out of sight and do just what I told you.'

Dasein ducked back into the nest.

Presently, he heard the door open and close. He looked at his wristwatch: five minutes to three a.m. Where had the time gone?

Could he believe Willa Burdeaux? he wondered.

There'd been something about that black pixie face, an intensity ... Dasein thought of compartments loaded with valuable food, all unlocked. Why should this evidence of a basic honesty alarm him? Perhaps it wasn't honesty. Fear could control behavior, too.

Could he believe Willa? Did he have a choice?

So this was a trysting place Cal Nis had made for the two of them. Why not? People in love usually wanted to be alone together.

Jenny knew what she was doing.

What did she know?

His mind felt clear and oiled, working at a furious pace. What was the danger in exposure to Jaspers? He thought of that dull-eyed line he'd glimpsed up there in the Co-op.

Was that what happened?

Dasein fought down a siege of trembling.

Ten minutes after three, the moment of decision, came more quickly than he wanted. He had no choice and knew it. His shoulder had gone stiff and there was a painful burning along his scraped chest and stomach. Favoring his shoulder, Dasein eased himself down off the storage pile.

The ramp door was unlocked as Willa had promised. He let himself out into a darkened side yard, hesitated. The stars overhead looked cold and close. It *was* cold. He felt goose pimples along his arms. There was no sign of a guard out here, but he glimpsed lights and motion far up on the hillside.

Lock the ramp door, she'd said.

Dasein locked the door, darted across the yard. It was a narrow gate in the chain fence. The hinges creaked and he thought the latch unnaturally loud. There was a hasp and padlock. He closed the lock.

A narrow path led along the fence to the road. There was the Inn across the way – dark, but inviting. A dim yellow light glowed through the double doors. Using the light as a beacon, Dasein limped down the path and across to the Inn.

The lobby was empty, most of its lights turned off. There was the sound of snoring from the switchboard room behind the desk.

Dasein slipped quietly across the lobby, up the stairs and down the hall to his room.

The key – had he turned it in or left it in the truck? No . . . here it was in his pocket. He opened the door softly, stepped into the darkness of his room. He'd spent only one night in this room but it suddenly was a haven.

The truck! It was still up there on the road to Porterville. The hell with it. He'd hire a ride up tomorrow and drive it down.

That Willa Burdeaux! Why had she done this?

Dasein began slipping out of his clothes. He wanted nothing more than a hot shower and bed. It was slow work undressing in the dark, but he knew a light might tell someone what time he'd returned.

What difference does that make? he asked himself. His clothing, torn, smeared with dirt, still stinking of the cave, was evidence enough of where he'd been and what he'd done.

Abruptly, he felt he no longer could sneak around.

Angry at himself, he turned on the light.

Directly ahead of him on the bedstand was a bottle of beer with a note attached to it. Dasein lifted the note, read it: 'This isn't much, but it's all I could get. You'll need it in the morning. I'll call Jenny and tell her you're all right. – Willa.'

Dasein picked up the bottle, looked at the label. There was a blue stamp on it: 'Exposed January 1959.'

5

A steady, loud pounding invaded Dasein's dream. He felt he was trapped inside a giant drum. Reverberations beat through his brain. Each drum-beat became a stab of pain along his temples, through his shoulders, across his stomach.

He was the drum! That was it!

His lips were dry. Thirst spread a scabby dustiness over his throat. His tongue was thick, fuzzy.

My God! Would the pounding never stop?

He awoke feeling he'd been caught in a caricature of a hangover. The blankets were twisted around his body, immobilizing his injured shoulder. The shoulder felt better, and that was a relief, but something had to be done about his head and that insane pounding.

His free arm was asleep. It tingled painfully when he tried to move it. Sunlight filtered through a tear in the curtain on the room's single window. One thin ray outlined in dust motes stabbed across the room. It dazzled him, hurt his eyes.

That damned pounding!

'Hey! Open up in there!'

It was a masculine voice from outside.

Dasein felt he knew that voice. Marden, the CHP captain? What was he doing here at this hour? Dasein lifted his wristwatch, stared at it – ten twenty-five.

The pounding resumed.

'Just a minute!' Dasein shouted. His own voice sent waves of pain through his head.

Blessedly, the pounding stopped.

Dasein gasped with relief, twisted himself out of the blankets, sat up. The room's walls began going around and around in a mad circle.

For the love of heaven! he thought. *I've heard of hangovers, but nothing like this.*

'Open the door, Dasein.'

That definitely was Marden.

'Right with you,' Dasein rasped.

What's wrong with me? he wondered. He knew he'd had no more than the beers with dinner. They couldn't possibly explain his present malaise. Could it be delayed reaction to the gas?

Beer.

There was something about beer.

Slowly so as not to dislocate his neck, Dasein turned his head toward the bedstand. Yes, there was a beer. Willa had thoughtfully provided an opener. He levered the cap off the bottle, drank hungrily.

Waves of soothing relief spread out from his stomach. He put down the empty bottle, stood up. *Hair of the dog,* he thought. *Hair of the Jaspers dog.* The bottle was redolent with the mushroom tang.

'Are you all right in there, Dasein?'

To hell with you, mister, Dasein thought. He tried to take a step, was rewarded with instant nausea and a wave of dizziness. He leaned against the wall breathing slowly, deeply.

I'm sick, he thought. *I've caught something.*

The beer felt as though it had begun to boil in his stomach.

'Open this door, Dasein! Now!'

All right – all right, Dasein thought. He stumbled to the door, unlocked it, stepped back.

The door was flung open to reveal Al Marden in uniform, the captain's bars glistening at his neck. His visored cap was pushed back to reveal a sweaty band of red hair.

'Well,' he said. 'Haven't we been the busy one?'

He stepped into the room, closed the door. He carried something round and chromed in his left hand – a thermos. What the devil was he doing here at this hour with a thermos? Dasein wondered.

One hand against the wall to steady himself, Dasein made his way back to the bed, sat on the edge.

Marden followed.

'I hope you're worth all this trouble,' he said.

Dasein looked up at the narrow, cynical face, remembering the glimpse he'd had of the high-wheeled bush buggy wheeling down the road out there with Marden steering, and the dogs beside him. That had been a proper setting for this man. There was an elevated look about him, a peering-down-at-the-world's-stupidity. What was it about him? Was it the Santaroga look? But what had the Porterville deputies seen, then? What had the man in the Chrysler seen?

Do I look that way? Dasein wondered.

'I brought you some coffee,' Marden said. 'You look like you could use it.' He opened the thermos, poured steaming amber liquid into the cup-top.

A rich smell of Jaspers rode on the steam from the cup. The smell set Dasein trembling, sent a pulsing, throbbing ache through his head. The ache seemed timed to a wavering reflection on the surface of the coffee as Marden presented it.

Dasein took the cup in both hands, tipped his head back and drank with a gulping eagerness. The coffee produced the same sensation of soothing as the beer.

Marden refilled the cup.

Dasein held it beneath his nose, inhaled the Jaspers rich steam. His headache began to fade. There was a hunger in him for the coffee that he realized went beyond the cravings from a hangover.

'Drink up,' Marden said.

Dasein sipped the coffee. He could feel it settling his stomach, his mind coming alert. Marden no longer appeared superior – only amused.

Why was a hangover amusing?

'The Jaspers, that's what gave me the screaming fantods, isn't it?' Dasein asked. He returned the cup.

Marden concentrated on restoring the cap to the thermos.

'A person can get too much of it, eh?' Dasein persisted, recalling what Willa Burdeaux had said.

'Overexposure too soon can cause a hangover,' Marden admitted. 'You'll be all right when you get used to it.'

'So you came up to play the good Samaritan,' Dasein said. He could feel the beginnings of anger.

'We found your truck up on the Porterville road and got worried about you,' Marden said. 'You can't abandon a vehicle like that.'

'I didn't abandon it.'

'Oh? What'd you do?'

'I went for a walk.'

'And caused one helluva lot of trouble,' Marden said. 'If you wanted a tour of the Co-op and the storage caves, all you had to do was ask.'

'And I'd have had a nice safe guided tour.'

'Any kind of tour you wanted.'

'So you came up to arrest me.'

'Arrest you? Don't talk stupid.'

'How'd you know where I was?'

Marden looked at the ceiling, shook his head. 'You're all alike, you young folks,' he said. 'That Willa's too damn' romantic, but she doesn't lie worth git all. None of us do, I guess.' He turned his glance full of cynical amusement on Dasein. 'You feeling better?'

'Yes!'

'Aren't we the intense one.' He pursed his lips. 'By the way, we broke into your truck and hot-wired it to drive it down. It's parked out front.'

'Gee, thanks.'

Dasein looked down at his hands. Anger and frustration twisted through him. He knew Marden wasn't a fit object for this anger ... nor Jenny ... nor Piaget ... No person or thing presented itself to him as an object for anger – yet the emotion remained. He trembled with it.

'You sure you're all right?' Marden asked.

'Yes, I'm all right!'

'Okay, okay,' Marden murmured. He turned away, but not before Dasein saw the smile forming on his lips.

The smile, not the man, brought Dasein's anger to focus. That smile! It embodied Santaroga – self-satisfied, superior, secretive. He jumped to his feet, strode to the window, whipped up the curtain.

Blazing sunshine on a flower garden, a small stream, and beyond that the flat with its broken edge dropping down into the redwoods. It was a day of brassy heat with the oaks sitting motionless, sun-drenched on the hillsides. He counted three plumes of smoke hanging on the still air, glimpsed a serpentine track of blue-green river in the distance.

This vale of pastoral beauty that was Santaroga, this was a fitting object for his anger, Dasein decided: Santaroga, this island of people in the wilderness. He pictured the valley as a swarming place behind a facade like a pyramid: solid, faceless, enduring. In there, behind the façade, Santaroga did something to its people. They lost personal identity and became masks for something that was the same in all of them.

He sensed a one-pointedness here such that every Santarogan became an extension of every other Santarogan. They were like rays spreading out from a pinhole in a black curtain.

What lay behind the black curtain?

There, he knew, was the real substance against which his anger was directed. The valley existed within an evil enchantment. The Santarogans had been trapped by a black sorcery, transmuted into the faceless pyramid.

With this thought, Dasein's anger faded. He realized he, too, had a place in this pyramid. It was like an ecological pyramid planted in the wilderness except for this gnome-change. The base of the pyramid had been firmly imbedded in the earth, extending roots deep into a moist, dank cave.

He could see the shape of his problem.

One thing set this valley apart – Jaspers. It brought Santarogans back as though they were addicted. He thought of his own craving reaction. It was the substance of the cave, the thing the pores drank and the lungs inhaled.

Marden stirred in the room behind him

Dasein turned, looked at the man.

Santarogans became extensions of that cave and its substance. There was a drug-effect at work in this valley. It was a material in a way similar to lysergic acid diethylamide – LSD.

How did it work? he wondered.

Did it shift the serotonin balance?

Dasein felt his mind working with remarkable clarity, sorting out possibilities, setting up avenues of investigation.

'If you're feeling all right now, I'll be running along,' Marden said. 'Before you get any more harebrained ideas for night excursions, let us know, huh?'

'Well, naturally,' Dasein said.

For some reason, this provoked a fit of laughter in Marden. He was still laughing as he let himself out.

'To hell with you, wise-guy Santarogan,' Dasein muttered.

He turned back to the window.

Objectivity was going to be a problem, he saw. He had no guinea pig except himself. What was the Jaspers effect on himself? An impression of heightened awareness? Could it be an actual heightened awareness in the pattern of LSD? This would require careful evaluation. What was the source of the morning-after symptoms? Withdrawal?

He began to focus on the Santaroga personality pattern, their alertness, their abrupt mannerisms, their apparent honesty. If awareness actually were heightened, would that explain the honest advertising? Could you be anything but bluntly honest with a wide-awake human being?

Avenues of attack opened all around. Barriers collapsed like sand walls before the waves of his new awareness, but the exposed vistas contained their own mysteries.

Jenny.

Again, Dasein recalled how she'd been dropped from the university's attempt to evaluate LSD. *No apparent reaction.* The ones running the tests had wanted to explore this phenomenon, but Jenny had refused. Why? She'd been written off, of course – 'a curious anomaly.' The evaluation had gone on to its natural end in the publicity fiasco.

Jenny.

Dasein went into the shower, humming to himself, his mind busy. His shoulder felt remarkably improved in spite of the way he'd mistreated it during the night . . . or perhaps because of that – the exercise.

I'll call Jenny, he thought, as he dressed. *Maybe we can meet for lunch.*

The prospect of seeing Jenny filled him with a wondering delight. He sensed his own protectiveness toward her, the mutual emotional dependence. Love, that was what it was. It was a sensation that wouldn't submit to analysis. It could only be experienced.

Dasein sobered.

His love for Jenny required that he save her from the Santaroga enchantment. She'd have to help him whether she knew it or not, whether she wanted it or not.

A brisk double knock sounded on his door.

'Come in,' he called.

Jenny slipped in, closed the door.

She wore a white dress, red scarf, red handbag and shoes. The outfit made her skin appear dark and exotic. She paused a moment at the door, her hand resting lightly on the knob, eyes wide and probing.

'Jen!' he said.

All in one swift dash, she was across the room into his arms, hugging him. Her lips were warm and soft on his. There was a clean spicy smell about her.

She pulled back, looked up at him. 'Oh, darling, I was so frightened. I kept imagining you driving off a cliff somewhere, your car wrecked, you in the wreckage. Then Willa called. Why would you do such a thing?'

He put a finger on the tip of her nose, pressed gently. 'I'm perfectly capable of taking care of myself.'

'I don't know about that. Do you feel all right now? I met Al in the lobby. He said he brought you some Jaspers coffee?'

'I've had my hair of the dog.'

'Your hair of . . . Oh. But why would you . . .'

'But me no buts. I'm sorry I worried you, but I have a job to do.'

'Oh, that!'

'I'm going to do the job I'm being paid to do.'

'You gave your word, I suppose?'

'That's only part of it.'

'Then they'll have to get something from you.'

'More than *something,* Jenny, m'love.'

She grinned. 'I like it when you call me your love.'

'Stop changing the subject.'

'But it's such a nice subject.'

'Agreed. Another time, though, eh?'

'How about tonight?'

'You're a forward wench, aren't you.'

'I know what I want.'

Dasein found himself studying her there in his arms. What had Willa said? *'Jenny knows what she's doing.'* Whatever it was, he couldn't doubt her love for him. It was there in her eyes and her voice, a radiance and vivacity that couldn't be mistaken.

Still, there was the certainty two men had died on this investigation – accidents! The fading pain in his shoulder and its implications couldn't be doubted either.

'You're so quiet suddenly,' Jenny said, looking up at him.

He took a deep breath. 'Can you get me some Jaspers?'

'I almost forgot,' she said. She pulled away, rummaged in her handbag. 'I brought you a square of cheese and some wheat crackers for your lunch today. They're from Uncle Larry's locker. I knew you'd need it because . . .' She broke off, produced a sack from the bag. 'Here they are.' She proffered a brown paper sack, stared at him. 'Gil! You said *Jaspers.*' There was a wary look in her eyes.

'Why not?' He took the bag. She was reluctant to part with it, her fingers trailing across the paper as he pulled it away.

'I don't want to trick you, darling,' she said.

'Trick me? How?'

She swallowed and her eyes glistened with unshed tears. 'We gave you an awfully strong dose last night, and then you went down into that stupid cave. Was it bad this morning?'

'I had quite a hangover, if that's what you mean.'

'I can just barely remember how it was when I was a child,' she said. 'When you're growing up, your body changing, there are some severe metabolic adjustments. At the school, when I took part in that crazy LSD test, I had a hangover the next morning.' She ran a finger along his forehead. 'Poor dear. I'd have been here this morning, but Uncle Larry needed me in the clinic. Anyway, he said you weren't in any danger; Willa got you out in time.'

'What would've happened if she hadn't got me out?'

Her eyes clouded as though with pain.

'What?' he insisted.

'You mustn't think about that.'

'About what?'

'It can't happen to you anyway. Uncle Larry says you're the wrong type.'

'Wrong type for what – turning into a zombie like those I saw in the Co-op?'

'Zombies? What're you talking about?'

He described what he'd glimpsed through the wide door.

'Oh ... them.' She looked away from him, her manner suddenly distant. 'Gilbert, are you going to put them in your report?'

'Maybe.'

'You mustn't.'

'Why not? Who are they? *What* are they?'

'We take care of our own,' she said. 'They're useful members of the community.'

'But not quite all there.'

'That's right.' She looked up at him with a fierce intensity. 'If the state takes them over, they'll be moved out of the valley – most of them. That can be very bad for Santarogans, Gilbert. Believe me.'

'I believe you.'

'I knew you would.'

'They're the failures, eh? The ones Jaspers ruined.'

'Gilbert!' she said. Then – 'It's not what you think. Jaspers is ... something wonderful. We call it a "Consciousness Fuel." It opens your eyes and your ears, it turns on your mind, it ...' She broke off, smiled at him. 'But you already know.'

'I know what it appears to be,' he said. He glanced at the bag in his hand. What did he hold here? Was it a paradisical gift for all mankind or something out of hell? Was it the evil enchantment he'd pictured, or an ultimate freedom?

'It's wonderful and you know it by now,' Jenny said.

'Then why aren't you all shouting it from the rooftops?' he demanded.

'Gil!' She stared at him accusingly.

Abruptly, Dasein thought of what Meyer Davidson's reaction would be ... Davidson and his cohorts, the eager young executives and the hard-eyed older men.

What he held here in his hand was their enemy.

To those men in their oddly similar dark suits, their cold eyes weighing and dismissing everything, the people of this valley were a foe to be defeated. As he thought of it, Dasein realized all customers were 'The Enemy' to these men. Davidson and his kind were pitted against each other, yes, competitive, but among themselves they betrayed that they were pitted more against the masses who existed beyond that inner ring of knowledgable financial operation.

The alignment was apparent in everything they did, in their words as well as their actions. They spoke of 'package grab-level' and 'container flash time'– of 'puff limit' and 'acceptance threshold.' It was an 'in' language of militarylike maneuvering and combat. They knew which height on a shelf was most apt to make a customer grab an item. They knew the 'flash time' – the shelf width needed for certain containers. They knew how much empty air could be 'puffed' into a package to make it appear a greater bargain. They knew how much price and package manipulation the customer would accept without jarring him into a 'rejection pattern.'

And we're their spies, Dasein thought. *The psychiatrists and psychologists – all the 'social scientists' – we're the espionage arm.*

He sensed the vast maneuvering of these armies, the conspiracy to maintain 'The Enemy' in a sleepy state of unawareness – malleable. Whatever the leaders of these armies did among themselves to each other, they maintained their inner code. No one betrayed the *real* war.

Dasein never before viewed the market-study world in quite this way. He thought of the brutal honesty in Santaroga's advertising, crumpled the neck of the paper bag in his hand.

What was this stuff doing to him? He turned away from Jenny to hide a surge of anger. It was making him imagine crazy things! Armies!

There was no way to avoid Jaspers here in Santaroga. The investigation required that he *not* avoid it.

I must insinuate myself into their minds, he reminded himself. *I must live their life, think as they think.*

He saw the situation then as Jenny and her fellow Santarogans must see it. They were involved in a form of guerrilla warfare. They had achieved a way of life which wouldn't be tolerated by the *outside*. Santaroga offered too much of a threat to the oligarchs of the money-industry world. The only hope for Santaroga lay in isolation and secrecy.

Shout it from the rooftops, indeed. No wonder she'd snapped at him in surprise.

Dasein turned, looked at Jenny standing there patiently waiting for him to think his way through the maze. She smiled encouragingly at him and he suddenly saw all Santarogans through her. They were the buffalo Indians, people who needed to get away by themselves, to live and hunt in the way their instincts told them. The trouble was, they lived in a world which couldn't be culturally neutral. That world out there would keep trying to make people – all people – be everywhere alike.

Straddling both worlds, thinking with the drug and thinking with his memories of the *outside*, he felt a deep sadness for Jenny. Santaroga would be destroyed – no doubt of that.

'I'm sure you see it,' Jenny said.

'Jaspers would be equated with LSD, with narcotics,' he said. 'It'd be legislated against as the Santaroga hashish. You'd be sneered out of existence, destroyed.'

'I never doubted you'd understand once you were exposed,' she said. She moved into his arms, leaned against him, hugging him fiercely. 'I trusted you, Gil. I knew I couldn't be wrong about you.'

He couldn't find words to answer her. A profound sadness held him. *Exposed.*

'You'll still have to do your report, of course,' she said. 'It wouldn't solve anything if you failed. They'd just find somebody else. We're getting kind of tired of it.'

'Yes – I'll have to do a report,' he said.

'We understand.'

Her voice sent a shudder through Dasein. '*We understand.*' That was the *We* which had searched his bag, had almost killed him . . . had actually killed two men.

'Why are you shivering?' Jenny asked.

'Just a chill,' he said.

He thought then of the *thing* he had sensed lurking just beyond his awareness, that restless, urgently peering ancient being which had risen within his consciousness like the neck of a dinosaur. It was still there, studying, waiting to judge.

'I only work half a day today,' Jenny said. 'Some of my friends have arranged a picnic at the lake. They want to meet you.' She leaned back, peered up at him. 'I want to show you off, too.'

'I . . . don't think I can go swimming,' he said.

'Your poor shoulder,' she said. 'I know. But the lake's beautiful this time of year. We'll have a bonfire tonight.'

Which We is that? he asked himself.

'It sounds wonderful,' he said.

And he wondered as he spoke why his stomach knotted with a congestion of fear. He told himself it wasn't Jenny he feared – not this warm and beautiful woman. It might be goddess-Jenny he feared, though . . . this was a thought that rose in his mind to leer at him.

Dasein sneered at himself then, thinking that he read too much into every nuance of this valley and its people. That was the psychoanalyst's disease, of course – seeing everything through a haze of reasoning.

'Get some rest and meet me downstairs at noon,' Jenny said.

She pulled away, went to the door, turned there to stare at him. 'You're acting very odd, Gil,' she said. 'Is something bothering you?'

Her voice carried a weighted probing that brought Dasein to sudden alertness. This wasn't the spontaneous Jenny worried about the man she loved. This was an ... an *observer* probing for something personally dangerous.

'Nothing food and rest won't cure,' he said. He tried to sound bantering, knew he'd failed.

'I'll see you in a little while,' she said, still in that distant tone.

Dasein watched the door close behind her. He had the feeling he'd been playing to a special kind of camera, one that pursued irrelevancies. An untethered thought wove through his mind: ... *the exposure of personality, method and character. Who wants to expose my personality, method and character?* Dasein asked himself. He felt this was a dangerous question, full of charge and countercharge.

The sack of food felt heavy in his hand. Dasein stared down at it, aware of his hunger, equally aware of the threat in this package. Did the Jaspers create irreversible change?

He tossed the sack onto his bed, went to the door, peered out into the hall. Empty. He stepped out, looked down the expanse of wall that concealed the TV room. It took a moment for him to realize something was wrong with that wall. It was like a dislocation of reality – a door occupied a space in that wall where no door had been.

As though pulled by strings, Dasein went to the door, stared at it. The door was framed in the same worn, polished wood that framed the other doors. Well-preserved age, that was the effect. This was a door that had always been here, that's what it said. The number plate carried a slight dent and a touch of tarnish at the edges where the maids' polishing rags had missed. There was a patina of long wear about the handle.

Dasein shook his head. He was tempted to try the door, resisted. He found himself frightened by what might lie beyond. Normalcy – a bed, a bath, desk and chairs – that would be the worst thing of all. The number plate–262 – fascinated him. He toyed with the eerie sensation that he'd seen it before ... right here. The door was too ordinary.

Abruptly, Dasein whirled back and into his room, threw open his window. A look through the windows from the porch roof would solve the mystery. He started to climb out, stopped. A man stood on a rose-bordered walk beyond the giant oak tree.

Dasein recognized Winston Burdeaux. He was pumping a hand sprayer that sent dust over the roses. As Dasein stared, Burdeaux looked up, waved.

Later, Dasein told himself. *I'll look later.*

He nodded to Burdeaux, withdrew, pulled the curtain.

So they'd cut a door through that wall, had they? What were they trying to do? Destroy his sense of reality?

The sack on the bed caught Dasein's attention. It drew him across the room. He saw it as an ultimate temptation. It was more than food. There was a hunger in him only the Jaspers could fulfill. Dasein felt abruptly that he was like Tennyson's Ulysses, his aim 'to strive, to seek, to find and not to yield.' Still, the thought of the Jaspers in that sack drew his hand. He felt the paper tear beneath his fingers.

Jaspers cheese. That tantalizing aroma lifted from it. With a feeling of spiritual helplessness, he found a bite of the cheese in his mouth. The food radiated a sensation of warmth as it went down his throat. He continued eating, hypnotized by his own actions.

Slowly, he sank back onto the bed, leaned against the pillow, gazed up at the ceiling. The wood grain in a beam wavered like the lifting and falling of the sea. It filled him with awe, undiluted and terrifying. He felt his own consciousness stood as a barrier opposing the external world, and that external world was a stupid mechanism without feeling or compassion.

His own identity became a narrowing beam of light, and he sensed a massive, streaming unconsciousness growing larger, larger ... larger ... building up an intolerable weight.

It's a psychedelic, he told himself. *Don't let go.*

But there was no stopping the movement now. His awareness, exploding up and out, riding a geyser of sense revelation, lifted him into a state of floating consciousness.

There was no inwardness now, only a timeless sense of being that existed without anxiety. Dasein found himself reveling in the sensation. His mind quested.

Where are the children? he asked himself.

It was a shocking sense of revelation for him to realize he'd seen no children or schools in the valley.

Where are the children? Why haven't any of the other investigators remarked on this?

The other investigators are dead, he reminded himself.

Death – that was an oddly nonfrightening thought. He felt he had risen through a consciousness decompression into a zone beyond all power struggles. The valley, the Jaspers, had become a condition of his being. The room full of probing sunlight, the leaves of the oak outside his window – all was beauty, innocent, uncluttered. The external universe had become translated into a part of himself, wise, compassionate.

Dasein marveled at the feeling. The universe *out there* – it was as though he had just created that universe. *Nama-Rupa*, he thought. *I am Nama-Rupa – name and form, creator of the universe in which I live.*

The pain of his injured shoulder occupied his drifting attention momentarily. Pain, a brief crisis, something against which to project memories of pleasure. The pain faded.

There came the sound of tires on gravel. He heard a bird singing. The sounds were a moire playing against his awareness. They danced and scintillated.

He remembered Jenny's probing stare.

This was an ugly, shocking memory that jerked him up short, compressed him. He found difficulty breathing. There was a sensation that he had been caught up in history, but it was a kind of history he'd never experienced, peopled by goddesses and creatures of terrifying powers. It was a history moving at an astonishing speed, defying all preconceived notions of slowness. It was like a series of events that he couldn't separate or distinguish. They flashed across his consciousness, leaving him irrevocably changed.

The Jaspers, he thought. *I cannot return ... to ... what ... I was ... before.*

Tears rolled down his cheeks.

He thought of the way his bag had been searched. A sob shook him. What did they want?

Dasein found himself believing there were demons around him, cunning, seeking his blood and being, hungry for his soul. They gibbered beyond the charmed circle of his lonely awareness. The sensation, primitive as a witch dance, refused to leave. They were robots, automata with grimacing malleable faces and headlight eyes.

He began to tremble, knew he was perspiring heavily, but it was a distant sensation, something happening to a foreign person.

Head whirling, Dasein heaved himself off the bed, lurched to his feet, stumbled across the room. At the wall, he turned, stumbled back – forth and back ... back and forth. No hiding place existed for him. Sunlight streaming in the window took on grotesque forms – lizards with human faces, silvery gnomes, insects with clock-face wings ...

He slumped to the floor, clawed at the rug. A red braided pattern extruded claws that reached for him. He retreated to the bed, fell across it. The ceiling undulated with inverted waves.

Somewhere, someone played a piano – Chopin.

Dasein felt abruptly that he was the piano. The sounds struck a crystal brilliance through him, plucking out his anguish. Glaring white clarity began to seep over him. He grew aware his clothes were soaked with perspiration. His palms were slippery. He sensed he had come a long distance through a dangerous passage. The journey had leeched all strength from him.

But he saw the room now with an uncluttered innocence. The ceiling beams were objects to be understood, their grain receding back into trees ... to seedlings ... to seeds ... to trees. Every artifact that met his vision extended into past and future for him. Nothing remained static.

All was motion and he was a part of that motion.

Waves of sleep began creeping from the back of his mind – higher ... higher ... higher.

Sleep enveloped him.

In the darkness of his sleep, something laughed and laughed and laughed and laughed ...

Dasein awoke with a feeling he'd been asleep for a long time – perhaps a lifetime. A chuckle lifted from his throat. He heard the noise coming from himself as from a stranger and it frightened him. A glance at his wristwatch told him he'd been asleep more than two hours.

Again, the stranger-chuckle teased his throat.

He pushed himself off the bed, wondering at his weakness. His shoulder felt better, though, the pain diminishing to a dull ache.

A rap sounded on his door.

'Yes?' Dasein called.

'It's Win Burdeaux, sir. Miss Jenny asked me to remind you she'll be here for you in about a half hour.'

'Oh ... thank you.'

'That's all right, sir. Hope you had a nice nap.'

Dasein stood staring at the door for a moment. *How did Burdeaux know I was asleep?*

Perhaps I snored.

No further sound came from the hall, but Dasein knew Burdeaux had gone away.

Thoughtful, Dasein stripped out of his wrinkled clothes, showered and changed. He felt angry, frustrated. They were watching him every minute. It would be so easy, he knew, to let his anger become rage. This was no time for rage, though.

He wondered then if there was a season for rage.

A sensation of wetness drew his attention to his right hand. He was surprised to find himself still holding a washrag. Innocent thing with a green and white braided edge. He threw it into the bathroom where it landed with a wet slap.

Another rap sounded on his door and he knew it was Jenny.

Decision gripped Dasein.

He strode across the room, threw open the door. She stood there in an orange jumper dress with white blouse, a smile deepening the dimple on her left cheek.

'I'm glad you're ready,' she said. 'Hurry up or we'll be late.'

As he allowed her to lead him out and down the stairs, Dasein wondered if imagination had played a trick on him, or had there been a brief moment of worry before she smiled?

Jenny carried on a continuing babble of unanswerable conversation as they went down the stairs, through the lobby onto the porch.

'You'll love the lake this time of year. I wish I could spend more time there. You're not favoring your shoulder as much as you did. I'll bet it's better. Uncle Larry wants you to stop by later for him to check you. All the gang are anxious to meet you. Here they are now.'

The gang occupied a stake truck.

Dasein recognized Willa Burdeaux's pixie face in the cab. She sat beside a blonde, rather craggy-faced youth with large innocent blue eyes. As he looked at her, she winked slowly, deliberately. At least a dozen couples stood in the back of the truck ... and there were odd singles: a tall, brown-haired man with fierce dark eyes – Walter Somebody; Dasein failed to catch the last name ... a set of twin young women, plump with long sandy hair, round faces – Rachel and Mariella.

Jenny performed the introductions too fast for Dasein to catch all the names, but he did focus on the fact that the young man with Willa Burdeaux was her fiancé, Cal Nis.

Reaching hands helped him into the back of the truck, pulled Jenny up beside him. There were boxes around the edges for seats. Dasein found himself crowded onto a box with Jenny snuggled beside him. He began to absorb the carnival air of the people around him – uninhibited laughter, bantering private jokes.

The truck rumbled into motion. Wind whipped them. Dasein had an impression of passing trees, patches of sky, lurching movement ... and the omnipresent laughter.

It grew on him that he and Jenny were being excluded from the laughter.

Was it a sense of delicacy in the group? Were they allowing the stranger time to acclimate himself?

He tried to see the situation as a psychologist, but his own involvement kept intruding. There was no way to focus his analytical eye on details without finding his own shadow across the scene. To cap it, his injured shoulder began to ache where Jenny pressed against it. Jenny's wind-tossed hair brushed his face. Each lurch of the truck sent a twinge through his shoulder.

The situation began to take on a nightmare quality.

Jenny stretched up, spoke into his ear: 'Oh, Gil – I've dreamed of this day . . . when you'd be here, one of us.'

One of us, Dasein thought. *Am I really one of them?*

Walter Somebody obviously had mistaken Jenny's move toward Dasein's ear. He waved and shouted from across the truck: 'Hey! No smooching before dark!'

This brought a short burst of laughter from the group, but no general shift in their attention. They continued to look and speak around Dasein and Jenny.

Smooching.

The word sent Dasein's mind into high gear. It was a word no longer in common use *outside*, a word out of its time and place. On this Walter's lips, though, it had carried the inflection of familiarity. It was a word they used here in the valley.

Dasein began to see Santaroga in a new light. They were conservatives here in the true sense of the word. They were clinging to the past, resisting change. He modified this thought: They resisted *some* change. They were people who had made a judgment that some things from the past should be maintained. This was what made them foreign. The world *outside* was moving away from them. The valley had become a preserve for conditions of another time.

The truck turned off onto another track through an avenue of overhanging sycamores. Great patches of maple-shaped leaves cast a green-gold aura over their world.

A jolting bump made Dasein wince with pain as Jenny lurched against his shoulder.

The truck emerged from the sycamores, passed through a stand of bull pine onto a grassy flat that merged into beach sand edging a cerulean lake.

Dasein stared out the open rear of the truck, hardly aware of the cascade of people leaping down to the grass, ignoring Jenny's urgings that they leave. Something about this lake – some sense of familiarity – had struck him with a feeling of beauty and menace.

A narrow floating walkway reached out from the beach to a float and diving platform – the wood all dark silver-gray from the sun. There were rowboats tied along one side of the diving float.

Beauty and menace.

The sensation passed and he wondered at himself. He was seeing phantoms, focusing too much inward.

'Is it your shoulder?' Jenny asked.

'It'll be all right,' Dasein said.

He followed her down off the truck, wishing he could let himself go, become a laughing part of this group. They were having fun here – carrying boxes to tables set under the trees, preparing fires in rock pits. Some wandered off into the trees, returned in bathing suits.

Jenny had attached herself to a group laying out picnic lunches on the tables. Presently, she joined the scampering movement toward the water, shedding her dress to reveal an orange one-piece bathing suit beneath. She was a naiad, limbs flashing brown and lithe in the sun.

She waved to him from the float, shouted: 'See you in a minute, darling!'

Dasein watched her dive into the lake with a feeling she was suddenly lost to him. He experienced an intense jealousy, imagining himself a decrepit old man surrounded by playing children, unable to join them in their happiness.

He looked around at lake and verging woods. There was a breeze across the water. The breeze had summer in it, fragrant with grass and evergreen needles. He wished suddenly for some drink with which to salute this breeze and day, some potion that would make him a part of the scene.

Slowly, Dasein walked down to the floating walk and out onto the boards. There were fleece clouds in the sky, and as he stared down at the water, he saw those clouds floating on the lake bottom. Waves shattered the illusion. Jenny swam up, leaned her elbows on the boards. Her face all dripping water, smiling, had never seemed more lovely.

'Darling, why don't you come out to the float and sun yourself while we swim?' she asked.

'All right,' he said. 'Maybe I can scull around in one of those boats.'

'You go easy on that shoulder or I'll tell Uncle Larry,' she said. She kicked away from the walk, swam lazily out toward the float.

Dasein followed, making his way through dripping swimmers running up and down the walk. It struck him as odd how this crowd saw him but didn't see him. They made way for him, but never looked at him. They shouted across him, but not to him.

He moved to the first boat in the line, untied its painter and prepared to get into it. Jenny was swimming some fifty feet out, a slow, smooth crawl that took her diagonally away from the float.

Dasein stood up, moved to step into the boat. As he stepped, something pushed him in the middle of the back. His foot kicked the gunwale, thrusting the boat out into the water. He saw he was going to fall into the lake, thought: *Oh, damn! I'll get my clothes all wet.* The stem of the boat was turning toward him and he thought of trying to reach for it, but his left foot on the dock slipped in a patch of wet wood. Dasein found himself turning sideways without any control over his motion.

The edge of the boat, seen out of the corner of an eye, rushed toward him. He tried to reach up, but that was the side of his bad shoulder. His arm wouldn't move fast enough.

There was an explosion of blackness in his head. Dasein felt himself sinking into an enveloping cold, soundless, all dark and inviting.

A part of his mind screamed: *Beauty! Menace!*

He thought that an odd combination.

There was a distant ache in his lungs and it was cold – terrifyingly cold. He felt pressure . . . and the cold . . . all distant and unimportant.

I'm drowning, he thought.

It was an unexciting thought – something that concerned another person.

They won't see me . . . and I'll drown.

The cold grew more immediate – wet.

Something turned him violently.

Still, everything remained remote – all happening to that *other* being which he knew to be himself, but which could not concern him.

Jenny's voice broke on him like a thunderclap: 'Help me! Please! Someone help me! Oh, God! Won't someone help me? I love him! Please help me!'

He grew aware suddenly of other hands, other voices.

'All right, Jen. We've got him '

'Please save him!' Her voice carried a sobbing intensity.

Dasein felt himself draped across something hard that pressed into his abdomen. Warmth gushed from his mouth. There was a blinding, terrible pain in his chest.

Abruptly, he began to cough – gasping, the pain tearing at his throat and bronchia.

'He swallowed a lot of water.' It was a man's voice, almost vacant of emotion.

Jenny's voice came pleading beside Dasein's ear: 'Is he breathing? Please don't let anything happen to him.' Dasein felt wetness on his neck, and still Jenny's voice pleading there beside him: 'I love him. Please save him.'

That same unemotional male voice answered: 'We understand, Jenny.'

And another voice, husky, feminine: 'There's only one thing to do, of course.'

'We're doing it!' Jenny screamed. 'Don't you understand?'

Even as hands picked Dasein up, began carrying him, Dasein wondered: *Doing what?*

His coughing had subsided, but the pain in his chest remained. It hurt when he breathed.

Presently, there was grass under his back. Something warm and confining was wrapped around him. It was an oddly womblike sensation.

Dasein opened his eyes, found himself staring up at Jenny, her dark hair framed by blue sky. She managed a trembling smile.

'Oh, thank God,' she whispered.

Hands lifted his shoulders. Jenny's face went away. A cup full of steaming brown liquid was pressed against his lips. Dasein experienced the almost overpowering smell of Jaspers, felt hot coffee burn down his throat.

Immediately, a sense of warmth and well-being began to seep outward through his body. The cup was pulled away, returned when he moved his mouth toward it.

Someone laughed, said something that Dasein couldn't quite catch. It sounded like, 'Take a full load.' But that didn't make sense and he rejected it.

The hands eased him gently back to the grass. That vacant masculine voice said: 'Keep him warm and quiet for awhile. He's okay.'

Jenny's face returned. Her hand stroked his head.

'Oh, darling,' she said. 'I looked at the dock and you were gone. I didn't see you fall, but I knew. And no one was paying any attention. It took me so long to get there. Oh, your poor head. Such a bruise.'

Dasein felt the throbbing then as though her words had turned it on – a pulsing ache at the temple and across his ear. *A blow like that – shouldn't I have X-rays?* he wondered. *How do they know I haven't a fractured skull ... or concussion?*

'Cal says the boat must've been tipping away from you as you hit it,' Jenny said. 'I don't think you've broken anything.'

Pain shot through him as she touched the bruise.

'It's just a bad bruise.'

Just a bad bruise! he thought. He was filled with abrupt anger at her. How could they be so casual?

Still, that feeling of warmth spread out through him, and he thought: *Of course I'm all right. I'm young, healthy. I'll heal. And I have Jenny to protect me. She loves me.*

Something about this train of thought struck him as profoundly wrong then. He blinked. As though that were the creative mechanism, his vision blurred, resolved into flashes of gemlike light, red, orange, yellow, brown, green, violet, blue light with offshooting crystal shards.

The light resolved into a membranous inward sensation, a perception of perception that reached out through his mind. He *saw* then strong pulses of his own heart, the tender brain sheathing that rose and fell with the pulse, the damaged area – just a bruise, skull intact.

Dasein grew aware then why the Santarogans showed so little concern for his injury. They *knew* the injury through him. If he were like them, he would tell them when he needed help.

Then why didn't they try to rescue me until Jenny came? Dasein asked himself. And the answer lay there to wonder at: *Because I didn't cry out for help in my thoughts!*

'You shouldn't sleep now, I don't think,' Jenny said.

She found his left hand, gripped it. 'Isn't there something about not sleeping after a head injury?'

Dasein stared up at her, seeing the dark wings of her hair disarrayed from rescuing him, the way her eyes seemed to touch him, so intense was her concentration. There was dampness on her lashes and he felt that he might look behind her eyes and find the way to a magic land.

'I love you,' he whispered.

She pressed a finger against his lips. 'I know.'

I am a Santarogan now, Dasein thought.

He lay there rolling the thought in his mind, filled by this odd awareness that let him reach out to Jenny even when she released his hand and left him alone there on the grass. There was nothing of telepathy in this awareness. It was more knowledge of mood in those around him. It was a lake in which they all swam. When one disturbed the water, the others knew it.

My God! What this Jaspers could do for the world! Dasein thought.

But this thought sent roiling waves through the lake of mutual awareness. There was storm in this thought. It was dangerous. Dasein recoiled from it.

He remembered then why he had come here and saw the conflict from a new perspective. The people who'd sent him – what did they want?

Proof, he thought.

He found he couldn't focus on what *they* wanted to prove. It was all tied up with Jersey Hofstedder's car and the blunt Yankee insularity of these people.

Jenny's friends were noticing him now, Dasein saw. They looked at him – directly at him. They spoke to him. And when he felt he wanted to get up and go to the big fire they'd built against the evening chill, strong hands came without bidding and helped him.

Night fell.

Dasein found himself seated on a blanket beside Jenny. Someone was playing a guitar in the darkness. Moon colored half the lake, leaving a great black stone of night against one side. Wind-wrinkled water lapped at the stone and he felt that if the blackness could only be moved it would blaze in light to reveal fairyland.

Jenny snuggled against him, murmured: 'You're feeling better. I know it.'

He agreed with her silently.

Torches flamed down by the lake – people securing the boats. Someone handed him a sandwich redolent with Jaspers. He ate, his attention on the torches and the fire – the trees around them gleaming red, grotesque shadows lurching, dove wings of smoke against the moon. Abruptly, Dasein secreted part of his sandwich in a pocket.

For no reason he could explain, Dasein remembered a time shortly after Jenny had left the school. It had rained. He remembered reaching out his window to feel the rain, seeing the wet sparkle of the lawn beneath a window, like a broken necklace scattered there.

Abruptly, the wind across the lake shifted, stung his eyes with smoke. He swallowed a mouthful of the smoke and it brought him to an intense awareness of the here and now, Jenny beside him ... waiting.

As he thought about her, she reached up, pulled his lips down on hers. It was a long kiss, full of guitar music, remembered rain and the taste of smoke.

How can I ever explain this? Dasein wondered. *Selador would think me mad.*

Jenny stirred against him at this thought, stroked his neck.

'Let's get married soon,' she whispered.

Why not? Dasein asked himself. *I'm a Santarogan now.*

But this thought brought a surge of fear that tightened his chest and made Jenny shiver. She pulled away, stared at him with worry in her eyes.

'Everything will be all right,' she whispered. 'You'll see.'

The worry remained in her voice, though. And Dasein sensed menace in the night. The guitarist struck a sour note, fell silent.

Dasein saw that moonlight had moved into the black area of the lake ... and it revealed no fairyland – only more lake, more trees.

The night was definitely cold now.

Once more, Jenny pressed her lips to his.

Dasein knew he still loved her. It was a real thing to which he could cling. But there was no more magic in this night. He felt that he had skirted madness and the thing had left its taint on him.

When she pulled away, he whispered: 'I want to marry you, Jenny. I love you ... but ... I need time. I need ...'

'I know, darling,' she said. She stroked his cheek. 'Take all the time you need.'

Her voice carried a withdrawing note compounded as she pulled back. Dasein felt the night's coldness then, the stillness of their companions.

Abruptly, there was a stirring in the people around them. They began moving toward the truck.

'It's time to go back,' Jenny said.

Back where? Dasein asked himself.

Jenny stood up, helped him to his feet. He stumbled in a brief spasm of dizziness. Jenny steadied him.

'Do you want Uncle Larry to look at your head tonight?' she asked.

Piaget, Dasein thought. That was the *back* at which he was aimed. Piaget. They would continue their trade of truths. The Jaspers change was forcing it.

'I'll see him in the morning,' Dasein said.

'Not tonight?'

In my own sweet time, Dasien thought. And he said: 'Not tonight.'

The answer seemed to trouble Jenny. She sat barely touching him on the ride back to town.

6

When they were gone, leaving Dasein standing alone behind his truck in the Inn yard, he stared up at the darkness of the sky, lost in thought. Jenny's good-night kiss – strained, trembling – still tingled on his lips. There was a smell of exhaust gases and oil in the air. From somewhere inside the building came the faint sound of music – a radio. The gravel of the driveway felt hard and immediate under his feet.

Slowly, Dasein brought his right hand from his pocket, opened it to stare at the small ball of matter there – an object indistinctly seen in the light from the Inn sign. Now, there was a strong smell of Jaspers around him.

Dasein studied the object in his hand – a compressed ball of bread, cheese and ham, a bit of one of the sandwiches from the picnic.

Did they know I secreted this? he wondered.

He debated going inside and changing his clothes. The pants and shirt he'd worn on the picnic, garments that had been soaked and allowed to dry on him, felt wrinkled and twisted against his body.

Dasein felt that his mind wandered around this decision: to change or not to change, that was the question. The object in his hand was more immediate, though. Selador. Yes, Selador had to get this and examine it.

I'm not thinking clearly, Dasein told himself.

He felt torn between extremes, between decisions of enormous moment. *The head injury?* he wondered. But he trusted the Jaspers-induced insight that told him the injury wasn't serious. Still ... decisions ...

With intense concentration, Dasein forced himself to get into his truck. He leaned against the steering wheel, put the compressed ball of the Jaspers sandwich on the seat beside him. There was warm wetness at his seat and he pulled his wallet from his hip pocket, felt the water trapped in it. The wallet went beside the bit of sandwich.

Now, Dasein told himself. *Now, I will go.*

But it was several minutes before he could muster the strength of decision to start the motor and pull out of the parking area and onto the road toward Porterville. He drove slowly, conscious of the blocking dullness inhibiting his motions.

The headlights picked out a wedge of flowing roadway and bordering trees – yellow center line, guard rails, driveways. Dasein opened his window, leaned out into the wind trying to clear his head. Now, he was on the winding road up out of the valley and the slowness of his mind grew like a deadly weight.

Headlights came toward him, passed.

Dark mass of rock beside the road – yellow center lines, twisting scars of repair lines on the paving . . . stars overhead . . . He came at last to the notch that led out through the black skeletons of burned trees.

Dasein felt something was drawing him back, ordering him to turn around and return to Santaroga. He fought it. Selador had to get that bit of food and analyze it. Duty. Promises. Had to get out to Porterville.

Somewhere in his mind, Dasein sensed a looming black shape, anonymous, terrifying. It studied him.

With an inner snapping sensation, Dasein felt his mind clear. The thing was so abrupt he almost lost control of the wheel, swerved across the center line and back, tires squealing.

The road, the night, the steering wheel, his foot on the accelerator – all slammed against his senses with a confused immediacy. Dasein hit the brakes, slowed almost to a crawl. Every nerve end yammered at him. His head whirled. Dasein clung to the wheel, concentrated on steering. Slowly, his senses sorted themselves out. He took a deep, trembling breath.

Drug reaction, he told himself. *Have to tell Selador.*

Porterville was the same dull street he had remembered – cars parked at the tavern, the single light beating down on the darkened gas station.

Dasein pulled to a stop beside the telephone booth, remembering the deputies who'd questioned him there, mistaking him for a Santarogan. Had they been premature? he wondered.

He gave the operator Selador's number, waited impatiently, tapping his finger against the wall. A faint and reedy woman's voice came on the line – 'Selador residence.'

Dasein leaned into the phone. 'This is Gilbert Dasein. Let me speak to Dr Selador.'

'I'm sorry. The Seladors are out for the evening. Is there a message?'

'Damn!' Dasein stared at the phone. He felt an irrational anger at Selador. It took a conscious effort of logic for Dasein to tell himself

Selador had no real reason to hang around the telephone. Life went on its normal way back in Berkeley.

'Is there a message, sir?' the reedy voice repeated.

'Tell him Gilbert Dasein called,' Dasein said. 'Tell him I'm sending him a package for chemical analysis.'

'A package for chemical analysis. Yes sir. Is that all?'

'That's all.'

Dasein replaced the receiver on its hook with a feeling of reluctance. He felt abandoned suddenly – alone up here with no one outside really caring whether he lived or died.

Why not chuck them all? he asked himself. *Why not marry Jenny, tell the rest of the world to go to hell?*

It was an intensely inviting prospect. He could feel himself sinking into quiet security back in the valley. Santaroga beckoned to him with that security. It was *safe* there.

That very sense of safety, though, was edged with danger. Dasein sensed it ... a lurking something in the outer darkness. He shook his head, annoyed at the tricks his mind was playing. The *vapors*, again!

He returned to the truck, found a jar in the back where he'd kept a store of matches. He dumped out the matches, put in the remains of the sandwich, sealed the jar, packaged it with the remnants of a cardboard grocery box and a scrap of wrapping paper, tied the whole thing with a length of fishline and addressed it to Selador. When it was done, he wrote a covering letter on a page from his notebook, listed his reactions there painstakingly – the drug effect, the *accident* at the lake and his own impressions of the group ... the wall they threw up to keep him at a distance ... Jenny's terror ...

It all went into the letter.

The effort of recalling the incidents made his head ache where he'd hit the edge of the boat. He found an envelope in his case, addressed the letter and sealed it.

With a sense of satisfaction, Dasein started up the truck, found a dark side street and parked. He locked the cab, climbed into the back and lay down to wait for morning when the Porterville post office would open.

They won't control the mail over here, he told himself. *Let Selador get the sample of Jaspers ... we'll soon know what it is.*

He closed his eyes and his lids became like a movie screen for a fantasy – Jenny cringing, crying out, pleading with him. Selador laughing. A gigantic Dasein figure stood bound like Prometheus, the eyes glazed ... panting with exertion.

Dasein's eyes popped open.

Waking fantasy!

He was over the hill – around the bend!

Hesitantly, he closed his eyes. Only darkness ... but there was sound in this darkness – Selador laughing.

Dasein pressed his hands over his ears. The sound changed to tolling bells, slow cadence ... mournful. He opened his eyes. The sound stopped.

He sat up, pushed himself back into a corner, eyes open. It was cold in the camper and there was a musty smell. He found his sleeping bag, wrapped it around him, sat there with his eyes open. There were cricket sounds outside, faint creakings in the truck's metal.

Slowly, sleep crept up on him His eyelids drooped, popped open.

How long would it take for the Jaspers effect to wear off? he wondered. Surely, this was drug effect.

His eyes closed.

Somewhere in an echoing box, Jenny whispered: 'Oh, Gil – I love you. Gil, I love you ...'

He went to sleep with her voice whispering to him.

7

Daylight found Dasein staring up at the camper's metal ceiling with a sense of disorientation. He recognized the ceiling, but couldn't locate it in space. His head and shoulder throbbed. Ceiling ... familiar ceiling.

A car horn honked. It brought him to the present and awareness. He threw off the twisted folds of his sleeping bag, climbed out into a gray, overcast day. His chin felt rough and stubbly. There was a sour taste in his mouth.

Two passing schoolboys stared at him, whispering.

I must look a sight, Dasein thought. He looked down at his clothes. They were twisted and wrinkled as though he had gone swimming in them and then slept in them until they dried. Dasein smiled to himself, thinking that was exactly what had happened.

He climbed into the cab, turned around and found the main street, drove down it until he saw the Post Office sign over the porch of a general store.

The postmaster had to finish selling candy to a girl before he could come around behind his caged counter to weigh Dasein's package and letter. The man was tall, pale with thinning black hair, darting, wary blue eyes. He sniffed once at Dasein, said: 'That'll be eighty-four for the package and five for the letter.'

Dasein pushed a dollar bill under the cage.

The man made change, looked once more at the package. 'What's in the package, mister?'

'Specimens for analysis at our laboratory,' Dasein said.

'Oh.'

The man didn't appear curious about specimens of what. 'Any return address?' he asked.

'Dr Gilbert Dasein, general delivery, Santaroga,' he said.

'Dasein,' the man said with sudden interest. 'Dasein ... seems I got a package for a Dasein. Just a minute.'

He disappeared into the back, returned in a moment with a box about

279

a foot square wrapped neatly and tied with heavy twine. Even from a distance, Dasein recognized Selador's precise script on the address.

Selador writing me here? Dasein wondered.

The air of conspiracy in this gave Dasein the abrupt sensation of being completely transparent to Selador. The man could send a package here and *know* it would be picked up. Immediately, Dasein told himself this was the simplest thing to figure – given the Santaroga Post Office situation as he'd described it to Selador.

There remained, though, the feeling he was a pawn and his every move was known to the masters of the game.

'Let's see your identification,' the postmaster said.

Dasein showed it.

'Sign here,' the man said.

Dasein signed, took the package. It felt heavy.

'Funny thing you Santarogans using my Post Office,' the postmaster said. 'Something wrong with your own?'

Santarogans ... plural, Dasein thought. He said: 'Is some other ... Santarogan using your Post Office?'

'Well – used to be,' the man said. 'Negro fellow over there ... Burdeaux, as I recollect. He used to send some mail from here. Got a package here once from Louisiana. Long time ago that was.'

'Oh, yes,' Dasein said, not knowing how else to acknowledge this information.

'Haven't seen Burdeaux in quite a spell,' the postmaster mused. 'Nice fellow. Hope he's all right.'

'Quite all right,' Dasein said. 'Well – thank you.' He took his package, went out to the truck.

With a feeling of caution he couldn't explain, Dasein left the package unopened on the seat beside him when he drove east on the road to Santaroga until he found a shady spot in which to pull off.

The box contained a .32 caliber automatic pistol with an extra clip and box of cartridges. Wired to the trigger guard was a note from Selador: 'Gilbert – This has been gathering dust in my bureau drawer for many years and I'm probably an old woman for sending it to you, but here it is. I think I'm sending it in the hope you won't have to use it. The situation you describe, however, has filled me with the oddest sensations of disquiet that I can remember. I hope you're being extremely cautious.'

On the reverse side of the note was a scrawled postscript: 'No news yet on the investigations you requested. These things move slowly. You give me hope, though, that we'll get the goods on these people.' It was signed: 'S.'

Dasein hefted the automatic, fought down an impulse to heave it out the window. The thing embodied ultimate menace. What had he said to prompt Selador to send it? Or was this part of some obscure motivational gambit Selador was setting up?

Could it be a reminder of duty? His bruised head ached with thought.

A line in Selador's note came back to him and he reread it: ' ... *get the goods on these people.*'

Is that what I'm, supposed to do? Dasein wondered. *Am I to set them up for prosecution?*

He remembered Marden alluding to the reasons an investigator had been sent.

Dasein swallowed. Selador's line, read once more, looked like a slip. Had the good doctor tipped his hand? Sending a gun wasn't like the man. In fact, Dasein realized if he'd been asked, he would've said Selador wasn't even the type to *own* a gun.

What to do with the damn' thing now that he had it?

Dasein checked it, found the clip full, no cartridge in the chamber. He resisted the impulse to shove it in the glove compartment and forget it. If the truck were searched. ...

Damn Selador!

Feeling foolish as he did it, Dasein slipped the gun into a hip pocket, pulled his coat over it. He'd settle with Selador later. Right now there was Piaget ... and Piaget had some answers to give.

8

Piaget was in his office with a patient when Dasein arrived. The gaunt, gray Sarah opened the door, allowed he could wait in the living room. With a grudging show of hospitality, she added that she would bring him some coffee if he wanted it.

With a stomach-gripping pang, Dasein realized he was ravenous with hunger. He wondered if he could mention this fact.

As though she'd read his mind, Sarah said. 'I'll bet you haven't eaten breakfast.' She looked him up and down. 'You look like you'd slept in those clothes. You doctors are all alike. Never care how you look.'

'As a matter of fact, I haven't eaten,' Dasein said.

'You're going to lead Jenny some life,' she said. But she softened her words with a smile.

Dasein stared in wonder at a double, whiteboned row of false teeth in the wrinkled face.

'Got a leftover apple roll and some Jaspers cream,' Sarah said. 'Bet you'd like that.'

She turned away, went out through the dining room into a glistening white kitchen, which Dasein glimpsed once through a swinging door. The door went slap-slap behind her.

Dasein thought about that smile, recalled Jenny saying Sarah liked him. On impulse, he followed her into the kitchen.

'Bet you don't like feeding people in the living room,' he said.

'Feed people wherever they have to be fed,' she said.

She put a dish on an oval table beside windows looking onto a flower garden brilliant in the morning sun. 'Sit here, young man,' she said. She poured a thick flow of cream from a pitcher onto the golden mound of crust in the dish.

Dasein inhaled a strong smell of Jaspers. His hand trembled as he picked up the spoon Sarah placed within his reach. The trembling stopped at his first swallow of the food.

The pastry was sweet and soothing, rich with apples.

With a detached feeling of shock, Dasein watched his hand guide the spoon into the pastry for another bite, saw the food conveyed to his mouth, felt himself swallow it.

Soothing.

I'm addicted to the stuff, he thought.

'Something wrong?' Sarah asked

'I ...' He put down his spoon. 'You've trapped me, haven't you?' he asked.

'What're you talking about?' Sarah asked.

'What's it ...' He nodded toward the pastry. '... doing to me?'

'You feel strange?' Sarah asked. 'Got a fluttery feeling behind your eyes?'

'I'm ...' He shook his head. Her words sounded insane. *Fluttery feeling behind his eyes!*

'I'll bring Doctor Larry,' Sarah said. She darted out a connecting door at the back of the kitchen and he saw her running along the covered walkway to the clinic.

Presently, she reappeared with Piaget in tow. The doctor's face wore a worried frown.

'What's this Sarah's telling me?' Piaget asked. He put a hand under Dasein's chin, stared into Dasein's eyes.

'What's she telling you what?' Dasein asked. The words sounded foolish as they spilled from his lips. He brushed Piaget's hand aside. The doctor's frown, the squinting eyes – he looked like an angry Buddha.

'You seem to be all right,' Piaget said. 'Any strange symptoms of ...'

'You've trapped me,' Dasein said. 'That's what I told her. You've trapped me.' He gestured at the plate in front of him. 'With this.'

'Is he just fighting it?' Sarah asked.

'Probably,' Piaget said.

'Don't make sense,' Sarah said.

'It happens,' Piaget said.

'I know, but ...'

'Will you two stop talking about me like I was a blob of something on a slide!' Dasein raged. He pushed away from the table, jumped to his feet. The motion sent his bowl of food sliding off the table with a crash.

'Now look what you've done!' Sarah said.

'I'm a human being,' Dasein said, 'not some sort of ...'

'Easy, lad, easy,' Piaget said.

Dasein whirled away, brushed past Piaget. He had to get away from this pair or be consumed by rage. Dasein's mind kept focusing on the weapon in his hip pocket.

Damn Selador!

'Here, now – wait a minute!' Piaget called.

Dasein paused in the kitchen door, turned to glare slit-eyed at Piaget. 'You can't leave like this,' Piaget said.

'Don't try to stop me,' Dasein growled. The gun felt large and cold against his hip.

Piaget fell silent – a stillness that Dasein imagined came up from the toes to stare out of measuring eyes. It was as though the man receded to become a figure seen through a reversed telescope – remote, secretive.

'Very well,' Piaget said. His voice came from that far away.

Deliberately, Dasein turned, went out the door, through the living room – out of the house. He felt his feet hitting the concrete of the front walk, the grass parking strip. His truck's door handle was cold under his hand. He started the motor, wondering at his own sensations – dreamlike.

A street flowed past, receded – signposts ... pavement crawling beneath his vision ... the Inn. He parked facing the long porch, an old green car on his left, make indeterminate, unimportant.

As though awakening, Dasein found his right hand on the Inn's front door – tugging, tugging. The door resisted. A sign on the center panel stared back at him.

'Closed.'

Dasein peered at the sign. *Closed?*

'Your luggage is right there by the steps, Dr Dasein.'

The voice Dasein recognized immediately – the infuriating Al Marden: *Authority ... Secrecy ... Conspiracy.*

Dasein turned, feeling himself bundled into a tight ball of consciousness. There was Marden standing halfway down the porch: red-haired, the narrow face, the green eyes, the tight-lipped mouth drawn into a straight line that could have signified any emotion from anger to amusement.

'So you're turning me out,' Dasein said.

'Hotel's closed,' Marden said. 'Health department.'

'The Inn, the restaurant, too?' Dasein asked.

'All closed.' It was a flat square of voice brooking no appeal.

'I can just go back where I came from, eh?' Dasein asked.

'Suit yourself.'

'You have other hotels,' Dasein said.

'Do we?'

'You must.'

'Must we?'

Dasein stared at the patrol captain, experiencing the same sensation he'd had with Piaget. The man receded.

'You can leave or go back to Dr Piaget's,' Marden said. 'He'll likely put you up.' So far away, that voice.

'Back to Piaget's,' Dasein said. 'How'd you know I just came from there?'

Marden remained silent, eyes withdrawn . . . distant.

'You move fast around here,' Dasein said.

'When we have to.'

Back to Piaget's? Dasein asked himself. He smiled, husbanding his tight ball of consciousness. *No!* They hadn't thought of everything. They hadn't thought of *quite* everything.

Still smiling, Dasein scooped up his suitcase from beside the steps, strode down to the truck, threw the bag into the cab, climbed behind the wheel.

'Best let people help you who know how,' Marden called.

There was just a faint trace of worry in his voice now. It broadened Dasein's smile, stayed with him as a satisfying memory as he drove back toward the town.

In the rear-view mirror, Dasein saw the patrol car following him. They wouldn't let him park in town, Dasein knew, but he remembered the map posted on a window of Scheler's service station. The map had shown a state park on the road west – Sand Hills State Park.

Down the main street he drove, Marden's patrol car right behind. There was the giant service station directly ahead. Dasein saw the telephone kiosk beside the parking area, swerved in so suddenly that Marden went past, screeched to a stop, backed up. Dasein already was out of the truck and at the kiosk.

Marden stopped the patrol car on the street, waited, staring at Dasein. The patrol car's motor seemed to rumble disapprovingly. Dasein turned, looked back at the service station – such a strange normality to the activity there: cars pulling in, out . . . no one paying the slightest attention to Marden or to the object of his attention.

Dasein shrugged, went into the booth, closed the door.

He put a dime in the slot, dialed the operator, asked for the Cooperative's number.

'If you want Jenny, Dr Dasein, she's already gone home.' Dasein stared at the telephone mouthpiece in front of him, letting the import of that supercilious female voice sink home. Not only did they know who was calling, they knew what he wanted before he could say it!

Dasein stared out at Marden, attention focused on the green eyes, the cynical green eyes.

Anger boiled in Dasein. He put it down. Damn them! Yes, he wanted to talk to Jenny. He'd talk to her in spite of them. 'I don't have Dr Piaget's number.'

A distinctly audible sigh came over the line.

Dasein looked at the telephone directory chained to the kiosk wall, felt a wave of guilt, unreasonable, damning, instantly repressed. He heard the operator dialing, the ring.

Jenny's voice answered.

'Jenny!'

'Oh, hello, Gilbert.'

Dasein experienced a cold sensation in his stomach. Her voice was so casual.

'You know they're trying to run me out of the valley, Jenny?' he asked.

Silence.

'Jenny?'

'I heard you.' Still that casual . . . distance in her tone.

'Is that all you have to say?' His voice betrayed hurt anger.

'Gilbert . . .' There was a long pause, then: ' . . . maybe it'd be . . . better . . . if you . . . just for a while, just for a while, went . . . well . . . outside.'

He sensed strain beneath the casual tone now.

'Jenny, I'm driving out to the Sand Hills Park and live in my camper. They're not running me out.'

'Gilbert, don't!'

'You . . . want me to leave?'

'I . . . Gilbert, please come back and talk to Uncle Larry.'

'I talked to Uncle Larry.'

'Please. For me.'

'If you want to see me, come out to the park.'

'I . . . don't dare.'

'You don't dare?' He was outraged. What pressure had they applied to her?

'Please don't ask me to explain.'

He hesitated, then: 'Jenny, I'm setting up camp in the park. To make my point. I'll be back after I make my point.'

'For the love of heaven, Gilbert – please be careful.'

'Careful of what?'

'Just . . . careful.'

Dasein felt the gun in his pocket, a heavy weight that brought his mind to bear on the nameless threats of this valley. That was the thing –

the threats were nameless. They lacked form. What use was a gun against a formless target?

'I'll be back, Jenny,' he said. 'I love you.'

She began crying. He heard the sobs distinctly before she broke the connection.

His muscles stiff with anger, Dasein marched back to his truck, pulled it around the police car and headed out the east road, Marden right behind.

Let the son-of-a-bitch follow, Dasein told himself. He could feel the reckless inanity of his actions, but there remained a driving current underneath that told him he had to do this. This was asking for a showdown. That was the thing. A showdown. Perhaps a showdown was needed to provide answers.

He crossed the river on a concrete bridge, glimpsed rows of greenhouses off to the left through the trees. The road climbed up through the trees, emerged into scrub country – madrone and mesquite. It twisted down through the scrub and again the land changed. In the distance there were tree-covered heights, but in between stretched low mounds of hills topped by gnarled bushes, scattered weedy growths with bare gray dirt and pools of black water, miasmic water untouched by growing things, in the low spots.

A smell of sulfur, dank and suffocating, hung over the land.

With almost a sense of recognition, Dasein realized these must be the sand hills. A broken sign came into view on the right. It dangled from one post. Another post leaned at a crazy angle.

Sand Hills State Park. Public camp ground.

Twin ruts led off through the sand to the right toward a fenced area with a doorless outhouse at one end and crumbling stone fireplaces spaced around the edge.

Dasein turned into the ruts. The truck lurched and growled its way to the parking area. He stopped beside one of the stone fireplaces, stared around. The place was outrageously drab.

A sound of wheels and laboring car engine brought Dasein's attention to the left. Marden pulled the patrol car to a stop beside him, leaned across to the open window.

'What're you stopping here for, Dasein?' There was just a touch of petulance in Marden's tone.

'This is a state park isn't it?' Dasein asked. 'Any law says I can't camp here?'

'Don't get smart with me, Dasein!'

'Unless you have a legal objection, I'm going to camp here,' Dasein said.

'Here?' Marden gestured at the desolation of the place.

'I find it relatively friendly after Santaroga,' Dasein said.

'What're you trying to prove, Dasein?'

Dasein answered him with a silent stare.

Marden pulled back into the patrol car. Dasein could see the man's knuckles white on the steering wheel. Presently, the patrol captain leaned back, glared up at Dasein. 'Okay, mister. It's your funeral.'

The patrol car leaped ahead, made a sand-spewing turn around the parking area, roared out to the highway and headed back toward town.

Dasein waited for the dust to settle before getting out. He climbed into the camper, checked his emergency larder – beans, powdered milk and powdered eggs, canned frankfurters, two bottles of ketchup, a can of syrup and a half empty box of prepared pancake mix . . . coffee, sugar . . . He sighed, sat down on the bunk.

The window opposite framed a view of the sand hills and the doorless outhouse. Dasein rubbed his forehead. There was an ache behind his eyes. The bruise on his head throbbed. The pitiless light beating down on the drab hills filled him with a sense of self-accusation.

For the first time since pointing his truck down into the valley, Dasein began to question his own actions. He felt there was an air of insanity around everything he had done. It was a mad pavane – Jenny . . . Marden . . . Burdeaux, Piaget, Willa, Scheler, Nis . . . It was mad, yet with its own kind of sense. His brushes with disaster became a part of the stately nonsense.

And there was Jersey Hofstedder's car – somehow the most significant thing of all.

He felt he had been down once more beneath the lake, rising now into a brutal honesty with himself. Jenny's 'We' lost some of its terrors. That was the *We* of the cave and the Jaspers, the *We* that waited patiently for him to make his decision.

The decision was his, he saw. No matter what the substance out of that dim red cave did to the psyche, the decision was his. It had to be his decision or the mad pavane lost all meaning.

I'm still fighting it, he thought. *I'm still afraid I'll wind up 'fluttery behind the eyes' and standing on a wrapping line at the Co-op.*

Restlessly, he climbed down out of the camper, stood on the sand absothing the mid-afternoon heat. A single crow flew overhead so close he heard the rushing harp sound of wind through its plumage.

Dasein gazed after the bird thinking how strange to see only one crow.

They were not a solitary bird. But here was this one – alone as he was alone.

What was I before that I cannot return to? he wondered. And he thought if he made the decision against Santaroga he'd be like that solitary crow, a creature without its own kind anywhere.

The problem, he knew, lay in a compulsion somewhere within him to make an honest report to those who'd hired him. The Jaspers clarity-of-being urged it. His own remembered sense of duty urged it. To do anything less would be a form of dishonesty, an erosion of selfdom. He felt a jealous possessiveness about this self. No smallest part of it was cheap enough to discard.

This self of his, old but newly seen, precious beyond anything he'd ever imagined, placed a terrifying burden on him, Dasein saw. He remembered the wildness of the Jaspers revelation, the gamut he'd run to come through to this peak.

The *had-I-but-known* quality of his immediate past settled on him then like a fog that chilled him in spite of the afternoon's heat. Dasein shivered. How pleasant it would be, he thought, to have no decisions. How tempting to allow that restlessly stirring *something* within his con-sciousness lift up its ancient snake's head and devour the disturbing parts of his awareness.

His view of the valley's people took on an Olympian cast. They stood beside him for a moment in ghostly ranks, godlike, masters of the primitive.

Are they testing me? he wondered.

Then why would Jenny say she dared not come here to him?

And where are the children?

A coldly rational part of his mind weighed his thinking and found the balance uncertain. *How much of what's in my mind is the drug thinking?* he asked himself.

At the fulcrum of any decision, that was the essential question. Where could he find solid ground upon which to stand and say, 'The things I'm to decide about are there ... and there ... and there ...?'

No one could help him find this ground, he knew. It must be a lonely search. If he made an honest report to Meyer Davidson's crew, that would doom Santaroga. But to make a false report would be to plant a cancer within himself.

He had separated himself from Santaroga in a definite way, like a knife stroke, Dasein realized. The Jaspers package he'd sent for analysis to Selador loomed in his mind. The cutting off had begun there.

It had been a gesture, nothing more. Symbolic. Some part of him had known even as he mailed it that the package would arrive with whatever Jaspers it had contained completely dissipated. He'd been sending a gesture of defiance to the Santaroga part of himself, Dasein realized.

Had Burdeaux done that? he wondered. What packages had Burdeaux exchanged with Louisiana?

The package to Selador – it had been like a thrown rock that could not reach its mark. He remembered as a child throwing a rock at a cat too far away to hit. Gray cat. He remembered the sudden bird silence in his aunt's garden, the gray cat slinking into view ... the rock landing short.

Piaget was the gray cat.

The cat in the garden had looked up, momentarily surprised by the sound, weighed the situation, and returned to its hunting with an insulting disdain for distant boys with distant rocks.

What had Piaget done?

Dasein experienced a sudden *deitgrasp*, an act of self-discovery in which the sky appeared to shimmer. He realized in this instant why he felt so terrifyingly lonely.

He had no group, no place in a hive of fellow-activity, nothing to shield him from personal decisions that might overwhelm him. Whatever decision he made, no matter the consequences, that was *his* decision. Selador might face the shame of his agent's failure. The school might lose its munificent grant. The unique *thing* that was Santaroga might be dissipated.

All because of a decision, a gesture really, by a lone man standing in a patch of barren sand hills, his mind caught up in fantasies about a solitary crow and a gray cat.

It was a moment for positive action, and all he could think to do was re-enter the camper and eat.

As he moved in the confining space preparing himself a powdered-egg mess in the frying pan, the truck emitted protesting creaks. Hunger gnawed at him, but he didn't want this food. He knew what he wanted – what he had fled here to escape, what his body craved until it was an ache at the core of him – Jaspers.

9

At full dark, Dasein switched on the camper's wall light, retreated into his notes. He felt he had to keep his mind occupied, but the fetid smell of the campground intruded. The camper was a tiny world with sharp boundaries, but it couldn't hold off the universe out there. Dasein peered out a window at stars: bright holes punched in blackness. They amplified his sense of loneliness. He jerked his gaze away.

The notes . . .

Always the same items floated to the surface:

Where were the children?

What failure of the Jaspers change produced zombies?

How could a whole community be ignited with the unconscious desire to kill a person?

What was the Jaspers essence? What was it? What did it do to the body's chemistry?

Dasein sensed the danger in putting his hand to these questions. They were questions and at the same time an answer. This probing – this was what ignited the community

He had to do it. Like a child poking at a sore, he had to do it. But once he had done it, could he turn then and tell the whole story to Meyer Davidson's crowd?

Even if he did find the answers and decided to make a full and honest report, would Santaroga permit it?

There were forces at work out there, Dasein realized, against which he was but a candle flickering in a gale.

He grew aware of footsteps crunching on the sand, turned off the light, opened the door and peered out.

A ghostly blur of a figure in the starlight, a woman in a light dress or a small man in a coat, was approaching along the tracks from the highway.

'Who's there?' Dasein called.

'Gil!'

'Jenny!'

He jumped down, strode to meet her. 'I thought you couldn't come out here. You told me ...'

'Please don't come any closer,' she said. She stopped about ten paces from him.

Such an oddly brittle quality to her voice – Dasein hesitated.

'Gil, if you won't come back to Uncle Larry's you must leave the valley,' she said.

'You want me to leave?'

'You must.'

'Why?'

'I ... they want you to go.'

'What have I done?'

'You're dangerous to us. We all know it. We can feel it. You're dangerous.'

'Jen ... do you think I'd hurt you?'

'I don't know! I just know you're dangerous.'

'And you want me to leave?'

'I'm ordering you to leave.'

'Ordering me?' He heard hysteria in her voice.

'Gil, please.'

'I can't go, Jen. I can't'

'You must.'

'I can't.'

'Then come back to Uncle Larry's. We'll take care of you.'

'Even if I turn into a zombie?'

'Don't say that!'

'It could happen, couldn't it?'

'Darling, we'll take care of you whatever happens!'

'You take care of your own.'

'Of course we do.'

'Jenny, do you know I love you?'

'I know,' she whispered.

'Then why are you doing this to me?'

'We're not doing anything to you.' She was crying, speaking through sobs. 'It's you who're doing ... whatever it is you're doing.'

'I'm only doing what I have to do.'

'You don't have to do anything.'

'Would you have me be dishonest ... lie?'

'Gil, I'm begging you. For my sake ... for your own sake, leave.'

'Or come back to Uncle Larry's?'

'Oh, please.'

'What'll happen to me if I don't?'

'If you really love me ... Oh, Gil, I couldn't stand it if ... if ...'

She broke off, crying too hard to speak.

He moved toward her. 'Jen, don't.'

The crying stopped abruptly and she began backing away, shaking her head at him. 'Stay away from me!'

'Jenny, what's wrong with you?'

She retreated even faster.

'Jenny, stop it.'

Suddenly, she whirled, began running down the track. He started to run after her, stopped. What was the use?

Her voice came back to him in a hysterical scream: 'Stay away from me! I love you! Stay away!'

He stood in shocked silence until he heard a car door slam out there on the highway. Lights came on; a car raced back toward town.

He remembered the soft moon of her face in the starlight, two black holes for eyes. It had been like a mask. He trudged back to the camper, his mind in turmoil. '*I love you! Stay away!*'

What do I really know about Jenny? he asked himself.

Nothing ... except that she loved him

Stay away?

Could that have been Jenny demanding, begging, ordering?

This speared his mind with a touch of madness. It transcended the irrationality of people in love.

'*You're dangerous. We all know it.*'

Indeed, they must.

In the Jaspers oneness he'd experienced at the lake, they must know him for a danger. If he could stay away from the stuff, kick it – would they know him then?

How could they help but know him then? His action would be the ultimate betrayal.

He thought of Santaroga then as a deceptive curtain of calmness over a pool of violence. Olympian-like, they'd surmounted the primitive – yes. But the primitive was still there, more explosive because it could not be recognized and because it had been held down like a coiled spring.

Jenny must sense it, he thought. Her love for him would give her a touch of clarity.

'*Stay away from me!*'

Her cry still rang in his ears.

And this was how the other investigators had died – releasing the explosion that was Santaroga.

Voices intruded on Dasein's reverie. They came from the other side of the camper away from the road. One voice definitely was that of a woman. He couldn't be sure about the other two. Dasein stepped around the camper, stared off toward the dank pools and sand hills. It was a shadowed starlit landscape with a suggestion of a glow in it.

A flashlight came into view across the hills. It wavered and darted. There were three black, lurching figures associated with the light. Dasein thought of Macbeth's witches. They walked and slid down a hill, skirted a pool and came on toward the campground.

Dasein wondered if he should call out. Perhaps they were lost. Why else would three people be out here in the night?

There was a burst of laughter from the group, vaguely childlike. The woman's voice came clearly out of the dark then: 'Oh, Petey! It's so good to have you with us.'

Dasein cleared his throat, said: 'Hello.' Then, louder: 'Hello!'

The light stabbed toward him. The lilting woman's voice said: 'Someone's in the campground.'

There was a masculine grunt.

'Who is it?' she asked.

'Just a camper,' Dasein said. 'Are you lost?'

'We've just been out frogging.' It sounded very like the voice of a young boy.

The trio came on toward him.

'Pretty poor place to camp,' the woman said.

Dasein studied the approaching figures. That was a boy on the left – definitely a boy. He appeared to be carrying a bow and a quiver of arrows. The woman had a long gigging pole, a bulky bag of some kind on one shoulder. The men carried the flashlight and a string of bullfrogs. They stopped beside the camper and the woman leaned against it to remove a shoe and pour sand from it.

'Been out to the pond,' she said.

'Hunh!' the man grunted.

'We got eight of them,' the boy said. 'Mom's gonna fry 'em for breakfast.'

'Petey had his heart set on it,' the woman said. 'I couldn't say no, not on his first day home.'

'I passed,' the boy said. 'Pop didn't pass, but I did.'

'I see,' Dasein said. He studied the man in the light reflected off the aluminum side of the camper. He was a tall man, slim, rather gawky.

Wisps of blonde hair protruded from a stocking cap. His eyes were as vacant as two pieces of blue glass.

The woman had put the shoe back on, now had the other one off emptying it. She was wrapped in a heavy coat that gave her the appearance of having been molded in a corrugated barrel. She was short, wouldn't stand any taller than the man's shoulder, but there was a purposeful air about her that reminded Dasein of Clara Scheler at the used-car lot.

'Bill's the first one in his family in eight generations didn't make it,' she said, restoring the shoe and straightening. 'They think it was something in his mother's diet before he was born. We were engaged before ... Why'm I telling you all this? I don't think I know you.'

'Dasein ... Gilbert Dasein,' he said. And he thought: *So this is how they take care of their own.*

'Jenny's fellow!' the woman said. 'Well, now.'

Dasein looked at the boy. *Petey.* He appeared to be no more than twelve, almost as tall as the woman. His face when the flashlight beam brushed it was a carbon copy of the man's. No denying parenthood there.

'Turn the light over here, Bill,' the woman said. She spoke carefully and distinctly as one might to a very young child. 'Over here, hon.'

'Over there, Pop.' The boy directed the man's uncertain hand.

'That's it, love,' the woman said. 'I think I got the gigging hook caught in my coat.' She fussed with a length of line at her side.

'Hunh,' the man said.

Dasein stared at him with a cold feeling of horror. He could see himself there, Jenny 'taking care' of him, their children helping.

'There,' the woman said, pulling the line free and attaching it to the gigging pole. 'Turn the light down toward the ground now, Bill. Toward the ground, hon.'

'Down this way, Pop,' the boy said, helping.

'That's a love,' the woman said. She reached out, patted the man's cheek.

Dasein felt something obscene in the gesture, wanted to turn away, couldn't.

'He's real good, Bill is,' the woman said.

The boy began playing with his bow, drawing it, releasing it.

'What you doing out here, Dr Dasein?' the woman asked.

'I ... wanted to be ... alone for awhile.' He forced himself to look at her.

'Well, this is a place to be alone all right,' she said. 'You feel all right? No ... *flutters* ... or anything?'

'Quite all right,' Dasein said. He shuddered.

The boy had knocked an arrow into the bow, was waving it about.

'I'm Mabel Jorick,' the woman said. 'This is Bill, my husband; our son, Petey. Petey's been ... you know, with Doc Piaget. Just got his bill of health.'

'I passed,' the boy said.

'Indeed you did, love.' She looked at Dasein. 'He's going outside to college next year.'

'Isn't he kind of young?' Dasein asked.

'Fifteen,' she said.

'Hunh,' the man said.

The boy had drawn the bow to its full arc, Dasein saw. The arrow tip glittered in the light from the flash.

Up, down ... right, left the arrow pointed.

Dasein moved uneasily as the tip traversed his chest – across, back. Sweat started on his forehead. He felt menace in the boy.

Instinctively, Dasein moved to put the man between himself and Petey, but Jorick moved back, stared off toward the highway.

'I think he hears the car,' the woman said. 'My brother, Jim, coming to pick us up.' She shook her head wonderingly. 'He has awful good hearing, Bill has.'

Dasein felt a crisis rushing upon him, dropped to his hands and knees. As he fell, he heard the bow twang, felt the wind of an arrow brush the back of his neck, heard it slam into the side of the camper.

'Petey!' the woman shouted. She snatched the bow from him. 'What're you doing?'

'It slipped, Ma.'

Dasein climbed to his feet studying these people narrowly.

'Hunh,' the man said.

The mother turned toward Dasein, the bow in her hand.

'He tried to kill me,' Dasein whispered.

'It was just an accident!' the boy protested.

The man lifted the flashlight, a menacing gesture.

Without looking at him, the woman said: 'Point it toward the ground, hon.' She pushed the light down, stared at Dasein. 'You don't think ...'

'It was an accident,' the boy said.

Dasein looked at the arrow. It had penetrated halfway through the camper's wall on a level with his chest. He tried to swallow in a dry throat. If he hadn't ducked at just that instant ... An accident. A regrettable accident. The boy was playing with a bow and arrow. It slipped.

Death by misadventure.

What warned me? Dasein wondered.

He knew the answer. It lay there in his mind, clearly readable. He had come to recognize the Santaroga pattern of menace. The means might differ, but the pattern carried a sameness – something lethal in an apparently innocent context.

'It was just an accident,' the woman whispered. 'Petey wouldn't harm a fly.'

She didn't believe it, Dasein saw.

And that was another thing. He was still connected by a tenuous thread to the Jaspers oneness. The warning message along that line was unmistakable. She'd received it, too.

'Wouldn't he?' Dasein asked. He looked once more at the arrow pro-truding from the camper.

The woman turned, grabbed her son's shoulder in one hand, shook the bow at him. 'You want to go back?' she demanded. 'Is that it?'

'Hunh,' the man said. He shuffled his feet uneasily.

'It was an accident,' the boy said. He obviously was near tears.

The woman turned a pleading look on Dasein. 'You wouldn't say anything to Doctor Larry, would you?'

'Say anything?' Dasein stared at her stupidly.

'He might . . . you know, misunderstand.'

Dasein shook his head. What was she talking about?

'It's so hard,' the woman said. 'After Bill, I mean. You know how it is over there.' She gestured vaguely with her head. 'The way they keep such a close watch on you, picking at every little symptom. It's so hard having a son there . . . knowing, seeing him only at visiting hours and . . . and never really being sure until . . .'

'I'm all right, Mom,' the boy said.

'Of course you are, love.' She kept her eyes on Dasein.

'I wouldn't deliberately hurt anyone,' Petey said.

'Of course you wouldn't, love.'

Dasein sighed.

'I passed,' the boy said. 'I'm not like Pop.'

'Hunh,' the man said.

Dasein felt like crying.

'You wouldn't say anything, would you?' the woman pleaded.

So Piaget had rewarding work for him here in the valley, Dasein thought. A clinic job . . . working with young people. And it was tied up with Jaspers, of course.

'Are they going to send me back?' Petey asked. There was fear in his voice.

'Dr Dasein, please . . .' the woman begged.

'It was an accident,' Dasein said. He knew it had not been an accident. The woman knew it. The arrow had been meant to kill. He said: 'Perhaps you'd better take the bow and arrows away from him for awhile.'

'Oh, don't you worry about that,' she said. There was a deep sighing of relief in her tone.

A car pulled to a stop on the highway at the entrance to the campground.

'There's Jim now,' the woman said. She turned away, her shoulder bag swinging toward Dasein. A rich aroma of Jaspers wafted across Dasein. It came from the bag.

Dasein stopped his right hand as it automatically reached toward the bag.

Mabel Jorick glanced back at him. 'I want to thank you for being so understanding,' she said. 'If there's ever anything . . .' She broke off, noting Dasein's attention on the bag. 'Bet you smelled the coffee,' she said. 'You want it?'

Dasein found himself unable to keep from nodding.

'Well, here.' She swung the bag around in front of her. 'Thermos is almost full. I just had one cup out at the pond. Spilled most of that. Petey, you run along, help your dad out to the car.'

'All right, Mom. Good night, Dr Dasein.'

Dasein was unable to take his gaze from the woman's hands pulling a shiny metal thermos from the bag.

'Take the thermos,' she said, holding it toward him. 'You can return it when you come back to town. We're only half a block from the clinic on Salmon Way.'

Dasein felt his fingers close around the corrugated sides of the thermos. He began trembling.

'You sure you're all right?' the woman asked.

'I'm . . . it's the aftereffect . . . shock, I guess,' he said.

'Sure. I'm so sorry.' She moved behind Dasein to the camper, broke off the protruding arrow. 'I'm going to give this to Petey as a reminder of how careful he should be.'

Dasein tore his attention away from the thermos, looked along the sand track. Petey and his father were almost halfway to the highway. The car's lights carved out a funnel of brilliance there. A horn honked once.

'If you're sure you're all right,' the woman said. 'I better be going.' She looked at the camper, glanced once more at Dasein. 'If there's ever anything we can do ...'

'I'll ... bring your thermos back as soon as I can,' Dasein said.

'Oh, no hurry; no hurry at all.' She pulled her coat tightly around her, trudged off toward the highway. About twenty paces away, she paused, turned. 'That was real sweet of you, Dr Dasein. I won't forget it.'

Dasein watched until the car turned back toward town. Before the car was out of sight, he was in the camper, the lid off the thermos, pouring himself a steaming cup of the coffee.

His hands trembled as he lifted the cup.

All the time and matter had been reduced to this moment, this cup, this Jaspers rich steam enveloping him. He drained the cup.

It was a sensation of rays spreading out from a pinhead spot in his stomach. Dasein groped his way to his bunk, wrapped the sleeping bag around him. He felt supremely detached, a transitory being. His awareness moved within a framework of glowing nets.

There was terror here. He tried to recoil, but the nets held him. *Where is the self that once I was?* he thought. He tried to hold onto a self that bore some familiarity, one he could identify. The very idea of a self eluded him. It became an ear-shaped symbol he interpreted as mind-in-action.

For a flickering instant he felt he had encountered the solid ground, a core of relative truth from which he could make his decisions and justify all his experiences. His eyes flew open. In the faint starlight reflected into the camper he saw something glittering on the wall, recognized the head of Petey's arrow.

There it was – the relative truth: an arrowhead. It had originated; it had ceased.

Everything with origin has cessation, he told himself.

He sensed the stirring in his consciousness then, the ancient *thing* abiding there, the mind eater. *Sleep,* Dasein told himself. There was an *atman* of sleep within him. It resisted awakening. It was infinite, circular. He lay spread on its rim.

Dasein slept.

10

Dawn light awakened him. The coffee in the thermos was cold and had lost its Jaspers savor. He sipped it anyway to ease the dryness in his throat.

There will be a place like a school, he thought. *A boarding school ... with visiting hours. It will have the Santaroga difference. It will be something besides a school.*

He stared at the thermos. It was empty. The bitter taste of its contents remained on his tongue, a reminder of his weakness in the night. The Jaspers had immersed him in nightmares. He remembered dreaming of glass houses, a shattering of glass that tumbled about him ... screaming.

House of glass, he thought. *Greenhouses.*

The sound of an approaching car intruded. Dasein stepped outside into chilly morning air. A green Chevrolet was bumping up the track toward him. It looked familiar. He decided the car either was Jersey Hofstedder's machine or its double.

Then he saw the beefy, gray-haired woman driving the car and he knew. It was Sam Scheler's mother – Clara, the car dealer.

She pulled to a stop beside Dasein, slid across the seat and got out his side.

'They told me you were here and by golly you are,' she said. She stood facing Dasein, a covered dish in her hands.

Dasein looked at the car. 'Did you drive clear out here to try to sell me that car again?' he asked.

'The car?' She looked around at the car as though it had appeared there by some form of magic. 'Oh, Jersey's car. Plenty of time for that ... later. I brought you some hair of the dog.' She presented the dish.

Dasein hesitated. Why should she bring him anything?

'Petey's my grandson,' she said. 'Mabel, my daughter, told me how nice you were last night.' She glanced at the stub of the arrow in the side of Dasein's camper, returned her attention to Dasein. 'Occurred to me maybe your problem's you don't realize how much we want you to be one of us. So I brought you some of my sour cream stew – plenty of Jaspers.'

She thrust the dish at him.

Dasein took it. Smooth, warm china under his hands. He fought down an unreasonable impulse to drop the dish and smash it. He was afraid suddenly. Perspiration made his palms slippery against the dish.

'Go on, eat it,' she said. 'It'll set you up for the day.'

I must not do it, Dasein told himself.

But that was irrational. The woman was just being kind, thoughtful ... Petey's grandmother. Thought of the boy brought the incident of the night flooding back into his mind.

School ... observation ... Jaspers ...

A whuffling noise from the green Chevrolet distracted him. A gray-muzzled old black-and-white border collie eased itself over onto the front seat, climbed down to the sand. It moved with the patient pain of old age, sniffed at Clara's heels.

She reached down, patted the dog's head. 'I brought Jimbo,' she said. 'He doesn't get out in the country much anymore. Dang nigh thirty-five years old and I think he's going blind.' She straightened, nodded to the dish in Dasein's hands. 'Go ahead, eat it.'

But Dasein was fascinated by the dog. Thirty-five? That was equivalent to more than two hundred years in a human. He put the dish on the camper's steps, bent to stare at the dog. *Jimbo.* Going blind, she said, but its eyes carried that same disturbing *Jaspers* directness he saw in all the humans.

'You like dogs?' Clara Scheler asked.

Dasein nodded. 'Is he really thirty-five?'

'Thirty-six in the spring ... if he lasts.'

Jimbo ambled across to Dasein, aimed the gray muzzle at his face, sniffed. Apparently satisfied, he curled up at the foot of the camper's steps, sighed, stared off across the sand hills.

'You going to eat or aren't you?' Clara asked.

'Later,' Dasein said. He was remembering how Jersey Hofstedder's car had figured in his thoughts – a key to Santaroga. Was it the car? he wondered. Or was the car just a symbol? Which was the important thing – the car or the symbol?

Seeing his attention on the car, Clara said: 'It's still priced at $650 if you want it.'

'I'd like to drive it,' Dasein said.

'Right now?'

'Why not?'

She glanced at the dish on the camper's step, said: 'That stew won't heat very well . . . and the Jaspers fades, you know.'

'I had your daughter's coffee last night,' Dasein said.

'No . . . aftereffects?'

It was a practical question. Dasein found himself probing his own bodily sensations – head injury fading, shoulder pain almost gone . . . a bit of latent anger over Petey's arrow, but nothing time wouldn't heal.

'I'm fine.'

'Well! You're coming around,' she said. 'Jenny said you would. Okay.' She gestured toward the green Chevrolet. 'Let's take a spin up the highway and back. You drive.' She climbed into the right-hand seat, closed the door.

The dog raised his head from his paws.

'You stay there, Jimbo,' she said 'We'll be right back.'

Dasein went around, climbed behind the wheel. The seat seemed to mould itself to his back.

'Comfortable, huh?' Clara asked.

Dasein nodded. He had an odd feeling of *déjà vu*, that he'd driven this car before. It felt right beneath his hands. The engine purred alive, settled into an almost noiseless motion. He backed the car around, eased it over the ruts and out the track to the highway, turned right away from town.

A touch on the throttle and the old Chevrolet leaped ahead – fifty . . . sixty . . . seventy. He eased back to sixty-five. It cornered like a sports car.

'Got torsion bars,' Clara said. 'Doesn't roll worth a sweet damn. Isn't she pretty?'

Dasein touched the brakes – no fading and the nose strayed not an inch. It was as though the car rode on tracks.

'This car's in better shape right now than the day it came off the assembly line,' Clara said.

Dasein silently agreed with her. It was a pleasure to drive. He liked the leather smell of the interior. The hand-finished wood of the dash glistened with a dull luster. There was no distraction from it, just a tight cluster of instruments set up high to be read easily without taking his eyes too long from the road.

'Notice how he padded the dash on this side,' Clara said. 'Inch-and-a-half thick and a thin roll of metal underneath. He cut the steering wheel about a third of the way back, offset it on a U-joint. Hit anything with this car and you won't have that wheel sticking out your back. Jersey was making safe cars before Detroit even heard the word.'

Dasein found a wide spot at a turn, pulled off, turned around and headed back to the campground. He knew he had to have this car. It was everything this woman said.

'Tell you what,' Clara said. 'I'll deliver the car over to the Doc's when I get back. We'll figure out the details later. You won't find me hard to deal with, though I can't give you much for that dunker of a truck.'

'I . . . don't know how I can pay for it,' Dasein said. 'But . . .'

'Say no more. We'll figure out something.'

The track into the campground came into view. Dasein slowed, turned off onto the ruts, shifted down to second.

'You really ought to use the seatbelt,' Clara said. 'I noticed you . . .' She broke off as Dasein stopped behind the camper. 'Something's wrong with Jimbo!' she said, and she was out of the car and across to the dog.

Dasein turned off the ignition, jumped out and ran around to her side.

The dog lay almost over on its back, feet stretched out stiff, neck curved backward, its mouth open and tongue extended.

'He's dead,' Clara said. 'Jimbo's dead.'

Dasein's attention went to the dish on the steps. Its cover had been pushed aside and the contents disturbed. There was a splash of gravy beside the lid. Again, he looked at the dog. The sand was scratched in a wide swirl around Jimbo.

Abruptly, Dasein bent to the dish of stew, sniffed it. Beneath the heavy odor of Jaspers there was a bitter aroma that curled his nostrils.

'Cyanide?' he asked. He stared accusingly at Clara Scheler.

She looked at the dish. 'Cyanide?'

'You were trying to kill me!'

She picked up the dish, smelled it. Her face went pale. She turned, stared wide-eyed at Dasein.

'Oh, my God! The paint bleach,' she said. She dropped the dish, whirled away, dashed to the car before Dasein could stop her. The Chevrolet leaped to life, turned in a whirl of sand and roared out the track to the highway. It made a skidding turn onto the highway, raced back toward town.

Dasein stared after her.

She tried to kill me, he thought. *Cyanide. Paint bleach.*

But he couldn't shake the memory of her pale, wide-eyed stare. She'd been surprised, as shocked as he was. *Paint bleach.* He stared down at the dead dog. Would she have left the dish there near her dog if she'd known it contained poison? Not likely. Then why had she run?

Paint bleach.

There was contaminated food at her house, Dasein realized. She was racing back to get it before it killed anyone.

I would've eaten the stew, Dasein thought.

An accident . . . another bloody accident.

He kicked the fallen dish aside, dragged the dog out of the way, got behind the wheel of his camper. The Ford's engine was a dismal, throbbing mess after Jersey's car. He maneuvered it gently out to the highway, turned toward town.

Accident, he thought.

A pattern was emerging, but he found it difficult to accept. There was a Holmesian flavor to his thought— '. . . *when you have eliminated the impossible, whatever remains, however improbable, must be the truth.*'

Jenny had screamed: 'Stay away from me. I love you.'

That was consistent. She did love him. Therefore, he had to stay away from her.

For the time being.

The road forked and he turned right, following the direction by a sign labeled: 'Greenhouses.'

There was a bridge over the river – an old-fashioned bridge that crowned in the middle . . . heavy planks rattling under the wheels. The river foamed and bunched itself over the shell-backs of smooth stones under the bridge.

Dasein slowed the truck at the far side, taken suddenly by a warning sense of caution which he had learned to trust.

The road followed the river's right bank. He paced the current, glanced upstream toward the bridge, found it hidden by a stand of willows.

It came over Dasein that there was something sliding and treacherous about the river. He thought of a liquid snake, venomous, full of evil energy. It contained a concentration of malevolence as it slipped down the rapids beside the road. And the sound – it laughed at him.

Dasein drew a sigh of relief when the road turned away from the river, wound over two low hills and down into a shallow valley. He glimpsed the glass through trees. It was an expanse of glistening green and covered a much larger area than he'd expected.

The road ended at a paved parking lot in front of a long stone building. More stone buildings – tile roofs, curtained windows – stepped in ranks up the hill beside the greenhouses.

A great many cars waited in the parking lot, a fact Dasein found curious – at least a hundred cars.

And there were people – men walking between the greenhouses, white-coated figures behind the glass, briskly striding women coming and going.

Dasein drove down the line of cars looking for a place to park. He found a slot beyond the end of the long stone building, pulled in to a stop and stared around.

Chanting.

Dasein turned toward the sound; it came from the ranks of buildings beyond the greenhouses. A troop of children came marching into view down a path between the buildings. They carried baskets. Three adults accompanied them. They counted a marching cadence. The troop wound out of sight down into the greenhouse level.

A tight feeling gripped Dasein's chest.

Footsteps sounded on his left. Dasein turned to find Piaget striding down the line of cars toward him. The doctor's bulky figure was accented by a long white smock. He was hatless, his hair wind mussed.

Piaget turned into the slot beside Dasein, stopped to stand looking in the truck's open window.

'Well,' he said. 'Jenny said there'd be an arriving.'

Dasein shook his head. There was almost meaning in Piaget's words, but the sense eluded him. He wet his lips with his tongue. 'What?'

Piaget scowled. 'Jenny knows rapport. She said you'd probably show up here.' His voice sounded suddenly full of effort.

An arriving, Dasein thought.

It was a label for an event, a statement withholding judgment. He studied Piaget's wide, bland face.

'I saw children,' Dasein said.

'What did you expect?'

Dasein shrugged. 'Are you going to run me off?'

'Al Marden says the ones that run get the fever,' Piaget said. 'The ones that watch get the benefit.'

'Count me among the watchers,' Dasein said.

Piaget grinned, opened the truck door. 'Come.'

Dasein remembered the river, hesitated. He thought of the torn carpet in the Inn's hallway, the open gas jet, the lake, the arrow ... the paint bleach. He thought of Jenny running away from him – '*Stay away from me! I love you.*'

'Come along,' Piaget said.

Still hesitating, Dasein said: 'Why're the children kept here?'

'We must push back at the surface of childhood,' Piaget said. 'It's a brutal, animate thing. But there's food growing.' He gestured at the expanse of greenhouses. 'There's educating. There's useful energy. Waste not; want not.'

Again, Dasein shook his head. *Almost-meaning.*

Push back at the surface of childhood?

It was like schizophrenic talk and he recalled the incident in the Blue Ewe, the haunting conversation of the young couple.

How could one hear a sunset?

'You ... you're not speaking English,' Dasein complained.

'I'm speaking,' Piaget said.

'But ...'

'Jenny says you'll be an understander.' Piaget scratched his cheek, a pensive look on his face. 'You have the training, Dasein.' Again, his voice took on that leaden effort. 'Where's your *Weltanschauung?* You do have a world view? The whole is greater than the sum of its parts. What is it?'

Piaget's arm swept out to include the greenhouse complex and the entire valley, the world and the universe beyond.

Dasein's mouth felt dry. The man was insane.

'You contain the Jaspers experience,' Piaget said. 'Digest it. Jenny says you can do it. Reality shoots through her words.'

The tight sensation was a pain in Dasein's chest. Thoughts tumbled through his mind without order or sense.

In a heavy voice, Piaget said: 'For approximately one in five hundred, the Jaspers cannot ...' He spread his arms, palms up. 'You are not one of those few. I stake a reputation on it. You will be an opening person.'

Dasein looked at the stone building, the hurrying people. All that action and purpose. He sensed it all might be like the dance of bees – motions designed to show him a direction. The direction escaped him.

'I will try to put it in the words of *outside*,' Piaget said. 'Perhaps then ...' He shrugged, leaned against the side of the door to bring his broad face close to Dasein. 'We sift reality through screens composed of ideas. These idea systems are limited by language. That is to say: language cuts the grooves in which our thoughts must move. If we seek new validity forms, we must step outside the language.'

'What's that have to do with the children?' Dasein nodded toward the greenhouses.

'Dasein! We have a common instinctive experience, you and I. What happens in the unformed psyche? As individuals, as cultures and societies, we humans reenact every aspect of the instinctive life that has accompanied our species for uncounted generations. With the Jaspers, we take off the binding element. Couple that with the brutality of childhood? No! We would have violence, chaos. We would have no society. It's simple, isn't it? We must superimpose a limiting order on the innate patterns of our nervous systems. We must have common interests.'

Dasein found himself grappling with these ideas, trying to see through them to some sense in Piaget's earlier words. *Push back at the surface of childhood? World view?*

'We must meet the survival needs of individuals,' Piaget said. 'We know the civilization-culture-society outside is dying. They *do* die, you know. When this is about to happen, pieces break off from the parent body. Pieces cut themselves free, Dasein. Our scalpel – that was Jaspers. Think, man! You've lived out there. It's a Virgilian autumn . . . the dusk of a civilization.'

Piaget stepped back, studied Dasein.

For his part, Dasein found himself suddenly fascinated by the doctor. There was a timeless essence in the man, powerful, intrusive on everything about him. Framed in the white smock's collar was an Egyptian head, strong cheeks and jaws, a nose out of Moses' time, white even teeth behind thin lips.

Piaget smiled, a deaf smile of ultimate stubborness, let a honeyed look flow across the landscape around them, the greenhouses, the people.

Dasein knew then why he'd been sent here. No mere market report had prompted this. Marden had nailed it. He was here to break this up, smash it.

The Santarogans were working their children here, training them. Child labor. Piaget seemed not to care how much he revealed.

'Come along,' Piaget said. 'I'll show you our school.'

Dasein shook his head. What would it be in there? An accidental push against broken glass? A child with a knife?

'I'm . . . I have to think,' Dasein said.

'Are you sure?' Piaget's words dropped on the air like a challenge.

Dasein thought of a fortress abbey in the Dark Ages, warrior monks. All this was contained in Piaget and his valley, in the confidence with which Santarogans defied the *outside*. Were they really confident? he wondered. Or were they actors hypnotized by their own performance?

'You've been a swimmer on the surface,' Piaget said. 'You haven't even seen the struggle. You haven't yet developed the innocent eye that sees the universe uncluttered by past assumptions. You were programmed and sent here to break us up.'

Dasein paled.

'To be programmed is to be prejudiced,' Piaget said. 'Because prejudice is selecting and rejecting and that is programming.' He sighed. 'Such pains we take with you because of our Jenny.'

'I came here with an open mind,' Dasein said.

'Not prejudiced?' Piaget raised his eyebrows.

307

'So you're contending with ... groups outside over what's the right way ...'

'Contending is too soft a word, Dasein. There's a power struggle going on over control of the human consciousness. We are a cell of health surrounded by plague. It's not men's minds that are at stake, but their consciousness, their awareness. This isn't a struggle over a market area. Make no mistake about it. This is a struggle over what's to be judged valuable in our universe. Outside, they value whatever can be measured, counted or tabulated. Here, we go by different standards.'

Dasein sensed threat in Piaget's voice. There was no longer a veneer of pretense here. The doctor was setting up the sides in a war and Dasein felt caught in the middle. He was, he knew, on more dangerous ground than he'd ever been before. Piaget and his friends controlled the valley. An ex-post-facto accident would be child's play for them.

'The ones who hired me,' Dasein said, 'they're men who believe ...'

'Men!' Piaget sneered. 'Out there ...' He pointed beyond the hills which enclosed the valley. ' ... they're destroying their environment. In the process, they're becoming not-men! We are men.' He touched his chest. 'They are not. Nature is a unified field. A radical change in environment means the inhabitants must change to survive. The not-men out there are changing to survive.'

Dasein gaped at Piaget. That was it, of course. The Santarogans were conservatives ... unchanging. He'd seen this for himself. But there was a fanatic intensity to Piaget, a religious fervor, that repelled Dasein. So it was a struggle over men's minds ...

'You are saying to yourself,' Piaget said, 'that these fool Santarogans have a psycheletic substance which makes them inhuman.'

It was so close to his thoughts that Dasein grew still with fear. Could they read minds? Was that a by-product of the Jaspers substance?

'You're equating us with the unwashed, sandaled users of LSD,' Piaget said. 'Kooks, you would say. But you are like them – unaware. We are aware. We have truly released the mind. We have a power medicine – just as whiskey and gin and aspirin and tobacco ... and, yes, LSD, just as these are power medicines. But you must see the difference. Whiskey and the other depressants, these keep their subjects docile. Our medicine releases the animal that has never been tamed ... up to now.'

Dasein looked at the greenhouses.

'Yes,' Piaget said. 'Look here. That is where we domesticate the human animal.'

With a shock of awareness, Dasein realized he had heard too much ever to be allowed out of the valley. They had passed a point of no return with him. In his present state of mind, there was only one answer for the Santarogans: they had to kill him. The only question remaining was: Did they know it? Was any of this conscious? Or did it truly operate at the level of instinct?

If he precipitated a crisis, Dasein knew he'd find out. Was there a way to avoid it? he wondered. As he hesitated, Piaget moved around the truck, climbed in beside him.

'You won't come with me,' he said. 'I'll go with you.'

'You'll go with me?'

'To my house; to the clinic.' He turned, studied Dasein. 'I love my niece, you understand? I'll not have her hurt if I can prevent it.'

'If I refuse?'

'Ahh, Gilbert, you would make the angels weep. We don't want weeping, do we? We don't want Jenny's tears. Aren't you concerned about her?'

'I've some anxiety about ...'

'When anxiety enters, inquiry stops. You have a hard head, Gilbert. A hard head makes a sore back. Let us go to the clinic.'

'What kind of death trap have you set up there?'

Piaget glared at him in outrage. 'Death trap?'

Holding as reasonable a tone as he could manage, Dasein said: 'You're trying to kill me. Don't deny it. I've ...'

'I'm disgusted with you, Gilbert. When have we tried to kill you?'

Dasein took a deep breath, held up his right hand, enumerated the *accidents*, dropping a finger for each one until his hand was clenched into a fist. He had left out only the incident with Petey Jorick ... and that because of a promise.

'Accidents!' Piaget said.

'As we both know,' Dasein said, 'there are very few real accidents in this world. Most of what we call accidents are unconscious violence. You say you've opened your mind. Use it.'

'Pah! Your thoughts are like muddy water!'

'Let the muddy water stand and it becomes clear,' Dasein said.

'You can't be serious.' He glared at Dasein. 'But I see that you are.' He closed his eyes momentarily, opened them. 'Well, would you believe Jenny?'

Stay away from me! I love you! Dasein thought.

'Let's go to your clinic,' Dasein said. He started the truck, backed out of the parking lot and headed toward town.

'Trying to kill you,' Piaget muttered. He stared out at the landscape rushing past them.

Dasein drove in silence ... thinking, thinking, thinking. The instant he headed toward Jenny, the old fantasies gripped him. Jenny and her valley! The place had enveloped him in its aura – crazy, crazy, crazy! But the pattern was emerging. It was going together with its own Santaroga kind of logic.

'So not everyone can take your ... power medicine?' Dasein asked. 'What happens to the ones who fail?'

'We take care of our own,' Piaget growled. 'That's why I keep hoping you'll stay.'

'Jenny's a trained psychologist. Why don't you use her?'

'She does her tour of duty.'

'I'm going to ask Jenny to leave with me,' Dasein said. 'You know that, don't you?'

Piaget sniffed.

'She can break away from your ... Jaspers,' Dasein said. 'Men go into the service from here. They must ...'

'They always come home when it's over,' Piaget said. 'That's in your notes. Don't you realize how unhappy they are out there?' He turned toward Dasein. 'Is that the choice you'd offer Jenny?'

'They can't be all that unhappy about leaving,' Dasein said. 'Otherwise you clever people would've found another solution.'

'Hmmph!' Piaget snorted. 'You didn't even do your homework for the people who hired you.' He sighed. 'I'll tell you, Gilbert. The draft rejects most of our young men – severe allergy reaction to a diet which doesn't include periodic administration of Jaspers. They can only get that here. The approximately six percent of our young people who go out do so as a duty to the valley. We don't want to call down the federal wrath on us. We have a political accommodation with the state, but we're not large enough to apply the same technique nationally.'

They've already decided about me, Dasein thought. *They don't care what they tell me.*

The realization brought a tight sensation of fear in the pit of his stomach.

He rounded a corner and came parallel with the river. Ahead stood the clump of willows and the long, down-sweeping curve to the bridge. Dasein recalled his projection of evil onto the river, stepped on the throttle to get this place behind him. The truck entered the curve. The road was banked nicely. The bridge came into view. There was a yellow truck parked off the road at the far side, men standing behind it drinking out of metal cups.

'Look out!' Piaget shouted.

In that instant, Dasein saw the reason for the truck – a gaping hole in the center of the bridge where the planks had been removed. That was a county work crew and they'd opened at least a ten foot hole in the bridge.

The truck sped some forty feet during the moment it took Dasein to realize his peril.

Now, he could see a two-by-four stretched across each end of the bridge, yellow warning flags tied at their centers.

Dasein gripped the steering wheel. His mind shifted into a speed of computation he had never before experienced. The effect was to slow the external passage of time. The truck seemed to come almost to a stop while he reviewed the possibilities –

Hit the brakes?

No. Brakes and tires were old. At this speed, the truck would skid onto the bridge and into the hole.

Swerve off the road?

No. The river waited on both sides – a deep cut in the earth to swallow them.

Aim for a bridge abutment to stop the truck?

Not at this speed and without seat belts.

Hit the throttle to increase speed?

That was a possibility. There was the temporary barrier to break through, but that was only a two-by-four. The bridge rose in a slight arc up and over the river. The hole had been opened in the center. Given enough speed, the truck could leap the hole.

Dasein jammed the throttle to the floorboards. The old truck leaped ahead. There came a sharp cracking sound as they smashed through the barrier. Planks clattered beneath the wheels. There came a breathless instant of flying, a spring-crushing lurch as they landed across the hole, the 'crack' of the far barrier.

He hit the brakes, came to a screeching stop opposite the workmen. Time resumed its normal pace as Dasein stared out at the crew – five men, faces pale, mouths agape.

'For the love of heaven!' Piaget gasped. 'Do you always take chances like that?'

'Was there any other way to get us out of that mess?' Dasein asked. He lifted his right hand, stared at it. The hand was trembling.

Piaget reflected a moment, then: 'You took what was probably the only way out . . . but if you hadn't been driving so damn' fast on a blind . . .'

'I will make you a bet,' Dasein said. 'I'll bet the work on that bridge wasn't necessary, that it was either a mistake or some sort of make-work.'

Dasein reached for his door handle, had to grope twice to get it in his hand, then found it took a conscious surge of effort to open the door. He stepped out, found his knees rubbery. He stood a moment, took several deep breaths, then moved around to the front of the truck.

Both headlights were smashed and there was a deep dent stretching across both fenders and the grill.

Dasein turned his attention to the workmen. One, a stocky, dark-haired man in a plaid shirt and dungarees stood a step ahead of the others. Dasein focused on the man, said: 'Why wasn't there a warning sign back there around the corner?'

'Good God, man!' the fellow said. His face reddened. 'Nobody comes down that road this time of day.'

Dasein walked down the road toward a pile of planks, dirt and oil on them testifying that they'd been taken from the bridge. They looked to be three-by-twelve redwood. He lifted the end of one, turned it over – no cracks or checks. It gave off the sharp sound of an unbroken board when he dropped it back to the pile.

He turned to see the workman he'd addressed approaching. Piaget was several paces behind the man.

'When did you get the order to do this work?' Dasein asked.

'Huh?' The man stopped, stared at Dasein with a puzzled frown.

'When did you get orders to repair this bridge?' Dasein asked.

'Well ... we decided to come up here about an hour ago. What the hell difference does it make? You've smashed the ...'

'You decided?' Dasein asked. 'Aren't you assigned to jobs?'

'I'm the road crew foreman in this valley, mister. I decide, not that it's any of your business.'

Piaget came to a stop beside the man, said: 'Dr Dasein, this is Josh Marden, Captain Marden's nephew.'

'Nepotism begins at home, I see,' Dasein said, his tone elaborately polite. 'Well, Mr Marden, or may I call you Josh?'

'Now, you look here, Dr Das ...'

'Josh, then,' Dasein said, still in that tone of calm politeness. 'I'm very curious, Josh. These appear to be perfectly sound planks. Why'd you decide to replace them?'

'What the hell diff ...'

'Tell him, Josh,' Piaget said. 'I confess to a certain curiosity of my own.'

Marden looked at Piaget, back to Dasein. 'Well ... we inspected the bridge ... We make regular inspections. We just decided to do a little preventive maintenance, put in new planks here and use the old ones on a bridge that doesn't get as much traffic. There's nothing unusual about ...'

'Is there any *urgent* road work in this valley?' Dasein asked. 'Is there some job you put off to come to this ...'

'Now, look here, Mister!' Marden took a step toward Dasein. 'You've no call to ...'

'What about the Old Mill Road?' Piaget asked. 'Are those pot holes still on the curve by the ditch?'

'Now, look, Doc,' Marden said, whirling toward Piaget. 'Not you, too. We decided ...'

'Easy does it, Josh,' Piaget said. 'I'm just curious. What about the Old Mill Road?'

'Aw, Doc. It was such a nice day and the ...'

'So that work still has to be done,' Piaget said.

'I win the bet,' Dasein said. He headed back toward his truck.

Piaget fell into step beside him

'Hey!' Marden shouted, 'You've broken county property and those boards you landed on are probably ...'

Dasein cut him off without turning. 'You'd better get that bridge repaired before somebody else has trouble here.'

He slid behind the wheel of his truck, slammed the door. Reaction was setting in now: his whole body felt tense with anger.

Piaget climbed in beside him. The truck rattled as he closed his door. 'Will it still run?' he asked.

'Accident!' Dasein said.

Piaget remained silent.

Dasein put the truck in gear, eased it up to a steady thirty-five miles an hour. The rear-view mirror showed him the crew already at work on the bridge, one of their number with a warning flag trudging back around the blind corner.

'Now, they send out a flagman,' Dasein said.

A corner cut off the view in the mirror Dasein concentrated on driving. The truck had developed new rattles and a front-end shimmy.

'They *have* to be accidents,' Piaget said. 'There's no other explanation.'

A stop sign came into view ahead. Dasein stopped for the main highway. It was empty of traffic. He turned right toward town. Piaget's protestations deserved no answer, he thought, and he gave no answer.

They entered the outskirts of town. There was Scheler's station on the left. Dasein pulled in behind the station, drove back to the large shed-roofed metal building labeled 'Garage.'

'What're you doing here?' Piaget asked. 'This machine isn't worth ...'

'I want it repaired sufficiently to get me out of Santaroga,' Dasein said.

The garage doors were open. Dasein nosed the truck inside, stopped, climbed out. There was a steady sound of work all around – clanging of metal, machinery humming. Lines of cars had been angled toward benches down both sides of the garage. Lights glared down on the benches.

A stocky, dark-skinned man in stained white coveralls came from the back of the garage, stopped in front of the truck. 'What the devil did you hit?' he asked.

Dasein recognized one of the quartet from the card game at the Inn – Scheler himself.

'Doctor Piaget here will tell you all about it,' Dasein said. 'I want some headlights put on this thing and you might have a look at the steering.'

'Why don't you junk it?' Scheler asked.

The truck door slammed and Piaget came up on the right. 'Can you fix it, Sam?' he asked.

'Sure, but it isn't worth it.'

'Do it anyway and put it on my bill. I don't want our friend here to think we're trying to trap him in the valley.'

'If you say so, Doc.'

Scheler turned around, shouted: 'Bill! Take that Lincoln off the rack and put this truck on. I'll write up a ticket.'

A young man in greasy blue coveralls came around from the left bends where he had been hidden by a Lincoln Continental lifted halfway up on a hoist. The young man had Scheler's build and dark skin, the same set of face and eyes: bright blue and alert.

'My son, Bill,' Scheler said. 'He'll take care of it for you.'

Dasein felt a twinge of warning fear, backed against the side of his truck. The garage around him had taken on the same feeling of concentrated malevolence he had sensed in the river.

Scheler started through the space between the Lincoln and an old Studebaker truck, called over his shoulder: 'If you'll sign the ticket over here, Dr Dasein, we'll get right at it.'

Dasein took two steps after him, hesitated. He felt the garage closing in around him

'We can walk to the clinic from here,' Piaget said. 'Sam will call when your rig's ready.'

Dasein took another step, stopped, glanced back. Young Bill Scheler was right behind him. The sense of menace was a pounding drumbeat in Dasein's head. He saw Bill reach out a friendly hand to guide him between the cars. There was no doubt of the innocent intention of that hand, the smiling face behind it, but Dasein saw the hand as the embodiment of danger. With an inarticulate cry, Dasein sprang aside.

The young mechanic, caught off balance with nothing ahead of his thrusting arm, lurched forward, stumbled, fell. As he fell, the hoist with the Lincoln on it came crashing down. It rocked twice, subsided. Bill Scheler lay halfway under it. One of his legs twitched, was still.

A pool of red began to flow from beneath the car.

Piaget dashed past him shouting for Scheler to raise the hoist.

A compressor began thumping somewhere in the background. The Lincoln jerked, began to rise. It exposed a body, its head smashed beyond recognition by one of the hoist's arms.

Dasein whirled away, ran out of the garage and was sick. *That could've been me,* he thought. *That was meant for me.* He grew aware of a great bustle of activity, the sound of a siren in the distance.

Two mechanics emerged from the garage with a pale-faced, staggering Sam Scheler between them.

It was his son, Dasein thought. He felt that this was of the deepest significance, but his shocked mind gave no explanation for that feeling.

He heard one of the mechanics with Scheler say: 'It was an accident, Sam. Nothing you could do.'

They went into the station with him.

A siren began giving voice in the distance. Its wailing grew louder. Dasein backed off to the edge of the station's parking area, stood against a low fence.

His truck, nosed into the garage, lurched into motion, was swallowed by the building.

The ambulance droned its way into the parking area, turned, backed into the garage. Presently, it emerged, drove away with its siren silent.

Piaget came out of the garage.

He was an oddly subdued man, indecisive in his walk – short strides, soft of step. He saw Dasein, approached with an air of diffidence. There was a smear of blood down the right side of his white smock, black grease at the hem, grease on the left arm.

Blood and grease – they struck Dasein as an odd combination but things out of which an entire scene could be reconstructed. He shuddered.

'I . . . I need a cup of coffee,' Piaget said. He closed his eyes briefly, opened them to stare pleadingly at Dasein. 'There's a café around the corner. Would you . . .' He broke off to take a deep, trembling breath. 'I brought that boy into the world.' He shook his head. 'Just when you think you're the complete doctor, immune to all personal involvement . . .'

Dasein experienced a surge of compassion for Piaget, stepped away from the fence to take the doctor's arm. 'Where's this café? I could use something myself.'

The café was a narrow brick building squeezed between a hardware store and a dark little shop labeled 'Bootery.' The screen door banged behind them. The place smelled of steam and the omnipresent Jaspers. One of Scheler's station attendants – dark green jacket and white hat – sat at a counter on the left staring into a cup of coffee. A man in a leather apron, horn-callused hands, gray hair, was eating a sandwich at the far end of the counter.

Dasein steered Piaget into a booth opposite the counter, sat down across from him.

The station attendant at the counter, turned, glanced at them. Dasein found himself confronted by a face he knew to be another Scheler – the same set to the blue eyes, the same blocky figure and dark skin. The man looked at Piaget, said: 'Hi, Doc. There was a siren.'

Piaget lifted his gaze from the tabletop, looked at the speaker. The glaze left Piaget's eyes. He took two shallow breaths, looked away, back to the man at the counter.

'Harry,' Piaget said, and his voice was a hoarse croak. 'I ... couldn't ...' He broke off.

The man slid off the counter stool. His face was a pale, frozen mask. 'I've been sitting here ... feeling ...' He brushed a hand across his mouth. 'It was ... Bill!' He whirled, dashed out of the café. The door slammed behind him.

'That's Scheler's other son,' Piaget said.

'He knew,' Dasein said, and he recalled the experience at the lake, the feeling of rapport.

Life exists immersed in a sea of unconsciousness, he reminded himself. *In the drug, these people gain a view of that sea.*

Piaget studied Dasein a moment, then: 'Of course he knew. Haven't you ever had a tooth pulled? Couldn't you feel the hole where it had been?'

A slender red-haired woman in a white apron, lines of worry on her face, came up to the booth, stood looking down at Piaget. 'I'll bring your coffee,' she said. She started to turn away, hesitated. 'I ... felt it ... and Jim next door came to the back to tell me. I didn't know how to tell Harry. He just kept sitting there ... getting lower and lower ... knowing really but refusing to face it. I ...' She shrugged. 'Anything besides coffee?'

Piaget shook his head. Dasein realized with a sense of shock the man was near tears.

The waitress left, returned with two mugs of coffee, went back to the kitchen – all without speaking. She, too, had sensed Piaget's emotions.

Dasein sighed, lifted his coffee, started to put the mug to his lips, hesitated. There was an odd bitter odor beneath the omnipresent Jaspers tang in the coffee. Dasein put his nose to the mug, sniffed. Bitter. A plume of steam rising from the dark liquid assumed for Dasein the shape of a hooded cobra lifting its fanged head to strike him.

Shakily, he returned the mug to the table, looked up to meet Piaget's questioning gaze.

'There's poison in that coffee,' Dasein rasped.

Piaget looked at his own coffee.

Dasein took the mug from him, sniffed at it. The bitter odor was missing. He touched his tongue to it – heat, the soothing flow of Jaspers ... coffee ...

'Is something wrong?'

Dasein looked up to find the waitress standing over him. 'There's poison in my coffee,' he said.

'Nonsense.' She took the mug from Dasein's hand, started to drink.

Piaget stopped her with a hand on her arm. 'No, Vina – this one.' He handed her the other mug.

She stared at it, smelled it, put it down, dashed for the kitchen. Presently, she returned carrying a small yellow box. Her face was porcelain white, freckles standing out across her cheeks and nose like the marks of some disease.

'Roach powder,' she whispered. 'I ... the box was spilled on the shelf over the counter. I ...' She shook her head.

Dasein looked at Piaget, but the doctor refused to meet his gaze.

'Another accident,' Dasein said, holding his voice even. 'Eh, doctor?'

Piaget wet his lips with his tongue.

Dasein slid out of the booth, pushing the waitress aside. He took the mug of poisoned coffee, poured it deliberately on the floor. 'Accidents will happen, won't they ... Vina?'

'Please,' she said. 'I ... didn't ...'

'Of course you didn't,' Dasein said.

'You don't understand,' Piaget said.

'But I *do* understand,' Dasein said. 'What'll it be next time? A gun accident? How about something heavy dropped from a roof? Accidentally, of course.' He turned, strode out of the cafe, stood on the sidewalk to study his surroundings.

It was such a *normal* town. The trees on the parking strip were so normal. The young couple walking down the sidewalk across from him – they were so normal. The sounds – a truck out on the avenue to his right, the cars there, a pair of jays arguing in the treetops, two women talking on the steps of a house down the street to his left – such an air of normalcy about it all.

The screen door slapped behind him. Piaget came up to stand at Dasein's side. 'I know what you're thinking,' he said.

'Do you, really?'

'I know how all this must look to you.'

'Is that so?'

'Believe me,' Piaget said, 'all this is just a terrible series of coincidences that ...'

'Coincidence!' Dasein whirled on him, glaring. 'How far can you stretch credulity, doctor? How long can you rationalize before you have to admit ...'

'Gilbert, I'd cut off my right arm rather than let anything happen to you. I'd break Jenny's heart to ...'

'You actually don't see it, do you?' Dasein asked, his voice filled with awe. 'You don't see it. You refuse to see it.'

'Dr Dasein?'

The voice came from his right. Dasein turned to find Harry – 'Scheler's other son' – standing there, hat in hand. He looked younger than he had in the café – no more than nineteen. There was a sad hesitancy in his manner.

'I wanted to ...' He broke off. 'My father said to tell you ... We know it wasn't your fault that ...' He looked into Dasein's eyes, a look that pleaded for help.

Dasein felt a pang of rapport for the young man. There was a basic decency at work here. In the midst of their own grief, the Schelers had taken time to try to ease Dasein's feelings.

They expected me to feel guilt about this, Dasein thought. The fact that he'd experienced no such feeling filled Dasein now with an odd questing sensation of remorse.

If I hadn't ... He aborted the thought. *If I hadn't what? That accident was meant for me.*

'It's all right, Harry,' Piaget said. 'We understand.'

'Thanks, Doc.' He looked at Piaget with relief. 'Dad said to tell you ... the car, Dr Dasein's truck ... The new headlights are in it. That's all we can do. The steering ... You'll just have to drive slow unless you replace the whole front end.'

'Already?' Dasein asked.

'It doesn't take long to put in headlights, sir.'

Dasein looked from the youth to Piaget. The doctor returned his stare with an expression that said as clearly as words: '*They want your truck out of there. It's a reminder ...*'

Dasein nodded. Yes. The truck would remind them of the tragedy. This was logical. Without a word, he set off for the garage.

Piaget sped up, matched his pace to Dasein's.

'Gilbert,' he said, 'I must insist you come over to the house. Jenny can...'

'Insist?'

'You're being very pig-headed, Gilbert.'

Dasein put down a surge of anger, said: 'I don't want to hurt Jenny any more than you do. That's why I'm going to direct my own steps. I don't really want you to know what I'm going to do next. I don't want any of you waiting there in my path with one of your ... accidents.'

'Gilbert, you *must* put that idea out of your mind! None of us want to hurt you.'

They were on the parking area between the station and the garage now. Dasein stared at the gaping door to the garage, overcome suddenly by the sensation that the door was a mouth with deadly teeth ready to clamp down on him The door yawned there to swallow him.

Dasein hesitated, slowed, stopped.

'What is it now?' Piaget asked.

'Your truck's just inside,' Harry Scheler said. 'You can drive it and ...'

'What about the bill?' Dasein asked, stalling for time.

'I'll take care of that,' Piaget said. 'Go get your truck while I'm settling up. Then we'll go to ...'

'I want the truck driven out here for me,' Dasein said. He moved to one side, out of the path of anything that might come spewing from that mouth-door.

'I can understand your reluctance to go back in there,' Piaget said, 'but really ...'

'You drive it out for me, Harry,' Dasein said.

The youth stared at Dasein with an oddly trapped look. 'Well, I have some ...'

'Drive the damn' car out for him!' Piaget ordered. 'This is nonsense!'

'Sir?' Harry looked at Piaget.

'I said drive the damn' car out here for him!' Piaget repeated. 'I've had as much of this as I can stomach!'

Hesitantly, the youth turned toward the garage door. His feet moved with a dragging slowness.

'See here, Gilbert,' Piaget said, 'you can't really believe we ...'

'I believe what I see,' Dasein said.

Piaget threw up his hands, turned away in exasperation.

Dasein listened to the sounds from the garage. They were subdued in there – voices, only a few mechanical noises, the whirring buzz of some machine.

A door slammed. It sounded like the door to the truck. Dasein recognized the grinding of his starter. The engine caught with its characteristic banging, as drowned immediately in a roaring explosion that sent a blast of flame shooting out the garage door.

Piaget leaped back with an oath.

Dasein ran diagonally past him to look into the garage. He glimpsed figures rushing out a door at the far end. His truck stood in the central traffic aisle at the core of a red-orange ball of flame. As he stared at the truck, a burning something emerged from the flames, staggered, fell.

Behind Dasein, someone screamed: 'Harry!'

Without consciously willing it, Dasein found himself dashing through the garage door to grab into the flames and drag the youth to safety. There were sensations of heat, pain. A roaring-crackling sound of fire filled the air around him. The smell of gasoline and char invaded Dasein's nostrils. He saw a river of fire reach toward him along the floor. A blazing beam crashed down where the youth had lain. There were shouts, a great scrambling confusion.

Something white was thrown over the figure he was dragging, engulfed the flames. Hands eased him aside. Dasein realized he was out of the garage, that Piaget was using his white smock to smother the fire on Harry.

Someone appeared to be doing something similar to both Dasein's arms and the front of his jacket, using a coat and a car robe. The coat and robe were pulled away. Dasein stared down at his own arms – black and red flesh, blisters forming. The sleeves of his shirt and jacket ended at the elbows in jagged edgings of char.

The pain began – a throbbing agony along the backs of both arms and hands. Through a world hazed by the pain, Dasein saw a station-wagon screech to a rocking stop beside him, saw men carry the smock-shrouded figure of Harry into the back of the wagon. More hands eased Dasein into the seat beside the driver.

There were voices: 'Easy there.' 'Get 'em to the clinic, Ed, and don't loiter.' 'Give us a hand here.' 'Here! Over here!'

There was a sound of sirens, the pounding throb of heavy truck engines.

Dasein heard Piaget's voice from the rear of the station-wagon: 'Okay, Ed. Let's get going.'

The wagon slipped into motion, dipped onto the street, turned, gathered speed. Dasein looked at the driver, recognized one of the station attendants, turned to peer into the back.

Piaget crouched there working over the injured youth.

'How bad is he?' Dasein asked.

'He was wearing long johns,' Piaget said. 'They helped. He seems to've protected his face by burying it in his cap, but his back is bad. So're his legs and arms and his hands.'

Dasein stared at the injured youth.

'Will he ...'

'I think we got to him in time,' Piaget said. 'I gave him a shot to put him out.' He looked at Dasein's arms. 'Do you want a needle?'

Dasein shook his head from side to side. 'No.'

What made me rush in there to save him? Dasein asked himself. It had been an instinctive reaction. Saving Harry had precipitated him into a semihelpless situation, needing medical attention himself, caught in a car with two Santarogans. Dasein probed at his embryo *Jaspers awareness*, the sixth sense which had warned him of danger. He found nothing. The threat appeared to have been withdrawn. *Is that why I acted to save Harry?* Dasein wondered. *Did I hope to propitiate Santaroga by saving one of their own even while they were trying to kill me?*

'Another accident,' Piaget said, and his voice carried a questioning tone of self-doubt.

Dasein met the doctor's probing gaze, nodded.

The station-wagon turned onto a tree-lined street, and Dasein recognized the broad, brown-shingled front of Piaget's house. They drove past it and onto a graveled driveway that curved around to the rear through a tall board fence and under a portico jutting from a two-storey brick building.

In spite of his pain, Dasein realized this building lay concealed from the street by the fence and a border planting of evergreens, that it must be part of the complex which included Piaget's house. It all seemed hazily significant.

White-coated attendants rushed a gurney out of the building, eased the burned youth from the rear of the station wagon. Piaget opened Dasein's door, said: 'Can you get out under your own power, Gilbert?'

'I ... think so.'

Dasein held his arms out in front of him, slid from the car. The pain and the motion required all his attention. There was a beginning ache along his forehead now and down the right side of his face. The brick building, a pair of swinging glass doors, hands gently guiding him – all seemed rather distant and receding.

I'm blacking out, he thought. He felt it might be extremely dangerous to sink into unconsciousness. With a start, he realized he had been eased into a wheelchair, that it was speeding down a green-walled hallway. The surge of awareness sent his senses crashing into the pain. He felt himself recoiling toward the blessed relief of unconsciousness. It was an almost physical thing, as though his body was bouncing between limiting walls – unconsciousness or pain.

Bright lights!

The light was all around him. He heard scissors snipping, looked down to see hands working the scissors. They were cutting the sleeves of his jacket and shirt, lifting the fabric away from seared flesh.

That's my flesh, Dasein thought. He tore his gaze away from it.

Dasein felt something cool at his left shoulder, a pricking sensation, a pulling. A hand holding a hypodermic moved across his plane of vision. The important thing to Dasein in this moment was that his vision was limited to a plane. There was light, a foggy glittering out of which hands moved and faces appeared. He felt himself being undressed. Something cool, soothing, sliding was being applied to his hands and arms, to his face.

They've given me a shot to put me out, he thought. He tried to think about danger then, about being totally helpless here. Consciousness refused to respond. He couldn't push his awareness through the glittering fog.

There were voices. He concentrated on the voices. Someone said: 'For the love of heaven! He was carrying a gun.' Another voice: 'Put that down!'

For some reason, this amused Dasein, but his body refused to laugh.

He thought then of his camper as he'd last seen it – a ball of orange flame. All his records had been in there, Dasein realized. Every bit of evidence he'd accumulated about Santaroga had gone up in that fire. *Evidence?* he thought. *Notes ... speculations ...* It was all still in his mind, subject to recall.

But memory is lost at death! he thought.

Fear galvanized a minuscule core of selfdom in him. He tried to shout. No sound came. He tried to move. Muscles refused to obey.

When the darkness came, it was like a hand that reached up and seized him.

11

Dasein awoke remembering a dream – a conversation with faceless gods.

'Dunghills rise and castles fall.' In the dream, something with an echo-box voice had said that. '*Dunghills rise and castles fall.*'

Dasein felt it important to remember all the dream. Yes. 'I'm the man who woke up.' That was what he'd tried to tell the faceless gods. 'I'm the man who woke up.'

The dream was a flowing pattern in his memory, a *process* that couldn't be separated from himself. It was full of pure deeds and anguish. There was a chronic frustration in it. He had tried to do something that was inherently impossible. What had he tried to do? It eluded him

Dasein remembered the hand of darkness that had preceded the dream. He caught his breath and his eyes popped open. Daylight. He was in a bed in a green-walled room. Out a window at his left he could see a twisted red branch of madrone, oily green leaves, blue sky. He felt his body then: bandages and pain along his arms, bandages across his forehead and his right cheek. His throat felt dry and there was a sourness on his tongue.

Still, the dream clung to him It was a disembodied *thing*. Disembodied. Death! That was a clue. He knew it. Dasein recalled Piaget speaking of 'a common instinctive experience.' What did instinct have to do with the dream? Instinct. Instinct. What was instinct? An innate pattern impressed on the nervous system. Death. Instinct.

'Look inward, look inward, oh Man, on thyself,' the faceless gods of the dream had said. He recalled that now, and felt like sneering.

It was the old know-thyself syndrome, the psychologist's disease. Inward, ever inward. The death instinct was in there with all the other instincts. Know thyself? Dasein sensed then he couldn't know himself without dying. Death was the background against which life could know itself.

A throat was cleared to Dasein's right.

He tensed, turned his head to look toward the sound.

Winston Burdeaux sat in a chair beside the door. The brown eyes staring out of Burdeaux's moorish face held a quizzical expression.

Why Burdeaux? Dasein wondered.

'I'm happy to see you're awake, sir,' Burdeaux said.

There was a soothing sense of companionship in the man's rumbling voice. Was that why Burdeaux had been brought in? Dasein wondered. Had Burdeaux been picked to soothe and lull the victim?

But I'm still alive, Dasein thought.

If they'd wanted to harm him, what better opportunity had presented itself? He'd been helpless, unconscious . . .

'What time is it?' Dasein asked. The movement of speaking hurt his burned cheek.

'It's almost ten o'clock of a beautiful morning,' Burdeaux said. He smiled, a flash of white teeth in the dark features. 'Is there anything you wish?'

At the question, Daselin's stomach knotted in a pang of hunger. He hesitated on the point of asking for breakfast. What might be in any food served here? he asked himself.

Hunger is more than an empty stomach, Dasein thought. *I can go without a meal.*

'What I wish,' Dasein said, 'is to know why you're here.'

'The doctor thought I might be the safest one,' Burdeaux said. 'I, myself, was an outsider once. I can recall how it was.'

'They tried to kill you, too?'

'Sir!'

'Well . . . did you have accidents?' Dasein asked.

'I do not share the doctor's opinion about . . . accidents,' Burdeaux said. 'Once . . . I thought – But I can see now how wrong I was. The people of this valley wish to harm no man.'

'Yet, you're here because the doctor decided you'd be the *safest*,' Dasein said. 'And you haven't answered my question: Did you have accidents?'

'You must understand,' Burdeaux said, 'that when you don't know the ways of the valley, you can get into . . . situations which . . .'

'So you *did* have accidents. Is that why you asked for secret packages from Louisiana?'

'Secret packages?'

'Why else did you have them sent to Porterville?'

'Oh, you know about that.' Burdeaux shook his head, chuckled. 'Haven't you ever hungered for the foods of your childhood? I didn't think my new friends would understand.'

'Is that what it was?' Dasein asked. 'Or did you wake up one morning

324

shaking with fear at what the Jaspers in the local food was doing to you?'

Burdeaux scowled, then: 'Sir, when I first came here, I was an ignorant *nigger.* Now, I'm an educated Negro ... *and* a Santarogan. I no longer have the delusions which I ...'

'So you *did* try to fight it!'

'Yes ... I fought it. But I soon learned how foolish that was.'

'A delusion.'

'Indeed; a delusion.'

To remove a man's delusions, Dasein thought, *is to create a vacuum. What rushes into that vacuum?*

'Let us say,' Burdeaux said, 'that I shared your delusions once.'

'It's normal to share the delusions of one's society,' Dasein murmured, half to himself. 'It's abnormal to develop private delusions.'

'Well put,' Burdeaux said

Again, he wondered: *What rushed into the vacuum? What delusions do Santarogans share?*

For one thing, he knew they couldn't see the unconscious violence which created *accidents* for outsiders. Most of them couldn't see this, he corrected himself. There was a possibility Piaget was beginning to understand. After all, he'd put Burdeaux in here. And Jenny – '*Stay away from me! I love you!*'

Dasein began to see Santarogans in a new light. There was something decorously Roman about them ... and Spartan. They were turned in upon themselves, unfriendly, insular, proud, cut off from exchange of ideas that might ... He hesitated on this thought, wondering about the TV room at the Inn.

'The room you tried to hide from me,' Dasein said. 'At the Inn – the room with the television receivers ...'

'We didn't really want to hide that from *you*,' Burdeaux said. 'In a way, we hide it from ourselves ... and from chance outsiders. There's something very alluring about the sickness that's poured over TV. That's why we rotate the watchers. But we cannot ignore it. TV is the key to the outside and its gods.'

'Its gods?' Dasein suddenly remembered his dream.

'They have very practical gods outside,' Burdeaux said.

'What's a practical god?' Dasein asked.

'A practical god? That's a god who agrees with his worshipers. This is a way to keep from being conquered, you see.'

Dasein turned away from Burdeaux to stare up at the green ceiling. *Conquer the gods?* Was that the dream's chronic frustration?

'I don't understand,' he murmured.

325

'You still carry some of the outside's delusions,' Burdeaux said. 'Outside, they don't really try to understand the universe. Oh, they say they do, but that's not really what they're up to. You can tell by what they do. They're trying to conquer the universe. Gods are part of the universe . . . even man-made gods.'

'If you can't beat 'em, join 'em,' Dasein said. 'To keep from being conquered, a practical god agrees with his attackers. Is that it?'

'You're just as perceptive as Jenny said you'd be,' Burdeaux said.

'So outsiders attack their gods,' Dasein said.

'Anything less than abject submission has to have some attack in it,' Burdeaux said. 'You try to change a god? What's that except accusing the god of not agreeing with you?'

'And you get all this from the TV?'

'All this from . . .' Burdeaux broke into a chuckle. 'Oh, no, Doctor Gil . . . You don't mind if I call you Doctor Gil?'

Dasein turned to stare at the questioning look on Burdeaux's face. *Doctor Gil.* To object would be to appear the stiffnecked fool. But Dasein felt that agreement would be a step backward, the loss of an important battle. He could see no way to object, though.

'Whatever you wish,' Dasein said. 'Just explain this about the TV.'

'That's . . . our *window* on the outside,' Burdeaux said. 'That whole world of the permanent expediency out there, that whole world is TV. And we watch it through . . .'

'Permanent expediency?' Dasein tried to raise himself on his elbows, but the effect set his burned arms to throbbing. He sank back, kept his gaze on Burdeaux.

'Why, of course, sir. The outside works on the temporary expedient, Doctor Gil. You must know that. And the temporary always turns into the permanent, somehow. The temporary tax, the necessary *little* war, the temporary brutality that will cease as soon as certain conditions end . . . the government agency created for the permanent *interim* . . .'

'So you watch the news broadcasts and get all this from . . .'

'More than the news, Doctor Gil. All of it, and our watchers write condensed reports that . . . You see, it's all TV out there – life, everything. Outsiders are spectators. They expect everything to happen *to* them and they don't want to do more than turn a switch. They want to sit back and let life happen to them. They watch the late-late show and turn off their TVs. Then they go to bed to sleep – which is a form of turning themselves off just like the TV. The trouble is, their late-late show is often later than they think. There's a desperation in not being able to recognize this, Doctor Gil. Desperation leads to violence. There comes a morning for almost every one of those poor people outside when they realize that life hasn't happened to them no matter how much TV they've watched. Life hasn't happened because they didn't take part in it. They've never been onstage, never had anything real. It was all illusion ... delusion.'

Dasein absorbed the intensity of the words, their meaning and what lay under them. There was a terrifying sense of truth in Burdeaux's words.

'So they get turned off,' Dasein murmured.

'It's all TV,' Burdeaux said.

Dasein turned his head, looked out the window.

'You really ought to eat something, Doctor Gil,' Burdeaux said.

'No.'

'Doctor Gil, you're a wise man in some things, but in others ...'

'Don't call me wise,' Dasein said. 'Call me experienced.'

'The food here is the very best,' Burdeaux said. 'I'll get it and serve you myself. You don't have to fear a ...'

'I've been burned enough times,' Dasein said.

'Fire won't crack a full pot, Doctor Gil.'

'Win, I admire you and trust you. You saved my life. I don't think you were supposed to, but you did. That's why Doctor Piaget sent you in here. But an *accident* could happen – even with you.'

'You hurt me to say that, Doctor Gil. I'm not the kind feeds you with the corn and chokes you with the cob.'

Dasein sighed. He'd offended Burdeaux, but the alternative ... It occurred to Dasein abruptly that he was sitting on a special kind of bomb. Santaroga had abated its attack on him, probably in part because of his present helplessness. But the community was capable of returning to the manufacture of *accidents* if and when he should ever want something not permitted here.

At the moment, Dasein wanted nothing more than to be far away from here. He wanted this desperately despite the certain knowledge this desire must be on the proscribed list.

The door beside Burdeaux opened. A nurse backed into the room pulling a cart. She turned. Jenny!

Dasein ignored his burns, lifted himself on his elbows.

Jenny stared at him with an oddly pained expression. Her full lips were thrust out almost in a pout. The long black hair had been tied back in a neat bun. She wore a white uniform, white stockings, white shoes – no cap.

Dasein swallowed.

'Miss Jenny,' Burdeaux said. 'What do you have on that cart?'

She spoke without taking her gaze from Dasein. 'Some food for this madman. I prepared it myself.'

'I've been trying to get him to eat,' Burdeaux said, 'but he says no.'

'Would you leave us for a while, Win?' she asked. 'I want ...'

'The doctor said I wasn't to let ...'

'Win, please?' She turned toward him, pleading.

Burdeaux swallowed. 'Well ... since it's you ...'

'Thank you, Win.'

'Twenty minutes,' Burdeaux said. 'I'll be right out in the hall where you can call me if you need.'

'Thank you, Win.' She turned her attention back to Dasein.

Burdeaux left the room, closed the door softly.

Dasein said: 'Jen, I ...'

'Be quiet,' she said. 'You're not to waste your strength. Uncle Larry said ...'

'I'm not eating here,' Dasein said.

She stamped a foot. 'Gil, you're being ...'

'I'm being a fool,' he said. 'But the important thing is I'm alive.'

'But look at you! Look at ...'

'How's Harry Scheler?'

She hesitated, then: 'He'll live. He'll have some scars, and for that matter so will you, but you ...'

'Have they figured out what happened?'

'It was an accident.'

'That's all? Just an accident?'

'They said something about the line from the fuel pump being broken ... a bad electrical connection to one of the lights and ...'

'An accident,' Dasein said. 'I see.' He sank back into his pillow.

'I've prepared you some coddled eggs and toast and honey,' Jenny said. 'You've got to eat something to keep up ...'

'No.'

'Gil!'

'I said no.'

'What're you afraid of?'

'Another accident.'

'But I prepared this myself!'

He turned his head, stared at her, spoke in a low voice: 'Stay away from me. I love you.'

'Gilbert!'

'You said it,' he reminded her.

Her face paled. She leaned against the cart, trembling. 'I know,' she whispered. 'Sometimes I can feel the ...' She looked up, tears streaming down her face. 'But I *do* love you. And you're hurt now. I want to take care of you. I *need* to take care of you. Look.' She lifted the cover from one of the dishes on the cart, spooned a bite of food into her mouth.

'Jenny,' Dasein whispered. The look of hurt on her face, the intensity of his love for her – he wanted to take her in his arms and ...

A wide-eyed look came over Jenny's face. She reached both hands to her throat. Her mouth worked, but no sound came forth.

'Jenny!'

She shook her head, eyes staring wildly.

Dasein threw back the covers of his bed, winced as movement increased the pain along his arms. He ignored the pain, slid his feet out to a cold tile floor, straightened. A wave of dizziness gripped him.

Jenny, hands still at her throat, backed toward the door.

Dasein started toward her, hospital nightshirt flopping around his knees. He found movement difficult, his knees rubbery.

Abruptly, Jenny slumped to the floor.

Dasein remembered Burdeaux, shouted: 'Help! Win! Help!' He staggered, clutched the edge of the cart. It started to roll.

Dasein found himself sitting helplessly on the floor as the door burst open. Burdeaux stood there glaring at him, looked down at Jenny who lay with her eyes closed, knees drawn up, gasping.

'Call the doctor,' Dasein husked. 'Something in the food. She ate some ...'

Burdeaux took one quick breath of awareness, whirled away down the hall, leaving the door open.

Dasein started to crawl toward Jenny. The room wavered and twisted around him. His arms throbbed. There was a whistle in Jenny's gasping breaths that made him want to dash to her, but he couldn't find the strength. He had covered only a few feet when Piaget rushed in with Burdeaux right behind.

Piaget, his round face a pale blank mask, knelt beside Jenny, motioned toward Dasein, said: 'Get him back in bed.'

'The food on the cart,' Dasein rasped. 'She ate something.'

A blonde nurse in a stiff white cap wheeled an emergency cart in the door, bent over Piaget's shoulder. They were cut from Dasein's view as Burdeaux scooped him up, deposited him on the bed.

'You stay there, Doctor Gil,' Burdeaux said. He turned, stared at the action by the door.

'Allergenic reaction,' Piaget said. 'Throat's closing. Give me a double tube; we'll have to pump her.'

The nurse handed something to Piaget, who worked over Jenny, his back obscuring his actions.

'Atropine,' Piaget said.

Again, he took something from the nurse.

Dasein found it difficult to focus on the scene. Fear tightened his throat. *Why am I so weak?* he wondered. Then: *Dear God, she can't die. Please save her.*

Faces of more hospital personnel appeared at the door, wide-eyed, silent.

Piaget glanced up, said: 'Get a gurney.'

Some of the faces went away. Presently, there was a sound of wheels in the corridor.

Piaget stood up, said: 'That's as much as I can do here. Get her on the gurney – head lower than her feet.' He turned to Dasein. 'What'd she eat?'

'She took . . .' Dasein pointed to the food cart. 'Whatever it is, she took the cover off. Eggs?'

Piaget took one stride to the cart, grabbed up a dish, sniffed at it. His movement opened the view to the door for Dasein. Two orderlies and a nurse were lifting Jenny there, carrying her out the door. There was one glimpse of her pale face with a tube dangling from the corner of her mouth.

'Was it a poison?' Burdeaux asked, his voice hushed.

'Of course it was a poison!' Piaget snapped. 'Acts like aconite.' He turned with the dish, rushed out.

Dasein listened to the sound of the wheels and swift footsteps receding down the hall until Burdeaux closed the door, shutting out the sound.

His body bathed in perspiration, Dasein lay unresisting while Burdeaux eased him under the blankets

'For one moment there,' Burdeaux said, 'I . . . I thought you'd hurt Jenny.'

She can't die, Dasein thought.

'I'm sorry,' Burdeaux said. 'I know you wouldn't hurt her.'

'She can't die,' Dasein whispered.

He looked up to see tears draw glistening tracks down Burdeaux's dark cheeks. The tears ignited an odd anger reaction in Dasein. He was aware of the anger swelling in him, but unable to stop it. Rage! It was directed not at Burdeaux, but at the disembodied essence of Santaroga, at the collective *thing* which had tried to use the woman he loved to kill him. He glared at Burdeaux.

'Doctor Larry won't let anything happen to Jenny,' Burdeaux said. 'He'll ...'

Burdeaux saw the expression in Dasein's eyes, instinctively backed away.

'Get out of here!' Dasein rasped.

'But the doctor said I was to ...'

'Doctor *Gil* says you get the hell out of here!'

Burdeaux's face took on a stubborn set. 'I'm not to leave you alone.'

Dasein sank back. What could he do?

'You had a very bad shock reaction last night,' Burdeaux said. 'They had to give you blood. You're not to be left alone.'

They gave me a transfusion? Dasein wondered. *Why didn't they kill me then? They were saving me for Jenny!*

'You all care so much for Jenny,' Dasein said. 'You'd let her kill me. It'd destroy her, but that doesn't make any difference, does it? Sacrifice Jenny, that's your verdict, you pack of ...'

'You're talking crazy, Doctor Gil.'

As quickly as it had come, the anger left Dasein. Why attack poor Win? Why attack any of them? They couldn't see the monkey on their back. He felt deflated. Of course this was crazy to Burdeaux. One society's reason was another's unreason.

Dasein cursed the weakness that had seized his body.

Bad shock reaction.

He wondered then what he would do if Jenny died. It was a curiously fragmented feeling – part of him wailing in grief at the thought, another part raging at the fate which had shunted him into this corner ... and part of him forever analyzing, analyzing ...

How much of the shock had been a Jaspers reaction? Had he become sensitized the way Santarogans were?

They'll kill me out of hand if Jenny dies, he thought.

Burdeaux said: 'I'll just sit here by the door. You be sure to tell me if you need anything.'

He sat down facing Dasein, folded his arms – for all the world like a guard.

Dasein closed his eyes, thought: *Jenny, please don't die.* He recalled Piaget telling how Harry Scheler had known of the brother's death.

An empty place.

Where do I sense Jenny? Dasein asked himself.

It bothered him that he couldn't probe within himself somewhere and be reassured by Jenny's presence. That kind of reassurance was worth any price. She had to be there. It was a thing any Santarogan could do.

But I'm not a Santarogan.

Dasein felt that he teetered on the razor's edge. One side held the vast unconscious sea of the human world into which he had been born. On the other side – there, it was like the green waters of a lake – serene, contained, every droplet knowing its neighbors.

He heard a door open, felt a storm begin in the unconscious sea, sensed a breeze stirring the surface of the lake. The sensation of balancing receded. Dasein opened his eyes.

Piaget stood in the middle of the room. He wore a stethoscope around his neck. There was a feeling of fatigue around his eyes. He studied Dasein with a puzzled frown.

'Jenny?' Dasein whispered.

'She'll live,' Piaget said. 'But it was close.'

Dasein closed his eyes, took a deep breath. 'How many more *accidents* like that can we take?' he asked. He opened his eyes, met Piaget's gaze.

Burdeaux came up beside Piaget, said: 'He's been talking crazy, Doctor Larry.'

'Win, would you leave us for a bit?' Piaget asked.

'You sure?' Burdeaux scowled at Dasein.

'Please,' Piaget said. He pulled up a chair, sat down beside the bed, facing Dasein.

'I'll be right outside,' Burdeaux said. He went out, closed the door.

'You've upset Win and that's rather difficult to do,' Piaget said.

'Upset ...' Dasein stared at him, speechless. Then: 'Is that your summation of what's happened?'

Piaget looked down at his own right hand, made a fist, opened it. He shook his head. 'I didn't mean to sound flippant, Gilbert. I ...' He looked up at Dasein. 'There must be some reasonable, rational explanation.'

'You don't think the word *accident* explains all this?'

'An accident prone ...'

'We both know there's no such thing as an accident prone in the popular sense of that label,' Dasein said.

Piaget steepled his hands in front of him, leaned back. He pursed his lips, then: 'Well, in the psychiatric view ...'

'Come off that!' Dasein barked. 'You're going to fall back on the old cliché about "a neurotic tendency to inflict self-injury," a defect in ego-control. Where did I have any control over the work on that bridge? Or the boy with the bow and arrow or ...'

'Boy with a bow and arrow?'

Dasein thought to hell with his promise, told about the incident at the park, added: 'And what about the garage hoist or the fire? For that matter, what about the poison in the food Jenny ... Jenny, of all people! the food that she ...'

'All right! You have grounds to ...'

'Grounds? I've an entire syndrome laid out in front of me. Santaroga is trying to kill me. You've already killed an apparently inoffensive young man. You've almost killed Jenny. What next?'

'In heaven's name, why would we ...'

'To eliminate a threat. Isn't that obvious? I'm a threat.'

'Oh, now really ...'

'Now, really! Or is it perfectly all right if I take Jenny out of this crazy valley and blow the whistle on you?'

'Jenny won't leave her ...' He paused. 'Blow the whistle? What do you mean?'

'Now, who's making the angels weep?' Dasein asked. 'You protest that you love Jenny and won't have her hurt. What more terrible thing is there than to have her be the instrument of my death?'

Piaget paled, drew two ragged breaths. 'She ... There must be ... What do you mean blow the whistle?'

'Has a Labor Department inspector ever looked into the child labor situation out at your *school*?' Dasein asked. 'What about the State Department of Mental Hygiene? Your records say no mental illness from Santaroga.'

'Gilbert, you don't know what you're talking about.'

'Don't I? What about the antigovernment propaganda in your newspaper?'

'We're not antigovernment, Gilbert, we're ...'

'What? Why, I've never seen such a ...'

'Allow me to finish, please. We're not antigovernment; we're anti-*outside*. That's a cat of quite different calico.'

'You think they're all ... insane?'

'We think they're all going to eat themselves up.'

Madness, madness, Dasein thought. He stared at the ceiling. Perspiration bathed his body. The intensity of emotion he'd put into the argument with Piaget ...

'Why did you send Burdeaux to watch over me?' Dasein asked.

Piaget shrugged. 'I ... to guard against the possibility you might be right in your ...'

'And you picked Burdeaux.' Dasein turned his eyes toward Piaget, studied the man. Piaget appeared to be warring with himself, nervously clenching and unclenching his fists.

'The reasons should be obvious,' he said.

'You can't let me leave the valley, can you?' Dasein asked.

'You're in no physical condition to ..'

'Will I ever be?'

Piaget met Dasein's gaze. 'How can I prove to you what we really ...'

'Is there any place here where I can protect myself from accidents?' Dasein asked.

'Protect yourself from ...' Piaget shook his head.

'You want to prove your honorable intentions,' Dasein said.

Piaget pursed his lips, then: 'There's an isolation suite, a penthouse on the roof – its own kitchen, facilities, everything. If you ...'

'Could Burdeaux get me up there without killing me?'

Piaget sighed. 'I'll take you up there myself as soon as I can get a ...'

'Burdeaux.'

'As you wish. You can be moved in a wheelchair.'

'I'll walk.'

'You're not strong enough to ...'

'I'll find the strength. Burdeaux can help me.'

'Very well. As to food, we can ...'

'I'll eat out of cans picked at random from a market's shelves. Burdeaux can shop for me until I'm ...'

'Now, see here ...'

'That's the way it's going to be, doctor. He'll get me a broad selection, and I'll choose at random from that selection.'

'You're taking unnecessary ...'

'Let's give it a try and see how many accidents develop.'

Piaget stared at him a moment, then: 'As you wish.'

'What about Jenny? When can I see her?'

'She's had a severe shock to her system and some intestinal trauma. I'd say she shouldn't have visitors for several days unless they ...'

'I'm not leaving that isolation suite until I've convinced you,' Dasein said. 'When can she come to see me?'

'It'll be several days.' He pointed a finger at Dasein. 'Now, see here, Gilbert – you're not going to take Jenny out of the valley. She'll never consent to ...'

'Let's let Jenny decide that.'

'Very well.' Piaget nodded. 'You'll see.' He went to the door, opened it. 'Win?'

Burdeaux stepped past Piaget into the room. 'Is he still talking crazy, Doctor Larry?'

'We're going to conduct an experiment, Win,' Piaget said. 'For reasons of Dr Dasein's health and Jenny's happiness, we're going to move him to the isolation suite.' Piaget jerked a thumb toward the ceiling. 'He wants you to move him.'

'I'll get a wheelchair,' Burdeaux said.

'Dr Dasein wants to try walking,' Piaget said.

'Can he do that?' Burdeaux turned a puzzled frown on Dasein. 'He was too weak to stand just a little ...'

'Dr Dasein appears to be relying on your strength,' Piaget said. 'Think you can manage?'

'I could carry him,' Burdeaux said, 'but that seems like a ...'

'Treat him with the same care you'd treat a helpless infant,' Piaget said.

'If you say so, Doctor Larry.'

Burdeaux crossed to the bed, helped Dasein to sit on the edge of the bed. The effort set Dasein's head to whirling. In the fuzzy tipping and turning of the room, he saw Piaget go to the door, open it and stand there looking at Burdeaux.

'I'll take my evil influence elsewhere for the time being,' Piaget said. 'You don't mind, do you, Gilbert, if I look in on you shortly – purely in a medical capacity?'

'As long as I have the final say on what you do to me,' Dasein said.

'It's only fair to warn you your bandages have to be changed,' Piaget said.

'Can Win do it?'

'Your trust in Win is very touching,' Piaget said. 'I'm sure he's impressed.'

'Can he ...'

'Yes, I'm certain he can – with my instruction.'

'All right then,' Dasein said.

With Burdeaux's help, Dasein struggled to his feet. He stood there panting, leaning on Burdeaux. Piaget went out, leaving the door open.

'You sure you can manage, sir?' Burdeaux asked.

Dasein tried to take a step. His knees were two sections of flexing rubber. He would have fallen had it not been for Burdeaux's support.

'Do we go by elevator?' Dasein asked.

'Yes, sir. It's right across the hall.'

'Let's get on with it.'

'Yes, sir. Excuse me, sir.' Burdeaux bent, lifted Dasein in his arms, turned to slip through the door.

Dasein glimpsed the startled face of a nurse walking down the hall. He felt foolish, helpless – stubborn. The nurse frowned, glanced at Burdeaux, who ignored her, punched the elevator button with an elbow. The nurse strode off down the hall, heels clicking.

Elevator doors slid open with a hiss.

Burdeaux carried him inside, elbowed a button marked 'P.'

Dasein felt his mouth go dry as the elevator doors closed. He stared up at a cream ceiling, a milky oblong of light, thinking: *They didn't hesitate to sacrifice Jenny. Why would they have a second thought about Burdeaux? What if the elevator's rigged to crash?*

A faint humming sounded. Dasein felt the elevator lift. Presently, the doors opened and Burdeaux carried him out. There was a glimpse of a cream-walled entrance foyer, a mahogany door labeled 'Isolation' and they were inside.

It was a long room with three beds, windows opening onto a black tar roof. Burdeaux deposited Dasein on the nearest bed, stepped back. 'Kitchen's in there,' he said, pointing to a swinging door at the end of the room. 'Bathroom's through that door there.' This was a door opposite the foot of Dasein's bed. There were two more doors to the right of this one. 'Other doors are a closet and a lab. Is this what you wanted, Doctor?'

Dasein met a measuring stare in Burdeaux's eyes, said: 'It'll have to do.' He managed a rueful smile, explained the eating arrangements.

'Canned food, sir?' Burdeaux asked.

'I'm imposing on you, I know,' Dasein said. 'But you were ... like me ... once. I think you sympathise with me ... unconsciously. I'm counting on that to ...' Dasein managed a weak shrug.

'Is this what Doctor Larry wants me to do?'

'Yes.'

'I just pick cans from the shelves ... at random?'

'That's right.'

'Well, it sounds crazy, sir ... but I'll do it.' He left the room, muttering.

Dasein managed to crawl under the blankets, lay for a moment regaining his strength. He could see a line of treetops beyond the roof – tall evergreens – a cloudless blue sky. There was a sense of quiet about the room. Dasein took a deep breath. Was this place really safe? A Santarogan had picked it. But the Santarogan had been off balance with personal doubts.

For the first time in days, Dasein felt he might relax. A profound lassitude filled him.

What is this unnatural weakness? he wondered.

It was far more than shock reaction or a result of his burns. This was like an injury to the soul, something that involved the entire being. It was a central command to all his muscles, a compulsion of inactivity.

Dasein closed his eyes.

In the red darkness behind his eyelids Dasein felt himself to be shattered, his ego huddled in a fetal crouch, terrified. One must not move, he thought. To move was to invite a disaster more terrible than death.

An uncontrollable shuddering shook his legs and hips, set his teeth chattering. He fought himself to stillness, opened his eyes to stare at the ceiling.

It's a Jaspers reaction, he thought.

There was a smell of it in the room. The aroma gnawed at his senses. He sniffed, turned toward a metal stand beside the bed, a partly-opened drawer. Dasein slid the drawer all the way out to a stop, rolled onto his side to peer at the space he'd exposed.

Empty.

But there'd been a Jaspers *something* in the drawer – and that recently. What?

Dasein swept his gaze around the room. Isolation suite, Piaget had said. Isolation of what? From what? For what?

He swallowed, sank back on the pillow.

The deliciously terrifying lassitude gripped him. Dasein sensed the green waters of unconsciousness ready to enfold him. By a desperate effort of will, he forced his eyes to remain open.

Somewhere, a cowering, fetal *something* moaned.

Faceless god chuckled.

The entrance door opened.

Dasein held himself rigidly unmoving, afraid if he moved his head to one side his face might sink beneath the upsurging unconsciousness, that he might drown in ...

Piaget came into his field of vision, peering down at him. The doctor thumbed Dasein's left eyelid up, studied the eye.

'Damned if you aren't still fighting it,' he said.

'Fighting what?' Dasein whispered.

'I was pretty sure it'd knock you out if you used that much energy at this stage,' Piaget said. 'You're going to have to eat before long, you know.'

Dasein was aware then of the pain – a demanding hollow within him. He held onto the pain. It helped fight off the enfolding green waves.

'Tell you what,' Piaget said. He moved from Dasein's range of vision. There came a scraping, a grunt. 'I'll just sit here and keep watch on you until Win gets back with something you'll stuff into that crazy face of yours. I won't lay a hand on you and I won't let anyone else touch you.

Your bandages can wait. More important for you to rest – sleep if you can. Stop fighting it.'

Sleep! Gods, how the lassitude beckoned.

Fighting what?

He tried to frame the question once more, couldn't find the energy. It took all of his effort merely to cling to a tiny glowing core of awareness that stared up at a cream-colored ceiling.

'What you're fighting,' Piaget said in a conversational tone, 'is the climb out of the morass. Mud clings to one. This is what leads me to suspect your theory may have a germ of truth in it – that some stain of violence still clings to us, reaching us on the blind side, as it were.'

Piaget's voice was a hypnotic drone. Phrases threaded their way in and out of Dasein's awareness.

'... experiment in domestication ...' ' ... removed from ex-stasis, from a fixed condition ...' ' ... must reimprint the sense of identity ...' ' ... nothing new: mankind's always in some sort of trouble ...' ' ... religious experience of a sort – creating a new order of theobotanists ...' ' ... don't shrink from life or from awareness of life ...' ' ... seek a society that changes smoothly, flowingly as the collective need requires ...'

One of the faceless gods produced a thundering whisper in Dasein's skull: '*This is my commandment given unto you: A poor man cannot afford principles and a rich man doesn't need them.*'

Dasein lay suspended in a hammock of silence.

Fear of movement dominated him.

He sensed a world-presence somewhere beneath him. But he lay stranded here above. Something beckoned. Familiar. He felt the familiar world and was repelled. The place seethed with disguises that tried to conceal a rubble of pretensions, devices, broken masks. Still, it beckoned. It was a place in which he could fit, shaped to him. He sensed himself reaching toward it with a feeling of exuberant self-gratification, drew back. The rubble. It was everywhere, a blanket over life, a creamy ennui – soothing, cajoling, saccharine.

Still, it beckoned.

The lure was inexhaustible, a brilliant bag of pyrotechnics, a palette flooded with gross colors.

It was all a trick.

He sensed this – all a trick, a mass of signal clichés and canned reflexes.

It was a hateful world.

Which world? he asked himself. *Was it Santaroga* ... or *the outside?*

Something grabbed Dasein's shoulder.

He screamed.

Dasein awoke to find himself moaning, mumbling. It took a moment to place himself. Where were the faceless gods?

Piaget leaned over him, a hand on Dasein's shoulder.

'You were having a nightmare,' Piaget said. He took his hand away. 'Win's back with the food – such as it is.'

Dasein's stomach knotted in pain.

Burdeaux stood at his right next to the adjoining bed. A box piled with canned food rested on the next bed.

'Bring me a can opener and a spoon,' Dasein said.

'Just tell me what you want and open it,' Burdeaux said.

'I'll do it,' Dasein said. He raised himself on his elbows, Movement set his arms to throbbing, but he felt stronger – as though he had tapped a strength of desperation.

'Humor him,' Piaget said as Burdeaux hesitated.

Burdeaux shrugged, went out the door across from the bed.

Dasein threw back the blankets, swung his feet out. He motioned Piaget back, sat up. His feet touched a cold floor. He took a deep breath, lurched across to the adjoining bed. His knees felt stronger, but Dasein sensed the shallowness of his reserves.

Burdeaux reappeared, handed Dasein a twist-handle can opener.

Dasein sat down beside the box, grabbed a fat green can out of it, not even looking at the label. He worked the opener around the can, took a proffered spoon from Burdeaux, lifted back the lid.

Beans.

An odor of Jaspers clamored at Dasein from the open can. He looked at the label: 'Packed by the Jaspers Cooperative.' There was a permit number, a date of a year ago and the admonition: 'Not for sale in interstate commerce. Exposed Dec. '64.'

Dasein stared at the can. *Jaspers?* It couldn't be. The stuff didn't ship. It couldn't be preserved out of . . .

'Something wrong?' Piaget asked.

Dasein studied the can: shiny, a glistening label.

'Beans with meat sauce and beef,' read the yellow letters.

Dasein ignored the lure of the aroma from the can, looked in the box. He tried to remember whether the can had given off the characteristic hiss of a vacuum seal breaking as it had been opened – couldn't remember.

'What's wrong?' Piaget insisted.

'Can't be anything wrong,' Burdeaux said. 'That's all private stock.'

Dasein looked up from the box. All the cans he could see bore the Co-op's label. *Private stock?*

'Here,' Piaget said. He took can and spoon from Dasein's hands, tasted a bite of beans, smiled. He returned the can and spoon to Dasein, who took them automatically.

'Nothing wrong there,' Piaget said.

'Better not be,' Burdeaux said. 'It came from Pete Maja's store, right off the private stock shelf.'

'It's Jaspers,' Dasein rasped.

'Of course it is,' Piaget said. 'Canned right here for local consumption. Stored here to preserve its strength. Won't keep long after it's opened, though, so you'd better start eating. Got maybe five, ten minutes.' He chuckled. 'Be thankful you're here. If you were *outside* and opened that can, wouldn't last more'n a few seconds.'

'Why?'

'Hostile environment,' Piaget said. 'Go ahead and eat. You saw me take some. Didn't hurt me.'

Dasein tested a bit of the sauce on his tongue. A soothing sensation spread across his tongue, down his throat. They were delicious. He spooned a full bite into his mouth, gulped it down.

The Jaspers went thump in his stomach.

Dasein turned, wide-eyed toward Burdeaux, met a look of wonder, dark brown eyes like African charms with butter-yellow flecks in them. The can drew Dasein's attention. He peered into it.

Empty

Dasein experienced a sensation of strange recall – like the fast rewind on a tape recorder, a screech of memory: his hand in a piston movement spooning the contents of the can into his mouth. Blurred gulpings.

He recognized the *thump* now. It had been a thump of awareness. He no longer was hungry.

My body did it, Dasein thought. A sense of wonder enfolded him. *My body did it.*

Piaget took the can and spoon from Dasein's unresisting fingers. Burdeaux helped Dasein back into bed, pulled the blankets up, straightened them.

My body did it, Dasein thought.

There'd been a trigger to action – knowledge that the Jaspers effect was fading . . . and consciousness had blanked out.

'There,' Piaget said.

'What about his bandages?' Burdeaux asked.

Piaget examined the bandage on Dasein's cheek, bent close to sniff, drew back. 'Perhaps this evening,' he said.

'You've trapped me, haven't you?' Dasein asked. He stared up at Piaget.

'There he goes again,' Burdeaux said.

'Win,' Piaget said, 'I know you have personal matters to take care of. Why don't you tend to them now and leave me with Gilbert? You can come back around six if you would.'

Burdeaux said: 'I could call Willa and have her ...'

'No need to bother your daughter,' Piaget said 'Run along and ...'

'But what if ...'

'There's no danger,' Piaget said.

'If you say so,' Burdeaux said. He moved toward the foyer door, paused there a moment to study Dasein, then went out.

'What didn't you want Win to hear?' Dasein asked.

'There he goes again,' Piaget said, echoing Burdeaux.

'Something must've ...'

'There's nothing Win couldn't hear!'

'Yet you sent him to watch over me ... because he was special,' Dasein said. He took a deep breath, feeling his senses clear, his mind come alert. 'Win was ... *safe* for me.'

'Win has his own life to live and you're interfering,' Piaget said. 'He ...'

'Why was Win *safe*?'

'It's your feeling, not mine,' Piaget said. 'Win saved you from falling. You've shown a definite empathy ...'

'He came from *outside*,' Dasein said. 'He was like me ... once.'

'Many of us came from outside,' Piaget said.

'You, too?'

'No, but ...'

'How does the trap really work?' Dasein asked.

'There is *no* trap!'

'What does the Jaspers do to one?' Dasein asked. 'Ask yourself that question.'

'Technically ... doctor?'

'Technically?'

'What does the Jaspers do?'

'Oh. Among other things, it speeds up catalysis of the chemical transmitters in the nervous system-5 hydroxytryptamine and serotonin.'

'Changes in the Golgi cells?'

'Absolutely not. Its effect is to break down blockage systems, to open the mind's image function and consciousness formulation processes. You *feel* as though you had a better ... an *improved* memory. Not true, of course, except in effect. Merely a side effect of the speed with which ...'

'Image function,' Dasein said. 'What if the person isn't capable of dealing with all his memories? There are extremely disagreeable, shameful ... dangerously traumatic memories in some ...'

'We have our failures.'

'Dangerous failures?'

'Sometimes.'

Dasein closed his mouth, an instinctive reaction. He drew in a deep breath through his nostrils. The odor of Jaspers assailed his senses. He looked toward the box of cans on the adjacent bed.

Jaspers. Consciousness fuel. Dangerous substance. Drug of ill omen. Speculative fantasies flitted through Dasein's mind. He turned, surprised a mooning look on Piaget's face.

'You can't get away from it here in the valley, can you?' Dasein asked.

'Who'd want to?'

'You're hoping I'll stay, perhaps help you with your failures.'

'There's certainly work to be done.'

Anger seized Dasein. 'How can I think?' he demanded. 'I can't get away from the smell of ...'

'Easy,' Piaget murmured. 'Take it easy, now. You'll get so you don't even notice it.'

Every society has its own essential chemistry, Dasein thought. *Its own aroma, a thing of profound importance, but least apparent to its own members.*

Santaroga had tried to kill him, Dasein knew. He wondered now if it could have been because he had a different smell. He stared at the box on the bed. Impossible! It couldn't be anything that close to the surface.

Piaget moved around to the box, tore a small, curling strip of paper from it, touched the paper to his tongue. 'This box has been down in storage,' he said. 'It's paper, organic matter. Anything organic becomes impregnated with Jaspers after a certain exposure.' He tossed the paper into the box.

'Will I be like that box?' Dasein asked. He felt he had a ghost at his heels, an essence he couldn't elude. The lurking presence stirred in his mind. 'Will I ...'

'Put such thoughts out of your mind,' Piaget said.

'Will I be one of the failures?' Dasein asked.

'I said stop that!'

'Why should I?'

Dasein sat up, the strength of fear and anger in him, his mind crowded

342

by suppositions, each one worse than its predecessor. He felt more exposed and vulnerable than a child running from a whipping.

With an abrupt shock of memory, Dasein fell back to the pillow. *Why did I choose this moment to remember that?* he asked himself. A painful incident from his childhood lay there, exposed to awareness. He remembered the pain of the switch on his back.

'You're not the failure type,' Piaget said.

Dasein stared accusingly at the odorous box.

Jaspers!

'You're the kind who can go very high,' Piaget said. 'Why do you really think you're here? Just because of that silly market report? Or because of Jenny? Ah, no. Nothing that isolated or simple. Santaroga calls out to some people. They come.'

Dasein looked sidelong at him

'I came so you people could get the chance to kill me,' Dasein said.

'We don't want to kill you!'

'One moment you suspect I may be right, the next you're denying it.'

Piaget sighed.

'I have a suggestion,' Dasein said.

'Anything.'

'You won't like it,' Dasein said.

Piaget glared at him. 'What's on your mind?'

'You'll be afraid to do it.'

'I'm not ...'

'It's something like a clinical test,' Dasein said. 'My guess is you'll try not to do it. You'll look for excuses, anything to get out of it or to discontinue it. You'll try to misunderstand me. You'll try to break away from ...'

'For the love of heaven! What's on your mind?'

'You may succeed.'

'Succeed in what?'

'Not doing what I suggest.'

'Don't try to crowd me into a corner, Gilbert.'

'Thus it starts,' Dasein said. He held up a hand as Piaget made as though to speak. 'I want you to let me hypnotize you.'

'What?'

'You heard me.'

'Why?'

'You're a native,' Dasein said, 'thoroughly conditioned to this ... consciousness fuel. I want to see what's under there, what kind of fears you ...'

'Of all the crazy ...'

'I'm not some amateur meddler asking to do this,' Dasein said. 'I'm a clinical psychologist well versed in hypnotherapy.'

'But what could you possibly hope to ...'

'What a man fears,' Dasein said. 'His fears are like a "homing beacon." Home in on a man's fears and you find his underlying motivations. Under every fear, there's a violence of no mean ...'

'Nonsense! I have no ...'

'You're a medical man. You know better than that.'

Piaget stared at him, silently measuring. Presently, he said: 'Well, every man has a death fear, of course. And ...'

'More than that.'

'You think you're some kind of god, Gilbert? You just go around ...'

'Doth the eagle mount up at thy command, and make her nest on high?' Dasein asked. He shook his head. 'What do you worship?'

'Oh ... religion.' Piaget took a deep breath of relief. 'Thou shalt not be afraid for the terror by night; nor for the arrow that flieth by day; nor for the pestilence that walketh in darkness; nor for the destruction that wasteth at noonday. Is that it? What do ...'

'That is *not* it.'

'Gilbert, I'm not ignorant of these matters, as you must realize. To stir up the areas you're suggesting ...'

'What would I stir up?'

'We both know that cannot be predicted with any accuracy.'

'You're doing things as a community ... a group, a society that you don't want me digging into,' Dasein said. 'What does that society really worship? With one hand, you say: "Look anywhere you like." With the other hand, you slam doors. In every action of ...'

'You really believe some of us tried to ... kill you ... for the community?'

'Don't you?'

'Couldn't there be some other explanation?'

'What?'

Dasein held a steady gaze on Piaget. The doctor was disturbed, no doubt of that. He refused to meet Dasein's eyes. He moved his hands about aimlessly. His breathing had quickened.

'Societies don't believe they can die,' Piaget said. 'It must follow that a society, as such, does not worship at all. If it cannot die, it'll never face a final judgment.'

'And if it'll never face judgment,' Dasein said, 'it can do things as a society that'd be too much for an individual to stomach.'

'Perhaps,' Piaget muttered. 'Perhaps.' Then: 'All right, then. Why examine me? I've never tried to harm you.'

Dasein looked away, taken aback by the question. Out of the window he could see through a frame of trees a stretch of hills which enclosed Santaroga. He felt himself enclosed by that line of hills, entangled here in a web of meanings.

'What about the people who have tried to kill me?' Dasein asked shortly. 'Would they be fit subjects?'

'The boy, perhaps,' Piaget said. 'I'll have to examine him anyway.'

'Petey, the Jorick boy,' Dasein said. 'A failure, eh?'

'I think not.'

'Another *opening person* ... like me?'

'You remember that?'

'Then, you said societies die, that you'd cut yourselves off here ... with Jaspers.'

'We had a speaking then, too, as I recall it,' Piaget said. 'Have you really opened now? Are you seeing? Have you become?'

Dasein abruptly remembered Jenny's voice on the telephone: 'Be careful.' And the fear when she'd said: 'They want you to leave.'

In this instant, Piaget became for him once more the gray cat in the garden, silencing the birds, and Dasein knew himself to be alone yet, without a group. He remembered the lake, the perception of perception – knowing his own body, that communal knowledge of mood, that sharing.

Every conversation he'd had with Piaget came back to Dasein then to be weighed and balanced. He felt his Santaroga experiences had been building – one moment upon another – to this instant.

'I'll get you some more Jaspers,' Piaget said. 'Perhaps then ...'

'You suspect I'm fluttery behind the eyes?' Dasein asked.

Piaget smiled. 'Sarah clings to the phrases of the past,' he said, 'before we systematized our dealings with Jaspers ... and with the outside. But don't laugh at her or her phrases. She has the innocent eye.'

'Which I haven't.'

'You still have some of the assumptions and prejudices of the not-men,' Piaget said.

'And I've heard too much, learned too much about you, ever to be allowed to leave,' Dasein said.

'Won't you even try to become?' Piaget asked.

'Become what?' Piaget's crazy, almost-schizophrenic talk enraged him. *A speaking! A seeing!*

'Only you know that,' Piaget said.

'Know what?'

Piaget merely stared at him.

'I'll tell you what I know,' Dasein said. 'I know you're terrified by my suggestion. You don't want to find out how Vina's roach powder got into the coffee. You don't want to know how Clara Scheler poisoned her stew. You don't want to know what prompted someone to push me off a float. You don't want to know why a fifteen-year-old boy would try to put an arrow through me. You don't want to know how Jenny poisoned the eggs. You don't want to know how a car was set up to crush me, or how my truck was rigged as a fire bomb. You don't want to ...'

'All right!'

Piaget rubbed his chin, turned away.

'I told you you might succeed,' Dasein said.

'"*Iti vuccati*"' Piaget murmured. '"Thus it is said: Every system and every interpretation becomes false in the light of a more complete system." I wonder if that's why you're here – to remind us no positive statement may be made that's free from contradictions.'

He turned, stared at Dasein.

'What're you talking about?' Dasein asked. Piaget's tone and manner carried a suddenly disturbing calmness.

'The inner enlightenment of all beings dwells in the self,' Piaget said. 'The self which cannot be isolated abides in the memory as a perception of symbols. We are conscious as a projection of self upon the receptive content of the senses. But it happens the self can be led astray – the self of a person or the self of a community. I wonder ...'

'Stop trying to distract me with gobbledygook,' Dasein said. 'You're trying to change the subject, avoid ...'

'A ... void,' Piaget said. 'Ah, yes. The void is very pertinent to this. Einstein cannot be confined to mathematics. All phenomenal existence is transitory, relative. No particular thing is real. It is passing into something else at every moment.'

Dasein pushed himself upright in the bed. Had the old doctor gone crazy?

'Performance alone doesn't produce the result,' Piaget said. 'You're grasping at absolutes. To seek any fixed thing, however, is to deal in false imagination. You're trying to strain soap from the water with your fingers. Duality is a delusion.'

Dasein shook his head from side to side. The man was making no sense at all.

'I see you are confused,' Piaget said. 'You don't really understand your own intellectual energy. You walk on narrow paths. I offer you new orbits of ...'

'You can stop that,' Dasein said. He remembered the lake then, the husky feminine voice saying: '*There's only one thing to do.*' And Jenny: '*We're doing it.*'

'You must adapt to conditional thought,' Piaget said. 'In that way, you'll be able to understand relative self-existence and express the relative truth of whatever you perceive. You have the ability to do it. I can see that. Your insight into the violent actions which surround ...'

'Whatever you're doing to me, you won't stop it, will you?' Dasein asked. 'You keep pushing and pushing and ...'

'Who pushes?' Piaget asked. 'Are you not the one exerting the greatest ...'

'Damn you! Stop it!'

Piaget looked at him silently.

'Einstein,' Dasein muttered. 'Relativity ... absolutes ... intellectual energy ... phenomenal ...' He broke off as his mind lurched momentarily into a speed of computation very like what he had experienced when deciding to hurdle the gap in the bridge.

It's sweep-rate, Dasein thought. *It's like hunting submarines – in the mind. It's how many search units you can put to the job and how fast they can travel.*

As quickly as it had come, the sensation was gone. But Dasein had never felt as shaken in his life. No immediate danger had triggered this ability ... not this time.

Narrow paths, he thought. He looked up at Piaget in wonder. There was more here than fell upon the ears. Could that be the way Santarogans thought? Dasein shook his head. It didn't seem possible ... or likely.

'May I elaborate?' Piaget asked.

Dasein nodded.

'You will have remarked the blunt way we state our relative truths for sales purposes,' Piaget said. 'Conditional thought rejects any other approach. Mutual respect is implicit, then, in conditional thought. Contrast the market approach of those who sent you to spy upon us. They have ...'

'How fast can you think?' Dasein asked.

'Fast?' Piaget shrugged. 'As fast as necessary.'

As fast as necessary, Dasein thought.

'May I continue?' Piaget asked.

Again, Dasein nodded.

'It has been noted,' Piaget said, 'that sewer-peak-load times tend to match station breaks on TV – an elementary fact you can recognize with only the briefest reflection. But it's only a short step from this elementary fact to the placement of flow meters in the sewers as a quite accurate check on the available listening units at any given moment. I've no doubt this already is being done; it's so obvious. Now, reflect a moment on the basic attitudes toward their fellowmen of people who would do this sort of thing, as opposed to those who could not find it in themselves to do it.'

Dasein cleared his throat. Here was the core of Santaroga's indictment against the *outside*. How did you use people? With dignity? Or did you tap their most basic functions for your own purposes? The *outside* began to appear more and more as a place of irritating emptiness and contrived blandishments.

I'm really beginning to see things as a Santarogan, Dasein thought. There was a sense of victory in the thought. It was what he had set out to do as part of his job.

'It isn't surprising,' Piaget said, 'to find the "N-square" law from warfare being applied to advertising and politics – other kinds of warfare, you see – with no real conversion problem from one field to the other. Each has its concepts of concentration and exposure. The mathematics of differentials and predictions apply equally well, no matter the field of battle.'

Armies, Dasein thought. He focused on Piaget's moving lips, wondering suddenly how the subject had been changed to such a different field. Had Piaget done it deliberately? They'd been talking about Santaroga's blind side, its fears ...

'You've given me food for speculation,' Piaget said. 'I'm going to leave you alone for a while and see if I can come up with something constructive. There's a call bell at the head of your bed. The nurses are not on this floor, but one can be here quite rapidly in an emergency. They'll look in on you from time to time. Would you like something to read? May I send you anything?'

Something constructive? Dasein wondered. *What does he mean?*

'How about some copies of our valley newspaper?' Piaget asked.

'Some writing paper and a pen,' Dasein said. He hesitated, then: 'And the papers – yes.'

'Very well. Try to rest. You appear to be regaining some of your strength, but don't overdo it.'

Piaget turned, strode out of the room.

Presently, a red-haired nurse bustled in with a stack of newspapers, a ruled tablet and a dark-green ballpoint pen. She deposited them on his nightstand, said: 'Do you want your bed straightened?'

'No, thanks.'

Dasein found his attention caught by her striking resemblance to Al Marden.

'You're a Marden,' he said.

'So what else is new?' she asked and left him.

Well, get her! Dasein thought.

He glanced at the stack of newspapers, remembering his search through Santaroga for the paper's office. They had come to him so easily they'd lost some of their allure. He slipped out of bed, found his knees had lost some of their weakness.

The canned food caught his eye.

Dasein rummaged in the box, found an applesauce, ate it swiftly while the food still was redolent with Jaspers. Even as he ate, he hoped this would return him to that level of clarity and speed of thought he'd experienced at the bridge and, briefly, with Piaget.

The applesauce eased his hunger, left him vaguely restless – nothing else.

Was it losing its kick? he wondered. Did it require more and more of the stuff each time? Or was he merely becoming acclimated?

Hooked?

He thought of Jenny pleading with him, cajoling. A *consciousness fuel. What in the name of God had Santaroga discovered?*

Dasein stared out the window at the path of boundary hills visible through the trees. A fire somewhere beneath his field of view sent smoke spiraling above the ridge. Dasein stared at the smoke, feeling an oddly compulsive mysticism, a deeply primitive sensation about that unseen fire. There was a spirit signature written in the smoke, something out of his own genetic past. No fear accompanied the sensation. It was, instead, as though he had been reunited with some part of himself cut off since childhood.

Pushing back at the surface of childhood, he thought.

He realized then that a Santarogan did not cut off his primitive past; he contained it within a membranous understanding.

How far do I go in becoming a Santarogan before I turn back? he wondered. *I have a duty to Selador and the ones who hired me. When do I make my break?*

The thought filled him with a deep revulsion against returning to the *outside*. But he had to do it. There was a thick feeling of nausea in his throat, a pounding ache at his temples. He thought of the irritant emptiness of the *outside* – piecemeal debris of lives, egos with sham patches, a world almost devoid of anything to make the soul rise and soar.

There was no substructure to life *outside*, he thought, no underlying sequence to tie it all together. There was only a shallow, glittering roadway signposted with flashy, hypnotic diversions. And behind the glitter – only the bare board structure of props ... and desolation.

I can't go back, he thought. He turned to his bed, threw himself across it. *My duty – I must go back. What's happening to me? Have I waited too long?*

Had Piaget lied about the Jaspers effect?

Dasein turned onto his back, threw an arm across his eyes. What was the chemical essence of Jaspers? Selador could be no help there; the stuff didn't travel.

I knew that, Dasein thought. *I knew it all along.*

He took his arm away from his eyes. No doubt of what he'd been doing: avoiding his own responsibility. Dasein looked at the doors in the wall facing him – kitchen, lab ...

A sigh lifted his chest.

Cheese would be the best carrier, he knew. It held the Jaspers essence longest. The lab ... and some cheese.

Dasein rang the bell at the head of his bed.

A voice startled him, coming from directly behind his head: 'Do you wish a nurse immediately?'

Dasein turned, saw a speaker grill in the wall. 'I'd ... like some Jaspers cheese,' he said.

'Oh ... Right away, sir.' There was delight in that feminine voice no electronic reproduction could conceal.

Presently, the red-haired nurse with the stamp of the Marden genes on her face shouldered her way into the room carrying a tray. She placed the tray atop the papers on Dasein's nightstand.

'There you are, doctor,' she said. 'I brought you some crackers, too.'

'Thanks,' Dasein said.

She turned at the doorway before leaving: 'Jenny will be delighted to hear this.'

'Jenny's awake?'

'Oh, yes. Most of her problem was an allergenic reaction to the aconite. We've purged the poison from her system and she's making a very rapid recovery. She wants to get up. That's always a good sign.'

'How'd the poison get in the food?' Dasein asked.

'One of the student nurses mistook it for a container of MSG. She ...'

'But how'd it get in the kitchen?'

'We haven't determined yet. No doubt it was some silly accident.'

'No doubt,' Dasein muttered.

'Well, you eat your cheese and get some rest,' she said. 'Ring if you need anything.'

The door closed briskly behind her.

Dasein looked at the golden block of cheese. Its Jaspers odor clamored at his nostrils. He broke off a small corner of the cheese in his fingers, touched it to his tongue. Dasein's senses jumped to attention. Without conscious volition, he took the cheese into his mouth, swallowed it: smooth, soothing flavor. A clear-headed alertness surged through him.

Whatever else happens, Dasein thought, *the world has to find out about this stuff.*

He swung his feet out of bed, stood up. A pulsing ache throbbed through his forehead. He closed his eyes, felt the world spin, steadied himself against the bed.

The vertigo passed.

Dasein found a cheese knife on the tray, cut a slice off the golden brick, stopped his hand from conveying the food to his mouth.

The body does it, he thought. He felt the strength of the physical demand, promised himself more of the cheese ... later. First – the lab.

It was pretty much as he'd expected: sparse, but sufficient. There was a good centrifuge, a microtome, a binocular microscope with controlled illumination, gas burner, ranks of clean test tubes – all the instruments and esoteria of the trade.

Dasein found a container of sterile water, another of alcohol, put bits of the cheese into solution. He started a culture flask, made a control slide and examined it under the microscope.

A threadlike binding structure within the cheese leaped into vision. As he raised magnification, the threads resolved into spirals of elongated structure that resembled cells which had been blocked from normal division.

Dasein sat back, puzzled. The thread pattern bore a resemblance to fungoid mycelium spawn. This agreed with his early surmise; he was dealing with a type of fungus growth.

What was the active agent, though?

He closed his eyes to think, realized he was trembling with fatigue.

Easy does it, he thought. *You're not a well man.*

Some of the experiments required time to mature, he told himself. They could wait. He made his way back to bed, stretched out on the blankets. His left hand reached out to the cheese, broke off a chunk.

Dasein became aware of his own action as he swallowed the cheese.

He looked at the crumbled specks on his fingers, rubbed them, felt the oily smoothness. A delicious sense of well-being spread through his body.

The body does it, Dasein thought. *Of itself, the body does it. Could the body go out and kill a man? Very likely.*

He felt sleep winding about his consciousness. The body needed sleep. The body would have sleep.

The mind, though, built a dream – of trees growing to gigantic size as he watched them. They leaped up with swift vitality. Their branches swept out, leafed, fruited. All basked under a sun the color of golden cheese.

12

Sunset was burning orange in the west when Dasein awoke. He lay, his head turned toward the windows, looking out at the blazing sky, his attention caught in a spell akin to ancient sun worship. The ship of life was headed down to its daily rest. Soon, steel darkness would claim the land.

A click sounded behind Dasein. Artificial light flooded the room. He turned, the spell broken.

Jenny stood just inside the door. She wore a long green robe that reached almost to her ankles. Green slippers covered her feet.

'It's about time you woke up,' she said.

Dasein stared at her as at a stranger. He could see it was the same Jenny he loved – her long black hair caught in a red ribbon, full lips slightly parted, dimple showing in her cheek – but furtive smoke drifted in her blue eyes. There was the calm of a goddess about her.

Something eternally of the past moved her body as Jenny stepped farther into the room.

A thrill of fear shot through Dasein. It was the fear an Attic peasant might have experienced before a priestess at Delphi. She was beautiful . . . and deadly.

'Aren't you going to ask how I am?' she asked.

'I can see you're all right,' he said.

She took another step toward him, said: 'Clara brought Jersey Hofstedder's car over and left it for you. It's down in the garage.'

Dasein thought of that beautifully machined automobile – another bauble to attract him.

'And what have you brought – this time?' he asked.

'Gil!'

'There's no food in your hands,' he said. 'Is it a poisoned hatpin, perhaps?'

Tears flooded her eyes.

'Stay away from me,' he said. 'I love you.'

She nodded. 'I do love you. And . . . I've felt how dangerous I could be . . . to you. There've been . . .' She shook her head. 'I knew I had to stay away from you. But not any more. Not now.'

'So it's all over,' he said. 'Let bygones be bygones. Wouldn't a gun be quicker?'

She stamped a foot. 'Gil, you're impossible!'

'*I'm* impossible?'

'Have you changed?' she whispered. 'Don't you feel any . . .'

'I still love you,' he said. 'Stay away from me. I love you.'

She bit her lip.

'Wouldn't it be kindest to do it while I'm asleep?' he asked. 'Never let me know who . . .'

'Stop it!'

Abruptly, she ripped off the green robe, revealing a white, lace-edged nightgown beneath. She dropped the robe, pulled the gown over her head, threw it on the floor, stood there naked, glaring at him.

'See?' she said. 'Nothing here but a woman! Nothing here but the woman who loves you.' Tears ran down her cheeks. 'No poison in my hands . . . Oh, Gil . . .' His name came out as a wail.

Dasein forced his gaze away from her. He knew he couldn't look at her – lovely, lithe, desirable – and retain any coolness of judgment. She was beautiful and deadly – the ultimate bait Santaroga offered.

There was a rustling of cloth near the door.

He whirled.

She stood once more clothed in the green robe. Her cheeks were scarlet, lips trembling, eyes downcast. Slowly, she raised her eyes, met his stare.

'I have no shame with you, Gil,' she said. 'I love you. I want no secrets between us at all – no secrets of the flesh . . . no secrets of any kind.'

Dasein tried to swallow past a lump in his throat. The goddess was vulnerable. It was a discovery that caused an ache in his chest.

'I feel the same way,' he said. 'Jen . . . you'd better leave now. If you don't . . . I might just grab you and rape you.'

She tried to smile, failed, whirled away and ran out of the room.

The door slammed. There was a moment's silence. The door opened. Piaget stood in the opening looking back into the foyer. The sound of the elevator doors closing came clearly to Dasein. Piaget came in, closed the door.

'What happened with you two?' he asked.

'I think we just had a fight and made up,' Dasein said. 'I'm not sure.'

Piaget cleared his throat. There was a look of confidence in his round face, Dasein thought. It was not a judgment he could be sure of, however, in the unmapped land of concentration. At any rate, the look was gone now, replaced by a wide-eyed stare of interest in Dasein.

'You're looking vastly improved,' Piaget said. 'You've a better color in your face. Feeling stronger?'

'As a matter of fact I am.'

Piaget glanced at the remains of the cheese on the night-stand, crossed and sniffed at it. 'Bit stale,' he said. 'I'll have a fresh block sent up.'

'You do that,' Dasein said.

'Care to let me look at your bandages?' Piaget asked.

'I thought we were going to let Burdeaux work on my bandages.'

'Win had a small emergency at home. His daughter's getting married tomorrow, you know. He'll be along later.'

'I didn't know.'

'Just getting the new couple's house built in time,' Piaget said. 'Bit of a delay because we decided to build four at once in the same area. Good location – you and Jenny might like one of them.'

'That's nice,' Dasein said. 'You all get together and build a house for the newlyweds.'

'We take care of our own,' Piaget said. 'Let's look at those bandages, shall we?'

'Let's.'

'Glad to see you're being more reasonable,' Piaget said. 'Be right back.' He went out the lab door, returned in a moment with a supply cart, stationed the cart beside Dasein's bed, began cutting away the head bandages.

'See you've been puttering around the lab,' Piaget said.

Dasein winced as air hit the burn on his cheek. 'Is that what I've been doing, puttering?'

'What have you been doing?' Piaget asked. He bent, examined Dasein's cheek. 'This is coming along fine. Won't even leave a scar, I do believe.'

'I'm looking for the active agent in Jaspers,' Dasein said.

'Been several attempts along that line,' Piaget said. 'Trouble is we all get too busy with more immediate problems.'

'You've had a try at it?' Dasein asked.

'When I was younger.'

Dasein waited for the head bandage to be tied off before asking: 'Do you have notes, any summary of . . .'

'No notes. Never had time '

Piaget began working on Dasein's right arm.

'But what did you find out?'

355

'Got a broth rich in amino acids,' Piaget said. 'Yeastlike. You're going to have a scar on this arm, nothing alarming, and you're healing rapidly. You can thank Jaspers for that.'

'What?' Dasein looked up at him, puzzled.

'Nature gives; nature takes away. The Jaspers change in body chemistry makes you more susceptible to allergenic reactions, but your body will heal five to ten times faster than it would *outside*.'

Dasein looked down at his exposed arm. Pink new flesh already covered the burned area. He could see the scar puckering Piaget had noted.

'What change in body chemistry?' Dasein asked.

'Well, mostly a better hormone balance,' Piaget said. 'Closer to what you find in an embryo.'

'That doesn't square with the allergy reactions,' Dasein protested.

'I'm not saying it's a simple thing,' Piaget said. 'Hold your arm out here. Steady now.'

Dasein waited for the bandage to be completed, then: 'What about structure and ...'

'Something between a virus and a bacteria,' Piaget said. 'Fungusoid in some respects, but ...'

'I saw cell structure in a sample under the microscope.'

'Yes, but no nucleus. Some nuclear material, certainly, but it can be induced to form virusoid crystals.'

'Do the crystals have the Jaspers effect?'

'No. They can, however, be introduced into the proper environment and after suitable development they will produce the desired effect.'

'What environment?'

'You know what environment, Gilbert.'

'The Co-op's cave?'

'Yes.' Piaget finished exposing Dasein's left arm. 'Don't think you'll have as much scar tissue on this side.'

'What's unique about the cave environment?' Dasein asked

'We're not certain.'

'Hasn't anybody ever tried to ...'

'We do have a great many *immediate* problems just to maintain ourselves, Gilbert,' Piaget said.

Dasein looked down, watched Piaget finish the bandage on the left arm. *Maintain themselves?* he wondered.

'Is there any objection to my looking into it?' Dasein asked.

'When you find time – certainly not.' Piaget restored instruments and material to the cart, pushed it aside. 'There. I think we'll be able to take the bandages off tomorrow. You're progressing beautifully.'

'Am I really?'

Piaget smiled at him. 'Insurance from the garage will take care of paying for your new car,' he said. 'I presume Jenny told you about the car.'

'She told me.'

'We're also replacing your clothing. Is there anything else?'

'How about replacing my freedom of choice?'

'You have freedom of choice, Gilbert, and a broader area from which to choose. Now, I have some ...'

'Keep your advice,' Dasein said.

'Advice? I was about to say I have some rather interesting information for you. Your suggestion that I look into the people you accuse of trying to kill you has borne some ...'

'My suggestion that *you* look?'

'I took the liberty of going ahead with your suggestion.'

'So you hypnotized some of them,' Dasein said. 'Did you prepare a Davis chart on their suscept ...'

'I did *not* hypnotize them,' Piaget snapped. 'Will you be silent and listen?'

Dasein sighed, looked at the ceiling.

'I've interviewed several of these people,' Piaget said. 'The boy, Petey Jorick, first because he's a primary concern of mine, having just been released from ... school. An extremely interesting fact emerges.'

'Oh?'

'Each of these persons has a strong unconscious reason to fear and hate the *outside*.'

'What?' Dasein turned a puzzled frown on Piaget.

'They weren't attacking you as Gilbert Dasein,' Piaget said. 'You were the *outsider*. There's a strong unresolved ...'

'You mean you consider this good and sufficient ...'

'The reasons are unconscious, as you suspected,' Piaget said. 'The structure of motivation, however ...'

'So Jenny both loves me and hates me ... as an *outsider*?'

'Get one thing straight, Gilbert. Jenny did not try to harm you. It was a student nurse who ...'

'Jenny told me herself she prepared ...'

'Only in the broadest sense is that true,' Piaget said. 'She did go to the diet kitchen and order your food and watch while it was prepared. However, she couldn't keep an eye on every- ...'

'And this ... this hate of *outsiders*,' Dasein said, 'you think this is why some of your people tried to get me?'

'It's clearly indicated, Gilbert.'

Dasein stared at him. Piaget believed this – no doubt of it.

'So all I have to watch out for as long as I live in Santaroga is people who hate outsiders?' Dasein asked.

'You have nothing to fear now at all,' Piaget said. 'You're no longer an outsider. You're one of us. And when you and Jenny marry ...'

'Of all the nonsense I've ever heard,' Dasein said. 'This takes all the honors! This ... this kid, Petey, he just wanted to put an arrow through me because ...'

'He has a pathological fear of leaving the valley for college outside,' Piaget said. 'He'll overcome this, of course, but the emotions of childhood have more ...'

'The roach powder in the coffee,' Dasein said. 'That was just ...'

'That's a very unhappy case,' Piaget said. 'She fell in love with an outsider at college – much as Jenny did, I might add. The difference is that her friend seduced her and left her. She has a daughter who ...'

'My god! You really believe this crap,' Dasein said. He pushed himself against the head of the bed, sat glaring at Piaget.

'Gilbert, I find this far easier to believe than I do your wild theory that Santaroga has mounted a concerted attack against you. After all, you yourself must see ...'

'Sure,' Dasein said. 'I want you to explain the accident at the bridge. I want to see how that ...'

'Easiest of all,' Piaget said. 'The young man in question was enamored of Jenny before you came on the scene.'

'So he just waited for the moment when ...'

'It was entirely on the unconscious level, that I assure you, Gilbert.'

Dasein merely stared at him. The structure of rationalisation Piaget had built up assumed for Dasein the shape of a tree. It was like the tree of his dream. There was the strong trunk protruding into daylight – consciousness. The roots were down there growing in darkness. The limbs came out and dangled prettily distracting leaves and fruit. It was a consistent structure despite its falsity.

There'd be no cutting it down, Dasein saw. The thing was too substantial. There were too many like it in the forest that was Santaroga. *'This is a tree, see? Doesn't it look like all the others?'*

'I think when you've had time to reflect,' Piaget said, 'you'll come to realize the truth of what ...'

'Oh, no doubt,' Dasein said.

'I'll uh . . . I'll send you up some more fresh cheese,' Piaget said. 'Special stock.'

'You do that,' Dasein said.

'I quite understand,' Piaget said. 'You think you're being very cynical and wise right now. But you'll come around.' He strode from the room.

Dasein continued to stare at the closed door long after Piaget had gone. The man couldn't see it, would never be capable of seeing it. No Santarogan could. Not even Jenny despite her love-sharpened awareness. Piaget's explanation was too easy to take. It'd be the official line.

I've got to get out of this crazy valley, Dasein thought.

He slipped out of bed just as the door opened and a hatless, chubby young student nurse entered with a tray.

'Oh, you're out of bed,' she said. 'Good.'

She took the old tray off the nightstand, put the new one in its place, set the old one on a chair.

'I'll just straighten up your bed while you're out of it,' she said.

Dasein stood to one side while she bustled about the bed. Presently, she left, taking the old tray with her.

He looked at what she had brought – a golden wedge of cheese, crackers, a glass and a bottle of Jaspers beer.

In a surge of anger, Dasein hurled the cheese against the wall. He was standing there staring at the mess when a soothing sensation on his tongue made him realize he was licking the crumbs off his fingers.

Dasein stared at his own hand as though it belonged to another person. He consciously forced himself not to bend and recover the cheese from the floor, turned to the beer. There was an opener behind the bottle. He poured it into the glass, drank in swift gulps. Only when the glass was drained did he grow aware of the rich bouquet of Jaspers in the remaining drops of beer.

Fighting down a fit of trembling, Dasein put the glass on the nightstand, crawled into the bed as though seeking sanctuary.

His body refused to be denied. People didn't take Jaspers, he thought. Jaspers took people. He felt the expanding effect within his consciousness, sensed the thunder of a host jarring across the inner landscape of his psyche. Time lost its normal flow, became compressed and explosive.

Somewhere in a hospital room there were purposeful footsteps. The toggles of a switch slammed away from their connections to create darkness. A door closed.

Dasein opened his eyes to a window and starshine. In its illumination he saw a fresh wedge of cheese on his nightstand. The mess had been cleaned from wall and floor. He remembered Jenny's voice – soft, musical, rippling like dark water over rocks, a plaintive tremor in it.

Had Jenny been here in the dark?

He sensed no answer.

Dasein groped for the call buzzer at the head of his bed, pressed it.

A voice sounded from the speaker: 'Do you wish a nurse?'

'What time is it?' Dasein asked.

'Three twenty-four a.m. Do you want a sleeping pill?'

'No ... thanks.'

He sat up, slid his feet to the floor, stared at the cheese.

'Did you just want the time?' the speaker asked

'What does a full round of Jaspers cheese weigh?' he asked.

'The weight?' There was a pause, then: 'They vary. The smaller ones weigh about thirty pounds. Why?'

'Send me a full round,' he said.

'A full ... Don't you have some now?'

'I want it for lab tests,' he said, and he thought: *There! Let's see if Piaget was being honest with me.*

'You want it when you get up in the morning?'

'I'm up now. And get me a robe and some slippers if you can.'

'Hadn't you better wait, doctor. If ...'

'Check with Piaget if you must,' Dasein said. 'I want that round now.'

'Very well.' She sounded disapproving.

Dasein waited sitting on the edge of the bed. He stared out the window at the night. Absently, he broke off a chunk of the cheese on his night-stand, chewed it and swallowed.

Presently, the foyer door produced a wedge of light. A tall, gray-haired nurse entered, turned on the room's lights. She carried a large wheel of golden cheese still glistening in its wax sealer.

'This is thirty-six pounds of prime Jaspers cheese,' she said. 'Where shall I put it?' There were overtones of outrage and protest in her voice.

'Find a place for it on one of the lab benches,' he said. 'Where are the robe and slippers?'

'If you'll be patient, I'll get them for you,' she said. She shouldered her way through the lab door, returned in a moment and crossed to a narrow door at the far end of the room, opened it to reveal a closet. From the closet she removed a green robe and a pair of black slippers which she dumped on the foot of Dasein's bed.

'Will that be all – sir?'

'That'll be all, for now.'

360

'Hmmmph.' She strode from the room, shut the foyer door with a final-comment thump

Dasein took another bite of the cheese from his nightstand, put on the robe and slippers, went into the lab. The nurse had left the lights on. The round of cheese lay on an open metal bench at his right.

Alcohol won't kill it, he thought. *Otherwise, it couldn't be incorporated in the local beer. What does destroy it? Sunlight?*

He recalled the dim red light of the Co-op's cave.

Well, there were ways of finding out. He rolled back the sleeves of his gown, set to work.

Within an hour he had three-fourths of the round reduced to a milky solution in a carboy, set about feeding it through the centrifuge.

The first test tubes came out with their contents layered in a manner reminiscent of a chromatograph. Near the top lay a thin silver-gray band of material.

Dasein poured off the liquid, burned a hole in the bottom of a test tube and removed the solids intact by blowing into the hole he'd created. A bit of the gray material went on a slide and he examined it under the microscope.

There was the mycelium structure, distorted but recognizable. He smelled the slide. It was redolent of Jaspers. He put a hand to the microscope's variable light control, watched the specimen while rotating the control. Abruptly, the specimen began to shrivel and crystallize before his eyes.

Dasein looked at the light control. It was the spectrum-window type and, at this moment, was passing light in the Angstrom range 4000–5800. It was cutting off the red end, Dasein noted.

Another look through the microscope showed the specimen reduced to a white crystalline mass.

Sunlight, then.

What would do the job? he wondered. A bomb to open the cave? A portable sunlamp?

As he thought this, Dasein felt that the darkness outside the hospital parted to reveal a shape, a monster rising out of a black lake.

He shuddered, turned to the carboy of milky solution. Working mechanically, he put the rest of the solution through the centrifuge, separated the silver-gray band, collected the material in a dark brown bottle. The solution produced almost a pint of the Jaspers essence.

Dasein smelled the bottle – sharp and definite odor of Jaspers. He emptied the bottle into a shallow dish, caught a bit of the substance on a spatula, touched it to his tongue.

An electrifying sensation of distant fireworks exploded from his tastebuds through his spine. He felt he could see with the tip of his tongue or the tip of a finger. Dasein sensed his core of awareness becoming a steely kernel surrounded by desolation. He concentrated his energy, forced himself to look at the dish of Jaspers essence.

Empty!

What had destroyed it? How could it be empty?

He looked at the palm of his right hand. How close it was to his face! There were specks of silver-gray against the pink flesh.

Tingling pulses of awareness began surging out from his throat and stomach, along his arms and legs. He felt that his entire skin came alight. There was a remote feeling of a body slipping to the floor, but he felt that the floor glowed wherever the body touched it.

I ate the entire dish of essence, he thought.

What would it do – the active agent from more than thirty pounds of Jaspers cheese? What would it do? What was it doing? Dasein felt this to be an even more interesting question.

What was it doing?

As he asked the question of himself, he experienced anguish. It wasn't fear, but pure anguish, a sense of losing his grip on reality.

The steely kernel of selfdom! Where was it?

Upon what fundament of reality did his selfdom sit? Frantically, Dasein tried to extend his awareness, experienced the direct sensation that he was projecting his own reality upon the universe. But there was a projection *of* the universe simultaneously. He followed the lines of this projection, felt them sweep through him as though through a shadow.

In this instant, he was lost, tumbling.

I was just a shadow, he thought.

The thought fascinated him. He remembered the shadow game, of his childhood, wondered what forms of shadows he could project by distorting the core of self. The wondering produced the effect of shapes. Dasein sensed a screen of awareness, a shapeless outline upon it. He willed the shape to change.

A muscled, breast-beating hero took form there.

Dasein shifted his emphasis.

The shadow became a bent-shouldered, myopic scientist in a long gown. Another shift: It was naked Apollo racing over a landscape of feminine figures.

And again – a plodder bent beneath a shapeless load.

With a gulping sensation of *deitgrasp* Dasein realized he was projecting the only limits his finite being could know. It was an act of self-discovery that gave birth to a feeling of hope. It was an odd sort of hope, unfixed, disoriented, but definite in its existence – not a hope of discernment, but pure hope without boundaries, direction or attachments.

Hope itself.

It was a profound instant permitting him to grasp for a fleeting instant the structureof his own existence, his possibilities as a being.

A twisted, dented and distorted *something* crossed the field of Dasein's awareness. He recognized the kernel of selfdom. The thing had lost all useful shape. He discarded it, chuckling.

Who discarded it? Dasein wondered.

Who chuckles?

There was a pounding sound – feet upon a floor.

Voices.

He recognized the tones of the gray-haired nurse, but there was a tingling of panic in the sounds she made.

Piaget.

'Let's get him on the bed,' Piaget said. The words were clear and distinct.

What was not distinct was the shape of a universe become blurred rainbows, nor the pressures of hands which blotted out the glowing sensation of his skin.

'It's difficult to become conscious about consciousness,' Dasein muttered.

'Did he say something?' That was the nurse.

'I couldn't make it out.' Piaget.

'Did you smell the Jaspers in there?' The nurse.

'I think he separated the essence out and took it.'

'Oh, my God! What can we do?'

'Wait and pray. Bring me a strait-jacket and the emergency cart.'

A strait-jacket? Dasein wondered. *What an odd request.*

He heard running footsteps. How loud they were! A door slammed. More voices. Such a rushing around!

His skin felt as though it were growing dark. Everything was being blotted out.

With an abrupt, jerking sensation, Dasein felt himself shrivel downward into an infant shape kicking, squalling, reaching outward, outward, fingers grasping.

'Give me a hand with him!' That was Piaget.

'What a mess!' Another male voice.

But Dasein already felt himself becoming a mouth, just a mouth. It blew out, out, out – such a wind. Surely, the entire world must collapse before this hurricane.

He was a board, rocking. A teeter-totter. Down and up – up and down.

A good run is better than a bad stand, he thought.

And he was running, running – breathless, gasping.

A bench loomed out of swirling clouds. He threw himself down on it, became the bench – another board. This one dipped down and down into a boiling green sea.

Life in a sea of unconsciousness, Dasein thought.

It grew darker and darker.

Death, he thought. *Here's the background against which I can know myself.*

The darkness dissolved. He was shooting upward, rebounding into a blinding glare.

Dark shapes moved in the glare.

'His eyes are open.' That was the nurse.

A shadow reduced the glare. 'Gilbert?' That was Piaget. 'Gilbert, can you hear me? How much Jaspers did you take?'

Dasein tried to speak. His lips refused to obey.

The glare came back.

'We'll just have to guess.' Piaget. 'How much did that cheese weigh?'

'Thirty-six pounds.' The nurse.

'The physical breakdown is massive.' Piaget. 'Have a respirator standing by.'

'Doctor, what if he ...' The nurse apparently couldn't complete the statement of her fear.

'I'm ... ready.' Piaget.

Ready for what? Dasein wondered.

By concentrating, he found he could make the glare recede. It resolved momentarily into a tunnel of clarity with Piaget at the far end of it. Dasein lay helplessly staring, unable to move as Piaget advanced on him carrying a boy that fumed and smoked.

Acid, Dasein thought, interpreting the nurse's words. *If I die, they'll dissolve me and wash me away down a drain. No body, no evidence.*

The tunnel collapsed.

The sensation of glare expanded, contracted.

Perhaps, I can no longer be, Dasein thought.

Perhaps, I cannot do, he thought.

Darker yet.

Perhaps, I cannot have, he thought.

Nothing.

13

'It was kill or cure,' the yellow god said.

'I wash my hands of you,' said the white god.

'What I offered, you did not want,' the red god accused.

'You make me laugh,' said the black god.

'There is no tree that's you,' the green god said.

'We are going now and only one of us will return,' the gods chorused.

There was a sound of a clearing throat.

'Why don't you have faces?' Dasein asked. 'You have color but no faces.'

'What?' It was a rumbling, vibrant voice.

'You're a funny sounding god,' Dasein said. He opened his eyes, looked up into Burdeaux's features, caught a puzzled scowl on the dark face.

'I'm no sort of god at all,' Burdeaux said. 'What're you saying, Doctor Gil? You having another nightmare?'

Dasein blinked, tried to move his arms. Nothing happened. He lifted his head, looked down at his body. He was bound tightly in a restraining jacket. There was a stink of disinfectants, of Jaspers and of something repellent and sour in the room. He looked around. It was still the isolation suite. His head fell back to the pillow.

'Why'm I tied down like this?' Dasein whispered.

'What did you say, sir?'

Dasein repeated his question.

'Well, Doctor Gil, we didn't want you to hurt yourself.'

'When ... when can I be released?'

'Doctor Larry said to free you as soon as you woke up.'

'I'm ... awake.'

'I know that, sir. I was just ...' He shrugged, began unfastening the bindings on the sleeves of the jacket.

'How long?' Dasein whispered.

'How long you been here like this?'

Dasein nodded.

'Three whole days now, and a little more. It's almost noon.'

The bindings were untied. Burdeaux helped Dasein to a sitting position, unlaced the back, slipped the jacket off.

Dasein's back felt raw and sensitive. His muscles responded as though they belonged to a stranger. This was an entirely new body, Dasein thought.

Burdeaux came up with a white hospital gown, slipped it onto Dasein, tied the back.

'You want the nurse to come rub your back?' he asked. 'You've a couple of red places there don't look too good.'

'No ... no thanks.'

Dasein moved one of the stranger's arms. A familiar hand came up in front of his face. It was his own hand. How could it be his own hand, he wondered, when the muscles of the arm belonged to a stranger?

'Doctor Larry said no one ever took that much Jaspers ever before all at once,' Burdeaux said. 'Jaspers is a good thing, sir, but everybody knows you can get too much.'

'Does ... is Jenny ..'

'She's fine, Doctor Gil. She's been worried sick about you. We all have.'

Dasein moved one of the stranger's legs, then the other until they hung over the edge of the bed. He looked down at his own knees. It was very odd.

'Here, now,' Burdeaux said. 'Best you stay in bed.'

'I've ... I ...'

'You want to go to the bathroom? Best I bring you the bedpan.'

'No ... I ...' Dasein shook his head. Abruptly, he realized what was wrong. The body was hungry.

'Hungry,' he said.

'Well, why didn't you say so? Got food right here waiting.'

Burdeaux lifted a bowl, held it in front of Dasein. The rich aroma of Jaspers enveloped him. Dasein reached toward the bowl, but Burdeaux said, 'Best let me feed you, Doctor Gil. You don't look too steady.'

Dasein sat patiently, allowed himself to be fed. He could feel strength gathering in the body. It was a bad fit, this body, he decided. It had been draped loosely on his psyche.

It occurred to him to wonder what the body was eating – in addition to the Jaspers, which surrounded him and pervaded him with its presence. Oatmeal, the tongue said. Jaspers honey and Jaspers cream.

'There's a visitor waiting to see you,' Burdeaux said when the bowl was empty.

'Jenny?'

'No ... a Doctor Selador.'

Selador! The name exploded on Dasein's conscience. Selador had trusted him, depended on him.

Selador had sent a gun through the mails.

'You feel up to seeing him?' Burdeaux asked.

'You ... don't mind if I see him?' Dasein asked.

'Mind? Why should I mind, sir?'

Burdeaux's not the you *I meant*, Dasein thought.

There arose in Dasein then an urge to send Selador away. Such an easy thing to do. Santaroga would insulate him from the Seladors of the world. A simple request to Burdeaux was all it would take.

'I'll ... uh, see him,' Dasein said. He looked around the room. 'Could you help me into a robe and ... is there a chair I could ...'

'Why don't I put you in a wheelchair, sir? Doctor Larry had one sent up for when you awakened. He didn't want you exerting yourself. You're not to get tired, understand?'

'Yes ... yes, I understand. A wheelchair.'

Presently, Dasein's bad-fit body was in the wheelchair. Burdeaux had gone to bring Selador, leaving the chair at the far end of the room from the foyer door. Dasein found himself facing a pair of French doors that opened onto a sundeck.

He felt he had been left alone in a brutally exposed position, his soul naked, wretched with fear. There was a heavy load on him, he thought. He felt embarrassment at the prospect of meeting Selador, and a special order of fright. Selador saw through pretense and sham. You could wear no mask before Selador. He was the psychoanalysts' psychoanalyst.

Selador will humiliate me, Dasein thought. *Why did I agree to see him? He will prod me and I will react. My reaction will tell him everything he wants to know about me ... about my failure.*

Dasein felt then his sanity had been corroded into a pitted shell, a thing of tinsel and fantasy. Selador would stamp upon it with the harsh, jolting dynamics of his aliveness.

The foyer door opened.

Slowly, forcing himself to it, Dasein turned his head toward the door.

Selador stood in the opening, tall, hawk-featured, the dark skin and wildness of India encased in a silver-gray tweed suit, a touch of the same silver at the temples. Dasein had the sudden blurred sensation of having seen this face in another life, the lancet eyes peering from beneath a turban. It had been a turban with a red jewel in it.

Dasein shook his head. Madness.

'Gilbert,' Selador said, striding across the room. 'In the name of heaven, what have you done to yourself now?' The precise accents of Oxford hammered each word into Dasein's ears. 'They said you were badly burned.'

And thus it starts, Dasein thought.

'I ... my arms and hands,' Dasein said. 'And a bit about the face.'

'I arrived only this morning,' Selador said. 'We were quite worried about you, you know. No word from you for days.'

He stopped in front of Dasein, blocking off part of the view of the sundeck.

'I must say you look a fright, Gilbert. There don't appear to be any scars on your face, though.'

Dasein put a hand to his cheek. It was his cheek suddenly, not a stranger's. The skin felt smooth, new.

'There's the damnedest musky smell about this place,' Selador said. 'Mind if I open these doors?'

'No ... no, go right ahead.'

Dasein found himself wrestling with the feeling that Selador was not Selador. There was a shallowness to the man's speech and mannerisms all out of character with the Selador of Dasein's memory. Had Selador changed in some way?

'Lovely sunny day,' Selador said. 'Why don't I wheel you out on this deck for a bit of air. Do you good.'

Panic seized Dasein's throat. That deck – it was a place of menace. He tried to speak; to object. They couldn't go out there. No words came.

Selador took the silence for agreement, wheeled Dasein's chair out the door. There was a slight jolt at the sill and they were on the deck.

Sunlight warmed Dasein's head. A breeze almost devoid of Jaspers washed his skin, cleared his head. He said: 'Don't you ...'

'Doesn't this air feel invigorating?' Selador asked. He stopped at a shallow parapet, the edge of the roof. 'There. You can admire the view and I can sit on this ledge.'

Selador sat down, put a hand on the back of Dasein's chair. 'I would imagine that ward is wired for sound,' Selador said. 'I do not believe they can have listening devices out here, however.'

Dasein gripped the wheels of his chair, afraid it might lurch forward, propel him off the roof. He stared down at a paved parking area, parked cars, lawn, strips of flowers, trees. The sense of Selador's words came to him slowly.

'Wired ... for ...' He turned, met amused inquiry in the dark eyes.

'Obviously, you're not quite yourself yet,' Selador said. 'Understandable. You've been through a terrible ordeal. That's obvious. I'll have you out of this place, though, as soon as you're able to travel. Set your mind at rest. You'll be safe in a *normal* hospital at Berkeley before the week's out.'

Dasein's emotions boiled, an arena of dispute. *Safe!* What a reassuring word. *Leave?* He couldn't leave! But he had to leave. *Outside? Go to that hideous place?*

'Have you been drugged, Gilbert?' Selador asked. 'You appear ... so ... so ...'

'I've ... I'm all right.'

'Really, you're behaving rather oddly. You haven't asked me once what we found on the leads you provided.'

'What ...'

'The source of their petrol proved to be a dud. All quite normal ... provided you appreciate their economic motives. Cash deal with an independent producer. The State Department of Agriculture gives their cheese and the other products of their Cooperative a clean bill of health. The real estate board, however, is interested that no one but Santarogans can buy property in the valley. It may be they've violated antidis-criminatory legislation with ...'

'No,' Dasein said. 'They ... nothing that obvious.'

'Ah, ha! You speak in the fashion of a man who has discovered the closeted skeleton. Well, Gilbert, what is it?'

Dasein felt he'd been seized by a vampire of duty. It would drain the blood from him Selador would feed on it. He shook his head from side to side.

'Are you ill, Gilbert? Am I wearying you?'

'No. As long as I take it slowly ... Doctor, you must understand, I've ...'

'Do you have notes, Gilbert? Perhaps I could read your report and ...'

'No ... fire.'

'Oh, yes. The doctor, this Piaget, said something about your truck burning. Everything up in smoke, I suppose?'

'Yes.'

'Well, then, Gilbert, we'll have to get it from your lips. Is there an opening we can use to break these people?'

Dasein thought of the greenhouses – child labor. He thought of the statistical few Santarogans Jaspers had destroyed. He thought of the narcotic implications in the Jaspers products. It was all there – destruc-tion for Santaroga.

'There must be something,' Selador said. 'You've lasted much longer than the others. Apparently, you've been given the freedom of the region. I'm sure you must have discovered something.'

Lasted much longer than the others, Dasein thought. There was naked revelation in the phrase. As though he had participated in them, Dasein saw the discussions which had gone into choosing him for this project. '*Dasein has connections in the valley – a girl. That may be the edge we need. Certainly, it gives us reason to hope he'll last longer than the others.*'

It had been something like that, Dasein knew. There was a callousness in it that repelled him.

'Were there more than two?' he asked

'Two? Two what, Gilbert?'

'Two other investigators . . . before me?'

'I don't see where that . . .'

'Were there?'

'Well . . . that's very discerning of you, Gilbert. Yes, there were more than two. Eight or nine, I suspect.'

'Why . . .'

'Why weren't you told? We wanted to imbue you with caution, but we saw no need to terrify you.'

'But you thought they were murdered here . . . by Santarogans?'

'It was all exceedingly mysterious, Gilbert. We were not at all sure.' He studied Dasein, eyes open wide and probing. 'That's it, eh? Murder. Are we in peril right now? Do you have the weapon I . . .'

'If it were only that simple,' Dasein said.

'In heaven's name, Gilbert, what is it? You must have found something. I had such high hopes for you.'

High hopes for me, Dasein thought. Again, it was a phrase that opened a door on secret conversations. How could Selador be that transparent? Dasein found himself shocked by the shallowness of the man. Where was the omnipotent psychoanalyst? How could he have changed so profoundly?

'You . . . you people were just using me,' Dasein said. As he spoke, he recalled Al Marden's accusation. Marden had seen this . . . yes.

'Now, Gilbert, that's no attitude to take. Why, just before I left to come here, Meyer Davidson was inquiring after you. You recall Davidson, the agent for the investment corporation behind the chain stores? He was very much taken with you, Gilbert. He told me he was thinking of making a place for you on his staff.'

Dasein stared at Selador. The man couldn't be serious.

'That would be quite a step up in the world for you, Gilbert.'

Dasein suppressed an urge to laugh. He had the odd sensation of being detached from his past and able to study a pseudoperson, a might-have-been creature who was himself. The other Dasein would have leaped at this offer. The new Dasein saw through the offer to the true opinion Selador and his cronies held for '*that useful, but not very bright person, Gilbert Dasein.*'

'Have you had a look at Santaroga?' Dasein asked. He wondered if Selador had seen Clara Scheler's used car lot or the advertisements in the store windows.

'This morning, while I was waiting for visiting hours with you, I drove around a bit,' Selador said.

'What did you think of the place?'

'My candid opinion? An odd sort of village. When I inquired directions of a native – their language is so brusque and ... odd. Not at all like ... well, it's not English, of course, full of Americanisms, but ...'

'They have a language like their cheese,' Dasein said. 'Sharp and full of tang.'

'Sharp! A very good choice of word.'

'A community of individuals, wouldn't you say?' Dasein asked.

'Perhaps ... but with a certain sameness to them. Tell me, Gilbert, does this have something to do with why you were sent here?'

'This?'

'These questions. I must say, you're talking like ... well, damned if you don't sound like a native.' A forced laugh escaped his dark lips. 'Have you gone native?'

The question, coming from that darkly eastern face, couched in that Oxford accent, struck Dasein as supremely amusing. Selador, of all people! To ask such a question.

Laughter bubbled from Dasein.

Selador misinterpreted the response. 'Well,' he said, 'I should hope you hadn't.'

'Humanity ought to be the first order of interest for humans,' Dasein said.

Again, Selador misinterpreted. 'Ah, and you studied the Santarogans like the excellent psychologist you are. Good. Well, then – tell it in your own way.'

'I'll put it another way,' Dasein said. 'To have freedom, you must know how to use it. There's a distinct possibility some people hunt freedom in such a way they become the slaves of freedom.'

'That's all very philosophical, I'm sure,' Selador said. 'How does it apply to finding justice for our sponsors?'

'Justice?'

'Certainly, justice. They were lured into this valley and cheated. They spent large sums of money here and got no return on it whatsoever. They're not people to take such treatment lightly.'

'Lured?' Dasein said. 'No one would sell to them, that I'm sure. How were they lured? For that matter, how did they acquire a lease on ...'

'This isn't pertinent, Gilbert.'

'Yes, it is. How'd they get a lease on Santaroga land?'

Selador sighed. 'Very well. If you insist. They forced a competetive bid on some excess State property and put in a bid ...'

'One they were sure no one else would match,' Dasein said. He chuckled. 'Did they have a market survey?'

'They had a good idea how many people live here.'

'But what kind of people?'

'What're you trying to say, Gilbert?'

'Santaroga's very like a Greek *polis*,' Dasein said. 'This is a community of individuals, not a collectivity. Santarogans are not anthill slaves to grubs and grubbing. This is a *polis*, small enough to meet human needs. Their first interest is in human beings. Now, as to justice for ...'

'Gilbert, you're talking very strangely.'

'Hear me, please, doctor.'

'Very well, but I hope you'll make some sense out of this ... this ...'

'Justice,' Dasein said. 'These sponsors you mention, and the government they control, are less interested in justice than they are in public order. They have stunted imaginations from too-long and too-intimate association with an ingrown system of self-perpetuating precedents. Do you want to know how they and their machinations appear to a Santarogan?'

'Let me remind you, Gilbert, this is one of the reasons you were sent here.'

Dasein smiled. Selador's accusatory tone brought not a twinge of guilt.

'Raw power,' Dasein said. 'That's how the *outside* appears to a Santarogan. A place of raw power. Money and raw power have taken over there.'

'Outside,' Selador said. 'What an interesting emphasis you give to that interesting word.'

'Raw power is movement without a governor,' Dasein said. 'It'll run wild and destroy itself with all about it. That's a civilization of battlefields out there. They have special names: market area, trade area, court, election, senate, auction, strike – but they're still battlefields. There's no denying it because every one can invoke the full gamut of weaponry from words to guns.'

'I do believe you're defending these Santaroga rascals,' Selador said.

'Of course I'm defending them! I've had my eyes opened here, I tell you. I lasted much longer, did I? You had such high hopes for me! How can you be so damn' transparent?'

'Now you see here, Gilbert!' Selador stood up, glared down at Dasein.

'You know what gets to me, really gets to me?' Dasein asked. 'Justice! You're all so damned interested in putting a cloak of justice and legality on your frauds! You give me a . . .'

'Doctor Gil?'

It was Burdeaux's voice calling from the doorway behind him. Dasein yanked back on his chair's left wheel, pushed on the right wheel. The chair whirled. All in the same instant, Dasein saw Burdeaux standing in the French doors, felt his chair hit something. He turned his head toward Selador in time to see a pair of feet disappear over the edge of the roof. There was a long, despairing cry terminated by the most sickening, wet thud Dasein had ever heard.

Burdeaux was suddenly beside him, leaning on the parapet to peer down at the parking area.

'Oh my goodness,' Burdeaux said. 'Oh, my goodness, what a terrible accident.'

Dasein lifted his hands, looked at them – his hands. *I'm not strong enough to've done that,* he thought. *I've been ill. I'm not strong enough.*

14

'A major contributing factor to the accident,' Piaget said, 'was the victim's own foolishness in standing that close to the edge of the roof.'

The inquest had been convened in Dasein's hospital room – 'Because it is at the scene of the accident and as a convenience to Doctor Dasein, who is not fully recovered from injuries and shock.'

A special investigator had been sent from the State Attorney General's office, arriving just before the inquest convened at ten a.m. The investigator, a William Garrity, obviously was known to Piaget. They had greeted each other 'Bill' and 'Larry' at the foot of Dasein's bed. Garrity was a small man with an appearance of fragility about him, sandy hair, a narrow face immersed in a mask of diffidence.

Presiding was Santaroga's Coroner, a Negro Dasein had not seen before this morning – Leroy Cos: kinky gray hair and a square, blocky face of remote dignity. He wore a black suit, had held himself apart from the preinquest bustle until the tick of ten o'clock when he had seated himself at a table provided for him, rapped once with a pencil and said: 'We will now come to order.'

Spectators and witnesses had seated themselves in folding chairs brought in for the occasion. Garrity shared a table with an Assistant District Attorney who, it developed, was a Nis, Swarthout Nis, a man with the family's heavy eyelids, wide mouth and sandy hair, but without the deeply cleft chin.

In the two days since the tragedy, Dasein had found his emotions embroiled with a growing anger against Selador – *the fool, the damned fool, getting himself killed that way.*

Piaget, seated in the witness chair, summed it up for Dasein.

'In the first place,' Piaget said, a look of stern indignation on his round face, 'he had no business taking Doctor Dasein outside. I had explained Doctor Dasein's physical condition quite clearly.'

Garrity, the State's investigator, was permitted a question: 'You saw the accident, Doctor Piaget?'

'Yes. Mr Burdeaux, having noted Doctor Selador wheel my patient onto the sundeck and knowing I considered this a physical strain on my patient, had summoned me. I arrived just in time to see Doctor Selador stumble and fall.'

'You saw him stumble?' Swarthout Nis asked.

'Definitely. He appeared to be reaching for the back of Doctor Dasein's wheelchair. I consider it fortunate he did not manage to grab the chair. He could have taken both of them over the edge.'

Selador stumbled? Dasein thought. A sense of opening relief pervaded him. *Selador stumbled! I didn't bump him. I knew I wasn't strong enough. But what did I bump? A loose board on the deck, perhaps?* For an instant, Dasein recalled his hands on the wheels of the chair, the firm, sure grip, the soft bump. *A board could feel soft,* he told himself.

Burdeaux was in the witness chair now corroborating Piaget's testimony.

It must be true then.

Dasein felt strength flow through his body. He began to see his Santaroga experience as a series of plunges down precipitous rapids. Each plunge had left him weaker until the final plunge had, through a mystic fusion, put him in contact with a source of infinite strength. It was that strength he felt now.

His life before Santaroga took on the aspects of a delicate myth held fleetingly in the mind. It was a tree in a Chinese landscape seen dimly through pastel mists. He sensed he had fallen somehow into a sequel, which by its existence had changed the past. But the present, here-and-now, surrounded him like the trunk of a sturdy redwood, firmly rooted, supporting strong branches of sanity and reason.

Garrity with his sleepy questions was a futile incompetent. 'You ran immediately to Dr Dasein's side?'

'Yes, sir. He was quite ill and weak. I was afraid he might try to get out of the wheelchair and fall himself.'

'And Dr Piaget?'

'He ran downstairs, sir, to see what he could do for the man who fell.'

Only the Santarogans in this room were fully conscious, Dasein thought. It occurred to him then that the more consciousness he acquired, the greater must be his unconscious content – a natural matter of balance. That would be the source of Santaroga's mutual strength, of course – a shared foundation into which each part must fit.

'Doctor Dasein,' the Coroner said.

They swore Dasein in then. The eyes in the room turned toward him. Only Garrity's eyes bothered Dasein – hooded, remote, concealing, *outsider eyes.*

'Did you see Dr Selador fall?'

'I . . . Mr Burdeaux called me. I turned toward him and I heard a cry. When I turned back . . . Doctor Selador's feet were going over the edge.'

'His feet?'

'That's all I saw.'

Dasein closed his eyes, remembering that moment of electric terror. He felt he was using a tunnel-vision effect in his memory, focusing just on those feet. An accident – a terrible accident. He opened his eyes, shut off the vision before memory reproduced that descending wail, the final punctuating thud.

'Had you known Dr Selador for a long time?'

'He was . . . yes.' What was Garrity driving at from behind those hooded eyes?

Garrity produced a sheet of paper from a briefcase on his table, glanced at it, said: 'I have here a page from Dr Selador's journal. It was forwarded to me by his wife. One passage interests me. I'll read it to . . .'

'Is this pertinent?' Coroner Cos asked.

'Perhaps not, sir,' Garrity said. 'Again, perhaps it is. I would like Dr Dasein's views. We are, after all, merely trying to arrive at the truth in a terrible tragedy.'

'May I see the passage?' That was Swarthout Nis, the Assistant District Attorney, his voice suavely questioning.

'Certainly.'

Nis took the paper, read it.

What is it? Dasein asked himself. *What did Selador write that his wife would send to a State investigator? Is this why Garrity came?*

Nis returned the paper to Garrity. 'Keeping in mind that Dr Selador was a psychiatrist, this passage could have many interpretations. I see no reason why Dr Dasein shouldn't have the opportunity to throw light upon it, however – if he can.'

'May I see this?' the Coroner asked.

Garrity stood, took the paper to Cos, waited while the Coroner read it.

'Very well,' Cos said, returning the paper to Garrity. 'The passage you've marked in red pencil presumably is what concerns you. You may question the witness about that passage if you wish.'

Garrity turned, the paper held stiffly before him, faced Dasein. With occasional glances at the page, he read: 'Dasein – a dangerous instrument for this project. They should be warned.'

He lowered the paper. 'What project, Dr Dasein?'

There was a hush in the room as thick as fog.

'I . . . when did he write this?'

'According to his wife, it's dated approximately a month ago. I repeat: what project?'

Dasein groped in his memory. *Project . . . dangerous?*

'The . . . only project . . .' He shook his head. The passage made no sense.

'Why did you come to Santaroga, Dr Dasein?'

'Why? My fiancée lives here.'

'Your fiancée . . .'

'My niece, Jenny Sorge,' Piaget interposed.

Garrity glanced at Piaget, who sat now in the front row of chairs, looked back to Dasein. 'Didn't you come here to make a market survey?'

'Oh, that – yes. But I don't see how I could be dangerous to that . . .' Dasein hesitated, weighing the time nicely. ' . . . unless he was afraid I'd have my mind too much on other things.'

A soft rustle of laughter whispered through the room. The Coroner rapped his pencil, said: 'I remind you this is a serious occasion. A man has died.'

Silence.

Garrity looked once more to the page in his hand. The paper seemed to have gained weight, pulling down.

'What else is on that page from his journal?' Dasein asked. 'Doesn't it explain what . . .'

'Who are the *they* who should be warned?' Garrity asked.

Dasein shook his head. 'I don't know – unless it could be the people who hired us for the market study.'

'You have prepared such a study?'

'I'll complete it as soon as I'm well enough to be released from the hospital.'

'Your injuries,' Garrity said, a note of anger in his voice. 'Something was said about burns. I'm not at all clear about . . .'

'Just a moment, please,' the Coroner said. 'Dr Dasein's injuries are not at issue here in any way other than now they bear on his being in a particular place at a particular time. We have had testimony that he was very weak and that Dr Selador had wheeled Dr Dasein's wheelchair out onto the sundeck.'

'How weak?' Garrity asked. 'And how dangerous?'

The Coroner sighed, glanced at Piaget, at Dasein, back to Garrity. 'The facts surrounding Dr Dasein's injuries are common knowledge in

Santaroga, Mr Garrity. There were more than a dozen witnesses. He was severely burned while saving a man's life. Dr Dasein is somewhat of a hero in Santaroga.'

'Oh.' Garrity returned to his seat at the table, put the page from Selador's journal on the briefcase. He obviously was angry, confused.

'I permit a considerable degree of informality in an inquiry such as this,' Cos said. 'Dr Dasein has asked a question about the surrounding contents of that page. I confess the entries make no sense to me, but perhaps ...' The Coroner left his question hanging there, his attention on Garrity.

'My office can add little,' Garrity said. 'There's an entry which obviously is a population figure; it's so labeled. There's a line ...' He lifted the page. '"Oil company checked out. Negative." There's a rather cryptic: "No mental illness." Except for the one entry referring to Dr Dasein ...'

'What about the rest of the journal?' the Coroner asked. 'Has your office investigated it?'

'Unfortunately, Mrs Selador says she obeyed her husband's testamentary wishes and burned his journal. It contained, she said, confidential data on medical cases. This one entry she preserved and sent to us ...' Garrity shrugged.

'I'm afraid the only man who could explain it is no longer living,' the Coroner said. 'If this was, however, a journal of medical data with reference to Dr Selador's psychiatric practice, then it would seem the entry in question might be explained easily in rather harmless terms. The word *dangerous* can have many interpretations in a psychiatric context. It may even be that Dr Dasein's interpretation is the correct one.'

Garrity nodded.

'Do you have any more questions?' the Coroner asked.

'Yes. One more.' Garrity looked at Dasein, a veiled, uncertain look. 'Were you and Dr Selador on friendly terms?'

Dasein swallowed. 'He was ... my teacher ... my friend. Ask anyone at Berkeley.'

A blank look of frustration came over Garrity's face.

He knows, Dasein thought. And immediately he wondered what it was Garrity *could* know. There was nothing to know. An accident. Perhaps he knew Selador's suspicions about Santaroga. But that was foolishness ... unless Garrity were another of the investigators looking into things that were none of his business.

Dasein felt his vision blur and, staring at Garrity, saw the man's face become a death's-head skull. The illusion vanished as Garrity shook his head, jammed Selador's journal page into the briefcase. A rueful smile appeared on his face. He glanced at the Coroner, shrugged.

'Something amuses you, Mr Garrity?' the Coroner asked.

The smile vanished.

'No, sir. Well ... my own thought processes sometimes. I've obviously allowed an unhappy woman, Mrs Selador, to send me on a wild goose chase.'

The investigator sat down, said: 'I've no more questions, sir.'

Abruptly, Dasein experienced a moment of insight; Garrity's thoughts had frightened the man! He'd suspected a vast conspiracy here in Santaroga. But that was too fantastic; thus, the smile.

The Coroner was closing his inquiry now – a brief summation: all the facts were in ... an allusion to the pathologist's gory details – 'massive head injuries, death instantaneous' – a notation that a formal inquest would be held at a date to be announced. Would Mr Garrity wish to return for it? Mr Garrity thought not.

It dawned on Dasein then that this had been a show for Garrity, something to set his mind at ease. Tiny bits of Piaget's preinquest conversation with Garrity returned to Dasein, fitted into a larger pattern. They'd been in school together – *outside!* Of course: old friends, Larry and Bill. One didn't suspect old friends of conspiracy. Reasonable.

It was over then – death by misadventure, an accident.

Garrity was shaking hands with Coroner Cos, with Piaget. Would Piaget be coming out to their class reunion? If his practice permitted ... but Garrity certainly must know how it was with country doctors. Garrity understood.

'This was a terrible thing,' Garrity said.

Piaget sighed. 'Yes, a terrible tragedy.'

Garrity was pausing at the foyer door now. There were knots of people behind him waiting for the elevator, a buzz of conversation. He turned, and Dasein thought he saw a look of angry speculation on the man's face.

Piaget bent over Dasein then, shutting off the view of the door. 'This has been a strain on you and I want you to get some rest now,' Piaget said. 'Jenny's coming in for a minute, but I don't want her staying too long.'

He moved aside.

The foyer doorway stood open and empty.

'Understand?' Piaget asked.

'Yes ... Jenny's coming.'

What was that look in Garrity's eyes? Dasein asked himself. A black savage in Africa might have peered that way into a white man's shiny city. Strange ... angry ... frustrated man. If Meyer Davidson and his crew chose Garrity for an investigator – there'd be a dangerous one. That'd be a bridge to cross in its own time, though ... if at all. Many things could happen to a man out there in the wide-wide world. Dasein could feel it – Santaroga was preparing itself to reach out there.

That's why I was chosen, he thought. *And Burdeaux ... and the others ... whoever they are. The only good defense is a good offense.*

This was a disturbing thought that sent trembling agitation through Dasein's stomach and legs.

Why am I trembling? he wondered.

He tried to recapture the thought that had disturbed him, failed. It was brief unimportant disturbance, a momentary ripple on a lake that otherwise was growing calmer and calmer. Dasein allowed the sensation of calm green waters to flow over and around him. He grew aware he was alone in the room with Jenny.

There was calmness personified: blue eyes with laugh wrinkes at their edges, full lips smiling at him. She wore an orange dress, an orange ribbon in her dark hair.

Jenny put a package on his nightstand, bent over and kissed him – warm lips, a deep sense of peace and sharing. She pulled away, sat down beside him, held his hand.

Dasein thought she had never looked more beautiful.

'Uncle Larry says you're to rest this afternoon, but you can be released from the hospital by Saturday,' she said.

Dasein reached out, ran his fingers through her hair – silky-smooth, sensuous hair. 'Why don't we get married Sunday?' he asked.

'Oh, darling ...'

Again, she kissed him, pulled back, looked prim. 'I better not do that anymore today. We don't want to weaken you.' The dimple flickered in her cheek. 'You want to be fully recovered and strong by Sunday.'

Dasein pulled her head down against his neck, stroked her hair.

'We can have one of the houses in the new section,' she whispered. 'We'll be near Cal and Willa. Darling, darling, I'm so happy.'

'So am I.'

She began describing the house to him, the garden space, the view ...

'You've chosen one of them already?'

'I was out there – dreaming, hoping ...'

The house was everything she'd ever longed for – it was important for a woman to have the right house in which to begin life with the man she loved. There was even a big garage with room for a shop ... and a lab.

Dasein thought of Jersey Hofstedder's car sitting in the garage she described. There was a sense of continuity in the thought, a peasant complacency involving 'good things' and 'vintage crops.'

His attention focused on the package Jenny had put on his nightstand.

'What's in the package?'

'Package?'

She lifted her head, turned to follow the direction of his gaze. 'Oh, that. The gang at the Co-op – they put together a "get-well" package for you.'

'Jaspers?'

'Of course.' She sat back, straightened her hair.

Dasein had a sudden vision of himself working in the wrapping line at the Co-op.

'Where will I work?' he asked.

'Uncle Larry wants you in the clinic, but we'll both get a month of honeymoon leave. Darling – it's going to be so long until Sunday.'

In the clinic, Dasein thought. *Not as a patient, thank God.* He wondered then which god he was thanking. It was a odd thought, without beginning and without end, a bit of string hanging in the green lake of his mind.

Jenny began unwrapping the package on the nightstand – a wedge of golden cheese, two bottles of beer, dark wheat crackers, a white container that sloshed when she moved it. He wondered when they had been exposed.

Dasein had the sudden feeling that he was a moth in a glass cage, a frantic thing fluttering against his barriers, lost, confused.

'Darling, I'm tiring you.' Jenny put her hand on his forehead. It soothed him, calmed him. The moth of his emotions settled on a strong green limb. The limb was attached to a tree. He felt the trunk of the tree as though it were himself – strong, an infinite source of strength.

'When will I see you?' he asked.

'I'll come by in the morning.'

She blew him a kiss, hesitated, bent over him – the sweet fragrance of Jaspers about her breath, a touch of lips.

Dasein stared after her until the foyer door closed.

A momentary anguish touched him, a fleeting sense that he'd lost his grip on reality, that this room was unreal without Jenny in it. Dasein grabbed a chunk of the golden cheese, stuffed it in his mouth, felt the soothing Jaspers presence, his awareness expanding, becoming firm and manageable.

What's reality, anyway? he asked himself. *It's as finite as a bit of cheese, as tainted by error as anything else with limits.*

He settled his mind firmly then onto thoughts of the home Jenny had described, pictured himself carrying her across the threshold – his wife. There'd be presents: Jaspers from 'the gang,' furniture ... Santaroga took care of its own.

It'll be a beautiful life, he thought. *Beautiful ... beautiful ... beautiful ...*

THE DOSADI EXPERIMENT

In memory of Babe
because she knew how to enjoy life

When the Calebans first sent us one of their giant metal 'beachballs,' communicating through this device to offer the use of jumpdoors for interstellar travel, many in the ConSentiency covertly began to exploit this gift of the stars for their own questionable purposes. Both the 'Shadow Government' and some among the Gowachin people saw what is obvious today: that instantaneous travel across unlimited space involved powers which might isolate subject populations in gross numbers.

This observation at the beginning of the Dosadi Experiment came long before Saboteur Extraordinary Jorj X. McKie discovered that visible stars of our universe were either Calebans or the manifestations of Calebans in ConSentient space. (See *Whipping Star*, an account of McKie's discovery thinly disguised as fiction.)

What remains pertinent here is that McKie, acting for his Bureau of Sabotage, identified the Caleban called 'Fannie Mae' as the visible star Thyone. This discovery of the Thyone-Fannie Mae identity ignited new interest in the Caleban Question and thus contributed to the exposure of the Dosadi Experiment – which many still believe was the most disgusting use of Sentients by Sentients in ConSentient history. Certainly, it remains the most gross psychological test of Sentient Beings ever performed, and the issue of informed consent has never been settled to everyone's satisfaction.

– From the first public account, the Trial of Trials

Justice belongs to those who claim it, but let the claimant beware lest he create new injustice by his claim and thus set the bloody pendulum of revenge into its inexorable motion.

– Gowachin aphorism

'Why are you so cold and mechanical in your Human relationships?'

Jorj X. McKie was to reflect on that Caleban question later. Had she been trying to alert him to the Dosadi Experiment and to what his investigation of that experiment might do to him? He hadn't even known about Dosadi at the time and the pressures of the Caleban communications trance, the accusatory tone she took, had precluded other considerations.

Still, it rankled. He didn't like the feeling that he might be a subject of her research into Humans. He'd always thought of that particular Caleban as his friend – if one could consider being friendly with a creature whose visible manifestation in this universe was a fourth-magnitude yellow sun visible from Central Central where the Bureau of Sabotage maintained its headquarters. And there was inevitable discomfort in Caleban communication. You sank into a trembling, jerking trance while they made their words appear in your consciousness.

But his uncertainty remained: had she tried to tell him something beyond the plain content of her words?

When the weather makers kept the evening rain period short, McKie liked to go outdoors immediately afterward and stroll in the park enclosure which BuSab provided for its employees on Central Central. As a Saboteur Extraordinary, McKie had free run of the enclosure and he liked the fresh smells of the place after a rain.

The park covered about thirty hectares, deep in a well of Bureau buildings. It was a scrambling hodgepodge of plantings cut by wide paths which circled and twisted through specimens from every inhabited planet of the known universe. No care had been taken to provide a particular area for any sentient species. If there was any plan to the park it was a maintenance plan with plants requiring similar conditions and care held in their own sectors. Giant Spear Pines from Sasak occupied a

389

knoll near one corner surrounded by mounds of Flame Briar from Rudiria. There were bold stretches of lawn and hidden scraps of lawn, and some flat stretches of greenery which were not lawns at all but mobile sheets of predatory leaf imprisoned behind thin moats of caustic water.

Rain-jeweled flowers often held McKie's attention to the exclusion of all else. There was a single planting of Lilium Grossa, its red blossoms twice his height casting long shadows over a wriggling carpet of blue Syringa, each miniature bloom opening and closing at random like tiny mouths gasping for air.

Sometimes, floral perfumes stopped his progress and held him in a momentary olfactory thralldom while his eyes searched out the source. As often as not, the plant would be a dangerous one – a flesh eater or poison-sweat variety. Warning signs in flashing Galach guarded such plantings. Sonabarriers, moats, and force fields edged the winding paths in many areas.

McKie had a favorite spot in the park, a bench with its back to a fountain where he could sit and watch the shadows collect across fat yellow bushes from the floating islands of Tandaloor. The yellow bushes thrived because their roots were washed in running water hidden beneath the soil and renewed by the fountain. Beneath the yellow bushes there were faint gleams of phosphorescent silver enclosed by a force field and identified by a low sign:

'Sangeet Mobilus, a blood-sucking perennial from Bisaj. Extreme danger to all sentient species. Do not intrude any portion of your body beyond the force field.'

As he sat on the bench, McKie thought about that sign. The universe often mixed the beautiful and the dangerous. This was a deliberate mixture in the park. The yellow bushes, the fragrant and benign Golden Iridens, had been mingled with Sangeet Mobilus. The two supported each other and both thrived. The ConSentient government which McKie served often made such mixtures ... sometimes by accident.

Sometimes by design.

He listened to the splashing of the fountain while the shadows thickened and the tiny border lights came on along the paths. The tops of the buildings beyond the park became a palette where the sunset laid out its final display of the day.

In that instant, the Caleban contact caught him and he felt his body slip into the helpless communications trance. The mental tendrils were immediately identified – Fannie Mae. And he thought, as he often had, what an improbable name that was for a star entity. He heard no sounds, but his hearing centers responded as to spoken words, and the inward glow was unmistakable. It was Fannie Mae, her syntax far more sophisticated than during their earliest encounters.

'You admire one of us,' she said, indicating his attention on the sun which had just set beyond the buildings.

'I try not to think of any star as a Caleban,' he responded. 'It interferes with my awareness of the natural beauty.'

'Natural? McKie, you don't understand your own awareness, nor even how you employ it!'

That was her beginning – accusatory, attacking, unlike any previous contact with this Caleban he'd thought of as friend. And she employed her verb forms with new deftness, almost as though showing off, parading her understanding of his language.

'What do you want, Fannie Mae?'

'I consider your relationships with females of your species. You have entered marriage relationships which number more than fifty. Not so?'

'That's right. Yes. Why do you ...'

'I am your friend, McKie. What is your feeling toward me?'

He thought about that. There was a demanding intensity in her question. He owed his life to this Caleban with an improbable name. For that matter, she owed her life to him. Together, they'd resolved the Whipping Star threat. Now, many Calebans provided the jumpdoors by which other beings moved in a single step from planet to planet, but once Fannie Mae had held all of those jumpdoor threads, her life threatened through the odd honor code by which Calebans maintained their contractual obligations. And McKie had saved her life. He had but to think about their past interdependence and a warm sense of camaraderie suffused him.

Fannie Mae sensed this.

'Yes, McKie, that is friendship, is love. Do you possess this feeling toward Human female companions?'

Her question angered him. Why was she prying? His private sexual relationships were no concern of hers!

'Your love turns easily to anger,' she chided.

'There are limits to how deeply a Saboteur Extraordinary can allow himself to be involved with anyone.'

'Which came first, McKie – the Saboteur Extraordinary or these limits?'

Her response carried obvious derision. Had he chosen the Bureau because he was incapable of warm relationships? But he really cared for

Fannie Mae! He admired her ... and she could hurt him because he admired her and felt ... felt *this way.*

He spoke out of his anger and hurt.

'Without the Bureau there'd be no ConSentiency and no need for Calebans.'

'Yes, indeed. People have but to look at a dread agent from BuSab and know fear.'

It was intolerable, but he couldn't escape the underlying warmth he felt toward this strange Caleban entity, this being who could creep unguarded into his mind and talk to him as no other being dared. If only he had found a woman to share that kind of intimacy ...

And this was the part of their conversation which came back to haunt him. After months with no contact between them, why had she chosen that moment – just three days before the Dosadi crisis burst upon the Bureau? She'd pulled out his ego, his deepest sense of identity. She'd shaken that ego and then she'd skewered him with her barbed question:

'*Why are you so cold and mechanical in your Human relationships?*'

Her irony could not be evaded. She'd made him appear ridiculous in his own eyes. He could feel warmth, yes ... even love, for a Caleban but not for a Human female. This unguarded feeling he held for Fannie Mae had never been directed at any of his marital companions. Fannie Mae had aroused his anger, then reduced his anger to verbal breast-beating, and finally to silent hurt. Still, the love remained.

Why?

Human females were bed partners. They were bodies which used him and which he used. That was out of the question with this Caleban. She was a star burning with atomic fires, her seat of consciousness unimaginable to other sentients. Yet, she could extract love from him. He gave this love freely and she knew it. There was no hiding an emotion from a Caleban when she sent her mental tendrils into your awareness.

She'd certainly known he would see the irony. That had to be part of her motive in such an attack. But Calebans seldom acted from a single motive – which was part of their charm and the essence of their most irritant exchanges with other sentient beings.

'McKie?' Softly in his mind.

'Yes.' Angry.

'I show you now a fractional bit of my feeling toward your node.'

Like a balloon being inflated by a swift surge of gas, he felt himself suffused by a projected sense of concern, of caring. He was drowning in it ... wanted to drown in it. His entire body radiated this white-hot sense of protective attention. For a whole minute after it was withdrawn, he still glowed with it.

A fractional bit?

'McKie?' Concerned.

'Yes.' Awed.

'Have I hurt you?'

He felt alone, emptied.

'No.'

'The full extent of my nodal involvement would destroy you. Some Humans have suspected this about love.'

Nodal involvement?

She was confusing him as she'd done in their first encounters. How could the Calebans describe love as . . . nodal involvement?

'Labels depend on viewpoint,' she said. 'You look at the universe through too narrow an opening. We despair of you sometimes.'

There she was again, attacking.

He fell back on a childhood platitude.

'I am what I am and that's all I am.'

'You may soon learn, friend McKie, that you're more than you thought.'

With that, she'd broken the contact. He'd awakened in damp, chilly darkness, the sound of the fountain loud in his ears. Nothing he did would bring her back into communication, not even when he'd spent some of his own credits on a Taprisiot in a vain attempt to call her.

His Caleban friend had shut him out.

We have created a monster – enormously valuable and even useful yet extremely dangerous. Our monster is both beautiful and terrifying. We do not dare use this monster to its full potential, but we cannot release our grasp upon it.

– *Gowachin assessment of the Dosadi Experiment*

A bullet went *spang!* against the window behind Keila Jedrik's desk, ricocheted and screamed off into the canyon street far below her office. Jedrik prided herself that she had not even flinched. The Elector's patrols would take care of the sniper. The patrols which swept the streets of Chu every morning would home on the sound of the shot. She held the casual hope that the sniper would escape back to the Rim Rabble, but she recognized this hope as a weakness and dismissed it. There were concerns this morning far more important than an infiltrator from the Rim.

Jedrik reached one hand into the corner of early sunlight which illuminated the contact plates of her terminal in the Master Accountancy computer. Those flying fingers – she could almost disassociate herself from them. They darted like insects at the waiting keys. The terminal was a functional instrument, symbol of her status as a Senior Liaitor. It sat all alone in its desk slot – grey, green, gold, black, white and deadly. Its grey screen was almost precisely the tone of her desk top.

With careful precision, her fingers played their rhythms on the keys. The screen produced yellow numbers, all weighted and averaged at her command – a thin strip of destiny with violence hidden in its golden shapes.

Every angel carries a sword, she thought.

But she did not really consider herself an angel or her weapon a sword. Her real weapon was an intellect hardened and sharpened by the terrible decisions her planet required. Emotions were a force to be diverted within the self or to be used against anyone who had failed to learn what Dosadi taught. She knew her own weakness and hid it carefully: she'd been taught by loving parents (who'd concealed their love behind exquisite cruelty) that Dosadi's decisions were indeed terrible.

Jedrik studied the numbers on her computer display, cleared the

394

screen and made a new entry. As she did this, she knew she took sustenance from fifty of her planet's Human inhabitants. Many of those fifty would not long survive this callous jape. In truth, her fingers were weapons of death for those who failed this test. She felt no guilt about those she slew. The imminent arrival of one Jorj X. McKie dictated her actions, precipitated them.

When she thought about McKie, her basic feeling was one of satisfaction. She'd waited for McKie like a predator beside a burrow in the earth. His name and identifying keys had been given to her by her chauffeur, Havvy, hoping to increase his value to her. She'd taken the information and made her usual investigation. Jedrik doubted that any other person on Dosadi could have come up with the result her sources produced: Jorj X. McKie was an adult Human who could not possibly exist. No record of him could be found on all of Dosadi – not on the poisonous Rim, not in Chu's Warrens, not in any niche of the existing power structure. McKie did not exist, but he was due to arrive in Chu momentarily, smuggled into the city by a Gowachin temporarily under her control.

McKie was the precision element for which she had waited. He wasn't merely a possible key to the God Wall (not a bent and damaged key like Havvy) but clean and certain. She'd never thought to attack this lock with poor instruments. There'd be one chance and only one; it required the best.

Thus fifty Dosadi Humans took their faceless places behind the numbers in her computer. Bait, expendable. Those who died by this act wouldn't die immediately. Forty-nine might never know they'd been deliberately submitted to early death by her deliberate choice. Some would be pushed back to the Rim's desperate and short existence. Some would die in the violent battles she was precipitating. Others would waste away in the Warrens. For most, the deadly process would extend across sufficient time to conceal her hand in it. But they'd been slain in her computer and she knew it. She cursed her parents (and the others before them) for this unwanted sensitivity to the blood and sinew behind these computer numbers. Those loving parents had taught her well. She might never see the slain bodies, need give not another thought to all but one of the fifty; still she sensed them behind her computer display ... warm and pulsing.

Jedrik sighed. The fifty were bleating animals staked out to lure a special beast onto Dosadi's poisonous soil. Her fifty would create a fractional surplus which would vanish, swallowed before anyone realized their purpose.

Dosadi is sick, she thought. And not for the first time, she wondered: *Is this really Hell?*

Many believed it.

We're being punished.

But no one knew what they'd done to deserve punishment.

Jedrik leaned back, looked across her doorless office to the sound barrier and milky light of the hall. A strange Gowachin shambled past her doorway. He was a frog figure on some official errand, a packet of brown paper clutched in his knobby hands. His green skin shimmered as though he'd recently come from water.

The Gowachin reminded her of Bahrank, he who was bringing McKie into her net, Bahrank who did her bidding because she controlled the substance to which he was addicted. More fool he to let himself become an addict to anything, even to living. One day soon Bahrank would sell what he knew about her to the Elector's spies; by then it would be too late and the Elector would learn only what she wanted him to learn when she wanted him to learn it. She'd chosen Bahrank with the same care she'd used at her computer terminal, the same care which had made her wait for someone precisely like McKie. And Bahrank was Gowachin. Once committed to a project, the frog people were notorious for carrying out their orders in a precise way. They possessed an inbred sense of order but understood the limits of law.

As her gaze traversed the office, the sparse and functional efficiency of the space filled her with quiet amusement. This office presented an image of her which she had constructed with meticulous care. It pleased her that she would be leaving here soon never to return, like an insect shedding its skin. The office was four paces wide, eight long. Twelve black metal rotofiles lined the wall on her left, dark sentinels of her methodical ways. She had reset their locking codes and armed them to destroy their contents when the Elector's toads pried into them. The Elector's people would attribute this to outrage, a last angry sabotage. It would be some time before accumulating doubts would lead them to reassessment and to frustrated questions. Even then they might not suspect her hand in the elimination of fifty Humans. She, after all, was one of the fifty.

This thought inflicted her with a momentary sense of unfocused loss. How pervasive were the seductions of Dosadi's power structure! How subtle! What she'd just done here introduced a flaw into the computer system which ruled the distribution of non-poisonous food in Dosadi's only city. Food – here was the real base of Dosadi's social pyramid, solid and ugly. The flaw removed her from a puissant niche in that pyramid.

She had worn the persona of Keila Jedrik-Liaitor for many years, long enough to learn enjoyment of the power system. Losing one valuable counter in Dosadi's endless survival game, she must now live and act only with the persona of Keila Jedrik-Warlord. This was an all-or-nothing move, a gambler's plunge. She felt the nakedness of it. But this gamble had begun long ago, far back in Dosadi's contrived history, when her ancestors had recognized the nature of this planet and had begun breeding and training for the individual who would take this plunge.

I am that individual, she told herself. *This is our moment.*

But had they truly assessed the problem correctly?

Jedrik's glance fell on the single window which looked out into the canyon street. Her own reflection stared back: a face too narrow, thin nose, eyes and mouth too large. Her hair could be an interesting black velvet helmet if she let it grow, but she kept it cropped short as a reminder that she was not a magnetic sex partner, that she must rely on her wits. That was the way she'd been bred and trained. Dosadi had taught her its cruelest lessons early. She'd grown tall while still in her teens, carrying more height in her body than in her legs so that she appeared even taller when seated. She looked down on most Gowachin and Human males in more ways than one. That was another gift (and lesson) from her *loving* parents and from their ancestors. There was no escaping this Dosadi lesson.

What you love or value will be used against you.

She leaned forward to hide her disquieting reflection, peered far down into the street. There, that was better. Her fellow Dosadis no longer were warm and pulsing people. They were reduced to distant movements, as impersonal as the dancing figures in her computer.

Traffic was light, she noted. Very few armored vehicles moved, no pedestrians. There'd been only that one shot at her window. She still entertained a faint hope that the sniper had escaped. More likely a patrol had caught the fool. The Rim Rabble persisted in testing Chu's defenses despite the boringly repetitive results. It was desperation. Snipers seldom waited until the day was deep and still and the patrols were scattered, those hours when even some among the most powerful ventured out.

Symptoms, all symptoms.

Rim sorties represented only one among many Dosadi symptoms which she'd taught herself to read in that precarious climb whose early stage came to climax in this room. It was not just a thought, but more a sense of familiar awareness to which she returned at oddly reflexive moments in her life.

We have a disturbed relationship with our past which religion cannot explain. We are primitive in unexplainable ways, our lives woven of the familiar and the strange, the reasonable and the insane.

It made some insane choices magnificently attractive.

Have I made an insane choice?

No!

The data lay clearly in her mind, facts which she could not obliterate by turning away from them. Dosadi had been designed from a cosmic grab bag: 'Give them one of these and one of these and one of these . . .'

It made for incompatible pairings.

The DemoPol with which Dosadi juggled its computer-monitored society didn't fit a world which used energy transmitted from a satellite in geosynchronous orbit. The DemoPol reeked of primitive ignorance, something from a society which had wandered too far down the path of legalisms – a law for everything and everything managed by law. The dogma that a God-inspired few had chosen Chu's river canyon in which to build a city insulated from this poisonous planet, and that only some twenty or so generations earlier, remained indigestible. And that energy satellite which hovered beneath the God Wall's barrier – that stank of a long and sophisticated evolution during which something as obviously flawed as the DemoPol would have been discarded.

It was a cosmic grab bag designed for a specific purpose which her ancestors had recognized.

We did not evolve on this planet.

The place was out of phase with both Gowachin and Human. Dosadi employed computer memories and physical files side by side for identical purposes. And the number of addictive substances to be found on Dosadi was outrageous. Yet this was played off against a religion so contrived, so gross in its demands for 'simple faith' that the two conditions remained at constant war. The mystics died for their 'new insights' while the holders of 'simple faith' used control of the addictive substances to gain more and more power. The only real faith on Dosadi was that you survived by power and that you gained power by controlling what others required for survival. Their society understood the medicine of bacteria, virus and brain control, but these could not stamp out the Rim and Warren Underground where *jabua* faith healers cured their patients with the smoke of burning weeds.

And they could not stamp out (not yet) Keila Jedrik because she had seen what she had seen. Two by two the incompatible things ebbed and flowed around her, in the city of Chu and the surrounding Rim. It was the same in every case: a society which made use of one of these things could not naturally be a society which used the other.

Not naturally.

All around her, Jedrik sensed Chu with its indigestible polarities. They had only two species: Human and Gowachin. Why two? Were there no other species in this universe? Subtle hints in some of Dosadi's artifacts suggested an evolution for appendages other than the flexible fingers of Gowachin and Human.

Why only one city on all of Dosadi?

Dogma failed to answer.

The Rim hordes huddled close, always seeking a way into Chu's insulated purity. But they had a whole planet behind them. Granted it was a poisonous planet, but it had other rivers, other places of potential sanctuary. The survival of both species argued for the building of more sanctuaries, many more than that pitiful hole which Gar and Tria thought they masterminded. No ... Chu stood alone – almost twenty kilometers wide and forty long, built on hills and silted islands where the river slowed in its deep canyon. At last count, some eighty-nine million people lived here and three times that number eked a short life on the Rim – pressing, always pressing for a place in the poison-free city.

Give us your precious bodies, you stupid Rimmers!

They heard the message, knew its import and defied it. What had the people of Dosadi done to be imprisoned here? What had their ancestors done? It was right to build a religion upon hate for such ancestors ... provided such ancestors were guilty.

Jedrik leaned toward the window, peered upward at the God Wall, that milky translucence which imprisoned Dosadi, yet through which those such as this Jorj X. McKie could come at will. She hungered to see McKie in person, to confirm that he had not been contaminated as Havvy had been contaminated.

It was a McKie she required now. The transparently contrived nature of Dosadi told her that there must be a McKie. She saw herself as the huntress, McKie her natural prey. The false identity she'd built in this room was part of her bait. Now, in the season of McKie, the underlying religious cant by which Dosadi's powerful maintained their private illusions would crumble. She could already see the beginnings of that dissolution; soon, everyone would see it.

She took a deep breath. There was a purity in what was about to happen, a simplification. She was about to divest herself of one of her two lives, taking all of her awareness into the persona of that other Keila Jedrik which all of Dosadi would soon know. Her people had kept her secret well, hiding a fat and sleazy blonde person from their fellow Dosadis, exposing just enough of that one to 'X' that the powers beyond the God Wall might react in the proper design. She felt cleansed by the fact that the disguise of that other life had begun to lose its importance. The whole of her could begin to surface in that other place. And Mckie had precipitated this metamorphosis. Jedrik's thoughts were clear and direct now:

Come into my trap, McKie. You will take me higher than the palace apartments of the Council Hills.

Or into a deeper hell than any nightmare has imagined.

How to start a war? Nurture your own latent hungers for power. Forget that only madmen pursue power for its own sake. Let such madmen gain power – even you. Let such madmen act behind their conventional masks of sanity. Whether their masks be fashioned from the delusions of defense or the theological aura of law, war will come.

– Gowachin aphorism

The odalarm awoke Jorj X. McKie with a whiff of lemon. For just an instant his mind played tricks on him. He thought he was on Tutalsee's gentle planetary ocean floating softly on his garlanded island. There were lemons on his floating island, banks of Hibiscus and carpets of spicy Alyssum. His bowered cottage lay in the path of perfumed breezes and the lemon . . .

Awareness came. He was not on Tutalsee with a loving companion; he was on a trained bedog in the armored efficiency of his Central Central apartment; he was back in the heart of the Bureau of Sabotage; he was back at work.

McKie shuddered.

A planet full of people could die today . . . or tomorrow.

It would happen unless someone solved this Dosadi mystery. Knowing the Gowachin as he did, McKie was convinced of it. The Gowachin were capable of cruel decisions, especially where their species pride was at stake, or for reasons which other species might not understand. Bildoon, his Bureau chief, assessed this crisis the same way. Not since the Caleban problem had such enormity crossed the ConSentient horizon.

But where was this endangered planet, this Dosadi?

After a night of sleep suppression, the briefings about Dosadi came back vividly as though part of his mind had remained at work sharpening the images. Two operatives, one Wreave and one Laclac, had made the report. The two were reliable and resourceful. Their sources were excellent, although the information was sparse. The two also were bucking for promotion at a time when Wreaves and Laclacs were hinting at discrimination against their species. The report required special scrutiny. No BuSab agent, regardless of species, was above some internal testing, a deception designed to weaken the Bureau and gain coup merits upon which to ride into the director's office.

However, BuSab was still directed by Bildoon, a PanSpechi in Human form, the fourth member of his creche to carry that name. It had been obvious from Bildoon's first words that he believed the report.

'McKie, this thing could set Human and Gowachin at each others' throats.'

It was an understandable idiom, although in point of fact you would go for the Gowachin abdomen to carry out the same threat. McKie already had acquainted himself with the report and, from internal evidence to which his long association with the Gowachin made him sensitive, he shared Bildoon's assessment. Seating himself in a grey chairdog across the desk from the director in the rather small, windowless office Bildoon had lately preferred, McKie shifted the report from one hand to the other. Presently, recognizing his own nervous mannerism, he put the report on the desk. It was on coded memowire which played to trained senses when passed through the fingers or across other sensitive appendages.

'Why couldn't they pinpoint this Dosadi's location?' McKie asked.

'It's known only to a Caleban.'

'Well, they'll ...'

'The Calebans refuse to respond.'

McKie stared across the desk at Bildoon. The polished surface reflected a second image of the BuSab director, an inverted image to match the upright one. McKie studied the reflection. Until you focused on Bildoon's faceted eyes (how like an insect's eyes they were), this Pan-Spechi appeared much like a Human male with dark hair and pleasant round face. Perhaps he'd put on more than the form when his flesh had been molded to Human shape. Bildoon's face displayed emotions which McKie read in Human terms. The director appeared angry.

McKie was troubled.

'Refused?'

'The Calebans don't deny that Dosadi exists or that it's threatened. They refuse to discuss it.'

'Then we're dealing with a Caleban contract and they're obeying the terms of that contract.'

Recalling that conversation with Bildoon as he awakened in his apartment, McKie lay quietly thinking. Was Dosadi some new extension of the Caleban Question?

It's right to fear what we don't understand.

The Caleban mystery had eluded ConSentient investigators for too long. He thought of his recent conversation with Fannie Mae. When you thought you had something pinned down, it slipped out of your grasp. Before the Calebans' gift of jumpdoors, the ConSentiency had been a relatively slow and understandable federation of the known sentient species. The universe had contained itself in a shared space of recognizable dimensions. The ConSentiency of those days had grown in a way likened to expanding bubbles. It had been linear.

Caleban jumpdoors had changed that with an explosive acceleration of every aspect of life. Jumpdoors had been an immediately disruptive tool of power. They implied infinite usable dimensions. They implied many other things only faintly understood. Through a jumpdoor you stepped from a room on Tutalsee into a hallway here on Central Central. You walked through a jumpdoor here and found yourself in a garden on Paginui. The intervening 'normal space' might be measured in light years or parsecs, but the passage from one place to the other ignored such old concepts. And to this day, ConSentient investigators did not understand how the jumpdoors worked. Concepts such as 'relative space' didn't explain the phenomenon; they only added to the mystery.

McKie ground his teeth in frustration. Calebans inevitably did that to him. What good did it do to think of the Calebans as visible stars in the space his body occupied? He could look up from any planet where a jumpdoor deposited him and examine the night sky. Visible stars: ah, yes. Those are Calebans. What did that tell him?

There was a strongly defended theory that Calebans were but a more sophisticated aspect of the equally mysterious Taprisiots. The ConSentiency had accepted and employed Taprisiots for thousands of standard years. A Taprisiot presented sentient form and size. They appeared to be short lengths of tree trunk cut off at top and bottom and with oddly protruding stub limbs. When you touched them they were warm and resilient. They were fellow beings of the ConSentiency. But just as the Calebans took your flesh across the parsecs, Taprisiots took your awareness across those same parsecs to merge you with another mind.

Taprisiots were a communications device.

But current theory said Taprisiots had been introduced to prepare the ConSentiency for Calebans.

It was dangerous to think of Taprisiots as merely a convenient means of communication. Equally dangerous to think of Calebans as 'transportation facilitators.' Look at the socially disruptive effect of jumpdoors! And when you employed a Taprisiot, you had a constant reminder of danger: the communications trance which reduced you to a twitching zombie while you made your call. No . . . neither Calebans nor Taprisiots should be accepted without question.

With the possible exception of the PanSpechi, no other species knew the first thing about Caleban and Taprisiot phenomena beyond their economic and personal value. They were, indeed, valuable, a fact reflected in the prices often paid for jumpdoor and long-call services. The PanSpechi denied that they could explain these things, but the PanSpechi were notoriously secretive. They were a species where each *individual* consisted of five bodies and only one dominant ego. The four reserves lay somewhere in a hidden creche. Bildoon had come from such a creche, accepting the communal ego from a creche-mate whose subsequent fate could only be imagined. PanSpechi refused to discuss internal creche matters except to admit what was obvious on the surface: that they could grow a simulacrum body to mimic most of the known species in the ConSentiency.

McKie felt himself overcome by a momentary pang of xenophobia.

We accept too damned many things on the explanations of people who could have good reasons for lying.

Keeping his eyes closed, McKie sat up. His bedog rippled gently against his buttocks.

Blast and damn the Calebans! Damn Fannie Mae!

He'd already called Fannie Mae, asking about Dosadi. The result had left him wondering if he really knew what Calebans meant by friendship.

'Information not permitted.'

What kind of an answer was that? Especially when it was the only response he could get.

Not permitted?

The basic irritant was an old one: BuSab had no real way of applying its 'gentle ministrations' to the Calebans.

But Calebans had never been known to lie. They appeared painfully, explicitly honest . . . as far as they could be understood. But they obviously withheld information. Not permitted! Was it possible they'd let themselves be accessories to the destruction of a planet and that planet's entire population?

McKie had to admit it was possible.

They might do it out of ignorance or from some stricture of Caleban morality which the rest of the ConSentiency did not share or understand. Or for some other reason which defied translation. They said they looked upon all life as 'precious nodes of existence.' But hints at peculiar exceptions remained. What was it Fannie Mae had once said?

'Dissolved well this node.'

404

How could you look at an individual life as a 'node'?

If association with Calebans had taught him anything, it was that understanding between species was tenuous at best and trying to understand a Caleban could drive you insane. In what medium did a node dissolve?

McKie sighed.

For now, this Dosadi report from the Wreave and Laclac agents had to be accepted on its own limited terms. Powerful people in the Gowachin Confederacy had sequestered Humans and Gowachin on an unlisted planet. Dosadi – location unknown, but the scene of unspecified experiments and tests on an imprisoned population. This much the agents insisted was true. If confirmed, it was a shameful act. The frog people would know that, surely. Rather than let their shame be exposed, they could carry out the threat which the two agents reported: blast the captive planet out of existence, the population and all of the incriminating evidence with it.

McKie shuddered.

Dosadi, a planet of thinking creatures – *sentients*. If the Gowachin carried out their violent threat, a living world would be reduced to blazing gases and the hot plasma of atomic particles. Somewhere, perhaps beyond the reach of other eyes, something would strike fire against the void. The tragedy would require less than a standard second. The most concise thought about such a catastrophe would require a longer time than the actual event.

But if it happened and the other ConSentient species received absolute proof that it had happened ... ahhh, then the ConSentiency might well be shattered. Who would use a jumpdoor, suspecting that he might be shunted into some hideous experiment? Who would trust a neighbor, if that neighbor's habits, language, and body were different from his own? Yes ... there would be more than Humans and Gowachin *at each other's throats*. These were things all the species feared. Bildoon realized this. The threat to this mysterious Dosadi was a threat to all.

McKie could not shake the terrible image from his mind: an explosion, a bright blink stretching toward its own darkness. And if the ConSentiency learned of it ... in that instant before their universe crumbled like a cliff dislodged in a lightning bolt, what excuses would be offered for the failure of reason to prevent such a thing?

Reason?

McKie shook his head, opened his eyes. It was useless to dwell on the worst prospects. He allowed the apartment's sleep gloom to invade his senses, absorbed the familiar presence of his surroundings.

I'm a Saboteur Extraordinary and I've a job to do.

It helped to think of Dosadi that way. Solutions to problems often depended upon the will to succeed, upon sharpened skills and multiple resources. BuSab owned those resources and those skills.

McKie stretched his arms high over his head, twisted his blocky torso. The bedog rippled with pleasure at his movements. He whistled softly and suffered the kindling of morning light as the apartment's window controls responded. A yawn stretched his mouth. He slid from the bedog and padded across to the window. The view stretched away beneath a sky like stained blue paper. He stared out across the spires and rooftops of Central Central. Here lay the heart of the domine planet from which the Bureau of Sabotage spread its multifarious tentacles.

He blinked at the brightness, took a deep breath.

The Bureau. The omnipresent, omniscient, omnivorous Bureau. The one source of unmonitored governmental violence remaining in the ConSentiency. Here lay the norm against which sanity measured itself. Each choice made here demanded utmost delicacy. Their common enemy was that never-ending sentient yearning for absolutes. And each hour of every waking workday, BuSab in all of its parts asked itself:

'What are we if we succumb to unbridled violence?'

The answer was there in deepest awareness:

'Then we are useless.'

ConSentient government worked because, no matter how they defined it, the participants believed in a common justice personally achievable. The *Government* worked because BuSab sat at its core like a terrible watchdog able to attack itself or any seat of power with a delicately balanced immunity. Government worked because there were places where it could not act without being chopped off. An appeal to BuSab made the individual as powerful as the ConSentiency. It all came down to the cynical, self-effacing behavior of the carefully chosen BuSab tentacles.

I don't feel much like a BuSab tentacle this morning, McKie thought.

In his advancing years, he'd often experienced such mornings. He had a personal way of dealing with this mood: he buried himself in work.

McKie turned, crossed to the baffle into his bath where he turned his body over to the programmed ministrations of his morning toilet. The psyche-mirror on the bath's far wall reflected his body while it examined and adjusted to his internal conditions. His eyes told him he was still a squat, dark-skinned gnome of a Human with red hair, features so large they suggested an impossible kinship with the frog people of the Gowa-chin. The mirror did not reflect his mind, considered by many to be the sharpest legal device in the ConSentiency.

The Daily Schedule began playing to McKie as he emerged from the bath. The DS suited its tone to his movements and the combined analysis of his psychophysical condition.

'Good morning, ser,' it fluted.

McKie, who could interpret the analysis of his mood from the DS tone, put down a flash of resentment. Of course he felt angry and concerned. Who wouldn't under these circumstances?

'Good morning, you dumb inanimate object,' he growled. He slipped into a supple armored pullover, dull green and with the outward appear-ance of cloth.

The DS waited for his head to emerge.

'You wanted to be reminded, ser, that there is a full conference of the Bureau Directorate at nine local this morning, but the ...'

'Of all the stupid ...' McKie's interruption stopped the DS. He'd been meaning for some time to reprogram the damned thing. No matter how carefully you set them, they always got out of phase. He didn't bother to bridle his mood, merely spoke the key words in full emotional spate: 'Now you hear me, machine: don't you ever again choose that buddy-buddy conversational pattern when I'm in this mood! I want nothing *less* than a reminder of that conference. When you list such a reminder, don't even suggest remotely that it's my wish. Understood?'

'Your admonition recorded and new program instituted, ser.' The DS adopted a brisk, matter of fact tone as it continued: 'There is a new reason for alluding to the conference.'

'Well, get on with it.'

McKie pulled on a pair of green shorts and matching kilt of armored material identical to that of the pullover.

The DS continued:

'The conference was alluded to, ser, as introduction to a new datum: you have been asked not to attend.'

McKie, bending to fit his feet into self-powered racing boots, hesitated, then:

'But they're still going to have a showdown meeting with all the Gowachin in the Bureau?'

'No mention of that, ser. The message was that you are to depart immediately this morning on the field assignment which was discussed with you. Code Geevee was invoked. An unspecified Gowachin Phylum has asked that you proceed at once to their home planet. That would be Tandaloor. You are to consult there on a problem of a legal nature.'

McKie finished fitting the boots, straightened. He could feel all of his accumulated years as though there'd been no geriatric intervention. Geevee invoked a billion kinds of hell. It put him on his own with but one shopside backup facility: a Taprisiot monitor. He'd have his own Taprisiot link sitting safely here on CC while he went out and risked his vulnerable flesh. The Taprisiot served only one function: to note his death and record every aspect of his final moments – every thought, every memory. This would be part of the next agent's briefing. And the next agent would get his own Taprisiot monitor etcetera, etcetera, etcetera ... BuSab was notorious for gnawing away at its problems. The Bureau never gave up. But the astronomical cost of such a Taprisiot monitor left the operative so gifted with only one conclusion: odds were not in his favor. There'd be no accolades, no cemetery rites for a dead hero ... probably not even the physical substance of a hero for private grieving.

McKie felt less and less heroic by the minute.

Heroism was for fools and BuSab agents were not employed for their foolishness. He saw the reasoning, though. He was the best qualified non-Gowachin for dealing with the Gowachin. He looked at the nearest DS voder.

'Was it suggested that someone doesn't want me at that conference?'

'There was no such speculation.'

'Who gave you this message?'

'Bildoon. Verified voiceprint. He asked that your sleep not be interrupted, that the message be given to you on awakening.'

'Did he say he'd call back or ask me to call him?'

'No.'

'Did Bildoon mention Dosadi?'

'He said the Dosadi problem is unchanged. Dosadi is not in my banks, ser. Did you wish me to seek more info ...'

'No! I'm to leave immediately?'

'Bildoon said your orders have been cut. In relationship to Dosadi, he said, and these are his exact words: "The worst is probable. They have all the motivation required."'

McKie ruminated aloud: 'All the motivation ... selfish interest or fear ...'

'Ser, are you inquiring of ...'

'No, you stupid machine! I'm thinking out loud. People do that. We have to sort things out in our heads, put a proper evaluation on available data.'

'You do it with extreme inefficiency.'

This startled McKie into a flash of anger. 'But this job takes a sentient, a *person*, not a machine! Only a person can make the responsible decision. And I'm the only agent who understands them sufficiently.'

'Why not set a Gowachin agent to ferret out their ...'

'So you've worked it out?'

'It was not difficult, even for a machine. Sufficient clues were provided. And since you'll get a Taprisiot monitor, the project involves danger to your person. While I do not have specifics about Dosadi, the clear inference is that the Gowachin have engaged in questionable activity. Let me remind McKie that the Gowachin do not admit guilt easily. Very few non-Gowachin are considered by them to be worthy of their company and confidence. They do not like to feel dependent upon non-Gowachin. In fact, no Gowachin enjoys any dependent condition, not even when dependent upon another Gowachin. This is at the root of their law.'

This was a more emotionally loaded conversation than McKie had ever before heard from his DS. Perhaps his constant refusal to accept the thing on a personal anthropomorphic basis had forced it into this adaptation. He suddenly felt almost shy with the DS. What it had said was pertinent, and more than that, vitally important in a particular way: chosen to help him to the extent the DS was capable. In McKie's thoughts, the DS was suddenly transformed into a valued confidante.

As though it knew his thoughts, the DS said:

'I'm still a machine. You are inefficient, but as you have correctly stated you have ways of arriving at accuracy which machines do not understand. We can only ... guess, and we are not really programmed to guess unless specifically ordered to do so on a given occasion. Trust yourself.'

'But you'd rather I were not killed?'

'That is my program.'

'Do you have any more helpful suggestions?'

'You would be advised to waste as little time as possible here. There was a tone of urgency in Bildoon's voice.'

McKie stared at the nearest voder. Urgency in Bildoon's voice? Even under the most urgent necessity, Bildoon had never sounded urgent to McKie. Certainly, Dosadi could be an urgent matter, but ... Why should that sound a sour note?

'Are you sure he sounded urgent?'

'He spoke rapidly and with obvious tensions.'

'Truthful?'

'The tone-spikes lead to that conclusion.'

McKie shook his head. Something about Bildoon's behavior in this matter didn't ring true, but whatever it was it escaped the sophisticated reading circuits of the DS.

And my circuits, too.

Still troubled, McKie ordered the DS to assemble a full travel kit and to read out the rest of the schedule. He moved to the tool cupboard beside his bath baffle as the DS began reeling off the schedule.

His day was to start with the Taprisiot appointment. He listened with only part of his attention, taking care to check the toolkit as the DS assembled it. There were plastipiks. He handled them gently as they deserved. A selection of stims followed. He rejected these, counting on the implanted sense/muscle amplifiers which increased the capabilities of senior BuSab agents. Explosives in various denominations went into the kit – raygens, pentrates. Very careful with these dangerous items. He accepted multilenses, a wad of uniflesh with matching mediskin, solvos, miniputer. The DS extruded a life-monitor bead for the Taprisiot linkage. He swallowed it to give the bead time to anchor in his stomach before the Taprisiot appointment. A holoscan and matching blanks were accepted, as were raptors and comparators. He rejected the adapter for simulation of target identities. It was doubtful he'd have time or facilities for such sophisticated refinements. Better to trust his own instincts.

Presently, he sealed the kit in its wallet, concealed the wallet in a pocket. The DS had gone rambling on:

'... and you'll arrive on Tandaloor at a place called Holy Running. The time there will be early afternoon.'

Holy Running!

McKie riveted his attention to this datum. A Gowachin saying skittered through his mind: *The Law is a blind guide, a pot of bitter water. The Law is a deadly contest which can change as waves change.*

No doubt of what had led his thoughts into that path. Holy Running was the place of Gowachin myth. Here, so their stories said, lived Mrreg, the monster who had set the immutable pattern of Gowachin character.

And now, McKie suspected he knew which Gowachin Phylum had summoned him. It could be any one of five Phyla at Holy Running, but he felt certain it'd be the worst of those five – the most unpredictable, the most powerful, the most feared. Where else could a thing such as Dosadi originate?

McKie addressed his DS:

'Send in my breakfast. Please record that the condemned person ate a hearty breakfast.'

The DS, programmed to recognize rhetoric for which there was no competent response, remained silent while complying.

All sentient beings are created unequal. The best society provides each with equal opportunity to float at his own level.

– The Gowachin Primary

By mid-afternoon, Jedrik saw that her gambit had been accepted. A surplus of fifty Humans was just the right size to be taken by a greedy underling. Whoever it was would see the possibilities of continuing – ten here, thirty there – and because of the way she'd introduced this *flaw*, the next people discarded would be mostly Humans, but with just enough Gowachin to smack of retaliation.

It'd been difficult carrying out her daily routine knowing what she'd set in motion. It was all very well to accept the fact that you were *going* into danger. When the actual moment arrived, it always had a different character. As the subtle and not so subtle evidence of success accumulated, she felt the crazy force of it rolling over her. Now was the time to think about her true power base, the troops who would obey her slightest hint, the tight communications linkage with the Rim, the carefully selected and trained lieutenants. Now was the time to think about McKie slipping so smoothly into her trap. She concealed elation behind a facade of anger. They'd expect her to be angry.

The evidence began with a slowed response at her computer terminal. Someone was monitoring. Whoever had taken her bait wanted to be certain she was expendable. Wouldn't want to eliminate someone and then discover that the eliminated someone was essential to the power structure. She'd made damned sure to cut a wide swath into a region which could be made non-essential.

The microsecond delay from the monitoring triggered a disconnect on her telltale circuit, removing the evidence of her preparations before anyone could find it. She didn't think there'd be that much caution in anyone who'd accept this gambit, but unnecessary chances weren't part of her plan. She removed the telltale timer and locked it away in one of the filing cabinets, there to be destroyed with the other evidence when the Elector's toads came prying. The lonely blue flash would be confined by metal walls which would heat to a nice blood red before lapsing into slag and ashes.

In the next stage, people averted their faces as they walked past her office doorway.

Ahhh, the accuracy of the rumor-trail.

The avoidance came so naturally: a glance at a companion on the other side, concentration on material in one's hands, a brisk stride with gaze fixed on the corridor's ends. Important business up there. No time to stop and chat with Keila Jedrik today.

By the Veil of Heaven! They were so transparent!

A Gowachin walked by examining the corridor's blank opposite wall. She knew that Gowachin: one of the Elector's spies. What would he tell Elector Broey today? Jedrik glared at the Gowachin in secret glee. By nightfall, Broey would know who'd picked up her gambit, but it was too small a bite to arouse his avarice. He'd merely log the information for possible future use. It was too early for him to suspect a sacrifice move.

A Human male followed the Gowachin. He was intent on the adjustment of his neckline and that, of course, precluded a glance at a Senior Liaitor in her office. His name was Drayjo. Only yesterday, Drayjo had made courting gestures, bending toward her over this very desk to reveal the muscles under his light grey coveralls. What did it matter that Drayjo no longer saw her as a useful conquest. His face was a wooden door, closed, locked, hiding nothing.

Avert your face, you clog!

When the red light glowed on her terminal screen, it came as anticlimax. Confirmation that her gambit had been accepted by someone who would shortly regret it. Communication flowed across the screen:

'Opp SD22240268523ZX.'

Good old ZX!

Bad news always developed its own coded idiom. She read what followed, anticipating every nuance:

'The Mandate of God having been consulted, the following supernumerary functions are hereby reduced. If your position screen carries your job title with an underline, you are included in the reduction.

'*Senior Liaitor.*'

Jedrik clenched her fists in simulated anger while she glared at the underlined words. It was done. Opp-Out, the good old Double-O. Through its pliable arm, the DemoPol, the Sacred Congregation of the Heavenly Veil had struck again.

None of her elation showed through her Dosadi controls. Someone able to see beyond immediate gain would note presently that only

Humans had received this particular good old Double-O. Not one Gowachin there. Whoever made that observation would come sniffing down the trail she'd deliberately left. Evidence would accumulate. She thought she knew who would read that accumulated evidence for Broey. It would be Tria. It was not yet time for Tria to entertain doubts. Broey would hear what Jedrik wanted him to hear. The Dosadi power game would be played by Jedrik's rules then, and by the time others learned the rules it'd be too late.

She counted on the factor which Broey labeled 'instability of the masses.' Religious twaddle! Dosadi's masses were unstable only in particular ways. Fit a conscious justification to their innermost unconscious demands and they became a predictable system which would leap into predictable actions – especially with a psychotic populace whose innermost demands could never be faced consciously by the individuals. Such a populace remained highly useful to the initiates. That was why they maintained the DemoPol with its mandate-of-God sample. The tools of government were not difficult to understand. All you needed was a pathway into the system, a place where what you did touched a new reality.

Broey would think himself the target of her action. More fool he.

Jedrik pushed back her chair, stood and strode to the window hardly daring to think about where her actions would truly be felt. She saw that the sniper's bullet hadn't even left a mark on the glass. These new windows were far superior to the old ones which had taken on dull streaks and scratches after only a few years.

She stared down at the light on the river, carefully preserving this moment, prolonging it.

I won't look up yet, not yet.

Whoever had accepted her gambit would be watching her now. Too late! Too late!

A streak of orange-yellow meandered in the river current: contaminants from the Warren factories . . . poisons. Presently, not looking too high yet, she lifted her gaze to the silvered layers of the Council Hills, to the fluting inverted-stalagmites of the high apartments to which the denizens of Chu aspired in their futile dreams. Sunlight gleamed from the power bulbs which adorned the apartments on the hills. The great crushing wheel of government had its hub on those hills, but the impetus for that wheel had originated elsewhere.

Now, having prolonged the moment while anticipation enriched it, Jedrik lifted her gaze to that region above the Council Hills, to the sparkling streamers and grey glowing of the barrier veil, to the God Wall which englobed her planet in its impenetrable shell. The Veil of Heaven looked the way it always looked in this light. There was no apparent change. But she *knew* what she had done.

Jedrik was aware of subtle instruments which revealed other suns and galaxies beyond the God Wall, places where other planets must exist, but her people had only this one planet. That barrier up there and whoever had created it insured this isolation. Her eyes blurred with quick tears which she wiped away with real anger at herself. Let Broey and his toads believe themselves the only objects of her anger. She would carve a way beyond them through that deadly veil. No one on Dosadi would ever again cower beneath the hidden powers who lived in the sky!

She lowered her gaze to the carpet of factories and Warrens. Some of the defensive walls were faintly visible in the layers of smoke which blanketed the teeming scramble of life upon which the city fed. The smoke erased fine details to separate the apartment hills from the earth. Above the smoke, the fluted buildings became more a part of sky than of ground. Even the ledged, set-back walls of the canyon within which Chu created its sanctuary were no longer attached to the ground, but floated separate from this place where people could survive to a riper maturity on Dosadi. The smoke dulled the greens of ledges and Rim where the Rabble waged a losing battle for survival. Twenty years was old out there. In that pressure, they fought for a chance to enter Chu's protective confines by any means available, even welcoming the opportunity to eat garbage from which the poisons of this planet had been removed. The worst of Chu was better than their best, which only proved that the conditions of hell were relative.

I seek escape through the God Wall for the same reasons the Rabble seeks entrance to Chu.

In Jedrik's mind lay a graph with an undulant line. It combined many influences: Chu's precious food cycle and economics, Rim incursions, spots which flowed across their veiled sun, subtle planetary movements, atmospheric electricity, gravitational flows, magnetronic fluctuations, the dance of numbers in the Liaitor banks, the seemingly random play of cosmic rays, the shifting colors in the God Wall ... and mysterious jolts to the entire system which commanded her most concentrated attention. There could be only one source for such jolts: a manipulative intelligence outside the planetary influence of Dosadi. She called that force 'X,' but she had broken 'X' into components. One component was a simulation model of Elector Broey which she carried firmly in her head, not needing any of the mechanical devices for reading such things.

'X' and all of its components were as real as anything else on the chart in her mind. By their interplay she read them.

Jedrik addressed herself silently to 'X':

By your actions I know you and you are vulnerable.

Despite all of the Sacred Congregation's prattle, Jedrik and her people knew the God Wall had been put there for a specific purpose. It was the purpose which pressed living flesh into Chu from the Rim. It was the purpose which jammed too many people into too little space while it frustrated all attempts to spread into any other potential sanctuary. It was the purpose which created people who possessed that terrifying mental template which could trade flesh for flesh ... Gowachin or Human. Many clues revealed themselves around her and came through that radiance in the sky, but she refused as yet to make a coherent whole out of that purpose. Not yet.

I need this McKie!

With a Jedrik-maintained tenacity, her people knew that the regions beyond the barrier veil were not heaven or hell. Dosadi was hell, but it was a *created* hell. *We will know soon ... soon.*

This moment had been almost nine Dosadi generations in preparation: the careful breeding of a specific individual who carried in one body the talents required for this assault on 'X,' the exquisitely detailed education of that weapon-in-fleshly-form ... and there'd been all the rest of it – whispers, unremarked observations in clandestine leaflets, help for people who held particular ideas and elimination of others whose concepts obstructed, the building of a Rim-Warren communications network, the slow and secret assembly of a military force to match the others which balanced themselves at the peaks of Dosadi power ... All of these things and much more had prepared the way for those numbers introduced into her computer terminal. The ones who appeared to rule Dosadi like puppets – those ones could be read in many ways and this time the rulers, both visible and hidden, had made one calculation while Jedrik had made another calculation.

Again, she looked up at the God Wall.

You out there! Keila Jedrik know you're there. And you can be baited, you can be trapped. You are slow and stupid. And you think I don't know how to use your McKie. Ahhh, sky demons, McKie will open your veil for me. My life's a wrath and you're the objects of my wrath. I dare what you would not.

Nothing of this revealed itself on her face nor in any movement of her body.

Arm yourself when the Frog God smiles.

– Gowachin admonition

McKie began speaking as he entered the Phylum sanctus: 'I'm Jorj X. McKie of the Bureau of Sabotage.'

Name and primary allegiance, that was the drill. If he'd been a Gowachin, he'd have named his Phylum or would've favored the room with a long blink to reveal the identifying Phylum tattoo on his eyelids. As a non-Gowachin, he didn't need a tattoo.

He held his right hand extended in the Gowachin peace sign, palm down and fingers wide to show that he held no weapon there and had not extended his claws. Even as he entered, he smiled, knowing the effect this would have on any Gowachin here. In a rare mood of candor, one of his old Gowachin teachers had once explained the effect of a smiling McKie.

'We feel our bones age. It is a very uncomfortable experience.'

McKie understood the reason for this. He possessed a thick, muscular body – a swimmer's body with light mahogany skin. He walked with a swimmer's rolling gait. There were Polynesians in his Old Terran ancestry, this much was known in the Family Annals. Wide lips and a flat nose dominated his face; the eyes were large and placidly brown. There was a final genetic ornamentation to confound the Gowachin: red hair. He was the Human equivalent of the greenstone sculpture found in every Phylum house here on Tandaloor. McKie possessed the face and body of the Frog God, the Giver of Law.

As his old teacher had explained, no Gowachin ever fully escaped feelings of awe in McKie's presence, especially when McKie smiled. They were forced to hide a response which went back to the admonition which every Gowachin learned while still clinging to his mother's back.

Arm yourselves! McKie thought.

Still smiling, he stopped after the prescribed eight paces, glanced once around the room, then narrowed his attention. Green crystal walls confined the sanctus. It was not a large space, a gentle oval of perhaps twenty meters in its longest dimension. A single oval window admitted

417

warm afternoon light from Tandaloor's golden sun. The glowing yellow created a contrived *spiritual ring* directly ahead of McKie. The light focused on an aged Gowachin seated in a brown chairdog which had spread itself wide to support his elbows and webbed fingers. At the Gowachin's right hand stood an exquisitely wrought wooden swingdesk on a scrollwork stand. The desk held one object: a metal box of dull blue about fifteen centimeters long, ten wide, and six deep. Standing behind the blue box in the servant-guard position was a red-robed Wreave, her fighting mandibles tucked neatly into the lower folds of her facial slit.

This Phylum was initiating a Wreave!

The realization filled McKie with disquiet. Bildoon had not warned him about Wreaves on Tandaloor. The Wreave indicated a sad shift among the Gowachin toward a particular kind of violence. Wreaves never danced for joy, only for death. And this was the most dangerous of Wreaves, a *female*, recognizable as such by the jaw pouches behind her mandibles. There'd be two males somewhere nearby to form the breeding triad. Wreaves never ventured from their home soil otherwise.

McKie realized he no longer was smiling. These damnable Gowachin! They'd known the effect a Wreave female would have on him. Except in the Bureau, where a special dispensation prevailed, dealing with Wreaves required the most delicate care to avoid giving offence. And because they periodically exchanged triad members, they developed extended families of gigantic proportions wherein offending one member was to offend them all.

These reflections did not sit well with the chill he'd experienced at sight of the blue box on the swingdesk. He still did not know the identity of this Phylum, but he knew what that blue box had to be. He could smell the peculiar scent of antiquity about it. His choices had been narrowed.

'I know you, McKie,' the ancient Gowachin said.

He spoke the ritual in standard Galach with a pronounced burr, a fact which revealed he'd seldom been off this planet. His left hand moved to indicate a white chairdog positioned at an angle to his right beyond the swingdesk, yet well within striking range of the silent Wreave.

'Please seat yourself, McKie.'

The Gowachin glanced at the Wreave, at the blue box, returned his attention to McKie. It was a deliberate movement of the pale yellow eyes which were moist with age beneath bleached green brows. He wore only a green apron with white shoulder straps which outlined crusted white chest ventricles. The face was flat and sloping with pale, puckered nostrils below a faint nose crest. He blinked and revealed the tattoos on his eyelids. McKie saw there the dark, swimming circle of the Running Phylum, that which legend said had been the first to accept Gowachin Law from the Frog God.

His worst fears confirmed, McKie seated himself and felt the white chairdog adjust to his body. He cast an uneasy glance at the Wreave, who towered behind the swingdesk like a red-robed executioner. The flexing bifurcation which served as Wreave legs moved in the folds of the robe, but without tension. This Wreave was not yet ready to dance. McKie reminded himself that Wreaves were careful in all matters. This had prompted the ConSentient expression, 'a Wreave bet.' Wreaves were noted for waiting for the sure thing.

'You see the blue box,' the old Gowachin said.

It was a statement of mutual understanding, no answer required, but McKie took advantage of the opening.

'However, I do not know your companion.'

'This is Ceylang, Servant of the Box.'

Ceylang nodded acknowledgment.

A fellow BuSab agent had once told McKie how to count the number of triad exchanges in which a Wreave female had participated.

'A tiny bit of skin is nipped from one of her jaw pouches by the departing companion. It looks like a little pockmark.'

Both of Ceylang's pouches were peppered with exchange pocks. McKie nodded to her, formal and correct, no offense intended, none given. He glanced at the box which she served.

McKie had been a Servant of the Box once. This was where you began to learn the limits of legal ritual. The Gowachin words for this novitiate translated as 'The Heart of Disrespect.' It was the first stage on the road to Legum. The old Gowachin here was not mistaken: McKie as one of the few non-Gowachin ever admitted to Legum status, to the practice of law in this planetary federation, would *see* that blue box and know what it contained. There would be a small brown book printed on pages of ageless metal, a knife with the blood of many sentient beings dried on its black surface, and lastly a grey rock, chipped and scratched over the millennia in which it'd been used to pound on wood and call Gowachin courts into session. The box and its contents symbolized all that was mysterious and yet practical about Gowachin Law. The book was ageless, yet not to be read and reread; it was sealed in a box where it could be thought upon as a thing which marked a beginning. The knife carried the bloody residue of many endings. And the rock – that came from the natural earth where things only changed, never beginning or ending. The entire assemblage, box and contents, represented a window into the soul of the Frog God's minions. And now they were educating a Wreave as Servant of the Box.

McKie wondered why the Gowachin had chosen a deadly Wreave, but dared not enquire. The blue box, however, was another matter. It said with certainty that a planet called Dosadi would be named openly here. The thing which BuSab had uncovered was about to become an issue in Gowachin Law. That the Gowachin had anticipated Bureau action spoke well of their information sources. A sense of careful choosing radiated from this room. McKie assumed a mask of relaxation and remained silent.

The old Gowachin did not appear pleased by this. He said:

'You once afforded me much amusement, McKie.'

That might be a compliment, probably not. Hard to tell. Even if it were a compliment, coming from a Gowachin it would contain signal reservations, especially in legal matters. McKie held his silence. This Gowachin was big power and no mistake. Whoever misjudged him would hear the Courtarena's final trumpet.

'I watched you argue your first case in our courts,' the Gowachin said. 'Betting was nine-point-three to three-point-eight that we'd see your blood. But when you concluded by demonstrating that eternal sloppiness was the price of liberty ... ahhh, that was a master stroke. It filled many a Legum with envy. Your words clawed through the skin of Gowachin Law to get at the meat. And at the same time you amused us. That was the supreme touch.'

Until this moment, McKie had not even suspected that there'd been amusement for anyone in that first case. Present circumstances argued for truthfulness from the old Gowachin, however. Recalling that first case, McKie tried to reassess it in the light of this revelation. He remembered the case well. The Gowachin had charged a Low Magister named Klodik with breaking his most sacred vows in an issue of justice. Klodik's crime was the release of thirty-one fellow Gowachin from their primary allegiance to Gowachin Law and the purpose of that was to qualify the thirty-one for service in BuSab. The hapless prosecutor, a much-admired Legum named Pirgutud, had aspired to Klodik's position and had made the mistake of trying for a direct conviction. McKie had thought at the time that the wiser choice would've been to attempt discrediting the legal structure under which Klodik had been arraigned. This would have thrown judgment into the area of popular choice, and there'd been no doubt that Klodik's early demise would've been popular. Seeing this opening, McKie had attacked the prosecutor as a legalist, a stickler, one who preferred Old Law. Victory had been relatively easy.

When it had come to the knife, however, McKie had found himself profoundly reluctant. There'd been no question of selling Pirgutud back to his own Phylum. BuSab had needed a non-Gowachin Legum ... the whole non-Gowachin universe had needed this. The few other non-Gowachin who'd attained Legum status were all dead, every last one of them in the Courtarena. A current of animosity toward the Gowachin worlds had been growing. Suspicion fed on suspicion.

Pirgutud had to die in the traditional, the formal, way. He'd known it perhaps better than McKie. Pirgutud, as required, had bared the heart area beside his stomach and clasped his hands behind his head. This extruded the stomach circle, providing a point of reference.

The purely academic anatomy lessons and the practice sessions on lifelike dummies had come to deadly focus.

'Just to the left of the stomach circle imagine a small triangle with an apex at the center of the stomach circle extended horizontally and the base even with the bottom of the stomach circle. Strike into the lower outside corner of this triangle and slightly upward toward the midline.'

About the only satisfaction McKie had found in the event was that Pirgutud had died cleanly and quickly with one stroke. McKie had not entered Gowachin Law as a 'hacker.'

What had there been in that case and its bloody ending to amuse the Gowachin? The answer filled McKie with a profound sense of peril.

The Gowachin were amused at themselves because they had so misjudged me! But I'd planned all along for them to misjudge me. That was what amused them!

Having provided McKie with a polite period for reflection, the old Gowachin continued:

'I'd bet against you, McKie. The odds, you understand? You delighted me nonetheless. You instructed us while winning your case in a classic manner which would've done credit to the best of us. That is one of the Law's purposes, of course: to test the qualities of those who choose to employ it. Now what did you expect to find when you answered our latest summons to Tandaloor?'

The question's abrupt shift almost caught McKie by surprise.

I've been too long away from the Gowachin, he thought. I can't relax even for an instant.

It was almost a palpable thing: if he missed a single beat of the rhythms in this room, he and an entire planet could fall before Gowachin judgment. For a civilization which based its law on the Courtarena where any participant could be sacrificed, anything was possible. McKie chose his next words with life-and-death care.

'You summoned me, that is true, but I came on official business of my Bureau. It's the Bureau's expectations which concern me.'

'Then you are in a difficult position because you're also a Legum of the Gowachin Bar subject to our demands. Do you know me?'

This was a Magister, a *Foremost-Speaker* from the 'Phylum of Phylums,' no doubt of it. He was a survivor in one of the most cruel traditions known to the sentient universe. His abilities and resources were formidable and he was on his home ground. McKie chose the cautious response.

'On my arrival I was told to come to this place at this time. That is what I know.'

The least thing that is known shall govern your acts. This was the course of evidence for the Gowachin. McKie's response put a legal burden on his questioner.

The old Gowachin's hands clutched with pleasure at the level of artistry to which this contest had risen. There was a momentary silence during which Ceylang gathered her robe tightly and moved even closer to the swingdesk. Now, there was tension in her movements. The Magister stirred, said:

'I have the disgusting honor to be High Magister of the Running Phylum, Aritch by name.'

As he spoke, his right hand thrust out, took the blue box, and dropped it into McKie's lap. 'I place the binding oath upon you in the name of the book!'

As McKie had expected, it was done swiftly. He had the box in his hands while the final words of the ancient legal challenge were ringing in his ears. No matter the ConSentient modifications of Gowachin Law which might apply in this situation, he was caught in a convoluted legal maneuvering. The metal of the box felt cold against his fingers. They'd confronted him with *the* High Magister. The Gowachin were dispensing with many preliminaries. This spoke of time pressures and a particular assessment of their own predicament. McKie reminded himself that he was dealing with people who found pleasure in their own failures, could be amused by death in the Courtarena, whose most consummate pleasure came when the currents of their own Law were changed artistically.

McKie spoke with the careful formality which ritual required if he were to emerge alive from this room.

'Two wrongs may cancel each other. Therefore, let those who do wrong do it together. That is the true purpose of Law.'

Gently, McKie released the simple swing catch on the box, lifted the lid to verify the contents. This must be done with precise attention to formal details. A bitter, musty odor touched his nostrils as the lid lifted. The box held what he'd expected: the book, the knife, the rock. It occurred to McKie then that he was holding the original of all such boxes. It was a thing of enormous antiquity – thousands upon thousands of standard years. Gowachin professed the belief that the Frog God had created this box, this *very* box, and its contents as a model, the symbol of 'the only workable Law.'

Careful to do it with his right hand, McKie touched each item of the box in its turn, closed the lid and latched it. As he did this, he felt that he stepped into a ghostly parade of Legums, names imbedded in the minstrel chronology of Gowachin history.

Bishkar who concealed her eggs . . .
Kondush the Diver . . .
Dritaik who sprang from the marsh and laughed at Mrreg . . .
Tonkeel of the hidden knife . . .

McKie wondered then how they would sing about him. Would it be *McKie the blunderer?* His thoughts raced through review of the necessities. The primary necessity was Aritch. Little was known about this High Magister outside the Gowachin Federation, but it was said that he'd once won a case by finding a popular bias which allowed him to kill a judge. The commentary on this coup said Aritch 'embraced the Law in the same way that salt dissolves in water.' To the initiates, this meant Aritch personified the basic Gowachin attitude toward their Law: 'respectful disrespect.' It was a peculiar form of sanctity. Every movement of your body was as important as your words. The Gowachin made it an aphorism.

'You hold your life in your mouth when you enter the Courtarena.'

They provided legal ways to kill any participant – judges, Legums, clients . . . But it must be done with exquisite legal finesse, with its justifications apparent to all observers, and with the most delicate timing. Above all, one could kill in the arena only when no other choice offered the same worshipful disrespect for Gowachin Law. Even while changing the Law, you were required to revere its sanctity.

When you entered the Courtarena, you had to feel that peculiar sanctity in every fiber. The forms . . . the forms . . . the forms . . . With that blue box in his hands, the deadly forms of Gowachin Law dominated every movement, every word. Knowing McKie was not Gowachin-born, Aritch was putting time pressures on him, hoping for an immediate flaw. They didn't want this Dosadi matter in the arena. That was the immediate contest. And if it did get to the arena . . . well, the crucial matter would be selection of the judges. Judges were chosen with great care. Both sides maneuvered in this, being cautious not to intrude a professional legalist onto the bench. Judges could represent those whom the Law had offended. They could be private citizens in any number satisfactory to the opposing forces. Judges could be (and often were) chosen for their special knowledge of a case at hand. But here you were forced to weigh the subtleties of prejudgment. Gowachin Law made a special distinction between prejudgment and bias.

McKie considered this.

The interpretation of bias was: 'If I can rule for a particular side I will do so.'

For prejudgment: 'No matter what happens in the arena I will rule for a particular side.'

Bias was permitted, but not prejudgment.

Aritch was the first problem, his possible prejudgments, his bias, his inborn and most deeply conditioned attitudes. In his deepest feelings, he would look down on all non-Gowachin legal systems as 'devices to weaken personal character through appeals to illogic, irrationality, and to ego-centered selfishness in the name of high purpose.'

If Dosadi came to the arena, it would be tried under modified Gowachin Law. The modifications were a thorn in the Gowachin skin. They represented concessions made for entrance into the ConSentiency. Periodically, the Gowachin tried to make their Law the basis for all ConSentient Law.

McKie recalled that a Gowachin had once said of ConSentient Law:

'It fosters greed, discontent, and competitiveness not based on excellence but on appeals to prejudice and materialism.'

Abruptly, McKie remembered that this was a quotation attributed to Aritch, High Magister of the Running Phylum. Were there even more deeply hidden motives in what the Gowachin did here?

Showing signs of impatience, Aritch inhaled deeply through his chest ventricles, said:

'You are now my Legum. To be convicted is to go free because this marks you as enemy of all government. I know you to be such an enemy, McKie.'

'You know me,' McKie agreed.

It was more than ritual response and obedience to forms, it was truth. But it required great effort for McKie to speak it calmly. In the almost fifty years since he'd been admitted to the Gowachin Bar, he'd served that ancient legal structure four times in the Courtarena, a minor record among the ordinary Legums. Each time, his personal survival had been in the balance. In all of its stages, this contest was a deadly battle. The loser's life belonged to the winner and could be taken at the winner's discretion. On rare occasions, the loser might be sold back to his own Phylum as a menial. Even the losers disliked this choice.

Better clean death than dirty life.

The blood-encrusted knife in the blue box testified to the more popular outcome. It was a practice which made for rare litigation and memorable court performances.

Aritch, speaking with eyes closed and the Running Phylum tattoos formally displayed, brought their encounter to its testing point.

'Now McKie, you will tell me what official matters of the Bureau of Sabotage bring you to the Gowachin Federation.'

Law must retain useful ways to break with traditional forms because nothing is more certain than that the forms of Law remain when all justice is gone.

– Gowachin aphorism

He was tall for a Dosadi Gowachin, but fat and ungroomed. His feet shuffled when he walked and there was a permanent stoop to his shoulders. A flexing wheezing overcame his chest ventricles when he became excited. He knew this and was aware that those around him knew it. He often used this characteristic as a warning, reminding people that no Dosadi held more power than he, and that power was deadly. All Dosadi knew his name: Broey. And very few misinterpreted the fact that he'd come up through the Sacred Congregation of the Heavenly Veil to his post as chief steward of Control: The Elector. His private army was Dosadi's largest, most efficient, and best armed. Broey's intelligence corps was a thing to invoke fear and admiration. He maintained a fortified suite atop his headquarters building, a structure of stone and plasteel which fronted the main arm of the river in the heart of Chu. Around this core, the twisting walled fortifications of the city stepped outward in concentric rings. The only entrance to Broey's citadel was through a guarded Tube Gate in a subbasement, designated TG One. TG One admitted the select of the select and no others.

In the forenoon, the ledges outside Broey's windows were a roosting place for carrion birds, who occupied a special niche on Dosadi. Since the Lords of the Veil forbade the eating of sentient flesh by sentient, this task devolved upon the birds. Flesh from the people of Chu and even from the Rim carried fewer of the planet's heavy metals. The carrion birds prospered. A flock of them strutted along Broey's ledge, coughing, squawking, defecating, brushing against each other with avian insolence while they watched the outlying streets for signs of food. They also watched the Rim, but it had been temporarily denied to them by a sonabarrier. Bird sounds came through a voder into one of the suite's eight rooms. This was a yellow-green space about ten meters long and six wide occupied by Broey and two Humans.

Broey uttered a mild expletive at the bird noise. The confounded creatures interfered with clear thinking. He shuffled to the window and silenced the voder. In the sudden quiet he looked out at the city's perimeter and the lower ledges of the enclosing cliffs. Another Rim foray had been repulsed out there in the night. Broey had made a personal inspection in a convoy of armored vehicles earlier. The troops liked it that he occasionally shared their dangers. The carrion birds already had cleaned up most of the mess by the time the armored column swept through. The flat back structure of Gowachin, who had no front rib cage, had been easily distinguishable from the white framework which had housed Human organs. Only a few rags of red and green flesh had marked where the birds had abandoned their feast when the sonabarriers herded them away.

When he considered the sonabarriers, Broey's thoughts grew hard and clear. The sonabarriers were one of Gar's damned affectations! *Let the birds finish it.*

But Gar insisted a few bodies be left around to make the point for the Rim survivors that their attacks were hopeless.

The bones by themselves would be just as effective.

Gar was bloody minded.

Broey turned and glanced across the room past his two Human companions. Two of the walls were taken up by charts bearing undulant squiggles in many colors. On a table at the room's center lay another chart with a single red line. The line curved and dipped, ending almost in the middle of the chart. Near this terminus lay a white card and beside it stood a Human male statuette with an enormous erection which was labeled 'Rabble.' It was a subversive, forbidden artifact of Rim origin. The people of the Rim knew where their main strength lay: breed, breed, breed ...

The Humans sat facing each other across the chart. They fitted into the space around them through a special absorption. It was as though they'd been initiated into the secrets of Broey's citadel through an esoteric ritual both forbidding and dangerous.

Broey returned to his chair at the head of the table, sat down, and quietly continued to study his companions. He experienced amusement to feel his fighting claws twitch beneath their finger shields as he looked at the two. Yes – trust them no more than they trusted him. They had their own troops, their own spies – they posed real threat to Broey but often their help was useful. Just as often they were a nuisance.

Quilliam Gar, the Human male who sat with his back to the windows, looked up as Broey resumed his seat. Gar snorted, somehow conveying that he'd been about to silence the voder himself.

Damned carrion birds! But they were useful . . . useful.

The Rim-born were always ambivalent about the birds.

Gar rode his chair as though talking down to ranks of the uninformed. He'd come up through the educational services in the Convocation before joining Broey. Gar was thin with an inner emaciation so common that few on Dosadi gave it any special notice. He had the hunter's face and eyes, carried his eighty-eight years as though they were twice that. Hairline wrinkles crawled down his cheeks. The bas-relief of veins along the backs of his hands and the grey hair betrayed his Rim origins, as did a tendency to short temper. The Labor Pool green of his clothing fooled very few, his face was that well known.

Across from Gar sat his eldest daughter and chief lieutenant, Tria. She'd placed herself there to watch the windows and the cliffs. She'd also been observing the carrion birds, rather enjoying their sounds. It was well to be reminded here of what lay beyond the city's outer gates.

Tria's face held too much brittle sharpness to be considered beautiful by any except an occasional Gowachin looking for an exotic experience or a Warren laborer hoping to use her as a step out of peonage. She often disconcerted her companions by a wide-eyed, cynical stare. She did this with an aristocratic sureness which commanded attention. Tria had developed the gesture for just this purpose. Today, she wore the orange with black trim of Special Services, but without a brassard to indicate the branch. She knew that this led many to believe her Broey's personal toy, which was true but not in the way the cynical supposed. Tria understood her special value: she possessed a remarkable ability to interpret the vagaries of the DemoPol.

Indicating the red line on the chart in front of her, Tria said, 'She has to be the one. How can you doubt it?' And she wondered why Broey continued to worry at the obvious.

'Keila Jedrik,' Broey said. And again: 'Keila Jedrik.'

Gar squinted at his daughter.

'Why would she include herself among the fifty who . . .'

'She sends us a message,' Broey said. 'I hear it clearly now.' He seemed pleased by his own thoughts.

Gar read something else in the Gowachin's manner.

'I hope you're not having her killed.'

'I'm not as quick to anger as are you Humans,' Broey said.

'The usual surveillance?' Gar asked.

'I haven't decided. You know, don't you, that she lives a rather celibate life? Is it that she doesn't enjoy the males of your species?'

'More likely they don't enjoy her,' Tria said.

'Interesting. Your breeding habits are so peculiar.'

Tria shot a measuring stare at Broey. She wondered why the Gowachin had chosen to wear black today. It was a robe-like garment cut at a sharp angle from shoulders to waist, clearing his ventricles. The ventricles revolted her and Broey knew this. The very thought of them pressing against her ... She cleared her throat. Broey seldom wore black; it was the happy color of priestly celebrants. He wore it, though, with a remoteness which suggested that thoughts passed through his mind which no other person could experience.

The exchange between Broey and Tria worried Gar. He could not help but feel the oddity that each of them tried to present a threatening view of events by withholding some data and coloring other data.

'What if she runs out to the Rim?' Gar asked.

Broey shook his head.

'Let her go. She's not one to stay on the Rim.'

'Perhaps we should have her picked up,' Gar said.

Broey stared at him, then:

'I've gained the distinct impression that you've some private plan in mind. Are you prepared to share it?'

'I've no idea what you ...'

'Enough!' Broey shouted. His ventricles wheezed as he inhaled.

Gar held himself very quiet.

Broey leaned toward him, noting that this exchange amused Tria.

'It's too soon to make decisions we cannot change! This is a time for ambiguity.'

Irritated by his own display of anger, Broey arose and hurried into his adjoining office, where he locked the door. It was obvious that those two had no more idea than he where Jedrik had gone to ground. But it was still his game. She couldn't hide forever. Seated once more in his office, he called Security.

'Has Bahrank returned?'

A senior Gowachin officer hurried into the screen's view, looked up.

'Not yet.'

'What precautions to learn where he delivers his cargo?'

'We know his entry gate. It'll be simple to track him.'

'I don't want Gar's people to know what you're doing.'

'Understood.'

'That other matter?'

'Pcharky may have been the last one. He could be dead, too. The killers were thorough.'

'Keep searching.'

Broey put down a sense of disquiet. Some very un-Dosadi things were happening in Chu . . . and on the Rim. He felt that things occurred which his spies could not uncover. Presently, he returned to the more pressing matter.

'Bahrank is not to be interfered with until afterward.'

'Understood.'

'Pick him up well clear of his delivery point and bring him to your section. I will interview him personally.'

'Sir, his addiction to . . .'

'I know the hold she has on him. I'm counting on it.'

'We've not yet secured any of that substance, sir, although we're still trying.'

'I want success, not excuses. Who's in charge of that?'

'Kidge, sir. He's very efficient in this . . .'

'Is Kidge available?'

'One moment, sir. I'll put him on.'

Kidge had a phlegmatic Gowachin face and rumbling voice.

'Do you want a status report, sir?'

'Yes.'

'My Rim contacts believe the addictive substance is derived from a plant called "tibac." We have no prior record of such a plant, but the outer Rabble has been cultivating it lately. According to my contacts, it's extremely addictive to Humans, even more so to us.'

'No record? What's its origin? Do they say?'

'I talked personally to a Human who'd recently returned from upriver where the outer Rabble reportedly has extensive plantations of this "tibac." I promised my informant a place in the Warrens if he provides me with a complete report on the stuff and a kilo packet of it. This informant says the cultivators believe tibac has religious significance. I didn't see any point in exploring that.'

'When do you expect him to deliver?'

'By nightfall at the latest.'

Broey held his silence for a moment. *Religious significance.* More than likely the plant came from beyond the God Wall then, as Kidge implied. But why? What were *they* doing?

'Do you have new instructions?' Kidge asked.

'Get that substance up to me as soon as you can.'

Kidge fidgeted. He obviously had another question, but was unwilling to ask it. Broey glared at him.

'Yes? What is it?'

'Don't you want the substance tested first?'

It was a baffling question. Had Kidge withheld vital information about the dangers of this tibac? One never knew from what quarter an attack might come. But Kidge was held in his own special bondage. He knew what could happen to him if he failed Broey. And Jedrik had handled this stuff. But why had Kidge asked this question? Faced with such unknowns, Broey tended to withdraw into himself, eyes veiled by the nictating membrane while he weighed the possibilities. Presently, he stirred, looked at Kidge in the screen.

'If there's enough of it, feed some to volunteers – both Human and Gowachin. Get the rest of it up to me immediately, even while you're testing, but in a sealed container.'

'Sir, there are rumors about this stuff. It'll be difficult getting real volunteers.'

'You'll think of something.'

Broey broke the connection, returned to the outer room to make his political peace with Gar and Tria. He was not ready to blunt that pair . . . not yet.

They were sitting just as he'd left them. Tria was speaking:

'. . . the highest probability and I have to go on that.'

Gar merely nodded.

Broey seated himself, nodded to Tria, who continued as though there'd been no hiatus.

'Clearly, Jedrik's a genius. And her Loyalty Index! That has to be false, contrived. And look at her decisions: one questionable decision in four years. One!'

Gar moved a finger along the red line on the chart. It was a curiously sensuous gesture, as though he were stroking flesh.

Broey gave him a verbal prod.

'Yes, Gar, what is it?'

'I was just wondering if Jedrik could be another . . .'

His glance darted ceilingward, back to the chart. They all understood his allusion to intruders from beyond the God Wall.

Broey looked at Gar as though awakening from an interrupted thought. What'd that fool Gar mean by raising such a question at this juncture? The required responses were so obvious.

'I agree with Tria's analysis,' Broey said. 'As to your question . . .' He gave a Human shrug. 'Jedrik reveals some of the classic requirements, but ...' Again, that shrug. 'This is still the world God gave us.'

Colored as they were by his years in the Sacred Congregation, Broey's words took on an unctuous overtone, but in this room the message was strictly secular.

'The others have been such disappointments,' Gar said. 'Especially Havvy.' He moved the statuette to a more central position on the chart.

'We failed because we were too eager,' Tria said, her voice snappish. 'Poor timing.'

Gar scratched his chin with his thumb. Tria sometimes disturbed him by that accusatory tone she took toward their failures. He said:

'But ... if she turns out to be one of *them* and we haven't allowed for it ...'

'We'll look through that gate when we come to it,' Broey said. '*If* we come to it. Even another failure could have its uses. The food factories will give us a substantial increase at the next harvest. That means we can postpone the more troublesome political decisions which have been bothering us.'

Broey let this thought hang between them while he set himself to identifying the lines of activity revealed by what had happened in this room today. Yes, the Humans betrayed unmistakable signs that they behaved according to a secret plan. Things were going well, then: they'd attempt to supersede him soon ... and fail.

A door behind Tria opened. A fat Human female entered. Her body bulbed in green coveralls and her round face appeared to float in a halo of yellow hair.

Her cheeks betrayed the telltale lividity of *dacon* addiction. She spoke subserviently to Gar.

'You told me to interrupt if ...'

'Yes, yes.'

Gar waved to indicate she could speak freely. The gesture's significance did not escape Broey. Another part of their set piece.

'We've located Havvy but Jedrik's not with him.'

Gar nodded, addressed Broey:

'Whether Jedrik's an agent or another puppet, this whole thing smells of something *they* have set in motion.'

Once more, his gaze darted ceilingward.

'I will act on that assumption,' Tria said. She pushed her chair back, arose. 'I'm going into the Warrens.'

Broey looked up at her. Again, he felt his talons twitch beneath their sheaths. He said:

'Don't interfere with them.'

Gar forced his gaze away from the Gowachin while his mind raced. Often, the Gowachin were difficult to read, but Broey had been obvious just then: he was confident that he could locate Jedrik and he didn't care who knew it. That could be very dangerous.

Tria had seen it, too, of course, but she made no comment, merely turned and followed the fat woman out of the room.

Gar arose like a folding ruler being opened to its limit. 'I'd best be getting along. There are many matters requiring my personal attention.'

'We depend on you for a great deal,' Broey said.

He was not yet ready to release Gar, however. Let Tria get well on her way. Best to keep those two apart for a spell. He said:

'Before you go, Gar. Several things still bother me. Why was Jedrik so precipitate? And why destroy her records? What was it that we were not supposed to see?'

'Perhaps it was an attempt to confuse us,' Gar said, quoting Tria. 'One thing's sure: it wasn't just an angry gesture.'

'There must be a clue somewhere,' Broey said.

'Would you have us risk an interrogation of Havvy?'

'Of course not!'

Gar showed no sign that he recognized Broey's anger. He said:

'Despite what you and Tria say, I don't think we can afford another mistake at this time. Havvy was ... well ...'

'If you recall,' Broey said, 'Havvy was not one of Tria's mistakes. She went along with us under protest. I wish now we'd listened to her.' He waved a hand idly in dismissal. 'Go see to your important affairs.' He watched Gar leave.

Yes, on the basis of the Human's behavior it was reasonable to assume he knew nothing as yet about this *infiltrator* Bahrank was bringing through the gates. Gar would've concealed such valuable information, would not have dared raise the issue of a God Wall intrusion ... Or would he? Broey nodded to himself. This must be handled with great delicacy.

We will now explore the particular imprint which various governments make upon the individual. First, be sure you recognize the primary governing force. For example, take a careful look at Human history. Humans have been known to submit to many constraints: to rule by Autarchs, by Plutarchs, by the power seekers of the many Republics, by Oligarchs, by tyrant Majorities and Minorities, by the hidden suasion of Polls, by profound instincts and shallow juvenilities. And always, the governing force as we wish you now to understand this concept was whatever the individual believed had control over his immediate survival. Survival sets the pattern of imprint. During much of Human history (and the pattern is similar with most sentient species), Corporation presidents held more survival in their casual remarks than did the figurehead officials. We of the ConSentiency cannot forget this as we keep watch on the Multiworld Corporations. We dare not even forget it of ourselves. Where you work for your own survival, this dominates your imprint, this dominates what you believe.

– *Instruction Manual*
Bureau of Sabotage

Never do what your enemy wants you to do, McKie reminded himself.

In this moment, Aritch was the enemy, having placed the binding oath of Legum upon an agent of BuSab, having demanded information to which he had no right. The old Gowachin's behavior was consistent with the demands of his own legal system, but it immediately magnified the area of conflict by an enormous factor. McKie chose a minimal response.

'I'm here because Tandaloor is the heart of the Gowachin Federation.'

Aritch, who'd been sitting with his eyes closed to emphasize the formal client-Legum relationship, opened his eyes to glare at McKie.

'I remind you *once* that I am your client.'

Signs indicating a dangerous new tension in the Wreave servant were increasing, but McKie was forced to concentrate his attention on Aritch.

'You name your *self* client. Very well. The client must answer truthfully such questions as the Legum asks when the legal issues demand it.'

Aritch continued to glare at McKie, latent fire in the yellow eyes. Now, the battle was truly joined.

McKie sensed how fragile was the relationship upon which his survival depended. The Gowachin, signatories to the great ConSentiency Pact binding the species of the known universe, were legally subject to certain BuSab intrusions. But Aritch had placed them on another footing. If the Gowachin Federation disagreed with McKie/Agent, they could take him into the Courtarena as a Legum who had wronged a client. With the entire Gowachin Bar arrayed against him, McKie did not doubt which Legum would *taste the knife*. His one hope lay in avoiding immediate litigation. That was, after all, the real basis of Gowachin Law.

Moving a step closer to specifics, McKie said:

'My Bureau has uncovered a matter of embarrassment to the Gowachin Federation.'

Aritch blinked twice.

'As we suspected.'

McKie shook his head. They didn't *suspect*, they knew. He counted on this: that the Gowachin understood why he'd answered their summons. If any Sentiency under the Pact could understand his position, it had to be the Gowachin. BuSab reflected Gowachin philosophy. Centuries had passed since the great convulsion out of which BuSab had originated, but the ConSentiency had never been allowed to forget that birth. It was taught to the young of every species.

'Once, long ago, a tyrannical majority captured the government. They said they would make all individuals equal. They meant they would not let any individual be better than another at doing anything. Excellence was to be suppressed or concealed. The tyrants made their government act with great speed "in the name of the people." They removed delays and red tape wherever found. There was little deliberation. Unaware that they acted out of an unconscious compulsion to prevent all change, the tyrants tried to enforce a grey sameness upon every population.

'Thus the powerful governmental machine blundered along at increasingly reckless speed. It took commerce and all the important elements of society with it. Laws were thought of and passed within hours. Every society came to be twisted into a suicidal pattern. People became unprepared for those changes which the universe demands. They were unable to change.

'It was the time of *brittle money*, "appropriated in the morning and gone by nightfall," as you learned earlier. In their passion for sameness, the tyrants made themselves more and more powerful. All others grew correspondingly weaker and weaker. New bureaus and directorates, odd ministries, leaped into existence for the most improbable purposes. These became the citadels of a new aristocracy, rulers who kept the giant wheel of government careening along, spreading destruction, violence, and chaos wherever they touched.

'In those desperate times, a handful of people (the Five Ears, their makeup and species never revealed) created the Sabotage Corps to slow that runaway wheel of government. The original corps was bloody, violent, and cruel. Gradually, the original efforts were replaced by more subtle methods. The governmental wheel slowed, became more manageable. Deliberation returned.

'Over the generations, that original Corps became a Bureau, the Bureau of Sabotage, with its present Ministerial powers, preferring diversion to violence, but ready for violence when the need arises.'

They were words from McKie's own teens, generators of a concept modified by his experiences in the Bureau. Now, he was aware that this directorate composed of all the known sentient species was headed into its own entropic corridors. Someday, the Bureau would dissolve or be dissolved, but the universe still needed them. The old imprints remained, the old futile seeking after absolutes of sameness. It was the ancient conflict between what the individual saw as personal needs for immediate survival and what the totality required if *any* were to survive. And now it was the Gowachin versus the Con-Sentiency, and Aritch was the champion of his people.

McKie studied the High Magister carefully, sensitive to the unrelieved tensions in the Wreave attendant. Would there be violence in this room? It was a question which remained unanswered as McKie spoke.

'You have observed that I am in a difficult position. I do not enjoy the embarrassment of revered teachers and friends, nor of their compatriots. Yet, evidence has been seen ...'

He let his voice trail off. Gowachin disliked dangling implications.

Aritch's claws slid from the sheaths of his webbed fingers.

'Your client wishes to hear of this evidence.'

Before speaking, McKie rested his hand on the latch of the box in his lap.

'Many people from two species have disappeared. Two species: Gowachin and Human. Singly, these were small matters, but these disappearances have been going on for a long time – perhaps twelve or fifteen generations by the old Human reckoning. Taken together, these disappearances are massive. We've learned that there's a planet called Dosadi where these people were taken. Such evidence as we have has been examined carefully. It all leads to the Gowachin Federation.'

Aritch's fingers splayed, a sign of acute embarrassment. Whether assumed or real, McKie could not tell.

'Does your Bureau accuse the Gowachin?'

'You know the function of my Bureau. We do not yet know the location of Dosadi, but we'll find it.'

Aritch remained silent. He knew BuSab had never given up on a problem.

McKie raised the blue box.

'Having thrust this upon me, you've made me guardian of your fate, client. You've no rights to inquire as to my methods. I will not follow *old* law.'

Aritch nodded.

'It was my argument that you'd react thus.'

He raised his right hand.

The rhythmic 'death flexion' swept over the Wreave and her fighting mandibles darted from her facial slit.

At the first movement from her, McKie whipped open the blue box, snatched out book and knife. He spoke with a firmness his body did not feel:

'If she makes the slightest move toward me, my blood will defile this book.' He placed the knife against his own wrist. 'Does your Servant of the Box know the consequences? The history of the Running Phylum would end. Another Phylum would be presumed to've accepted the Law from its Giver. The name of this Phylum's *last* High Magister would be erased from living thought. Gowachin would eat their own eggs at the merest hint that they had Running Phylum blood in their veins.'

Aritch remained frozen, right hand raised. Then:

'McKie, you are revealed as a sneak. Only by spying on our most sacred rituals could you know this.'

'Did you think me some fearful, pliable dolt, client? I am a true Legum. A Legum does not have to sneak to learn the Law. When you admitted me to your Bar you opened every door.'

Slowly, muscles quivering, Aritch turned and spoke to the Wreave: 'Ceylang?'

She had difficulty speaking while her poison-tipped fighting mandibles remained extruded.

'Your command?'

'Observe this Human well. Study him. You will meet again.'

'I obey.'

'You may go, but remember my words.'

'I remember.'

McKie, knowing the death dance could not remain uncompleted, stopped her.

'Ceylang!'

Slowly, reluctantly, she looked at him.

'*Do* observe me well, Ceylang. I am what you hope to be. And I warn you: unless you shed your Wreave skin you will never be a Legum.' He nodded in dismissal. 'Now, you may go.'

In a fluid swish of robes she obeyed, but her fighting mandibles remained out, their poison tips glittering. Somewhere in her triad's quarters, McKie knew, there'd be a small feathered pet which would die presently with poison from its mistress burning through its veins. Then the death dance would be ended and she could retract her mandibles. But the hate would remain.

When the door had closed behind the red robe, McKie restored book and knife to the box, returned his attention to Aritch. Now, when McKie spoke, it was really Legum to client without any sophistry, and they both knew it.

'What would tempt the High Magister of the renowned Running Phylum to bring down the Arch of Civilization?'

McKie's tone was conversational, between equals.

Aritch had trouble adjusting to the new status. His thoughts were obvious. If McKie had witnessed a Cleansing Ritual, McKie had to be accepted as a Gowachin. But McKie was not Gowachin. Yet he'd been accepted before the Gowachin Bar ... and if he'd seen that most sacred ritual ...

Presently, Aritch spoke.

'Where did you see the ritual?'

'It was performed by the Phylum which sheltered me on Tandaloor.'

'The Dry Heads?'

'Yes.'

'Did they know you witnessed?'

'They invited me.'

'How did you shed your skin?'

'They scraped me raw and preserved the scrapings.'

Aritch took some time digesting this. The Dry Heads had played their own secret game of Gowachin politics and now the secret was out. He had to consider the implications. What had they hoped to gain? He said:

'You wear no tattoo.'

'I've never made formal application for Dry Heads membership.'

'Why?'

'My primary allegiance is to BuSab.'

'The Dry Heads know this?'

'They encourage it.'

'But what motivated them to ...'

McKie smiled.

Aritch glanced at a veiled alcove at the far end of the sanctum, back to McKie. A likeness to the Frog God?

'It'd take more than that.'

McKie shrugged.

Aritch mused aloud:

'The Dry Heads supported Klodik in his crime when you ...'

'Not crime.'

'I stand corrected. You won Klodik's freedom. And after your victory the Dry Heads invited you to the Cleansing Ritual.'

'A Gowachin in BuSab cannot have divided allegiance.'

'But a Legum serves only the Law!'

'BuSab and Gowachin Law are not in conflict.'

'So the Dry Heads would have us believe.'

'Many Gowachin believe it.'

'But Klodik's case was not a true test.'

Realization swept through McKie: Aritch regretted more than a lost bet. He'd put his money with his hopes. It was time then to redirect this conversation.

'I am your Legum.'

Aritch spoke with resignation.

'You are.'

'Your Legum wishes to hear of the Dosadi problem.'

'A thing is not a problem until it arouses sufficient concern.' Aritch glanced at the box in McKie's lap. 'We're dealing with differences in values, changes in values.'

McKie did not believe for an instant this was the tenor of Gowachin defense, but Aritch's words gave him pause. The Gowachin combined such an odd mixture of respect and disrespect for their Law and all government. At the root lay their unchanging rituals, but above that everything remained as fluid as the seas in which they'd evolved. Constant fluidity was the purpose behind their rituals. You never entered any exchange with Gowachin on a sure-footed basis. They did something different every time ... religiously. It was their nature. *All ground is temporary. Law is made to be changed.* That was their catechism. *To be a Legum is to learn where to place your feet.*

'The Dry Heads did something different,' McKie said.

This plunged Aritch into gloom. His chest ventricles wheezed, indicating he'd speak *from the stomach.*

'The people of the ConSentiency come in so many different forms: Wreaves (a flickering glance doorward), Sobarips, Laclacs, Calebans, PanSpechi, Palenki, Chithers, Taprisiots, Humans, we of the Gowachin ... so many. The unknowns between us defy counting.'

'As well count the drops of water in a sea.'

Aritch grunted, then:

'Some diseases cross the barriers between species.'

McKie stared at him. Was Dosadi a medical experiment station? Impossible! There would be no reason for secrecy then. Secrecy defeated the efforts to study a common problem and the Gowachin knew it.

'You are not studying Gowachin-Human diseases.'

'Some diseases attack the psyche and cannot be traced to any physical agent.'

McKie absorbed this. Although Gowachin definitions were difficult to understand, they permitted no aberrant behavior. Different behavior, yes; aberrant behavior, no. You could challenge the Law, not the ritual. They were compulsive in this regard. They slew the ritual deviant out of hand. It required enormous restraint on their part to deal with another species.

Aritch continued:

'Terrifying psychological abrasions occur when divergent species confront each other and are forced to adapt to new ways. We seek new knowledge in this arena of behavior.'

McKie nodded.

One of his Dry Head teachers had said it: 'No matter how painful, life must adapt or die.'

It was a profound revelation about how Gowachin applied their insight to themselves. Law changed, but it changed on a foundation which could not be permitted the slightest change. 'Else, how do we know where we are or where we have been?' But encounters with other species changed the foundation. Life adapted ... willingly or by force.

McKie spoke with care.

'Psychological experiments with people who've not given their informed consent are still illegal ... even among the Gowachin.'

Aritch would not accept this argument.

'The ConSentiency in all of its parts has accumulated a long history of scientific studies into behavioral and biomedical questions where people are the final test site.'

McKie said:

'And the first issue when you propose such an experiment is "How great is the known risk to the subjects?"'

'But, my dear Legum, *informed consent* implies that the experimenter knows all the risks and can describe them to his test subjects. I ask you: how can that be when the experiment goes beyond what you already know? How can you describe risks which you cannot anticipate?'

'You submit a proposal to many recognized experts in the field,' McKie said. 'They weigh the proposed experiment against whatever value the new knowledge is expected to uncover.'

'Ahh, yes. We submit our proposal to fellow researchers, to people whose *mission*, whose very view of their own personal identity is controlled by the belief that they can improve the lot of all sentient beings. Tell me, Legum: do review boards composed of such people reject many experimental proposals?'

McKie saw the direction of the argument. He spoke with care.

'They don't reject many proposals, that's true. Still, you didn't submit your Dosadi protocol to any outside review. Was that to keep it secret from your own people or from others?'

'We feared the fate of our proposal should it run the gauntlet of other species.'

'Did a Gowachin majority approve your project?'

'No. But we both know that having a majority set the experimental guidelines gives no guarantee against dangerous projects.'

'Dosadi has proved dangerous?'

Aritch remained silent for several deep breaths, then:

'It has proved dangerous.'

'To whom?'

'Everyone.'

It was an unexpected answer, adding a new dimension to Aritch's behavior. McKie decided to back up and test the revelation. 'This Dosadi project was approved by a minority among the Gowachin, a minority willing to accept a dangerous risk-benefit ratio.'

'You have a way of putting these matters, McKie, which presupposes a particular kind of guilt.'

'But a majority in the ConSentiency might agree with my description?'

'Should they ever learn of it.'

'I see. Then, in accepting a dangerous risk, what were the future benefits you expected?'

Aritch emitted a deep grunt.

'Legum, I assure you that we worked only with volunteers and they were limited to Humans and Gowachin.'

'You evade my question.'

'I merely defer an answer.'

'Then tell me, did you explain to your volunteers that they had a choice, that they could say "no"? Did you tell them they might be in danger?'

'We did not try to frighten them ... no.'

'Was any one of you concerned about the free destiny of your *volunteers*?'

'Be careful how you judge us, McKie. There is a fundamental tension between science and freedom – no matter how science is viewed by its practitioners nor how freedom is sensed by those who believe they have it.'

McKie was reminded of a cynical Gowachin aphorism: *To believe that you are free is more important than being free*. He said:

'Your volunteers were lured into this project.'

'Some would see it that way.'

McKie reflected on this. He still did not know precisely what the Gowachin had done on Dosadi, but he was beginning to suspect it'd be something repulsive. He could not keep this fear from his voice.

'We return to the question of expected benefits.'

'Legum, we have long admired your species. You gave us one of our most trusted maxims: *No species is to be trusted farther than it is bound by its own interests.*'

'That's no longer sufficient justification for ...'

'We derive another rule from your maxim: *It is wise to guide your actions in such a way that the interests of other species coincide with the interests of your species.*'

McKie stared at the High Magister. Did this crafty old Gowachin seek a Human-Gowachin conspiracy to suppress evidence of what had been done on Dosadi? Would he dare such a gambit? Just how bad was this Dosadi fiasco?

To test the issue, McKie asked:

'What benefits did you expect? I insist.'

Aritch slumped. His chairdog accommodated to the new position. The High Magister favored McKie with a heavy-lidded stare for a long interval, then:

'You play this game better than we'd ever hoped.'

'With you, Law and Government are always a game. I come from another arena.'

'Your Bureau.'

'And I was trained as a Legum.'

'Are you *my* Legum?'

'The binding oath is binding on me. Have you no faith in ...'

McKie broke off, overwhelmed by a sudden insight. Of course! The Gowachin had known for a long time that Dosadi would become a legal issue.

'Faith in what?' Aritch asked.

'Enough of these evasions!' McKie said. 'You had your Dosadi problem in mind when you trained me. Now, you act as though you distrust your own plan.'

Aritch's lips rippled.

'How strange. You're more Gowachin than a Gowachin.'

'What benefits did you expect when you took this risk?'

Aritch's fingers splayed, stretching the webs.

'We hoped for a quick conclusion and benefits to offset the natural animosities we knew would arise. But it's now more than twenty of your generations, not twelve or fifteen, that we've grasped the firebrand. Benefits? Yes, there are some, but we dare not use them or free Dosadi from bondage lest we raise questions which we cannot answer without revealing our ... source.'

'The benefits!' McKie said. 'Your *Legum* insists.'

Aritch exhaled a shuddering breath through his ventricles.

'Only the Caleban who guards Dosadi knows its location and she is charged to give access without revealing that place. Dosadi is peopled by Humans and Gowachin. They live in a single city they call Chu. Some ninety million people live there, almost equally divided between the two species. Perhaps three times that number live outside Chu, on the Rim, but they're outside the experiment. Chu is approximately eight hundred square kilometers.'

The population density shocked McKie. Millions per kilometer. He had difficulty visualizing it. Even allowing for a city's vertical dimension ... and burrowing ... There'd be some, of course, whose power bought them space, but the others ... Gods! Such a city would be crawling with people, no escaping the pressure of your fellows anywhere except on that unexplained Rim. McKie said as much to Aritch.

The High Magister confirmed this.

'The population density is very great in some areas. The people of Dosadi call these areas "Warrens" for good reason.' 'But why? With an entire planet to live on ...'

'Dosadi is poisonous to our forms of life. All of their food comes from

443

carefully managed hydroponics factories in the heart of Chu. Food factories and the distribution are managed by warlords. Everything is under a quasi-military form of management. But life expectancy in the city is four times that outside.'

'You said the population outside the city was much larger than . . .'

'They breed like mad animals.'

'What possible benefits could you have expected from . . .'

'Under pressure, life reveals its basic elements.'

McKie considered what the High Magister had revealed. The picture of Dosadi was that of a seething mass. Warlords . . . He visualized walls, some people living and working in comparative richness of space while others . . . Gods! It was madness in a universe where some highly habitable planets held no more than a few thousand people. His voice brittle, McKie addressed himself to the High Magister.

'These basic elements, the *benefits* you sought . . . I wish to hear about them.'

Aritch hitched himself forward.

'We have discovered new ways of association, new devices of motivation, unsuspected drives which can impose themselves upon an entire population.'

'I require specific and explicit enumeration of these discoveries.'

'Presently, Legum . . . presently.'

Why did Aritch delay? Were the so-called benefits insignificant beside the repulsive horror of such an experiment? McKie ventured another tack.

'You say this planet is poisonous. Why not remove the inhabitants a few at a time, subject them to memory erasure if you must, and feed them out into the ConSentiency as new . . .'

'We dare not! First, the inhabitants have developed an immunity to erasure, a by-product of those poisons which do get into their diet. Second, given what they have become on Dosadi . . . How can I explain this to you?'

'Why don't the people just leave Dosadi? I presume you deny them jumpdoors, but rockets and other mechanical . . .'

'We will not permit them to leave. Our Caleban encloses Dosadi in what she calls a "tempokinetic barrier" which our test subjects cannot penetrate.'

'Why?'

'We will destroy the entire planet and everything on it rather than loose this population upon the ConSentiency.'

444

'What are the people of Dosadi that you'd even contemplate such a thing?'

Aritch shuddered.

'We have created a monster.'

Every government is run by liars and nothing they say should be
believed.
                                    – *Attributed to an ancient Human journalist*

As she hurried across the roof of the adjoining parking spire at mid-
afternoon of her final day as a Liaitor, Jedrik couldn't clear her mind of
the awareness that she was about to shed another mark of rank. Stacked
in the building beneath her, each one suspended by its roof grapples on
the conveyor track, were the vehicles of the power merchants and their
minions. The machines varied from the giant *jaigers* heavy with armor
and weapons and redundant engine systems, of the ruling few, down to
the tiny black skitters assigned to such as herself. Ex-minion Jedrik knew
she was about to take a final ride in the machine which had released her
from the morning and evening crush on the underground walkways.

She had timed her departure with care. The ones who rode in the
jaigers would not have reassigned her *skitter* and its driver. That driver,
Havvy, required her special attentions in this last ride, this narrow time
slot which she had set aside for dealing with him.

Jedrik sensed events rushing at their own terrible pace now. Just that
morning she had loosed death against fifty Humans. Now, the avalanche
gathered power.

The parking spire's roof pavement had been poorly repaired after the
recent explosive destruction of three Rim guerrillas. Her feet adjusted to
the rough paving as she hurried across the open area to the drop chute.
At the chute, she paused and glanced westward through Chu's enclosing
cliffs. The sun, already nearing its late afternoon line on the cliffs, was a
golden glow beyond the God Wall's milky barrier. To her newly sensitized
fears, that was not a sun but a malignant eye which peered down at her.

By now, the rotofiles in her office would've been ignited by the clumsy
intrusion of the LP toads. There'd be a delay while they reported this,
while it was bucked up through the hierarchy to a level where somebody
dared make an important decision.

Jedrik fought against letting her thoughts fall into trembling shadows.
After the rotofiles, other data would accumulate. The Elector's people

would grow increasingly suspicious. But that was part of her plan, a layer with many layers.

Abruptly, she stepped into the chute, dropped to her parking level, stared across the catwalks at her *skitter* dangling among the others. Havvy sat on the sloping hood, his shoulders in their characteristic slouch. Good. He behaved as expected. A certain finesse was called for now, but she expected no real trouble from anyone as shallow and transparent as Havvy. Still, she kept her right hand in the pocket where she'd secreted a small but adequate weapon. Nothing could be allowed to stop her now. She had selected and trained lieutenants, but none of them quite matched her capabilities. The military force which had been prepared for this moment needed Jedrik for that extra edge which could pluck victory from the days ahead of them.

For now, I must float like a leaf above the hurricane.

Havvy was reading a book, one of those pseudodeep things he regularly affected, a book which she knew he would not understand. As he read, he pulled at his lower lip with thumb and forefinger, the very picture of a deep intellectual involvement with important ideas. But it was only a picture. He gave no sign that he heard Jedrik hurrying toward him. A light breeze flicked the pages and he held them with one finger. She could not yet see the title, but assumed this book would be on the contraband list as was much of his reading. That was about the peak of Havvy's risk taking, not great but imbued with a certain false glamor. Another picture.

She could see him quite distinctly now in readable detail. He should have looked up by now but still sat absorbed in his book. Havvy possessed large brown eyes which he obviously believed he employed with deceptive innocence. The real innocence went far beyond his shallow attempts at deception. Jedrik's imagination easily played the scene should one of Broey's people confront Havvy in this pose.

'A contraband book?' Havvy would ask, playing his brown eyes for all their worthless innocence. 'I didn't think there were any more of those around. Thought you'd burned them all. Fellow handed it to me on the street when I asked what he was reading.'

And the Elector's spy would conceal a sneer while asking, 'Didn't you question such a gift?'

Should it come to that, things would grow progressively stickier for Havvy along the paths he could not anticipate. His *innocent* brown eyes would deceive one of the Elector's people no more than they deceived her. In a view of this, she read other messages in the fact that Havvy had

447

produced her key to the God Wall – this Jorj X. McKie. Havvy had come to her with his heavy-handed conspiratorial manner:

'The Rim wants to send in a new agent. We thought you might . . .'

And every datum he'd divulged about this oddity, every question he'd answered with his transparent candor, had increased her tension, surprise, and elation.

Jedrik thought upon these matters as she approached Havvy.

He sensed her presence, looked up. Recognition and something unexpected – a watchfulness half-shielded – came over him. He closed his book.

'You're early.'

'As I said I'd be.'

This new manner in Havvy set her nerves on edge, raised old doubts. No course remained for her except attack.

'Only toads don't break routine,' she said.

Havvy's gaze darted left, right, returned to her face. He hadn't expected this. It was a bit more open risk than Havvy relished. The Elector had spy devices everywhere. Havvy's reaction told her what she wanted to know, however. She gestured to the *skitter*.

'Let's go.'

He pocketed his book, slid down, and opened her door. His actions were a bit too brisk. The button tab on one of his green-striped sleeves caught a door handle. He freed himself with an embarrassed flurry.

Jedrik slipped into the passenger harness. Havvy slammed the door a touch too hard. Nervous. Good. He took his place at the power bar to her left, kept his profile to her when he spoke.

'Where?'

'Head for the apartment.'

A slight hesitation, then he activated the grapple tracks. The skitter jerked into motion, danced sideways, and slid smoothly down the diveway to the street.

As they emerged from the parking spire's enclosing shadows, even before the grapple released and Havvy activated the skitter's own power, Jedrik firmed her decision not to look back. The Liaitor building had become part of her past, a pile of grey-green stones hemmed by other tall structures with, here and there, gaps to the cliffs and the river's arms. That part of her life she now excised. Best it were done cleanly. Her mind must be clear for what came next. What came next was war.

It wasn't often that a warrior force lifted itself out of Dosadi's masses to seek its place in the power structure. And the force she had groomed would strike fear into millions. It was the fears of only a few people that concerned her now, though, and the first of these was Havvy.

He drove with his usual competence, not overly proficient but adequate. His knuckles were white on the steering arms, however. It was still the Havvy she knew moving those muscles, not one of the evil identities who could play their tricks in Dosadi flesh. That was Havvy's usefulness to her and his failure. He was Dosadi-flawed, corrupted. That could not be permitted with McKie.

Havvy appeared to have enough good sense to fear her. Jedrik allowed this emotion to ferment in him while she studied the passing scene. There was little traffic and all of that was armored. The occasional tube access with its sense of weapons in the shadows and eyes behind the guard slits – all seemed normal. It was too soon for the hue and cry after an errant Senior Liaitor.

They went through the first walled checkpoint without delay. The guards were efficiently casual, a glance at the skitter and the identification brassards of the occupants. It was all routine.

The danger with routines, she told herself, was that they very soon became boring. Boredom dulled the senses. That was a boredom which she and her aides constantly guarded against among their warriors. This new force on Dosadi would create many shocks.

As Havvy took them up the normal ring route through the walls, the streets became wide, more open. There were garden plantings in the open here, poisonous but beautiful. Leaves were purple in the shadows. Barren dirt beneath the bushes glittered with corrosive droplets, one of Dosadi's little ways of protecting territory. Dosadi taught many things to those willing to learn.

Jedrik turned, studied Havvy, the way he appeared to concentrate on his driving with an air of stored-up energy. That was about as far as Havvy's learning went. He seemed to know some of his own deficiencies, must realize that many wondered how he held a driver's job, even for the middle echelons, when the Warrens were jammed with people violently avaricious for any step upward. Obviously, Havvy carried valuable secrets which he sold on a hidden market. She had to nudge that hidden market now. Her act must appear faintly clumsy, as though events of this day had confused her.

'Can we be overheard?' she asked.

That made no difference to her plans, but it was the kind of clumsiness which Havvy would misinterpret in precisely the way she now required.

'I've disarmed the transceiver the way I did before,' he said. 'It'll look like a simple-breakdown if anyone checks.'

To no one but you, she thought.

449

But it was the level of infantile response she'd come to expect from Havvy. She picked up his gambit, probing with real curiosity.

'You expected that we'd require privacy today?'

He almost shot a startled look at her, caught himself, then:

'Oh, no! It was a precaution. I have more information to sell you.'

'But you *gave* me the information about McKie.'

'That was to demonstrate my value.'

Oh, Havvy! Why do you try?

'You have unexpected qualities,' she said, and marked that he did not even detect the first level of her irony. 'What's this information you wish to sell?'

'It concerns this McKie.'

'Indeed?'

'What's it worth to you?'

'Am I your only market, Havvy?'

His shoulder muscles bunched as his grip grew even tighter on the steering arms. The tensions in his voice were remarkably easy to read.

'Sold in the right place my information could guarantee maybe five years of easy living – no worries about food or good housing or anything.'

'Why aren't you selling it in such a place?'

'I didn't say I *could* sell it. There are buyers and then there are buyers.'

'And then there are the ones who just take?'

There was no need for him to answer and it was just as well. A barrier dropped in front of the skitter, forcing Havvy to a quick stop. For just an instant, fear gripped her and she felt her reflexes prevent any bodily betrayal of the emotion. Then she saw that it was a routine stop while repair supplies were trundled across the roadway ahead of them.

Jedrik peered out the window on her right. The interminable repair and strengthening of the city's fortifications was going on at the next lower level. Memory told her this was the eighth layer of city protection on the southwest. The noise of pounding rock hammers filled the street. Grey dust lay everywhere, clouds of it drifting. She smelled burnt flint and that bitter metallic undertone which you never quite escaped any-where in Chu, the smell of the poison death which Dosadi ladled out to its inhabitants. She closed her mouth and took shallow breaths, noted absently that the labor crew was all Warren, all Human, and about a third of them women. None of the women appeared older than fifteen. They already had that hard alertness about the eyes which the Warren-born never lost.

A young male strawboss went by trailing a male assistant, an older man with bent shoulders and straggly grey hair. The older man walked with slow deliberation and the young strawboss seemed impatient with him, waving the assistant to keep up. The important subtleties of the relationship thus revealed were entirely lost on Havvy, she noted. The strawboss, as he passed one of the female laborers, looked her up and down with interest. The worker noted his attention and exerted herself with the hammer. The strawboss said something to his assistant, who went over and spoke to the young female. She smiled and glanced at the strawboss, nodded. The strawboss and assistant walked on without looking back. The obvious arrangement for later assignation would have gone without Jedrik's conscious notice except that the young female strongly resembled a woman she'd once known ... dead now as were so many of her early companions.

A bell began to ring and the barrier lifted.

Havvy drove on, glancing once at the strawboss as they passed him. The glance was not returned, telling Jedrik that the strawboss had assessed the skitter's occupants much earlier.

Jedrick picked up the conversation with Havvy where they'd left it.

'What makes you think you could get more from me than from someone else?'

'Not more ... It's just that there's less risk with you.'

The truth was in his voice, that innocent instrument which told so much about Havvy. She shook her head.

'You want me to take the risk of selling higher up?'

After a long pause, Havvy said:

'You know a safer way for me to operate?'

'I'd have to use you somewhere along the line for verification.'

'But I'd be under your protection then.'

'Why should I protect you when you're no longer of value?'

'What makes you think this is all the information I can get?'

Jedrik allowed herself a sigh, wondered why she continued this empty game.

'We might both run into a taker, Havvy.'

Havvy didn't respond. Surely, he'd considered this in his foolish game plan.

They passed a squat brown building on the left. Their street curved upward around the building and passed through a teeming square at the next higher level. Between two taller buildings on the right, she glimpsed a stretch of a river channel, then it was more buildings which enclosed them like the cliffs of Chu, growing taller as the skitter climbed.

As she'd known, Havvy couldn't endure her silence.

'What're you going to do?' he asked.

'I'll pay one year of such protection as I can offer.'

'But this is . . .'

'Take it or leave it.'

He heard the finality but, being Havvy, couldn't give up. It was his one redeeming feature.

'Couldn't we even discuss a . . .'

'We won't discuss anything! If you won't sell at my price, then perhaps I should become a taker.'

'That's not like you!'

'How little you know. I can buy informants of your caliber far cheaper.'

'You're a hard person.'

Out of compassion, she ventured a tiny lesson. 'That's how to survive. But I think we should forget this now. Your information is probably something I already know, or something useless.'

'It's worth a lot more than you offered.'

'So you say, but I know you, Havvy. You're not one to take big risks. Little risks sometimes, big risks never. Your information couldn't be of any great value to me.'

'If you only knew.'

'I'm no longer interested, Havvy.'

'Oh, that's great! You bargain with me and then pull out after I've . . .'

'I was *not* bargaining!' Wasn't the fool capable of anything?

'But you . . .'

'Havvy! Hear me with care. You're a little tad who's stumbled onto something you believe is important. It's actually nothing of great importance, but it's big enough to frighten you. You can't think of a way to sell this information without putting your neck in peril. That's why you came to me. You presume to have me act as your agent. You presume too much.'

Anger closed his mind to any value in her words.

'I take risks!'

She didn't even try to keep amusement from her voice. 'Yes, Havvy, but never where you think. So here's a risk for you right out in the open. Tell me your valuable information. No strings. Let me judge. If I think it's worth more than I've already offered I'll pay more. If I already have this information or it's otherwise useless, you get nothing.'

'The advantage is all on your side!'

'Where it belongs.'

Jedrik studied Havvy's shoulders, the set of his head, the rippling of muscles under stretched fabric as he drove. He was supposed to be pure Labor Pool and didn't even know that silence was the guardian of the

LP: *Learning silence, you learn what to hear.* The LP seldom volunteered anything. And here was Havvy, so far from that and other LP traditions that he might never have experienced the Warren. *Had* never experienced it until he was too old to learn. Yet he talked of friends on the Rim, acted as though he had his own conspiratorial cell. He held a job for which he was barely competent. And everything he did revealed his belief that all of these things would not tell someone of Jedrik's caliber the essential facts about him.

Unless his were a marvelously practiced act.

She did not believe such a marvel, but there was a cautionary element in recognizing the remote possibility. This and the obvious flaws in Havvy had kept her from using him as a key to the God Wall.

They were passing the Elector's headquarters now. She turned and glanced at the stone escarpment. Her thoughts were a thorn thicket. Every assumption she made about Havvy required a peculiar protective reflex. A non-Dosadi reflex. She noted workers streaming down the steps toward the tube entrance of the Elector's building. Her problem with Havvy carried an odd similarity to the problem she knew Broey would encounter when it came to deciding about an ex-Liaitor named Keila Jedrik. She had studied Broey's decisions with a concentrated precision which had tested the limits of her abilities. Doing this, she had changed basic things about herself, had become oddly non-Dosadi. They would no longer find Keila Jedrik in the DemoPol. No more than they'd find Havvy or this McKie there. But if she could do this ...

Pedestrian traffic in this region of extreme caution had slowed Havvy to a crawl. More of the Elector's workers were coming up from the Tube Gate One exit, a throng of them as though released on urgent business. She wondered if any of her fifty flowed in that throng.

I must not allow my thoughts to wander.

To float like an *aware* leaf was one thing, but she dared not let herself enter the hurricane ... not yet. She focused once more on the silent, angry Havvy.

'Tell me, Havvy, did you ever kill a person?'

His shoulders stiffened.

'Why do you ask such a question?'

She stared at his profile for an adequate time, obviously reflecting on this same question.

'I presumed you'd answer. I understand now that you will not answer. This is not the first time I've made that mistake.'

Again, Havvy missed the lesson.

'Do you ask many people that question?'

'That doesn't concern you now.'

She concealed a profound sadness.

Havvy hadn't the wit to read even the most blatant of the surface indicators. He compounded the useless.

'You can't justify such an intrusion into my . . .'

'Be still, little man! Have you learned nothing? Death is often the only means of evoking an appropriate answer.'

Havvy saw this only as an utterly unscrupulous response as she'd known he would. When he shot a probing stare at her, she lifted an eyebrow in a cynical shrug. Havvy continued to divide his attention between the street and her face, apprehensive, fearful. His driving degenerated, became actively dangerous.

'Watch what you're doing, you fool!'

He turned more of his attention to the street, presuming this the greater danger.

The next time he glanced at her, she smiled, knowing Havvy would be unable to detect any lethal change in this gesture. He already wondered if she would attack, but guessed she wouldn't do it while he was driving. He doubted, though, and his doubts made him even more transparent. Havvy was no marvel. One thing certain about him: he came from beyond the God Wall, from the lands of 'X,' from the place of McKie. Whether he worked for the Elector was immaterial. In fact, it grew increasingly doubtful that Broey would employ such a dangerous, a *flawed* tool. No pretense at foolhardy ignorance of Dosadi's basic survival lessons could be this perfect. The pretender would not survive. Only the truly ignorant could have survived to Havvy's age, allowed to go on living as a curiosity, a possible source of interesting data . . . *interesting* data, not necessarily useful.

Having left resolution of the Havvy Problem to the ultimate moment, wringing every last bit of usefulness from him, she knew her course clearly. Whoever protected Havvy, her questions placed the precisely modulated pressure upon them and left her options open.

'What is your valued information?' she asked.

Sensing now that he bought life with every response, Havvy pulled the skitter to the curb at a windowless building wall, stopped, and stared at her.

She waited.

'McKie . . .' He swallowed. 'McKie comes from beyond the God Wall.'

She allowed laughter to convulse her and it went deeper than she'd anticipated. For an instant, she was helpless with it and this sobered her. Not even Havvy could be permitted such an advantage.

Havvy was angry.

'What's funny?'

'You are. Did you imagine for even a second that I wouldn't recognize someone alien to Dosadi? Little man, how *have* you survived?'

This time, he read her correctly. It threw him back on his only remaining resource and it even answered her question.

'Don't underestimate my value.'

Yes, of course: the unknown value of 'X.' And there was a latent threat in his tone which she'd never heard there before. Could Havvy call on protectors from beyond the God Wall? That didn't seem possible, given his circumstances, but it had to be considered. It wouldn't do to approach her larger problem from a narrow viewpoint. People who could enclose an entire planet in an impenetrable barrier would have other capabilities she had not even imagined. Some of these creatures came and went at will, as though Dosadi were merely a casual stopping point. And the travelers from 'X' could change their bodies; that was the single terrible fact which must never be forgotten; that was what had led her ancestors to breed for a Keila Jedrik.

Such considerations always left her feeling almost helpless, shaken by the ultimate unknowns which lay in her path. Was Havvy still Havvy? Her trusted senses answered: yes. Havvy was a spy, a diversion, an amusement. And he was something else which she could not fathom. It was maddening. She could read every nuance of his reactions, yet questions remained. How could you ever understand these creatures from beyond the Veil of Heaven? They were transparent to Dosadi eyes, but that transparency itself confused one.

On the other hand, how could the people of 'X' hope to understand (and thus anticipate) a Keila Jedrik? Every evidence of her senses told her that Havvy saw only a surface Jedrik which she wanted him to see. His spying eyes reported what she wanted them to report. But the enormous interests at stake here dictated a brand of caution beyond anything she'd ever before attempted. The fact that she saw this arena of explosive repercussions, however, armed her with grim satisfaction. The idea that a Dosadi *puppet* might rebel against 'X' and fully understand the nature of such rebellion, surely that idea lay beyond their capabilities. They were overconfident while she was filled with wariness. She saw no way of hiding her movements from the people beyond the God Wall as she hid from her fellow Dosadis. 'X' had ways of spying that no one completely evaded. They would know about the two Keila Jedriks. She counted on only one thing: that they could not see her deepest thoughts, that they'd read only that surface which she revealed to them.

Jedrik maintained a steady gaze at Havvy while these considerations flowed through her mind. Not by the slightest act did she betray what went on in her mind. That, after all, was Dosadi's greatest gift to its survivors.

'Your information is valueless,' she said.

He was accusatory. 'You already knew!'

What did he hope to catch with such a gambit? Not for the first time, she asked herself whether Havvy might represent the best that 'X' could produce? Would they knowingly send their dolts here? It hardly seemed possible. But how could Havvy's childish incompetence command such tools of power as the God Wall implied? Were the people of 'X' the decadent descendants of greater beings?

Even though his own survival demanded it, Havvy would not remain silent.

'If you didn't already know about McKie ... then you ... you don't believe me!'

This was too much. Even for Havvy it was too much and she told herself: *despite the unknown powers of 'X,' he will have to die. He muddies the water. Such incompetence cannot be permitted to breed.*

It would have to be done without passion, not like a Gowachin male weeding his own tads, but with a kind of clinical decisiveness which 'X' could not misunderstand.

For now, she had arranged that Havvy take her to a particular place. He still had a role to perform. Later, with discreet attention to the necessary misdirections, she would do what had to be done. Then the next part of her plan could be assayed.

All persons act from beliefs they are conditioned not to question, from a set of deeply seated prejudices. Therefore, whoever presumes to judge must be asked: 'How are you affronted?' And this judge must begin there to question inwardly as well as outwardly.

– 'The Question' from Ritual of the Courtarena Guide to
Servants of the Box

'One might suspect you of trying to speak under water,' McKie accused.

He still sat opposite Aritch in the High Magister's sanctus, and this near-insult was only one indicator marking the changed atmosphere between them. The sun had dropped closer to the horizon and its *spiritual ring* no longer outlined Aritch's head. The two of them were being more direct now, if not more candid, having explored individual capacities and found where profitable discourse might be directed.

The High Magister flexed his thigh tendons.

Knowing these people from long and close observation, McKie realized the old Gowachin was in pain from prolonged inactivity. That was an advantage to be exploited. McKie held up his left hand, enumerated on his fingers:

'You say the original volunteers on Dosadi submitted to memory erasure, but many of their descendants are immune to such erasure. The present population knows nothing about our ConSentient Universe.'

'As far as the present Dosadi population comprehends, they are the only people on the only inhabited planet in existence.'

McKie found this hard to believe. He held up a third finger.

Aritch stared with distaste at the displayed hand. *There were no webs between the alien fingers!*

McKie said, 'And you tell me that a DemoPol backed up by certain religious injunctions is the primary tool of government there?'

'An original condition of our experiment,' Aritch said.

It was not a comprehensive answer, McKie observed. Original conditions invariably changed. McKie decided to come back to this after the High Magister had submitted to more muscle pain.

'Do the Dosadi know the nature of the Caleban barrier which encloses them?'

'They've tried rocket probes, primitive electromagnetic projections. They understand that those energies they can produce will not penetrate their "God Wall."'

'Is that what they call the barrier?'

'That or "The Heavenly Veil." To some degree, these labels measure their attitude toward the barrier.'

'The DemoPol can serve many governmental forms,' McKie said. 'What's the basic form of their government?'

Aritch considered this, then:

'The form varies. They've employed some eighty different governmental forms.'

Another nonresponsive answer. Aritch did not like to face the fact that their experiment had assumed warlord trappings. McKie thought about the DemoPol. In the hands of adepts and with a population responsive to the software probes by which the computer data was assembled, the DemoPol represented an ultimate tool for manipulation of a populace. The ConSentiency outlawed its use as an assault on individual rights and freedoms. The Gowachin had broken this prohibition, yes, but a more interesting datum was surfacing: Dosadi had employed some eighty different governmental forms without rejecting the DemoPol. That implied frequent changes.

'How often have they changed their form of government?'

'You can divide the numbers as easily as I,' Aritch said. His tone was petulant.

McKie nodded. One thing had become quite clear.

'Dosadi's masses know about the DemoPol, but you won't let them remove it!'

Aritch had not expected this insight. He responded with revealing sharpness which was amplified by his muscle pains.

'How did you learn that?'

'You told me.'

'I?'

'Quite plainly. Such frequent change is responsive to an irritant – the DemoPol. They change the forms of government, but leave the irritant. Obviously, they cannot remove the irritant. That was clearly part of your experiment – to raise a population resistant to the DemoPol.'

'A resistant population, yes,' Aritch said. He shuddered.

'You've fractured ConSentient Law in many places,' McKie said.

'Does my Legum presume to judge me?'

'No. But if I speak with a certain bitterness, please recall that I am a Human. I embrace a profound sympathy for the Gowachin, but I remain Human.'

'Ahhhh, yes. We must not forget the long Human association with DemoPols.'

'We survive by selecting the best decision makers,' McKie said.

'And a DemoPol elevates mediocrity.'

'Has that happened on Dosadi?'

'No.'

'But you wanted them to try many different governmental forms?'

The High Magister shrugged, remained silent.

'We Humans found that the DemoPoi does profound damage to social relationships. It destroys preselected portions of a society.'

'And what could we hope to learn by *damaging* our Dosadi society?'

'Have we arrived back at the question of expected benefits?'

Aritch stretched his aching muscles.

'You are persistent, McKie. I will say that.'

McKie shook his head sadly.

'The DemoPol was always held up to us as the ultimate equalizer, a source of decision-making miracles. It was supposed to produce a growing body of knowledge about what a society really needed. It was thought to produce justice in all cases despite any odds.'

Aritch was irritated. He leaned forward, wincing at the pain of his old muscles.

'One might make the same accusations about the *Law* as practiced everywhere except on Gowachin worlds!'

McKie suppressed a sharp response. Gowachin training had forced him to question assumptions about the uses of law in the ConSentiency, about the inherent rightness of any aristocracy, any power bloc whether majority or minority. It was a BuSab axiom that all power blocs tended toward aristocratic forms, that the descendants of decision makers dominated the power niches. BuSab never employed offspring of their agents.

Aritch repeated himself, a thing Gowachin seldom did.

'Law is delusion and fakery, McKie, everywhere except on the Gowachin worlds! You give your law a theological aura. You ignore the ways it injures your societies. Just as with the DemoPol, you hold up your law as the unvarying source of justice. When you ...'

'BuSab has ...'

'No! If something's wrong in your societies, what do you do? You create new law. You never think to remove law or disarm the law. You make more law! You create more legal professionals. We Gowachin sneer at you! We always strive to reduce the number of laws, the number of Legums. A Legum's first duty is to avoid litigation. When we create new Legums, we always have specific problems in mind. We anticipate the ways that laws damage our society.'

It was the opening McKie wanted.

'Why are you training a Wreave?'

Belatedly, Aritch realized he had been goaded into revealing more than he had wanted.

'You are good, McKie. Very good.'

'Why?' McKie persisted. 'Why a Wreave?'

'You will learn why in time.'

McKie saw that Aritch would not expand on this answer, but there were other matters to consider now. It was clear that the Gowachin had trained him for a specific problem: Dosadi. To train a Wreave as Legum, they'd have an equally important problem in mind . . . perhaps the same problem. A basic difference in the approach to law, species differentiated, had surfaced, however, and this could not be ignored. McKie well understood the Gowachin disdain for all legal systems, including their own. They were educated from infancy to distrust any community of professionals, especially legal professionals. A Legum could only tread their religious path when he completely shared that distrust.

Do I share that distrust?

He thought he did. It came naturally to a BuSab agent. But most of the ConSentiency still held its professional communities in high esteem, ignoring the nature of the intense competition for new achievements which invariably overcame such communities: *new* achievements, *new* recognition. But the *new* could be illusion in such communities because they always maintained a peer review system nicely balanced with peer pressures for ego rewards.

'Professional always means power,' the Gowachin said.

The Gowachin distrusted power in all of its forms. They gave with one hand and took with the other. Legums faced death whenever they used the Law. To make *new* law in the Gowachin Courtarena was to bring about the elegant dissolution of old law with a concomitant application of justice.

Not for the first time, McKie wondered about the unknown problems a High Magister must face. It would have to be a delicate existence indeed. McKie almost formed a question about this, thought better of it. He shifted instead to the unknowns about Dosadi. *God Wall? Heavenly Veil?*

'Does Dosadi often accept a religious oligarchy?'

'As an outward form, yes. They currently are presided over by a supreme Elector, a Gowachin by the name of Broey.'

'Have Humans ever held power equal to Broey's?'

'Frequently.'

It was one of the most responsive exchanges that McKie had achieved with Aritch. Although he knew he was following the High Magister's purpose, McKie decided to explore this.

'Tell me about Dosadi's *social* forms.'

'They are the forms of a military organization under constant attack or threat of attack. They form certain cabals, certain power enclaves whose influences shift.'

'Is there much violence?'

'It is a world of constant violence.'

McKie absorbed this. Warlords. Military society. He knew he had just lifted a corner of the real issue which had brought the Gowachin to the point of obliterating Dosadi. It was an area to be approached with extreme caution. McKie chose a flanking approach.

'Aside from the military forms, what are the dominant occupations? How do they perceive guilt and innocence? What are their forms of punishment, of absolution? How do they . . .'

'You do not confuse me, McKie. Consider, Legum: there are better ways to answer such questions.'

Brought up short by the Magister's chiding tone, McKie fell into silence. He glanced out the oval window, realizing he'd been thrown onto the defensive with exquisite ease. McKie felt the nerves tingling along his spine. Danger! Tandaloor's golden sun had moved perceptibly closer to the horizon. That horizon was a blue-green line made hazy by kilometer after kilometer of hair trees whose slender female fronds waved and hunted in the air. Presently, McKie turned back to Aritch.

Better ways to answer such questions.

It was obvious where the High Magister's thoughts trended. The experimenters would, of course, have ways of watching their experiment. They could also influence their experiment, but it was obvious there were limits to this influence. A population resistant to outside influences? The implied complications of this Dosadi problem daunted McKie. Oh, the circular dance the Gowachin always performed!

Better ways.

Aritch cleared his ventricle passages with a harsh exhalation, then:

'Anticipating the possibility that others would censure us, we gave our test subjects the Primary.'

Devils incarnate! The Gowachin set such store on their damned Primary!

Of course all people were created unequal and had to find their own level!

McKie knew he had no choice but to plunge into the maelstrom.

'Did you also anticipate that you'd be charged with violating sentient rights on a massive scale?'

Aritch shocked him by a brief puffing of jowls, the Gowachin shrug.

McKie allowed himself a warning smile.

'I remind the High Magister that *he* raised the issue of the Primary.'

'Truth is truth.'

McKie shook his head sharply, not caring what this revealed. The High Magister couldn't possibly have that low an estimation of his Legum's reasoning abilities. *Truth indeed!*

'I'll give you truth: the ConSentiency has laws on this subject to which the Gowachin are signatories!'

Even as the words fell from his lips, McKie realized this was precisely where Aritch had wanted him to go. *They've learned something from Dosadi! Something crucial!*

Aritch massaged the painful muscles of his thighs, said, 'I remind *you*, Legum, that we peopled Dosadi with volunteers.'

'Their descendants volunteered for nothing!'

'Ancestors always volunteer their descendants – for better or for worse. Sentient rights? Informed consent? The Con- Sentiency has been so busy building law upon law, creating its great illusion of rights, that you've almost lost sight of the Primary's guiding principle: to develop our capacities. People who are never challenged never develop *survival* strengths!'

Despite the perils, McKie knew he had to press for the answer to his original question: *benefits.*

'What've you learned from your monster?'

'You'll soon have a complete answer to that question.'

Again, the implication that he could actually watch Dosadi. But first it'd be well to disabuse Aritch of any suspicion that McKie was unaware of the root implications. The issue had to be met head on.

'You're not going to implicate me.'

'Implicate you?' There was no mistaking Aritch's surprise.

'No matter how you use what you've learned from Dosadi, you'll be suspected of evil intent. Whatever anyone learns from . . .'

'Oh, that. New data gives one power.'

'And *you* do not confuse *me*, Aritch. In the history of every species there are many examples of places where new data has been gravely abused.'

Aritch accepted this without question. They both knew the background. The Gowachin distrusted power in all of its forms, yet they used power with consummate skill. The trend of McKie's thoughts lay heavily in this room now. To destroy Dosadi would be to hide whatever the Gowachin had learned there. McKie, a non-Gowachin, therefore, would learn these things, would share the mantle of suspicion should it be cast. The historical abuses of new data occurred between the time that a few people learned the important thing and the time when that important thing became general knowledge. To the Gowachin and to BuSab it was the 'Data Gap,' a source of constant danger.

'We would not try to hide *what* we've learned,' Aritch said, 'only how we learned it.'

'And it's just an academic question whether you destroy an entire planet and every person on it!'

'Ahh, yes: academic. What you don't know, McKie, is that one of our test subjects on Dosadi has initiated, all on her own, a course of events which will destroy Dosadi very quickly whether we act or not. You'll learn all about this very soon when, like the good Legum we know you to be, you go there to experience this monster with your own flesh.'

In the name of all that we together hold holy I promise three things to the sacred congregation of people who are subject to my rule. In the first place, that the holy religion which we mutually espouse shall always preserve their freedom under my auspices; secondly, that I will temper every form of rapacity and inequity which may inflict itself upon us all; and thirdly, that I will command swift mercy in all judgments, that to me and to you the gracious Lord may extend His Recognition.

– The Oath of Power,
Dosadi Sacred Congregation papers

Broey arose from prayer, groped behind him for the chair, and sank into it. Enclosed darkness surrounded him. The room was a shielded bubble attached to the bottom of his Graluz. Around the room's thick walls was the warm water which protected his females and their eggs. Access to the bubble was through a floor hatch and a twisting flooded passage from the Graluz. Pressure in the bubble excluded the water, but the space around Broey smelled reassuringly of the Graluz. This helped reinforce the mood he now required.

Presently, the God spoke to him. Elation filled Broey. God spoke to him, only to him. Words hissed within his head. Scenes impinged themselves upon his vision centers.

Yes! Yes! I keep the DemoPol!

God was reassured and reflected that reassurance.

Today, God showed him a ritual Broey had never seen before. The ritual was only for Gowachin. The ritual was called Laupuk. Broey saw the ritual in all of its gory details, felt the *rightness* of it as though his very cells accepted it.

Responsibility, expiation – these were the lessons of Laupuk. God approved when Broey expressed understanding.

They communicated by words which Broey expressed silently in his thoughts, but there were other thoughts which God could not perceive. Just as God no doubt held thoughts which were not communicated to Broey. God used people, people used God. Divine intervention with cynical overtones. Broey had learned the Elector's role through a long and painful apprenticeship.

I am your servant, God.

As God admonished, Broey kept the secret of his private communion. It suited his purpose to obey, as it obviously suited God's purpose. There were times, though, when Broey wanted to shout it:

'*You fools! I speak with the voice of God!*'

Other Electors had made that mistake. They'd soon fallen from the seat of power. Broey, drawing on several lifetimes of assembled experiences, knew he must keep this power if he ever were to escape from Dosadi.

Anyway, the fools did his bidding (and therefore God's) without divine admonition. All was well. One presented a selection of thoughts to God ... being careful always where and when one reviewed private thoughts. There were times when Broey felt God within him when there'd been no prayer, no preparations here in the blackness of this bubble room. God might peer out of Broey's eyes at any time – softly, quietly – examining His world and its works through mortal senses.

'I guard My servant well.'

The warmth of reassurance which flowed through Broey then was like the warmth of the Graluz when he'd still been a tad clinging to his mother's back. It was a warmth and sense of safety which Broey tempered with a deep awareness of that other Graluz time: a giant grey-green adult male Gowachin ravening through the water, devouring those tads not swift enough, alert enough to escape.

I was one of the swift.

Memory of that plunging, frantic flight in the Graluz had taught Broey how to behave with God.

In his bubble room's darkness, Broey shuddered. Yes, the ways of God were cruel. Thus armed, a servant of God could be equally cruel, could surmount the fact that he knew what it was to be both Human and Gowachin. He need only be the pure servant of God. This thought he shared.

Beware, McKie. God has told me whence you come. I know your intentions. Hold fast to the narrow path, McKie. You risk my displeasure.

Behavioral engineering in all of its manifestations always degenerates into merciless manipulation. It reduces all (manipulators and manipulated alike) to a deadly 'mass effect.' The central assumption, that manipulation of individual personalities can achieve uniform behavioral responses, has been exposed as a lie by many species but never with more telling effect than by the Gowachin on Dosadi. Here, they showed us the 'Walden Fallacy' in ultimate foolishness, explaining: 'Given any species which reproduces by genetic mingling such that every individual is a unique specimen, all attempts to impose a decision matrix based on assumed uniform behavior will prove lethal.'

– *The Dosadi Papers,*
BuSab reference

McKie walked through the jumpdoor and, as Aritch's aides had said, found himself on sand at just past Dosadi's midmorning. He looked up, seeking his first real-time view of the God Wall, wanting to share the Dosadi feeling of that enclosure. All he saw was a thin haze, faintly silver, disappointing. The sun circle was more defined than he'd expected and he knew from the holographic reproductions he'd seen that a few of the third-magnitude stars would be filtered out at night. What else he'd expected, McKie could not say, but somehow this milky veil was not it. Too thin, perhaps. It appeared insubstantial, too weak for the power it represented.

The visible sun disk reminded him of another urgent necessity, but he postponed that necessity while he examined his surroundings.

A tall white rock? Yes, there it was on his left.

They'd warned him to wait beside that rock, that he'd be relatively safe there. Under no circumstances was he to wander from this contact point.

'We can tell you about the dangers of Dosadi, but words are not enough. Besides, the place is always developing new threats.'

Things he'd learned in the briefing sessions over the past weeks reinforced the warning. The rock, twice as tall as a Human, stood only a few paces away, massive and forbidding. He went over and leaned against it. Sand grated beneath his feet. He smelled unfamiliar perfumes and acridities. The sun-warmed surface of the rock gave its energy to his flesh through the thin green coveralls they'd insisted he wear.

McKie longed for his armored clothing and its devices to amplify muscles, but such things were not permitted. Only a reduced version of his toolkit had been allowed and that reluctantly, a compromise. McKie had explained that the contents would be destroyed if anyone other than himself tried to pry into the kit's secrets. Still, they'd warned him never to open the kit in the presence of a Dosadi native.

'The most dangerous thing you can do is to underestimate any of the Dosadi.'

McKie, staring around him, saw no Dosadi.

Far off across a dusty landscape dotted with yellow bushes and brown rocks, he identified the hazy spires of Chu rising out of its river canyon. Heat waves dizzied the air above the low scrub, giving the city a magical appearance.

McKie found it difficult to think about Chu in the context of what he'd learned during the crash course the Gowachin had given him. Those magical fluting spires reached heavenward from a muck where 'you can buy anything ... anything at all.'

Aritch's aides had sewn a large sum in Dosadi currency into the seams of his clothing but, at the same time, had forced him to digest hair-raising admonitions about 'any show of unprotected wealth.'

The jumpdoor attendants had recapitulated many of the most urgent warnings, adding:

'You may have a wait of several hours. We're not sure. Just stay close to that rock where you'll be relatively safe. We've made protective arrangements which should work. Don't eat or drink anything until you get into the city. You'll be faintly sick with the diet change for a few days, but your body should adjust.'

'*Should* adjust?'

'Give it time.'

He'd asked about specific dangers to which he should be most alert.

'Stay clear of any Dosadi natives except your contacts. Above all, don't even appear to threaten anyone.'

'What if I get drowsy and take a nap?'

They'd considered this, then:

'You know, that might be the safest thing to do. Anyone who'd dare to nap out there would have to be damned well protected. There'd be some risk, of course, but there always is on Dosadi. But they'd be awfully leery of anyone casual enough to nap out there.'

Again, McKie glanced around.

Sharp whistlings and a low rasp like sand across wood came from behind the tall rock. Quietly, McKie worked his way around to where he could see the sources of these noises. The whistling was a yellow lizard almost the color of the bushes beneath which it crouched. The rasp came from a direction which commanded the lizard's attention. Its source appeared to be a small hole beneath another bush. McKie thought he detected in the lizard only a faint curiosity about himself. Something about that hole and the noise issuing from it demanded a great deal of concentrated attention.

Something stirred in the hole's blackness.

The lizard crouched, continued to whistle.

An ebony creature about the size of McKie's fist emerged from the hole, darted forward, saw the lizard. Wings shot from the newcomer's sides and it leaped upward, but it was too late. With a swiftness which astonished McKie, the lizard shot forward, balled itself around its prey. A slit opened in the lizard's stomach, surrounded the ebony creature. With a final rasping, the black thing vanished into the lizard.

All this time, the lizard continued to whistle. Still whistling it crawled into the hole from which its prey had come.

'Things are seldom what they seem to be on Dosadi,' McKie's teachers had said.

He wondered now what he had just seen.

The whistling had stopped.

The lizard and its prey reminded McKie that, as he'd been warned, there had not been time to prepare him for every new detail on Dosadi. He crouched now and, once more, studied his immediate surroundings.

Tiny jumping things like insects inhabited the narrow line of shade at the base of the white rock. Green (blossoms?) opened and closed on the stems of the yellow bushes. The ground all around appeared to be a basic sand and clay, but when he peered at it closely he saw veins of blue and red discoloration. He turned his back on the distant city, saw far away mountains: a purple graph line against silver sky. Rain had cut an arroyo in that direction. He saw touches of darker green reaching from the depths. The air tasted bitter.

Once again, McKie made a sweeping study of his surroundings, seeking any sign of threat. Nothing he could identify. He palmed an instrument from his toolkit, stood casually and stretched while he turned toward Chu. When he stole a glance at the instrument, it revealed a sonabarrier at the city. Absently scratching himself to conceal the motion, he returned the instrument to his kit. Birds floated in the silver sky above the sonabarrier.

468

Why a sonabarrier? he wondered.

It would stop wild creatures, but not people. His teachers had said the sonabarrier excluded pests, vermin. The explanation did not satisfy McKie.

Things are seldom what they seem.

Despite the God Wall, that sun was hot. McKie sought the shady side of the rock. Seated there, he glanced at the small white disk affixed to the green lapel at his left breast: OP40331-D404. It was standard Galach script, the lingua franca of the ConSentiency.

'They speak only Galach on Dosadi. They may detect an accent in your speech, but they won't question it.'

Aritch's people had explained that this badge identified McKie as an open-contract worker, one with slightly above average skills in a particular field, but still part of the Labor Pool and subject to assignment outside his skill.

'This puts you three hierarchical steps from the Rim,' they'd said.

It'd been his own choice. The bottom of the social system always had its own communications channels flowing with information based on accurate data, instinct, dream stuff, and what was fed from the top with deliberate intent. Whatever happened here on Dosadi, its nature would be revealed in the unconscious processes of the Labor Pool. In the Labor Pool, he could tap that revealing flow.

'I'll be a weaver,' he'd said, explaining that it was a hobby he'd enjoyed for many years.

The choice had amused his teachers. McKie had been unable to penetrate the reason for their amusement.

'It is of no importance right now. One choice is as good as another.'

They'd insisted he concentrate on what he'd been doing at the time, learning the signal mannerisms of Dosadi. Indeed, it'd been a hectic period on Tandaloor after Aritch's insistence (with the most reasonable of arguments) that the best way for his Legum to proceed was to go personally to Dosadi. In retrospect, the arguments remained persuasive, but McKie had been surprised. For some reason which he could not now identify, he had expected a less involved *overview* of the experiment, watching through instruments and the spying abilities of the Caleban who guarded the place.

McKie was still not certain how they expected him to pull this hot palip from the cooker, but it was clear they expected it. Aritch had been mysteriously explicit:

'You are Dosadi's best chance for survival and our own best chance for ... understanding.'

They expected their Legum to save Dosadi while exonerating the Gowachin. It was a Legum's task to win for his client, but these had to be the strangest circumstances, with the client retaining the absolute power of destruction over the threatened planet.

On Tandaloor, McKie had been allowed just time for short naps. Even then, his sleep had been restless, part of his mind infernally aware of where he lay: the bedog strange and not quite attuned to his needs, the odd noises beyond the walls – water gurgling somewhere, always water.

When he'd trained there as a Legum, that had been one of his first adjustments: the uncertain rhythms of disturbed water. Gowachin never strayed far from water. The Graluz – that central pool and sanctuary for females, the place where Gowachin raised those tads which survived the ravenous *weeding* by the male parent – the Graluz always remained a central fixation for the Gowachin. As the saying put it:

'If you do not understand the Graluz, you do not understand the Gowachin.'

As such sayings went, it was accurate only up to a point.

But there was always the water, contained water, the nervous slapping of wavelets against walls. The sound conveyed no fixed rhythms, but it was a profound clue to the Gowachin: contained, yet always different.

For all short distances, swimming tubes connected Gowachin facilities. They traversed long distances by jumpdoor or in hissing jetcars which moved on magnetic cushions. The comings and goings of such cars had disturbed McKie's sleep during the period of the crash course on Dosadi. Sometimes, desperately tired, his body demanding rest, he would find himself awakened by voices. And the subtle interference of the other sounds – the cars, the waves – made eavesdropping difficult. Awake in the night, McKie would strain for meaning. He felt like a spy listening for vital clues, seeking every nuance in the casual conversations of people beyond his walls. Frustrated, always frustrated, he had retreated into sleep. And when, as happened occasionally, all sound ceased, this brought him to full alert, heart pounding, wondering what had gone wrong.

And the odors! What memories they brought back to him. Graluz musk, the bitter pressing of exotic seeds, permeated every breath. Fern tree pollen intruded with its undertones of citrus. And the caraeli, tiny, froglike pets, invaded your sleep at every dawning with their exquisite belling arias.

During those earlier days of training on Tandaloor, McKie had felt more than a little lost, hemmed in by threatening strangers, constantly aware of the important matters which rode on his success. But things were different after the interview with Aritch. McKie was now a trained, tested, and proven Legum, not to mention a renowned agent of BuSab. Yet there were times when the mood of those earlier days intruded. Such intrusions annoyed him with their implication that he was being maneuvered into peril against his will, that the Gowachin secretly laughed as they prepared him for some ultimate humiliation. They were not above such a jest. Common assessment of Gowachin by non-Gowachin said the Frog God's people were so ultimately civilized they had come full circle into a form of primitive savagery. Look at the way Gowachin males slaughtered their own newborn tads!

Once, during one of the rare naps Aritch's people permitted him, McKie had awakened to sit up and try to shake off that depressing mood of doom. He told himself true things: that the Gowachin flattered him now, deferred to him, treated him with that quasireligious respect which they paid to all Legums. But there was no evading another truth: the Gowachin had groomed him for their Dosadi problem over a long period of time, and they were being less than candid with him about that long process and its intentions.

There were always unfathomed mysteries when dealing with Gowachin.

When he'd tried returning to sleep that time, it was to encounter disturbing dreams of massed sentient flesh (both pink and green) all naked and quite defenseless before the onslaughts of gigantic Gowachin males.

The dream's message was clear. The Gowachin might very well destroy Dosadi in the way (and for similar reasons) that they winnowed their own tads – searching, endlessly searching, for the strongest and most resilient survivors.

The problem they'd dumped in his lap daunted McKie. If the slightest inkling of Dosadi leaked into common awareness without a concurrent justification, the Gowachin Federation would be hounded unmercifully. The Gowachin had clear and sufficient reason to destroy the evidence – or to let the evidence destroy itself.

Justification.

Where was that to be found? In the elusive benefits which had moved the Gowachin to mount this experiment?

Even if he found that justification, Dosadi would be an upheaval in the ConSentiency. It'd be the subject of high drama. More than twenty generations of Humans and Gowachin surfacing without warning! Their lonely history would titillate countless beings. The limits of language would be explored to wring the last drop of emotive essence from this revelation.

No matter how explained, Gowachin motives would come in for uncounted explorations and suspicions.

Why did they *really* do it? What happened to their original volunteers?

People would look backward into their own ancestry – Human and Gowachin alike. 'Is that what happened to Uncle Elfred?' Gowachin phylum records would be explored. 'Yes! Here are two – gone without record!'

Aritch's people admitted that 'a very small minority' had mounted this project and kept the lid on it. Were they completely sane, this Gowachin cabal?

McKie's short naps were always disturbed by an obsequious Gowachin bowing over his bedog, begging him to return at once to the briefing sessions which prepared him for survival on Dosadi.

Those briefing sessions! The implied prejudices hidden in every one raised more questions than were answered. McKie tried to retain a reasoned attitude, but irritants constantly assailed him.

Why had the Gowachin of Dosadi taken on Human emotional characteristics? Why were Dosadi's Humans aping Gowachin social compacts? Were the Dosadi truly aware of why they changed governmental forms so often?

The bland answer to these frequent questions enraged McKie.

'All will be made clear when you experience Dosadi for yourself.'

He'd finally fallen into a counterirritant patter:

'You don't really know the answer, do you? You're hoping I'll find out for you!'

Some of the data recitals bored McKie. While listening to a Gowachin explain what was known about Rim relationships, he would find himself distracted by people passing in the multisentient access way outside the briefing area.

Once, Ceylang entered and sat at the side of the room, watching him with a hungry silence which rubbed McKie's sensibilities to angry rawness. He'd longed for the blue metal box then, but once the solemn investment had pulled the mantle of Legumic protection around him, the box had been removed to its sacred niche. He'd not see it again unless this issue entered the Courtarena. Ceylang remained an unanswered question among many. Why did that dangerous Wreave female haunt this room without contributing one thing? He suspected they allowed Ceylang to watch him through remote spy devices. Why did she choose that once to come in person? To let him know he was being observed?

It had something to do with whatever had prompted the Gowachin to train a Wreave. They had some future problem which only a Wreave could solve. They were grooming this Wreave as they'd groomed him. Why? What Wreave capabilities attracted the Gowachin? How did this Wreave female differ from other Wreaves? Where were her loyalties? What was the 'Wreave Bet'?

This led McKie into another avenue never sufficiently explored: what Human capabilities had led the Gowachin to him? Dogged persistence? A background in Human law? The essential individualism of the Human?

There were no sure answers to these questions, no more than there were about the Wreave. Her presence continued to fascinate him, however. McKie knew many things about Wreave society not in common awareness outside the Wreave worlds. They were, after all, integral and valued partners in BuSab. In shared tasks, a camaraderie developed which often prompted intimate exchanges of information. Beyond the fact that Wreaves required a breeding triad for reproduction, he knew that Wreaves had never discovered a way to determine in advance which of the Triad would be capable of nursing the offspring. This formed an essential building stone in Wreave society. Periodically, this person from the triad would be exchanged for a like person from another triad. This insured their form of genetic dispersion and, of equal importance, built countless linkages throughout their civilization. With each such linkage went requirements for unquestioning support in times of trouble.

A Wreave in the Bureau had tried to explain this:

'Take, for example, the situation where a Wreave is murdered or, even worse, deprived of essential vanity. The guilty party would be answerable *personally* to millions upon millions of us. Wherever the triad exchange has linked us, we are required to respond intimately to the insult. The closest thing you have to this, as I understand it, is familial responsibility. We have this familial responsibility for vendetta where such affronts occur. You have no idea how difficult it was to release those of us in BuSab from this ... this bondage, this network of responsibility.'

The Gowachin would know this about the Wreaves, McKie thought. Had this characteristic attracted the Gowachin or had they chosen in spite of it, making their decision because of some other Wreave aspect? Would a Wreave Legum continue to share that network of familial responsibility? How could that be? Wreave society could only offend a basic sensibility of the Gowachin. The Frog God's people were even more ... more *exclusive* and individual than Humans. To the Gowachin, family remained a private thing, walled off from strangers in an isolation which was abandoned only when you entered your chosen phylum.

As he waited beside the white rock on Dosadi, McKie reflected on these matters, biding his time, listening. The alien heat, the smells and unfamiliar noises, disturbed him. He'd been told to listen for the sound of an internal combustion engine. Internal combustion! But the Dosadi used such devices outside the city because they were more powerful (although much larger) than the beamed impulse drivers which they used within Chu's walls.

'The fuel is alcohol. Most of the raw materials come from the Rim. It doesn't matter how much poison there is in such fuel. They ferment bushes, trees, ferns ... anything the Rim supplies.'

A sleepy quiet surrounded McKie now. For a long time he'd been girding himself to risk the thing he knew he would have to do once he were alone on Dosadi. He might never again be this alone here, probably not once he was into Chu's Warrens. He knew the futility of trying to contact his Taprisiot monitor. Aritch, telling him the Gowachin knew BuSab had bought 'Taprisiot insurance,' had said:

'Not even a Taprisiot call can penetrate the God Wall.'

In the event of Dosadi's destruction, the Caleban contract ended. McKie's Taprisiot might even have an instant to complete the death record of McKie's memories. Might. That was academic to McKie in his present circumstances. The Calebans owed him a debt. The Whipping Star threat had been as deadly to Calebans as to any other species which had ever used jump-doors. The threat had been real and specific. Users of jump-doors and the Caleban who controlled those jumpdoors had been doomed. 'Fannie Mae' had expressed the debt to McKie in her own peculiar way:

'The owing of me to thee connects to no ending.'

Aritch could have alerted his Dosadi guardian against any attempt by McKie to contact another Caleban. McKie doubted this. Aritch had specified a ban against Taprisiot calls. But all Calebans shared an awareness at some level. If Aritch and company had been lulled into a mistaken assumption about the security of their barrier around Dosadi ...

Carefully, McKie cleared his mind of any thoughts about Taprisiots. This wasn't easy. It required a Sufi concentration upon a particular *void*. There could be no accidental thrust of his mind at the Taprisiot waiting in the safety of Central Central with its endless patience. Everything must be blanked from awareness except a clear projection toward Fannie Mae.

McKie visualized her: the star Thyone. He recalled their long hours of mental give and take. He projected the warmth of emotional attachment, recalling her recent demonstration of 'nodal involvement.'

Presently, he closed his eyes, amplified that internal image which now suffused his mind. He felt his muscles relax. The warm rock against his back, the sand beneath him, faded from awareness. Only the glowing presence of a Caleban remained in his mind.

'Who calls?'

The words touched his auditory centers, but not his ears.

'It's McKie, friend of Fannie Mae. Are you the Caleban of the God Wall?'

'I am the God Wall. Have you come to worship?'

McKie felt his thoughts stumble. Worship? The projection from this Caleban was echoing and portentous, not at all like the probing curiosity he always sensed in Fannie Mae. He fought to regain that first clear image. The inner glow of a Caleban contact returned. He supposed there might be something worshipful in this experience. You were never absolutely certain of a Caleban's meaning.

'It's McKie, friend of Fannie Mae,' he repeated.

The glow within McKie dimmed, then: 'But you occupy a point upon Dosadi's wave.'

That was a familiar kind of communication, one to which McKie could apply previous experience in the hope of a small understanding, an approximation.

'Does the God Wall permit me to contact Fannie Mae?'

Words echoed in his head:

'One Caleban, all Caleban.'

'I wish converse with Fannie Mae.'

'You are not satisfied with your present body?'

McKie felt his body then, the trembling flesh, the zombie-like trance state which went with Caleban or Taprisiot contact. The question had no meaning to him, but the body contact was real and it threatened to break off communication. Slowly, McKie fought back to that tenuous mind-presence.

'I am Jorj X. McKie. Calebans are in my debt.'

'All Calebans know this debt.'

'Then honor your debt.'

He waited, trying not to grow tense.

The glow within his head was replaced by a new presence. It insinuated itself into McKie's awareness with penetrating familiarity – not full mental contact, but rather a playing upon those regions of his brain where sight and sound were interpreted. McKie recognized this new presence.

'Fannie Mae!'

'What does McKie require?'

For a Caleban, it was quite a direct communication. McKie, noting this, responded more directly:

'I require your help.'

'Explain.'

'I may be killed here ... ahh, have an end to my node here on Dosadi.'

'Dosadi's wave,' she corrected him.

'Yes. And if that happens, if I die here, I have friends on Central Central ... on Central Central's wave ... friends there who must learn everything that's in my mind when I die.'

'Only Taprisiot can do this. Dosadi contract forbids Taprisiots.'

'But if Dosadi is destroyed ...'

'Contract promise passes no ending, McKie.'

'You cannot help me?'

'You wish advice from Fannie Mae?'

'Yes.'

'Fannie Mae able to maintain contact with McKie while he occupies Dosadi's wave.'

Constant trance? McKie was shocked.

She caught this.

'No trance. McKie's nexus known to Fannie Mae.'

'I think not. I can't have any distractions here.'

'Bad choice.'

She was petulant.

'Could you provide me with a personal jumpdoor to ...'

'Not with node ending close to ending for Dosadi wave.'

'Fannie Mae, do you know what the Gowachin are doing here on Dosadi? This ...'

'Caleban contract, McKie.'

Her displeasure was clear. You didn't question the honor of a Caleban's word-writ. The Dosadi contract undoubtedly contained specific prohibitions against any revelations of what went on here. McKie was dismayed. He was tempted to leave Dosadi immediately.

Fannie Mae got this message, too.

'McKie can leave now. Soon, McKie cannot leave in his own body/node.'

'Body/node?'

'Answer not permitted.'

Not permitted!

'I thought you were my friend, Fannie Mae!'

Warmth suffused him.

'Fannie Mae possesses friendship for McKie.'

'Then why won't you help me?'

'You wish to leave Dosadi's wave in this instant?'

'No!'

'Then Fannie Mae cannot help.'

Angry, McKie began to break the contact.

Fannie Mae projected sensations of frustration and hurt. 'Why does McKie refuse advice? Fannie Mae wishes . . .'

'I must go. You know I'm in a trance while we're in contact. That's dangerous here. We'll speak another time. I appreciate your wish to help and your new clarity, but . . .'

'Not clarity! Very small hole in understanding but Human keeps no more dimension!'

Obvious unhappiness accompanied this response, but she broke the contact. McKie felt himself awakening, his fingers and toes trembling with cold. Caleban contact had slowed his metabolism to a dangerous low. He opened his eyes.

A strange Gowachin clad in the yellow of an armored vehicle driver stood over him. A tracked machine rumbled and puffed in the background. Blue smoke enveloped it. McKie stared upward in shock.

The Gowachin nodded companionably.

'You are ill?'

We of the Sabotage Bureau remain legalists of a special category. We know that too much law injures a society; it is the same with too little law. One seeks a balance. We are like the balancing force among the Gowachin: without hope of achieving heaven in the society of mortals, we seek the unattainable. Each agent knows his own conscience and why he serves such a master. That is the key to us. We serve a mortal conscience for immortal reasons. We do it without hope of praise or the sureness of success.

– The early writings of Bildoon,
PanSpechi Chief of BuSab

They moved out onto the streets as soon as the afternoon shadows gloomed the depths of the city, Tria and six carefully chosen companions, all of them young Human males. She'd musked herself to key them up and she led them down dim byways where Broey's spies had been eliminated. All of her troop was armored and armed in the fashion of an ordinary sortie team.

There'd been rioting nearby an hour earlier, not sufficiently disruptive to attract large military attention, but a small Gowachin salient had been eliminated from a Human enclave. A sortie team was the kind of thing this Warren could expect after such a specific species adjustment. Tria and her six companions were not likely to suffer attack. None of the rioters wanted a large-scale mopping up in the area.

A kind of hushed, suspenseful waiting pervaded the streets.

They crossed a wet intersection, green and red ichor in the gutters. The smell of the dampness told her that a Graluz had been broached and its waters freed to wash through the streets.

That would attract retaliation. Some Human children were certain to be killed in the days ahead. An old pattern.

The troop crossed the riot area presently, noting the places where bodies had fallen, estimating casualties. All bodies had been removed. Not a scrap remained for the birds.

They emerged from the Warrens soon afterward, passing through a Gowachin-guarded gate, Broey's people. A few blocks along they went through another gate, Human guards, all in Gar's pay. Broey would learn of her presence here soon, Tria knew, but she'd said she was going into the Warrens. She came presently to an alleyway across from a Second Rank building. The windowless grey of the building's lower floors presented a blank face broken only by the lattice armor of the entrance gate. Behind the gate lay a dimly lighted passage. Its deceptively plain walls concealed spy devices and automatic weapons.

Holding back her companions with a hand motion, Tria waited in the dark while she studied the building entrance across from her. The gate was on a simple latch. There was one doorguard in an alcove on the left near the door which was dimly visible beyond the armorwork of the gate. A building defense force stood ready to come at the doorguard's summons or at the summons of those who watched through the spy devices.

Tria's informants said this was Jedrik's bolt hole. Not in the deep Warrens at all. Clever. But Tria had maintained an agent in this building for years, as she kept agents in many buildings. A conventional precaution. Everything depended on timing now. Her agent in the building was poised to eliminate the inner guards at the spy device station. Only the doorguard would remain. Tria waited for the agreed upon moment.

The street around her smelled of sewage: an open reclamation line. Accident? Riot damage? Tria didn't like the feeling of this place. What was Jedrik's game? Were there unknown surprises built into this guarded building? Jedrik must know by now that she was suspected of inciting the riot – and of other matters. But would she feel safe there in her own enclave? People tended to feel safe among their own people. She couldn't have a very large force around her, though. Still, some private plot worked itself through the devious pathways of Jedrik's mind, and Tria had not yet fathomed all of that plot. There were surface indicators enough to risk a confrontation, a parley. It was possible that Jedrik flaunted herself here to attract Tria. The potential in that possibility filled Tria with excitement.

Together, we'd be unbeatable!

Yes, Jedrik fitted the image of a superb agent. With the proper organization around her ...

Once more, Tria glanced left and right. The streets were appropriately empty. She checked the time. Her moment had come. With hand motions, she sent flankers out left and right and another young male probing straight across the street to the gate. When they were in place, she slipped across with her three remaining companions in a triangular shield ahead.

The doorguard was a Human with grey hair and a pale face which glistened yellow in the dim light of the passage. His lids were heavy with a recent dose of his personal drug, which Tria's agent had supplied.

Tria opened the gate, saw that the guard carried a round dead-man switch in his right hand as expected. His grin was gap toothed as he held the switch toward her. She knew he'd recognized her. Much depended now on her agent's accuracy.

'Do you want to die for the frogs?' Tria asked.

He knew about the rioting, the trouble in the streets. And he was Human, with Human loyalties, but he knew she worked for Broey, a Gowachin. The question was precisely calculated to fill him with indecision. Was she a turncoat? He had his Human loyalties and a fanatic's dependence upon this guard post which kept him out of the depths. And there was his personal addiction. All doorguards were addicted to something, but this one took a drug which dulled his senses and made it difficult for him to correlate several lines of thought. He wasn't supposed to use his drug on duty and this troubled him now. There were so many matters to be judged, and Tria had asked the right question. He didn't want to die for the frogs.

She pointed to the dead-man switch, a question.

'It's only a signal relay,' he said. 'No bomb in this one.'

She remained silent, forcing him to focus on his doubts.

The guard swallowed. 'What do you ...'

'Join us or die.'

He peered past her at the others. Things such as this happened frequently in the Warrens, not very often here on the slopes which led up to the heights. The guard was not a one trusted with full knowledge of whom he guarded. He had explicit instructions and a dead-man relay to warn of intruders. Others were charged with making the more subtle distinctions, the real decisions. That was this building's weak point.

'Join who?' he asked.

There was false belligerency in his voice, and she knew she had him then.

'Your own kind.'

This locked his drug-dulled mind onto its primary fears. He knew what he was supposed to do: open his hand. That released the alarm device in the dead-man switch. He could do this of his own volition and it was supposed to deter attackers from killing him. A dead man's hand opened anyway. But he'd been fed with suspicions to increase his doubts. The device in his hand might not be a simple signal transmitter. What if it actually were a bomb? He'd had many long hours to wonder about that.

'We'll treat you well,' Tria said.

She put a companionable arm around his shoulder, letting him get the full effect of her musk while she held out her other hand to show that it carried no weapon. 'Demonstrate to my companion here how you pass that to your relief.'

One of the young males stepped forward.

The guard showed how it was done, explaining slowly as he passed the device. 'It's easy once you get the trick of it.'

When her companion had the thing firmly in hand, she raised her arm from the guard's shoulder, touched his carotid artery with a poisoned needle concealed in a fingernail. The guard had only time to draw one gasping breath, his eyes gaping, before he sank from her embrace.

'I treated him well,' she said.

Her companions grinned. It was the kind of thing you learned to expect from Tria. They dragged the body out of sight into the guard alcove, and the young male with the signal device took his place at the door. The others protected Tria with their bodies as they swept into the building. The whole operation had taken less than two minutes. Everything was working smoothly, as Tria's operations were expected to work.

The lobby and its radiating hallways were empty.

Good.

Her agent in this building deserved a promotion.

They took a stairway rather than trust an elevator. It was only three short flights. The upper hallway also was empty. Tria led the way to the designated door, used the key her agent had supplied. The door opened without a sound and they surged into the room.

Inside, the shades had been pulled, and there was no artificial illumination. Her companions took up their places at the closed door and along both flanking walls. This was the most dangerous moment, something only Tria could handle.

Light came from thin strips where shades did not quite seal a south window. Tria discerned dim shapes of furniture, a bed with an indeterminate blob of darkness on it.

'Jedrik?' A whisper.

Tria's feet touched soft fabric, a sandal.

'Jedrik?'

Her shin touched the bed. She held a weapon ready while she felt for the dark blob. It was only a mound of bedding. She turned.

The bathroom door was closed, but she could make out a thin slot of light at the bottom of the door. She skirted the clothing and sandal on the floor, stood at one side, and motioned a companion to the other side. Thus far they had operated with a minimum of sound.

Gently, she turned the knob, thrust open the door. There was water in a tub and a body face down, one arm hanging flaccidly over the edge, fingers dangling. A dark purple welt was visible behind and beneath the left ear. Tria lifted the head by the hair, stared at the face, lowered it gently to avoid splashing. It was her agent, the one she'd trusted for the intelligence to set up this operation. And the death was characteristic of a Gowachin ritual slaying: that welt under the ear. A Gowachin talon driven in there to silence the victim before drowning? Or had it just been made to appear like a Gowachin slaying?

Tria felt the whole operation falling apart around her, sensed the uneasiness of her companions. She considered calling Gar from where she stood, but a feeling of fear and revulsion came over her. She stepped out into the bedroom before opening her communicator and thumbing the emergency signal.

'Central.' The voice was tense in her ear.

She kept her own voice flat. 'Our agent's dead.'

Silence. She could imagine them centering the locator on her transmission, then: 'There?'

'Yes. She's been murdered.'

Gar's voice came on: 'That can't be. I talked to her less than an hour ago. She ...'

'Drowned in a tub of water,' Tria said. 'She was knocked out first – something sharp driven in under an ear.'

There was silence again while Gar absorbed this data. He would have the same uncertainties as Tria.

She glanced at her companions. They had taken up guard positions facing the doorway to the hall. Yes, if attack came, it would come from there.

The channel to Gar remained open, and now Tria heard a babble of terse orders with only a few words intelligible: ' ... team ... don't let ... time ...' Then, quite clearly: 'They'll pay for this!'

Who will pay? Tria wondered.

She was beginning to make a new assessment of Jedrik.

Gar came back on: 'Are you in immediate danger?'

'I don't know.' It was a reluctant admission.

'Stay right where you are. We'll send help. I've notified Broey.'

So that was the way Gar saw it. Yes. That was most likely the proper way to handle this new development. Jedrik had eluded them. There was no sense in proceeding alone. It would have to be done Broey's way now.

Tria shuddered as she issued the necessary orders to her companions. They prepared to sell themselves dearly if an attack came, but Tria was beginning to doubt there'd be an immediate attack. This was another message from Jedrik. The trouble came when you tried to interpret the message.

The military mentality is a bandit and raider mentality. Thus, all military represents a form of organized banditry where the conventional mores do not prevail. The military is a way of rationalizing murder, rape, looting, and other forms of theft which are always accepted as part of warfare. When denied an outside target, the military mentality always turns against its own civilian population, using identical rationalizations for bandit behavior.

> *– BuSab Manual, Chapter Five:*
> *'The Warlord Syndrome'*

McKie, awakening from the communications trance, realized how he must've appeared to this strange Gowachin towering over him. Of course a Dosadi Gowachin would think him ill. He'd been shivering and mumbling in the trance, perspiration rolling from him. McKie took a deep breath.

'No, I'm not ill.'

'Then it's an addiction?'

Recalling the many substances to which the Dosadi could be addicted, McKie almost used this excuse but thought better of it. This Gowachin might demand some of the addictive substance.

'Not an addiction,' McKie said. He lifted himself to his feet, glanced around. The sun had moved perceptibly toward the horizon behind its streaming veil.

And something new had been added to the landscape – that gigantic tracked vehicle, which stood throbbing and puffing smoke from a vertical stack behind the Gowachin intruder. The Gowachin maintained a steady, intense concentration on McKie, disconcerting in its unwavering directness. McKie had to ask himself: was this some threat, or his Dosadi contact? Aritch's people had said a vehicle would be sent to the contact point, but . . .

'Not ill, not an addiction,' the Gowachin said. 'Is it some strange condition which only Humans have?'

'I *was* ill,' McKie said. 'But I'm recovered. The condition has passed.'

'Do you often have such attacks?'

'I can go years without a recurrence.'

'Years? What causes this . . . condition?'

'I don't know.'

'I . . . ahhhh.' The Gowachin nodded, gestured upward with his chin. 'An affliction of the Gods, perhaps.'

'Perhaps.'

'You were completely vulnerable.'

McKie shrugged. Let the Gowachin make of that what he could.

'You were not vulnerable?' Somehow, this amused the Gowachin, who added: 'I am Bahrank. Perhaps that's the luckiest thing which has ever happened to you.'

Bahrank was the name Aritch's aides had given as McKie's first contact.

'I am McKie.'

'You fit the description, McKie, except for your, ahhh, condition. Do you wish to say more?'

McKie wondered what Bahrank expected. This was supposed to be a simple contact handing him on to more important people. Aritch was certain to have knowledgeable observers on Dosadi, but Bahrank was not supposed to be one of them. The warning about this Gowachin had been specific.

'Bahrank doesn't know about us. Be extremely careful what you reveal to him. It'd be very dangerous to you if he were to learn that you came from beyond the God Veil.'

The jumpdoor aides had reinforced the warning.

'If the Dosadi penetrate your cover, you'll have to return to your pickup point on your own. We very much doubt that you could make it. Understand that we can give you little help once we've put you on Dosadi.'

Bahrank visibly came to a decision, nodding to himself.

'Jedrik expects you.'

That was the other name Aritch's people had provided. 'Your cell leader. She's been told that you're a new infiltrator from the Rim. Jedrik doesn't know your true origin.'

'Who does know?'

'We cannot tell you. If you don't know, then that information cannot be wrested from you. We assure you, though, that Jedrik isn't one of our people.'

McKie didn't like the sound of that warning. ' . . . wrested from you.' As usual, BuSab sent you into the tiger's mouth without a full briefing on the length of the tiger's fangs.

Bahrank gestured toward his tracked vehicle. 'Shall we go?'

McKie glanced at the machine. It was an obvious war device, heavily armored with slits in its metal cab, projectile weapons protruding at odd angles. It looked squat and deadly. Aritch's people had mentioned such things.

'We saw to it that they got only primitive armored vehicles, projectile weapons and relatively unimportant explosives, that sort of thing. They've been quite resourceful in their adaptations of such weaponry, however.'

Once more, Bahrank gestured toward his vehicle, obviously anxious to leave.

McKie was forced to suppress an abrupt feeling of profound anxiety. What had he gotten himself into? He felt that he had awakened to find himself on a terrifying slide into peril, unable to control the least threat. The sensation passed, but it left him shaken. He delayed while he continued to stare at the vehicle. It was about six meters long with heavy tracks, plus other wheels faintly visible within the shadows behind the tracks. It sported a conventional antenna at the rear for tapping the power transmitter in orbit beneath the barrier veil, but there was a secondary system which burned a stinking fuel. The smoke of that fuel filled the air around them with acridity.

'For what do we wait?' Bahrank demanded. He glared at McKie with obvious fear and suspicion.

'We can go now,' McKie said.

Bahrank turned and led the way swiftly, clambering up over the tracks and into a shadowed cab. McKie followed, found the interior a tightly cluttered place full of a bitter, oily smell. There were two hard metal seats with curved backs higher than the head of a seated Human or Gowachin. Bahrank already occupied the seat on the left, working switches and dials. McKie dropped into the other seat. Folding arms locked across his chest and waist to hold him in place; a brace fitted itself to the back of his head. Bahrank threw a switch. The door through which they'd entered closed with a grinding of servomotors and the solid clank of locks.

An ambivalent mood swept over McKie. He had always felt faint agoraphobia in open places such as the area around the rock. But the dim interior of this war machine, with its savage reminders of primitive times, touched an atavistic chord in his psyche and he fought an urge to claw his way outside. This was a trap!

An odd observation helped him overcome the sensation. There was glass over the slits which gave them their view of the outside. Glass. He felt it. Yes, glass. It was common stuff in the ConSentiency – strong yet fragile. He could see that this glass wasn't very thick. The fierce appearance of this machine had to be more show than actuality, then.

Bahrank gave one swift, sweeping glance to their surroundings, moved levers which set the vehicle into lurching motion. It emitted a grinding rumble with an overriding whine.

A track of sorts led from the white rock toward the distant city. It showed the marks of this machine's recent passage, a roadway to follow. Glittering reflections danced from bright rocks along the track. Bahrank appeared very busy with whatever he was doing to guide them toward Chu.

McKie found his own thoughts returning to the briefings he'd received on Tandaloor.

'Once you enter Jedrik's cell you're on your own.'

Yes ... he felt very much alone, his mind a clutter of data which had little relationship to any previous experience. And this planet could die unless he made sense out of that data plus whatever else he might learn here.

Alone, alone ... If Dosadi died there'd be few sentient watchers. The Caleban's tempokinetic barrier would contain most of that final destructive flare. The Caleban would, in fact, feed upon the released energy. That was one of the things he'd learned from Fannie Mae. One consuming blast, a *meal* for a Caleban, and BuSab would be forced to start anew and without the most important piece of physical evidence – Dosadi.

The machine beneath McKie thundered, rocked, and skidded, but always returned to the track which led toward Chu's distant spires.

McKie studied the driver covertly. Bahrank showed uncharacteristic behavior for a Gowachin: more direct, more Human. That was it! His Gowachin instincts had been contaminated by contact with Humans. Aritch was sure to despise that, fear it. Bahrank drove with a casual expertise, using a complex control system. McKie counted eight different levers and arms which the Gowachin employed. Some were actuated by knees, others by his head. His hands reached out while an elbow deflected a lever. The war machine responded.

Bahrank spoke presently without taking his attention from driving.

'We may come under fire on the second ledge. There was quite a police action down there earlier.'

McKie stared at him.

'I thought we had safe passage through.'

'You Rimmers are always pressing.'

McKie peered out the slits: bushes, barren ground, that lonely track they followed.

Bahrank spoke.

'You're older than any Rimmer I ever saw before.'

Aritch's people had warned McKie about this as a basic flaw in his cover, the need to conceal the subtle signs of age.

They'd provided him with some geriatric assistance and an answer to give when challenged. He used that answer now.

'It ages you in a hurry out here.'

'It must.'

McKie felt that something in Bahrank's response eluded him, but dared not pursue this. It was an unproductive exchange. And there was that reference to a 'police action.' McKie knew that the Rim Rabble, excluded from Chu, tried periodic raids, most often fruitless. Barbaric!

'What excuse did you use to come out here?' McKie asked.

Bahrank shot a probing glance at him, raised one webbed hand from the controls to indicate a handle in the roof over his head. The handle's purpose was unknown to McKie, and he feared he had already betrayed too much ignorance. But Bahrank was speaking.

'Officially, I'm scouting this area for any hidden surprises the Rimmers may have stored out here. I often do that. Unofficially, everyone thinks I've a secret pond out here full of fertile females.'

A pond . . . not a Graluz. Again, it was a relatively fruitless exchange with hidden undertones.

McKie stared silently ahead through a slit. Their dusty track made a slow and wide sweep left, abruptly angled down onto a narrow ledge cut from red rock walls. Bahrank put them through a series of swift changes in speed: slow, fast, slow, fast. The red rock walls raced past. McKie peered out and downward on his side. Far below lay jungle verdure and, in the distance, the smoke and spires of Chu – fluted buildings ranked high over dim background cliffs.

The speed changes appeared purposeless to McKie. And the dizzy drop off the cliff on his side filled him with awe. Their narrow ledge hugged the cliff, turning as the cliff turned – now into shadows and now into light. The machine roared and groaned around him. The smell of oil made his stomach heave. And the faraway city seemed little closer than it had from the cliff top, except that it was taller, more mysterious in its smoky obscurity.

'Don't expect any real trouble until we reach the first ledge,' Bahrank said.

McKie glanced at him. First ledge? Yes, that'd be the first elevation outside the city's walls. The gorge within which Chu had been raised came down to river level in broad steps, each one numbered. Chu had been anchored to island hills and flats where the river slowed and split into many arms. And the hills which had resisted the river were almost solid iron ore, as were many of the flanking ledges.

'Glad to get off there,' Bahrank said.

Their narrow ledge had turned at right angles away from the cliff onto a broad ramp which descended into grey-green jungle. The growth enclosed them in abrupt green shadows. McKie, looking out to the side, identified hair fronds and broad leaf ficus, giant spikes of barbed red which he had never before seen. Their track, like the jungle floor, was grey mud. McKie looked from side to side; the growth appeared an almost equal mixture of Terran and Tandaloor, interspersed with many strange plants.

Sunlight made him blink as they raced out of the overhanging plants onto a plain of tall grass which had been trampled, blasted, and burned by recent violence. He saw a pile of wrecked vehicles off to the left, twisted shards of metal with, here and there, a section of track or a wheel aimed at the sky. Some of the wrecks looked similar to the machine in which he now rode.

Bahrank skirted a blast hole at an angle which gave McKie a view into the hole's depths. Torn bodies lay there. Bahrank made no comment, seemed hardly to notice.

Abruptly, McKie saw signs of movement in the jungle, the flitting presence of both Humans and Gowachin. Some carried what appeared to be small weapons – the glint of a metal tube, bandoliers of bulbous white objects around their necks. McKie had not tried to memorize all of Dosadi's weaponry; it was, after all, primitive, but he reminded himself now that primitive weapons had created these scenes of destruction.

Their track plunged again into overhanging growth, leaving the battle-field behind. Deep green shadows enclosed the lurching, rumbling machine. McKie, shaken from side to side against the restraints, carried an odor memory with him: deep, bloody musks and the beginnings of rot. Their shaded avenue made a sharp right turn, emerged onto another ledge slashed by a plunging cut into which Bahrank took them, turning onto another cliff-hugging ledge.

McKie stared across Bahrank through the slits. The city was nearer now. Their rocking descent swept his gaze up and down Chu's towers, which lifted like silvery organ pipes out of the Council Hills. The far cliff was a series of misted steps fading into purple grey. Chu's Warrens lay smokey and hazed all around the fluted towers. And he could make out part of the city's enclosing outer wall. Squat forts dotted the wall's top, offset for enfilading fire. The city within the wall seemed so tall. McKie had not expected it to appear so tall – but that spoke of the population pressures in a way that could not be misunderstood.

Their ledge ended at another battlefield plain strewn with bodies of metal and flesh, the death stink an inescapable vapor. Bahrank spun his vehicle left, right, dodged piles of torn equipment, avoided craters where mounds of flesh lay beneath insect blankets. Ferns and other low growth were beginning to spring upright after the monstrous trampling. Grey and yellow flying creatures sported in the ferntops, uncaring of all that death. Aritch's aides had warned McKie that Dosadi's life existed amidst brutal excesses, but the actuality sickened him. He identified both Gowachin and Human forms among the sprawled corpses. The sleek green skin of a young Gowachin female, orange fertility marks prominent along her arms, especially revolted him. McKie turned sharply away, found Bahrank studying him with tawny mockery in the shining Gowachin eyes. Bahrank spoke as he drove.

'There're informers everywhere, of course, and after this . . .' His head nodded left and right. ' . . . you'll have to move with more caution than you might've anticipated.'

A brittle explosion punctuated his words. Something struck the vehicle's armor on McKie's side. Again they were a target. And again. The clanging of metal against metal came thickly, striking all around them, even on the glass over the view slits.

McKie suppressed his shock. That thin glass did not shatter. He knew about thick shields of tempered glass, but this put a new dimension on what he'd been told about the Dosadi. Quite resourceful, indeed!

Bahrank drove with apparent unconcern.

More explosive attacks came from directly in front of them, flashes of orange in the jungle beyond the plain.

'They're testing,' Bahrank said. He pointed to one of the slits. 'See? They don't even leave a mark on that new glass.'

McKie spoke from the depths of his bitterness.

'Sometimes you wonder what all this proves except that our world runs on distrust.'

'Who trusts?'

Bahrank's words had the sound of a catechism.

McKie said:

'I hope our friends know when to stop testing.'

'They were told we couldn't take more'n eighty millimeter.'

'Didn't they agree to pass us through?'

'Even so, they're expected to try a few shots if just to keep me in good graces with my superiors.'

Once more, Bahrank put them through a series of dazzling speed changes and turns for no apparent reason. McKie lurched against the restraints, felt bruising pain as an elbow hit the side of the cab. An explosion directly behind rocked them up onto the left track. As they bounced, Bahrank spun them left, avoided another blast which would've landed directly on them along their previous path. McKie, his ears ringing from the explosions, felt the machine bounce to a stop, reverse as more explosions erupted ahead. Bahrank spun them to the right, then left, once more charged full speed ahead right into an unbroken wall of jungle. With explosions all around, they crashed through greenery, turned to the right along another shadowed muddy track. McKie had lost all sense of direction, but the attack had ceased.

Bahrank slowed them, took a deep breath through his ventricles.

'I knew they'd try that.'

He sounded both relieved and amused.

McKie, shaken by the brush with death, couldn't find his voice.

Their shadowy track snaked through the jungle for a space, giving McKie time to recover. By then, he didn't know what to say. He couldn't understand Bahrank's amusement, the lack of enduring concern over such violent threat.

Presently, they emerged onto an untouched, sloping plain as smooth and green as a park lawn. It dipped gently downward into a thin screen of growth through which McKie could see a silver-green tracery of river. What caught and held McKie's attention, however, was a windowless, pock-walled grey fortress which lifted from the plain in the middle distance. It towered over the growth screening the river. Buttressed arms reached toward them to enclose a black metal barrier.

'That's our gate,' Bahrank said.

Bahrank turned them left, lined up with the center of the buttressed arms. 'Gate Nine and we're home through the tube,' he said.

McKie nodded. Walls, tubes, and gates: those were the keys to Chu's defenses. They had 'barrier and fortress minds' on Dosadi. This tube would run beneath the river. He tried to place it on the map which Aritch's people had planted in his mind. He was supposed to know the geography of this place, its geology, religions, social patterns, the intimate layout of each island's walled defenses, but he found it hard to locate himself now on that mental map. He leaned forward to the slit, peered upward as the machine began to gather speed, saw the great central spire with its horizontal clock. All the hours of map briefing snicked into place.

'Yes, Gate Nine.'

Bahrank, too busy driving, did not reply.

McKie dropped his gaze to the fortress, stifled a gasp.

The rumbling machine was plunging downslope at a frightening pace, aimed directly toward that black metal barrier. At the last instant, when it seemed they would crash into it, the barrier leaped upward. They shot through into a dimly illuminated tube. The gate thundered closed behind them. Their machine made a racketing sound on metal grating beneath the tracks.

Bahrank slowed them, shifted a lever beside him. The machine lifted onto wheels with an abrupt reduction in noise which made McKie feel that he'd been deafened. The feeling was heightened by the realization that Bahrank had said the same thing to him several times.

'Jedrik says you come from beyond the far mountains. Is that true?'

'Jedrik says it.' He tried to make it sound wry, but it came out almost questioning.

Bahrank was concentrating on a line of thought, however, as he drove them straight down the grating floor of the dim tube.

'There's a rumor that you Rimmers have started a secret settlement back there, that you're trying to build your own city.'

'An interesting rumor.'

'Isn't it, though?'

The single line of overhead lights in the tube left the cab's interior darker than it'd been outside, illuminated by only the faint reflections from instruments and dials. But McKie had the odd sensation that Bahrank saw him clearly, was studying every expression. Despite the impossibility of this, the thought persisted. What was behind Bahrank's probing?

Why do I feel that he sees right through me?

These disquieting conjectures ended as they emerged from the tube onto a Warren street. Bahrank spun them to the right along a narrow alleyway in deep grey shadows.

Although he'd seen many representations of these streets the actuality deepened McKie's feelings of misgiving. So dirty ... oppressive ... so many people. They were everywhere!

Bahrank drove slowly now on the silent wheels, the tracks raised off the paving. The big machine eased its way through narrow little streets, some paved with stone, some with great slabs of gleaming black. All the streets were shaded by overhanging upper stories whose height McKie could not judge through the slits. He saw shops barred and guarded. An occasional stairway, also guarded, led up or down into repellent darkness. Only Humans occupied these streets, and no casual, pedestrian expressions on any of them. Jaws were set on grim mouths. Hard, questioning eyes peered at the passing vehicle. Both men and women wore the universal dark, one-piece clothing of the Labor Pool.

Noting McKie's interest, Bahrank spoke.

'This is a Human enclave and you have a Gowachin driver.'

'Can they see us in here?'

'They know. And there's trouble coming.'

'Trouble?'

'Gowachin against Human.'

This appalled McKie, and he wondered if this were the source of those forebodings which Aritch and aides would not explain: destruction of Dosadi from within. But Bahrank continued:

'There's a growing separation between Humans and Gowachin, worse than it's ever been. You may be the last Human to ride with me.'

Aritch and company had prepared McKie for Dosadi's violence, hunger, and distrust, but they'd said nothing about species against species ... only that someone they refused to name could destroy the place from within. What was Bahrank trying to say? McKie dared not expose his ignorance by probing, and this inability dismayed him.

Bahrank, meanwhile, nosed their machine out of a narrow passage onto a wider street which was crowded by carts, each piled with greenery. The carts moved aside slowly as the armored vehicle approached, hatred plain in the eyes of the Humans who moved with the carts. The press of people astonished McKie: for every cart (and he lost count of them within a block) there were at least a hundred people crowding around, lifting arms high, shouting at the ring of people who stood shoulder to shoulder around each cart, their backs to the piled contents and obviously guarding those contents.

McKie, staring at the carts, realized with a shocked sense of recognition that he was staring at carts piled with garbage. The crowds of people were buying garbage.

Again, Bahrank acted the part of tour guide.

'This is called the Street of the Hungry. That's very select garbage, the best.'

McKie recalled one of Aritch's aides saying there were restaurants in Chu which specialized in garbage from particular areas of the city, that no poison-free food was wasted.

The passing scene compelled McKie's attention: hard faces, furtive movements, the hate and thinly suppressed violence, all of this immersed in a *normal* commercial operation based on garbage. And the numbers of these people! They were everywhere around: in doorways, guarding and pushing the carts, skipping out of Bahrank's path. New smells assaulted McKie's nostrils, a fetid acridity, a stink such as he had never before experienced. Another thing surprised him: the appearance of antiquity in this Warren. He wondered if all city populations crowded by threats from outside took on this ancient appearance. By ConSentient standards, the population of Chu had lived here only a few generations, but the city looked older than any he'd ever seen.

With an abrupt rocking motion, Bahrank turned their machine down a narrow street, brought them to a stop. McKie, looking out the slit on his right, saw an arched entry in a grimy building, a stairway leading downward into gloom.

'Down there's where you meet Jedrik,' Bahrank said. 'Down those stairs, second door on your left. It's a restaurant.'

'How'll I know her?'

'Didn't they tell you?'

'I ...' McKie broke off. He'd seen pictures of Jedrik during the Tandaloor briefings, realized now that he was trying to delay leaving Bahrank's armored cocoon.

Bahrank appeared to sense this.

'Have no fear, McKie. Jedrik will know you. And McKie ...'

McKie turned to face the Gowachin.

'... go directly to the restaurant, take a seat, wait for Jedrik. You'll not survive long here without her protection. Your skin's dark and some Humans prefer even the green to the dark in this quarter. They remember Pylash Gate here. Fifteen years isn't long enough to erase that from their minds.'

Nothing about a Pylash Gate had been included in McKie's briefings and now he dared not ask.

Bahrank moved the switch which opened McKie's door. Immediately, the stink of the street was amplified to almost overpowering proportions. Bahrank, seeing him hesitate, spoke sharply.

'Go quickly!'

McKie descended in a kind of olfactory daze, found himself standing on the side of the street, the object of suspicious stares from all around. The sight of Bahrank driving away was the cutting of his last link to the ConSentiency and all the familiar things which might protect him. Never in his long life had McKie felt this much alone.

No legal system can maintain justice unless every participant – magisters, prosecutors, Legums, defendants, witnesses, all – risks life itself in whatever dispute comes before the bar. Everything must be risked in the Courtarena. If any element remains outside the contest and without personal risk, justice inevitably fails.

— *Gowachin Law*

Near sunset there was a fine rain which lasted well into darkness, then departed on the gorge wind which cleared Dosadi's skies. It left the air crystalline, cornices dripping puddles in the streets. Even the omnipresent Warren stink was diluted and Chu's inhabitants showed a predatory lightness as they moved along the streets.

Returning to headquarters in an armored troop carrier which carried only his most trusted Gowachin, Broey noted the clear air even while he wondered at the reports which had brought him racing from the Council Hills. When he entered the conference room, Broey saw that Gar already was there standing with his back to the dark window which looked out on the eastern cliffs. Broey wondered how long Gar had been there. No sign of recognition passed between Gowachin and Human, but this only emphasized the growing separation of the species. They'd both seen the reports which contained that most disturbing datum: the killing of a Human double agent under circumstances which pointed at Broey himself.

Broey crossed to the head of the conference table, flipped the toggle which activated his communicator, addressed the screen which only he could see.

'Assemble the Council and link for conference.'

The response came as a distorted buzz filtered through scramblers and suppressed by a privacy cone. Gar, standing across the room, could make no sense out of the noises coming from the communicator.

While he waited for the Council members to come on the conference link, Broey seated himself at the communicator, summoned a Gowachin aide to the screen, and spoke in a low voice masked by the privacy cone.

'Start a security check on all Humans in positions where they might threaten us. Use Plan D.'

Broey glanced up at Gar. The Human's mouth worked silently. He was annoyed by the privacy cone and his inability to tell exactly what Broey was doing. Broey continued speaking to his aide.

'I'll want the special force deployed as I told you earlier ... Yes ...'

Gar pointedly turned his back on this conversation, stared out at the night.

Broey continued to address his aide in the screen.

'No! We must include even the Humans in this conference. Yes, that's the report Gar made to me. Yes, I also received that information. Other Humans can be expected to riot and drive out their Gowachin neighbors, and there'll be retaliations. Yes, that was my thought when I saw the report.'

Broey turned off the privacy cone and scrambler. Tria had just come onto his screen with an override, interrupting the conversation with his security aide. She spoke in a low, hurried voice with only a few words intelligible to Gar across the room. But Broey's suspicions were becoming obvious. He heard Tria out, then:

'Yes ... it would be logical to suppose that such a killing was made to look like Gowachin work for ... I see. But the scattered incidents which ... Indeed? Well, under the circumstances ...'

He left the thought incomplete, but his words drew a line between Human and Gowachin, even at the highest levels of his Advisory Council.

'Tria, I must make my own decisions on this.'

While Broey was speaking, Gar brought up a chair and placed it near the communicator, then sat down. Broey had finished his conversation with Tria and restored the privacy circuits, however, and even though he sat nearby Gar could not penetrate their protective screen. He was close enough now, though, to hear the buzzing of the privacy system and the sound annoyed Gar. He did not try to conceal his annoyance.

Broey saw Gar, but gave no indication that he approved or disapproved Gar's nearness.

'So I understand,' Broey said. 'Yes ... I'll issue those orders as soon as I've finished here. No ... Agreed. That would be best.' He closed the circuit. The annoying buzz stopped.

'Jedrik means to set Gowachin against Human, Human against Gowachin,' Gar said.

'If so, it's been a long time in secret preparation,' Broey said.

His words implied many things: that there was conspiracy in high places, that the situation had achieved dangerous momentum without being detected, that all of the inertial forces could not now be anticipated.

'You expect it to get worse,' Gar said.

'Hopefully.'

Gar stared at him for a long period, then:

'Yes.'

It was clear that Broey wanted a well-defined condition to develop, one which would provide clear predictions of the major consequences. He was prepared for this. When Broey understood the situation to his own satisfaction, he'd use his own undeniable powers to gain as much as possible during a period of upset.

Gar broke the silence.

'But if we've misunderstood Jedrik's intent—'

'It helps us when the innocent suffer,' Broey said, paraphrasing part of an old axiom which every Dosadi knew.

Gar completed the thought for him.

'But who's innocent?'

Before Broey could respond, his screen came alight with the assembled faces of his Council, each face in its own little square. Broey conducted the conference quickly, allowing few interruptions. There were no house arrests, no direct accusations, but his words and manner divided them by species. When he was through, Gar imagined the scrambling which must be going on right then in Chu while the powerful assembled their defenses.

Without knowing how he sensed this, Gar felt that this was exactly what Jedrik had wanted, and that it'd been a mistake for Broey to increase the tensions.

After turning off the communicator, Broey sat back and addressed himself to Gar with great care.

'Tria tells me that Jedrik cannot be found.'

'Didn't we expect that?'

'Perhaps.' Broey puffed his jowls. 'What I don't understand is how a simple Liaitor could elude my people *and* Tria.'

'I think we've underestimated this Jedrik. What if she comes from ...' His chin jerked ceilingward.

Broey considered this. He'd been supervising the interrogation of Bahrank at a secure post deep in the Council Hills when the summons to headquarters had interrupted. The accumulating reports indicated a kind of trouble Chu had known at various times, but never at this magnitude. And Bahrank's information had been disappointing. He'd delivered this Rim infiltrator named McKie to such and such an address. (Security had been unable to check this in time because of the riots.)

Bahrank's beliefs were obvious. And perhaps the Rimmers *were* trying to build their own city beyond the mountains. Broey thought this unlikely. His sources in the Rim had proved generally trustworthy and his special source was always trustworthy. Besides, such a venture would require gigantic stocks of food, all of it subject to exposure in the regular accounting. That, after all, was the Liaitor function, why he had . . . No, that was not probable. The Rim subsisted on the lowest of Chu's leavings and whatever could be wrested from Dosadi's poisonous soil. No . . . Bahrank was wrong. This McKie was peculiar, but in quite another way. And Jedrik must've known this before anyone else – except himself. The paramount question remained: who'd helped her?

Broey sighed.

'We have a long association, Gar. A person of your powers who has worked his way from the Rim through the Warrens . . .'

Gar understood. He was being told that Broey looked upon him with active suspicion. There'd never been any real trust between them, but this was something else: nothing openly spoken, nothing direct or specific, but the meaning clear. It was not even sly; it was merely Dosadi.

For a moment, Gar didn't know which way to turn. There'd always been this possibility in his relationship with Broey, but long acceptance had lulled Gar into a dangerous dependency. Tria had been his most valuable counter. He needed her now, but she had other, much more demanding, duties at this juncture.

Gar realized now that he would have to precipitate his own plans, calling in all of the debts and dependencies which were his due. He was distracted by the sound of many people hurrying past in the outer hall. Presumably, things were coming to a head faster than expected.

Gar stood up, stared vaguely out the windows at those dark shadows in the night which were the Rim cliffs. While waiting for Broey, Gar had watched darkness settle there, watched the spots of orange appear which were the Rim's cookfires. Gar knew those cookfires, knew the taste of the food which came from them, knew the flesh-dragging dullness which dominated existence out there. Did Broey expect him to flee back to that? Broey would be astonished at the alternatives open to Gar.

'I will leave you now,' Broey said. He arose and waddled from the room. What he meant was: 'Don't be here when I return.'

Gar continued to stare out the windows. He seemed lost in angry reverie. Why hadn't Tria reported yet? One of Broey's Gowachin aides came in, fussed over papers on a corner table.

It was actually no more than five minutes that Gar remained standing thus. He shook himself presently, turned, and let himself out of the room.

Scarcely had he set foot in the outer passage than a troop of Broey's Gowachin shouldered their way past him into the conference room. They'd been waiting for him to leave.

Angry with himself for what he knew he must do, Gar turned left, strode down the hall to the room where he knew he'd find Broey. Three Gowachin wearing Security brassards followed him, but did not interfere. Two more Gowachin guarded Broey's door, but they hesitated to stop him. Gar's power had been felt here too long. And Broey, not expecting Gar to follow, had failed to issue specific orders. Gar counted on this.

Broey, instructing a group of Gowachin aides, stood over a table cluttered with charts. Yellow light from fixtures directly overhead played shifting shadows on the charts as the aides bent over the table and made notes. Broey broke off at the intrusion, his surprise obvious.

Gar spoke before Broey could order him removed.

'You still need me to keep you from making the worst mistake of your life.'

Broey straightened, did not speak, but the invitation for Gar to continue was there.

'Jedrik's playing you like a fine instrument. You're doing precisely what she wants you to do.'

Broey's cheeks puffed. The shrug angered Gar.

'When I first came here, Broey, I took certain precautions to insure my continued health should you ever consider violence against me.'

Again, Broey gave that maddening Gowachin shrug. This was all so mundane. Why else did this fool Human continue alive and at liberty?

'You've never been able to discover what I did to insure myself against you,' Gar said. 'I have no addictions. I'm a prudent person and, naturally, have means of dying before your experts on pain could overcome my reason. I've done all of the things you might expect of me ... and something more, something you now need *desperately* to know.'

'I have my own precautions, Gar.'

'Of course, and I admit I don't know what they are.'

'So what do you propose?'

Gar gave a little laugh, not quite gloating.

'You know my terms.'

Broey shook his head from side to side, an exquisitely Human gesture.

'Share the rule? I'm astonished at you, Gar.'

'Your astonishment hasn't reached its limits. You don't know what I've really done.'

'Which is?'

'Shall we retire to a more private place and discuss it?'

Broey looked around at his aides, waved for them to leave.

'We will talk here.'

Gar waited until he heard the door close behind him on the last of the departing aides.

'You probably know about the death fanatics we've groomed in the Human enclaves.'

'We are prepared to deal with them.'

'Properly motivated, fanatics can keep great secrets, Broey.'

'No doubt. Are you now going to reveal such a secret?'

'For years now, my fanatics have lived on reduced rations, preserving and exporting their surplus rations to the Rim. We have enough, megatons of food out there. With a whole planet in which to hide it, you'll never find it. City food, every bit of it and we will . . .'

'Another city!'

'More than that. Every weapon the city of Chu has, we have.'

Broey's ventricle lips went almost green with anger.

'So you never really left the Rim?'

'The Rim-born cannot forget.'

'After all that Chu has done for you . . .'

'I'm glad you didn't mention blasphemy.'

'But the Gods of the Veil gave us a mandate!'

'Divide and rule, subdivide and rule even more powerfully, fragment and rule absolutely.'

'That's not what I meant.' Broey breathed deeply several times to restore his calm. 'One city and only one city. That is our mandate.'

'But the other city will be built.'

'Will it?'

'We've dug in the factories to provide our own weapons and food. If you move against our people inside Chu, we'll come at you from the outside, shatter your walls and . . .'

'What do you propose?'

'Open cooperation for a separation of the species, one city for Gowachin, one for Human. What you do in Chu will be your own business then, but I'll tell you that we of the new city will rid ourselves of the DemoPol and its aristocracy.'

'You'd create another aristocracy?'

'Perhaps. But my people will die for the vision of freedom we share. We no longer provide our bodies for Chu!'

'So that's why your fanatics are all Rim-born.'

'I see that you don't yet understand, Broey. My people are not merely Rim-born; they are willing, even *eager*, to die for their vision.'

Broey considered this. It was a difficult concept for a Gowachin, whose Graluz guilt was always transformed into a profound respect for the survival drive. But he saw where Gar's words must lead, and he built an image in his mind of fleshly Human waves throwing themselves onto all opposition without inhibitions about pain, death, or survival in any respect. They might very well capture Chu. The idea that countless Rim immigrants lived within Chu's walls in readiness for such sacrifice filled him with deep disquiet. It required strong self-control to conceal this reaction. He did not for an instant doubt Gar's story. It was just the kind of thing this dry-fleshed Rimmer would do. But why was Gar revealing this now?

'Did Jedrik order you to prepare me for ...'

'Jedrik isn't part of our plan. She complicates matters for us, but the kind of upset she's igniting is just the sort of thing we can exploit better than you.'

Broey weighed this with what he knew about Gar, found it valid as far as it went, but it still did not answer the basic question.

'Why?'

'I'm not ready to sacrifice my people,' Gar said.

That had the ring of partial truth. Gar had shown many times that he could make hard decisions. But numbered among his fanatic hordes there doubtless were certain skills he'd prefer not losing – not yet. Yes, that was the way Gar's mind worked. And Gar would know the profound respect for life which matured in a Gowachin breast after the weeding frenzy. Gowachin, too, could make bloody decisions, but the guilt ... oh, the guilt ... Gar counted on the guilt. Perhaps he counted too much.

'Surely, you don't expect me to take an open and active part in your Rim city project?'

'If not open, then passive.'

'And you insist on sharing the rule of Chu?'

'For the interim.'

'Impossible!'

'In substance if not in name.'

'You have been my advisor.'

'Will you precipitate violence between us with Jedrik standing there to pick up whatever she can gain from us?'

'Ahhhhhh . . .' Broey nodded.

So that was it! Gar was not part of this Jedrik thing. Gar was afraid of Jedrik, more afraid of her than he was of Broey. This gave Broey cause for caution. Gar was not easily made fearful. What did he know of this Jedrik that Broey did not know? But now there was a sufficient reason for compromise. The unanswered questions could be answered later.

'You will continue as my chief advisor,' Broey said.

It was acceptable. Gar signified his consent by a curt nod.

The compromise left an empty feeling in Broey's digestive nodes, though. Gar knew he'd been manipulated to reveal his fear of Jedrik. Gar could be certain that Broey would try to neutralize the Rim city project. But the magnitude of Gar's plotting went far beyond expectations, leaving too many unknowns. One could not make accurate decisions with insufficient data. Gar had given away information without receiving an equal exchange. That was not like Gar. Or was that a correct interpretation of what'd happened here? Broey knew he had to explore this, risking one piece of accurate information as bait.

'There's been a recent increase of mystical experiences by Gowachin in the Warrens.'

'You know better than to try that religious nonsense on me!'

Gar was actually angry.

Broey concealed his amusement. Gar did not know then (or did not accept) that the God of the Veil sometimes created illusions in his flock, that God spoke truly to his anointed and would even answer some questions.

Much had been revealed here, more than Gar suspected. Bahrank had been right. And Jedrik would know about Gar's Rim city. It was possible that Jedrik wanted Broey to know and had maneuvered Gar into revealing the plot. If Gar saw this, that would be enough to make him fearful.

Why didn't the God reveal this to me? Broey wondered. *Am I being tested?*

Yes, that had to be the answer, because there was one thing certain now:

This time, I'll do what the God advises.

People always devise their own justifications. Fixed and immovable Law merely provides a convenient structure within which to hang your justifications and the prejudices behind them. The only universally acceptable law for mortals would be one which fitted every justification. What obvious nonsense. Law must expose prejudice and question justification. Thus, Law must be flexible, must change to fit new demands. Otherwise, it becomes merely the justification of the powerful.

– *Gowachin Law*
(The BuSab Translation)

It required a moment after Bahrank drove away for McKie to recover his sense of purpose. The buildings rose tall and massive over him, but through a quirk of this Warren's growth, an opening to the west allowed a spike of the silvery afternoon sunlight to slant into the narrow street. The light threw hard shadows on every object, accented the pressure of Human movement. McKie did not like the way people looked at him: as though everyone measured him for some private gain.

Slowly, McKie pressed through the passing throng to the arched entry, observing all he could without seeming to do so. After all those years in BuSab, all of the training and experience which had qualified him for such a delicately powerful agency, he possessed superb knowledge of the ConSentiency's species. He drew on that knowledge now, sensing the powerful secrecy which governed these people. Unfortunately, his experience also was replete with knowledge of what species could do to species, not to mention what a species could do to itself. The Humans around him reminded him of nothing more than a mob about to explode.

Moving with a constant readiness to defend himself, he went down a short flight of stairs into cool shadows where the foot traffic was lighter but the smells of rot and mold were more pronounced.

Second door on the left.

He went to the doorway to which Bahrank had directed him, peered into the opening: another stairway down. Somehow, this dismayed him. The picture of Chu growing in his mind was not at all what Aritch's people had drawn. Had they deliberately misled him? If so, why? Was it possible they really didn't understand their monster? The array of answers to his questions chilled him. What if a few of the observers sent here by Aritch's people had chosen to capitalize on whatever power Dosadi provided?

In all of his career, McKie had never before come across a world so completely cut off from the rest of the universe. This planet was *alone*, without many of the amenities which graced the other ConSentient worlds: no common access to jumpdoors, no concourse of the known species, none of the refined pleasures nor the sophisticated traps which occupied the denizens of other worlds. Dosadi had developed its own ways. And the instructors on Tandaloor had returned time and again to that constant note of warning – that these lonely *primitives* would take over the ConSentiency if released upon the universe.

'Nothing restrains them. Nothing.'

That was, perhaps, an overstatement. Some things did restrain the Dosadi physically. But they were not held back by the conventions or mores of the ConSentiency. Anything could be purchased here, any forbidden depravity which the imagination might conceive. This idea haunted McKie. He thought of this and of the countless substances to which many Dosadi were addicted. The power leverage such things gave to the unprincipled few was terrifying.

He dared not pause here wrestling with his indecisions, though. McKie stepped into the stairwell with a boldness which he did not feel, following Bahrank's directions because he had no choice. The bottom landing was a wider space in deep shadows, one dim light on a black door. Two Humans dozed in chairs beside the door while a third squatted beside them with what appeared to be a crude projectile weapon in his hands.

'Jedrik summoned me,' McKie said.

The guard with the weapon nodded for him to proceed.

McKie made his way past them, glanced at the weapon: a length of pipe with a metal box at the back and a flat trigger atop the box held by the guard's thumb. McKie almost missed a step. The weapon was a dead-man bomb! Had to be. If that guard's thumb relaxed for any reason, the thing no doubt would explode and kill everyone in the stairwell. McKie glanced at the two sleepers. How could they sleep in such circumstances?

The black door with its one dim light commanded his attention now. A strong smell of highly seasoned cooking dominated the other stinks here. McKie saw that it was a heavy door with a glittering spyeye at face level. The door opened at his approach. He stepped through into a large low room crowded – *jammed!* – with people seated on benches at trestle tables. There was barely room for passage between the benches. And everywhere that McKie looked he saw people spooning food into their mouths from small bowls. Waiters and waitresses hurried through the narrow spaces slapping down bowls and removing empties.

The whole scene was presided over by a fat woman seated at a small desk on a platform at his left. She was positioned in such a way that she commanded the entry door, the entire room, and swinging doors at the side through which the serving people flowed back and forth. She was a monstrous woman and she sat her perch as though she had never been anywhere else. Indeed, it was easy for McKie to imagine that she could not move from her position. Her arms were bloated where they squeezed from the confines of short-sleeved green coveralls. Her ankles hung over her shoe tops in folds.

Take a seat and wait.

Bahrank had been explicit and the warning clear.

McKie looked for an opening on the benches. Before he could move, the fat woman spoke in a squeaky voice.

'Your name?'

McKie's gaze darted toward those beady eyes in their folds of fat.

'McKie.'

'Thought so.'

She raised a dimpled finger. From somewhere in the crush a young boy came hurrying. He could not have been over nine years old but his eyes were cold with adult wisdom. He looked up to the fat woman for instructions.

'This is the one. Guide him.'

The boy turned and, without looking to see if McKie followed, hurried down the narrow pathway where the doors swung back and forth to permit the passage of the servitors. Twice, McKie was almost run down by waiters. His guide was able to anticipate the opening of every door and skipped aside.

At the end of this passage, there was another solid black door with spyeye. The door opened onto a short passage with closed doors on both sides, a blank wall at the end. The blank wall slid aside for them and they descended into a narrow, rock-lined way lighted by widely spaced bulbs overhead. The walls were damp and evil smelling. Occasionally, there were wide places with guards. They passed through several guarded doors, climbed up and went down. McKie lost track of the turns, the doors, and guard posts. After a time, they climbed to another short hallway with doors along its sides. The boy opened the second door on the right, waited for McKie to enter, closed the door. It was all done without words. McKie heard the boy's footsteps recede.

The room was small and dimly lighted by windows high in the wall opposite the door. A trestle table about two meters long with benches down both sides and a chair at each end almost filled the space. The walls were grey stone and unadorned. McKie worked his way around to the chair at the far end, sat down. He remained seated there silently for several minutes, absorbing this place. It was cold in the room: Gowachin temperature. One of the high windows behind him was open a crack and he could hear street noises: a heavy vehicle passing, voices arguing, many feet. The sense of the Warren pressing in upon this room was very strong. Nearer at hand from beyond the single door, he heard crockery banging and an occasional hiss as of steam.

Presently, the door opened and a tall, slender woman entered, slipping through the door at minimal opening. For a moment as she turned, the light from the windows concentrated on her face, then she sat down at the end of the right-hand bench, dropping into shadows.

McKie had never before seen such hard features on a woman. She was brittle rock with ice crystal eyes of palest blue. Her black hair was closely cropped into a stiff bristle. He repressed a shudder. The rigidity of her body amplified the hard expression on her face. It was not the hardness of suffering, not that alone, but something far more determined, something anchored in a kind of agony which might explode at the slightest touch. On a ConSentient world where the geriatric arts were available, she could have been any age between thirty-five and one hundred and thirty-five. The dim light into which she had seated herself complicated his scrutiny, but he suspected she was younger than thirty-five.

'So *you* are McKie.'

He nodded.

'You're fortunate Adril's people got my message. Broey's already searching for you. I wasn't warned that you were so dark.'

He shrugged.

'Bahrank sent word that you could get us all killed if we're not careful with you. He says you don't have even rudimentary survival training.'

This surprised McKie, but he held his silence.

She sighed. 'At least you have the good sense not to protest. Well ... welcome to Dosadi, McKie. Perhaps be able to keep you alive long enough for you to be of some use to us.'

Welcome to Dosadi!

'I'm Jedrik as you doubtless already know.'

'I recognize you.'

This was only partly true. None of the representations he'd seen had conveyed the ruthless brutality which radiated from her.

A hard smile flickered on her lips, was gone.

'You don't respond when I welcome you to our planet.'

McKie shook his head. Aritch's people had been specific in their injunction:

'She doesn't know your origin. Under no circumstances may you reveal to her that you come from beyond the God Wall. It could be immediately fatal.'

McKie continued to stare silently at her.

A colder look came over Jedrik's features, something in the muscles at the corners of the mouth and eyes.

'We shall see. Now: Bahrank says you carry a wallet of some kind and that you have currency sewn into your clothing. First, hand me the wallet.'

My toolkit?

She reached an open hand toward him.

'I'll warn you once, McKie. If I get up and walk out of here you'll not live more than two minutes.'

Every muscle quivering protest, he slipped the toolkit from its pocket, extended it.

'And I'll warn you, Jedrik: I'm the only person who can open this without being killed and the contents destroyed.'

She accepted the toolkit, turned its flat substance over in her hands. 'Really?'

McKie had begun to interest her in a new way. He was less than she'd expected, yet more. Naive, of course, incredibly naive. But she'd already known that of the people from beyond the God Wall. It was the most suitable explanation. Something was profoundly wrong in the Dosadi situation. The people beyond the Veil would have to send their best here. This McKie was their best? Astonishing.

She arose, went to the door, rapped once.

McKie watched her pass the toolkit to someone outside, heard a low-voiced conversation, neither half of it intelligible. In a flashing moment of indecision, he'd considered trying for some of the toolkit's protective contents. Something in Jedrik's manner and the accumulation of unknowns all around had stopped him.

Jedrik returned to her seat empty-handed. She stared at him a moment, head cocked to one side, then:

'I'll say several things to you. In a way, this is a test. If you fail, I guarantee you'll not survive long on Dosadi. Understood?'

When McKie failed to respond, she pounded a fist on the table.

'Understood?'

'Say what you have to say.'

'Very well. It's obvious to me that those who instructed you about Dosadi warned you not to reveal your true origin. Yet, most of those who've talked to you for more than a few seconds suspect you're not one of us – not from Chu, not from the Rim, not from anywhere on Dosadi.' Her voice took on a new harshness. 'But I know it. Let me tell you, McKie, that there's not even a child among us who's failed to realize that the people imprisoned on Dosadi did not originate here!'

McKie stared at her, shocked.

Imprisoned.

As she spoke, he knew she was telling him the truth. Why hadn't Aritch or the others warned him? Why hadn't he seen this for himself? Since Dosadi was poison to both Human and Gowachin, rejected them, of course they'd know they hadn't originated here.

She gave him time to absorb this before continuing. 'There are others among us from your realm, perhaps some we've not identified, better trained. But I was taught to act only on certainty. Of you I'm certain. You do not originate on Dosadi. I've put it to the question and I've the present confirmation of my own senses. You come from beyond the God Wall. Your actions with Bahrank, with Adril, with me . . .' She shook her head sadly.

Aritch set me up for this!

This thought brought back a recurrent question which continued to nag McKie; BuSab's discovery of the Dosadi experiment. Were the Gowachin that clumsy? Would they make such slips? The original plan to conceal this project must have been extensive. Yet, key facts had leaked to BuSab agents. McKie felt overwrought from asking himself the same questions over and over without satisfaction. And now, Jedrik's pressures compounded the burden. The only suitable answer was that Aritch's people had done everything with the intent of putting him in this position. They'd deliberately leaked information about Dosadi. And McKie was their target.

To what purpose?

'Can we be overheard?' he asked.

'Not by my enemies on Dosadi.'

He considered this. She'd left open the question of whether anyone from beyond the God Wall might eavesdrop. McKie pursed his lips with indecision. She'd taken his toolkit with such ridiculous ease . . . yet, what choice had he? They wouldn't get anything from the kit and someone out there, one of Jedrik's underlings, would die. That could have a useful effect on Jedrik. He decided to play for time.

'There're many things I could tell you. So many things. I hardly know where to begin.'

'Begin by telling me how you came through the God Wall.'

Yes, he might be able to confuse her with a loose description of Calebans and jumpdoors. Nothing in her Dosadi experience could've prepared Jedrik for such phenomena. McKie took a deep breath. Before he could speak there was a rap on the door.

Jedrik raised a hand for silence, leaned over, and opened the door. A skinny young man with large eyes beneath a high forehead and thin blond hair slipped through, placed McKie's toolkit on the table in front of Jedrik.

'It wasn't very difficult,' he said.

McKie stared at the kit in shock. It lay open with all of its contents displayed in perfect order.

Jedrik gestured the youth to the seat opposite her. She reached for a raygen.

McKie could no longer contain himself.

'Careful! That's dangerous!'

'Be still, McKie. You know nothing of danger.'

She removed the raygen, examined it, replaced it neatly, looked at the young man.

'All right, Stiggy. Tell me.'

The youth began removing the items from the toolkit one by one, handling each with a knowledgeable correctness, speaking rapidly.

McKie tried hard to follow the conversation, but it was in a code he could not understand. The expressions on their faces were eloquent enough, however. They were elated. Whatever Stiggy was saying about the dangerous toys in McKie's toolkit, his revelations profited both of them.

The uncertainties which had begun during McKie's ride with Bahrank reached a new intensity. The feeling had built up in him like a sickness: disquiet stomach, pains in his chest, and, lastly, an ache across his forehead. He'd wondered for a time if he might be the victim of some new disease native to Dosadi. It could not be the planet's food because he'd eaten nothing yet. The realization came over him as he watched Jedrik and Stiggy that his reactions were his own reasoning system trying to reject something, some assumption or set of assumptions which he'd accepted without question. He tried to empty his mind, not asking any questions in particular. Let come into his awareness what may. It would all have a fresh appraisal.

Dosadi requires you to be coldly brutal in all of your decisions. No exceptions.

Well . . . he'd let go of the toolkit in the belief that someone would die trying to open it. But he'd issued a warning. That warning could've helped them. Probably did.

I must become exactly like them or I cannot survive – let alone succeed.

At last, McKie felt Aritch's fear of Dosadi, understood the Gowachin desperation. What a terrible training ground for the recognition and use of power!

Jedrik and Stiggy finished their conversation over the toolkit. Stiggy closed the kit, arose with it in one hand, speaking at last in words McKie understood.

'Yes, we must lose no time.'

Stiggy left with the kit.

Jedrik faced McKie. The toolkit and its contents had helped answer the most obvious question about McKie and his kind. The people beyond the God Wall were the degenerate descendants of those who'd invented such devices. It was the only workable explanation. She felt almost sorry for this poor fool. But that was not a permissible emotion. He must be made to understand that he had no choice but to obey her.

'Now, McKie, you will answer all of my questions.'

'Yes.'

It was utter submission and she knew it.

'When you've satisfied me in all matters,' she said, 'then we'll eat and I'll take you to a place where you'll be reasonably safe.'

The Family/Clan/Factions of the Rim are still responding to their defeat in the mass attempt on our defenses of last Decamo. They appear severely chastened. Small police actions are all that we need anticipate over the next planning period. Further, our operatives in the Rim find no current difficulties in steering the F/C/F toward a natural and acceptable cultural rejection of economic developments which might lead them to improved food production.

— *From a Dosadi Bureau of Control document*

An angry Broey, full out and uninhibited anger, was something to see and quite a number of his Gowachin aides had seen this emotional display during the night. It was now barely dawn. Broey had not slept in two days; but the fourth group of his aides stood before him in the sanctum to receive the full spate of his displeasure. The word had already gone out through their ranks and they, like the others, did not try to hide their fear or their anxious eagerness to restore themselves in Broey's good graces.

Broey stood near the end of the long table where, earlier, he had met with Gar and Tria. The only visible sign of his long sleepless hours was a slight pitting of the fatty nodes between his ventricles. His eyes were as sharp as ever and his voice had lost none if its bite.

'What I'd like explained is how this could happen without a word of warning. And it's not just that we failed to detect this, but that we continued to grind out complacent reports, reports which went exactly contrary to what actually was happening.'

The aides massed at the other end of the table, all standing, all fidgeting, were not assuaged by Broey's use of 'we.' They heard him clearly. He was saying: 'You! You! You!'

'I will be satisfied by nothing less than an informant,' Broey said. 'I want a Human informant, either from Chu or from the Rim. I don't care how you get this informant. We must find that store of city food. We must find where they have started their blasphemous Rim city.'

One of his aides, a slender young Gowachin in the front rank, ventured a cautious question which had been repeated several times by other chastened aides during the night.

'If we move too strongly against Humans in the Warrens, won't that feed the unrest that ...'

'We'll have more riots, more turning of Gowachin against Human and Human against Gowachin,' Broey agreed. 'That's a consequence we are prepared to accept.'

This time they understood that Broey used the royal 'we.' Broey would accept the consequences. Some of his aides, however, were not ready to accept a war between the species within the city's walls. One of the aides farther back in the ranks raised an arm.

'Perhaps we should use only Human troops in the Warrens. If we ...'

'Who would that fool?' Broey demanded. 'We have taken the proper steps to maintain our hold on Chu. You have one task and one task only: find that store of food and those hidden factories. Unless we find them we're finished. Now, get out of here. I don't want to see any of you until you can report success!'

They filed out silently.

Broey stood looking down at the blank screen of his communicator. Alone at last, he allowed his shoulders to slump, breathed heavily through both mouth and ventricles.

What a mess! What a terrible mess.

He knew in his node of nodes that he was behaving precisely as Jedrik wanted him to behave. She had left him no alternatives. He could only admire her handling of the situation while he waited for the opening which he knew must come. But what a magnificent intellect operated in that Human head. And a female at that! Gowachin females never developed such qualities. Only on the Rim were Gowachin females used as other than breeders. Human females, on the other hand, never ceased to amaze him. This Jedrik possessed real leadership qualities. Whether she was the one to take over the Electorship remained to be seen.

Broey found himself recalling those first moments of terrible awareness in the Graluz. Yes, this was the way of the world. If one chose the survivors by other than a terrible testing process, all would die. It would be the end of both species. At least, it would be the end of them on Dosadi and only Dosadi mattered.

He felt bereft, though. He felt betrayed by his God. Why had God failed to warn him? And when questioned, how could God respond that only evil could penetrate the mind of a fanatic? Wasn't God omnipotent? Could any awareness be closed to God? How could God be *God* then?

I am your God!

He could never forget that voiceless voice reverberating in his head.

Was that a lie?

The idea that they were puppets of a false god was not a new one. But if this were the case, then the other uses of those like Pcharky eluded him. What was the purpose of being a Gowachin in Human form or vice versa if not to elude the God of the Veil? Quite obviously, Jedrik operated on such a premise. What other motive could she have than to prolong her own life? As the City was to the Rim, so was the power to elude the God (false God or true) to those of the City. No other assumption fitted a Dosadi justification.

We are plagued by a corrupt polity which promotes unlawful and/or immoral behavior. Public interest has no practical significance in every-day behavior among the ruling factions. The real problems of our world are not being confronted by those in power. In the guise of public service, they use whatever comes to hand for personal gain. They are insane with and for power.

– From a clandestine document circulated on Dosadi

It was dark when a disguised Jedrik and undisguised McKie emerged onto the streets. She led them down narrow passages, her mind full of things McKie had revealed. Jedrik wore a blonde wig and puff-out disguise which made her appear heavy and hunched.

As they passed an open courtyard, McKie heard music. He almost stumbled. The music came from a small orchestra – delicate tympany, soft strings, and a rich chorus of wind instruments. He did not recognize the melody, but it moved him more deeply than any other music of his experience. It was as though the music were played only for him. Aritch and company had said nothing about such magnificent music here.

People still thronged the streets in numbers which astonished him. But now they appeared to pay him little notice.

Jedrik kept part of her attention on McKie, noting the fools with their musical dalliance, noting how few people there were on the streets – little more than her own patrols in this quarter. She'd expected that, but the actuality held an eerie mood in the dim and scattered illumination from lighted corners.

She had debated providing McKie with a crude disguise, but he obviously didn't have the cunning to carry off the double deception she required. She'd begun to sense a real intelligence in him, though. McKie was an enigma. Why had he never encountered the opportunities to sharpen that intelligence? Sensing the sharpness in him, she could not put off the thought that she had missed something vital in his accounts of that social entity which he called the ConSentiency. Whether this failure came from actual concealment by McKie or through his inadequacies, she was not yet willing to judge. The enigma set her on edge.

And the mood in the streets did nothing to ease her emotions. She was glad when they crossed the line into the area completely controlled by her own personal cell.

The bait having been trailed through the streets by one who would appear a tame underling, Jedrik allowed herself a slight relaxation. Broey would have learned by this time about the killing of Tria's double agent. He would react to that and to the new bait. It was almost time for phase two of her design for Broey.

McKie followed her without question, acutely aware of every strange glance cast their way. He was emptied of all resistance, knowing he could not survive if he failed to follow Jedrik through the smelly, repellent darkness of her streets.

The food from the restaurant sat heavily in his stomach. It had been tasty: a stew of odd shapes full of shredded greenery, and steaming hot. But he could not shake the realization that his stew had been compounded of someone's garbage.

Jedrik had left him very little. She hadn't learned of the Taprisiot, or the bead in his stomach which probably would not link him to the powers of the ConSentiency if he died. She had not learned of the standard BuSab implantation devices which amplified his senses. And, oddly, she had not explored many of his revelations about BuSab. She'd seemed much more interested in the money hidden about his person and had taken possession of all of it. She'd examined the currency carefully.

'This is real.'

He wasn't sure, but he thought she'd been surprised.

'This was given to you *before* you were sent to Dosadi?'

'Yes.'

She was a while absorbing the implications, but appeared satisfied. She'd given him a few small currency tokens from her own pockets.

'Nobody'll bother you for these. If you need anything, ask. We may be able to gratify some of your needs.'

It was still dark, lighted only by illumination at corners, when they came to the address Jedrik sought. Grey light suffused the street. A young Human male of about ten squatted with his back against the stone wall at the building's corner. As Jedrik and McKie approached, he sprang up, alert. He nodded once to Jedrik.

She did not acknowledge, but by some hidden signal the boy knew she had received his message. He relaxed once more against the wall.

When McKie looked back a few paces beyond where the boy had signaled, he was gone. No sound, no sign – just gone.

Jedrik stopped at a shadowed entryway. It was barred by an openwork metal gate flanked by two armed guards. The guards opened the gate without words. Beyond the gate there was a large, covered courtyard illuminated by glowing tubes on right and left. Three of its sides were piled to the courtyard cover with boxes of various sizes – some taller than a Human and narrow, others short and fat. Set into the stacks as though part of the courtyard's walls was one narrow passage leading to a metal door opposite the gateway.

McKie touched Jedrik's arm.

'What's in the boxes?'

'Weapons.' She spoke as though to a cretin.

The metal door was opened from within. Jedrik led McKie into a large room at least two stories tall. The door clanged shut behind them. McKie sensed several Humans along the courtyard wall on both sides of him, but his attention had been captured by something else.

Dominating the room was a gigantic cage suspended from the ceiling. Its bars sparkled and shimmered with hidden energies. A single Gowachin male sat cross-legged in a hammock at the cage's center. McKie had seldom seen a ConSentient Gowachin that aged. His nose crest was fringed by flaking yellow crusts. Heavy wrinkles wormed their way beneath watery eyes beginning to glaze with the degeneration which often blinded Gowachin who lived too long away from water. His body had a slack appearance, with loose muscles and pitted indentations along the nodes between his ventricles. The hammock suspended him off the cage floor and that floor shimmered with volatile energies.

Jedrik paused, divided her attention between McKie and the old Gowachin. She seemed to expect a particular reaction from McKie, but he wasn't certain she found what she sought.

McKie stood a moment in silent examination of the Gowachin. Prisoner? What was the significance of that cage and its shimmering energies? Presently, he glanced around the room, recording the space. Six armed Human males flanked the door through which he and Jedrik had entered. A remarkable assortment of objects crammed the room's walls, some with purpose unknown to him but many recognizable as weapons: spears and swords, flame-throwers, garish armor, bombs, pellet projectors . . .

Jedrik moved a pace closer to the cage. The occupant stared back at her with faint interest. She cleared her throat.

'Greetings, Pcharky. I have found my key to the God Wall.'

The old Gowachin remained silent, but McKie thought he saw a sparkle of interest in the glazed eyes.

Jedrik shook her head slowly from side to side, then: 'I have a new datum, Pcharky. The Veil of Heaven was created by creatures called Calebans. They appear to us as suns.'

Pcharky's glance flickered to McKie, back to Jedrik. The Gowachin knew the source of her new datum.

McKie renewed his speculations about the old Gowachin. That cage must be a prison, its walls enforced by dangerous energies. Bahrank had spoken of conflict between the species. Humans controlled this room. Why did they imprison a Gowachin? Or ... was this caged Gowachin, this Pcharky, another agent from Tandaloor? With a tightening of his throat, McKie wondered if his own fate might be to live out his days in such a cage.

Pcharky grunted, then:

'The God Wall is like this cage but more powerful.'

His voice was a husky croaking, the words clear Galach with an obvious Tandaloor accent. McKie, his fears reinforced, glanced at Jedrik, found her studying him. She spoke.

'Pcharky has been with us for a long time, very long. There's no telling how many people he has helped to escape from Dosadi. Soon, I may persuade him to be of service to me.'

McKie found himself shocked to silence by the possibilities glimpsed through her words. Was Dosadi in fact an investigation of the Caleban mystery? Was that the secret Aritch's people concealed here? McKie stared at the shimmering bars of Pcharky's cage. Like the God Wall? But the God Wall was enforced by a Caleban.

Once more, Jedrik looked at the caged Gowachin.

'A sun confines enormous energies, Pcharky. Are your energies inadequate?'

But Pcharky's attention was on McKie. The old voice croaked.

'Human, tell me: Did you come here willingly?'

'Don't answer him,' Jedrik snapped.

Pcharky closed his eyes. Interview ended.

Jedrik, accepting this, whirled and strode to the left around the cage.

'Come along, McKie.' She didn't look back, but continued speaking. 'Does it interest you that Pcharky designed his own cage?'

'He designed it? Is it a prison?'

'Yes.'

'If he designed it ... how does it hold him?'

'He knew he'd have to serve my purposes if he were to remain alive.'

She had come to another door which opened onto a narrow stairway. It climbed to the left around the cage room. They emerged into a long hallway lined with narrow doors dimly lighted by tiny overhead bulbs. Jedrik opened one of these doors and led the way into a carpeted room about four meters wide and six long. Dark wood panels reached from floor to waist level, shelves loaded with books above. McKie peered closely: books ... actual paper books. He tried to recall where he'd ever before seen such a collection of primitive ... But, of course, these were not primitive. These were one of Dosadi's strange recapitulations.

Jedrik had removed her wig, stopped midway in the room to turn and face McKie.

'This is my room. Toilet there.' She pointed to an opening between shelves. 'That window ...' Again, she pointed, this time to an opening opposite the toilet door. ' ... is one-way to admit light, and it's our best. As Dosadi measures such things, this is a relatively secure place.'

He swept his gaze around the room.

Her room?

McKie was struck by the amount of living space, a mark of power on Dosadi; the absence of people in the hall. By the standards of this planet, Jedrik's room, this building, represented a citadel of power.

Jedrik spoke, an odd note of nervousness in voice and manner.

'Until recently, I also had other quarters: a prestigious apartment on the slopes of the Council Hills. I was considered a climber with excellent prospects, my own skitter and driver. I had access to all but the highest codes in the master banks, and that's a powerful tool for those who can use it. Now ...' She gestured. ' ... this is what I have chosen. I must eat swill with the lowest. No males of rank will pay the slightest attention to me. Broey thinks I'm cowering somewhere, a pallet in the Warrens. But I have this ...' Again, that sweeping gesture. ' ... and this.' One finger tapped her head. 'I need nothing more to bring those Council Hills crashing down.'

She stared into McKie's eyes.

He found himself believing her.

She was not through speaking.

'You're definitely male Human, McKie.'

He didn't know what to make of that, but her air of braggadocio fascinated him.

'How did you lose that other ...'

'I didn't lose it. I threw it away. I no longer needed it. I've made things move faster than our precious Elector, or even your people, can anticipate. Broey thinks to wait for an opening against me?' She shook her head.

Captivated, McKie watched her cross to the window, open a ventilator above it. She kicked a wooden knob below the adjoining bookshelves, pulled out a section of paneling which trailed a double bed. Standing across the bed from McKie, she began to undress. She dropped the wig to the floor, slipped off the coveralls, peeled the bulging inner disguise from her flesh. Her skin was pale cream.

'McKie, I am your teacher.'

He remained silent. She was long waisted, slim, and graceful. The creamy skin was marked by two faint scars to the left of the pubic wedge.

'Take off your clothes,' she said.

He swallowed.

She shook her head.

'McKie, McKie, to survive here you must become Dosadi. You don't have much time. Get your clothes off.'

Not knowing what to expect, McKie obeyed.

She watched him carefully.

'Your skin is lighter than I expected where the sun has not darkened you. We will bleach the skin of your face and hands tomorrow.'

McKie looked at his hands, at the sharp line where his cuffs had protected his arms. Dark skin. He recalled Bahrank talking of dark skin and a place called Pylash Gate. To mask the unusual shyness he felt, he looked at Jedrik, asked about Pylash Gate.

'So Bahrank mentioned that? Well, it was a stupid mistake. The Rim sent in shock troops and foolish orders were given for the gate's defenses. Only one troop survived there, all dark-skinned like you. The suspicion of treachery was natural.'

'Oh.'

He found his attention compelled toward the bed. A dark maroon spread covered it.

Jedrik approached him around the foot of the bed. She stopped less than a hand's width away from him ... creamy flesh, full breasts. He looked up into her eyes. She stood half a head over him, an expression of cold amusement on her face.

McKie found the musky smell of her erotically stimulating. She looked down, saw this, laughed, and abruptly hurled him onto the bed. She landed with him and her body was all over him, hot and hard and demanding.

It was the strangest sexual experience of McKie's life. Not lovemaking, but violent attack. She groaned, bit at him, clawed. And when he tried to caress her, she became even more violent, frenzied. Through it all, she was oddly careful of his pleasure, watching his reactions, reading him. When it was over, he lay back, spent. Jedrik sat up on the edge of the bed. The blankets were a twisted mess. She grabbed a blanket, threw it across the room, stood up, whirled back to look down at him.

'You are very sly and tricky, McKie.'

He drew in a trembling breath, remained silent.

'You tried to catch me with softness,' she accused. 'Better than you have tried that with me. It will not work.'

McKie marshalled the energy to sit up and restore some order to the bed. His shoulder pained him where she'd scratched. He felt the ache of a bite on his neck. He crawled into the bed, pulled the blankets up to his chin. She was a madwoman, absolutely mad. Insane.

Presently, Jedrik stopped looking at him. She recovered the blanket from across the room, spread it on the bed, joined him. He was acutely conscious of her staring at him with an openly puzzled frown.

'Tell me about the relationships between men and women on your worlds.'

He recounted a few of the love stories he knew, fighting all the while to stay awake. It was difficult to stifle the gaping yawns. She kept punching his shoulder.

'I don't believe it. You're making this up.'

'No ... no. It's true.'

'You have women of your own there?'

'Women of my ... Well, it's not like that, not ownership ... ahhh, not possession.'

'What about children?'

'What about them?'

'How're they treated, educated?'

He sighed, sketched in some details from his own childhood.

After a while she let him go to sleep. He awakened several times during the night, conscious of the strange room and bed, of Jedrik breathing softly beside him. Once, he thought he felt her shoulders shaking with repressed sobs.

Shortly before dawn, there was a scream in the next block, a terrifying sound of agony loud enough to waken all but the most hardened or the most fatigued. McKie, awake and thinking, felt Jedrik's breathing change. He lay tense and watchful, awaiting a repetition or another sound which might explain that eerie scream. A threatening silence gripped the night. McKie built an image in his mind of what could be happening in the buildings around them: some people starting from sleep not knowing (perhaps not caring) what had awakened them; lighter sleepers grumbling and sinking back into restless slumber.

Finally, McKie sat up, peered into the room's shadows. His disquiet communicated itself to Jedrik. She rolled over, looked up at him in the pale dawn light now creeping into the shadows.

'There are many noises in the Warrens that you learn to ignore,' she said.

Coming from her, it was almost conciliatory, almost a gesture of apology, of friendship.

'Someone screamed,' he said.

'I knew it must be something like that.'

'How can you sleep through such a sound?'

'I didn't.'

'But how can you ignore it?'

'The sounds you ignore are those which aren't immediately threatening to you, those which you can do nothing about.'

'Someone was hurt.'

'Very likely. But you must not burden your soul with things you cannot change.'

'Don't you want to change ... that?'

'I am changing it.'

Her tone, her attitude were those of a lecturer in a schoolroom, and now there was no doubt that she was being deliberately helpful. Well, she'd said she was his teacher. And he must become completely Dosadi to survive.

'How're you changing things?'

'You're not capable of understanding yet. I want you to take it one step at a time, one lesson at a time '

He couldn't help asking himself then:

What does she want from me now?

He hoped it was not more sex.

'Today,' she said, 'I want you to meet the parents of three children who work in our cell.'

If you think of yourselves as helpless and ineffectual, it is certain that you will create a despotic government to be your master. The wise despot, therefore, maintains among his subjects a popular sense that they are helpless and ineffectual.

– *The Dosadi Lesson: A Gowachin Assessment*

Aritch studied Ceylang carefully in the soft light of his green-walled relaxation room. She had come down immediately after the evening meal, responsive to his summons. They both knew the reason for that summons: to discuss the most recent report concerning McKie's behavior on Dosadi.

The old Gowachin waited for Ceylang to seat herself, observing how she pulled the red robe neatly about her lower extremities. Her features appeared composed, the fighting mandibles relaxed in their folds. She seemed altogether a figure of secure competence, a Wreave of the ruling classes – not that Wreaves recognized such classes. It disturbed Aritch that Wreaves tested for survival only through a complex understanding of sentient behavior, rigid performance standards based on ancient ritual, whose actual origins could only be guessed; there was no written record.

But that's why we chose her.

Aritch grunted, then:

'What can you say about the report?'

'McKie learns rapidly.'

Her spoken Galach had a faint sibilance.

Aritch nodded.

'I would say rather that he *adapts* rapidly. It's why we chose him.'

'I've heard you say he's more Gowachin than the Gowachin.'

'I expect him soon to be more Dosadi than the Dosadi.'

'If he survives.'

'There's that, yes. Do you still hate him?'

'I have never hated him. You do not understand the spectrum of Wreave emotions.'

'Enlighten me.'

'He has violated my essential pride of self. This requires a specific reaction in kind. Hate would only dull my abilities.'

'But *I* was the one who gave you the orders which had to be countermanded.'

'My oath of service to the Gowachin contains a specific injunction, that I cannot hold any one of my teachers responsible for either understanding or obeying the Wreave protocols of courtesy. It is the same injunction which frees us to serve McKie's Bureau.'

'You do not consider McKie one of your teachers?'

She studied him for a moment, then:

'Not only do I exclude him, but I know him to be one who has learned much about our protocols.'

'What if I were to say he is one of your teachers?'

Again, she stared at him.

'I would revise my estimations of him – and of you.'

Aritch took a deep breath.

'Yet, you must learn McKie as though you lived in his skin. Otherwise, you will fail us.'

'I will not fail you. I know the reasons you chose me. Even McKie will know in time. He dares not spill my blood in the Courtarena, or even subject me to public shame. Were he to do either of these things, half the Wreave universe would go hunting him with death in their mandibles.'

Aritch shook his head slowly from side to side.

'Ceylang! Didn't you hear him, warn you that you must shed your Wreave skin?'

She was a long time responding and he noted the subtle characteristics which he'd been told were the Wreave adjustments to anger: a twitching of the jowls, tension in the pedal bifurcations ...

Presently, she said:

'Tell me what that means, Teacher.'

'You will be charged with performing under *Gowachin* Law, performing as though you were another McKie. He adapts! Haven't you observed this? He is capable of defeating you – and us – in such a way, *in such a way* that your Wreave universe would shower him with adulation for his victory. That cannot be permitted. Too much is at stake.'

Ceylang trembled and showed other signs of distress.

'But I am Wreave!'

'If it comes to the Courtarena, you no longer can be Wreave.'

She inhaled several shallow breaths, composed herself.

'If I become too much McKie, aren't you afraid I might hesitate to slay him?'

'McKie would not hesitate.'

She considered this.

'Then there's only one reason you chose me for this task.'

He waited for her to say it.

'Because we Wreaves are the best in the universe at learning the behavior of others – both overt and covert.'

'And you dare not rely on any supposed inhibitions he may or may not have!'

After a long pause, she said:

'You are a better teacher than I'd suspected. Perhaps you're even better than *you* suspected.'

'Their law! It is a dangerous foundation for nonauthentic traditions. It is no more than a device to justify false ethics!'
— *Gowachin comment on ConSentient Law*

While they dressed in the dim dawn light coming through the single window, McKie began testing what Jedrik meant by being his teacher.

'Will you answer any question I ask about Dosadi?'

'No.'

Then what areas would she withhold from him? He saw it at once: those areas where she gained and held personal power.

'Will anyone resent it that we . . . had sex together?'

'Resent? Why should anyone resent that?'

'I don't . . .'

'Answer my question!'

'Why do I have to answer your every question?'

'To stay alive.'

'You already know everything I . . .'

She brushed this aside.

'So the people of your ConSentiency sometimes resent the sexual relationships of others. They are not sure, then, how they use sex to hold power over others.'

He blinked. Her quick, slashing analysis was devastating.

She peered at him.

'McKie, what can you do here without me? Don't you know yet that the ones who sent you intended you to die here?'

'Or survive in my own peculiar way.'

She considered this. It was another idea about McKie which she had put aside for later evaluation. Indeed, he might well have hidden talents which her questions had not yet exposed. What annoyed her now was the sense that she didn't know enough about the ConSentiency to explore this. Could not take the time right now to explore it. His response disturbed her. It was as though everything she could possibly do had already been decided for her by powers of which she knew next to nothing. They were leading her by the nose, perhaps, just as she led Broey

. . . just as those mysterious Gowachin of the ConSentiency obviously had led McKie . . . poor McKie. She cut this short as unprofitable speculation. Obviously, she had to begin at once to search out McKie's talent. Whatever she discovered would reveal a great deal about his ConSentiency.

'McKie, I hold a great deal of power among the Humans and even among some Gowachin in the Warrens – and elsewhere. To do this, I must maintain certain fighting forces, including those who fight with physical weapons.'

He nodded. Her tone was that of lecturing to a child, but he accepted this, recognizing the care she took with him.

'We will go first,' she said, 'to a nearby training area where we maintain the necessary edge on one of my forces.'

Turning, she led him out into the hall and down a stairway which avoided the room of the cage. McKie was reminded of Pcharky, though, thinking about that gigantic expenditure of space with its strange occupant.

'Why do you keep Pcharky caged?' he asked, addressing Jedrik's back.

'So I can escape.'

She refused to elaborate on this odd answer.

Presently, they emerged into a courtyard nestled into the solid walls of towering buildings. Only a small square of sky was visible directly overhead and far away. Artificial lighting from tubes along the walls provided an adequate illumination. It revealed two squads facing each other in the center of the courtyard. They were Humans, both male and female; all carried weapons: a tube of some sort with a wandlike protrusion from the end near their bodies. Several other Humans stood at observation positions around the two squads. There was a guard station with a desk at the door through which McKie and Jedrik had emerged.

'That's an assault force,' Jedrik said, indicating the squads in the courtyard. She turned and consulted with the two young men at the guard station.

McKie made a rough count of the squads: about two hundred. It was obvious that everything had stopped because of Jedrik's presence. He thought the force was composed of striplings barely blooded in Dosadi's cruel necessities. This forced him to a reevaluation of his own capabilities.

From Jedrik's manner with the two men, McKie guessed she knew them well. They paid close attention to everything she said. They, too, struck him as too young for responsibility.

The training area was another matter. It bore a depressing similarity

THE DOSADI EXPERIMENT

to other such facilities he'd seen in the backwaters of the ConSentiency. War games were a constant lure among several species, a lure which BuSab had managed thus far to channel into such diversions as weapons fetishes.

Through the omnipresent stink, McKie smelled the faint aroma of cooking. He sniffed.

Turning to him, Jedrik spoke:

'The trainees have just been fed. That's part of their pay.'

It was as though she'd read his mind, and now she watched him for some reaction.

McKie glanced around the training area. They'd just been fed here? There wasn't a scrap or crumb on the ground. He thought back to the restaurant, belatedly aware of a fastidious care with food that he'd seen and passed right over.

Again, Jedrik demonstrated the ease with which she read his reactions, his very thoughts.

'Nothing wasted,' she said.

She turned away.

McKie looked where her attention went. Four women stood at the far side of the courtyard, weapons in their hands. Abruptly, McKie focused on the woman to the left, a competent-looking female of middle years. She was carrying a . . . it couldn't be, but . . .

Jedrik headed across the courtyard toward the woman. McKie followed, peered closely at the woman's weapon. It was an enlarged version of the pentrate from his kit! Jedrik spoke briefly to the woman.

'Is that the new one?'

'Yes. Stiggy brought it up this morning.'

'Useful?'

'We think so. It focuses the explosion with somewhat more concentration than our equipment.'

'Good. Carry on.'

There were more training cadre near the wall behind the women. One, an older man with one arm, tried to catch Jedrik's attention as she led McKie toward a nearby door. 'Could you tell us when we . . .'

'Not now.'

In the passage beyond the door, Jedrik turned and confronted McKie.

'Your impressions of our training? Quick!'

'Not sufficiently versatile.'

She'd obviously probed for his most instinctive reaction, demanding the gut response unmonitored by reason. The answer brought a glowering expression to her face, an emotional candor which he was not to appreciate until much later. Presently, she nodded.

'They are a commando. More functions of a commando should be interchangeable. Wait here.'

She returned to the training area. McKie, watching through the open door, saw her speak to the woman with the pentrate. When Jedrik returned, she nodded to McKie with an expression of approval.

'Anything else?'

'They're awfully damned young. You should have a few seasoned officers among them to put a rein on dangerous impetuosity.'

'Yes, I've already set that in motion. Hereafter, McKie, I want you to come out with me every morning for about an hour. Watch the training, but don't interfere. Report your reactions to me.'

He nodded. Clearly, she considered him useful and that was a step in the right direction. But it was an idiotic assignment. These violent infants possessed weapons which could make Dosadi uninhabitable. There was an atavistic excitement in the situation, though. He couldn't deny that. Something in the Human psyche responded to mass violence – really, to violence of any sort. It was related to Human sexuality, an ancient stirring from the most primitive times.

Jedrik was moving on, however.

'Stay close.'

They were climbing an inside stairway now and McKie, hurrying to keep up, found his thoughts locked on that pentrate in the hands of one of Jedrik's people. The speed with which they'd copied and enlarged it dazzled him. It was another demonstration of why Aritch feared Dosadi.

At the top of the stairs, Jedrik rapped briefly at a door. A male voice said, 'Come in.'

The door swung open, and McKie found himself presently in a small, unoccupied room with an open portal at the far wall into what appeared to be a larger, well-lighted area. Voices speaking so softly as to be unintelligible came from there. A low table and five cramped chairs occupied the small room. There were no windows, but a frosted overhead fixture provided shadowless illumination. A large sheet of paper with colored graph lines on it covered the low table.

A swish of fabric brought McKie's attention to the open portal. A short, slender woman in a white smock, grey hair, and the dark, penetrating stare of someone accustomed to command entered, followed by a slightly taller man in the same white. He looked older than the woman, except his hair remained a lustrous black. His eyes, too, held that air of command. The woman spoke.

'Excuse the delay, Jedrik. We've been changing the summation. There's now no point where Broey can anticipate and change the transition from riots to full-scale warfare.'

McKie was surprised by the abject deference in her voice. This woman considered herself to be far below Jedrik. The man took the same tone, gesturing to chairs.

'Sit down, please. This chart is our summation.'

As the woman turned toward him, McKie caught a strong whiff of something pungent on her breath, a not unfamiliar smell. He'd caught traces of it several times in their passage through the Warrens. She went on speaking as Jedrik and McKie slipped into chairs.

'This is not unexpected.' She indicated the design on the paper.

The man intruded.

'We've been telling you for some time now that Tria is ready to come over.'

'She's trouble,' Jedrik said.

'But Gar ...'

It was the woman, arguing, but Jedrik cut her off.

'I know: Gar does whatever she tells him to do. The daughter runs the father. He thinks she's the most wonderful thing that ever happened, able to ...'

'Her abilities are not the issue,' the man said.

The woman spoke eagerly.

'Yes, it's her influence on Gar that ...'

'Neither of them anticipated my moves,' Jedrik said, 'but I anticipated their moves.'

The man leaned across the table, his face close to Jedrik's. He appeared suddenly to McKie like a large, dangerous animal – dangerous because his actions could never be fully predicted. His hands twitched when he spoke.

'We've told you every detail of our findings, every source, every conclusion. Now, are you saying you don't share our assessment of ...'

'You don't understand,' Jedrik said.

The woman had drawn back. Now, she nodded.

Jedrik said:

'It isn't the first time I've had to reassess your conclusions. Hear me: Tria will leave Broey when she's ready, not when he's ready. It's the same for anyone she serves, even Gar.'

They spoke in unison:

'Leave Gar?'

'Leave anyone. Tria serves only Tria. Never forget that. Especially don't forget it if she comes over to us.'

The man and woman were silent.

McKie thought about what Jedrik had said. Her words were another indication that someone on Dosadi might have other than personal aims. Jedrik's tone was unmistakable: she censured and distrusted Tria because Tria served *only* selfish ambition. Therefore, Jedrik (and this other pair by inference) served some unstated mutual purpose. Was it a form of patriotism they served, species-oriented? BuSab agents were always alert for this dangerous form of tribal madness, not necessarily to suppress it, but to make certain it did not explode into a violence deadly to the ConSentiency.

The white-smocked woman, after mulling her own thoughts, spoke:

'If Tria can't be enlisted for ... what I mean is, we can use her own self-serving to hold her.' She corrected herself. 'Unless you believe we cannot convince her we'll overcome Broey.' She chewed at her lip, a fearful expression in her eyes.

A shrewd look came over Jedrik's face.

'What is it you suspect?'

The woman pointed to the chart on the table.

'Gar still shares in the major decisions. That shouldn't be, but it is. If he ...'

The man spoke with subservient eagerness.

'He has some hold on Broey!'

The woman shook her head.

'Or Broey plays a game other than the one we anticipated.'

Jedrik looked at the woman, the man, at McKie. She spoke as though to McKie, but McKie realized she was addressing the air.

'It's a specific thing. Gar has revealed something to Broey. I know what he's revealed. Nothing else could force Broey to behave this way.' She nodded at the chart. 'We *have* them!'

The woman ventured a question.

'Have we done well?'

'Better than you know.'

The man smiled, then:

'Perhaps this is the time to ask if we could have larger rooms. The damn' children are always moving the furniture. We bump ...'

'Not now!'

Jedrik arose. McKie followed her example.

'Let me see the children,' Jedrik said.

The man turned to the open portal.

'Get out here, you! Jedrik wants you!'

Three children came scurrying from the other room. The woman didn't even look at them. The man favored them with an angry glare. He spoke to Jedrik.

'They've brought no food into this house in almost a week.'

McKie studied the children carefully as he saw Jedrik was doing. They stood in a row just inside the room and, from their expressions, it was impossible to tell their reaction to the summons. They were two girls and a boy. The one on the right, a girl, was perhaps nine; on the left, another girl, was five or six. The boy was somewhat older, perhaps twelve or thirteen. He favored McKie with a glance. It was the glance of a predator who recognizes ready prey, but who already has eaten. All three bore more resemblance to the woman than to the man, but the parentage was obvious: the eyes, the set of the ears, nose . . .

Jedrik had completed her study. She gestured to the boy.

'Start sending him to the second training team.'

'About time,' the woman said. 'We'll be glad to get him out of here.'

'Come along, McKie.'

In the hall, Jedrik said:

'To answer your question, they're pretty typical.'

McKie, who had only wondered silently, swallowed in a dry throat. The petty goals of these people: to get a bigger room where they could live without bumping into furniture. He'd sensed no affection for each other in that couple. They were companions of convenience. There had been not the smallest hint of emotion for each other when they spoke. McKie found it difficult to imagine them making love, but apparently they did. They had produced three children.

Realization came like an explosion in his head. Of course they showed no emotion! What other protection did they have? On Dosadi, anything cared for was a club to beat you into somebody else's line. And there was another thing.

McKie spoke to Jedrik's back as they went down the stairs.

'That couple – they're addicted to something.'

Surprisingly, Jedrik stopped, looked back up at him.

'How else do you think I hold such a pair? The substance is called *dis*. It's very rare. It comes from the far mountains, far beyond the . . . far beyond. The Rim sends parties of children as bearers to obtain *dis* for me. In a party of fifty, thirty can expect to die on such a trek. Do you get the measure of it, McKie?'

Once more, they headed down the stairs.

McKie, realizing she'd taken the time to teach him another lesson about Dosadi, could only follow, stunned, while she led him into a room where technicians bleached the sun-darkened areas of his skin.

When they emerged, he no longer carried the stigma of Pylash Gate.

When the means of great violence are widespread, nothing is more
dangerous to the powerful than that they create outrage and injustice,
for outrage and injustice will certainly ignite retaliation in kind.

– BuSab Manual

'It is no longer classifiable as rioting,' the aide said.

He was a short Gowachin with pinched features, and he looked across
the room to where Broey sat facing a dead communicator. There was a
map on the wall behind the aide, its colors made brilliant by harsh
morning light coming in the east windows. Below the map, a computer
terminal jutted from the wall. Occasionally it clicked.

Gar came into the room from the hall, peered around as though
looking for someone, left.

Broey noted the intrusion, glanced at the map.

'Still no sign of where she's gone to ground?'

'Nothing certain.'

'The one who paraded McKie through the streets . . .'

'Clearly an expendable underling.'

'Where did they go?'

The aide indicated a place on the map, a group of buildings in the
Warrens to the northwest.

Broey stared at the blank face of his communications screen. He'd
been tricked again. He knew it. That damnable Human female! Violence
in the city teetered on the edge of full-scale war: Gowachin against
Human. And still nothing, not even a hint at the location of Gar's Rim
stores, the blasphemous factories. It was an unstable condition which
could not continue much longer.

His communications screen came alive with a report: violent fighting
near Gate Twenty-One. Broey glanced at the map. That made it more
than one hundred clearly defined battles between the species along an
unresolved perimeter. The report spoke of new weapons and unsuc-
cessful attempts to capture specimens.

Gate Twenty-One?

That wasn't far from the place where McKie had been paraded through . . .

Several things slipped into a new relationship in Broey's mind. He looked at his aide, who stood waiting obediently at the map.

'Where's Gar?'

Aides were summoned, sent running. Gar was not to be found.

'Tria?'

She, too, was unavailable.

Gar's fanatics remained neutral, but more of Jedrik's pattern was emerging. Everything pointed to an exquisite understanding of the weakness implicit in the behavior of Gar and Tria.

And I thought I was the only one who saw that!

Broey hesitated.

Why would the God not speak to him other than to say 'I am watched.'

Broey felt tricked and betrayed in his innermost being. This had a cleansing effect on his reason. He could only depend on himself. And he began to sense a larger pattern in Jedrik's behavior. Was it possible that Jedrik shared *his* goals? The possibility excited him.

He looked at the aides who'd come running with the negative information about Gar and Tria, began to snap orders.

'Get our people out of all those Warrens, except that corridor to the northeast. Reinforce that area. Everyone else fall back to the secondary walls. Let no Humans inside that perimeter. Block all gates. Get moving!'

This last was shouted as his aides hesitated.

Perhaps it already was too late. He realized now that he'd allowed Jedrik to bait and distract him. It was clear that she'd created in her mind an almost perfect simulation model of Broey. And she'd done it from a Liaitor position! Incredible. He could almost feel sorry for Gar and Tria. They were like puppets dancing to Jedrik's strings.

I was no better.

It came over him that Jedrik's simulation probably encompassed this very moment of realization. Admiration for her permeated him.

Superb!

Quietly, he issued orders for the sequestering of Gowachin females within the inner Graluz bastions which he'd had the foresight to prepare. His people would thank him for that.

Those who survived the next few hours.

The attack by those who want to die – this is the attack against which you cannot prepare a perfect defense.

– Human aphorism

By the third morning, McKie felt that he might have lived all of his life on Dosadi. The place demanded every element of attention he could muster.

He stood alone in Jedrik's room, staring absently at the unmade bed. She expected him to put the place in order before her return. He knew that. She'd told him to wait here and had gone away on urgent business. He could only obey.

Concerns other than an unmade bed distracted him, though. He felt now that he understood the roots of Aritch's fears. The Gowachin of Tandaloor might very well destroy this place, even if they knew that by doing so they blasted open that bloody region where every sentient hid his most secret fears. He could see this clearly now. How the Running Phylum expected him to avoid that monstrous decision was a more elusive matter.

There were secrets here.

McKie sensed Dosadi like a malignant organism beneath his feet, jealously keeping those secrets from him. This place was the enemy of the ConSentiency, but he found himself emotionally siding with Dosadi. It was betrayal of BuSab, of his Legum oath, everything. But he could not prevent that feeling or recognition of it. In the course of only a few generations, Dosadi had become a particular thing. Monstrous? Only if you held to your own precious myths. Dosadi might be the greatest cleansing force the ConSentiency had ever experienced.

The whole prospect of the ConSentiency had begun to sicken him. And Aritch's Gowachin. Gowachin Law? Stuff Gowachin Law!

It was quiet in Jedrik's room. Painfully quiet.

He knew that out on the streets of Chu there was violent warfare between Gowachin and Human. Wounded had been rushed through the training courtyard while he was there with Jedrik. Afterward, she'd taken him to her command post, a room across the hall and above

Pcharky's cage. He'd stood nearby, watched her performance as though she were a star on an entertainment circuit and he a member of the audience. It was fascinating. Broey will do this. Broey will give that order. And each time, the reports revealed how precisely she had anticipated her opponent.

Occasionally, she mentioned Gar or Tria. He was able to detect the subtle difference in her treatment of that pair.

On their second night together, Jedrik had aroused his sexual appetites softly, deftly. She had treated him to a murmurous compliance, and afterward had leaned over him on an elbow to smile coldly.

'You see, McKie: I can play your game.'

Shockingly, this had opened an area of awareness within him which he'd not even suspected. It was as though she'd held up his entire previous life to devastating observation.

And *he* was the observer!

Other beings formed lasting relationships and operated from a secure emotional base. But he was a product of BuSab, the Gowachin ... and much that had gone before. It had become increasingly obvious to him why the Gowachin had chosen him to groom for this particular role.

I was damaged and they could rebuild me the way they wanted!

Well, the Gowachin could still be surprised by what they produced. Dosadi was evidence of that. They might not even suspect what they'd actually produced in McKie.

He was bitter with a bitterness he knew must've been fermenting in him for years. The loneliness of his own life with its central dedication to BuSab had been brought to a head by the loneliness of this imprisoned planet. An incredible jumble of emotions had sorted themselves out, and he felt new purpose burning within him.

Power!

Ahhhh ... that was how it felt to be Dosadi!

He'd turned away from Jedrik's cold smile, pulled the blankets around his shoulder.

Thank you, loving teacher.

Such thoughts roamed through his mind as he stood alone in the room the following day and began to make the bed. After her revelation, Jedrik had resumed her interest in his memories, napping only to awaken him with more questions.

In spite of his sour outlook, he still felt it his duty to examine her behavior in every possible light his imagination could produce. Nothing about Dosadi was too absurd. He had to build a better picture of this society and its driving forces.

Before returning to Jedrik's room, he'd made another tour of the training courtyard with her. There'd been more new weapons adapted from his kit, and he'd realized the courtyard was merely Jedrik's testing ground, that there must be many more training areas for her followers.

McKie had not yet revealed to her that Aritch's people might terminate Dosadi's people with violence. She'd been centering on this at dawn. Even while they shared the tiny toilet cubicle off her room she'd pressed for answers.

For a time, McKie had diverted her with questions about Pcharky. What were the powers in that cage? At one point, he'd startled her.

'Pcharky knows something valuable he hopes to trade for his freedom.'

'How'd you know?'

'It's obvious. I'll tell you something else: he came here of his own free will . . . for whatever purpose.'

'You learn quickly, McKie.'

She was laughing at him and he glared at her.

'All right! I don't know that purpose, but it may be that you only think you know it.'

For the briefest flicker, something dangerous glared from her eyes, then:

'Your *jumpdoors* have brought us many fools, but Pcharky is one of the biggest fools. I know why he came. There've been many like him. Now . . . there is only one. Broey, for all of his power, cannot search out his own Pcharky. And Keila Jedrik is the one who frustrates him.'

Too late, she realized that McKie had goaded her into this performance. How had he done that? He'd almost found out too much too soon. It was dangerous to underestimate this naive intruder from beyond the God Wall.

Once more, she'd begun probing for things he had not yet revealed. Time had protected him. Aides had come urging an early inspection of the new weapons. They were needed.

Afterward, they'd gone to the command post and then to breakfast in a Warren dining room. All through breakfast, he'd plied her with questions about the fighting. How extensive was it? Could he see some of the prisoners? Were they using the weapons built from the patterns in his kit? Were they winning?

Sometimes she merely ignored his questions. Most of her answers were short, distracted. Yes. No. No. Yes. McKie realized she was answering in monosyllables to fend him off. He was a distraction. Something important had been communicated to her and he'd missed it. Although this angered him, he tried to mask the emotion, striving to penetrate her wall of concern. Oddly, she responded when he changed his line of questioning to the parents of the three children and the conversation there.

'You started to designate a particular place: "Beyond the ..." Beyond what?'

'It's something Gar thinks I don't know. He thinks only his death fanatics have that kind of rapport with the Rim.'

He stared at her, caught by a sudden thought. By now, he knew much about Gar and Tria. She answered his questions about them with candor, often using him openly to clarify her own thoughts. But – death fanatics?

'Are these fanatics homosexual?'

She pounced.

'How'd you know?'

'A guess.'

'What difference would it make?'

'Are they?'

'Yes.'

McKie shuddered.

She was peremptory.

'Explain!'

'When Humans for any reason go terminal where survival of their species is concerned, it's relatively easy to push them the short step further into *wanting* to die.'

'You speak from historical evidence?'

'Yes.'

'Example.'

'With rare exceptions, primitive Humans of the tribal eras reserved their homosexuals as the ultimate shock troops of desperation. They were the troops of last resort, sent into battle as berserkers who expected, who *wanted*, to die.'

She had to have the term *berserkers* explained, then showed by her manner that she believed him. She considered this, then:

'What does your ConSentiency do about this susceptibility?'

'We take sophisticated care to guide all natural sexual variants into constructive survival activities. We protect them from the kinds of pressures which might tip them over into behavior destructive of the species.'

Only later had McKie realized she had not answered his question: *beyond what?* She'd rushed him off to a conference room where more than twenty Humans were assembled, including the two parents who'd made the chart about Tria and Gar. McKie realized he didn't even know their names.

It put him at a disadvantage not knowing as many of these people by sight and name as he should. They, of course, had ready memories of everyone important around them and, when they used a name, often did it with such blurred movement into new subjects that he was seldom sure who had been named. He saw the key to it, though. Their memories were anchored in explicit references to relative abilities of those around them, relative dangers. And it wasn't so much that they concealed their emotions as that they *managed* their emotions. Nowhere in their memories could there be any emotive clouding such as thoughts of love or friendship. Such things weakened you. Everything operated on the strict basis of *quid pro quo*, and you'd better have the cash ready – whatever that cash might be. McKie, pressed all around by questions from the people in the conference room, knew he had only one real asset: he was a key they might use to open the God Wall. Very important asset, but unfortunately owned by an idiot.

Now, they wanted his information about death fanatics. They milked him dry, then sent him away like a child who has performed for his elders but is sent to his room when important matters are brought up for discussion.

> The more control, the more that requires control. This is the road to chaos.
>
> *– PanSpechi aphorism*

By the fourth morning of the battle for Chu, Tria was in a vile humor. Her forces had established lines holding about one-eighth of the total Warren territory, mostly low buildings, except along Broey's corridor to the Rim. She did not like the idea that Jedrik's people held an unobstructed view down onto most of the death fanatics' territory. And most of those leaders who'd thrown in their lot with Tria were beginning to have second thoughts, especially since they'd come to realize that this enclave had insufficient food production facilities to maintain itself. The population density she'd been forced to accept was frightening: almost triple the Warren norm.

Thus far, neither Broey nor Jedrik had moved in force against her. Tria had finally been brought to the inescapable conclusion that she and Gar were precisely where Jedrik wanted them. They'd been cut out of Broey's control as neatly and cleanly as though by a knife. There was no going back. Broey would never accept Human help under present circumstances. That, too, spoke of the exquisite care with which Jedrik had executed her plan.

Tria had moved her command post during the night to a high building which faced the canyon walls to the north. Only the river, with a single gate under it, separated her from the Rim. She'd slept badly, her mind full of worries. Chief among her worries was the fact that none of the contact parties she'd sent out to the Rim had returned. There'd been no fires on the Rim ledges during the night. No word from any of her people out there.

Why?

Once more, she contemplated her position, seeking some advantage, any advantage. One of her lines was anchored on Broey's corridor to the Rim, one line on the river wall with its single gate, and the rest of her perimeter meandered through a series of dangerous salients from the fifth wall to the river.

She could hear sounds of battle along the far side of Broey's corridor. Jedrik's people used weapons which made a great deal of noise. Occasionally, an explosive projectile landed in Tria's enclave. These were rare, but she'd taken casualties and the effect on morale was destructive. That was a major problem with fanatics: they demanded to be used, to be wasted.

Tria stared down at the river, aware of the bodies drifting on its poison currents – both Human and Gowachin bodies, but more Gowachin than Human. Presently, she turned away from the scene, padded into the next room, and roused Gar.

'We must contact Jedrik,' she said.

He rubbed sleep from his eyes.

'No! We must wait until we make contact with our people on the Rim. Then we can . . .'

'Faaaaa!'

She'd seldom showed that much disgust with him.

'We're not going to make contact with our people on the Rim. Jedrik and Broey have seen to that. It wouldn't surprise me if they were cooperating to isolate us.'

'But we've . . .'

'Shut up, Father!' She held up her hands, stared at them. 'I was never really good enough to be one of Broey's chief advisors. I always suspected that. I always pressed too hard. Last night, I reviewed as many of my decisions as I could. Jedrik deliberately made me look good. She did it oh so beautifully!'

'But our forces on the Rim . . .'

'May not be ours! They may be Jedrik's.'

'Even the Gowachin?'

'Even the Gowachin.'

Gar could hear a ringing in his ears. Contact Jedrik? Throw away all of their power?

'I'm good enough to recognize the weakness of a force such as ours,' Tria said. 'We can be goaded into spending ourselves uselessly. Even Broey didn't see that, but Jedrik obviously did. Look at the salients along her perimeter!'

'What have salients . . .'

'They can be pinched off and obliterated! Even *you* must see that.'

'Then pull back and . . .

'Reduce our territory?' She stared at him, aghast. 'If I even intimate I'm going to do that, our auxiliaries will desert wholesale. Right now they're . . .'

'Then attack!'

'To gain what?'

Gar nodded. Jedrik would fall back across mined areas, blast the fanatics out of existence. She held enough territory that she could afford such destruction. Clearly, she'd planned on it.

'Then we must pinch off Broey's corridor.'

'That's what Jedrik wants us to do. It's the only negotiable counter we have left. That's why we must contact Jedrik.'

Gar shook his head in despair.

Tria was not finished, though.

'Jedrik might restore us to a share of power in the Rim city if we bargain for it now. Broey would never do that. Do you understand now the mistake you made with Broey?'

'But Broey was going to . . .'

'You failed to follow my orders, Father. You must see now why I always tried to keep you from making independent decisions.'

Gar fell into abashed silence. This was his daughter, but he could sense his peril.

Tria spoke.

'I will issue orders presently to all of our commanders. They will be told to hold at all costs. They will be told that you and I will try to contact Jedrik. They will be told why.'

'But how can . . .'

'We will permit ourselves to be captured.'

QUESTION: Who governs the governors?
ANSWER: Entropy.

– Gowachin riddle

Many things conspired to frustrate McKie. Few people other than Jedrik answered his questions. Most responded as though to a cretin. Jedrik treated him as though he were a child of unknown potential. At times, he knew he amused her. Other times, she punished him with an angry glance, by ignoring him, or just by going away – or worse, sending him away.

It was now late afternoon of the fifth day in the battle for Chu, and Broey's forces still held out in the heart of the city with their slim corridor to the Rim. He knew this from reports he'd overheard. He stood in a small room off Jedrik's command post, a room containing four cots where, apparently she and/or her commanders snatched occasional rest. One tall, narrow window looked out to the south Rim. McKie found it difficult to realize that he'd come across that Rim just six days previously.

Clouds had begun to gather over the Rim's terraced escarpments, a sure sign of a dramatic change in the weather. He knew that much, at least, from his Tandaloor briefings. Dosadi had no such thing as weather control. Awareness of this left him feeling oddly vulnerable. Nature could be so damnably capricious and dangerous when you had no grip on her vagaries.

McKie blinked, held his breath for a moment.

Vagaries of nature.

The vagaries of sentient nature had moved the Gowachin to set up this experiment. Did they really hope to control that vast, seething conglomerate of motives? Or had they some other reason for Dosadi, a reason which he had not yet penetrated? Was this, after all, a test of Caleban mysteries? He thought not.

He knew the way Aritch and aides *said* they'd set up this experiment. Observations here bore out their explanations. None of that data was consistent with an attempt to understand the Calebans. Only that brief encounter with Pcharky, a thing which Jedrik no longer was willing to discuss.

No matter how he tried, McKie couldn't evade the feeling that something essential lay hidden in the way this planet had been set upon its experimental course; something the Gowachin hadn't revealed, something they perhaps didn't even understand themselves. What'd they done at the beginning? They had this place, Dosadi, the subjects, the Primary yes, the Primary. The inherent inequality of individuals dominated Gowachin minds. And there was that damnable DemoPol. How had they mandated it? Better yet: how did they maintain that mandate?

Aritch's people had hoped to expose the inner workings of sentient social systems. So they said. But McKie was beginning to look at that explanation with Dosadi eyes, with Dosadi scepticism. What had Fannie Mae meant about not being able to leave here in his own body/node? How could he be Jedrik's *key* to the God Wall? McKie knew he needed more information than he could hope to get from Jedrik. Did Broey have this information? McKie wondered if he might in the end have to climb the heights to the Council Hills for his answers. Was that even possible now?

When he'd asked for it, Jedrik had given him almost the run of this building, warning:

'Don't interfere.'

Interfere with what?

When he'd asked, she'd just stared at him.

She had, however, taken him around to familiarize everyone with his status. He was never quite sure what that status might be, except that it was somewhere between guest and prisoner.

Jedrik had required minimal conversation with her people. Often, she'd used only hand waves to convey the necessary signals of passage. The whole traverse was a lesson for McKie, beginning with the door-guards.

'McKie.' Pointing at him.

The guards nodded.

Jedrik had other concerns.

'Team Nine?'

'Back at noon.'

'Send word.'

Everyone subjected McKie to a hard scrutiny which he felt certain would let them identify him with minimal interruption.

There were two elevators: one an express from a heavily guarded street entrance on the side of the building, the other starting above the fourth level at the ceiling of Pcharky's cage. They took this one, went up, pausing at each floor for guards to see him.

When they returned to the cage room, McKie saw that a desk had been installed just inside the street door. The father of those three wild children sat there watching Pcharky, making occasional notations in a notebook. McKie had a name for him now, Ardir.

Jedrik paused at the desk.

'McKie can come and go with the usual precautions.'

McKie, addressing himself finally to Jedrik, had said:

'Thanks for taking this time with me.'

'No need to be sarcastic, McKie.'

He had not intended sarcasm and reminded himself once more that the usual amenities of the ConSentiency suffered a different inter-pretation here.

Jedrik glanced through Ardir's notes, looked up at Pcharky, back to McKie. Her expression did not change.

'We will meet for dinner.'

She left him then.

For his part, McKie had approached Pcharky's cage, noting the tension this brought to the room's guards and observers. The old Gowachin sat in his hammock with an indifferent expression on his face. The bars of the cage emitted an almost indiscernible hissing as they shimmered and glowed.

'What happens if you touch the bars?' McKie asked.

The Gowachin jowls puffed in a faint shrug.

McKie pointed.

'There's energy in those bars. What is that energy? How is it main-tained?'

Pcharky responded in a hoarse croaking.

'How is the universe maintained? When you first see a thing, is that when it was created?'

'Is it a Caleban thing?'

Shrug.

McKie walked around the cage, studying it. There were glistening bulbs wherever the bars crossed each other. The rods upon which the hammock was suspended came from the ceiling. They penetrated the cage top without touching it. The hammock itself appeared to be fabric. It was faintly blue. He returned to his position facing Pcharky.

'Do they feed you?'

No answer.

Ardir spoke from behind him.

'His food is lowered from the ceiling. His excreta are hosed into the reclamation lines.'

McKie spoke over his shoulder.

'I see no door into the cage. How'd he get in there?'

'It was built around him according to his own instructions.'

'What are the bulbs where the bars cross?'

'They came into existence when he activated the cage.'

'How'd he do that?'

'We don't know. Do you?'

McKie shook his head from side to side.

'How does Pcharky explain this?'

'He doesn't.'

McKie had turned away to face Ardir, probing, moving the focus of questions from Pcharky to the planetary society itself. Ardir's answers, especially on matters of religion and history, were banal.

Later, as he stood in the room off the command post reviewing the experience, McKie found his thoughts touching on a matter which had not even come into question.

Jedrik and her people had known for a long time that Dosadi was a Gowachin creation. They'd known it long before McKie had appeared on the scene. It was apparent in the way they focused on Pcharky, in the way they reacted to Broey. McKie had added one significant datum: that Dosadi was a Gowachin *experiment*. But Jedrik's people were not using him in the ways he might expect. She said he was the key to the God Wall, but how was he that key?

The answer was not to be found in Ardir. That one had not tried to evade McKie's questions, but the answers betrayed a severely limited scope to Ardir's knowledge and imagination.

McKie felt deeply disturbed by this insight. It was not so much what the man said as what he did not say when the reasons for speaking openly in detail were most demanding. Ardir was no dolt. This was a Human who'd risen high in Jedrik's hierarchy. Many speculations would've crossed his mind. Yet he made no mention of even the more obvious speculations. He raised no questions about the way Dosadi history ran to a single cutoff point in the past without any trace of evolutionary beginnings. He did not appear to be a religious person and even if he were, Dosadi would not permit the more blatant religious inhibitions. Yet Ardir refused to explore the most obvious discrepancies in those overt religious attitudes McKie had been told to expect. Ardir played out the right attitudes, but there was no basis for them underneath. It was all surface.

Mckie suddenly despaired of ever getting a deep answer from any of these people – even from Jedrik.

An increase in the noise level out in the command post caught McKie's attention. He opened the door, stood in the doorway to study the other room.

A new map had been posted on the far wall. There was a position board, transparent and covered with yellow, red, and blue dots, over the map. Five women and a man – all wearing earphones – worked the board, moving the colored markers. Jedrik stood with her back to McKie, talking to several commanders who'd just come in from the streets. They still carried their weapons and packs. It was their conversation which had attracted McKie. He scanned the room, noted two communications screens at the left wall, both inactive. They were new since his last view of the room and he wondered at their purpose.

An aide leaned in from the hallway, called out:

'Gate Twenty-One just reported. Everything has quieted there. They want to know if they should keep their reserves on the alert.'

'Have them stand down,' Jedrik said.

'The two prisoners are being brought here,' the aide added.

'I see it,' Jedrik said.

She nodded toward the position board.

McKie, following the direction of her gaze, saw two yellow markers being moved with eight blue companions. Without knowing how he understood this, he saw that this must be the prisoners and their escort. There were tensions in the command post which told him this was an important event. Who were those prisoners?

One of Jedrik's commanders spoke.

'I saw the monitor at ...'

She was not listening to him and he broke off. Two people on the position board exchanged places, trading earphones. The messenger who'd called out the information about the gate and the prisoners had gone. Another messenger came in presently, conferred in a soft voice with people near the door.

In a few moments, eight young Human males entered carrying Gar and Tria securely trussed with what appeared to be shining wire. McKie recognized the pair from Aritch's briefings. The escort carried their prisoners like so much meat, one at each leg and each arm.

'Over here,' Jedrik said, indicating two chairs facing her.

McKie found himself suddenly aware, in an extremely Dosadi way, of many of the nuances here. It filled him with elation.

The escort crossed the room, not bothering to steer clear of all the furniture. The messenger from the hallway delayed his departure, reluctant to leave. He'd recognized the prisoners and knew something important was about to happen.

Gar and Tria were dumped into the two chairs.

'Release their bindings,' Jedrik said.

The escort obeyed.

Jedrik waited, staring across at the position board. The two yellow and eight blue markers had been removed. She continued to stare at the board, though. Something there was more important than these two prisoners. She pointed to a cluster of red markers in an upper corner.

'See to that.'

One of her commanders left the room.

McKie took a deep breath. He'd spotted the flicker of her movement toward the commander who'd obeyed. So that was how she did it! McKie moved farther into the room to put Jedrik in profile to him. She made no response to his movement, but he knew she was aware of him. He stepped closer to what he saw as the limit of her tolerance, noted a faint smile as she turned toward the prisoners.

There was an abrupt silence, one of those uncomfortable moments when people realize there are things they must do, but everyone is reluctant to start. The messenger still stood by the door to the hall, obviously wanting to see what would happen here. The escort who'd brought the prisoners remained standing in a group at one side. They were almost huddled, as though seeking protection in their own numbers.

Jedrik glanced across at the messenger.

'You may go.'

She nodded to the escort.

'And you.'

McKie held his cautious distance, waiting, but Jedrik took no notice of him. He saw that he not only would be allowed to stay, but that he was expected to use his wits, his off-world knowledge. Jedrik had read things in his presence: a normal distrust, caution, patience. And the fears, of course.

Jedrik took her time with the prisoners. She leaned forward, examined first Tria, then Gar. From the way she looked at them, it was clear to McKie she weighed many possibilities on how to deal with this pair. She was also building the tensions and this had its effect. Gar broke.

'Broey has a way of describing people such as you,' Gar said. 'He calls you "rockets," which is to say you are like a display which shoots up into the sky – and falls back.'

Jedrik grinned.

McKie understood. Gar was not managing his emotions very well. It was a weakness.

'Many rockets in this universe must die unseen,' Jedrik said.

Gar glared at her. He didn't like this response, glanced at Tria, saw from her expression that he had blundered.

Tria spoke now, smiling faintly.

'You've taken a personal interest in us, Jedrik.'

To McKie, it was as though he'd suddenly crossed a threshold into the understanding of another language. Tria's was a Dosadi statement, carrying many messages. She'd said that Jedrik saw an opportunity for personal gain here and that Tria knew this. The faint smile had been the beginning of the statement. McKie felt a new awe at the special genius of the Dosadi awareness. He moved a step closer. There was something else about Tria ... something odd.

'What is that one to you?'

Tria spoke to Jedrik, but a flicker of the eyes indicated McKie.

'He has a certain utility,' Jedrik said.

'Is that the reason you keep him near you?'

'There's no single reason.'

'There've been certain rumors ...'

'One uses what's available,' Jedrik said.

'Did you plan to have children by him?'

Jedrik shook with silent mirth. McKie understood that Tria probed for weaknesses, found none.

'The breeding period is so incapacitating for a female,' Tria said.

The tone was deliberately goading, and McKie waited for a response. Jedrik nodded.

'Offspring produce many repercussions down through the generations. Never a casual decision for those of us who understand.'

Jedrik looked at Gar, forcing McKie to shift his attention.

Gar's face went suddenly bland, which McKie interpreted as shock and anger. The man had himself under control quickly, however. He stared at McKie, directed a question to Jedrik.

'Would his death profit us?'

Jedrik glanced at McKie.

Shocked by the directness of the question, McKie was at least as intrigued by the assumptions in Gar's question. '*Us!*' Gar assumed that he and Jedrik had common cause. Jedrik was weighing that assumption and McKie, filled with elation, understood. He also recognized something else and realized he could now repay all of Jedrik's patient teaching.

Tria!

Something about Tria's way of holding her head, the inflections in her spoken Galach, struck a chord in McKie's memory. Tria was a Human who'd been trained by a PanSpechi – that way of moving the eyes before the head moved, the peculiar emphasis in her speech mannerisms. But there were no PanSpechi on Dosadi. Or were there?

None of this showed on McKie's face. He continued to radiate distrust, caution, patience. But he began to ask himself if there might be another loose thread in this Dosadi mystery. He saw Jedrik looking at him and, without thinking about it, gave her a purely Dosadi eye signal to follow him, returned to the adjoining room. It was a measure of how she read him that she came without question.

'Yes?'

He told her what he suspected.

'These PanSpechi, they are the ones who can grow a body to simulate that of another species?'

'Except for the eyes. They have faceted eyes. Any PanSpechi who could act freely and simulate another species would be only the surface manifestation. The freely moving one is only one of five bodies; it's the holder of the ego, the identity. This passes periodically to another of the five. It's a PanSpechi crime to prevent that transfer by surgically fixing the ego in only one of the bodies.'

Jedrik glanced out the doorway. 'You're sure about her?'

'The pattern's there.'

'The faceted eyes, can that be disguised?'

'There are ways: contact lenses or a rather delicate operation. I've been trained to detect such things, however, and I can tell you that the one who trained her is not Gar.'

She looked at him.

'Broey?'

'A Graluz would be a great place to conceal a creche but ...' He shook his head. ' ... I don't think so. From what you tell me about Broey ...'

'Gowachin,' she agreed. 'Then who?'

'Someone who influenced her when she was quite young.'

'Do you wish to interrogate the prisoners?'

'Yes, but I don't know their potential value.'

She stared at him in open wonder. His had been an exquisitely penetrating Dosadi-style statement. It was as though a McKie she thought she knew had been transformed suddenly right in front of her eyes. He was not yet sufficiently Dosadi to trust completely, but she'd never expected him to come this far this quickly. He did deserve a more detailed assessment of the military situation and the relative abilities of Tria and Gar. She delivered this assessment in the Dosadi way: barebones words, swift, clipped to an essential spareness which assumed a necessary broad understanding by the listener.

Absorbing this, McKie sensed where she limited her recital, tailoring it for his abilities. In a way, it was similar to a response by his Daily Schedule back on Central Central. He could see himself in her attitudes, read her assessment of him. She was favoring him with a limited, grudging respect tempered by a certain fondness as by a parent toward a child. And he knew that once they returned to the other room, the fondness would be locked under a mask of perfect concealment. It was there, though. It was there. And he dared not betray her trust by counting on that fondness, else it would be locked away forever.

'I'm ready,' he said.

They returned to the command post, McKie with a clearer picture of how to operate here. There was no such thing as mutual, unquestioning trust. You always questioned. You always managed. A sort of grudging respect was the nearest they'd reveal openly. They worked together to survive, or when it was overwhelmingly plain that there was personal advantage in mutual action. Even when they united, they remained ultimate individualists. They suspected any gift because no one gave away anything freely. The safest relationships were those in which the niches of the hierarchy were clear and solidly held — minimum threat from above and from below. The whole thing reminded McKie of stories told about behavior in Human bureaucracies of the classical period before deep space travel. And many years before he had encountered a multispecies corporation which had behaved similarly until the ministrations of BuSab had shown them the error of their ways. They'd used every dirty trick available: bribing, spying and other forms of covert and overt espionage, fomenting dissent in the opposition, assassination, blackmail, and kidnapping. Few in the ConSentiency had not heard of InterRealm Supply, now defunct.

McKie stopped three paces from the prisoners.

Tria spoke first.

'Have you decided what to do with us?'

'There's useful potential in both of you,' McKie said, 'but we have other questions.'

The 'we' did not escape Tria or Gar. They both looked at Jedrik, who stood impassively at McKie's shoulder.

McKie addressed himself to Gar.

'Is Tria really your daughter, your natural child?'

Tria appeared surprised and, with his new understanding, McKie realized she was telling him she didn't care if he saw this reaction, that it suited her for him to see this. Gar, however, had betrayed a flicker of shock. By Dosadi standards, he was dumbfounded. Then Tria was not his natural daughter, but until this moment, Tria had never questioned their relationship.

'Tell us,' McKie said.

The Dosadi spareness of the words struck Gar like a blow. He looked at Jedrik. She gave every indication of willingness to wait forever for him to obey, which was to say that she made no response either to McKie's words or Gar's behavior.

Visibly defeated, Gar returned his attention to McKie.

'I went with two females, only the three of us, across the far mountains. We tried to set up our own production of pure food there. Many on the Rim tried that in those days. They seldom came back. Something always happens: the plants die for no reason, the water source runs dry, something steals what you grow. The Gods are jealous. That's what we always said.'

He looked at Tria, who studied him without expression.

'One of the two women died the first year. The other was sick by the following harvest season, but survived through the next spring. It was during that harvest ... we went to the garden ... ha! The garden! This child was there. We had no idea of where she'd come from. She appeared to be seven or eight years old, but her reactions were those of an infant. That happens often enough on the Rim – the mind retreats from something too terrible to bear. We took her in. Sometimes you can train such a child back to usefulness. When the woman died and the crop failed, I took Tria and we headed back to the Rim. That was a very bad time. When we returned ... I was sick. Tria helped me then. We've been together ever since.'

McKie found himself deeply touched by this recital and hard put to conceal his reaction. He was not positive that he did conceal it. With his new Dosadi awareness, he read an entire saga into that sparse account of events which probably were quite ordinary by Rim standards. He found himself enraged by the other data which could be read into Gar's words.

PanSpechi trained!

That was the key. Aritch's people had wanted to maintain the purity of their experiment: only two species permitted. But it would be informative to examine PanSpechi applications. Simple. Take a Human female child. Put her exclusively under PanSpechi influence for seven or eight years. Subject that child to selective memory erasure. Hand her over to convenient surrogate parents on Dosadi.

And there was more: Aritch lied when he said he knew little about the Rim, that the Rim was outside the experiment.

As these thoughts went through his head, McKie returned to the small adjoining room. Jedrik followed. She waited while he assembled his thoughts.

Presently, McKie looked at her, laid out his deductions. When he finished, he glanced at the doorway.

'I need to learn as much as I can about the Rim.'

'Those two are a good source.'

'But don't you require them for your other plans, the attack on Broey's corridor?'

'Two things can go forward simultaneously. You will return to their enclave with them as my lieutenant. That'll confuse them. They won't know what to make of that. They will answer your questions. And in their confusion they'll reveal much that they might otherwise conceal from you.'

McKie absorbed this. Yes ... Jedrik did not hesitate to put him into peril. It was an ultimate message to everyone. McKie would be totally at the mercy of Gar and Tria. Jedrik was saying, 'See! You cannot influence me by any threat to McKie.' In a way, this protected him. In an extremely devious Dosadi way, this removed many possible threats to McKie, and it told him much about what her true feelings toward him could be. He spoke to this.

'I detest a cold bed.'

Her eyes sparkled briefly, the barest touch of moisture, then, arming him:

'No matter what happens to me, McKie – free us!'

Given the proper leverage at the proper point, any sentient awareness may be exploded into astonishing self-understanding.

– from an ancient Human mystic

'Unless she makes a mistake, or we find some unexpected advantage, it's only a matter of time until she overruns us,' Broey said.

He sat in his aerie command post at the highest point of the dominant building on the Council Hills. The room was an armored oval with a single window about fifteen meters away directly in front of Broey looking out on sunset through the river's canyon walls. A small table with a communicator stood just to his left. Four of his commanders waited near the table. Maps, position boards, and the other appur-tenances of command, with their attendants, occupied most of the room's remaining space.

Broey's intelligence service had just brought him the report that Jedrik had taken Gar and Tria captive.

One of his commanders, slender for a Gowachin and with other deprivation marks left from birth on the Rim, glanced at his three companions, cleared his throat.

'Is it time to capitulate?'

Broey shook his head in a Human gesture of negation.

It's time I told them, he thought.

He felt emptied. God refused to speak to him. Nothing in his world obeyed the old mandates.

We've been tricked.

The Powers of the God Wall had tricked him, had tricked his world and all of its inhabitants. They'd ...

'This McKie,' the commander said.

Broey swallowed, then:

'I doubt if McKie has even the faintest understanding of how she uses him.'

He glanced at the reports on his communicator table, a stack of reports about McKie. Broey's intelligence service had been active.

'If we captured or killed him ...' the commander ventured.

554

'Too late for that,' Broey said.

'Is there a chance we won't have to capitulate?'

'There's always that chance.'

None of the four commanders liked this answer. Another of them, fat and silky green, spoke up:

'If we have to capitulate, how will we know the . . .'

'We must never capitulate, and we must make certain she knows this,' Broey said. 'She means to exterminate us.'

There! He'd told them.

They were shocked but beginning to understand where his reasoning had led him. He saw the signs of understanding come over their faces.

'The corridor . . .' one of them ventured.

Broey merely stared at him. The fool must know they couldn't get more than a fraction of their forces onto the Rim before Jedrik and Tria closed off that avenue. And even if they could escape to the Rim, what could they do? They hadn't the faintest idea of where the damned factories and food stores were buried.

'If we could rescue Tria,' the slim commander said.

Broey snorted. He'd prayed for Tria to contact him, to open negotiations. There'd been not a word, even after she'd fallen back into that impossible enclave. Therefore, Tria had lost control of her people outside the city. All the other evidence supported this conclusion. There was no contact with the Rim. Jedrik's people had taken over out there. Tria would've sent word to him the minute she recognized the impossibility of her position. Any valuable piece of information, any counter in this game would've leaped into Tria's awareness, and she'd have recognized who the highest bidder must be.

Who was the highest bidder? Tria, after all, was Human.

Broey sighed.

And McKie – an idiot savant from beyond the God Wall, a *weapons* expert. Jedrik must've known. But how? Did the Gods talk to her? Broey doubted this. Jedrik gave every evidence of being too clever to be sucked in by trickster Gods.

More clever, more wary, more Dosadi than I.

She deserved the victory.

Broey arose and went to the window. His commanders exchanged worried glances behind him. Could Broey *think* them out of this mess?

A corner of his slim corridor to the Rim was visible to Broey. He could not hear the battle, but explosive orange blossoms told him the fighting continued. He knew the gamble Jedrik took. Those Gowachin beyond the God Wall, the ones who'd created this hellish place, were slow –

terrifyingly slow. But eventually they would be unable to misunderstand Jedrik's intentions. Would they step in, those mentally retarded Gowachin out there, and try to stop Jedrik? She obviously thought they would. Everything she did told Broey of the care with which Jedrik had prepared for the stupids from Outside. Broey almost wished her success, but he could not bear the price he and his people would have to pay.

Jedrik had the time-edge on him. She had McKie. She had played McKie like a superb instrument. And what would McKie do when he realized the final use Jedrik intended to make of him? Yes ... McKie was a perfect tool for Jedrik. She'd obviously waited for that perfect instrument, had known when it arrived.

Gods! She was superb!

Broey scratched at the nodes between his ventricles. Well, there were still things a trapped people could do. He returned to his commanders.

'Abandon the corridor. Do it quietly, but swiftly. Fall back to the prepared inner walls.'

As his commanders started to turn away, Broey stopped them.

'I also want some carefully selected volunteers. The fix we're in must be explained to them in such a way that there's no misunderstanding. They will be asked to sacrifice themselves in a way no Gowachin has ever before contemplated.'

'How?'

It was the slender one.

Broey addressed himself to this one. A Gowachin born on the Rim should be the first to understand.

'We must increase the price Jedrik's paying. Hundreds of their people for every *one* of ours.'

'Suicide missions,' the slender one said.

Broey nodded, continued:

'One more thing. I want Havvy brought up here and I want orders issued to increase the food allotment to those Humans we've held in special reserve.'

Two of his commanders spoke in unison:

'They won't sacri ...'

'I have something else in mind for them.'

Broey nodded to himself. Yes indeed. Some of those Humans could still serve his purposes. It wasn't likely they could serve him as McKie served Jedrik, but there was still a chance ... yes, a chance. Jedrik might not be certain of what Broey could do with his Humans. Havvy, for example. Jedrik had certainly considered and discarded Havvy. In itself, that might be useful. Broey waved for his commanders to leave and execute his orders. They'd seen the new determination in him. They'd pass that along to the ones beneath them. That, too, would serve his purposes. It would delay the moment when his people might suspect that he was making a desperate gamble.

He returned to his communicator, called his search people, urged them to new efforts. They might still achieve what Jedrik obviously had achieved with Pcharky . . . if they could find a Pcharky.

Knowledge is the province of the Legum, just as knowledge is a source of crime.

– *Gowachin Law*

McKie told himself that he might've known an assignment from Jedrik could not be simple. There had to be Dosadi complications.

'There can be no question in their minds that you're really my lieutenant.'

'Then I must be your lieutenant.'

This pleased her, and she gave him the bare outline of her plan, warning him that the upcoming encounter could not be an act. He must respond as one who was fully aware of this planet's demands.

Night fell over Chu while she prepared him and, when they returned to the command post where Gar and Tria waited, the occasion presented itself as Jedrik had told him it would. It was a sortie by Broey's people against Gate Eighteen. Jedrik snapped the orders at him, sent him running.

'Find the purpose of that!'

McKie paused only to pick up four waiting guards at the command post door, noting the unconcealed surprise in Gar and Tria. They'd formed a particular opinion of McKie's position and now had to seek a new assessment. Tria would be most upset by this, confused by self-doubts. McKie knew Jedrik would immediately amplify those doubts, telling Gar and Tria that McKie would go with them when he returned from Gate Eighteen.

'You must consider his orders as my orders.'

Gate Eighteen turned out to be more than a minor problem. Broey had taken the gate itself and two buildings. One of the attackers, diving from an upper window into one of Jedrik's best units, had blown himself up with a nasty lot of casualties.

'More than a hundred dead,' a breathless courier told him.

McKie didn't like the implications of a suicide attack, but couldn't pause to assess it. They had to eliminate this threat. He gave orders for two feints while a third force blasted down one of the captured buildings, smothering the gate in rubble. That left the other captive building isolated. The swiftness of this success dazzled Jedrik's forces, and the commanders snapped to obedience when McKie issued orders for them to take captives and bring those captives to him for interrogation.

At McKie's command, one of his original four guards brought a map of the area, tacked it to a wall. Less than an hour had passed since he'd left Jedrik, but McKie felt that he'd entered another world, one even more primitive than that surrounding the incredible woman who'd set all of this in motion. It was the difference between second- and third-hand reports of action and the physical feeling of that action all around him. Explosions and the hissing of flamers down on the streets jarred his awareness.

Staring at the map, McKie said, 'This has all the marks of a trap. Get all but a holding force out of the area. Tell Jedrik.'

People scurried to obey.

One of the guards and two sub-commanders remained. The guard spoke.

'What about this place?'

McKie glanced around him. It was a square room with brown walls. Two windows looked out on the street away from the battle for the isolated building near the gate. He'd hardly looked at the room when they'd brought him here to set up his command post. Four streets with isolated holdouts cushioned him from the main battle. They could shoot a cable bridge to another building if things became hot here. And it'd help morale if he remained in the danger area.

He spoke to one of the sub-commanders:

'Go down to the entry. Call all the elevators down there and disable all but one. Stand by that one with a holding force and put guards in the stairway. Stand by yourself to bring up captives. Comment?'

'I'll send up two cable teams and make sure the adjoining buildings are secure.'

Of course! McKie nodded.

Gods! How these people reacted in emergencies. They were as direct and cutting as knives.

'Do it,' McKie said.

He had less than a ten-minute wait before two of Jedrik's special security troops brought up the first captive, a young Gowachin whose eyelids bore curious scars – scroll-like and pale against the green skin.

The two security people stopped just inside the doorway. They held the Gowachin firmly, although he did not appear to be struggling. The sub-commander who'd brought them up closed the door as he left.

One of the captors, an older man with narrow features, nodded as he caught McKie's attention.

'What'll we do with him?'

'Tie him in a chair,' McKie instructed.

He studied the Gowachin as they complied.

'Where was he captured?'

'He was trying to escape from that building through a perimeter sewage line.'

'Alone?'

'I don't know. He's the first of a group of prisoners. The others are waiting outside.'

They had finished binding the young Gowachin, now took up position directly behind him.

McKie studied the captive. He wore black coveralls with characteristic deep vee to clear the ventricles. The garment had been cut and torn in several places. He'd obviously been searched with swift and brutal thoroughness. McKie put down a twinge of pity. The scar lines on the prisoner's eyelids precluded anything but the most direct Dosadi necessities.

'They did a poor job removing your Phylum tattoos,' McKie said. He'd already recognized the scar lines: Deep Swimmers. It was a relatively unimportant Phylum, small in numbers and sensitive about their status.

The young Gowachin blinked. McKie's opening remark had been so conversational, even-toned, that the shock of his words came after. Shock was obvious now in the set of the captive's mouth.

'What is your name, please?' McKie asked, still in that even, conversational way.

'Grinik.'

It was forced out of him.

McKie asked one of the guards for a notebook and stylus, wrote the Gowachin's name in it, adding the Phylum identification.

'Grinik of the Deep Swimmers,' he said. 'How long have you been on Dosadi?'

The Gowachin took a deep, ventricular breath, remained silent. The security men appeared puzzled. This interrogation wasn't going as they'd expected. McKie himself did not know what to expect. He still felt himself recovering from surprise at recognition of the badly erased Phylum tattoos.

'This is a very small planet,' McKie said. 'The universe from which we both come is very big and can be very cruel. I'm sure you didn't come here expecting to die.'

If this Grinik didn't know the deadly plans of his superiors, that would emerge shortly. McKie's words could be construed as a personal threat beyond any larger threat to Dosadi as a whole. It remained to see how Grinik reacted.

Still, the young Gowachin hesitated.

When in doubt, remain silent.

'You appear to've been adequately trained for this project,' McKie said. 'But I doubt if you were told everything you should know. I even doubt if you were told things essential to you in your present position.'

'Who are you?' Grinik demanded. 'How dare you speak here of matters which ...' He broke off, glanced at the two guards standing at his shoulders.

'They know all about us,' McKie lied.

He could smell the sweet perfume of Gowachin fear now, a floral scent which he'd noted only on a few previous occasions. The two guards also sensed this and showed faint smiles to betray that they knew its import.

'Your masters sent you here to die,' McKie said. 'They may very well pay heavily for this. You ask who I am? I am Jorj X McKie, Legum of the Gowachin Bar, Saboteur Extraordinary, senior lieutenant of Jedrik who will shortly rule all of Dosadi. I make formal imposition upon you. Answer my questions for the Law is at stake.'

On the Gowachin worlds, that was a most powerful motivator. Grinik was shaken by it.

'What do you wish to know?'

He barely managed the words.

'Your mission on Dosadi. The precise instructions you were given and who gave them to you.'

'There are twenty of us. We were sent by Mrreg.'

That name! The implications in Gowachin lore stunned McKie. He waited, then:

'Continue.'

'Two more of our twenty are out there.'

Grinik motioned to the doorway, clearly pleading for his captive associates.

'Your instructions?'

'To get our people out of this terrible place.'

'How long?'

'Just ... sixty hours remain.'

McKie exhaled slowly. So Aritch and company had given up on him. They were going to eliminate Dosadi.

'Where are the other members of your party?'

'I don't know.'

'You were, of course, a reserve team trained and held in readiness for this mission. Do you realize how poorly you were trained?'

Grinik remained silent.

McKie put down a feeling of despair, glanced at the two guards. He understood that they'd brought him this particular captive because this was one of three who were not Dosadi. Jedrik had instructed them, of course. Many things became clearer to him in this new awareness. Jedrik had put sufficient pressure on the Gowachin beyond the God Wall. She still had not imagined the extremes to which those Gowachin might go in stopping her. It was time Jedrik learned what sort of fuse she'd lighted. And Broey must be told. Especially Broey – before he sent many more suicide missions.

The outer door opened and the sub-commander leaned in to speak.

'You were right about the trap. We mined the area before pulling back. Caught them nicely. The gate's secure now, and we've cleared out that last building.'

McKie pursed his lips, then:

'Take the prisoners to Jedrik. Tell her we're coming in.'

A flicker of surprise touched the sub-commander's eyes.

'She knows.'

Still the man hesitated.

'Yes?'

'There's one Human prisoner out here you should question before leaving.'

McKie waited. Jedrik knew he was coming in, knew what had gone on here, knew about the Human prisoner out there. She wanted him to question this person. Yes ... of course. She left nothing to chance ... by her standards. Well, her standards were about to change, but she might even know that.

'Name?'

'Havvy. Broey holds him, but he once served Jedrik. She says to tell you Havvy is a reject, that he was contaminated.'

'Bring him in.'

Havvy surprised him. The surface was that of a bland-faced nonentity, braggadocio clearly evident under a mask of secret knowledge. He wore a green uniform with a driver's brassard. The uniform was wrinkled, but there were no visible rips or cuts. He'd been treated with more care than the Gowachin who was being led out of the room. Havvy replaced the Gowachin in the chair. McKie waved away the bindings.

Unfocused questions created turmoil in McKie's mind. He found it difficult to delay. Sixty hours! But he felt that he could almost touch the solution to the Dosadi mystery, that in only a few minutes he would know names and real motives for the ones who'd created this monster. Havvy? He'd served Jedrik. In what way? Why rejected? Contaminated?

Unfocused questions, yes.

Havvy sat in watchful tension, casting an occasional glance around the room, at the windows. There were no more explosions out there.

As McKie studied him more carefully, certain observations emerged. Havvy was small but solid, one of those Humans of lesser stature who concealed heavy musculature which could surprise you if you suddenly bumped into them. It was difficult to guess his age, but he was not Dosadi. A member of Grinik's team? Doubtful. Clearly not Dosadi, though. He didn't examine those around him with an automatic status assessment. His reactions were slow. Too much that should remain under shutters flowed from within him directly to the surface. Yes, that was the ultimate revelation. It bothered McKie that so much went unseen beneath the surface here, so much for which Aritch and company had not prepared him. It would take a lifetime to learn all the nuances of this place, and he had less than sixty hours remaining to him.

All of this flowed through McKie's mind in an eyeblink. He reached his decision, motioned the guards and others to leave.

One of the security people started to protest, but McKie silenced him with a glance, pulled up a chair, and sat down facing the captive.

The door closed behind the last of the guards.

'You were sent here deliberately to seek me out,' McKie said.

It was not the opening Havvy had expected. He stared into McKie's eyes. A door slammed outside. There was the sound of several doors opening and shutting, the shuffling of feet. An amplified voice called out:

'Move these prisoners out!'

Havvy chewed at his upper lip. He didn't protest. A deep sigh shook him, then:

'You're Jorj X. McKie of BuSab?'

McKie blew out through pursed lips. Did Havvy doubt the evidence of his own senses? Surprising. McKie shook his head, continued to study the captive.

'You can't be McKie!' Havvy said.

'Ahhhhhh . . .' It was pressed out of McKie.

Something about Havvy: the body moved, the voice spoke, but the eyes did not agree.

McKie thought about what the Caleban, Fannie Mae, had said. *A light*

563

touch. He was overtaken by an abrupt certainty: someone other than Havvy looked out through the man's eyes. Yessss. Aritch's people controlled the Caleban who maintained the barrier around Dosadi. The Caleban could contact selected people here. She'd have a constant updating on everything such people learned. There must be many such spies on Dosadi, all trained not to betray the Caleban contact – no twitching, no lapses into trance. No telling how many agents Aritch possessed here.

Would all the other people on Dosadi remain unaware of such a thing, though? That was a matter to question.

'But you must be McKie,' Havvy said. 'Jedrik's still working out of ...' He broke off.

'You must've provided her with some amusement by your bumbling,' McKie said. 'I assure you, however, that BuSab is *not* amused.'

A gloating look came over Havvy's face.

'No, she hasn't made the transfer yet.'

'Transfer?'

'Haven't you figured out yet how Pcharky's supposed to buy his freedom?'

McKie felt off balance at this odd turn.

'Explain.'

'He's supposed to transfer your identity into Jedrik's body and her identity into your body. I think she was going to try that with me once, but ...'

Havvy shrugged.

It was like an explosion in McKie's newly sensitized awareness. Rejected! Contaminated! Body exchange! McKie was accusatory!

'Broey sent you !'

'Of course.' Offensive.

McKie contained his anger. The Dosadi complexities no longer baffled him as once they had. It was like peeling back layer upon layer of concealment. With each new layer you expected to find *the* answer. But that was a trap the whole universe set for the unwary. It was the ultimate mystery and he hated mystery. There were those who said this was a necessary ingredient for BuSab agents. You eliminated that which you hated. But everything he'd uncovered about this planet showed him how little he'd known previously about any mystery. Now, he understood something new about Jedrik. There was little doubt that Broey's Human messenger told the truth.

Pcharky had penetrated the intricacies of PanSpechi ego transfer. He'd done it without a PanSpechi as his subject, unless ... yes ... that expanded the implications in Tria's history. Their PanSpechi experiment had assumed even more grotesque proportions.

'I will speak directly to your Caleban monitor,' McKie said.

'My what?'

It was such obvious dissimulation that McKie only snorted. He leaned forward.

'I will speak directly to Aritch. See that he gets this message without any mistakes.'

Havvy's eyes became glassy. He shuddered.

McKie felt the inner tendrils of an attempted Caleban contact in his own awareness, thrust them aside.

'No! I will speak openly through your agent. Pay close attention, Aritch. Those who created this Dosadi horror cannot run far enough, fast enough, or long enough to escape. If you wish to make every Gowachin in the universe a target for violence, you are proceeding correctly. Others, including BuSab, can employ mass violence if you force it upon them. Not a pleasant thought. But unless you adhere to your own Law, to the honored relationship between Legum and Client, your shame will be exposed. Innocent Gowachin as well as you others whose legal status has yet to be determined – all will pay the bloody price.'

Havvy's brows drew down in puzzlement.

'Shame?'

'They plan to blast Dosadi out of existence.'

Havvy pressed back into the chair, glared at McKie.

'You're lying.'

'Even you, Havvy, are capable of recognizing a truth. I'm going to release you, pass you back through the lines to Broey. Tell him what you learned from me.'

'It's a lie! They're not going to ...'

'Ask Aritch for yourself.'

Havvy didn't ask 'Aritch who?' He lifted himself from the chair.

'I will.'

'Tell Broey we've less than sixty hours. None of us who can resist mind erasure will be permitted to escape.'

'Us?'

McKie nodded, thinking: *Yes, I am Dosadi now.* He said:

'Get out of here.'

It afforded him a measure of amusement that the door was opened by the sub-commander just as Havvy reached it.

'See to him yourself,' McKie said, indicating Havvy. 'I'll be ready to go in a moment.'

Without any concern about whether the subcommander understood the nature of the assignment, McKie closed his eyes in thought. There remained the matter of Mrreg, who'd sent twenty Gowachin from Tandaloor to get *his people* off the planet. Mrreg. That was the name of the mythical monster who'd tested the first primitive Gowachin people almost to extinction, setting the pattern of their deepest instincts.

Mrreg?

Was it code, or did some Gowachin actually use that name? Or was it a role that some Gowachin filled?

Does a populace have informed consent when a ruling minority acts in secret to ignite a war, doing this to justify the existence of the minority's forces? History already has answered that question. Every society in the ConSentiency today reflects the historical judgment that failure to provide full information for informed consent on such an issue represents an ultimate crime.

– from The Trial of Trials

Less than an hour after closing down at Gate Eighteen, McKie and his escort arrived back at Jedrik's headquarters building. He led them to the heavily guarded side entrance with its express elevator, not wanting to pass Pcharky at this moment. Pcharky was an unnecessary distraction. He left the escort in the hallway with instructions to get food and rest, signaled for the elevator. The elevator door was opened by a small Human female of about fifteen years who nodded him into the dim interior.

McKie, his natural distrust of even the young on this planet well masked, nevertheless kept her under observation as he accepted the invitation. She was a gamin child with dirty face and hands, a torn grey single garment cut off at the knees. Her very existence as a Dosadi survivor said she'd undoubtedly sold her body many times for scraps of food. He realized how much Dosadi had influenced him when he found that he couldn't raise even the slightest feeling of censure at this knowledge. You did what the conditions around you demanded when those conditions were overwhelming. It was an ultimate question: this or death? And certainly some of them chose death.

'Jedrik,' he said.

She worked her controls and he found himself presently in an unfamiliar hallway. Two familiar guards stood at a doorway down the hall, however. They betrayed not the slightest interest in him as he opened the door between them swiftly and strode through.

It was a tiny anteroom, empty, but another door directly in front of him. He opened this with more confidence than he felt, entered a larger space full of projection-room gloom with shadowed figures seated facing a holographic focus on his left. McKie identified Jedrik by her profile, slipped into a seat beside her.

She kept her attention on the h-focus where a projection of Broey stood looking out at something over their shoulders. McKie recognized the subtle slippage of computer simulation. That was not a flesh-and-blood Broey in the focus.

Someone on the far side of the room stood up and crossed to sit beside another figure in the gloom. McKie recognized Gar as the man moved through one of the projection beams.

McKie whispered to Jedrik, 'Why simulation?'

'He's beginning to do things I didn't anticipate.'

The suicide missions. McKie looked at the simulation, wondered why there was no sync-sound. Ahhh, yes. They were lip-reading, and it was silent to reduce distractions, to amplify concentration. Yes, Jedrik was reworking the simulation model of Broey which she carried in her head. She would also carry another model, even more accurate than the one of Broey, which would give her a certain lead time on the reactions of one Jorj X. McKie.

'Would you really have done it?' he asked.

'Why do you distract me with such nonsense?'

He considered. Yes, it was a good question. He already knew the answer. She would have done it: traded bodies with him and escaped outside the God Wall as McKie. She might still do it, unless he could anticipate the mechanics of the transfer.

By now, she knew about the sixty-hour limit and would suspect its significance. Less than sixty hours. And the Dosadi could make extremely complex projections from limited data. Witness this Broey simulation.

The figure in the focus was talking to a fat Human female who held a tube which McKie recognized as a communicator for field use.

Jedrik spoke across the room to Gar.

'She still with him?'

'Addicted.'

A two-sentence exchange, and it condensed an entire conversation about possible uses of that woman. McKie did not ask addicted to what. There were too many such substances on Dosadi, each with peculiar characteristics, often involving odd monopolies with which everyone seemed familiar. This was a telltale gap in Aritch's briefings: the monopolies and their uses.

As McKie absorbed the action in the focus, the reasons behind this session became more apparent. Broey was refusing to believe the report from Havvy.

And there was Havvy in the focus.

Jedrik favored McKie with one flickering glance as Havvysimulation appeared. Certainly. She factored McKie into her computations.

McKie compressed his lips. She knew Havvy would contaminate me. They couldn't say 'I love you' on this damned planet. Oh, no. They had to create a special Dosadi production number.

'Most of the data for this originated before the breakup,' McKie said. 'It's useless. Rather than ask the computer to play pretty pictures for us, why don't we examine our own memories? Surely, somewhere in the combined experiences with Broey . . .'

A chuckle somewhere to the left stopped him.

Too late, McKie saw that every seat in the room had an arm keyed to the simulations. They were doing precisely what he'd suggested, but in a more sophisticated way. The figures at the focus were being adjusted to the combined memories. There was such a keyed arm at McKie's right hand. He suddenly realized how tactless and lecturing he still must appear to these people. They didn't waste energy on unnecessary words. Anyone who did must be subnormal, poorly trained or . . . or not from Dosadi.

'Does he always state the obvious?' Gar asked.

McKie wondered if he'd blown his lieutenancy, lost the opportunity to explore the mystery of the Rim, but . . . no, there wasn't time for that now. He'd have to penetrate the Rim another way.

'He's new,' Jedrik said. 'New is not necessarily naive, as you should know.'

'He has you doing it now,' Gar said.

'Guess again.'

McKie put a hand to the simulation controls under his right hand, tested the keys. He had it in a moment. They were similar to such devices in the ConSentiency, an adaptation from the DemoPol inputs, no doubt. Slowly, he changed the Broey at the focus, heavier, the sagging jowls and node wattles of a breeding male Gowachin. McKie froze the image.

'Tentative?' Gar asked.

Jedrik answered for him.

'It's knowledge he brought here with him.' She did something to her controls, stopped the projection, and raised the room lights.

McKie noted that Tria was nowhere in the room.

'The Gowachin have sequestered their females somewhere,' McKie said. 'That somewhere should not be difficult to locate. Send word to Tria that she must not mount her attack on Broey's corridor just yet.'

'Why delay?' Gar demanded.

'Broey will have all but evacuated the corridor by now,' McKie said. Gar was angry and showing it.

'Not a single one of them has gone through that Rim gate.'

'Not to the Rim,' Jedrik said.

It was clear to her now. McKie had supplied the leverage she needed. It was time now to employ him as she'd always intended. She glanced at McKie.

'We have unfinished business. Are you ready?'

He held his silence. How could he answer such a Dosadi-weighted question? There were so many things left unspoken on this planet, only the native-born could understand them all. McKie felt once more that he was a dull outsider, a child of dubious potential among normal adults.

Jedrik arose, looked across at Gar.

'Send word to Tria to hold herself in readiness for another assignment. Tell Broey. Call him on an open line. We now have an excellent use for your fanatics. If only a few of your people fight through to that Graluz complex, it'll be enough and Broey will know it.'

McKie noted that she spoke to Gar with a familiar teaching emphasis. It was the curiously weighted manner she'd once used with McKie, but no longer found necessary. His recognition of this amused her.

'Come along, McKie. We haven't much time.'

Does a population have informed consent when that population is not taught the inner workings of its monetary system, and then is drawn, all unknowing, into economic adventures?

– from The Trial of Trials

For almost an hour after the morning meal, Aritch observed Ceylang as she worked with the McKie simulator. She was pushing herself hard, believing Wreave honor at stake, and had almost reached the pitch Aritch desired.

Ceylang had set up her own simulator situation: McKie interviewing five of Broey's Gowachin. She had the Gowachin come to McKie in surrender, hands extended, the webbed fingers exposed to show that the talons were withdrawn.

Simulator-McKie merely probed for military advantages.

'Why does Broey attack in this fashion?'

Or he'd turn to some places outside the h-focus of the simulator.

'Send reinforcements into that area.'

Nothing about the Rim.

Earlier, Ceylang had tried the issue with a prisoner simulation where the five Gowachin tried to confuse McKie by presenting a scenario in which Broey massed his forces at the corridor. The makings of a breakout to the Rim appeared obvious.

Simulator-McKie asked the prisoners why they lied.

Ceylang cleared the simulator and sat back. She saw Aritch at the observation window, opened a channel to him.

'Something has to be wrong in the simulation. McKie cannot be led into questioning the purposes of the Rim.'

'I assure you that simulation is remarkable in its accuracy. Remarkable.'

'Then why ...'

'Perhaps he already knows the answer. Why don't you try him with Jedrik? Here ...' Aritch operated the controls at the observer station. 'This might help. This is a record of McKie in recent action on Dosadi.'

The simulator presented a view down a covered passage through a building. Artificial light. Darkness at the far end of the passage. McKie, two blocky guards in tow, approached the viewers.

Ceylang recognized the scene. She'd watched this action at Gate Eighteen from several angles, had seen this passage empty before the battle, acquainting herself with the available views. As she'd watched it then, the passage had filled with Human defenders. There was a minor gate behind the viewer and she knew the viewer itself to be only a bright spot, a fleck of glittering impurity in an otherwise drab brick over the gate's archway.

Now, the long passage seemed strange to Ceylang without its throng of defenders. There were only a few workmen along its length as McKie passed. The workmen repaired service pipes in the ceiling. A cleanup crew washed down patches of blood at the far end of the passage, the high-water mark of the Gowachin attack. An officer leaned against a wall near the viewer, a bored expression on his face which did not mislead Ceylang. He was there to watch McKie. Three soldiers squatted nearby rolling hexi-bones for coins which lay in piles before each man. Every now and then, one of the gamblers would pass a coin to the watching officer. A repair supervisor stood with his back to the viewer, notebook in hand, writing a list of supplies to complete the job. McKie and his guards were forced to step around these people. As they passed, the officer turned, looked directly into the viewer, smiled.

'That officer,' Ceylang said. 'One of your people?'

'No.'

The viewpoint shifted, looking down on the gate itself, McKie in profile. The gatekeeper was a teenager with a scar down his right cheek and a broken nose. McKie showed no signs of recognition, but the youth knew McKie.

'You go through on request.'

'When did she call?'

'Ten.'

'Let us through.'

The gate was opened. McKie and his guards went through, passed beyond the viewer's focus.

The youthful gatekeeper stood up, smashed the viewer. The h-focus went blank.

Aritch looked down from his observation booth for a moment before speaking.

'Who called?'

'Jedrik?' Ceylang spoke without thinking.

'What does that conversation tell you? Quickly!'

'That Jedrik anticipated his movements, was observing him all the time.'

'What else?'

'That McKie ... knows this, knows she can anticipate him.'

'She carries a better simulation of him in her head than we have ... there.'

Aritch pointed at the h-focus area.

'But they left so much unspoken!' Ceylang said.

Aritch remained silent.

Ceylang closed her eyes. It was like mind reading. It confused her.

Aritch interrupted her musings.

'What about that officer and the gatekeeper?'

She shook her head.

'You're wise to use living observers there. They all seem to know when they're being watched. And how it's done.'

'Even McKie.'

'He didn't look at the viewers.'

'Because he assumed from the first that we'd have him under almost constant observation. He's not concerned about the mechanical intrusions. He has built a simulation McKie of his own who acts on the surface of the real McKie.'

'That's your assumption?'

'We arrived at this from observation of Jedrik in her dealings with McKie. She peels away the simulation layers one at a time, coming closer and closer to the actuality at the core.'

Another observation bothered Ceylang.

'Why'd the gatekeeper shut down that viewer just then?'

'Obviously because Jedrik told him to do that.'

Ceylang shuddered.

'Sometimes I think those Dosadi play us like a fine instrument.'

'But of course! That's why we sent them our McKie.'

The music of a civilization has far-reaching consequences on consciousness and thus, influences the basic nature of a society. Music and its rhythms divert and compel the awareness, describing the limits within which a consciousness, thus fascinated, may operate. Control the music, then, and you own a powerful tool with which to shape the society.

– The Dosadi Analysis, BuSab Documents

It was a half-hour before Jedrik and McKie found themselves in the hallway leading to her quarters. McKie, aware of the effort she was expending to conceal a deep weariness, watched her carefully. She concentrated on presenting a show of vitality, her attention glued on the prospect ahead. There was no way of telling what went on in her mind. McKie did not attempt to break the silence. He had his own worries.

Which was the real Jedrik? How was she going to employ Pcharky? Could he resist her?

He knew he was close to a solution of the Dosadi mystery, but the prospect of the twin gambles he was about to take filled him with doubts.

On coming from the projection room, they'd found themselves in a strange delaying situation, as though it were something planned for their frustration. Everything had been prepared for their movement – guards warned, elevator waiting, doors opened. But every time they thought the way clear, they met interference. Except for the obvious importance of the matters which delayed them, it was easy to imagine a conspiracy.

A party of Gowachin at Gate Seventy wanted to surrender, but they demanded a parley first. One of Jedrik's aides didn't like the situation. Something about the assessment of the offer bothered her, and she wanted to discuss it with Jedrik. She stopped them halfway down the first hall outside the projection room.

The aide was an older woman who reminded McKie vaguely of a Wreave lab worker at BuSab, one who'd always been suspicious of computers, even antagonistic toward them. This Wreave had read every bit of history he could find about the evolution of such instruments and liked to remind his listeners of the misuses of the DemoPol. Human history had provided him with abundant ammunition, what with its periodic revolts against 'enslavement by machines.' Once, he'd cornered McKie.

'Look here! See this sign: "Gigo." That's a very old sign that was hung above one of your ancient computers. It's an acronym: "Garbage In, Garbage Out." You see! They knew.'

Yes. Jedrik's female aide reminded him of that Wreave.

McKie listened to her worries. She roamed all around a central disquiet, never settling on a particular thing. Aware of Aritch's deadline and Jedrik's fatigue, McKie felt the pressures bearing down upon him. The aide's data was accurate. Others had checked it. Finally, he could hold his impatience no longer.

'Who fed this data into your computer?'

The aide was startled at the interruption, but Jedrik turned to him, waiting.

'I think it was Holjance,' the aide said. 'Why?'

'Get him in here.'

'Her.'

'Her, then! Make sure she's actually the one who fed in that data.'

Holjance was a pinch-faced woman with deep wrinkles around very bright eyes. Her hair was dark and wiry, skin almost the color of McKie's. Yes, she was the one who'd fed the data into the computer because it had arrived on her shift, and she'd thought it too important to delegate.

'What is it you want?' she demanded.

He saw no rudeness in this. It was Dosadi directness. Important things were happening all around. *Don't waste time.*

'You saw this assessment of the surrender offer?' he asked.

'Yes.'

'Are you satisfied with it?'

'The data went in correctly.'

'That's not my question.'

'Of course I'm satisfied!'

She stood ready to defend herself against any charge that she'd slighted her job.

'Tell me, Holjance,' he said, 'if you wanted the Gowachin computers to produce inaccurate assessments, what would you do?'

She thought about this a moment, blinked, glanced almost furtively at Jedrik who appeared lost in thought. 'Well, sir, we have a regular filtering procedure for preventing ...'

'That's it,' Jedrik said. 'If I were a Gowachin, I would not be doing that right now.'

Jedrik turned, barked orders to the guards behind her.

'That's another trap! Take care of it.'

As they emerged from the elevator on Jedrik's floor, there was another delay, one of the escort who'd been with McKie at Gate Eighteen. His name was Todu Pellas and McKie addressed him by name, noting the faint betrayal of pleasure this elicited. Pellas, too, had doubts about carrying out a particular order.

'We're supposed to back up Tria's move by attacking across the upper parkway, but there are some trees and other growth knocked down up there that haven't been moved for two days.'

'Who knocked down those trees?' McKie asked.

'We did.'

McKie understood. You feinted. The Gowachin were supposed to believe this would provide cover for an attack, but there'd been no attack for two days.

'They must be under pretty heavy strain,' Jedrik said.

McKie nodded. That, too, made sense. The alternative Gowachin assumption was that the Humans were trying to fake them into an attack at that point. But the cover had not been removed by either side for two days.

Jedrik took a deep breath.

'We have superior firepower and when Tria ... well, you should be able to cut right through there to ...'

McKie interrupted.

'Call off that attack.'

'But ...'

'Call it off!'

She saw the direction of his reasoning. Broey had learned much from the force which Gar and Tria had trained. And Jedrik herself had provided the final emphasis in the lesson. She saw there was no need to change her orders to Pellas.

Pellas had taken it upon himself to obey McKie, not waiting for Jedrik's response, although she was his commander. He already had a communicator off his belt and was speaking rapidly into it.

'Yes! Dig in for a holding action.'

He spoke in an aside to Jedrik.

'I can handle it from here.'

In a few steps, Jedrik and McKie found themselves in her room. Jedrik leaned with her back against the door, no longer trying to conceal her fatigue.

'McKie, you're becoming very Dosadi.'

He crossed to the concealing panels, pulled out the bed.

'You need rest.'

'No time.'

Yes, she knew all about the sixty-hour deadline – less than fifty-five hours now. Dosadi's destruction was a reaction she hadn't expected from 'X,' and she blamed herself.

He turned, studied her, saw that she'd passed some previously defined limit of personal endurance. She possessed no amplifiers of muscles or senses, none of the sophisticated aids McKie could call upon in emergencies. She had nothing but her own magnificent mind and body. And she'd almost run them out. Still, she pressed on. This told him a great deal about her motivation.

McKie found himself deeply touched by the fact that she'd not once berated him for hiding that ultimate threat which Aritch held over Dosadi. She'd accepted it that someone in Aritch's position could erase an entire planet, that McKie had been properly maneuvered into concealing this.

The alternative she offered filled McKie with misgivings.

Exchange bodies?

He understood now that this was Pcharky's function, the price the old Gowachin paid for survival. Jedrik had explained.

'He will perform this service one more time. In exchange, we release him from Dosadi.'

'If he's one of the original . . . I mean, why doesn't he just leave?'

'We haven't provided him with a body he can use.'

McKie had suppressed a feeling of horror. But the history of Dosadi which Jedrik unfolded made it clear that a deliberate loophole had been left in the Caleban contract which imprisoned this planet. Fannie Mae had even said it. He could leave in another body. That was the basic purpose behind this experiment.

New bodies for old!

Aritch had expected this to be the ultimate enticement, luring McKie into the Gowachin plot, enlisting McKie's supreme abilities and his powerful position in BuSab.

A new body for his old one.

All he'd have to do would be to cooperate in the destruction of a planet, conceal the real purpose of this project, and help set up another body-trade planet better concealed.

But Aritch had not anticipated what might be created by Jedrik plus McKie. They now shared a particular hate and motivation.

Jedrik still stood at the door waiting for him to decide.

'Tell me what to do,' he said.

'You're sure that you're willing to . . .'

'Jedrik!'

He thought he saw the beginning of tears. It wasn't that she hid them, but that they reached a suppression level barely visible and she defied them. She found her voice, pointed.

'That panel beside the bed. Pressure latch.'

The panel swung wide to reveal two shimmering rods about two centimeters in diameter. The rods danced with the energies of Pcharky's cage. They emerged from the floor, bent at right angles about waist height and, as the panel opened, they rotated to extend into the room – two glowing handles about a meter apart.

McKie stared at them. He felt a tightness in his breast. What if he'd misread Jedrik? Could he be sure of any Dosadi? This room felt as familiar to him now as his quarters on CC. It was here that Jedrik had taught him some of the most essential Dosadi lessons. Yet . . . he knew the old pattern of what she proposed. The discarded body with its donor ego had always been killed immediately. Why?

'You'll have your answer to that question when we've done this thing.'

A Dosadi response, ambiguous, heavy with alternatives.

He glanced around the room, found it hard to believe that he'd known this place only these few days. His attention returned to the shimmering rods. Another trap?

He knew he was wasting precious time, that he'd have to go through with this. But what would it be like to find himself in Jedrik's flesh, wearing her body as he now wore his own? PanSpechi transferred an ego from body to body. But something unspeakable which they would not reveal happened to the donor.

McKie took a trembling breath.

It had to be done. He and Jedrik shared a common purpose. She'd had many opportunities to use Pcharky simply to escape or to extend her life . . . the way, he realized now, that Broey had used the Dosadi secret. The fact that she'd waited for a McKie forced him to believe her. Jedrik's followers trusted her – and they were Dosadi. And if he and Jedrik escaped, Aritch would find himself facing a far different McKie from the one who'd come so innocently across the Rim. They might yet stay Aritch's hand.

The enticement had been real, though. No doubting that. Shed an old body, get a new one. And the Rim had been the major source of *raw material:* strong, resilient bodies. Survivors.

'What do I do?' he asked.

He felt a hand on his shoulder, and she spoke from beside him.

'You are very Dosadi, McKie. Astonishing.'

He glanced at her, saw what it had cost her to move here from the door. He slipped a hand around her waist, eased her to a sitting position on the bed and within reach of the rods.

'Tell me what to do.'

She stared at the rods, and McKie realized it was rage driving her, rage against Aritch, the embodiment of 'X,' the embodiment of a contrived fate. He understood this. The solution of the Dosadi mystery had left him feeling empty, but on the edges there was such a rage as he'd never before experienced. He was still BuSab, though. He wanted no more bloodshed because of Dosadi, no more Gowachin justifications.

Jedrik's voice interrupted his thoughts and he saw that she also shared some of his misgivings.

'I come from a long line of heretics. None of us doubted that Dosadi was a crime, that somewhere there was a justice to punish the criminals.'

McKie almost sighed. Not the old Messiah dream! Not that! He would not fill that role, even for Dosadi.

It was as though Jedrik read his mind. Perhaps, with that simulation model of him she carried in her head, this was exactly what she did.

'We didn't expect a hero to come and save us. We knew that whoever came would suffer from the same deficiencies as the other non-Dosadi we saw here. You were so . . . slow. Tell me, McKie, what drives a Dosadi?'

He almost said, 'Power.'

She saw his hesitation, waited.

'The power to change your condition,' he said.

'You make me very proud, McKie.'

'But how did you know I was . . .'

'McKie!'

He swallowed, then: 'Yes, I guess that was the easiest part for you.'

'It was much more difficult finding your abilities and shaping you into a Dosadi.'

'But I might've been . . .'

'Tell me how I did it, McKie.'

It was a test. He saw that. How had she known absolutely that he was the one she needed?

'I was sent here in a way that evaded Broey.'

'And that's not easy.' Her glance flickered ceilingward. 'They tried to bait us from time to time. Havvy . . .'

'Compromised, contaminated . . .'

'Useless. Sometimes, a stranger looks out of Havvy's eyes.'

'My eyes are my own.'

'The first thing Bahrank reported about you.'

'But even before that ...'

'Yes?'

'They used Havvy to tell you I was coming ... and he told you that you could use my body. He had to be truthful with you up to a point. You could read Havvy! How clever they thought they were being! I had to be vulnerable ... really vulnerable.'

'The first thing ...'

'... you found out about me.' He nodded. 'Suspicions confirmed. All of that money on my person. Bait. I was someone to be eliminated. I was a powerful enemy of your enemies.'

'And you were angered by the right things.'

'You saw that?'

'McKie, you people are so easy to read. So *easy*!'

'And the weapons I carried. You were supposed to use those to destroy yourselves. The implications ...'

'I would've seen that if I'd had first-hand experience of Aritch. You *knew* what he intended for us. My mistake was to read your fears as purely personal. In time ...'

'We're wasting time.'

'You fear we'll be too late?'

Once more, he looked at the shimmering rods. What was it Pcharky did? McKie felt events rushing over him, engulfing him. What bargain had Jedrik really driven with Pcharky? She saw the question on his face.

'My people knew all along that Pcharky was just a tool of the God who held us prisoner. We forced a bargain on that God – that Caleban. Did you think we would not recognize the identity between the powers of that cage and the powers of our God Wall? No more delays, McKie. It's time to test our bargain.'

Geriatric or other life extension for the powerful poses a similar threat to a sentient species as that found historically in the dominance of a self-perpetuating bureaucracy. Both assume prerogatives of immortality, collecting more and more power with each passing moment. This is power which draws a theological aura about itself. the unassailable Law, the God-given mandate of the leader, manifest destiny. Power held too long within a narrow framework moves farther and farther away from the adaptive demands of changed conditions. The leadership grows ever more paranoid, suspicious of inventive adaptations to change, fearfully protective of personal power and, in the terrified avoidance of what it sees as risk, blindly leads its people into destruction.

– BuSab Manual

'Very well, I'll tell you what bothers me,' Ceylang said. 'There are too many things about this problem that I fail to understand.'

From her seated position, she looked across a small, round room at Aritch, who floated gently in a tiny blue pool. His head at the pool's lip was almost on a level with Ceylang's. Again, they had worked late into the night. She understood the reasons for this, the time pressures were quite apparent, but the peculiar Gowachin flavor of her training kept her in an almost constant state of angry questioning.

This whole thing was so un-Wreave!

Ceylang smoothed the robe over her long body. The robe was blue now, one step away from Legum black. Appropriately, there was blue all around her: the walls, the floor, the ceiling, Aritch's pool.

The High Magister rested his chin on the pool's edge to speak.

'I require specific questions before I can even hope to penetrate your puzzlement.'

'Will McKie defend or prosecute? The simulator ...'

'Damn the simulator! Odds are that he'll make the mistake of prosecuting. Your own reasoning powers should ...'

'But if he doesn't?'

'Then selection of the judicial panel becomes vital.'

Ceylang twisted her body to one side, feeling the chairdog adjust for her comfort. As usual, Aritch's answer only deepened her sense of uncertainty. She voiced that now.

'I continue to have this odd feeling that you intend me to play some role which I'm not supposed to discover until the very last instant.'

Aritch breathed noisily through his mouth, splashed water onto his head.

'This all may be moot. By this time day after tomorrow, Dosadi *and* McKie may no longer exist.'

'Then I will not advance to Legum?'

'Oh, I'm fairly certain you'll be a Legum.'

She studied him, sensing irony, then:

'What a delicate line you walk, High Magister.'

'Hardly. My way is wide and clear. You know the things I cannot countenance. I cannot betray the Law or my people.'

'I have similar inhibitions. But this Dosadi thing – so tempting.'

'So dangerous! Would a Wreave don Human flesh to learn the Human condition? Would you permit a Human to penetrate Wreave society in this ...'

'There are some who might conspire in this! There are even Gowachin who ...'

'The opportunities for misuse are countless.'

'Yet you say that McKie already is more Gowachin than a Gowachin.'

Aritch's webbed hands folded over the pool's edge, the claws extended.

'We risked much in training him for this task.'

'More than you risk with me?'

Aritch withdrew his hands, stared at her, unblinking.

'So that's what bothers you.'

'Precisely.'

'Think, Ceylang, how near the core of Wreavedom you would permit me to come. Thus far and no farther will we permit you.'

'And McKie?'

'May already have gone too far for us to permit his continued existence.'

'I heed your warning, Aritch. But I remain puzzled as to why the Calebans couldn't prevent ...'

'They profess not to understand the ego transfer. But who can understand a Caleban, let alone control one in a matter so delicate? Even this one who created the God Wall ...'

'It's rumored that McKie understands Calebans.'

'He denies it.'

She rubbed her pocked left jowl with a prehensile mandible, felt the many scars of her passage through the Wreave triads. Family to family to family until it was a single gigantic family. Yet, all were Wreave. This Dosadi thing threatened a monstrous parody of Wreavedom. Still . . .

'So fascinating,' she murmured.

'That's its threat.'

'We should pray for the death of Dosadi.'

'Perhaps.'

She was startled.

'What . . .'

'This might not die with Dosadi. Our sacred bond assures that you will leave here with this knowledge. Many Gowachin know of this thing.'

'And McKie.'

'Infections have a way of spreading,' Aritch said. 'Remember *that* if this comes to the Courtarena.'

There are some forms of insanity which, driven to an ultimate expression, can become the new models of sanity.

– BuSab Manual

'McKie?'

It was the familiar Caleban presence in his awareness, as though he heard and felt someone (or some*thing*) which he knew was not there.

The preparation had been deceptively simple. He and Jedrik clasped hands, his right hand and her left, and each grasped one of the shimmering rods with the other hand.

McKie did not have a ready identity for this Caleban and wondered at the questioning in her *voice*. He agreed, however, that he was indeed McKie, shaping the thought as subvocalized conversation. As he spoke, McKie was acutely aware of Jedrik beside him. She was more than just another person now. He carried a tentative simulation model of her, sometimes anticipating her responses.

'You make mutual agreement?' the Caleban asked.

McKie sensed Pcharky then: a distant presence, the monitor for this experience. It was as though Pcharky had been reduced to a schematic which the Caleban followed, a set of complex rules, many of which could not be translated into words. Some part of McKie responded to this as though a monster awakened within him, a sleeping monster who sat up full of anger at being aroused thus, demanding:

'Who is it that dares awaken me?'

McKie felt his body trembling, felt Jedrik trembling beside him. The Caleban/Taprisiot-trembling, the sweaty response to trance! He saw these phenomena now in a different light. When you walked at the edge of this abyss . . .

While these thoughts passed through his mind, he felt a slight shift, no more than the blurred reflection of something which was not quite movement. Now, while he still felt his own flesh around him, he also felt himself possessed of an inner contact with Jedrik's body and knew she shared this experience.

Such a panic as he had not thought possible threatened to overwhelm

584

him. He felt Jedrik trying to break the contact, to stop this hideous sharing, but they were powerless in the grip of a force which would not be stopped.

No time sense attached itself to this experience, but a fatalistic calm overcame them almost simultaneously. McKie felt awareness of Jedrik/flesh deepen. Curiosity dominated him now.

So this is woman!

This is man?

They shared the thoughts across an indistinct bridge.

Fascination gripped McKie. He probed deeper.

He/She could feel himself/herself breathing. And the differences! It was not the genitalia, the presence or lack of breasts. She felt bereft of breasts. He felt acutely distressed by their presence, self-consciously aware of profound implications. The sense of difference went back beyond gamete McKie/Jedrik.

McKie sensed her thoughts, her reactions.

Jedrik: 'You cast your sperm upon the stream of time.'

McKie: 'You enclose and nurture ...'

'I cast/I nurture.'

It was as though they looked at an object from opposite sides, aware belatedly that they both examined the same thing.

'We cast/we, nurture.'

Obscuring layers folded away and McKie found himself in Jedrik's mind, she in his. Their thoughts were one entity.

The separate Dosadi and ConSentient experiences melted into a single relationship.

'Aritch ... ah, yes. You see? And your PanSpechi friend, Bildoon. Note that. You suspected, but now you know ...'

Each set of experiences fed on the other, expanding, refining ... condensing, discarding, creating ...

So that's the training of a Legum.

Loving parents? Ahhh, yes, loving parents.

'I/we will apply pressure there ... and there ... They must be man-euvered into choosing that one as a judge. Yes, that will give us the required leverage. Let them break their own code.'

And the awakened monster stirred within them. It had no dimension, no place, only existence. They felt its power.

'*I do what I do!*'

The power enveloped them. No other awareness was permitted. They sensed a primal current, unswerving purpose, a force which could override any other thing in their universe. It was not God, not Life, not any particular species. It was something so far beyond such articulations that Jedrik/McKie could not even contemplate it without a sense that the next instant would bring obliteration. They felt a question hurled at their united, fearful awareness. The question was framed squarely in anger, astonishment, cold amusement, and threat.

'For *this* you awaken *me*?'

Now, they understood why the old body and donor-ego had always been slain immediately. This terrible sharing made a . . . made a noise. It awakened a questioner.

They understood the question without words, knowing they could never grasp the full meaning and emotive thrust, that it would burn them out even to try. Anger . . . astonishment . . . cold amusement . . . threat. The question as their own united mind(s) interpreted it represented a limit. It was all that Jedrik/McKie could accept.

The intrusive questioner receded.

They were never quite sure afterward whether they'd been expelled or whether they'd fled in terror, but the parting words were burned into their combined awareness.

'*Let the sleeper sleep.*'

They walked softly in their minds then. They understood the warning, but knew it could never be translated in its fullest threat for any other sentient being.

Concurrent: McKie/Jedrik felt a projection of terror from the God Wall Caleban, unfocused, unexplained. It was a new experience in the male-female collective memory. Caleban Fannie Mae had not even projected this upon original McKie when she'd thought herself doomed.

Concurrent: McKie/Jedrik felt a burntout fading from Pcharky. Something in that terrible contact had plunged Pcharky into his death spiral. Even as McKie/Jedrik realized this, the old Gowachin died. It was a slammed door. But this came after a blazing realization by McKie/Jedrik that Pcharky had shared the original decision to set up the Dosadi experiment.

McKie found himself clothed in living, breathing flesh which routed its messages through his awareness. He wasn't sure which of their two bodies he possessed, but it was distinct, separate. It wrapped him in Human senses: the taste of salt, the smell of perspiration, and the omnipresent Warren stink. One hand held cold metal, the other clasped the hand of a fellow Human. Perspiration drenched this body, made the clasped hands slippery. He felt that knowing which hand held another hand was of utmost importance, but he wasn't ready to face that knowledge. Awareness of self, this new self, and a whole lifetime of new memories, demanded all of the attention he could muster.

Focus: A Rim city, never outside Jedrik's control because she had fed the signals through to Gar and Tria with exquisite care, and because those who gave the orders on the Rim had shared in the generations of selective breeding which had produced Jedrik. She was a biological weapon whose sole target was the God Wall.

Focus: Loving parents can thrust their child into deadly peril when they know everything possible has been done to prepare that child for survival.

The oddity to McKie was that he felt such things as personal memories. 'I did that.'

Jedrik suffered the throes of similar experiences.

Which body?

So that was the training of a BuSab agent. Clever ... almost adequate. Complex and full of much that she found to be new, but why did it always stop short of a full development?

She reviewed the sessions with Aritch and Ceylang. A matched pair. The choice of Ceylang and the role chosen for her appeared obvious. How innocent! Jedrik felt herself free to pity Ceylang. When allowed to run its course, this was an interesting emotion. She had never before felt pity in uncolored purity.

Focus: McKie actually loved her. She savored this emotion in its ConSentient complexity. The straight flow of selected emotions fascinated her. They did not have to be bridled!

In and out of this creative exchange there wove an intimacy, a pure sexuality without inhibitions.

McKie, savoring the amusement Jedrik had felt when Tria had suggested a McKie/Jedrik breeding, found himself caught by demanding male eroticism and knew by the sensation that he retained his old body.

Jedrik, understanding McKie's long search for a female to complete him, found her amusement converted to the desire to demonstrate that completion. As she turned toward him, releasing the dull rod which had once shimmered in contact with Pcharky, she found herself in McKie's flesh looking into her own eyes.

McKie gasped in the mirror experience.

Just as abruptly, driven by shock, they shifted back into familiar flesh: McKie male, Jedrik female. Instantly, it became a thing to explore – back – and forth. Eroticism was forgotten in this new game.

'We can be either sex/body at will!'

It was something beyond Taprisiots and Calebans, far more subtle than the crawling progression of a PanSpechi ego through the bodies from its creche.

They knew the source of this odd gift even as they sank back on the bed, content to be familiar male and female for a time.

The sleeping monster.

This was a gift with barbs in it, something *loving parents* might give their child in the knowledge that it was time for this lesson. Yet they felt revitalized, knowing they had for an instant tapped an energy source without limits.

A pounding on the door interrupted this shared reverie.

'Jedrik! Jedrik!'

'What is it?'

'It's Broey. He wishes to talk to McKie.'

They were off the bed in an instant.

Jedrik glanced at McKie, knowing she had not one secret from him, that they shared a reasoning base. Out of the mutual understanding in this base, she spoke for both of them.

'Does he say why?'

'Jedrik . . .'

They both recognized the voice of a trusted aide and heard the fear in it.

'. . . it's midmorning and there is no sun. God has turned off the sun!'

'Sealed us in . . .'

'. . . to conceal the final blast.'

Jedrik opened the door, confronted the frightened aide.

'Where is Broey?'

'Here – in your command post. He came alone without escort.'

She glanced at McKie. 'You will speak for us.'

Broey waited near the position board in the command post. Watchful Humans stood within striking distance. He turned as McKie and Jedrik entered. McKie noted that the Gowachin's body was, indeed, heavy with breeding juices as anticipated. Unsettling for a Gowachin.

'What are your terms, McKie?'

Broey's voice was guttural, full of heavy breathing.

McKie's features remained Dosadi-bland, but he thought: *Broey thinks I'm responsible for the darkness. He's terrified.*

McKie glanced at the threatening black of the windows before speaking. He knew this Gowachin from Jedrik's painstaking study. Broey was a sophisticate, a collector of sophistication who surrounded himself with people of the same stripe. He was a professional sophisticate who read everything through that peculiar Dosadi screen. No one could come into his circle who didn't share this pose. All else remained outside and inferior. He was an ultimate Dosadi, a distillation, almost as Human as Gowachin because he'd obviously once worn a Human body. He was Gowachin at his origins, though – no doubt of it.

'You followed my scent,' McKie said.

'Excellent!'

Broey brightened. He had not expected a Dosadi exchange, pared to the nonemotional essentials.

'Unfortunately,' McKie said, 'You have no position from which to negotiate. Certain things will be done. You will comply willingly, your compliance will be forced, or we will act without you.'

It was a deliberate goading on McKie's part, a choice of non-Dosadi forms to abbreviate this confrontation. It said more than anything else that McKie came from beyond the God Wall, that the darkness which held back the daylight was the least of his resources.

Broey hesitated, then:

'So?'

The single word fell on the air with countless implications: an entire exchange discarded, hopes dashed, a hint of sadness at lost powers, and still with that sophisticated reserve which was Broey's signature. It was more subtle than a shrug, more powerful in its Dosadi overtones that an entire negotiating session.

'Questions?' McKie asked.

Broey glanced at Jedrik, obviously surprised by this. It was as though he appealed to her: they were both Dosadi, were they not? This outsider came here with his gross manners, his lack of Dosadi understanding. How could one speak to such one? He addressed Jedrik.

'Have I not already stated my submission? I came alone, I ...'

Jedrik picked up McKie's cue.

'There are certain ... peculiarities to our situation.'

'Peculiarities?'

Broey's nictating membrane blinked once.

Jedrik allowed her manner to convey a slight embarrassment.

'Certain delicacies of the Dosadi condition must be overlooked. We are now, all of us, abject supplicants ... and we are dealing with people who do not speak as we speak, act as we act ...'

'Yes.' He pointed upward. 'The mentally retarded ones. We are in danger then.'

It was not a question. Broey peered upward, as though trying to see through the ceiling and intervening floors. He drew in a deep breath.

'Yes.'

Again, it was compressed communication. Anyone who could put the God Wall there could crush an entire planet. Therefore, Dosadi and all of its inhabitants had been brought to a common subjection. Only a Dosadi could have accepted it this quickly without more questions, and Broey was an ultimate Dosadi.

McKie turned to Jedrik. When he spoke, she anticipated every word, but she waited him out.

'Tell your people to stop all attacks.'

He faced Broey.

'And your people.'

Broey looked from Jedrik to McKie, back to Jedrik with a puzzled expression openly on his face, but he obeyed.

'Which communicator?'

Where pain predominates, agony can be a valued teacher.
— *Dosadi aphorism*

McKie and Jedrik had no need to discuss the decision. It was a choice which they shared and knew they shared through a memory-selection process now common to both of them. There was a loophole in the God Wall and even though that wall now blanketed Dosadi in darkness, a Caleban contract was still a Caleban contract. The vital question was whether the Caleban of the God Wall would respond.

Jedrik in McKie's body stood guard outside her own room while a Jedrik-fleshed McKie went alone into the room to make the attempt. Who should he try to contact? Fannie Mae? The absolute darkness which enclosed Dosadi hinted at an absolute withdrawal of the guardian Caleban. And there was so little time.

McKie sat cross-legged on the floor of the room and tried to clear his mind. The constant strange discoveries in the female body he now wore interfered with concentration. The moment of exchange left an aftershock which he doubted would ever diminish. They had but to share the desire for the change now and it occurred. But this different body – ahh, the multiplicity of differences created its own confusions. These went far beyond the adjustments to different height and weight. The muscles of his/her arms and hips felt wrongly attached. The bodily senses were routed through different unconscious processes. Anatomy created its own patterns, its own instinctual behavior. For one thing, he found it necessary to develop consciously monitored movements which protected his/her breasts. The movements were reminiscent of those male adjustments by which he prevented injury to testes. These were movements which a male learned early and relegated to an automatic behavior pattern. The problem in the female body was that he had to *think* about such behavior. And it went far beyond the breast-testes interlock.

As he tried to clear his mind for the Caleban contact, these webbed clusters of memory intruded. It was maddening. He needed to clear away bodily distractions, but this female body demanded his attention.

In desperation, he hyperventilated and burned his awareness into a pineal focus whose dangers he knew only too well. This was the way to permanent identity loss if the experience were prolonged. It produced a sufficient clarity, however, that he could fill his awareness with memories of Fannie Mae.

Silence.

He sensed time's passage as though each heartbeat were a blow.

Fear hovered at the edges of the silence.

It came to him that something had put a terrible fear into the God Wall Caleban.

McKie felt anger.

'Caleban! You owe me!'

'McKie?'

The response was so faint that he wondered whether it might be his hopes playing tricks on him.

'Fannie Mae?'

'Are you McKie?'

That was stronger, and he recognized the familiar Caleban presence in his awareness.

'I am McKie and you owe me a debt.'

'If you are truly McKie ... why are you so ... strange ... changed?'

'I wear another body.'

McKie was never sure, but he thought he sensed consternation. Fannie Mae responded more strongly then.

'I remove McKie from Dosadi now? Contract permits.'

'I will share Dosadi's fate.'

'McKie!'

'Don't argue with me, Fannie Mae. I will share Dosadi's fate unless you remove another node/person with me.'

He projected Jedrik's patterns then, an easy process since he shared all of her memories.

'She wears McKie's body!'

It was accusatory.

'She wears *another* body,' McKie said. He knew the Caleban saw his new relationship with Jedrik. Everything depended now on the interpretation of the Caleban contract.

'Jedrik is Dosadi,' the Caleban protested.

'So am I Dosadi ... now.'

'But you are McKie!'

'And Jedrik is also McKie. Contact her if you don't believe me.'

He broke the contact with an angry abruptness, found himself sprawled on the floor, still twitching. Perspiration bathed the female body which he still wore. The head ached.

Would Fannie Mae do as he'd told her? He knew Jedrik was as capable of projecting his awareness as he was of projecting hers. How would Fannie Mae interpret the Dosadi contract?

Gods! The ache in this head was a burning thing. He felt alien in Jedrik's body, misused. The pain persisted and he wondered if he'd done irreparable harm to Jedrik's brain through that intense pineal focus.

Slowly, he pushed himself upright, got to his feet. The Jedrik legs felt weak beneath him. He thought of Jedrik outside that door, trembling in the zombielike trance required for this mind-to-mind contact. What was taking so long? Had the Calebans withdrawn?

Have we lost?

He started for the door but before he'd taken the second step, light blazed around him. For a fractional heartbeat he thought it was the final fire to consume Dosadi, but the light held steady. He glanced around, found himself in the open air. It was a place he recognized immediately: the courtyard of the Dry Head compound on Tandatoor. He saw the familiar phylum designs on the surrounding walls: green Gowachin script on yellow bricks. There was the sound of water splashing in the corner pool. A group of Gowachin stood in an arched entry directly ahead of him and he recognized one of his old teachers. Yes – this was a Dry Head sanctum. These people had protected him, trained him, introduced him to their most sacred secrets.

The Gowachin in the shadowed entry were moving excitedly into the courtyard, their attention centered on a figure sprawled near them. The figure stirred, sat up.

McKie recognized his own body there.

Jedrik!

It was an intense mutual need. The body exchange required less than an eyeblink. McKie found himself in his own familiar body, seated on cool tiles. The approaching Gowachin bombarded him with questions.

'McKie, what is this?'

'You fell through a jumpdoor!'

'Are you hurt?'

He waved the questions away, crossed his legs, and fell into the long-call trance focused on that bead in his stomach. That bead Bildoon had never expected him to use!

As it was paid to do, the Taprisiot waiting on CC enfolded his awareness. McKie rejected contact with Bildoon, made six calls through the responsive Taprisiot. The calls went to key agents in BuSab, all of them ambitious and resourceful, all of them completely loyal to the agency's mandate. He transmitted his Dosadi information in full bursts, using the technique derived from his exchanges with Jedrik – mind-to-mind.

There were few questions and those easily answered.

'The Caleban who holds Dosadi imprisoned plays God. It's the letter of the contract.'

'Do the Calebans approve of this?'

That question came from a particularly astute Wreave agent sensitive to the complications implicit in the fact that the Gowachin were training Ceylang, a Wreave female, as a Legum.

'The concepts of approval or disapproval are not applicable. The role was necessary for that Caleban to carry out the contract.'

'It was a game?'

The Wreave agent was outraged.

'Perhaps. There's one thing certain: the Calebans don't understand harmful behavior and ethics as we understand them.'

'We've always known that.'

'But now we've really learned it.'

When he's made the six calls, McKie sent his Taprisiot questing for Aritch, found the High Magister in the Running Phylum's conference pool.

'Greetings, Client.'

McKie projected wry amusement. He sensed the Gowachin's shock.

'There are certain things which your Legum instructs you to do under the holy seal of our relationship,' McKie said.

'You will take us into the Courtarena, then?'

The High Magister was perceptive and he was a beneficiary of Dosadi's peculiar gifts, but he was not a Dosadi. McKie found it relatively easy to manipulate Aritch now, enlisting the High Magister's deepest motivations. When Aritch protested against cancelling the God Wall contract, McKie revealed only the first layer of stubborn determination.

'You will not add to your Legum's difficulties.'

'But what will keep them on Dosadi?'

'Nothing.'

'Then you will defend rather than prosecute?'

'Ask your pet Wreave,' McKie said. 'Ask Ceylang.'

He broke the contact then, knowing Aritch could only obey him. The High Magister had few choices, most of them bad ones. And Gowachin Law prevented him from disregarding his Legum's orders once the pattern of the contest was set.

McKie awoke from the call to find his Dry Head friends clustered around Jedrik. She was explaining their predicament. Yes . . . There were advantages to having two bodies with one purpose. McKie got to his feet. She saw him, spoke.

'My head feels better.'

'It was a near thing.' And he added:

'It still is. But Dosadi is free.'

In the classical times of several species, it was the custom of the powerful to nudge the power-counters (money or other economic tabulators, status points, etc.) into occasional violent perturbations from which the knowledgeable few profited. Human accounts of this experience reveal edifying examples of this behavior (for which, see Appendix G). Only the PanSpechi appear to have avoided this phenomenon, possibly because of creche slavery.

– Comparative History, The BuSab Text

McKie made his next series of calls from the room the Dry Heads set aside for him. It was a relatively large room reserved for Human guests and contained well-trained chairdogs and a wide bedog which Jedrik eyed with suspicion despite her McKie memories of such things. She knew the things had only a rudimentary brain, but still they were *alive.*

She stood by the single window which looked out on the courtyard pool, turning when she heard McKie awaken from his Taprisiot calls.

'Suspicions confirmed,' he said.

'Will our agent friends leave Bildoon for us?' she asked.

'Yes.'

She turned back to the window.

'I keep thinking how the Dosadi sky must look now . . . without a God Wall. As bright as this.' She nodded toward the courtyard seen through the window. 'And when we get jumpdoors . . .'

She broke off. McKie, of course, shared such thoughts. This new intimacy required considerable adjustment.

'I've been thinking about your training as a Legum,' she said.

McKie knew where her thoughts had gone.

The Gowachin chosen to train him had all appeared open in their relationship. He had been told that his teachers were a select group, chosen for excellence, the best available for the task: making a Gowachin Legum out of a non-Gowachin.

A silk purse from a sow's ear!

His teachers had appeared to lead conventional Gowachin lives, keeping the usual numbers of fertile females in family tanks, weeding the Graluz tads with necessary Gowachin abandon. On the surface of it, the whole thing had assumed a sense of the ordinary. They had introduced him to intimate aspects of their lives when he'd inquired, answered his questions with disarming frankness.

McKie's Jedrik-amplified awareness saw this in a different light now. The contests between Gowachin phylums stood out sharply. And McKie knew now that he had not asked the right questions, that his teachers had been selected by different rules than those revealed to him at the time, that their private instructions from their Gowachin superiors contained nuances of vital importance which had been hidden from their student.

Poor Ceylang.

These were unsettling reflections. They changed his understanding of Gowachin honor, called into question all of those inadvertent comparisons he'd made between Gowachin forms and the mandate of his own BuSab. His BuSab training came in for the same questioning examination.

Why ... why ... why ... why ...

Law? Gowachin Law?

The value in having a BuSab agent as a Legum of the Gowachin had gained a new dimension. McKie saw these matters now as Jedrik had once seen through the God Wall. There existed other forces only dimly visible behind the visible screen. An unseen power structure lay out there – people who seldom appeared in public, decision makers whose slightest whim carried terrible import for countless worlds. Many places, many worlds would be held in various degrees of bondage. Dosadi had merely been an extreme case for a special purpose.

New bodies for old. Immortality. And a training ground for people who made terrible decisions.

But none of them would be as completely Dosadi as this Jedrik-amplified McKie.

He wondered where the Dosadi decision had been made. Aritch had not shared in it; that was obvious. There were others behind Aritch – Gowachin and non-Gowachin. A shadowy power group existed. It could have its seat on any world of the ConSentiency. The power merchants would have to meet occasionally, but not necessarily face to face. And never in the public eye. Their first rule was secrecy. They would employ many people who lived at the exposed fringes of their power, people to carry out shadowy commands – people such as Aritch.

And Bildoon.

What had the PanSpechi hoped to gain? A permanent hold on his creche's ego? Of course. That ... plus new bodies – Human bodies, undoubtedly, and unmarked by the stigmata of his PanSpechi origins.

Bildoon's behavior – and Aritch's – appeared so transparent now. And there'd be a Mrreg nearby creating the currents in which Aritch swam. Puppet leads to Puppet Master.

Mrreg.

That poor fool, Grinik, had revealed more than he thought.

And Bildoon.

'We have two points of entry,' McKie said.

She agreed.

'Bildoon and Mrreg. The latter is the more dangerous.'

A crease beside McKie's nose began to itch. He scratched at it absently, grew conscious that something had changed. He stared around, found himself standing at the window and clothed in a female body.

Damn! It happened so easily.

Jedrik stared up at him with his own eyes. She spoke with his voice, but the overtones were pure Jedrik. They both found this amusing.

'The powers of your BuSab.'

He understood.

'Yes, the watchdogs of justice.'

'Where were the watchdogs when my ancestors were lured into this Dosadi trap?'

'Watchdogs of justice, very dangerous role,' he agreed.

'You know our feelings of outrage,' she said.

'And I know what it is to have loving parents.'

'Remember that when you talk to Bildoon.'

Once more, McKie found himself on the bed, his old familiar body around him.

Presently, he felt the mental tendrils of a Taprisiot call, sensed Bildoon's awareness in contact with him. McKie wasted no time. The shadow forces were taking the bait.

'I have located Dosadi. The issue will come to the Court-arena. No doubt of that. I want you to make the preliminary arrangements. Inform the High Magister Aritch that I make the formal imposition of the Legum. One member of the judicial panel must be a Gowachin from DoSadi. I have a particular Gowachin in mind. His name is Broey.'

'Where are you?'

'On Tandaloor.'

'Is that possible?'

McKie masked his sadness. *Ahhh, Bildoon, how easily you are read.*

'Dosadi is temporarily out of danger. I have taken certain retaliatory precautions.'

McKie broke the contact.

Jedrik spoke in a musing voice.

'Ohh, the perturbations we spread.'

McKie had no time for such reflections.

'Broey will need help, a support team, an extremely reliable troop which I want you to select for him.'

'Yes, and what of Gar and Tria?'

'Let them run free. Broey will pick them up later.'

Communal/managed economics have always been more destructive of their societies than those driven by greed. This is what Dosadi says: Greed sets its own limits, is self-regulating.

— The Dosadi Analysis/BuSab Text

McKie looked around the Legum office they'd assigned him. Afternoon smells from Tandaloor's fern jungles came in an open window. A low barrier separated him from the Courtarena with its ranks of seats all around. His office and adjoining quarters were small but fitted with all requisite linkages to libraries and the infrastructure to summon witnesses and experts. It was a green-walled space so deceptively ordinary that its like had beguiled more than one nonGowachin into believing he knew how to perform here. But these quarters represented a deceptive surface riding on Gowachin currents. No matter that the ConSentient Pact modified what the Gowachin might do here, this was Tandaloor, and the forms of the frog people dominated.

Seating himself at the single table in the office space, McKie felt the chairdog adjust itself beneath him. It was good to have a chairdog again after Dosadi's unrelenting furniture. He flipped a toggle and addressed the Gowachin face which appeared on the screen inset into his table.

'I require testimony from those who made the actual decision to set up the Dosadi experiment. Are you prepared to meet this request?'

'Do you have the names of these people?'

Did this fool think he was going to blurt out: 'Mrreg'?

'If you force me to it,' McKie warned, 'I will bind Aritch to the Law and extract the names from him.'

This had no apparent effect on the Gowachin. He addressed McKie by name and title, adding:

'I leave the formalities to you. Any witness I summon must have a name.'

McKie suppressed a smile. Suspicions confirmed. This was a fact which the watchful Gowachin in the screen was late recognizing. Someone else had read the interchange correctly, however. Another, older, Gowachin face replaced the first one on the screen.

'What're you doing, McKie?'

'Determining how I will proceed with this case.'

'You will proceed as a Legum of the Gowachin Bar.'

'Precisely.'

McKie waited.

The Gowachin peered narrowly at him from the screen.

'Jedrik?'

'You are speaking to Jorj X. McKie, a Legum of the Gowachin Bar.'

Belatedly, the older Gowachin saw something of the way the Dosadi experience had changed McKie.

'Do you wish me to place you in contact with Aritch?'

McKie shook his head. They were so damned obvious, these underlings.

'Aritch didn't make the Dosadi decision. Aritch was chosen to take the blow if it came to that. I will accept nothing less than the one who made that ultimate decision which launched the Dosadi experiment.'

The Gowachin stared at him coldly, then:

'One moment. I will see what I can do.'

The screen went blank, but the audio remained. McKie heard the voices.

'Hello ... Yes, I'm sorry to interrupt at this time.'

'What is it?'

That was a deep and arrogant Gowachin voice, full of annoyance at the interruption. It was also an accent which a Dosadi could recognize in spite of the carefully overlaid masking tones. Here was one who'd used Dosadi.

The voice of the older Gowachin from McKie's screen continued:

'The Legum bound to Aritch has come up with a sensitive line of questioning. He wishes to speak to you.'

'To me? But I am preparing for Laupuk.'

McKie had no idea what Laupuk might be, but it opened a new window on the Gowachin for him. Here was a glimpse of the rarified strata which had been concealed from him all of those years. This tiny glimpse confirmed him in the course he'd chosen.

'He is listening to us at this time.'

'Listening ... why?'

The tone carried threats, but the Gowachin who'd intercepted McKie's demands went on, unwavering:

'To save explanations. It's clear that he'll accept nothing less than speaking to you. This caller is McKie, but ...'

'Yes?'

'You will understand.'

'I presume you have interpreted things correctly. Very well. Put him on.'

McKie's screen flickered, revealed a wide view of a Gowachin room such as he'd never before seen. A far wall held spears and cutting weapons, streamers of colorful pennants, glistening rocks, ornate carvings in a shiny black substance. All of this was backdrop for a semireclining chairdog occupied by an aged Gowachin who sat spraddle-legged being anointed by two younger Gowachin males. The attendants poured a thick, golden substance onto the aged Gowachin from green crystal flasks. The flasks were of a spiral design. The contents were gently massaged into the Gowachin's skin. The old Gowachin glistened with the stuff and when he blinked – no Phylum tattoos.

'As you can see,' he said, 'I'm being prepared for . . .'

He broke off, recognizing that he spoke to a non-Gowachin. Certainly, he'd known this. It was a slow reaction for a Dosadi.

'This is a mistake,' he said.

'Indeed.' McKie nodded pleasantly. 'Your name?'

The old Gowachin scowled at this gaucherie, then chuckled.

'I am called Mrreg.'

As McKie had suspected. And why would a Tandaloor Gowachin assume the name, no, the *title* of the mythical monster who'd imbued the frog people with a drive toward savage testing? The implications went far beyond this planet, colored Dosadi.

'You made the decision for the Dosadi experiment?'

'Someone had to make it.'

That was not a substantive answer, and McKie decided to take it to issue. 'You are not doing me any favors! I now know what it means to be a Legum of the Gowachin Bar and I intend to employ my powers to their limits.'

It was as though McKie had worked some odd magic which froze the scene on his screen. The two attendants stopped pouring unguent, but did not look toward the pickup viewer which was recording their actions for McKie. As for Mrreg, he sat utterly still, his eyes fixed unblinking upon McKie.

McKie waited.

Presently, Mrreg turned to the attendant on his left.

'Please continue. There is little time.'

McKie took this as though spoken to himself.

'You're my client. Why did you send a proxy?'

Mrreg continued to study McKie.

'I see what Ekris meant.' Then, more briskly: 'Well, McKie, I followed your career with interest. It now appears I did not follow you closely enough. Perhaps if we had not ...'

He left the thought incomplete.

McKie picked up on this.

'It was inevitable that I escape from Dosadi.'

'Perhaps.'

The attendants finished their work, departed, taking the oddly shaped crystal flasks with them.

'Answer my question,' McKie said.

'I am not required to answer your question.'

'Then I withdraw from this case.'

Mrreg hunched forward in sudden alarm. 'You cannot! Aritch isn't ...'

'I have no dealings with Aritch. My client is that Gowachin who made the Dosadi decision.'

'You are engaging in strange behavior for a Legum. Yes, bring it.' This last was addressed to someone offscreen. Another attendant appeared, carrying a white garment shaped somewhat like a long apron with sleeves. The attendant proceeded to put this onto Mrreg, who ignored him, concentrating on McKie.

'Do you have any idea what you're doing, McKie?'

'Preparing to act for my client.'

'I see. Who told you about me?'

McKie shook his head.

'Did you really believe me unable to detect your presence or interpret the implications of what my own senses tell me?'

McKie saw that the Gowachin failed to see beneath the surface taunting. Mrreg turned to the attendant who was tying a green ribbon at the back of the apron. The old Gowachin had to lean forward for this. 'A little tighter,' he said.

The attendant retied the ribbon.

Addressing McKie, Mrreg said, 'Please forgive the distraction. This must proceed at its own pace.'

McKie absorbed this, assessed it Dosadi fashion. He could see the makings of an important Gowachin ritual here, but it was a new one to him. No matter. That could wait. He continued speaking, probing this Mrreg.

'When you found your own peculiar uses for Dosadi ...'

'Peculiar? It's a universal motivation, McKie, that one tries to reduce the competition.'

'Did you assess the price correctly, the price you might be asked to pay?'

'Oh, yes. I knew what I might have to pay.'

There was a clear tone of resignation in the Gowachin's voice, a rare tone for his species. McKie hesitated. The attendant who'd brought the apron left the room, never once glancing in McKie's direction, although there had to be a screen to show whatever Mrreg saw of his caller.

'You wonder why I sent a proxy to hire the Legum?' Mrreg asked.

'Why Aritch?'

'Because he's a candidate for ... greater responsibilities. You know, McKie, you astonish me. Undoubtedly you know what I could have done to you for this impertinence, yet that doesn't deter you.'

This revealed more than Mrreg might have intended, but he remained unaware (or uncaring) of what McKie saw. For his part, McKie maintained a bland exterior, as blank as that of any Dosadi.

'I have a single purpose,' McKie said. 'Not even my client will sway me from it.'

'The function of a Legum,' Mrreg said.

The attendant of the white apron returned with an unsheathed blade. McKie glimpsed a jeweled handle and glittering sweep of cutting edge about twenty centimeters long. The blade curved back upon itself in a tight arc at the tip. The attendant, his back to McKie, stood facing Mrreg. The blade no longer was visible.

Mrreg, his left side partly obscured from McKie by the attendant, leaned to the right and peered up at the screen through which he watched McKie.

'You've never been appraised of the ceremony we call Laupuk. It's very important and we've been remiss in leaving this out of your education. Laupuk was essential before such a ... project as Dosadi could be set in motion. Try to understand this ritual. It will help you prepare your case.'

'What was your Phylum?' McKie asked.

'That's no longer important but ... very well. It was Great Awakening. I was High Magister for two decades before we made the Dosadi decision.'

'How many Rim bodies have you used up?'

'My final one. That, too, is no longer important. Tell me, McKie, when did you suspect Aritch was only a proxy?'

'When I realized that not all Gowachin were born Gowachin.'

'But Aritch ...'

'Ahh, yes: Aritch aspires to greater responsibilities.'

'Yes ... of course. I see. The Dosadi decision had to go far beyond a few phylums or a single species. There had to be a ... I believe you Humans call it a "High Command." Yes, that would've become obvious to one as alert as you now appear. Your many marriages deceived us, I think. Was that deliberate?'

Secure behind his Dosadi mask, McKie decided to lie.

'Yes.'

'Ahhhhhhhhh.'

Mrreg seemed to shrivel into himself, but rallied.

'I see. We were made to believe you some kind of dilettante with perverted emotions. It'd be judged a flaw which we could exploit. Then there's another High Command and we never suspected.'

It all came out swiftly, revealing the wheels within wheels which ruled Mrreg's view of the ConSentient universe. McKie marveled at how much more was said than the bare words. This one had been a long time away from Dosadi and had not been born there, but there were pressures on Mrreg now forcing him to the limits of what he'd learned on Dosadi.

McKie did not interrupt.

'We didn't expect you to penetrate Aritch's role, but that was not our intent, as you know. I presume ...'

Whatever Mrreg presumed, he decided not to say it, musing aloud instead.

'One might almost believe you were born on Dosadi.'

McKie remained silent, allowing the fear in that conjecture to fill Mrreg's consciousness.

Presently, Mrreg asked, 'Do you blame all Gowachin?'

Still, McKie remained silent.

Mrreg became agitated.

'We are a government of sorts, my High Command. People can be induced not to question a government.'

McKie decided to press this nerve.

'Governments always commit their entire populations when the demands grow heavy enough. By their passive acceptance, these populations become accessories to whatever is done in their name.'

'You've provided free use of jumpdoors for the Dosadi?'

McKie nodded. 'The Calebans are aware of their obligation. Jedrik has been busy instructing her compatriots.'

'You think to loose the Dosadi upon the ConSentiency and hunt down my High Command? Have a care, McKie. I warn you not to abandon your duties as a Legum, or to turn your back on Aritch.'

McKie continued silent.

'Don't make that error, McKie. Aritch is your client. Through him you represent all Gowachin.'

'A Legum requires a responsible client,' McKie said. 'Not a proxy, but a client whose acts are brought into question by the case being tried.'

Mrreg revealed Gowachin signs of deep concern.

'Hear me, McKie. I haven't much time.'

In a sudden rush of apprehension, McKie focused on the attendant with the blade who stood there partly obscuring the seated Gowachin. Mrreg spoke in a swift spill of words.

'By our standards, McKie, you are not yet very well educated in Gowachin necessities. That was our error. And now your ... impetuosity has put you into a position which is about to become untenable.'

The attendant shifted slightly, arms moving up. McKie glimpsed the blade tip at the attendant's right shoulder.

'Gowachin don't have families as do Humans or even Wreaves,' Mrreg said. 'We have graduated advancement into groups which hold more and more responsibility for those beneath them. This was the pattern adopted by our High Command. What you see as a Gowachin family is only a breeding group with its own limited rules. With each step up in responsibility goes a requirement that we pay an increasing price for failure. You ask if I know the price? Ahhh, McKie. The breeding male Gowachin makes sure that only the swiftest, most alert of his tads survive. A Magister upholds the forms of the Law. The High Command answers to a ... Mrreg. You see? And a Mrreg must make only the best decisions. No failures. Thus ... Laupuk.'

As he spoke the final word, the blade in the attendant's hands flashed out and around in a shimmering arc. It caught the seated Gowachin at the neck. Mrreg's head, neatly severed, was caught in the loop at the blade's tip, lifted high, then lowered onto the white apron which now was splashed with green gore.

The scene blanked out, was replaced by the Gowachin who had connected McKie with Mrreg.

'Aritch wishes to consult his Legum,' the Gowachin said.

In a changing universe, only a changing species can hope to be immortal and then only if its eggs are nurtured in widely scattered environments. This predicts a wealth of unique individuals.
> *– Insights (a glimpse of early Human philosophy), BuSab Text*

Jedrik made contact with McKie while he waited for the arrival of Aritch and Ceylang. He had been staring absently at the ceiling, evaluating in a profoundly Dosadi way how to gain personal advantage from the upcoming encounter, when he felt the touch of her mind on his.

McKie locked himself in his body.

'No transfer.'

'Of course not.'

It was a tiny thing, a subtle shading in the contact which could have been overlooked by anyone with a less accurate simulation model of Jedrik.

'You're angry with me,' McKie said.

He projected irony, knew she'd read this correctly.

When she responded, her anger had been reduced to irritation. The point was not the shading of emotion, it was that she allowed such emotion to reveal itself.

'You remind me of one of my early lovers,' she said.

McKie thought of where Jedrik was at this moment: safely rocked in the flower-perfumed air of his floating island on the planetary sea of Tutalsee. How strange such an environment must be for a Dosadi – no threats, fruit which could be picked and eaten without a thought of poisons. The memories she'd taken from him would coat the island with familiarity, but her flesh would continue to find that a strange experience. His memories – yes. The island would remind her of all those wives he'd taken to the honeymoon bowers of that place.

McKie spoke from this awareness.

'No doubt that early lover failed to show sufficient appreciation of your abilities, outside the bedroom, that is. Which one was it . . .'

And he named several accurate possibilities, lifting them from the memories he'd taken from Jedrik.

Now, she laughed. He sensed the untainted response, real humor and unchecked.

McKie was reminded in his turn of one of his early wives, and this made him think of the breeding situation from which Jedrik had come – no confusions between a choice for breeding mate and a lover taken for the available enjoyment of sex. One might even actively dislike the breeding mate.

Lovers ... wives ... What was the difference, except for the socially imprinted conventions out of which the roles arose? But Jedrik did remind him of that one particular woman, and he explored this memory, wondering if it might help him now in his relationship with Jedrik. He'd been in his midthirties and assigned to one of his first personal BuSab cases, sent out with no oldtimer to monitor and instruct him. The youngest Human agent in the Bureau's history ever to be released on his own, so it was rumored. The planet had been one of the Ylir group, very much unlike anything in McKie's previous experience: an ingrown place with deep entryways in all of the houses and an oppressive silence all around. No animals, no birds, no insects just that awesome silence within which a fanatic religion was reported forming. All conversations were low voiced and full of subtle intonations which suggested an inner communication peculiar to Ylir and somehow making sport with all outsiders not privy to their private code. Very like Dosadi in this.

His wife of the moment, safely ensconced on Tutalsee, had been quite the opposite: gregarious, sportive, noisy.

Something about that Ylir case had sent McKie back to this wife with a sharpened awareness of her needs. The marriage had gone well for a long time, longer than any of the others. And he saw now why Jedrik reminded him of that one: they both protected themselves with a tough armor of femininity, but were extremely vulnerable behind that facade. When the armor collapsed, it collapsed totally. This realization puzzled McKie because he read his own reaction clearly: he was frightened.

In the eyeblink this evaluation took, Jedrik read him:

'We have not left Dosadi. We've taken it with us.'

So that was why she'd made this contact, to be certain he mixed this datum into his evaluations. McKie looked out the open window. It would be dusk soon here on Tandaloor. The Gowachin home planet was a place which had defied change for thousands of standard years. In some respects, it was a backwater.

The ConSentiency will never be the same.

The tiny trickle of Dosadi which Aritch's people had hoped to cut off was now a roaring cataract. The people of Dosadi would insinuate themselves into niche after niche of ConSentient civilization. What could resist even the lowliest Dosadi? Laws would change. Relationships would assume profound and subtle differences. Everything from the most casual friendship to the most complex business relationship would take on some Dosadi character.

McKie recalled Aritch's parting question as Aritch had sent McKie to the jumpdoor which would put him on Dosadi.

'Ask yourself if there might be a price too high to pay for the Dosadi lesson.'

That had been McKie's first clue to Aritch's actual motives and the word *lesson* had bothered him, but he'd missed the implications. With some embarrassment, McKie recalled his glib answer to Aritch's question:

'It depends on the lesson.'

True, but how blind he'd been to things any Dosadi would have seen. How ignorant. Now, he indicated to Jedrik that he understood why she'd called such things to his attention. 'Aritch didn't look much beyond the uses of outrage and injustice ...'

'And how to turn such things to personal advantage.'

She was right, of course. McKie stared out at the gathering dusk. Yes, the species tried to make everything its own. If the species failed, then forces beyond it moved in, and so on, *ad infinitum*.

I do what I do.

He recalled those words of the sleeping monster with a shudder, felt Jedrik recoil. But she was proof even against this. 'What powers your ConSentiency had.'

Past tense, right. And not *our* ConSentiency because that already was a thing of the past. Besides ... she was Dosadi. 'And the illusions of power,' she said.

He saw at last what she was emphasizing, and her own shared memories in his mind made the lesson doubly impressive. She'd known precisely what McKie's personal ego-focus might overlook. Yet, this was one of the glues which held the ConSentiency together.

'Who can imagine himself immune from any retaliation?' he quoted.

It was right out of the BuSab Manual.

Jedrik made no response.

McKie needed no more emphasis from her now. The lesson of history was clear. Violence bred violence. If this violence got out of hand, it ran a course depressing in its repetitive pattern. More often than not, that course was deadly to the innocent, the so-called 'enlistment phase.' The ex-innocents ignited more violence and more violence until either reason prevailed or all were destroyed. There were a sufficient number of cinder blocks which once had been planets to make the lesson clear. Dosadi had come within a hair of joining that uninhabited, uninhabitable list.

Before breaking contact, Jedrik had another point to make.

'You recall that in those final days, Broey increased the rations for his Human auxiliaries, his way of saying to them: "You'll be turned out onto the Rim soon to fend for yourselves."'

'A *Dosadi* way of saying that.'

'Correct. We always held that thought in reserve: that we should breed in such numbers that some would survive no matter what happened. We would thus begin producing species which could survive there without the city of Chu ... or any other city designed solely to produce nonpoisonous foods.'

'But there's always a bigger force waiting in the wings.'

'Make sure Aritch understands that.'

Choose containable violence when violence cannot be avoided. Better
this than epidemic violence.

– Lessons of Choice, The BuSab Manual

The senior attendant of the Courtarena, a squat and dignified Gowachin
of the Assumptive Phylum, confronted McKie at the arena door with a
confession:

'I have delayed informing you that some of your witnesses have been
excluded by Prosecution challenge.'

The attendant, whose name was Darak, gave a Gowachin shrug,
waited.

McKie glanced beyond the attendant at the truncated oval of the arena
entrance which framed a lower section of the audience seats. The seats
were filled. He had expected some such challenge for this first morning
session of the trial, saw Darak's words as a vital revelation. They were
accepting his gambit. Darak had signaled a risky line of attack by those
who guided Ceylang's performance. They expected McKie to protest. He
glanced back at Aritch, who stood quietly submissive three steps behind
his Legum. Aritch gave every appearance of having resigned himself to
the arena's conditions.

'*The forms must be obeyed.*'

Beneath that appearance lay the hoary traditions of Gowachin Law –
*The guilty are innocent. Governments always do evil. Legalists put their
own interests first. Defense and prosecution are brother and sister. Suspect
everything.*

Aritch's Legum controlled the initial posture and McKie had chosen
defense. It hadn't surprised him to be told that Ceylang would prosecute.
McKie had countered by insisting that Broey sit on a judicial panel which
would be limited to three members. This had caused a delay during
which Bildoon had called McKie, probing for any betrayal. Bildoon's
approach had been so obvious that McKie had at first suspected a feint
within a feint.

'McKie, the Gowachin fear that you have a Caleban at your command.
That's a force which they ...'

'The more they fear the better.'

McKie had stared back at the screen-framed face of Bildoon, observing the signs of strain. Jedrik was right: the non-Dosadi were very easy to read.

'But I'm told you left this Dosadi in spite of a Caleban contract which prohibited ...'

'Let them worry. Good for them.'

McKie watched Bildoon intently without betraying a single emotion. No doubt there were others monitoring this exchange. Let them begin to see what they faced. Puppet Bildoon was not about to uncover what those shadowy forces wanted. They had Bildoon here on Tandaloor, though, and this told McKie an essential fact. The PanSpechi chief of BuSab was being offered as bait. This was precisely the response McKie sought.

Bildoon had ended the call without achieving his purpose. McKie had nibbled only enough to insure that Bildoon would be offered again as bait. And the puppet masters still feared that McKie had a Caleban at his beck and call.

No doubt the puppet masters had tried to question their God Wall Caleban. McKie hid a smile, thinking how that conversation must have gone. The Caleban had only to quote the letter of the contract, and if the questioners became accusatory the Caleban would respond with anger, ending the exchange. And the Caleban's words would be so filled with terms subject to ambiguous translation that the puppet masters would never be certain of what they heard.

As he stared at the patiently waiting Darak, McKie saw that they had a problem, those shadowy figures behind Aritch. Laupuk had removed Mrreg from their councils and his advice would have been valuable now. McKie had deduced that the correct reference was 'The Mrreg' and that Aritch headed the list of possible successors. Aritch might be Dosadi-trained but he was not Dosadi-born. There was a lesson in this that the entire ConSentiency would soon learn.

And Broey as a judge in this case remained an unchangeable fact. Broey was Dosadi-born. The Caleban contract had kept Broey on his poison planet, but it had not limited him to a Gowachin body. Broey knew what it was to be both Human and Gowachin. Broey knew about the Pcharkys and their use by those who'd held Dosadi in bondage. And Broey was now Gowachin. The forces opposing McKie dared not name another Gowachin judge. They must choose from the other species. They had an interesting quandary. And without a Caleban assistant, there were no more Pcharkys to be had on Dosadi. The most valuable *coin* the puppet masters had to offer was lost to them. They'd be desperate. Some of the older ones would be very desperate.

Footsteps sounded around the turn of the corridor behind Aritch. McKie glanced back, saw Ceylang come into view with her attendants. McKie counted no less than twenty leading Legums around her. They were out in force. Not only Gowachin pride and integrity, but their sacred view of Law stood at issue. And the desperate ones stood behind them, goading. McKie could almost see those shadowy figures in the shape of this entourage.

Ceylang, he saw, wore the black robes and white-striped hood of Legum Prosecutor, but she'd thrown back the hood to free her mandibles. McKie detected tension in her movements. She gave no sign of recognition, but McKie saw her through Dosadi eyes.

I frighten her. And she's right.

Turning to address the waiting attendant and speaking loudly to make sure that the approaching group heard, McKie said:

'Every law must be tested. I accept that you have given me formal announcement of a limit on my defense.'

Darak, expecting outraged protest and a demand for a list of the excluded witnesses, showed obvious confusion.

'Formal announcement?'

Ceylang and entourage came to a stop behind Aritch.

McKie went on in the same loud voice:

'We stand here within the sphere of the Courtarena. All matters concerning a dispute in the arena are formal in this place.'

The attendant glanced at Ceylang, seeking help. This response threatened him. Darak, hoping someday to be a High Magister, should now be recognizing his inadequacies. He would never make it in the politics of the Gowachin Phyla, especially not in the coming Dosadi age.

McKie explained as though to a neophyte:

'Information to be verified by my witnesses is known to me in its entirety. I will present the evidence myself.'

Ceylang, having stooped to hear a low-voiced comment from one of her Gowachin advisors, showed surprise at this. She raised one of her ropey tendrils, called, 'I protest. The Defense Legum cannot give ...'

'How can you protest?' McKie interrupted. 'We stand here before no judicial panel empowered to rule on any protest.'

'I make *formal* protest!' Ceylang insisted, ignoring an advisor on her right who was tugging at her sleeve.

McKie permitted himself a cold smile.

'Very well. Then we must call Darak into the arena as witness, he being the only party present who is outside our dispute.'

The edges of Aritch's jaws came down in a Gowachin grimace.

'At the end, I warned them not to go with the Wreave,' he said. 'They cannot say they came here unwanted.'

Too late, Ceylang saw what had happened. McKie would be able to question Darak on the challenges to the witnesses. Some of those challenges were certain to be overturned. At the very least, McKie would know who the Prosecution feared. He would know it in time to act upon it. There would be no delays valuable to Prosecution. Tension, fear, and pride had made Ceylang act precipitately. Aritch had been right to warn them, but they counted on McKie's fear of the interlocked Wreave triads. Let them count. Let them blunt their awareness on that and on a useless concern over the excluded witnesses.

McKie motioned Darak through the doorway into the arena, heard him utter an oath. The reason became apparent as McKie pressed through in the crowded surge of the Prosecutor's party. The instruments of Truth-by-Pain had been arrayed on their ancient rack below the judges. Seldom brought out of their wrappings even for display to visiting dignitaries these days, the instruments had not been employed in the arena within the memory of a living witness. McKie had expected this display. It was obvious that Darak and Ceylang had not. It was interesting to note the members of Ceylang's entourage who were watching for McKie's response.

He gave them a grin of satisfaction.

McKie turned his attention to the judicial panel. They had given him Broey. The ConSentiency, acting through BuSab, held the right of one appointment. Their choice delighted McKie. Bait, indeed! Bildoon occupied the seat on Broey's right. The PanSpechi chief of bureau sat there all bland and reserved in his unfamiliar Gowachin robes of water green. Bildoon's faceted eyes glittered in the harsh arena lighting. The third judge had to be the Gowachin choice and undoubtedly maneuvered (as Bildoon had been) by the puppet masters. It was a Human and McKie, recognizing him, missed a step, recovered his balance with a visible effort.

What were they doing?

The third judge was named Mordes Parando, a noted challenger of BuSab actions. He wanted BuSab eliminated – either outright or by removing some of the bureau's key powers. He came from the planet Lirat, which provided McKie with no surprises. Lirat was a natural cover for the shadowy forces. It was a place of enormous wealth and great private estates guarded by their own security forces. Parando was a man of somewhat superficial manners which might conceal a genuine sophisticate, knowledgeable and erudite, or a completely ruthless autocrat of Broey's stamp. He was certainly Dosaditrained. And his features bore the look of the Dosadi Rim.

There was one more fact about Parando which no one outside Lirat was supposed to know. McKie had come upon it quite by chance while investigating a Palenki who'd been an estate guard on Lirat. The turtlelike Palenki were notoriously dull, employed chiefly as muscle. This one had been uncommonly observant.

'Parando makes advice on Gowachin Law.'

This had been responsive to a question about Parando's relationship with the estate guard being investigated. McKie, not seeing a connection between question and answer, had not pursued the matter, but had tucked this datum away for future investigation. He had been mildly interested at the time because of the rumored existence of a legalist enclave on Lirat and such enclaves had been known to test the limits of legality.

The people behind Aritch would expect McKie to recognize Parando. Would they expect Parando to be recognized as a legalist? They were certain to know the danger of putting Parando on a Gowachin bench. Professional legalists were absolutely prohibited from Gowachin judicial service.

'Let the people judge.'

Why would they need a legalist here? Or were they expecting McKie to recognize the Rim origins of Parando's body? Were they warning McKie not to raise *that* issue here? Body exchange and the implications of immortality represented a box of snakes no one wanted to open. And the possibility of one species spying on another ... There was fragmentation of the ConSentiency latent in this case. More ways than one.

If I challenge Parando, his replacement may be more dangerous. If I expose him as a legalist after the trial starts ... Could they expect me to do that? Let us explore it.

Knowing he was watched by countless eyes, McKie swept his gaze around the arena. Above the soft green absorbent oval where he stood were rank on rank of benches, every seat occupied. Muted morning light from the domed translucent ceiling illuminated rows of Humans, Gowachin, Palenki, Sobarips ... McKie identified a cluster of Ferret Wreaves just above the arena, limber thin with a sinuous flexing in every movement. They would bear watching. But every species and faction in the ConSentiency would be represented here. Those who could not come in person would watch these proceedings via the glittering transmitter eyes which looked down from the ceiling's edges.

Now, McKie looked to the right at the witness pen set into the wall beneath the ranked benches. He identified every witness he'd called, even the challenged ones. The forms were being obeyed. While the ConSentient Covenant required certain modifications here, this arena was still dominated by Gowachin Law. To accent that, the blue metal box from the Running Phylum occupied the honor place on the bench in front of the judicial panel.

Who will taste the knife here?

Protocol demanded that Prosecutor and Defense approach to a point beneath the judges, abase themselves, and call out acceptance of the arena's conditions. The Prosecutor's party, however, was in disarray. Two of Ceylang's advisors were whispering excited advice to her.

The members of the Judicial panel conferred, glancing at the scene below them. They could not act formally until the obeisance.

McKie passed a glance across the panel, absorbed Broey's posture. The Dosadi Gowachin's enlightened greed was like an anchor point. It was like Gowachin Law, changeable only on the surface. And Broey was but the tip of the Dosadi advisory group which Jedrik had approved.

Holding his arms extended to the sides, McKie marched forward, abased himself face down on the floor, stood and called out:

'I accept this arena as my friend. The conditions here are my conditions but Prosecution has defiled the sacred traditions of this place. Does the court give me leave to slay her outright?'

There was an exclamation behind him, the sound of running, the sudden flopping of a body onto the arena's matted floor. Ceylang could not address the court before this obeisance and she knew it. She and the others now also knew something else just as important – that McKie was ready to slay her despite the threat of Wreave vendetta.

In a breathless voice, Ceylang called out her acceptance of the arena's conditions, then:

'I protest this trick by Defense Legum!'

McKie saw the stirring of Gowachin in the audience. A trick? Didn't Ceylang know yet how the Gowachin dearly loved legal tricks?

The members of the judicial panel had been thoroughly briefed on the surface demands of the Gowachin forms, though it was doubtful that Bildoon understood sufficiently what went on beneath those forms. The PanSpechi confirmed this now by leaning forward to speak.

'Why does the senior attendant of this court enter ahead of the Legums?'

McKie detected a fleeting smile on Broey's face, glanced back to see Darak standing apart from the prosecution throng, alone and trembling.

McKie took one step forward.

'Will the court direct Darak to the witness pen? He is here because of a formal demand by the Prosecutor.'

'This is the senior attendant of your court,' Ceylang argued. 'He guards the door to ...'

'Prosecution made formal protest to a matter which occurred in the presence of this attendant,' McKie said. 'As an attendant, Darak stands outside the conflicting interests. He is the only reliable witness.'

Broey stirred, looked at Ceylang, and McKie realized how strange the Wreave must appear to a Dosadi. This did not deter Broey, however.

'Did you protest?'

It was a direct question from the bench. Ceylang was required to answer. She looked to Bildoon for help but he remained silent. Parando also refused to help her. She glanced at Darak. The terrified attendant could not take his attention from the instruments of pain. Perhaps he knew something specific about their presence in the arena.

Ceylang tried to explain.

'When Defense Legum suggested an illegal ...'

'Did you protest?'

'But the ...'

'This court decides on all matters of legality. Did you protest?'

'I did.'

It was forced out of her. A fit of trembling passed over the slender Wreave form.

Broey waved Darak to the witness pen, had to add a vocal order when the frightened attendant failed to understand. Darak almost ran to the shelter of the pen.

Silence pervaded the arena. The silence of the audience was an explosive thing. They sat poised in the watching ovals, all of those species and factions with their special fears. By now, they'd heard many stories and rumors. Jumpdoors had spread the Dosadi emigres all across the ConSentiency. Media representatives had been excluded from Dosadi and this court on the Gowachin argument that they were 'prey to uninformed subjective reactions,' but they would be watching here through the transmitter eyes at the ceiling.

McKie looked around at nothing in particular but taking in every detail. There were more than three judges in this arena and Ceylang certainly must realize that. Gowachin Law turned upon itself, existing 'only to be changed.' But that watching multitude was quite another matter. Ceylang must be made to understand that she was a sacrifice of the arena. ConSentient opinion stood over her like a heavy sledge ready to smash down.

It was Parando's turn.

'Will opposing Legums make their opening arguments now?'

'We can't proceed while a formal protest is undecided,' McKie said.

Parando understood. He glanced at the audience, at the ceiling. His actions were a direct signal: Parando knew which *judges* really decided here. To emphasize it, he ran a hand from the front of his neck down his chest, the unique Rim Raider's salute from Dosadi signifying 'Death before surrender.' Subtle hints in the movement gave McKie another datum: Parando was a Gowachin in a Human body. They'd dared put two Gowachin on that panel!

With Dosadi insight, McKie saw why they did this. They were prepared to produce the Caleban contract here. They were telling McKie that *they* would expose the body-exchange secret if he forced them to it. All would see that loophole in the Caleban contract which confined the Dosadi-born, but released outsiders in Dosadi flesh.

They think I'm really Jedrik in this flesh!

Parando revealed even more. His people intended to find the Jedrik body and kill it, leaving this *McKie* flesh forever in doubt. He could protest his McKie identity all he wanted. They had but to demand that he prove it. Without the other person ... What had their God Wall Caleban told them?

'He is McKie, she is McKie. He is Jedrik, she is Jedrik.'

His mind in turmoil, McKie wondered if he dared risk an immediate mind contact with Jedrik. Together, they'd already recognized this danger. Jedrik had hidden herself on McKie's hideaway, a floating island on Tutalsee. She was there with a special Taprisiot contract prohibiting unwanted calls which might inadvertently reveal her location.

The judges, led by Parando, were acting, however, moving for an immediate examination of Darak. McKie forced himself to perform as a Legum.

His career in ruins, the attendant answered like an automaton. In the end, McKie restored most of his witnesses. There were two notable exceptions: Grinik (that flawed thread which might have led to The Mrreg) and Stiggy. McKie was not certain why they wanted to exclude the Dosadi weapons genius who'd transformed a BuSab wallet's contents into instruments of victory. Was it that Stiggy had broken an *unbreakable* code? That made sense only if Prosecution intended to play down the inherent Dosadi superiority.

Still uncertain, McKie prepared to retire and seek a way to avoid Parando's gambit, but Ceylang addressed the bench.

'The issue of witnesses having been introduced by Defense,' she said, 'Prosecution wishes to explore this issue. We note many witnesses from Dosadi called by Defense. There is a noteworthy omission whose name has not yet been introduced here. I refer to a Human by the name of Jedrik. Prosecution wishes to call Keila Jedrik as . . .'

'One moment!'

McKie searched his mind for the forms of an acceptable escape. He knew that his blurted protest had revealed more than he wanted. But they were moving faster than he'd expected. Prosecution did not really want Jedrik as a witness, not in a Gowachin Courtarena where the roles were never quite what they appeared to non-Gowachin. This was a plain message to McKie.

'*We're going to find her and kill her.*'

With Bildoon and Parando concurring, a jumpdoor was summoned and Ceylang played her trump.

'Defense knows the whereabouts of witness Keila Jedrik.'

They were forcing the question, aware of the emotional bond between McKie and Jedrik. He had a choice: argue that a personal relationship with the witness excluded her. But Prosecution and all the judges had to concur. They obviously would not do this – not yet. A harsh lock on his emotions, McKie gave the jumpdoor instructions.

Presently, Jedrik stepped onto the arena floor, faced the judges. She'd been into the wardrobe at his bower cottage and wore a yellow and orange sarong which emphasized her height and grace. Open brown sandals protected her feet. There was a flame red blossom at her left ear. She managed to look exotic and fragile.

Broey spoke for the judges.

'Do you have knowledge of the issues at trial here?'

'What issues are at trial?'

She asked it with a childlike innocence which did not even fool Bildoon. They were forced to explain, however, because of those other *judges* to whom every nuance here was vital. She heard them out in silence.

'An alleged experiment on a sentient population confined to a planet called Dosadi . . . lack of informed consent by subject population charged . . . accusations of conspiracy against certain Gowachin and others not yet named . . .'

Two fingers pressed to his eyes in the guise of intense listening, McKie made contact with Jedrik, suggesting, conferring. They had to find a way out of this trap! When he looked up, he saw the suspicions in Parando's face: *Which body, which ego? McKie? Jedrik?*

In the end, Ceylang hammered home the private message, demanding whether Jedrik had 'any personal relationship with Defense Legum?'

Jedrik answered in a decidedly un-Dosadi fashion.

'Why ... yes. We are lovers.'

In itself, this was not enough to exclude her from the arena unless Prosecution and the entire judicial panel agreed. Ceylang proposed the exclusion. Bildoon and Parando were predictable in their agreement. McKie waited for Broey.

'Agreed.'

Broey had a private compact with the shadow forces then. Jedrik and McKie had expected this, but had not anticipated the form confirmation would take.

McKie asked for a recess until the following morning.

With the most benign face on it, this was granted. Broey announced the decision, smiling down at Jedrik. It was a measure of McKie's Dosadi conditioning that he could not find it in himself to blame Broey for wanting personal victory over the person who had beaten him on Dosadi.

Back in his quarters, Jedrik put a hand on McKie's chest, spoke with eyes lowered.

'Don't blame yourself, McKie. This was inevitable. Those judges, none of them, would've allowed any protest from you before seeing me in person on that arena floor.'

'I know.'

She looked up at him, smiling.

'Yes ... of course. How like one person we are.'

For a time after that, they reviewed the assessment of the aides chosen for Broey. Shared memories etched away at minutiae. Could any choice be improved? Not one person was changed – Human or Gowachin. All of those advisors and aides were Dosadi-born. They could be depended upon to be loyal to their origins, to their conditioning, to themselves individually. For the task assigned to them, they were the best available.

McKie brought it to a close.

'I can't leave the immediate area of the arena until the trial's over.'

She knew that, but it needed saying.

There was a small cell adjoining his office, a bedog there, communications instruments, Human toilet facilities. They delayed going into the bedroom, turned to a low-key argument over the advisability of a body exchange. It was procrastination on both sides, outcome

620

known in advance. Familiar flesh was familiar flesh, less distracting. It gave each of them an edge which they dared not sacrifice. McKie could play Jedrik and Jedrik could play McKie, but that would be dangerous play now.

When they retired, it was to make love, the most tender experience either had known. There was no submission, only a giving, sharing, an open exchange which tightened McKie's throat with joy and fear, sent Jedrik into a fit of un-Dosadi sobbing.

When she'd recovered, she turned to him on the bed, touched his right cheek with a finger.

'McKie.'

'Yes?'

'I've never had to say this to another person, but ...' She silenced his attempted interruption by punching his shoulder, leaning up on an elbow to look down at him. It reminded McKie of their first night together, and he saw that she had gone back into her Dosadi shell ... but there was something else, a difference in the eyes.

'What is it?'

'Just that I love you. It's a very interesting feeling, especially when you can admit it openly. How odd.'

'Stay here with me.'

'We both know I can't. There's no safe place here for either of us, but the one who ...'

'Then let's ...'

'We've already decided against an exchange.'

'Where will you go?'

'Best you don't know.'

'If ...'

'No! I wouldn't be safe as a witness; I'm not even safe at your side. We both ...'

'Don't go back to Dosadi.'

'Where is Dosadi? It's the only place where I could ever feel at home, but Dosadi no longer exists.'

'I meant ...'

'I know.'

She sat up, hugged her knees, revealing the sinewy muscles of her shoulders and back. McKie studied her, trying to fathom what it was she hid in that Dosadi shell. Despite the intimacy of their shared memories, something about her eluded him. It was as though he didn't want to learn this thing. She would flee and hide, of course, but ... He listened carefully as she began to speak in a faraway voice.

'It'd be interesting to go back to Dosadi someday. The differences ...'

She looked over her shoulder at him

'There are those who fear we'll make over the ConSentiency in Dosadi's image. We'll try, but the result won't be Dosadi. We'll take what we judge to be valuable, but that'll change Dosadi more than it changes you. Your masses are less alert, slower, less resourceful, but you're so numerous. In the end, the ConSentiency will win, but it'll no longer be the ConSentiency. I wonder what it'll be when ...'

She laughed at her own musings, shook her head.

'And there's Broey. They'll have to deal with Broey and the team we've given him. Broey Plus! Your ConSentiency hasn't the faintest grasp of what we've loosed among them.'

'The predator in the flock.'

'To Broey, your people are like the Rim – a natural resource.'

'But he has no Pcharkys.'

'Not yet.'

'I doubt if the Calebans ever again will participate in ...'

'There may be other ways. Look how easy it is for us.'

'But we were printed upon each other by ...'

'Exactly! And they continue to suspect that you're in my body and I'm in yours. Their entire experience precludes the free shift back and forth, one body to another ...'

'Or this other thing ...'

He caressed her mind.

'Yes! Broey won't suspect until too late what's in store for him. They'll be a long time learning there's no way to sort you from ... me!'

This last was an exultant shout as she turned and fell upon him. It was a wild replay of their first night together. McKie abandoned himself to it. There was no other choice, no time for the mind to dwell on depressing thoughts.

In the morning, he had to tap his implanted amplifiers to bring his awareness to the required pitch for the arena. The process took a few minutes while he dressed.

Jedrik moved softly with her own preparations, straightened the bedog and caressed its resilient surface. She summoned a jumpdoor then, held him with a lingering kiss. The jumpdoor opened behind her as she pushed away from him.

McKie smelled familiar flowers, glimpsed the bowers of his Tutalsee island before the door blinked out of existence, hiding Jedrik and the island from him. Tutalsee? The moment of shocked understanding delayed him. She'd counted on that! He recovered, sent his mind leaping after her.

I'll force an exchange! By the Gods . . .

His mind met pain, consuming, blinding pain. It was agony such as he'd not even imagined could exist.

Jedrik!

His mind held an unconscious Jedrik whose awareness had fled from pain. The contact was so delicate, like holding a newborn infant. The slightest relaxation and he knew he would lose her to . . . He felt that terrifying monster of the first exchange hovering in the background, but love and concern armed him against fear.

Frantic, McKie held that tenuous contact while he called a jumpdoor. There was a small delay and when the door opened, he saw through the portal the black, twisted wreckage which had been his bower island. A hot sun beat down on steaming cinders. And in the background, a warped metal object which might have been one of Tutalsee's little four-place flitters rolled over, gurgled, and sank. The visible wreckage said the destructive force had been something like a pentrate, swift and all-consuming. The water around the island still bubbled with it. Even while he watched, the island began breaking up, its cinders drifting apart on the long, low waves. A breeze flattened the steaming smoke. Soon, there'd be nothing to show that beauty had floated here. With a pentrate, there would be nothing to recover . . . not even bodies to . . .

He hesitated, still holding his fragile grasp on Jedrik's unconscious presence. The pain was only a memory now. Was it really Jedrik in his awareness, or only his remembered imprint of her? He tried to awaken the sleeping presence, failed. But small threads of memory emerged, and he saw that the destruction had been Jedrik's doing, response to attack. The attackers had wanted a live hostage. They hadn't anticipated that violent, unmistakable message.

'You won't hold *me* over McKie's head!'

But if there were no bodies . . .

Again, he tried to awaken that unconscious presence. Her memories were there, but she remained dormant. The effort strengthened his grip upon her presence, though. And he told himself it had to be Jedrik, or he wouldn't know what had happened on the bower island.

Once more, he searched the empty water. Nothing.

A pentrate would've torn and battered everything around it. Shards of metal, flesh reduced to scattered cinders . . .

She's dead. She has to be dead. A pentrate . . .

But that familiar presence lay slumbering in his mind.

623

The door clacker interrupted his reverie. McKie released the jumpdoor, turned to look through the bedside viewer at the scene outside his Legum quarters. The expected deputation had arrived. Confident, the puppet masters were moving even before confirmation of their Tutalsee gambit. They could not possibly know yet what McKie knew. There could be no jumpdoor or any other thread permitted to connect this group to Tutalsee.

McKie studied them carefully, keeping a bridle on his rage. There were eight of them, so contained, so well schooled in Dosadi self-control. So transparent to a Jedrik-amplified McKie. They were four Humans and four Gowachin. Overconfident. Jedrik had seen to that by leaving no survivors.

Again, McKie tried to awaken that unconscious presence. She would not respond.

Have I only built her out of my memories?

There was no time for such speculation. Jedrik had made her choice on Tutalsee. He had other choices to make here and now – for both of them. That ghostly presence locked in his mind would have to wait.

McKie punched the communicator which linked him to Broey, gave the agreed-upon signal.

'It's time.'

He composed himself then, went to the door.

They'd sent no underlings. He gave them that. But they addressed him as Jedrik, made the anticipated demands, gloated over the hold they had upon him. It was only then that McKie saw fully how well Jedrik had measured these people; and how she had played upon her McKie in those last hours together like an exquisitely tuned instrument. Now, he understood why she'd made that violent choice.

As anticipated, the members of the delegation were extremely surprised when Broey's people fell upon them without warning.

For the Gowachin, to stand alone against all adversity is the most sacred moment of existence.

— The Gowachin, a BuSab analysis

The eight prisoners were dumped on the arena floor, bound and shackled. McKie stopped near them, waiting for Ceylang to arrive. It was not yet dawn. The ceiling above the arena remained dark. A few of the transmitter eyes around the upper perimeter glittered to reveal that they were activated. More were coming alive by the moment. Only a few of the witness seats were occupied, but people were streaming in as word was passed. The judicial bench remained empty.

The outer areaway was a din of Courtarena security forces coming and going, people shouting orders, the clank of weapons, a sense of complete confusion there which gradually resolved itself as Broey led his fellow judges up onto their bench. The witness pen was also filling, people punching sleep from their eyes, great gaping yawns from the Gowachin.

McKie looked to Broey's people, the ones who'd brought in the prisoners. He nodded for the captors to leave, giving them a Dosadi hand signal to remain available. They left.

Ceylang passed them as she entered, still fastening her robe. She hurried to McKie's side, waited for the judges to be seated before speaking.

'What is the meaning of this? My attendants . . .'

Broey signaled McKie.

McKie stepped forward to address the bench, pointed to the eight bound figures who were beginning to stir and push themselves upright.

'Here you see my client.'

Parando started to speak, but Broey silenced him with a sharp word which McKie did not catch. It sounded like 'frenzy.'

Bildoon sat in fearful fascination, unable to wrest his attention from the bound figures, all of whom remained silent. Yes, Bildoon would recognize those eight prisoners. In his limited, ConSentient fashion, Bildoon was sharp enough to recognize that he was in personal danger.

Parando, of course, knew this immediately and watched Broey with great care.

Again, Broey nodded to McKie.

'A fraud has been perpetrated upon this court,' McKie said. 'It is a fraud which was perpetrated against those great and gallant people, the Gowachin. Both Prosecution and Defense are its victims. The Law is its ultimate victim.'

It had grown much quieter in the arena. The observer seats were jammed, all the transmitter eyes alive. The faintest of dawn glow touched the translucent ceiling. McKie wondered what time it was. He had forgotten to put on any timepiece.

There was a stir behind McKie. He glanced back, saw attendants belatedly bringing Aritch into the arena. Oh, yes – they would have risked any delay to confer with Aritch. Aritch was supposed to be the other McKie expert. Too bad that this Human who looked like McKie was no longer the McKie they thought they knew.

Ceylang could not hold her silence. She raised a tendril for attention. 'This Tribunal . . .'

McKie interrupted.

'. . . is composed of three people. Only three.'

He allowed them a moment to digest this reminder that Gowachin trial formalities still dominated this arena, and were like no other such formalities in the ConSentiency. It could've been fifty judges up there on that bench. McKie had witnessed Gowachin trials where people were picked at random off the streets to sit in judgment. Such jurists took their duties seriously, but their overt behavior could lead another sentient species to question this. The Gowachin chattered back and forth, arranged parties, exchanged jokes, asked each other rude questions. It was an ancient pattern. The jurists were required to become 'a single organism.' Gowachin had their own ways of rushing that process.

But this Tribunal was composed of just three judges, only one of them visibly Gowachin. They were separate entities, their actions heavy with mannerisms foreign to the Gowachin. Even Broey, tainted by Dosadi, would be unfamiliar to the Gowachin observers. No 'single organism' here holding to the immutable forms beneath Gowachin Law. That had to be deeply disturbing to the Legums who advised Ceylang.

Broey leaned forward, addressed the arena.

'We'll dispense with the usual arguments while this new development is explored.'

Again, Parando tried to interrupt. Broey silenced him with a glance.

'I call Aritch of the Running Phylum,' McKie said.

He turned.

Ceylang stood in mute indecision. Her advisors remained at the back of the arena conferring among themselves. There seemed to be a difference of opinion among them.

Aritch shuffled to the death-focus of the arena, the place where every witness was required to stand. He glanced at the instruments of pain arrayed beneath the judicial bench, cast a wary look at McKie. The old High Magister appeared harried and undignified. That hurried conference to explore this development must've been a sore trial to the old Gowachin.

McKie crossed to the formal position beside Aritch, addressed the judges.

'Here we have Aritch, High Magister of the Running Phylum. We were told that if guilt were to be found in this arena, Aritch bore that guilt. He, so we were led to believe, was the one who made the decision to imprison Dosadi. But how can that be so? Aritch is old, but he isn't as old as Dosadi. Then perhaps his alleged guilt is to be found in concealing the imprisonment of Dosadi. But Aritch summoned an agent of BuSab and sent that agent openly to Dosadi.'

A disturbance among the eight shackled prisoners interrupted McKie. Several of the prisoners were trying to get to their feet, but the links of the shackles were too short.

On the judicial bench, Parando started to lean forward, but Broey hauled him back.

Yes, Parando and others were recalling the verities of a Gowachin Courtarena, the constant reversals of concepts common throughout the rest of the ConSentiency.

To be guilty is to be innocent. Thus, to be innocent is to be guilty.

At a sharp command from Broey, the prisoners grew quiet.

McKie continued.

'Aritch, conscious of the sacred responsibilities which he carried upon his back as a mother carries her tads, was deliberately named to receive the punishment blow lest that punishment be directed at all Gowachin everywhere. Who chose this innocent High Magister to suffer for all Gowachin?'

McKie pointed to the eight shackled prisoners.

'Who are these people?' Parando demanded.

McKie allowed the question to hang there for a long count. Parando knew who these eight were. Did he think he could divert the present course of events by such a blatant ploy?

Presently, McKie spoke.

'I will enlighten the court in due course. My duty, however, comes first. My client's *innocence* comes first.'

'One moment.'

Broey held up a webbed hand.

One of Ceylang's advisors hurried past McKie, asked and received permission to confer with Ceylang. A thwarted Parando sat like a condemned man watching this conversation as though he hoped to find reprieve there. Bildoon had hunched forward, head buried in his arms. Broey obviously controlled the Tribunal.

The advisor Legum was known to McKie, one Lagag of a middling reputation, an officer out of breeding. His words to Ceylang were low and intense, demanding.

The conference ended, Lagag hurried back to his companions. They now understood the tenor of McKie's *defense*. Aritch must have known all along that he could be sacrificed here. The ConSentient Covenant no longer permitted the ancient custom where the Gowachin audience had poured into the arena to kill with bare hands and claws the *innocent* defendant. But let Aritch walk from here with the brand of innocence upon him; he would not take ten paces outside the arena's precincts before being torn to pieces.

There'd been worried admiration in the glance Lagag had given McKie in passing. Yes . . . now they understood why McKie had maneuvered for a small and vulnerable judicial panel.

The eight prisoners began a new disturbance which Broey silenced with a shout. He signaled for McKie to continue.

'Aritch's design was that I expose Dosadi, return and defend him against the charge that he had permitted illegal psychological experiments upon an unsuspecting populace. He was prepared to sacrifice himself for others.'

McKie sent a wry glance at Aritch. Let the High Magister try to fight in half-truths in that defense!

'Unfortunately, the Dosadi populace was *not* unsuspecting. In fact, forces under the command of Keila Jedrik had moved to take control of Dosadi. Judge Broey will affirm that she had succeeded in this.'

Again, McKie pointed to the shackled prisoners.

'But these conspirators, these people who designed and profited from the Dosadi Experiment, ordered the death of Keila Jedrik! She was murdered this morning on Tutalsee to prevent my using her at the proper moment to prove Aritch's *innocence*. Judge Broey is witness to the truth of what I say. Keila Jedrik was brought into this arena yesterday only that she might be traced and killed!'

McKie raised both arms in an eloquent gesture of completion, lowered his arms.

Aritch looked stricken. He saw it. If the eight prisoners denied the charges, they faced Aritch's fate. And they must know by now that Broey wanted them *Gowachin-guilty*. They could bring in the Caleban contract and expose the body-exchange plot, but that risked having McKie defend or prosecute them because he'd already locked them to his actual *client*, Aritch. Broey would affirm this, too. They were at Broey's mercy. If they were *Gowachin-guilty*, they walked free only here on Tandaloor. *Innocent*, they died here.

As though they were one organism, the eight turned their heads and looked at Aritch. Indeed! What would Aritch do? If he agreed to sacrifice himself, the eight might live. Ceylang, too, focused on Aritch.

Around the entire arena there was a sense of collective held breath.

McKie watched Ceylang. How candid had Aritch's people been with their Wreave? Did she know the full Dosadi story?

She broke the silence, exposing her knowledge. She chose to aim her attack at McKie on the well-known dictum that, when all else failed, you tried to discredit the opposing Legum.

'McKie, is this how you defend these eight people whom only *you* name as client?' Ceylang demanded.

Now, it was delicate. Would Broey go along?

McKie countered her probe with a question of his own.

'Are you suggesting that you'd prosecute these people?'

'I didn't charge them! You did.'

'To prove Aritch's innocence.'

'But you call them client. Will you defend them?'

A collective gasp arose from the cluster of advisors behind her near the arena doorway. They'd seen the trap. If McKie accepted the challenge, the judges had no choice but to bring the eight into the arena under Gowachin forms. Ceylang had trapped herself into the posture of prosecutor against the eight. She'd said, in effect, that she affirmed their guilt. Doing so, she lost her case against Aritch and her life was immediately forfeit. She was caught.

Her eyes glittered with the unspoken question.

What would McKie do?

Not yet, McKie thought. *Not yet, my precious Wreave dupe.*

He turned his attention to Parando. Would they dare introduce the Caleban contract? The eight prisoners were only the exposed tip of the shadowy forces, a vulnerable tip. They could be sacrificed. It was clear that they saw this and didn't like it. No Gowachin Mrregs here with that iron submission to responsibility! They loved life and its power, especially the ones who wore Human flesh. How precious life must be for those who'd lived many lives! *Very* desperate, indeed.

To McKie's Dosadi-conditioned eyes, it was as though he read the prisoners' thoughts. They were safest if they remained silent. Trust Parando. Rely on Broey's enlightened greed. At the worst, they could live out what life was left to them here on Tandaloor, hoping for new bodies before the flesh they now wore ran out of vitality. As long as they still lived they could hope and scheme. Perhaps another Caleban could be hired, more Pcharkys found . . .

Aritch broke, unwilling to lose what had almost been his.

The High Magister's Tandaloor accent was hoarse with protest.

'But I did supervise the tests on Dosadi's population!'

'To what tests do you refer?'

'The Dosadi . . .'

Aritch fell silent, seeing the trap. More than a million Dosadi Gowachin already had left their planet. Would Aritch make targets of them? Anything he said could open the door to proof that the Dosadis were superior to non-Dosadis. Any Gowachin (or Human, for that matter) could well become a target in the next few minutes. One had only to denounce a selected Human or Gowachin as Dosadi. ConSentient fears would do the rest. And any of his arguments could be directed into exposure of Dosadi's real purpose. He obviously saw the peril in that, had seen it from the first.

The High Magister confirmed this analysis by glancing at the Ferret Wreaves in the audience. What consternation it would create among the secretive Wreaves to learn that another species could masquerade successfully as one of their own!

McKie could not leave matters where they stood, though. He threw a question at Aritch.

'Were the original transportees to Dosadi apprised of the nature of the project?'

'Only *they* could testify to that.'

'And their memories were erased. We don't *even* have historical testimony on this matter.'

Aritch remained silent. Eight of the original designers of the Dosadi project sat near him on the arena floor. Would he denounce them to save himself? McKie thought not. A person deemed capable of performing as The Mrreg could not possess such a flaw. Could he? Here was the real point of no return.

The High Magister confirmed McKie's judgment by turning his back on the Tribunal, the ages-old Gowachin gesture of submission. What a shock Aritch's performance must have been for those who'd seen him as a possible Mreg. A poor choice except at the end, and that'd been as much recognition of total failure as anything else.

McKie waited, knowing what had to happen now. Here was Ceylang's moment of truth.

Broey addressed her.

'You have suggested that you would prosecute these eight prisoners. The matter is in the hands of Defense Legum.'

Broey shifted his gaze.

'How say you, Legum McKie?'

The moment to test Broey had come. McKie countered with a question.

'Can this Courtarena suggest another disposition for these eight prisoners?'

Ceylang held her breath.

Broey was pleased. He had triumphed in the end over Jedrik. Broey was certain in his mind that Jedrik did not occupy this Legum body on the arena floor. Now, he could show the puppet masters what a Dosadi-born could do. And McKie saw that Broey intended to move fast, much faster than anyone had expected.

Anyone except Jedrik, and she was only a silent (memory?) in McKie's awareness.

Having given the appearance of deliberation, Broey spoke.

'I can order these eight bound over to ConSentient jurisdiction if McKie agrees.'

The eight stirred, subsided.

'I agree,' McKie said. He glanced at Ceylang. She made no protest, seeing the futility. Her only hope now lay in the possible deterrent presence of the Ferret Wreaves.

'Then I so order it,' Broey said. He spared a triumphant glance for Parando. 'Let a ConSentient jurisdiction decide if these eight are guilty of murder and other conspiracy.'

He was well within the bounds of the Covenant between the Con-Sentiency and Gowachin, but the Gowachin members of his audience didn't like it. Their Law was best! Angry whistlings could be heard all around the arena.

Broey rose half-out of his seat, pointed at the instruments of pain arrayed beneath him. Gowachin in the audience fell silent. They, better than anyone, knew that no person here, not even a member of the audience, was outside the Tribunal's power. And many understood

clearly now why those bloody tools had been displayed here. Thoughtful people had anticipated the problem of keeping order in this
arena.

Responding to the silent acceptance of his authority, Broey sank back
into his seat.

Parando was staring at Broey as though having just discovered the
presence of a monster in this Gowachin form. Many people would be
reassessing Broey now.

Aritch held his attitude of complete submission.

Ceylang's thoughts almost hummed in the air around her. Every way
she turned, she saw only a tangle of unmanageable tendrils and a blocked
passage.

McKie saw that it was time to bring matters to a head. He crossed to
the foot of the judicial bench, lifted a short spear from the instruments
there. He brandished the barbed, razor-edged weapon.

'Who sits on this Tribunal?'

Once, Aritch had issued such a challenge. McKie, repeating it, pointed
with the spear, answered his own question.

'A Gowachin of my choice, one supposedly wronged by the Dosadi
project. Were you wronged, Broey?'

'No.'

McKie faced Parando.

'And here we have a Human from Lirat. Is that not the case, Parando?'

'I am from Lirat, yes.'

McKie nodded.

'I am prepared to bring a parade of witnesses into this arena to testify
as to your occupation on Lirat. Would you care to state that occupation?'

'How dare you question this Tribunal?'

Parando glared down at McKie, face flushed.

'Answer his question.'

It was Broey.

Parando looked at Bildoon, who still sat with face concealed in his
arms, face down on the bench. Something about the PanSpechi repelled
Parando, but he knew he had to have Bildoon's vote to overrule Broey.
Parando nudged the PanSpechi. Inert flesh rolled away from Parando's
hand.

McKie understood.

Facing doom, Bildoon had retreated into the creche. Somewhere, an
unprepared PanSpechi body was being rushed into acceptance of that
crushed identity. The emergence of a new Bildoon would require considerable time. They did not have that time. When the creche finally

brought forth a functioning persona, it would not be heir to Bildoon's old powers in BuSab.

Parando was alone, exposed. He stared at the spear in McKie's hand.

McKie favored the arena with a sweeping glance before speaking once more to Parando.

'I quote that renowned expert on Gowachin Law, High Magister Aritch: "ConSentient Law always makes aristocrats of its practitioners. Gowachin Law stands beneath that pretension. Gowachin Law asks: Who knows the people? Only such a one is fit to judge in the Courtarena." That is Gowachin Law according to High Magister Aritch. That is the law in this place.'

Again, McKie gave Parando a chance to speak, received only silence.

'Perhaps you are truly fit to judge here,' McKie suggested. 'Are you an artisan? A philosopher? Perhaps you're a humorist? An artist? Ahhh, maybe you are that lowliest of workmen, he who tends an automatic machine?'

Parando remained silent, gaze locked on the spear.

'None of these?' McKie asked. 'Then I shall supply the answer. You are a professional legalist, one who gives legal advice, even to advice on Gowachin Law. You, a Human, not even a Legum, dare to speak of Gowachin Law!'

Without any muscular warning signal, McKie leaped forward, hurled the spear at Parando, saw it strike deeply into the man's chest.

One for Jedrik!

With bubbling gasp, Parando sagged out of sight behind the bench.

Broey, seeing the flash of anger in McKie's effort, touched the blue box in front of him.

Have no fear, Broey. Not yet. I still need you.

But now, more than Broey knew it was really McKie in this flesh. Not Jedrik. Those members of the shadow force watching this scene and able to plot would make the expected deduction because they did not know how freely and completely Jedrik and McKie had shared. To the shadow force, McKie would've known Parando's background. They'd trace out that mistake in short order. So this was McKie in the arena. But he'd left Dosadi. There could be only one conclusion in the plotters' minds.

McKie had Caleban help!

They had Calebans to fear.

And McKie thought: *You have only McKie to fear.*

He grew aware that grunts of Gowachin approval were sounding all around the arena. They accepted him as a Legum, thus they accepted his argument. Such a judge deserved killing.

Aritch set the precedent. McKie improved on it.

Both had found an approved way to kill a flawed judge, but McKie's act had etched a Gowachin precedent into the ConSentient legal framework. The compromise which had brought Gowachin and ConSentient Law into the Covenant of shared responsibility for the case in this arena would be seen by the Gowachin as a first long step toward making their Law supreme over all other law.

Aritch had half-turned, looking toward the bench, a glittering appraisal in his eyes which said the Gowachin had salvaged something here after all.

McKie strode back to confront Ceylang. He faced her as the forms required while he called for judgment.

'Bildoon?'

Silence.

'Parando?'

Silence.

'Broey?'

'Judgment for Defense.'

The Dosadi accent rang across the arena. The Gowachin Federation, only member of the ConSentiency which dared permit a victim to judge those accused of victimizing him, had received a wound to its pride. But they'd also received something they would consider of inestimable value – a foothold for their Law in the ConSentiency, plus a memorable court performance which was about to end in the drama they loved best.

McKie stepped to within striking distance of Ceylang, extended his right hand straight out to the side, palm up.

'The knife.'

Attendants scurried. There came the sound of the blue box being opened. Presently, the knife handle was slapped firmly into McKie's palm. He closed his fingers around it, thinking as he did so of all those countless others who had faced this moment in a Gowachin Courtarena.

'Ceylang?'

'I submit to the ruling of this court.'

McKie saw the Ferret Wreaves rise from their seats as one person. They stood ready to leap down into the arena and avenge Ceylang no matter the consequences. They could do nothing else but carry out the role which the Gowachin had designed for them. Few in the arena had misunderstood their presence here. No matter the measurement of the wound, the Gowachin did not suffer such things gladly.

An odd look of camaraderie passed between Ceylang and McKie then. Here they stood, the only two non-Gowachin in the ConSentient universe who had passed through that peculiar alchemy which transformed a person into a Legum. One of them was supposed to die immediately, and the other would not long survive that death. Yet, they understood each other the way siblings understand each other. Each had shed a particular *skin* to become something else.

Slowly, deliberately, McKie extended the tip of his blade toward Ceylang's left jowl, noting the myriad pocks of her triad exchanges there. She trembled but remained firm. Deftly, with the swiftest of flicking motions, McKie added another pock to those on her left jowl.

The Ferret Wreaves were the first to understand. They sank back into their seats.

Ceylang gasped, touched a tendril to the wound. Many times she had been set free by such a wound, moving on to new alliances which did not completely sunder the old.

For a moment, McKie thought she might not accept, but the increasing sounds of approval all around the arena overcame her doubts. The noise of that approval climbed to a near deafening crescendo before subsiding. Even the Gowachin joined this. How dearly they loved such legal nuances!

Pitching his voice for Ceylang alone, McKie spoke.

'You should apply for a position in BuSab. The new director would look with favor upon your application.'

'You?'

'Make a Wreave bet on it.'

She favored him with the grimace which passed for a smile among Wreaves, spoke the traditional words of triad farewell.

'We were well and truly wed.'

So she, too, had seen the truth in their unique closeness.

McKie betrayed the extent of his esoteric knowledge by producing the correct response.

'By my mark I know you.'

She showed no surprise. A good brain there, not up to Dosadi standards, but good.

Well and truly wed.

Keeping a firm lock on his emotions (the Dosadi in him helped), McKie crossed to confront Aritch.

'Client Aritch, you are innocent.'

McKie displayed the fleck of Wreave blood on the knife tip.

'The forms have been obeyed and you are completely exonerated. I rejoice with all of those who love justice.'

At this point in the old days, the jubilant audience would've fallen on the hapless client, would've fought for bloody scraps with which to parade through the city. No doubt Aritch would've preferred that. He was a traditionalist. He confirmed that now.

'I am glad to quit these times, McKie.'

McKie mused aloud.

'Who will be the Mrreg now that you're ... disqualified? Whoever it is, I doubt he'll be as good as the one he replaces. It will profit that next Mrreg to reflect upon the fragile and fugitive value to be gained from the manipulation of others.'

Glowering, Aritch turned and shambled toward the doorway out of the arena.

Some of the Gowachin from the audience already were leaving, no doubt hoping to greet Aritch outside. McKie had no desire to witness that remnant of an ancient ritual. He had other concerns.

Well and truly wed.

Something burned in his eyes. And still he felt that soft and sleeping presence in his awareness.

Jedrik?

No response.

He glanced at Broey who, true to his duty as a judge, would be the last to leave the arena. Broey sat blandly contemplating this place where he'd displayed the first designs of his campaign for supremacy in the ConSentiency. He would accept nothing less short of his own death. Those shadowy puppet masters would be the first to feel his rule.

That fitted the plan McKie and Jedrik had forged between them. In a way, it was still the plan of those who'd bred and conditioned Jedrik for the tasks she'd performed so exquisitely.

It was McKie's thought that those nameless, faceless Dosadis who stood in ghostly ranks behind Jedrik had made a brave choice. Faced with the evidence of body exchange all around, they'd judged that to be a deadly choice – the conservatism of extinction. Instead, they'd trusted sperm and ova, always seeking the new and better, the changed, the adapted. And they'd launched their simultaneous campaign to eliminate the Pcharkys of their world, reserving only that one for their final gamble.

It was well that this explosive secret had been kept here. McKie felt grateful to Ceylang. She'd known, but even when it might've helped her, she'd remained silent. BuSab would now have time to forge ways of dealing with this problem. Ceylang would be valuable there. And perhaps more would be learned about PanSpechi, Calebans, and Taprisiots. If only Jedrik ...

He felt a fumbling in his memories.

'If only Jedrik what?'

She spoke laughingly in his mind as she'd always spoken there.

McKie suppressed a fit of trembling, almost fell.

'Careful with our body,' she said. 'It's the only one we have now.'

'Whose body?'

She caressed his mind.

'Ours, love.'

Was it hallucination? He ached with longing to hold her in his arms, to feel her arms around him, her body pressed to him.

'That's lost to us forever, love, but see what we have in exchange.'

When he didn't respond, she said:

'One can always be watching while the other acts . . . or sleeps.'

'But where are you?'

'Where I've always been when we exchanged. See?'

He felt her parallel to him in the shared flesh and, as he voluntarily drew back, he came to rest in contact with her mutual memories, still looking from his own eyes but aware that someone else peered out there, too, that someone else turned this body to face Broey.

Fearful that he might be trapped here, McKie almost panicked, but Jedrik gave him back the control of their flesh.

'Do you doubt me, love?'

He felt shame. There was nothing she could hide from him. He knew how she felt, what she'd been willing to sacrifice for him.

'You'd have made their perfect Mrreg.'

'Don't even suggest it.'

She went pouring through his arena memories then and her joy delighted him.

'Oh, marvelous, McKie. Beautiful! I couldn't have done it better. And Broey still doesn't suspect.'

Attendants were taking the eight prisoners out of the arena now, all of them still shackled. The audience benches were almost empty.

A sense of joy began filtering through McKie.

I lost something but I gained something.

'You didn't lose as much as Aritch.'

'And I gained more.'

McKie permitted himself to stare up at Broey then, studying the Gowachin judge with Dosadi eyes and two sets of awareness. Aritch and the eight accused of murder were things of the past. They and many others like them would be dead or powerless before another ten-day. Broey already had shown the speed with which he intended to act. Supported by his troop of Jedrik-chosen aides, Broey would occupy the seats of power, consolidating lines of control in that shadow government, eliminating every potential source of opposition he could touch. He believed Jedrik dead and, while McKie was clever, McKie and BuSab were not a primary concern. One struck at the real seats of power. Being Dosadi, Broey could not act otherwise. And he'd been almost the best his planet had ever produced. Almost.

Jedrik-within chuckled.

Yes, with juggernaut certainty, Broey would create a single target for BuSab. And Jedrik had refined the simulation pattern by which Broey could be anticipated. Broey would find McKie waiting for him at the proper moment.

Behind McKie would be a new BuSab, an agency directed by a person whose memories and abilities were amplified by the one person superior to Broey that Dosadi had ever produced.

Standing there in the now silent arena, McKie wondered:

When will Broey realize he does our work for us?

'When we show him that he failed to kill *me!*'

In the purest obedience to Gowachin forms, without any sign of the paired thoughts twining through his mind, McKie bowed toward the surviving jurist, turned, and left. And all the time, Jedrik-within was planning ... plotting ... planning ...

If you've enjoyed these books and would like to read more, you'll find literally thousands of classic Science Fiction & Fantasy titles through the **SF Gateway**

For the new home of Science Fiction & Fantasy . . .

For the most comprehensive collection of classic SF on the internet . . .

Visit the SF Gateway

www.sfgateway.com

Frank Hebert (1920–1986)

Frank Herbert was born in Tacoma, Washington in 1920 and worked as a reporter, and later editor, of a number of West Coast newspapers before becoming a full-time writer. His first Science Fiction story was published in 1952 but he achieved fame more than ten years later with the publication in *Analog* of *Dune World* and *The Prophet of Dune*, which were amalgamated into the novel *Dune* in 1965. Winner of both the *Nebula* and the *Hugo* awards, it is the best selling SF novel of all time.